MW01235827

The Justus Scrolls

Recollections of an Almost Apostle

The Justus *Scrolls*

Recollections of an Almost Apostle

Paul David Morris

and Bonnie Gaffney Morris

Inspiring Voices®
A Service of Guideposts

Copyright © 2013 Paul David Morris.

All rights reserved. No part of this book may be used or reproduced by any means, graphic, electronic, or mechanical, including photocopying, recording, taping or by any information storage retrieval system without the written permission of the publisher except in the case of brief quotations embodied in critical articles and reviews.

Inspiring Voices books may be ordered through booksellers or by contacting:

Inspiring Voices
1663 Liberty Drive
Bloomington, IN 47403
www.inspiringvoices.com
1-(866) 697-5313

Because of the dynamic nature of the Internet, any web addresses or links contained in this book may have changed since publication and may no longer be valid. The views expressed in this work are solely those of the author and do not necessarily reflect the views of the publisher, and the publisher hereby disclaims any responsibility for them.

Any people depicted in stock imagery provided by Thinkstock are models, and such images are being used for illustrative purposes only. Certain stock imagery © Thinkstock.

ISBN: 978-1-4624-0525-1 (sc)
ISBN: 978-1-4624-0526-8 (e)

Library of Congress Control Number: 2013902499

Printed in the United States of America

Inspiring Voices rev. date: 3/7/2013

For All My Children.

Acknowledgements

If you are an athlete, and on scoring a victory, you just may get down on one knee and bow your head. If you swim for the gold and win, you lift your eyes and point to the ceiling; and if you are interviewed by a sportsperson, you may start by saying, "First, giving thanks to God..."

Well, in this attempt at literary arts, I make no claim at winning anything, but in this book, I have run the race and completed it. For this pleasure alone, I lift my heart in praise, worship and gratitude to God. Like the seventeen-year Cicada, this work has finally reached its molting. Seventeen years buried in the earth in its cocoon, it is finally ready and because God has been its Provocateur, Overseer and Cultivator, he does indeed warrant first thanks. It has been a privilege and honor to be a part of it.

Second, and almost as close to the top as God, is my wife Bonnie. Like me, she has agonized over every word. She has edited, argued and construed. She has added a bit here and a bit there. No one can use literary scissors like her, much to my pain; and then when I see her finished work, to my immense joy. Incredibly, more important than her investment of hundreds of hours with this book, was her encouragement and her belief in me. She actually thinks I can write, silly girl. It is beyond my reach to say how much I truly appreciate all of this, or how very much it has contributed to the finished work.

We walked a precarious path, she, advising me on what a reader might enjoy, and what not; I, remonstrating on the presumption of how her efforts could possibly improve on what I had already written. She won most of these elephantine struggles, as she well should have. I shall take to eternity the vision of her broad smile and dancing eyes, when I, at length announced, "The deed is done!" No man on earth could possibly have such a nourishing life partner. For this, my debt of gratitude to God knows no bounds.

To David, my son and professional advisor, I owe an enormous debt. Awash in thanksgiving for the support and attentions of such a son, I am honored that David has been, and will remain my stalwart. He has helped form this book, sometimes even when he didn't know it.

Dr. Louis Tharp, psychologist and professor of Philosophy and Religion, has thundered at me incessantly to get this project done, not because he thought me a procrastinator, which, of course, I am, but because he believes in its message. I have known him for almost forty years. We have laughed together, sailed together, argued together, gone to the dinner theater together, eaten in Mexican restaurants together, and along with his beautiful wife, Anna, for a time, lived in the same house (his) together. Without Lou's thudding and prodding, this book might still be lying in fragments on my computer. He helped in its formation, and especially helped make its completion possible.

Linda Lashley, English professor and dearest friend, proved invaluable in providing important, professional editorial support. She examined each comma, each quotation mark, caught spelling errors and made extremely helpful suggestions regarding the use of specific words. In other words, she did the job of a top-notch, professional editor. In going through her work on the manuscript, I was awed and humbled by her gracious gift of time, talent and training. So much was Linda's contribution that with her oversight the work has immensely benefitted. Thank you, Linda for your help.

Thanks also to Nancy Stockton who was extremely helpful in this regard.

Our daughter, Pamela Tinsley, was kind enough to allow me to use her warm, heartfelt thoughts of her newborn son, and in this story, they found their way into Mary's thoughts of her newborn Son. There are so many others to thank: Rod Pejsar and his marvelous twin daughters, Robin and Karen, who provided graphic arts support. For Ray Bailey, whose enthusiasm, moral and technical support, I am deeply grateful. To all my family and friends who have tolerated my emails requesting feedback on this passage or that, thank you.

For each person mentioned here, and for all who impacted this work without knowing they were doing so, I offer my thanksgiving to God. I earnestly hope you find the result something of which you can be proud.

—Paul Morris

How can we present Jesus Christ to the world in a way that is simultaneously authentic and relevant? A double discipline seems to be needed, negative and positive. The negative is to rid our minds of all preconceptions and prejudices, and resolutely to renounce any attempt to force Jesus into our pre-determined mould. In other words we must repent of Christian 'procrusteanism.' Procrustes, in Greek mythology, was a brutal robber who compelled his victims to fit the dimensions of his iron bed. If they were too short, he stretched them. If they were too long, he chopped off their feet. The Christian "Procrustes' exhibits a similar inflexibility, forcing Jesus into his way of thinking and resorting to ruthless measures in order to secure his conformity. From Procrustes and all his disciples, good Lord deliver us!

John R.W. Stott
The Incomparable Christ

My task which I am trying to achieve is, by the power of the written word to make you hear, to make you feel—it is before all, to make you see. That—and no more, and it is everything. If I succeed, you shall find there according to your deserts: encouragement, consolation, fear, charm—all you demand—and, perhaps also that glimpse of truth for which you have forgotten to ask.

Joseph Conrad

Speaking Personally

Let us understand one thing: if we love him and believe in him, God does not deal with us according to the bad things we do, nor the persistent penchant itching deep in our psyche to do them. The consequence of the gospel is as simple as that.

Then are you not struck by this appeal . . ?

> *"Come to me, all you who are weary and burdened, and I will give you rest. Take my yoke upon you and learn of me, for I am gentle and humble in heart, and you will find rest for your souls. For my yoke is easy and my burden is light."*

For me, these words are a galvanizing invitation. They are so palatable and nonthreatening. They call me to a lifetime of connectedness to the Person who stands solitary, demarcating time as we know it. One does not squander one's time considering the One by whom time is measured. One does not abuse one's time following him whose thought, words and deeds have so deeply framed human history. No king, president, general, scientist, mogul of commerce or philosopher has so shaped civilization as has the power of those 1,000 or so days in which this simple Peasant moved among us. A Carpenter, whose only brush with the halls of civil power stood in the capacity of a criminal condemned to death. And that is the paradox. The events which surrounded him, his teachings, or even the cataclysmic days of his death, burial and resurrection; none of these things wrought this compelling supremacy. While each of these events demands preemptive significance, it was his patently audacious claims of *identity—who he is*—that credentialed them.

Such words as these call me to a life of reaching transcendence, an existential extension of being. Unfortunately, my assorted foibles preclude my lingering long in such airs. Still, I cannot resist such an appeal. This presentation is a result of my response to this invitation. In it you will discover my own prejudices and biases. *I am responsible for every error in thinking and for none of the truth.* This present volume was not written to replace the sacred page. Let me be clear: It is only within the pages of the *Original Autographs*, that one will find the unadulterated, written revelation of God. That said and affirmed, should this volume provoke interest in the scriptures, it will have served its purpose.

I began this book in the fall of 1995. The first draft was completed on August 23, 2003. It has been simultaneously, the most difficult writing task in my seven plus decades of life and the most sublime. Contained in those moments of pattering away on my keyboard were the most precious times I have ever known with God. The intensity of spiritual intimacy often evoked tears of joy, gratitude and satisfaction. More so than counseling, more so than teaching and preaching, more so than the sweet fellowship I have had with other believers. Apart from giving life to and raising three extraordinary human beings, this book is for me the most important thing I have ever done in my expenditure of human effort and energy.

Should this work ever be published or read by a population other than my family and close friends, I fear the consequences. I think I have managed to offend just about every religious denomination and sect. I wish them to know that this was not deliberate or intentional. I meant them no harm. I comfort myself with the truth that Jesus himself was, on occasion, not inoffensive. On the other hand, the crucible of merit for this work lies not in its acceptance by the major denominations or theological academe, but in acceptance by prostitutes, those imprisoned, the immoral, profane, destitute and unchurched of this world. Certainly no condescension intended, but these may well be the "little ones" of whom Jesus spoke, the ones for whom drowning would be preferred rather than to offend them. To these, "the least of my brethren," I humbly commit these pages.

You must remember that you are looking over my shoulder as I, like others before me, struggle with God. Sometimes in tears. Sometimes in happiness. Sometimes in stony silence. It is as if you are sitting with me in the closet of my heart and sharing with me the rich Cognac of Truth. As Mr. Emerson has eloquently put it...

> *The argument which has not power to reach my own practice,...will fail to reach yours. But* [I have done my best

to] *take Sidey's maxim: "Look in thy heart, and write." He that writes to himself, writes to an eternal public.*[1]

So here is the glass, my friend. Swirl gently this shimmering, agéd liquid gold and savor the bouquet. Taste and see that it is good.

—Paul Morris

1 Emerson, Ralph Waldo, Selected Essays, *Spiritual Laws,* People's Book Club, Chicago. MCMXLIX. P.103 [The insertion is my own.]

Truncated

October, A.D. 60

Creaking under the weight of a copper-sheathed wooden box and the elderly man it carried, a makeshift wagon bumped and rumbled its way across a cobbled-stoned quay. The driver held loosely to the reins as the sweating mule moved wagon, driver, passenger and box, down the jarring quay where a ship was being laded. Recently, the ship had sailed from Alexandria, and after a circuitous voyage of more than two thousand miles, would thence return. Or, at least, that was the intention of its owner, and the obligation of its captain. But these leagues were yet ahead of its prow, and who is to know the future or, who is to know what lurks in the mists of the deep?

A dock worker, his full, red beard matted with dried spittle, approached the wagon; his body thick, hands like a troll, covered with hair, two fingers missing along with several yellow teeth, one eye was closed. "Oove y' 'orse over 'ere," he commanded, dropping his consonants, and pointing what remained of his fingers to a spot on the wharf. A large hawser hung from the wooden beam of a crane, an iron hook attached to its business end. As the wagon pulled into position, the dock-walloper yanked the heavy hawser to suspend directly over the box, now strapped with ropes in order to lift it. He slipped the hook into the O-ring and turned to the crane operator, giving a universal, thumbs-up sign.

"Careful how you handle that box!" cried the old gentleman. "It contains precious, fragile cargo."

"Min' yer own earwax, yer ol' mule-fart!" replied the dockman, "an I'll min' mine!" The copper box swung up and over the gunwale of the ship, and down into the blackness of the hold. The old man looked concerned, but turned and made his way up the gangplank.

"Yes," muttered the object of the dockman's scorn. *A mule-fart?* thought he. *More like a fly-fart in a gale. Such is the consequence of my life.* He had no justifiable reason to take such a view of himself. He was a man of honor and integrity. In fact, he had done much in his life for which to take satisfaction, and much for which to feel pride. Yet, he was continually nagged by the notion that he was unworthy. He was met at the gunwale by the ship's clerk who examined his credentials, checking them against the ship's manifest, and who advised him of his assigned berth.

After stowing his gear, the elderly gentleman wandered out again on deck. It was a beautiful day on a substantial ship, perhaps 230 feet long and 75 feet from beam to beam. White clouds scudded through bright blue skies. She was constructed of mortised plankings, cedar and other woods, using treenails (a wooden dowel pin that swells when wet) to fasten them together, and pitch for caulking the seams, in the manner of superb Egyptian artisanship. Two masts, a large one set just forward of amidships, and another smaller set aft of the foc'sle, a single canvas on each mast. Above her prow, curved the neck of a white swan, crafted to the very image of the real thing pushing through serene waters, perhaps a talisman to conjure a promise of smooth sailing. Together, there were ample quarters for almost 300 souls, including the rowers below decks, and 30 tons of cargo. Most of that, it seemed, was great stores of wheat.

He stood at the rail, adjusting his robes, when a disturbance occurred on the quay. Three soldiers and a centurion, by the look of him, were escorting a man toward the gangplank. There was a crowd, shouting and surging around the man. Some seemed to favor him, others in angry opposition. The old man narrowed his eyes. A vague awareness of recognition came over him. Looking deeper into the crowd, he recognized a second person. The first was the celebrated evangelist, Paul, formerly known as Saul of Tarsus, and the other was Lucian, the physician. Although he was not shackled or in chains, Paul was clearly in the custody of the Roman centurion. They were surrounded by a mob of thirty or forty men, shouting and shoving. The soldiers had their hands full.

The centurion strode up the gangway and addressed the ship's clerk at the rail, "I am Julian, centurion to Caesar." The clerk dipped his head in respect. "I bring with me Saul of Tarsus, also known as Paul, a leader of the Christian sect. He is my prisoner and I escort him to Rome for audience with Caesar."

"Prisoner?" inquired the clerk, somewhat frightened. "Why is he not in irons?"

"This prisoner is no flight risk, nor is he a threat to anyone. He is but an expounder of annoying words." The centurion seemed impatient with the clerk's question. "He will cause no trouble aboard ship. Here are my credentials for passage." He handed the clerk his documents. Again, the clerk examined his manifest.

"It says here that the prisoner is to be manacled and quartered in the brig."

"He will not be manacled while in my custody," said the centurion flatly.

"Nor will he be quartered in the ship's gaol. He remains with me, in my sight at all times."

"You will be mindful, sir, that the Captain of this vessel will make such decisions."

The centurion smiled sardonically. "Then you will summon him here." The clerk appeared unsettled and confused. "Now!" Then the ship's man found the good sense to know that he had heard the voice of authority.

Still, he hesitated, "I must…"

"Move!"

The clerk disappeared toward the aft cabin. In a moment he returned with a burly looking fellow, full-bearded and with the epaulets of captaincy on his shoulders. He took one look and the centurion and cried, "Julian! What in the name of the fires of hell are you doing on my vessel?" The captain was grinning as though he had encountered a long, lost friend. Which, indeed, he had.

αΘω

As he adjusted his robes, he could not help but notice how threadbare they had become, how gray from repeated washings. Thoughts came at random. He thought of the events which had led him to this hour, this place. He had spent the last fifteen years of his life writing about it or, was it sixteen? He couldn't remember. It had started one day when he reminisced, enjoying a few memories of his time with the Master. He remembered that it was evening and growing dark outside, that he had lit a few candles, retrieved some blank parchment, dipped his quill and begun to write. So long ago, it seemed, and the memories he penned? Even longer.

Now, as the ship's prow pointed southwest, sails filled with wind, and as the quay receded in the distance, his mind returned to this amazing coincidence of being on the same ship with the man called Paul. He believed, that with God, there were no "coincidences." This inevitable encounter had to be divinely arranged. He wondered where it would go? *A step at a time…We'll see…*The horizon beckoned, winds soft, almost non-existent; an occasional luff in the sails, the ship creaked gently, the splash of its prow a comforting sound.

The day passed uneventfully. The next day, the day after that and the day after that. Sight of land was lost, but at the imperceptible rate the ship sailed, it couldn't be far off to starboard. Myra, the point of embarkation, had disappeared days ago. The ship continued to loll about in almost calm waters. Sails, ruffling. Seabirds hanging motionless in the air. Sweating men straining against oars dipping rhythmically, biting the sea. Lethargically, the ship loitered through the waters.

At length, a breeze picked up, sails filled and the white swan dipped her breast into dancing whitecaps. Headway began. But then the wind shifted. The ship jibed. The wind shifted. The ship tacked. The wind shifted yet again. Waves, confused by the changing wind, crashed into one another. The ship lurched and wallowed. Strong winds, navigable, but strong, began to blow. Unrelenting, they shifted yet again, and again after that. Going was difficult, perhaps, impossible. Ship, passengers and cargo were getting nowhere. After days of seeming floundering, the island of Crete was sighted in the distance. Tiller angled for land, oarsmen commanded to pull, and at length, the ship put in at Good Harbor, which served the town of Lacea.

Almost everyone disembarked, glad and grateful to get their feet accustomed once again to solid ground. The elderly passenger stayed aboard ship. "Come, old fellow!" said one of the departing crew to him, "Come, and let us rest from this infernal sea. Come, and break a skin of good wine."

"You go, sir. Enjoy yourself. I stay aboard ship until I reach my destination."

"And where might that be?"

"Alexandria, Egypt."

"Alexandria! By way of Italy? This ship sails for Rome, old friend. You will be sick of her by then. You should be sick of her now!"

"I have cargo," replied the old man. "I do not wish to leave it." Mumbling to himself about the shrunken world of the elderly, the crewman made his way down the gangplank to the quay.

He did, indeed, ask himself why he had chosen such a circuitous route to his destination, instead of the more direct route across the Great Sea. It was hard to determine a good reason. He loved life on board ship and often wondered why he did not choose a life at sea. But, with favorable winds, this voyage should only take a little over two weeks of actual sailing, not counting time in ports of call. He looked forward to the journey and the smell of sea and salt.

And then he thought of what he had done. He often wondered how God valued what he had done. It was the culmination of his entire life, especially his those four years with his Lord and friend. Now, it was all recorded. These scrolls and the time he had invested in them meant more to him in terms of the purpose of his life, than anything else he had done. It was, he believed, God's intention and purpose for his existence.

Now, for their preservation, he was taking them to the great library at Alexandria, Egypt. Of course, he knew that the library had burned thanks to the carelessness of Julius Caesar over a hundred years ago. Caesar had deliberately set fire to his own ships in an attempt to thwart the treachery of one of his own generals. The fire from one of the ships docked too close to the library, accidentally setting the great repository of ancient literature afire. Countless documents had been destroyed, but not all. Many priceless scrolls were saved and stored in a Temple known as the *Serapeum* where scholars continued to labor among the cherished texts. It was among these that he thought to place his own. *This is the place they should live,* thought he. *Here, in this daughter library, they will be preserved until someday, perhaps, someday…*

αΘω

Owing to the season, (the autumn solstice had passed), they anticipated treacherous seas. Wintering on the sea was not a pleasant prospect. There was much discussion among the crew as to whether to winter in the harbor or continue on. The prisoner, Paul, who was not being treated like a prisoner, weighed in on the issue: "Cast out to sea, and the ship is doomed. We will all perish, every mother's son of us." This made us all feel better.

The ship's captain rolled his eyes and looked at the man of God with the tolerance one gives a child who believes he can command the waves on the beach. "What do you think?" asked the centurion of the captain. "I think I prefer the opinion of a sea-faring professional, than that of a religious philosopher."

"He is right about one thing," said the captain. "The going will be rough. Still, I have never seen the storm that could best me and my crew; not to speak of my ship. She's Egyptian. She can deal with any Euroclydon this sea can offer. The swan will guide us. We sail at daybreak!"

αΘω

Religious philosopher! The thought provoked disdain in the old man's mind. *This man Paul is more than a religious philosopher. He may be the 13th apostle! Or, so some think.*

"May I intrude on your thoughts?" The question interrupted his reverie as he had been watching the swelling waves, watching the seabirds hover, watching the clouds scudding darker and darker. He turned to see who had spoken.

You!

"I may be a prisoner, sir, but I will not harm you. It is for what I preach that I am in the custody of Rome. I am not a robber, thief, or a murderer—*at least not anymore,"* he thought quietly.

He calmed himself after the initial shock that the apostle had spoken to him. "I know you to be none of these things, sir. I know who you are."

"Have we met? You do seem familiar."

"We have not met. At least not formally. I was present when you were introduced to the apostles in Antioch. We barely made eye-contact."

"Yes! You were there! I remember seeing you. You were…we both were younger then." The old man smiled at the apostle's observation.

"I am older than you might think, Paul of the Epiphany. I know how you have served the Lord all these years. I know you bear his scars; scars I am ashamed to say, I have not borne."

"The disfigurement and scabs I bear, dear friend, are but badges of honor in my service to Jesus Christ. And your shame is unfounded, sir. Though I bear in my body the marks of the Lord Jesus, that you have none is no sign that you are one whit of less importance to him, or God forbid, that you are loved less."

"I long most to be his servant; no matter the cost, no matter the consequence."

"Paul of the Epiphany?" responded the apostle with a smile. "So you know of my experience on the highway to Damascus." It was a statement, not a question. "Then, indeed, you were there when I met the twelve. You know of James, the Lord's brother. You know of Peter, John and the others."

"Yes, I not only know of them, brother, I know them all personally and intimately. Or, at least, I thought I did." His eyes turned down and away.

"I take it then, that you are a follower of The Way."

"If that is what you wish to call it, yes."

"What would you call it?"

The old man seemed lost in thought for a moment. Pensive. Observing, evaluating the undulating horizon as if it had something to say. "I am a follower of Jesus of Nazareth, sir. He is my King, my Lord, my Savior and my God. He was, he is my friend, my brother, my kinsman."

"Then we have much of which to speak."

"Perhaps, sir, but not now." The old man rose from his seat, leaned on his staff which he used to steady himself and began to move away. "These bones are old, stiff and sore. The brain I carry in my head is tired. I need rest." And with that Paul the apostle was left to wonder.

αΘω

Beneath the baggage, and buried under other assorted passenger paraphernalia, the copper-encased box rested. Three feet square, the box was completely encased with copper, a durable, but malleable metal. There was a lid, or a cover, which separated from the main body of the box about eight inches down from the top, the seam being filled with molten tin and allowed to harden. In order to open the box, the tin had to be melted again with an iron, heated to red-hot. The flashpoint of the wood beneath the seam, had only to be slightly lower than the tin. This was an excellent method of sealing the wood beneath a coating of copper. It would allow no entry of insect, rodent or pest, or humidity, or even briny water. It was, indeed, effectively sealed.

Inside the box, packed in washed sand, there stood fixed a large, impressively adorned urn, its lid tightly sealed with resin. And inside the urn, wrapped in dry cloths, was the old man's treasure of memories, more important to him than his own life.

Sails fill again with whistling wind. Whitecaps send ocean spray into the air. *Taste the salt on your lips.* There are fewer trailing seagulls. Swells in the water become larger. Troughs deeper. Clouds darker. There is a serious, almost ominous tension among the crew. The captain is often seen observing the weather, a look of concern, if not worry, on his face. Were you standing near him, you would strain to hear him say, perhaps sense him thinking, *"Euroclydon."*

αΘω

A knock on the door of his cabin. The apostle looked at the opaque passageway. "Come," said he. The door opened and the old man entered the small room that served as quarters for the apostle's voyage. Paul smiled. It was good to have a brother believer with him. Perhaps they could talk. Perhaps they could pray together. Without waiting to be invited, the old man sat down at the table, his gaze looking deep into the eyes of the famous prisoner.

"Why do you do it?"

"Why do I do what?" responded Paul, a bit nonplussed at the old man's directness.

"Why do you go about organizing believers? Why bishops and elders? Why do you place men in authority among the sheep? Are they not all sheep? And do flocks of sheep have bishops among them?" Paul's eyebrows lifted. The questions did not seem accusatory. The old gentleman seemed truly curious. Still, Paul felt his emotions shift. The questions elicited a measure of discomfort. The ship lurched.

"Flocks of sheep need a shepherd," replied Paul.

"True, but the shepherd is not a sheep. Did not Jesus declare himself to be the Shepherd?" The older man was not done. "And why men with short hair, and women with long hair? What possible relevance can the length of one's hair have to one's relationship with God? And, why, if, in the beginning, God created man and woman to become one flesh, do you relegate marriage to a secondary, or an inferior way of life? And why, after accusing Peter of dissembling, did you do the same thing with our brother, Timothy?

"You appear to know me better than I know you." The apostle's brow furrowed. "You have read my writings. Then you must know, I am not a perfect man. I am not our Lord Jesus."

"Apparently."

"I am the chief of sinners."

"No, brother Paul, you are not. You are no more or less a sinner than any of us." The apostle did not know whether to be indignant and defensive, or to face these issues squarely, or to feel comforted.

"Since you know me so well," Paul's tone tainted not without an edge of sarcasm, "please advise me of what I really am."

His visitor did not hesitate. "You are likely the most brilliant and spiritually sensitive follower of Jesus Christ among us. You have seen things, whether in body or in spirit, that no one else has seen. You are one of God's chosen servants. You bear in your body the marks, the cost of following our Lord. I deeply admire you, respect you, and brother, though we are just beginning to know one another, I feel deep affection and love for you."

"Then why do you question my teachings?"

"Are my questions not legitimate? Are you not a man? By your own words you confess to being a sinner like the rest of us. Do not sinners sin?"

"I sin. I sin indeed. Every day, it seems, I deal with sins I cannot shake. But if you have read my letters, then you know that I trust in his grace and forgiveness. I believe his strength is made perfect in my weakness." The wind outside the cabin shrieked through the rigging. Thc shipped heaved and rolled. Shouts outside, interrupted and truncated by things crashing, shattering, splintering on deck.

"I do know that, dear friend. I also trust in his grace and forgiveness. Like you, I have also written words of him, and I often struggle with the likelihood that I have written things prompted by my own biases, than prompted by the Spirit of God."

At this, the apostle smiled. "Then, with all my heart, I embrace you, old friend." Paul's eyes seemed as if they were about to fill with tears, as if finding at last a brother who understood both his writings, and himself. "It has just occurred to me, I do not yet know your name."

"I am Joseph, son of Sabbas. My friends call me Justus."

PROLOGUE

Joseph bar Sabbas[2]

2 Acts 1:21-26

Shadows on the wall dance in syncopated rhythms with the flickering of lamps I have spread before me. I have several, you see. My eyes are failing somewhat and the light they provide enable me to the write with legibility, if not clarity. The shadows have become friends. They seem alive and energized with silent force, watching me write words that speak of him. It is about all there is left that I can do. Once I held forth in preaching and teaching. Once men listened to me instruct them of him. Some were important men, supposedly. Governors. Senators. Others appointed to high office by Rome. But no more. I speak no more. I am applauded and appreciated by crowds—no more.

I confess to you that I am not bitter. I can say that without rancor and in honesty with myself. Admittedly, I often long for another platform, especially when I hear others speak, some better, most worse than I did. I am ashamed to say that I am truly fond of the plaudits, of the well-wishers, of the expressions of gratitude. But they are gone now and it is not constructive to linger among such memories, not to speak of useless.

I have a new profession now: word craft. I love to find just the precise word to express meaning, feeling, intelligence. I want my reader to enjoy the pleasure they bring. Just reading the word itself will produce a quality of pleasure or pain. And if by God's eternal grace they breed closeness with him, then I have chosen well. I know, because I read and reread these words myself, desiring to choose an even better word, a more eloquent phrase, a paragraph potentate. In this reading and rereading, I often weep.

The words I write tell of him. There are no words, in any language, equal to this task. Words written of him are holy, set apart from the usual concourse of words. And as this scribbling chronicles the hours he moved among us, I deeply sense that it is not I who scratches away beneath the shadows in some lonely vigil, but some *Other*. Whether my sensing has any connection with reality or not, I do not know. He has not chosen to let me know that I speak for him. But I can tell you this: from the day I first met him, from that day until my last breath—I am his servant, if he will have me. If not, then I spend my life wishing to possess what I am denied.

I clearly am not selected to be among his choicest servants, although

I knew him from the beginning. From the day I saw with my own eyes the feathered embodiment of the Spirit light upon him, I knew that I must follow him. I knew then that I would rather cease to exist than be without him. It is an amazing consternation to me that such devotion can be affirmed or disenfranchised by casting lots. But so it was. And so it is. So now in these fading days, I comfort myself with words.

– Joseph, bar Sabbas, called Justus

Gone Forever

October, A.D. 60

From the Diary of Joseph bar Sabbas, called Justus...

The wind shrieked through the rigging like a raging, maniacal spirit that appears as a sign that all who hear her voice are about to die. Sails rent, torn in tatters flailed in the stinging, howling, rain-swept gale. Despite anchors thrown from the stern of the ship, the vessel careened in the storm like desultory flotsam tossed by relentless, swelling surges. The anchors caught and held, lines snapping taut and rigid. The storm bore down from the northeast and by anchoring from the stern, the prow of the ship pointed downwind southwest, directly toward land. The crew feared that should the lines break, we would with certainty, founder on the rocks. A mammoth wall of water assaulted our stern, lifting it high in the air and then crashing down into into the trailing sea-trough. As the aft-end of the ship descended, another undulating surge loomed above, lifting it precipitously, straining the lines to the anchors. Suddenly, there was a sharp, vibrating *twang!,* as one of the four lines snapped. The other lines, absorbing the strain from the broken line, quickly gave way as if the wind and the waves had severed them with a razor. The ship surged with the waves, free of restraint.

Timbers creaked loudly. Hemp lines cascaded across the decks in chaotic array. Mountains of water fell athwart the beams. Spars and yardarms dipped, as if yearning, seeking to find comfort in the sea. Loud thumps, crashes from the ship's hold gave verdict to loose and tumbling cargo slamming against weakening bulkheads. A shattering thud! Dull noise of cracking timbers. For a split second, there was no movement—no movement at all—a shock of eerie silence amidst raging cacophony. Arrested momentum threw the bodies of crew members and passengers alike against bulkheads with jarring force. Screams of panic and despair. The ship was doomed, barely four hundred yards from the shores of Malta.

Recovering my consciousness and adjusting from that terrible, bone-crushing halt, we wallowed perilously amongst the waves. It took no intelligence to discern that the ship had struck a rock, or rocks—and we were going down. I rushed to the port side and stared into the rain, driven by black, angry clouds and gale-force winds from above, trying to see what I hoped was land close by. What I saw was a gigantic rock protuberance impelling itself from the depths thirty feet into the air above the churning surface, its top painted white with seagull droppings. This is what we struck. Another massive bank of water slammed the wreck hard against the rock and when it had passed, the ship began to slip back into the ocean, its port rail, where I was standing dipping low, bending for the water.

Instantly I leaped back, in pathetic effort to save myself from drowning. The deck tilted into an unscalable wall. My foot slid on the wet. I grabbed for something, anything to hold onto and save myself. My fingers wrapped around the edges of a container, a wooden box, or a lid of a box, I couldn't tell. Yet another mountain of water struck the ship, driving it up once again against the rock. More bursting timbers. The lid came loose and in seconds I skidded across the deck untethered, and into the dark maw of cascading depths. The wood jerked from my grip as I impacted the water and plunged beneath the waves. In a moment I emerged, my lungs afire, sputtering and choking on salt water. Not a soul in sight. The ship heaved ominously above me, a giant shadow of impending death. Something bumped and I turned to see the lid of the box which had, thankfully, pursued me into the water. I reached and grasped it with both hands, pulled it against my chest and held on for the dearest moments of my life.

The sea was relentless, tossing wave after wave, and tossing me into a somersault and away from the ship. As my head emerged from the water again, I watched in horror as the vessel broke free of the rock and was blown toward land—now lost to sight, I was alone with my solitary piece of debris, my old flesh and bones screaming agony and affliction. The water was ungodly cold and I seemed to drift in and out of consciousness. I saw the ship one last time as I drove past her on my life-saving box-lid. She had run aground, her prow stuck firmly in whatever sand or clay that counted for an ocean bottom in these waters. She was breaking up. Men were scampering into boats and jumping overboard. I wondered how many would survive. Surely I would, myself, perish, and my treasure; my precious treasure would find its permanent home at the bottom of the sea, forever sealed from the eyes of those I had yearned to behold it. My cherished cargo, my Gospel of my Lord, gone forever.

June, 1993 A.D.

On June 23, 1993, Raul Maduse, in full scuba gear, scudded across the bottom of St. Paul's Bay on the island of Malta, his girlfriend, Serena, close by his side. He glanced quickly at the depth gauge on his wrist; 27.4 metres. He noticed a large crab making its way across the bottom. Removing the knife from its sheath strapped to his leg, he plunged the blade through the crustacean, killing it instantly. Such an act revealed gross immaturity and ignorance, yet he felt compelled to impress Serena, to whom he held up his victim for her to approve. She did not.

It had been named "St. Paul's Bay," owing to the fact that Biblical scholars identified it as the body of water in which the apostle Paul's ship foundered, almost 2,000 years previously. It is now a bustling resort, where its year-round population of 16,000 swells in the summertime to over 60,000. On this day in June, a boat filled with scuba-diving tourists who were exploring the depths of the bay in search of adventure and spear fishing. Some hoped, perhaps, to find ancient relics from civilizations inhabiting the island in lost millennia past.

But such thoughts were remote to the minds of the young couple 15 fathoms down, quietly examining the reefs and underwater flora, their exhalations floating softly to the kelp bed above. Gigantic kelp stalks spring from the bottom creating forests of green beneath azure waters. Through these stalks swim myriads of bright denizens, including moray, shark and an occasional misguided jellyfish. Among them today swam Raul and Serena. Raul looked at his watch to check his bottom-time, noted that they had about 12 minutes dive time left, and motioned for Serena to follow him. He swam close to the rock whose base, at this depth seemed beyond measure. Inspecting the crevasses for spectacular fish, or whatever he may find, he saw an odd-shaped rock protruding several centimeters above the bottom sand and pointing like a pyramid to the surface.

Owing to its odd shape, he stopped to look. Brushing the fine sea-bottom sand away into a small cloud, he saw the pyramid shape emerge. On closer inspection, he discovered that it was not a rock at all. Once again taking his knife from its sheath on his leg, he scratched at its surface. It resisted the blade, yet yielded a spoonful of accumulated debris. He tried a second time; this time with a little more force, and a chunk of the debris loosened and fell away, leaving a glint of the color of copper where the point of the knife had struck. It was then that Raul Maduse knew that he and Serena, might become famous.

The First Scroll

Let There Be Light

In the beginning, God created the heavens and the earth. Now the earth was formless and empty, darkness was over the surface of the deep, and the Spirit of God was hovering over the waters. And God said, "let there be light," and there was light. God saw that the light was good, and he separated the light from the darkness. God called the light "day," and the darkness he called "night." And there was evening, and there was morning—the first day.

—*Genesis 1:1-5 NIV*

I

6 B.C.

Censer Priest

Being a priest is not all it is said to be. This thought amongst others of less magnitude addled the old man's brain as he shuffled toward the Temple. He resented the designation, *"idiot-priest,"* accorded to him and others like him by rabbis, scribes and interpreters of the Law. Benign contempt? *Hah! Consummate fools! Condescending...*He thought for a moment, searching for the appropriate word, then smiled with satisfaction...*Pig droppings!* Then laughing cynically to himself added, *diarrheic pig droppings!* He had been a priest of the Division of Abijah for his entire life and now wondered if he had wasted his time here on earth. For years, decades, had he stood quietly by and seen other men chosen. Older men when he was young. Younger men now that he was advanced in years. Never him. Random chance made choosing a Censer-priest fall to God himself. Didn't it? *Randomness* as the very purpose, the absurd protocol for giving God his way! Isn't that how we settle how God thinks? The whole fashion nauseated him.

To be chosen as Censer-priest only occurred once in one's lifetime. The natural inference that to be chosen at all is tacitly equivalent to God's setting his seal of approval on you, that God thought you of importance, that God recognized you as a man of character and worth. It lessened the taunt of the rabbis. To be chosen while you are young implies that you are anointed, destined for greatness. Many priests live their entire lives never to be chosen.

There is no record that this particular priest had ever violated his trust in office. Those who cared enough to observe him thought him "righteous." He, of course, knew differently. So did God. That is why, he concluded, he had never been chosen. Not to be chosen logically provoked the ominous question, "What is wrong with you that God has not chosen you?" Cruel question; richly undeserved. It wasn't difficult for him to imagine why God had not chosen him. He, himself, knew well of his sins.

Elizabeth understood. How grateful I am for her. His wife believed in him, loved him, encouraged him when all others failed him. Like all priests he had married, seemingly, he thought for his entire life. *How long have we been together? God help me! I think I have forgotten.* He did not regret one moment of it. Elizabeth! The only person in the world who he knew loved him, despite the shame that they had no children. Almost everyone blamed her. *Elizabeth is barren!* Supposed friends said this in sometimes not so hushed tones. Again, he knew better. It was not she. It was he. God had rejected him. That is why his prayers for a child, a son, had gone unanswered, unheard. *Idiot-priest, indeed!* Perhaps the rabbinic fools were right.

αΘω

The time had come once again for his division, the Division of Abijah, to care for the priestly services of the Temple. The lot is taken to select the Censer-priest whose duty is to burn incense on the altar in the Temple of God. Once, the altar stood before the Veil in the Temple of God. No more, not in these days in Herod's Temple. The altar did not stand even in the Holy Place. Different times; nothing stayed the same. Incense, supposedly, symbolized the prayers of the nation to God. Indeed, the Censer-priest came to offer such prayers. Two relatives assisted him, one to remove what remained of the previous day's sacrifice, the other to rearrange the live coals on the altar of incense. Zechariah had long since laid aside any expectations. Too often he had wondered why God had granted him life. Why live, especially as a priest, when one is not allowed to serve? Why live when your life would end, leaving no son, no purpose? Why live at all?

Once, he looked forward to the lot, hoping to be chosen, wishing to be chosen, living for the day when he would be chosen. Not anymore. Today, as in recent years, he thought it all tedious, a wearisome, vexing bother. He was too old to bother, too decrepit to care. His knees ached. There were shooting pains in his hip. He wearied with life. There was no thought, no expectation at all that he would be chosen.

Hence, on this day he was.

αΘω

At first, the realization that it had happened amused him. *Well,* he thought, *the old man finally gets his day.* He thought it not unlike eulogies at funerals. Since you are dead, how can you enjoy them? He was less than impressed.

When the reality of his doing the services of Censer-priest began to seep into the cisterns of his self-esteem, tired cynicism yielded to childlike joy opening the dawn of a percipient day. Like the taste of exquisite wine, he rolled it around in his brain, letting it bring to life the calloused taste buds of jaded emotions. He allowed himself to enjoy the inebriation—at least, partially. The other pain, that at his age he would never see a son, he did not think about, at least not today. It was pleasant and perhaps more significant, after a manner of speaking, to be chosen when you are old. Could it be an endorsement of his years? The rationalization amused him; perhaps all had not been a waste. For now, he would humbly serve. This provided him a semblance of peace.

The first week of October, Zechariah stood facing the altar. At his left, stood the table of showbread. To his right, the seven-branched candlestick. Before him stood the golden altar of incense on which red coals glowed. Deep notes of the Magrephah filled distant corners of the Temple summoning priests and people to whatever holy service awaited them. Still the old priest waited as were his instructions, until the signal came to spread incense on the coals. The signal came; the incense spread and rich aromas filled the candlelit room. *Is it not odd,* thought Zechariah, *that sensate faculties in one's nostrils titillate one's sense of worship?* The whole scene struck him as sublime and absurd at the same time. The warm musical notes, the smells, the stunning visionary beauty of the altar, the candlesticks; the hidden mystery of the Veil. *Since God lives in the heart,* thought he, *of what worth are these trifles? Does the Creator have the slightest interest in the smell of pleasant odors?* Despite his doubts, he loved everything about this service.

αΘω

It became for Zechariah, a wondrous ceremony; an old man who had long since lost his capacity for awe. His head bowed, his eyes closed, his hands postured in prayer, when involuntarily—he blinked. A soft glow, brighter than that warranted by the candlestick, illumined the marble floor where his gaze fell. His pupils focused for the slightest of instants as if examining the masonry patterns in the floor. *Whence comes this light?* Anxiety elevated as slowly, he lifted his head.

αΘω

A man stood between the golden altar of incense and the candlestick. Clearly, he appeared no ordinary man, his clothing iridescent as a prism dancing rainbows on the walls, his expression serene and in command, his bearing unnatural. He felt his knees begin to weakly tremble.

"Do not be afraid, Zechariah." Instantly, his spirit was comforted. At these simple words, the old priest felt his heart enlarge, his blood pound, his lungs fill. Every nerve in his body resonated. His posture strengthened.

Their eyes engaged!

Suddenly, and for the first time in decades, his arms felt as if he could bend steel. In tones soft and holy, the man continued, "I am sent to tell you that God has heard your prayers." The priest tried to digest this. "Your wife, Elizabeth, will bear you a son." Despite his empowerment, the old man's heart staggered.

Merciful God!

The man continued. "You will call his name John."

Merciful God!

"He will give you gladness and many will celebrate his birth. He will be great in the eyes of the Lord. As Samuel and Sampson, he will be a Nazirite and will never drink wine or strong spirits. While he is yet in his mother's womb, the Holy Spirit will fill him. He will turn the hearts of many in Israel to the Lord their God. He will act with the spirit and power of Elijah and he will prepare the people for the Lord."

Zechariah listened but absorbed none of this. He was much too stunned to absorb anything beyond the simple—*preposterous!*—announcement that he may have a son.

"How can this be?" The priest had found his tongue. "Don't you see? I - I am an old man. My wife has long since passed the age of bearing a child." Conflicting thoughts invaded his brain. *Could the miracle done for Abrahams's Sarah happen again? Those were holy times, with holy men of old. Such miracles no longer happen!* He shook his head. He is hallucinating. His mind is finally going. This cannot be happening. He needed something to drink; a strong spirit would do nicely. He wanted to believe but he was too old. He had been kicked in the groin too many times. Again and again he had prayed. A thousand times again. "Perhaps a sign? Perhaps something miraculous that I can see? Some credentials? Please?" He was whining he knew. *I need something to hold on to...*

αΘω

"I am *Gabriel!*" The sentence seemed laughable to the old priest, yet it compelled him to take note of the obvious and, at the same time, announced a hidden reality. *"I stand in the presence of El Shaddai! I am sent to speak to you!"* The daring pronouncement provoked him but he remained unconvinced. Why would God wish to speak to him? He was not illiterate. He knew the scriptures. Is this man, for all of his distinction, claiming to be *that* Gabriel? "I am sent to tell you wonderful news," he continued, "but since you cannot accept it, your sign will be this: you will be unable to speak until the day your son is born."

"Poor Zechariah," his friends gossiped, "he was so overcome at being Censer-priest that he can no longer speak."

Elizabeth, however, became pregnant.

II

Mary's Place

Nazareth did not fit. An independent-minded community, considered with some scorn by stricter Jews, Nazareth annoyed the religious climate. Residents took perverse pride in being different. This irritated the religious leadership as far away as Jerusalem. Nazareth was a creature to itself, a rogue community. It lay outside the mainstream of Israelite life. Except for several trade routes that ran near the town, it stood to itself, alone and outcast. Located midway between the Sea of Galilee and Mt. Carmel and just south of both, the village lay along the slopes of the lower hills of the Lebanon range quietly overlooking a spreading plain.

A short walk from Nazareth, a clear, cold spring seeped through a precipitous embankment and formed a small pool. Surrounded by trees that gave shade; moss, fern and lilies flourished. Here, morning wetness and gentle mists greet awakening dawn. Here, dew mantles the meadow with glistening drops of crystal. Here, sunlight dances in innumerable droplets of condensation. In evening hours, familiar, unbroken sounds of small creatures announce the creeping softness of approaching silence. Here, in the afternoons, she came.

This was Mary's place; a solitary place where she came when she felt the need for quiet meditation, for closeness with God. Here in late afternoon, she smiled at bright butterflies bouncing in puffs of gentle summer zephyrs. A small beauty with blue streaks in butter-yellow wings lit upon her hand as if stopping to gossip. Captivated, she watched as it sat between her thumb and forefinger, slowly moving its wings to some silent rhythm. Nature often accommodates the delight of those who hold her in awe. Mary wondered at the bees buzzing above the blossoms, legs heavy with pollen. She spread herself on the grass gazing at giant white cumulus explosions in the sky, thinking about how it would be to soar among them like the eagle, imagining their shapes with people that were familiar to her. "That one looks like old Uncle Elimelech," she laughed. And here, in early morning or evening vesper hours she came to pray; this place, hidden in the hills, her private sanctuary.

Evening airs still and cool. She stood where the slopes fell sharply to the Plain of Esrdraelon, watching lights below reflect in the deepening panoply above, the light of day fleeing to the place opposing from whence it will come in the morning. Waters from the spring gurgle into a pool so clear it seems invisible, trickling down lush slopes, forming part of a watershed quenching the thirsts of caravans on Roman roads below.

Still lights twinkling in the valley plain and in the deepening vault above. Sweet Jasmine fragrances. The urgency of parental concern flitted about her consciousness tugging at her thoughts, at her compulsive want to stay in this place. "Oh God," her heart exclaimed, "Let me live here forever." She did not expect an answer, but one came.

"Mary."

αΘω

The man simply appeared. He had not approached by foot. She had heard no one coming and surely she would have. He appeared there as if he had preceded her, waiting for her. But she had not seen him, or heard him. She was afraid. She wanted to flee but her legs would not move. He made no attempt to touch her, he just stood there, looking at her as if— as if it were she and not he, who had suddenly and mysteriously appeared, as if it were she who were the apparition to be feared, as if she, not he, were the subject of awe. *What beautiful eyes;* Mary thought without fear.

He spoke, "Be comforted, child." He appeared to be about ten years her senior. Not a man of ancient years, although he was. Not a man of maturity and command, although he was that, too. He bore no semblance of opulence, no airs, no attitude of superiority. He was simply a man, unspectacular, unassuming. Intuitively, Mary knew this was no ordinary man. "God has chosen you above all women, Mary," he said quietly. He waited as the soft sound of the brook splashed and rippled. It was an appropriate sound, making itself heard with poignant moment. "In this you are highly honored. You are favored as no other." The magnitude of this simple declaration did not register for the child.

"I - I do not understand," she stammered. "Who are you?" Even more important, her heart inquired, *What are you?* Unanswering, his eyes danced with the twilight. He smiled. Whatever anxiety may have stalked her retreated, replaced with expectancy. *Why have you come?* A question of thought, reluctant to make its way to her tongue.

Sensing her expectancy he said, "I have splendid news for you, child."

He spoke to her as a father, yet he was not. He waited. He wanted her to hunger, to seek, to demand what he had to say. It did not take long.

In the pressing necessity of her heart, she begged, peremptorily: *Please!*

αΘω

He had thought of a thousand ways in which what he had to say could be said. He wanted to announce it to the sound of trumpets and the race of stars across the heavens. He wanted to make an *event* of it. These urgings stirred powerfully in his heart but in the end he stated simply, "You are to bear a child." Mary's heart stopped. Questions, unformed, unintelligible, bubbled in her mind. "A son. You will call his name—*Jesus!*" She had been standing but at this, she dropped to her knees and then sat on the grass. She was confused, undone and terrified. It was not his appearance, nor the tone of his voice that unsettled her, but the import in his speech. Weakly, she stammered,

"I cannot..."

"Mary," he continued, each syllable in sweet velvet, "Your son will be very great. He will be the Son of the Most High God." And then the man appeared to succumb to transcendent ecstasy and uttered words that seemed to her as lyrics of a song, soaring beyond her comprehension,

"And the Lord God
will give to him
the throne of his father, David.
He will reign
over the house of Jacob forever
and of his kingdom
there shall be no end!"

It was then that Mary realized that this man is something other than a man. An intimation? A subtle emanation? A verisimilitude of superhuman life? However construed, it caused her to cry out within herself, *"He is an angel of God!"*

"Um!" She swallowed hard in adolescent agitation. *"Um!"* Again. The emotion of the moment took her voice away. Questions came hard into exclamations, "I have never been with—a man!" This, the premise upon which all else was considered. Mary, just preparing to visit her sixteenth

year, knew how babies were made. *I am betrothed!* Instantly, she thought of Joseph. Whatever the angel meant, she somehow understood that Joseph was not a part of it. "How can this happen?" said she. *How can this be?* She inquired not of the possibility, but of the process. But in her heart, she visited deference and in that submission, discovered acceptance.

He, as actuated by emotion as she. This, his highest moment, the zenith of the purpose for which he had been created in lost millennia past. However restive his exultation, his words did not betray him. With perfect lucidity he proclaimed, "The Holy Spirit shall come upon you, child. And the power of the Highest will overshadow you." He took a deep breath, "That *holy thing* born of you shall be called the Son of God." Mary could not speak. A moment passed. They sat quietly. The soothing stillness of evening, like a mother's reassuring hand, extended its calm.

He spoke again in words more subdued. "The wife of Zechariah the priest has conceived a son. She is already in her sixth month." *Elizabeth? I've not seen or heard in months . . ?* He took a few steps and sat upon a rock. Resting his hands on his knees he continued, "She is very old. For how many years has she been taunted as barren by ignorant, unfeeling people! Now she is with child. You must believe, Mary, nothing is impossible with God."

The child had nothing to say, nothing to ask. She felt compassion for this sweet man, this angelic creature who had brought her such words. Silent moments passed between them, he, sitting on the rock, she upon the grass. In her face one could see signs of resignation. Hesitating, she put her hand out to him, touching him, "Let it be done to me as you have said. I wait on the Lord—as a bride—waits for her husband." Only the Father could know what Mary was thinking. How would she become impregnated? It no longer mattered. If this is what God wanted, if He chose to honor her in this manner, she was ready. She withdrew her hand. His head lowered, hands squeezing his knees, relaxing and then squeezing again. "What is your name?" She asked softly. He lifted his eyes and looked at her, seeing the light of love in her eyes. She smiled, as sweet as rain upon a violet.

He sat erect and as if answering the question of royalty instead of that of a peasant girl. He spoke, "My name is *Gabriel*." And with that, he was gone.

αΘω

Mary's thoughts flickered through her mind like the butterflies she loved. *How* was *this to happen? When?* How would she explain it to her mother? Her father? And Joseph? How would he—*how could he!*—react to news like this? She felt trapped between unspeakable ecstasy and terrible convolution.

A quiet girl, yet playful, quick to laugh, content with simple things; the angelic visit still vivid in her thoughts, she relived, she tasted each delicious word. She found herself repeating over and over *"How can this be?"* Her eyes lay softly upon the stars peeking through purpling evening song hushed. She wondered what lived beyond the stars.

It was not abrupt, nor disruptively sudden, but it *was* instantaneous. Softly, tenderly, Mary felt warmth surround her as if her mother had just covered her with a blanket on a winter's night. In her body, in her soul, in the very focus of her being—that eternal part of her—now touched *Something* beyond anything she had known or ever would know again.

Beyond the stars, from a point somewhere in Eternity, he moved toward earth. The world, life and human history waited. It would never be the same.

Jacob was once touched like this and became a cripple. Mary became pregnant, knowing only that she had been known.

αΘω

Her mother's worried eyes. Her father's frown. Of course they had worried. She would herself one day understand what it was like to fret over the disappearance of a child. Her mother's chiding words were, of course, compulsory, but distant and ineffectual. She quickly sensed her child's serenity and yielded the need to disapprove. Questions could wait until morning. Mary was home and safe. That was all that mattered.

Just before slumber claimed the child, as her eyes watched the crescent moon through her window rise toward its zenith, a thought came. The fulfillment of all time had begun, *in her.*

Her secret was secure for the moment.

III

Disgrace

"She is a harlot!" Shrill accusation. "Stone her!" Swift judgment. She had been only eleven when she watched the men in town kill Zephorah. The memory survived through the years with poignant terror.

As girls do, she had combed and braided Mary's hair many times in their moments together. Mary had come to look upon her as an older sister. They lived in adjoining houses. Their families had often dined together, especially on feast days. Although they had played together since Mary's toddler days, they were actually quite different. Mary seemed shy, deferential and demure; Zephorah daring, inquisitive, assertive. It struck some quite odd that two so different should become so close. Rarely had they argued, Mary content to let the older girl decide what games they would play, or what they would do on any given day. This resulted more often than not in daily trips to the town well, a popular place for adolescents to meet and discuss their interests, which almost always concerned the opposite sex.

Zephorah, a shapely fifteen-year-old, flirted and blushed, playfully teasing the young men loitering there, a lively sport for all concerned. Her olive skin, brown almond eyes, lush auburn hair, clothes which clung to her shapely form; she had become the main event among the young stallions at the well. On the way home she amused and entertained the younger girl with lengthy biographies of each boy. It seemed to Mary that Zephorah knew *something* about every young male in Nazareth. "We must not speak of such things, Zepha," spoke Mary, uncomfortably titillated with her friends' romantic fantasies. But the older girl just rolled her eyes and giggled.

"Just wait, little one. One day you will understand."

αΘω

Mary had not understood. What had happened? How did her friend suddenly turn "bad?" How could she have run away with this boy and leave her family to grieve? Three days later she came home alone, afraid and ashamed. Her lover had returned the day before with a good story to tell his friends. He would be admired now. He would be thought manly—experienced. To his father, of course, he told of how she had seduced him. He was a good boy from a good family, his father a priest. So the boy would not suffer. No punishment greater than a sacrifice offered. With that, it would be over. "Why is it," thought Mary, remembering this event years later, "that when a man has his way with a girl, he is thought manly, but when a girl does it, she is a harlot?"

Who would throw the first stone? This honor naturally fell to the one who had been violated. Since he was a mere boy, his father took stone in hand, a broken, jagged piece of thick pottery. But instead of casting the piece himself, the older man thought for a moment and then handed it to his son. This confused the boy, frightening him. The eyes of his father-priest, however, were demanding, unforgiving. His son looked at Zephorah weeping in the street where she had been harshly thrown, her hair filthy with dust, her eyes streaming dark tears, pleading. Somewhere in the back of the crowd which stood more than ten deep, a mother screamed, "She is but a child!" The eyes of the boy's father prevailed. With a force strengthened by fear, his hand traced the arc. The stone struck between the eyes just above the nose. Blood spurted. Zephorah fell. Seconds later, dozens of stones rained on the girl. A heavy stone struck her in the head, mercifully crushing her skull. The boy watched. Someday, he would be a priest himself.

αΘω

The basket fell from her hands as Mary shuddered, remembering the brutal death of her friend. Her mother had reacted to the news of her encounter with the angel in disbelief. She was now two weeks late and the questions were tense and fearful. When she told her mother that she had been chosen by God, she was met with anger and tears; but how could a mother be expected to understand a thing like this? "And that is not all, Mother." Mary continued tearfully, "The angel said that Elizabeth is also with child—and she is *old!*"

Her mother looked at her, stunned. "Hush, child! We do not speak of such things." Mary's mother thought, *How could she have known? My cousin has been in seclusion for more than six months.* Elizabeth had not publicly announced her condition. Nine months is a long time to wait for a promise. Anything could happen. Only trusted friends and relatives knew. Of course, her mother knew of the special circumstances of her cousin's pregnancy. *But*

Mary could not possibly know, unless . . ? As the truthfulness of her daughter's claims found credence in her heart, she reached for the child and held her to her breast. "You shall *not* be judged, my lamb. No indeed," she held her tighter, smiling through wet diamonds, "you shall not be judged."

Abruptly she ended the embrace and held her daughter tightly by the shoulders as if she might escape. Mary's eyes widened. "You must go to her!" With urgency. "Yes! That *is* the thing to do! You must go to her now. I will get your things." Instantly her mother began preparing Mary's things. She continued talking, instructing, "You're not to worry about anything. You will be safe there. You will be in a priest's own house!" Words cascaded. "I'll deal with your father--*and Joseph. I'll see to them both!*" Her mother was now in command. "*Hurry!*"

Mary, dumfounded at her mother's actions, and frightened.

αΘω

In a letter to her cousin Elizabeth, Mary's mother wrote:

> *My Dear Cousin,*
> *Please be kind to accept my daughter into your home.*
> *She is with child…*

The letter explained all that Mary's mother knew, all that her daughter had revealed. The dispatch-bearer left ahead of Mary and would reach the house of Zechariah well before the girl's entourage. Elizabeth would be waiting, anticipating her arrival.

The trip took almost a week and the path, as always, arduous and chafing. Down into the Esdraelon Plain, across the Jordan fords to avoid Samaria, down the eastern bank of the river, crossing again at Jericho, the climb back up to and through Jerusalem and out into the Judean hill-country until the house of Zechariah came into view. The strain of the trip evaporated as hopeful expectations rose in Mary. Barely within hearing, she began shouting *"Elizabeth! Elizabeth!"*

At first, the sound was as faint as that of a distant bird. Then at last, she clearly discerned her name, *"Elizabeth!"* in a girl-child's voice. The swelling in her stomach visibly moved. Her body responded in an enchanting sensate awareness of something rich and full and beautiful. Ecstasy seized her. When at last her aged eyes saw her young cousin she shouted. *"Oh, Mary! How blessed you are among all women! And blessed is the child you are to bear!* The two women met and embraced. Tears of consummate joy for Elizabeth. Tears of relief and comfort for Mary. An old woman and a child. A woman long past childbearing yet with child, and a woman who has not known a man also with child. Wondrous *enceinte!*

Elizabeth took Mary's face in her hands and said, "And how is it permitted me that the mother of my Lord should come to me? Hm?" Mary's eyes glistened. "Did you know that the moment I heard your voice the babe within me leaped for joy?" She paused to let the words have their effect. "Oh my child, your mother has revealed to me all that has happened to you. I am so proud of you for believing the things that were told to you by the Lord. You are so richly and deservedly blessed!"

Mary at last found her speech, *"Cousin Elizabeth!"* Letting her hands meet in front of her, the girl-child erupted, *"My heart is exploding!"* A not un-butterfly-like pirouette. She flounced to her knees. *"Oh how I love the Lord! Oh God my Savior, how my spirit soars!"* Everything was an exclamation. *"He's chosen me, Elizabeth! Me! I am nobody! I am not a princess! I am poor. How is it that he has chosen me!? Elizabeth!"* She reached for the older woman embracing her vigorously, *"Elizabeth, the angel told me that from this time forth all generations will call me blessed! Can you imagine? God has done a great thing to me! Holy is his Name!"*

Beyond her understanding of historical and national events and far beyond her adolescent comprehension, using her voice, her lips, the Spirit within her exulted in jubilant song…

"His mercy goes forth to all who love him
from age to age to age!
He has shown his strength
by scattering the tyrants
in all their imaginations.
"He has put down mighty men
and exalted a poor woman-child.

"He has filled the hungry
with good things
and sent the rich away empty.
"In remembrance of his mercy,
he has come to Israel
as he promised to Abraham
and his seed forever."

IV

Forerunner

Elizabeth, *barren* Elizabeth, elderly Elizabeth gave birth to a son. Over the past several months she and Mary shared their feelings, their experiences with God; and held long conversations about their soon to be born babies.

Early before the sun had begun to awaken the skies, Elizabeth awakened Mary. "It is time," she whispered. "Go, find Alethea." Mary, her blood pounding, driving sleep from her eyes, dressed quickly and ran to wake the midwife.

She observed, carefully, every detail as she busied herself being useful. Hours drained the color from Elizabeth's face as Mary watched her stomach rise and then relax, her body pushing the babe into place. She watched as Elizabeth rested between pains. She watched as the baby's head began to show and then suddenly made his entry into the sunlit room of mid-morning. She watched the cutting of the cord and heard the first cries as his little pink body was washed and wrapped tightly in soft blankets.

The infant was handed to exhausted Elizabeth. Tears of joy filled her wrinkled cheeks, falling into the baby's tiny hand. As he wriggled inside his blanket, she felt the same movements that she'd felt for months inside her body. "I know you," she smiled as his tiny eyes gazed, unfocused, into hers in seeming wonder.

Zechariah had been watching patiently, but could wait no longer. He went to Elizabeth, kissed her on the forehead and put out his arms to hold his son. Elizabeth laid the baby in his awkward old arms. He thought his breath was being drawn from him. He held the baby high over his head. The reality had struck him like a sudden wind. *This --this is my son! I have a son! I have a son!* Had he been able to speak, he would have been heard all through Judea and into the next country. Alas, his heart soared in silent gratitude to God for his mercy to an old man such as he. He staggered at the reality of new life.

Sensing the private intimacy between the new father and mother, Mary made motion to leave the room. "Wait," spoke Elizabeth softly. And then to her husband, "Give the child to Mary for a moment, my husband, and come, sit here next to me. It's been a trying day for both of us."

Mary held the child tightly. *How small and perfect he is,* she thought, wondering what her own baby would look like. As he stretched his little body against the tight blankets, Mary felt a flutter in her stomach for the first time. Not wanting to take anything from this special day for Elizabeth and Zechariah, she said nothing. *"Cousins,"* she thought and smiled knowingly.

Elizabeth's friends, confidants and relatives came to be happy with her. The secret of this astounding event was out. The word had spread. Ancient Elizabeth, thought well past the time of childbearing, has given birth to a son. They brought food and wine. They danced and played. Women clucked and cooed over the infant. Those first days took the shape of a week. The child would be circumcised tomorrow.

In the Temple, the babe shrieked as the priests performed the service of Abraham. "My," quoth one of the women in great humor, "young Zechariah has the voice of an ass."

Everyone at the Temple service laughed. Elizabeth, her voice as clear and uncompromising as steel, said simply, "His name is John! His voice will proclaim the coming of the Lord!" Her tone arrested attention.

Laughter ceased. In the embarrassed silence that followed, a close relative said quietly and with respect, "Elizabeth…come now; there is no one in the family by that name."

Zechariah sat mute as all had come to expect of him. Still, he was this child's father. They gestured to him. Ignorance is monstrously embarrassing. Zechariah could hear every word everyone had said. Though he could not speak, he could hear as well as any of them. It is remarkable, he thought, how people think that because one cannot speak, one also cannot hear. Stupidly, they made signs at him. They mouthed the question, "What will you name the child?" hoping he might understand their question. Zechariah dropped his head in exasperated resignation. He rubbed his eyes. He had not spoken a syllable in nine long months. He gestured with his hands to make way. The people parted to allow him room to maneuver. On the wooden table lay a tablet. Taking a writing instrument the doddering old man wrote, "His name is John!" He held it high over his head passing through each point of the compass. More embarrassed silence followed until he completed the circle, all eyes on the arc of the tablet.

Then came a shout, *"His name is John! Praise to God Almighty!"* an exclamation of commanding power.

αΘω

To say that all were surprised is to understate the case. They were dumfounded and frightened. Zechariah's shout had forced the issue of the tangible, miraculous *Presence!* And to Jews who were not permitted so much as to speak or write his name, this was a fearsome thing.

How *does* one speak or write of such things? Not even the Scriptures can adequately explain the awful fear that came upon the prophets of Baal when, *alas,* the fire fell. Who can describe the terrible angst of the Egyptians as they furiously drove through towering walls of water in futile pursuit of the Hebrews? Or the thoughts of King Saul when a solitary stone from a boy's sling struck down the giant? When the miraculous unfolds, when the unfamiliar and unexpected comes before one's very eyes, fear is rational.

Yet, an elderly woman giving birth to an infant, or an old man's speech after more than nine months of silent muteness; these things are hardly on the magnitude of parting the Red Sea. Is it because these friends, these well wishers, these celebrants had never in their lifetimes seen such things? Here we chronicle angelic visitations and the impregnation of old women and virgins, and speech withheld and speech released in paeans of praise. Are these things mere tremors of the earthshaking to come? Perhaps rather, it is the question that provokes fear, What do these things mean?

V

Prophet of the Highest

The ancient priest was not done. Lifting his hands to heaven and gazing at the ceiling he said,

> *Blessed be the Lord God of Israel, for he has redeemed and visited his people! Salvation has come to us from the house of his servant, David—just as he promised it would. We will be saved from those that hate us.*

No one doubted the prophetic character of Zechariah's oration. This priest had always been a quiet man, not given to mere self-aggrandizing showmanship. All conceded that the Holy Spirit possessed him. The news had an effervescent effect. Smiles appeared. Elation accompanied thoughts of deliverance from Roman rule. *Is this child the long-promised Messiah?* Then the old man's prophecy took a different turn.

> *There is purpose to this deliverance! There is reason! There is rationale! We are to become a merciful people. Remember his holy covenant that he swore to Abraham our father? He has saved us from our enemies, yes! But he has saved us to serve him without fear, in righteousness and holiness for the rest of our lives on earth.*

Zechariah spoke with power and certainty. As long as he spoke of God and his mercy, those who heard were attentive. But when the subject turned to personal responsibility for mercy, when it turned to the people themselves, thoughts turned elsewhere. They were wondering what all this had to do with the birth of his son. *"What of the child?" they cried.*

It did not take much to persuade Zechariah to be taken with his son. He lifted the infant in his arms and held him to his breast. Then he held him at arm's length. Gazing happily at the baby's face he proclaimed,

My son! My little one! You will be called the prophet of the Highest. You will go before him. You will prepare the hearts of the people to receive him. You will reveal the heart of God's mercy in bringing Salvation to deliver us.

In benediction, the old man turned to those standing by and proclaimed,

The Dayspring on high has dawned upon us; to give light to those who sit in darkness and in the shadow of death; to guide our feet into the way of peace.

Dayspring! Such a magnificent word!

A story is told of a caravan lost in the wilderness of the desert sand. Its constituents, overtaken by the blackness of night, sit down to wait for death. Hopelessness drones through the cold. Helpless hours in darkness; when suddenly their eyes behold a spectacle of matchless beauty. A daystar springs from the eastern horizon and begins its climb toward the heavens. As it does, the sky following it brightens, and the great orb of shining gold takes its first glimpse of a prescient day, bringing illumination and warmth upon the earth. The caravan, encouraged, rises with this Dayspring star, this brilliant antecedent of coming dawn, and goes its way, and over the rise, over the crest of the hill, they find that for which their hearts have longed—Zion, the City of their God.

Without full understanding, Zechariah was telling that his child, his Dayspring, refers not to Jesus Messiah, but to John. He it is who brings the hope of dawn to a people who sit in darkness and the shadow of death. With the rising sun, this lovely morning star is obliterated and is seen no more. Such is the story of our beloved John who himself declared, *"He must increase, but I must decrease!"*

The old priest turned prophet sat down. *"Water!"* he muttered. His eyes focused on something distant, on nothing, on everything. He appeared stunned. Someone brought him a cup of water. Zechariah wept.

αΘω

She sat still in the night. The house quiet. The babe had awakened, cried and then quieted at Elizabeth's swollen breast. All were asleep, except this young, pregnant virgin. Her belly had begun to increase in size, for this was her sixth month. In these quiet hours of very early morning, she thought of Joseph, she thought of her parents, she thought of Nazareth, she thought of her quiet place by the spring and what had happened there. It was time to go home.

αΘω

The days that followed stretched into years of happiness for Elizabeth and Zechariah. Almost from his birth little John lived and breathed in the ambiance of the Hebrew Scriptures. Since the events surrounding the angelic visitation, Zechariah had become more than zealous in raising his only child as God intended. A razor never touched his hair and it grew until it fell to his waist. John did not grow up as did the other children. As one in preparation to be a Nazirite, from the beginning his differentness alienated him from friends he might otherwise enjoy. He seemed withdrawn and sad to those who didn't know him well. If the truth of the matter be told, he laughed and enjoyed himself more than most. His parents thought him happy and well adjusted. John simply didn't need to be around others as much as other boys needed their peers. Content to draw his companionship from within himself and from his feeling of God's care for him, John's character formed into a pillar of internal rectitude. After his parents died, he left the family home to live a solitary existence in the wilderness of Judea. They would never know how their son came to his grim end at the scheming of Herodias, her daughter Salome and the cowardice of Herod Antipas.

VI

The Dream

How could she have done this? Who has she been seeing? What should I do? He thought in the dark, agitated and pained by the discovery of his beloved's pregnancy. His head hurt. Terrible, jealous thoughts of her with another man flooded his brain, relentless and torturing. Impossible to sleep! He knew that to make much of this would accomplish nothing but embarrassment and disgrace. Despite the shock, the agony, the humiliation, he loved her still. He felt robbed. He felt robbed of his rights as a husband. He felt robbed of her virginity. He felt robbed of his wife. He felt robbed of the very love of his life. In his pain and his rage he thought, *She has done enough already to disgrace herself—and me!* The possibility of stoning entered his head. This he could not endure. He considered a quiet divorce. He would have to write a letter. He would need at least two witnesses. Who? What would become of her? What does a pregnant woman with no husband do?

Joseph made things from wood. Over the years of working with his father, he had become an extraordinary craftsman who could make a beautiful toy for a child, or a prized piece of furniture for a Roman home. Carpentry was his talent, but it was also his business. Joseph's trade, as long as he was healthy, guaranteed his income. He was not rich, but neither was he among the poor. The best thing that had ever happened to him was this lovely v*irgin,* the most beautiful, gentle creature he had ever known. Mary possessed his heart, his every thought. The desire to build her a home and for her to have his children consumed him. Knowledge of her pregnancy staggered him beyond endurance, shattering his dreams and along with his dreams, his heart. His mind tortured and pained, drew him into a vacuum of agonizing loneliness. The pit in his stomach turned into stone, and from stone into the excruciating lava of pain.

αΘω

Shattered dreams are the cruelest torturers. They lurk behind visions of contentment as hungry scavengers. They sear the heart with agony unimagined. They destroy life. They make one pull away from something good for fear that it will be taken away. It is easier and less painful to pull away from your dreams yourself than to have them ripped from you. It is easier to avoid the risk of rejection than to actually be rejected. That is why so few dare to dream, dare to risk, dare to try.

Woman? She is hardly more than a child. *What is wrong with me? I thought she loved me. Why would she seek comfort in the arms of another?* Outside a cricket chirped. Stars leisurely pirouetted, preparing to meet the dawn. Wearily, his body shifted into a position of quiet, somniferous breathing...

"Joseph, son of David?"

Words that made his eyelids tremble. He glanced toward the casement before closing his eyes again. *Still dark outside. Not yet time to get up.* He felt himself sink deeper into his bed. At last it felt good, like a womb. In a moment his hypnotic breathing returned.

"Joseph, son of David!"

Son of David? He hadn't thought of himself in those terms for years. The words comforted him. His breathing deepened. Words whispered quietly into his dreams.

Words emitting no sounds, only thoughts. Words permeating his mind.

"Joseph, son of David!"

Strange thoughts formed as he slept,

"Take Mary to yourself...as your wife...not to fear that she is with child...

The corners of his lips teased into a questioned smile.

> *What is conceived in her is of the Holy Spirit...*
> *She will give birth to a son. God's Son—your son...*
> *You will give him a name...give him the name, Jesus, He will save his people from their sins...*
> *Remember the words of the prophet Isaiah...'A virgin will conceive and be with child and will give birth to a son, and they will call him Immanuel,' which means, "God with us..."'*
> *...your son, Joseph...*

He awoke with an enormous sense of release and peace. *Mary still a virgin?* He loved her more intensely than ever before. *Can it be?* More than life, he wanted her to be his. He needed no further encouragement to do what his dreams had released him to do.

Dreams do have a way of colliding with judgment.

αΘω

Mary's mother opened the door to let in the morning air. There stood Joseph. The surprise of his unannounced presence provoked her. Their last conversation had been tense, accusative. Despite wanting to believe her daughter's story, she had wondered if, in truth, Joseph and Mary had yielded to their sexual urges. Now look at the mess they had on their hands! Joseph, of course, had been overwhelmed at the news of Mary's pregnancy and outraged at her mother's accusations regarding his integrity and his good intentions. He had left the house in anger and hadn't returned until now.

"I am sorry to startle you." Joseph ventured, "but I wanted to tell you that I know that Mary is with your cousin, Elizabeth." The mother's hand went to her mouth in alarm. "I am leaving this morning to get her. Please make the wedding plans while I am gone." She took a deep breath that betrayed her relief. Her face allowed a cautious smile. She knew the law. She knew that Joseph could easily put Mary away, voiding the contract between them, perhaps even have her stoned, if he had chosen.

"Dear mother," he continued, "an angel came to me in a dream last night. He told me that this child is of the Holy Spirit. That it is a boy and that his name shall be called,

"Jesus!" They spoke the same word at the same time. Each stared at the other, aghast. She had told no one of the baby's name, especially Joseph. Knowing, deeply knowing that a thing is true, despite all contrary natural evidence, is indeed, a thing of awe. This was such a moment. This was a moment of knowing.

"He will be born into the house of David," Joseph spoke as though the statement was prophetic. After a long reflective pause, he put his hand on her shoulder and smiled. The tension between them had evaporated. "I'll be back in about two weeks with Mary—*and your grandson."*

αΘω

So Joseph took Mary as his wife—*gladly!* He knew that he loved her and that was exactly what God required of him. Joseph and Mary were quietly married. He took her to his home and there they waited as her middle continued to swell. Though his desire was to share pleasure with his wife, they had no union until she gave birth to her son—*his son.*

VII

Rome: The Senate Chambers

My Uncle Julius!" Octavian surmised. "One of his most…what shall I say?…elegant accomplishments?" He referred to the *descripto orbis,* the Great Registration ordered by Julius Caesar which had taken thirty-two years to complete. Octavian also held the title, *Caesar.* Under that title, he had actually finished his uncle's work. Under that title, he had defeated the forces of Mark Antony and Cleopatra. Now he had been accorded the designation, "Augustus Caesar," emperor for life.

"It is in our obvious interest, don't you think, that the empire should be appraised as to the extent of its tax resources?" The Roman Senate robed in white trimmed in gold and red, reclined in their respective places of honor. "The precedent has been set by Caesar himself. I shall therefore build on this precedent by ordering a decree that every male in the empire be valued as to his profession, his fortune, and as to his wards."

This decree came to be known as the *Breviarium totius imperii,* written on skin parchment in Augustus' own hand. In addition to the number of citizens, both freedmen and slaves, it provided information on the empire's allies under arms, the nature and composition of the fleets, of the kingdoms, provinces, and of the *tributes,* or taxes. When Augustus died some fourteen years later, the actual count of this registration was made public for the first time. The Roman Empire, vast beyond comprehension, counted more than twenty million souls, yet had no sense of humanitarian function. There were problems. Chieftains, Clan leaders, Sheiks, Shamans, Satraps and Kings tended to rebel or have their own way of caring for these matters of state. Of these, a powerful king in the region of the Hebrews, Herod the Great, enjoyed the greatest power and influence.

The states under the rule of Herod were among the allied kingdoms, or *Regina reddita.* However influential his reach, he could not have refused to submit to and be a cooperative part of this registration. All of the coin in Herod's states bore the image of Caesar. He had no choice. He must comply.

Augustus continued, "I shall appoint twenty of the most able and trusted officials who are rigidly devoted to administrative procedure, to accomplish this task. They shall travel to every state governed by Caesar (referring to himself) and shall cause to be registered every male in his home with his property. They shall assemble the required staff necessary to accomplish this task and shall do so under the decree and authority of Caesar."

"What of Herod?" This from one of the senators representing the eastern provinces.

"What of Herod?" replied Augustus. He considered the question by repeating it. "What of that disingenuous old fool? How many wives has he had?"

"I think the latest count is ten," remarked another. Laughter.

"And how many of them has he had killed?" asked Caesar cynically. "And his sons! How many of his sons did he dispatch?"

"Three! He has killed three of his own issue."

"Poor bastards," replied Caesar. "I'd rather be Herod's pig than his son." More laughter. "Do you anticipate a problem?" He remembered with no small revulsion the Jewishness of the Hebrew potentate. Though Herod was not a Jew in the strictest sense of that term, he was thought of as such by Roman authorities. "He may be insane, but is he not a Roman ally?" The implied threat was clear.

"Just a complication, Caesar. He will want to carry out the registration of the Hebrews as they have done it for generations."

Augustus appeared irritated. He looked at his polished fingernails disinterestedly. "And just how is that, Pontius? I am sure you are expert in such matters?"

"Eminent Emperor," responded the senator acidly, "I am merely your servant, but yes, I have lived among the Jews."

"You are to be envied, Pontius." A twitter of laughter.

Ignoring the slight, the senator continued, "The Hebrews return to their place of birth for such things. They like to connect their odd existence to their ancestral roots."

"How the census is taken is of small importance to me, Senator. However, I do require thoroughness and accuracy. Let Herod do it his way, but I will instruct the field governor to watch him. Enough of this! Let it be done! Bring me the seal." And thus it was that the decree went out from Caesar ugustus that the entire world should be registered.

VIII

Labor Begins

No one completed the trip from Galilee to Judea in less than three days. With a pregnant woman approaching the birth of her infant, it took much longer. She did not complain but the expression on her face betrayed her. The lurching of the ass caused her back to spasm. Tributaries of pain explored her muscles as she stiffened against the motion. Her husband walked beside her, his hand massaging the small of her back. Often she laid her arm across his shoulders for support at which time their faces met and lip touched the lip in a gentle caress. When it became unbearable, she walked. This helped for a time but soon she felt exhausted and once again mounted the donkey. Even in the cool of winter, sweat dripped from Joseph's brow as concern for Mary grew.

At the Jericho fords, inns and commercial eating establishments crowded with travelers; so many people, returning to their place of heritage. Herod had ordered it, or was it Caesar? As if everyone in the country was on a forced holiday; camels, carts, asses and oxen trampled dense dust into rasping lungs. Damp cloths draped or held over dry, parched lips. Walkers. Thousands of Jews walked great distances to be registered so Caesar could fill his coffers.

Joseph's career as a carpenter had yet to materialize. His father had not given him much to get started. His family was not rich, but Joseph's "inheritance" had been unnecessarily meager. His father thought him foolish to marry a woman already with child. "I cannot invest in a son so given to throwing away his life. What do you think will become of your business when others discover your wife's *adultery*?" His father's generosity truncated, Joseph left with nothing but the tools of his trade, a solitary ass, modest clothing and enough money he had saved over the years to—hopefully—begin a new life for himself, Mary and the child. The inns along the way had taken most of what he had. He hoped it wouldn't be too difficult to set up shop in Bethlehem; if not Bethlehem, Jerusalem. He preferred the smaller community of Bethlehem. *Yes, Bethlehem, the city of my fathers, be kind to me.* But would it support him and his family? Such questions haunt the thoughts of young adventurers.

αΘω

The uphill journey from Jericho to Jerusalem had taken its usual toll. Mary felt faint. Through the city and out the western gate, Joseph walked beside her, shoulders sagging. The sun settled quietly, golden and red, its radiant crown disappearing over the rising horizon. Deepening twilight crept across the Judean countryside. A soft glow from the light of Bethlehem lay in the distance. A welcome sight to both of them. "There it is my darling," said Joseph quietly. "Our new home. I hope there are enough consumers and critics of wood in this town to support us."

"God will support us, Joseph," scolded Mary playfully. Exhausted Mary. How could she laugh? "Where is your faith? Do you think He would ever abandon his Son?" A prophetic question, ominous with portent.

Joseph, of course, could not have recognized any prophetic portent. "I am glad to see you are still in light spirits," he smiled. Mary smiled back. Smiles were becoming to her. Despite her distended abdomen, perhaps because of it, her smiles were radiant and beautiful.

The lights of Bethlehem drew closer. You could hear laughter now. Torches penetrating the night. People moving about. Though the day crept toward evening, the crowds were restive. Family and friends who hadn't seen each other for months or years were joyfully reuniting. Merchants and concessionaires, followers and hangers-on of human traffic, hawked their wares. The surrounding countryside spoke of peace and solicitude. The city spoke activity, energy and commerce. "Now to find a place to spend the night," said Joseph with the naive expectation of a young, inexperienced traveler.

"Oh!" from Mary. Joseph, alarmed at her tone, looked at her quizzically. Mary grasped her abdomen. "Oh!" again. Her face grimaced. Joseph did not need to be told what was happening. "Oh Joseph!" this time in anguish, "My water!" Each word, each syllable she spoke was an exclamation followed by sucking breath. He could see the clear liquid dripping from the flanks of the ass. Abruptly, Mary's eyes rolled up into her head with the intensity of the first sharp pain, "Oh my Lord God! Joseph! Please! Hurry!" Joseph looked at her as all men look at their wives at this moment, helpless and afraid.

αΘω

No one along the road seemed to notice what was happening. No one stopped to help. No one paid attention to the young woman on the ass, leaning against her husband lest she fall. No family, no aunts or uncles, no grandparents, not even a supportive friend. No one to hold them up. No one to sustain them. Mary and Joseph were alone, lost in a world of humanity scurrying about their own concerns. She began to weep. "Please, God?" she whimpered. Joseph was no veteran father. He, too, was young and inexperienced in these things. He was not much help. Slowly, the instruction of Elizabeth came seeping through the walls of pain and loneliness. "Joseph, we must find a place for me to lie down. Now!" Her dazed husband looked at her again, as if wondering how she could be rational at a time like this.

αΘω

"An inn!" Joseph's reason asserted itself. "I must find an inn." He reeled forward, yanking the reins of the ass to make it walk faster. Mary lurched, but held on.

As it is in so many towns and cities, places to stay the night were erected near the perimeter of the city. One of the first structures they approached happened to be an inn. Joseph entered the door and found an innkeeper sitting at a table pushing around tablets and looking stressed. "I need a room for the night," said Joseph, "My wife is..."

"You will not find a room in this town tonight, young man. Can't you see Bethlehem is flooded with travelers? This is David's city. Everybody wants to be of the house and lineage of David," he went on with practiced disdain. The shock on Joseph's face did not register with the innkeeper, bewildered and stupefied by the question, *What to do!?*

"My wife," he stammered, "My wife is with child." Then urgency gripped him. "Please," he implored the innkeeper, "My wife is giving birth to a baby. She is in pain. *My God, man, isn't there something you can do?"*

The innkeeper sobered thoughtfully, not a heartless man, but what could he do? "Already I am overcrowded. I cannot take away someone's room who has already paid. I'm sorry, there is not much I can do for you." An embarrassed pause. "I don't know what to say." Resignation. He hoped Joseph could comprehend the obvious.

"You have nothing? Nothing at all?" *This cannot be happening*, thought Joseph anxious and panicked.

"Not unless you want the stable," responded the innkeeper lifting his hands, shrugging his shoulders as if explaining an absurdity. Joseph saw no absurdity at all.

"Yes!" he said in relief, "Yes! The stable! How much?" The innkeeper just stared at Joseph. It was only a few seconds but to Joseph, it seemed longer. "How much?" he demanded.

"Keep your money," from the innkeeper. "You can stay there without charge." Not a man lacking in kindness, *Young people!* He thought, as he rose from the table shaking his head, "Follow me." Joseph did as instructed. He plodded through the door and around the corner of the building, Joseph in his train. A low structure loomed in the darkness. For all the troubling features of this scene, the innkeeper felt a satisfying sense of warmth. *God help them*, a prayer again, of mere thought.

αΘω

It appeared incongruous for an inn to boast of a stable. Stables were usually the province of farmers and shepherds, housing animals of the field and pasture. The more popular inns, however, maintained such stables for the animals of their guests. They were populated with the usual conveyances, camels, donkeys, an occasional ox. Located at the rear of the inn, this stable stood separate from the main building, adjoining it a large sheepfold where shepherds lodged their sheep for the night. The air hung heavy with the usual smells of animal waste, hay and the body odors of the animals, smells both pleasant and unpleasant. It was a stable. Creatures crowded, both inside and outside. Three camels lay squatting on the ground around the entrance to the stable, their nostrils blowing cloud puffs into the cold evening air. Within, Joseph found a small enclosure, filled it with fresh hay, spread robes and blankets on the hay and there Mary, with difficulty, laid herself down.

An hour passed. Then two. The scurrying about outside in the streets had subsided to an occasional inebriated soul who had imbibed too much wine. Dust from the day had settled. Airs grew cooler, a blessing not lost on the birthing young mother whose brow beaded with sweat. People asleep. Inside the stable it was warmer. Not much, but enough. The body heat from the asses and oxen made life slightly more comfortable. An occasional chicken perched here and there with peeping eyes signifying an end to the day's scratching and clucking. Quiet scurries of small creatures. Mary lay sweating and wincing, her chest heaving, her abdomen contracting.

IX

Shepherd's Campfire

Coals from the campfire glow hot and red from yellow flames recently fallen. Bright flickers still spurt here and there, settling softly among the embers. Still the fire crackled, sending sparks like tiny shooting stars. The air adorned pleasantly with the smell of burning cedar. Lemuel hugged his thick wool cloak around his shoulders, his eyelids drooping with approaching sleep. Stars hung above with uncommon presence against purplish black velvet. Lemuel, however, was not thinking about stars. His head nodded with thoughts envisioning the lovely Sheililah. He thought of her eyes, her golden hair, the fullness of her lips and just as his thoughts began to consider the rest of this quean beauty, Ahiam spoke,

"Aaah!" It was loud enough to open Lemuel's eyes and twitter his heart. The first thought of a startled shepherd is, *An attack!* His hand reached with automatic practice for his staff. But it was not an attack. Ahiam, who was not preoccupied with blood-surging dreams of Sheililah, was taken rather with what appeared to be an anomaly in the heavens. Ahiam's exclamation sounded as if the breath were knocked out of him. *No alarm amongst the sheep,* Lemuel's second thought. An eerie incandescence enveloped them. It was not soft and glowing. It burst upon them, bright and abrasive. Gleaming. Frightening.

Young Jesse, a mere boy, emitted a high-pitched wail. Lemuel stared at him, agitated. Veteran shepherd that he was, he felt his presence of mind slipping. He thought he might urinate. The fourth member of the group, Elieazar, began to flee. Unheard of among shepherds. Shepherds were known to die protecting their flock. Elieazar suddenly stopped, confronted by an apparition which nailed him to the earth. His muscles could not work. He froze where he stood.

Lemuel had seen just about everything his calling had to offer. He had confronted and defeated predators of every description, animal and human. Lemuel was not easily awed by the events around him. There was the time for example, when a drunken centurion attempted to make sport of him. The officer had drawn his short sword as if to decapitate him. Lemuel stood straight, galvanizing the man with his eyes, almost daring him to strike. When the blow came, Lemuel caught the soldier's wrist with his hand and held it as if in a vise. Then abruptly, he laughed. The officer's colleagues saw the humor of the event and also laughed. The embarrassed soldier desisted and lowered his sword. Lemuel was not a man of whom one easily made sport.

This light, however, jolted him. He did not rise to the moment with detached coolness. He, too, was afraid. His stomach recoiled in a wave of mild nausea. Perspiration wept through trembling, clammy skin. What he saw was totally unknown to him—indeed, unknown to all living men.

The "apparition" that had so arrested Elieazar emanated a brilliance that permeated this theater on the hillside. It was human in appearance, yet inhuman. A man. A creature. A source of unimaginable light. After a moment of silence, it spoke. *"Do not be frightened."* Despite his appearance, despite the supernatural tension of the moment, his words, indeed, were soothing. If it is possible to go from intense fear to calm expectancy in an instant of time, it happened in the terror-stricken hearts of these peasant shepherds. *"I bring you good news of immense joy."*

αΘω

Joy is the result and the essence of a love fulfilled. It is one of the many reasons for the gift of life. We may count it useful or productive to live one's life in the service of another, or of God. This is another reason for the gift of life. But it is the simple things of joy, the smile and laughter of a grandchild, the lifting of a cloud to the heavens, the smell of jasmine, the announcement of a birth; all of these also are reasons for life and living.

"What is this news? For whom is it intended?" The words struggled to emerge from Lemuel's mouth. Despite his dumbfounded condition, somewhere in the back of his consciousness lurked the question, *"Why is a messenger from God bringing news to insignificant, unknown shepherds?"*

Why indeed? Why does God invest himself in the insignificant? With the whole of Creation from which to choose, why choose earth? From among all the peoples of the earth, why choose a tiny sect called Jews? Why choose Abraham? Moses? Elijah? Why choose a slight youth to slay a threatening giant? Why choose Bethlehem? Why choose a manger, a stable of animal smells, in which to birth his Son? Why does God, as he moves events among men, have the perversity to make small men large and large men small? Why this delight in the unimpressive, the insignificant? Why his strength made perfect in weakness? Is it because he is attracted to humility and put off by the proud strutting of human arrogance? God holds sway over the heavens. Men of power and influence have no power or influence with him.

This is perhaps exciting news to the disenfranchised, the governed, for those whose lives are dramatically affected by the whims of other men, men who except for status are just like them. But that is hardly the point. It could be argued that the impoverished have stronger character, are less pretentious and full of themselves. Alas, character flaws, pretentiousness and pride are as ubiquitous among the poor as among the rich. The poor are as quick to take unwarranted advantage of a weaker neighbor as are the rich. There is no honor among beasts, whether rich or poor.

It is, nonetheless, a fact that pain is greater among those without the resources to make life more pleasant. Suffering is more prevalent. Babies die quicker and more often. More violence and murder. Hunger. The nagging feeling of being in need greater. The struggle for survival more intense. The malaise of will and determination more accepted and understood. More of their lives spent in prisons. Though many cry out against the terrible Fate that decreed their poverty, God is still more readily received among such people. They seek him for they have discovered that mankind does not love them, does not know what to do with them. They have no place else to go. If God does not help them, they will perish.

Of course, the verdict of the affluent and sufficient is that these pathetic creatures need a God. They invent something, someone larger than themselves, larger than anything they know in order to help them survive in an adversarial, competitive world. Poor things. That is obviously why their God favors them, is it not?

Lemuel, however, could not think beyond *Why?* Simple man. For him there was none of this insufferable, pedantic reasoning. Lemuel, a man of whom not even Rome made sport, was afraid.

αΘω

...news of great joy to all people. For unto you is born this day in the city of David, a Savior who is Christ, the Lord!

The words had yet to have much meaning to Lemuel and his friends. They were still reeling from the spectacle of the angel's appearance. While God's angel spoke of peace and comfort, while he spoke of the coming of a Savior, their hearts pounded with excitement. When suddenly, there was with the angel myriads of heavenly creatures. The scene caused the three men and the boy to fall to the ground. Ahaim cried out, "God help us! We shall be slain!" But they were not slain. The heavenly beings instead began to sing,

> *Glory to God in the highest, and on earth, peace and goodwill toward men!*

And as suddenly as they appeared, the angel and the heavenly creatures were gone. The happy angelic rejoicing hushed. Sounds of night quickly descended. Fire coals snapped. Sheep heads lowered. A frog croaked in a distant stream, the sound carrying to their ears as they looked at one another, each clinging to the ground as if they would fly off it, their minds so dazzled they were sore. "Will they come back?" whimpered the boy.

The question hung unanswered for a passing respite until Lemuel spoke, "I think they have left us." Silence settled upon them like a sweet syrup. "Now," he whispered, "Gather the sheep. We go to see this great thing that has come to pass."

Lemuel, Ahaim, Elieazar and Jesse with their combined flocks of sheep descended the grassy slopes of the hills surrounding Bethlehem. In the darkness of early morning, the wooly creatures bleated their way into the sheepfold adjoining the stable. There they found Mary and Joseph, cuddled together in the hay, and the baby sleeping next to them.

αΘω

From the Sanctuary of Eternity
He came.
From hallowed halls of holy heights
He came.
Through Andromeda, Pisces and Orion,
Through Sun and Moon this Scion
Of Omnipotence came.

Only shepherds were told.
In the night wintry and cold,
They nestled their flocks
As the embers glowed
And angels knocked
At the hearts of children,
He came.

To a stable small,
To hay and smells
Of animal tells,
He came.

To a virgin, to a man,
To all men He came.

What shall we then do?
How then, shall we answer?

αΘω

X

The Birth of Jesus

The shepherds could not be contained. They told everyone they saw about what happened to them the night before in the hills and finding the child in the stable. Most laughed at them. Too many nights in the wilderness make men odd. Some did listen and came to see for themselves. Those who came found the stable busy with people scurrying about. The birth of a child was a big event. Women now attended Mary. They helped bathe the infant and wrapped him in blankets. As the first day of the child's life stretched into the next, the news spread. A special child, born in the inn's stable in the town of Bethlehem. A remarkable star had appeared overhead. An omen of rare and significant beauty. Who might this child be? Eight days later, Joseph presented him to the priests to be circumcised and, as the angel had said, they called his name

JESUS.

αΘω

Despite their silent compliance, Jewish women did not always consider being "unclean" for bodily functions over which they had no control a compliment. Since the birth of Jesus, Mary and Joseph had been received in the home of Julia and Hermas, two compassionate people who would not hear of Mary and the child "spending one more hour in that horrible stable." Hermas ben David had lived in Bethlehem all his life, his father a Jew, his mother gentile. He had married a Roman woman, not an uncommon practice for Jewish men. Yet they lived as Jews. Julia more tolerated Judaism than embraced it. She had little patience for some Jewish teachings, especially as they regarded women. Still, they were a devout family, and hospitable.

For the first week of Jesus' life, his mother was considered ceremonially unclean until his circumcision. While her unclean status found its basis in Moses, and ceremony, and in the eyes of those who were not unclean, there was no substantial difference between Mary's condition and that of a leper.

Julia found this unnecessarily cruel for someone who had just gone through nine months of discomfort and braved the pain of childbirth. "Shameful," she would say, "Even God gets his day of rest, but for us women? Not so much as a grunt of appreciation from the so-called righteous men of this world. Shameful, I say."

Hermas smiled at his wife's complaint. "She's right, you know." He remarked to Joseph. "It is much more difficult in this world to be a woman than to be a man."

"It does seem insufferable that women should be so demeaned as to be considered 'unclean' for any reason connected to childbirth. I do not understand the ways of priests and Levites," agreed Joseph. *Especially for this child,* Joseph thought.

His mind still recoiling from the previous night's events. It did not seem right for his son to be born in *this* way. Mary should have had the best midwife in the village. Her mother should have been here. He struggled with some guilt, as any man would, for not doing more for his wife at this delicate time.

But there was no midwife, no women to assist her or care for her needs, to talk with her during her labor or about their own, no mother to encourage her. Only the dim memories of Elizabeth's labor and, of course, Joseph.

αΘω

It is not appropriate for men to be present at the time of childbirth. It is just not done. But besides Joseph, there was no one else. Despite this cultural disgrace, another feeling consumed him, a deep inner secret spoken to him by an angel in a dream he would never forget. He had, out of sheer necessity, taken part in the most amazing thing in his young life. The birth of his son. He had been the first to see him—even before Mary. Joseph was all too aware of the origins of this child, but now he was also his son!

For an additional thirty days Mary was forbidden to touch hallowed things and in that time was not permitted even to enter the Temple. After forty days, she was required to offer sacrifice for her purification. *Purification?* She thought. *Purification from what? For having this child?* The incongruity appalled her. Purification after a birth required a sacrificial lamb, or if a family could not afford that, two turtledoves or two young pigeons. Joseph, ever mindful of his dwindling purse, watched as the priest broke the necks of the birds and offered them to God. *Now,* he mused acidly, *she is clean!* Joseph found the whole process revolting.

At this time also, Jesus, as their firstborn son, would be presented to the Lord for service as a priest. According to tradition and ceremony, they would then "buy him back," or redeem him for the price of five shekels. Joseph rolled his eyes heavenward at the Levitical considerations that had brought the young family to the Temple in Jerusalem when Jesus was barely six weeks old. They dutifully deposited their shekels in the third Trumpet near the raised dais where ordinarily the women worshiped.

αΘω

As they turned to leave, a man robed in religious vestments stopped them. It was difficult to tell from his clothing, or his manner, what he was doing there, but he seemed as if he belonged to the Temple. The robe was drawn over his head so that its shadow fell over his face. His dress gave the appearance of an official. His demeanor, however, was different. "Please," he said unobtrusively, "just a small moment of your time." There was something in his voice. Age? "May I please look upon your child?" When Mary nodded approval, tentatively, tenderly, he reached his hand and removed the baby's blanket, exposing the infant's face. At the same time, the hood fell from the man's head exposing his face as well. The wrinkles in the corners of his eyes deepened as pleasure splashed over his face. Lines from years of life deepened into exhilaration, his almost white beard of grand length trembled. His voice, choked with emotion rattled, "May I hold him?" Without reluctance, Mary held Jesus out to him. He held the babe close to his breast, hugging him. Jesus smiled back in obvious delight, his little hand unconsciously grasping the old man's beard. Old eyes lifted toward heaven and closed. Wet streams coursed down his cheeks as he whispered, "Now Lord, let your servant depart in peace."

Strange comment, thought Joseph. *What could he mean? Who is this old gentleman?*

"My name is Simeon." It was a simple, quiet declaration. "I live here... well, I almost live here—in the Temple. The Rabbis and priests treat me as if I were a candlestick," he said with a not so wry grin. He looked at the child he held as his finger touched his face. "I have spent years praying for this, waiting for this, hoping for this." He smiled at the young parents. Then again he lifted his face to heaven and said, "And now *my eyes have seen* your Salvation!" The sparkle in his eyes danced the dance of a field of yellow poppies swaying in the wind. It seemed as if welling emotion would burst from his veins. "Oh," with embarrassment, "I must be making a fool of myself. Please, you must humor an old man," as he gently shifted the child back into Mary's arms.

As Mary held the baby close to her breast, Simeon placed his right hand on the child's brow. He looked first at Joseph and then gazed directly into the eyes of the young mother. "Your son is appointed for the fall and rise of many in Israel," he stated. His features sobered. His wrinkles worked in concert with his mouth as he spoke, "This child will be a sign against which men will speak." Mary's eyes widened. His veined hand lifted from the face of the babe to caress the face of the mother, "My sweet daughter," he said, "A sword shall pierce your own heart also." Mary's breath drew in and caught. "That the thoughts of many hearts may be revealed..." She heard nothing else. Her eyes, even her thoughts had blinded at his words. As suddenly as the old man had appeared, he was gone.

"Where . . ?" she whispered. Joseph put his arm around his wife and guided her away.

XI

Anna

Making their way out of the Court of Women, they approached an ancient woman sitting at the base of a marble column near a series of stairs leading away from the Temple. Although she had the appearance of a beggar, she did not hold out her hand, she asked for nothing. She did not cry for alms. Her name was Anna and she had sat in this very spot every day since time past remembering. Some said she was over a hundred years old. Here in the Temple, she fasted and prayed, a woman of deep faith. Like Simeon, she waited.

When she saw Joseph and Mary approaching, holding the child, she held up her hand as if asking them to stop. While the young couple was anxious to leave, the commanding presence of this elderly woman compelled them to stop yet again. Stiffly, with no small difficulty, she stood. One hand propped against the column, she beckoned with the other for them to come nearer. Warily, they did. "I wish to see the child," she croaked, her voice weak with years.

She made no attempt to hold Jesus. Her balance would not have permitted that. Yet the urge to do so compelled her to reach forth her hand to touch the infant's cheek. And with that solitary touch her face radiated pleasure. Eyes of amazing blue, clear of the onslaught of age, gleamed at the baby. Her expression changed to one of wonder. Suddenly, inexplicably, she began to sing with the voice of a songbird,

You are Holy, O Lord!
Let now your Light
Precede the flight of angels
To ease the affliction of
Your children.

The notes floated with such crystal clarity that all who heard stopped to listen. The delicate sweetness of each note, punctuated with stately elegance lifted the hearts of all who heard. Amazing incongruity, that a voice which only croaked above a whisper, could sing in such lovely triumph. One by one, others started to join the paeans of praise. Mary and Joseph looked about ill at ease at the attention. Those who sang with Anna did not know to whom or of what the notes pealed. Still, the sanctity and force of the old woman's song caught them up. She knew. And that, it seemed, was all that mattered.

αΘω

The trip back to Bethlehem from Jerusalem was short—about two hours. On the way, Joseph thought once again of work. Concern for generating income nagging at his thoughts almost preempted the wonder of being a father. When they arrived at the home of Hermas ben David, the women discussed the baby and the events in Jerusalem. Joseph and Hermas spoke of other things.

Hermas ben David was a man of some means. He was known up and down the caravan routes as a merchant of oils, fine fabrics and wines. Gold often crossed his hands, silver and fine jewelry. He and Julia had one child, a son eight years old named Urbanus. He dreamed of being a soldier when he grew up.

"Stay with me, my young friend," he said to Joseph. "Stay with me until you are established. With your skills, I see no reason why you shouldn't soon flourish."

Joseph found it difficult to believe that a stranger, especially one who is half gentile, would make such an offer. It wasn't that Joseph hated Romans; it was that he had learned what treatment to expect from them. Hermas could see the wary embarrassment in the eyes of his new friend. Being almost ten years his senior, perhaps a firm elder brother approach might be effective.

"I quite insist, Joseph," he ventured. "You have no choice but to stay with me and Julia. Mary and the baby need Julia's help at this difficult time." Joseph had to agree. "Further, I would enjoy assisting you in setting up shop. It's been a long time since I've helped start a business." He sat back as if the arrangement had been concluded. Joseph remained silent. "Joseph," said Hermas almost pleading, "Let me help you. For the sake of the Lord God, for the sake of that wondrous child, let me help you. Do not be blind to the possibility that God has put me in position to care for you." Joseph buried his face in his hands and nodded his head. He didn't know how to express his gratitude.

αΘω

Aside from being the birthplace of King David, Bethlehem was also known as the burial place of Rachel, beloved wife of Jacob ben Isaac, and mother of Joseph and Benjamin. The town and its environs were often called "the land of Benjamin." When Rachel died, Jacob erected a stone edifice there later to be known as the pillar of Rachel. Of this place Jeremiah prophesied,

> *Thus speaks the LORD: "A voice is heard in Ramah, lamentation and bitter weeping, Rachel weeping for her children, refusing to be comforted, because they are no more."*

These words burned fiercely in the hearts of all Israelites who longed for hope in the promise that followed:

> *Thus speaks the LORD: "Refrain your voice from weeping, and your eyes from tears; for your work shall be rewarded, says the LORD, and they shall come back from the land of the enemy. There is hope in your future, says the LORD, that your children shall come back to their own border.*

The people of Judea, indeed all Israelites began to view themselves as the "children of Rachel" and waited for the promised deliverance. And when the prophet Micah prophesied,

> *"But you, Bethlehem Ephrathah, though you are small among the thousands of Judah, yet out of you shall come forth to Me the One who is to be Ruler in Israel, whose goings forth are from of old, from everlasting."*

It was not an impossible leap of logic for the Rabbis and teachers to conclude that Bethlehem would be the birthplace of Messiah, the One to deliver Rachel's children from the terrible bitterness of her tears.

Joseph wandered to the edge of town. Later people would know, or thought they knew, the precise spot where Rachel was buried. But in Joseph's time, they knew only that it was "a little distance" from Bethlehem in the town's surrounding environs. "Somewhere out here," he thought, "is where Mother Rachel is buried. Oh, if she only knew, if she only knew." His thoughts began to excite as his feelings enlarged. "This is it!" he exclaimed. "This is the place where, with Hermas' help—with God's help—I will build my home, where I will earn my bread with the skill in my hands." *I will take upon me the trait of Mother Rachel. I will never give up! I will not despair!* The story of Ruth took place here. Nearby was where Samuel anointed David. So, Joseph dreamed and planned. Such is the way with men—but not with God. As it is with most men, he was not really aware of what God was doing. Above him in the eastern sky, a distant star glinted unnoticed.

XII

King Astrologers

Sands shift softly in hissing winds. Night falls cool upon the desert. Scurrying creatures of darkness venture from their lairs, obtain a quick meal and hurry back to the familiar amenity of hole, cave or crevasse. Flames dance and coals glow as learned men gather around the firelight, peering over parchments. "There is no such star listed in any of our charts," one of them observed.

"Do you always feel the need to state the obvious," responded a colleague. Sarcasm and irritability were inevitable. They were embarrassed. They were educated men who had encountered something within their field of expertise they could not explain. Such an event was close to shameful. Intellectual arrogance has forever been the hallmark of men of science. Often they speak with insufferable objectivity of the "things we know" and the "things we don't know." Yet no matter how absolute their answers on either side of that equation, time all too often proves them wrong and they are embarrassed. It is unacceptable for those who deal with natural phenomena to be mistaken.

They could not surmise the origin of this unnatural phenomenon. It was at first thought to be a "meteor" tracing a trail of flames and vapor across the expanse of early evening. A wondrous thing to most, to these men? No. Watchers of the sky as they were, they had observed meteors many times. The uniqueness of size and shape, the distinctness of its flaming trail challenged their expertise. Of course, it held some portent. Such an event happened not without some meaning to interpret. Then something spectacular occurred. The "meteor" slowed in the sky and then stopped, as if the Creator were adding a new ornament to an already glittering meadow of lights. It might have blended with the rest of the stars of the night sky, but for its brilliance. And something else: If you stood absolutely still, you could see distinct and uncomplicated movement. Pulsating, as if it were alive.

Many were drawn by the phenomenon, but only these astrologers chose to heed. Only they followed, their caravan auspicious but modest in size. Their raiment laced with gold and silver. Jewels on their fingers, around their necks, affixed to their robes. Harnesses of their camels richly appointed. They were First Advisors to the King, Magi, magicians, scholars of the night. The celestial anomaly was something that evoked curiosity in the sophisticated and fear in the superstitious. Thus the caravan consisted of men far above the mass of curious onlookers. These men represented an elite. They were wise. Shaman, Savants they were. They would not be followed, yet many wondered what they would discover.

αΘω

Time. Much too little time to prepare. What to take with them? How long would they travel? How much to provision? Since they were carrying treasure they required protection, a military cohort. The caravan had begun to swell with soldiers, camel attendants, slaves, tents and all the accouterments necessary to a long journey. Because the phenomenon could be observed better at night, that is when they traveled, stopping only for an occasional conference which usually determined their next move. When they moved, the "star" moved. When they stopped, the star stopped. It led them west and south. The familiar sound of the camel's feet plodding on sand and earth, labored breathing, sweat dampening stinking flanks. No matter the night cool, travel by camel back was work for rider and ridden alike. Hours passed in silence. Swaying, creaking, lost in reverie and time. What were they looking for? What lay ahead of them? Where was this star leading them? How would they be received along the way?

αΘω

"I never believed omens could be so compelling!" The exclamation mixed with the sounds of the train. These men knew that much of their art was pure chicanery. They were not fools. The notion that stellar phenomena foretold anything concerning human endeavor held little credibility in their disciplined minds. For all of their genius, however, they were practical men. Men of the world. They knew what royalty wanted to hear. And since it was royalty that held the power and gold, it was prudent to regale them with wonders of magic intended, of course, to enhance the royal persona.

"It is no simple matter to discover a new star. One must use one's imagination. A simple stratagem to make us richer—and no doubt, safer."

"That is why they call us wise men, is it not?"

Others were not amused. This was no cleverly invented canard, no practical joke to play on a witless king. They knew that the star they followed reached for them, leading them, nourishing them. It waited upon them more certain and pure than the sun and moon.

αΘω

He had spent the last hour preparing the caravan to be on its way yet once more. He could hear the gurgle of the Jordan waters nearby as he observed the star—or whatever it was—hanging low in the western sky just above the horizon. He watched pensively as his slave cinched the saddle on the dirty beast upon which he had ridden this far. He was weary. He despaired of ever finding whatever it was they were looking for, wherever this thing was leading them. Perhaps they had been foolish. Perhaps the study of astrology, however ancient, was a hoax. Yet, he mounted the camel and tried to steady himself against being jerked back and forth, as the animal got to its feet. He fixed his eyes on the star, as they had come to call it, and spurred the beast into line. The caravan was on its way again. Although his eyes followed the star, he didn't think about it. He had long since become accustomed to its presence and no longer felt anything at all about it. His mind wandered without direction or purpose, and while in its promenade, the star concluded its movement.

He watched for several minutes more. For months, the brilliant phenomenon had distinctly moved in relation to their travels. Now it appeared stationary. Having left the small town of Jericho behind them, they moved up the steady incline toward the Jewish city of Jerusalem. He spurred his camel and pulled abreast of the caravan's leader.

"Welcome, my brother, the night is yet interminable and my bones ache beyond description."

"They may not need ache much longer; look."

The other man glanced again at the familiar star and remarked, "So?"

"Look closely."

Abruptly, he reined his camel. Since he led the caravan, all stopped. Weariness vanished as his face frowned and then relaxed in quiet elation. "It is stilled," he whispered.

The star came and stood over where the young child was.

αΘω

Although less than an hour into this night's journey, the decision was quickly made to halt the caravan and reassess the approach to the mission. Night had fallen softly upon the countryside. Clouds above reflected light from Jerusalem causing eerie vapors to seem luminescent. Unseen shepherds, one standing solitary, watchful and alone tending sheep in the distance, the others asleep waiting their watch.

"We shall abide here until morning."

As the slaves began building a fire, men of science and wisdom conferred together once again.

"This is the land of the Jews. How shall we approach them? How can we learn why we have come among such a people? How shall we explain ourselves?" The astrologers were not unfamiliar with Jews. Indeed, many Jews lived in their own country, descendants of an ancient captivity.

Flames flickered brightly. Settling themselves upon cushions arranged in a semi-circle by slaves, food was served. Figs, grapes, olives, assorted meats, wine and goat's milk. Perhaps no feast to these wealthy men, but to the hungry it might appear over-indulgent. This did not concern them.

"I have studied much on Jews," one of them ventured. "They have been a part of our own culture since the days of Nebuchadnezzar."

"Have you studied their Book?" asked another.

"You refer, of course, to the writings of Moses," said his companion, as if the question were absurd.

"They call it their Torah, God's Law."

"Do they not have books of poetry also?"

"The writings of David, Solomon and others. Other prophets arose during the time of captivity. Then of course, there was Daniel. He looms larger than all in our history, yet he was a Jew. Yes, and I have studied their rabbinical writings, Hillel and Shammai as well."

"And now our star has led us to their land."

"A king, then, is born among them?"

"Exactly. And their God whom Nebuchadnezzar, Darius the Mede, Cyrus the Great and Ahasueras, all acknowledged, has brought us here to honor him."

"You jest." Flat. Cynical.

"I do not jest."

"Merely honor, or worship?" More cynicism.

"We do not know. Perhaps we will find out when we find him."

"And just how shall we do that? We can't parade the whole caravan aimlessly through Jerusalem." This seemed a legitimate, practical consideration. Having come this far, they were now faced with the issue of how to approach dwellers in a land foreign to them. Language was not the problem. Each of them spoke fluent Aramaic. But their dress, the armed guard, the ostentation, the impression they would make would skew, or perhaps mitigate, any meaningful information they might gather.

"We stay here. We do not bring the caravan into the city just yet. We send our Aramaic-speaking slaves among the people. Let them inquire. Surely, the common folk will know. Then we follow."

It took some arguing and deliberation but, at length, they agreed on this procedure and slaves went out among the streets of Jerusalem asking, *"Where is he that is born king of the Jews?"*

XIII

Herod the Great

Herod the Great is King of the Jews. That title accorded him by Mark Antony himself and confirmed by the Roman Senate without a dissenting voice.

Word of the travelers spread like the wind among the inhabitants of Jerusalem. Priests and Levites were alarmed. The whole city was troubled. Inquiries from the astrologers slaves did not take long to reach Herod's ears.

"From whence did they come!" demanded Herod.

"It seems they are Armenian Magi, my king. It seems they seek one recently born king of the Jews."

"They would travel this far for that?" he asked. "Why, for God's sake? What possible interest could they have in a Jewish king?" He paused as if considering the question. *War?* Their armed cohort was clearly defensive… obviously to ward off robbers. *Gifts? Treasure?* The thought passed through his mind that they might have come to honor *him*! But then he remembered the qualification, *"born"* King of the Jews. They were seeking a child, perhaps an infant. Possessing a natural distaste for children, the thought disgusted him.

"By God, *I* am the Jewish king!" An advisor, an elderly scribe, then made a mistake. Turning to a colleague, he mumbled something indistinct to the king's ears. Herod did, however, hear the word, *"Messiah!"* The king was incredulous. "What did you say?"

The scribe had lived too long to be much impressed with a king's self-importance. Evenly, he replied, "I said, majesty, that perhaps they are scholars investigating our scriptures."

"You said, *'Messiah!'*"

"I did, majesty. It is possible they know of him. It is possible they seek him."

Herod stared at the scribe as if weighing the impertinence. His initial thought was to insult the old man. Then the plausibility of his suggestion intrigued him. *"The Blessed One? Now?"* He was not ignorant of the prophecy;

no Jew was. Herod considered himself a Jew, despite the fact that his mother was Arab. He did not, however, care enough to know the details. *I am not ready for this!* "How can you suggest such a thing? It is not yet time! *Is it?*" This king could not know. His massive ego could never permit him to give it serious thought. "Where exactly is this Messiah to be born?"

"In Judean Bethlehem, my king."

Herod was aghast. The town was practically within the environs of Jerusalem. He paced back and forth, his mind scheming. At last, he ordered, "Send the palace guard! Bring these star-struck fools to me immediately!"

"Is that wise, my king?" asked the chief priest, demurely. These men had compelling reason to fear Herod. He had once put the entire Sanhedrin to death. Although this religious body had been reconstituted under the king's watchful eye, he mercilessly intimidated them, yet they enjoyed a certain royal sanctuary. So on occasion what appeared to be an unseemly presumption was allowed.

"Wise?" the king reacted. "Have I not a reputation for wisdom?" The priest lowered his eyes in deference. "No matter. How is it, as you say, unwise? Why should I not command that these strangers be brought before me?"

"It is known that they have soldiers themselves," the chief priest continued. "No doubt, ours will overcome them, but there will be an engagement. You can be sure Rome will look into that. There will be an official inquiry."

Herod laughed loudly. These blind idiots would never grasp the reality that as far as the Jews were concerned, he held Rome in his hand. He was a friend with both Augustus and Mark Antony. Although he was not pleased with the latter's cavorting with *that mongrel bitch* in Egypt. "Accompanied by a contingent of military, you say? That can only mean that they are important, or that they carry treasure." His eyes narrowed. "Perhaps you are right." As Procurator of the region, Herod held no fear at all of a small security force. With two Roman legions at his command, he held little fear of an invading army. He could and would destroy these Magi should he possess the whim to do so. They did not call him "The Great" for nothing.

"No!" commanded the king, changing his mind. "Send a secret messenger," Herod continued ignoring the priest. "*Ask* these Armenian adventurers to come to my palace. I desire an audience with them."

αΘω

Urbanus, son of Hermas, had also heard of the Armenian caravan. His father maintained a rented room in Jerusalem from which he conducted most of his business. Since the room often contained considerable amounts of denarii, Eh-Ret, a Nubian slave, stood guard at the door while customers came and went. In addition to being a large, powerful man, Eh-Ret was also friend to young Urbanus. Often he entertained the boy with stories of his homeland in the desert south of the land of Egypt.

"My people are archers," he told the boy. "By the time the testicles of our sons descend, they are able to split a grape at twenty paces." The eyes of the boy widened. He had never held a bow, let alone actually used one. "When I was fifteen, I killed a lion with my bow. Shot him in the eye as he was killing a goat. See, I still wear his fang." He touched the polished, gold encrusted lion's tooth suspended from a gold necklace around his neck. Urbanus listened, entranced.

"Even girls?" he asked.

"What?"

"Can girls kill lions, too?"

"Why do you ask such a thing? Women do not touch the bow. This is a man's skill. In Nubia, women are not persons. They are women." Eh-Ret said this without emotion, as though it were the natural order of things.

"But you marry them. They are the mothers of your children."

"I've had many wives," said Eh-Ret irritably, "and even more children. Some are older than you. Warriors."

Urbanus thought about that. He knew the Romans sometimes had more than one wife. Almost all of the Roman men had other women with whom they dallied, to the sometimes not so quiet chagrin of the women to whom they were married.

"Do you ever divorce?" The boy's curiosity seemed inexhaustible.

"We do not divorce our wives," said the Nubian. "We care for them as long as they live. If we tire of them, we simply get another wife." Eh-Ret was smiling now. "But we do not send them away. That would be cruel. They would die of starvation."

The boy responded, "That is a very strange custom."

"If you lived among my people, you would think differently."

"If I lived among your people, I could split a grape at twenty paces," laughed Urbanus. "I could kill a lion!"

"You will kill, my little friend," spoke the slave. "In your time. In your place."

αΘω

"You seek him who is born king of the Jews?" It was a statement couched as a question. Its irony was not lost on Herod. He hoped it was not lost on these opulently dressed intruders. He had asked the question with a smile, patronizingly, condescendingly, and if the feeling in his heart was known, contemptuously.

"We have followed his star from the east. We have been traveling for many months."

"How many months? *Exactly* when did the star appear to you?" Herod's desire for accuracy seemed odd to the astrologers. The star had been there for all to see. Surely, news of the phenomenon in the east had traveled this far. Of what was this Jewish king so curious?

"We are not certain of exactness, King Herod," this was a lie. These men could tell you to the portion of the hour when the orb was first seen. "After our first observation, there was some deliberation in the decision to follow it. That took time. Those chosen to journey took time. Preparation took time. We had no concept of how long we might be away, so we prepared for the worst. All of this took time. Now we have been traveling these eight months in diminishing hope that we might ever reach our destination."

Herod was ignorant of the potential for precision from these magicians. Herod was ignorant of much. He did not trust them. Men such as Herod the Great were very frightened men. Nervous men, agitated by any possible—real or imagined—threat to their security and power. "It is said in our scriptures that a messiah will be born, we know not when, in Bethlehem of Judea, a short distance from where we now stand. Perhaps you will investigate. And perhaps you will be kind to come back and inform me of this great event—should it actually have happened." *A Messiah from such a place as Bethlehem! How utterly disinteresting!* Herod paused; hoping yet not hoping the astrologers would surmise his incredulity. "Of course, I should wish to pay him homage as well. *Of course* ," he muttered quietly.

αΘω

It was still there. Quiet. Pulsating. Magnificent. Returning to the caravan, the Magi moved south and west, following their obsession. Their hearts pounding in anticipation, the distance to Bethlehem seemed invisible. Its beams reaching for the ground, the star locked in stillness, as if to select the very dwelling of its resolve. At last, the caravan halted.

The house and the nearby structures bathed in light. The wise men did not call upon their wisdom to know that they had reached, at last, the end of their long trek. Even the camels seemed to know as they settled awkwardly to their bellies without being commanded to do so.

Men of erudition, men of fame, men whose wisdom had the ears of kings and princes, these were the men who entered the modest but well-appointed home in Bethlehem, viewed the babe suckling at the breast of his young mother and fell to their knees in worship. They had come a long distance; they had come anticipating this very moment. However rampant the stories of celestial omens regarding the birth of kings, never in recorded or oral history had it been seen or heard that a star—or whatever it was—would lead men such as them to the feet of a babe such as this.

They brought their treasures. A chest filled with the gold of the realm. For such a child, for such a king, it was no extravagance.

Frankincense. These were men of prayer. Scholars, some of whom had studied the Hebrew Scriptures. They knew the stories of the ancient kings of their country, Nebuchadnezzar, Darius the Mede and Cyrus the Great, Ahasuerus. All of the prophecies of Daniel had happened. This they accepted as fact. To each of them, this new king might well be a priest, a Messiah sent by the Hebrew God. Frankincense, a gift appropriate to that possibility.

The physician among them brought a tankard of the oil of myrrh, considered by Jews to be the balm of Gilead, an expensive perfume, used by kings and lovers. It had other uses, but these were not in the intentions of the Magi. To them myrrh was apropos owing to its value, in some cases, exceeding that of gold.

To the young family, these gifts were welcome. The financial benefit alone stunned them. The gold and myrrh were enough to sustain them through the next few years of their lives. Enough to establish Joseph in his trade. Being an anesthetic, myrrh would sooth the red rash so common to infants who frequently soiled their clothes. It was used in this manner by the very rich.

αΘω

Bel-Tar slept fitfully that night. The visit with the child and his parents had left a penetrating impression in his Eastern mind. To some, it might have seemed anticlimactic to see a mere infant after so long a journey of anticipation. But for Bel-Tar, it was a most satisfying end to their trip. The baby had actually smiled at him and held his finger. And in those child-eyes, he had seen something that he had never seen in the eyes of such a small person. What it was exactly, he could not say; perhaps unusual intelligence, perhaps something deeper and more personal, perhaps; *was it recognition?* Whatever it was, it made him deliriously happy. It filled him with a triumph he could not form words to describe. He could see that the others were similarly affected.

Just when it seemed that slumber would claim him, a vision flooded his mind that compelled every atom of thought. An enraged Herod the Great in the presence of the child. The king meant to harm the child, not pay him homage. *Herod? Pay homage to a child? Herod the Great…Pariah?* Not likely. Instantly he knew, they must not report back to this monster, this sadist. Suddenly, every fiber in his body tingled with urgency. Sleep was now impossible. He thought of the king's guard coming to demand their presence. He could envision their being escorted back to the palace.

His senses gathering in alarm he went to each of his companions. "Arise," he demanded softly, shaking each one, "Awake, We must be off—*now!*"

αΘω

Joseph's sleep was also troubled. He had slept through the noise of the departing caravan, but now his mind seemed alert to the nuances of the night. A creeping sense of dread paralyzed his breathing. Next to the sleeping young mother, the babe twisted and flailed.

"Joseph."

It was not a sound, yet his eyes fluttered as if he had heard something.

"Joseph, arise!" The voice was urgent, irresistible. Joseph could not yet open his eyes, yet he could hear and comprehend. *"Herod is conspiring to kill your son. You must go away—far away. Far enough that the king will not attempt to follow you."* Joseph listened to each syllable, the spit evaporating in his mouth. His limbs twitched. He tried to move, to get up; to run but he could not. In his dream, he poured all his energy into action, but felt as though locked in muck. *"You must escape to Egypt!"*

He awakened, his night clothing damp with perspiration. He glanced first at the child and then at Mary. Both were slumbering comfortably. He started to dismiss the nightmare…some intuition coerced him to investigate. His mind fell upon the caravan, the camels, the Magi. He arose and plodded his way to the door of the house. Peering outside into the small hours of the night, he could still smell the animals, but they were gone. No one was in sight. They had vanished.

You must escape to Egypt!

The urgency of the appeal, no; the *authority* of it frightened him. *Why Egypt?* Questioning confused him.

While Herod the king had assisted Julius Caesar in conquering the reaches of Egypt, his memory of Cleopatra's hatred held him from further adventures there. Though dead now these thirty years, yet she lived in the hearts of all Egyptians, however subjected to Roman rule. Herod also knew that he could not trifle with the Roman Empire, however secure his position in Israel.

Joseph, young peasant that he was, of course, knew none of this. He had no way of knowing that Herod would not dare follow them to Egypt. The agitation he felt bewildered him. *Where did they go?* He could not understand why the Magi would leave without telling him. *The baby!* He hurried back to where the child lay. The infant was asleep on his pallet next to his mother. Joseph considered the peaceful scene of child and mother and wondered how he could have been so fortunate. *This beautiful and special Child,* he thought. *Herod seeks to destroy him? Why?* The sense of dread had not left him. He moved closer to his wife. He was not sure if he should wake her or go back to sleep himself. He lay back down. His eyes open. He tried to close them. He tried to sleep. At length, he turned to Mary. Shaking her gently he said, "Awake, my darling."

Before the first rays of light tiptoed through the night, another caravan departed in the cool quiet of darkness. Against a backdrop of starlight, an ass carried a mother and child, an ass carried a father and an ass carried their provisions. Egypt awaited them, for the herald of holiness has spoken, *"Out of Egypt have I called my Son."*

αΘω

Crashing against palace wall, dark liquid forming explosive patterns on stone, a wine goblet disintegrated into a thousand shards. The chief priest and other members of the Sanhedrin cowered. Slaves stood immobile, invisible, which was the way they wanted it. Filling his hands with folds of silk drapes, he yanked them from the wall, cascading around his feet soiled in spilled wine. Screaming incomprehensible epithets against the Magi, against God, against anything and anyone that entered his inflamed brain.

Spittle formed at the corners of his mouth. Eyes bulged. Veins protruded. Sweat flowed. Herod the Great succumbed to madness.

"Sons of swine!" he screamed. "Dog vomit! Ass droppings!" On he railed. His mind searched in futility for the vilest names he could conceive. His vitriolic rampage knew no boundary. He could think of nothing that would sate his hurt, nothing that would absolve the insult. At length he fell silent, sitting on his throne, black clouds brooding in his eyes. No one spoke. No one moved. No one attempted to comfort him in the fear that he might suddenly resume venting his spleen. Nothing good could come of this. Herod was a tyrant of ungodly adolescent passions. This night, blood would be spilled.

"Leave me." It was a subdued, mumbled command, but a royal command nonetheless. The priests, his advisors, the slaves all left him alone. Herod brooded darkly. Hours paraded with little pomp and ceremony into the night all the way to the first grey light of dawn. The king slept not. His temples pounded with scheming outrage. His nostrils dilated, went dry and sent him into spasms of sneezing. His anxiety knew no respite. He screamed and his personal aide appeared.

"Fetch me the Captain of the Guard." His eyes were red, but not from weeping. His voice low, even, malicious. *"Fetch him out of bed. Fetch him from the joint of his bitch's thighs! Fetch him before me this instant! Fetch him now!"* The aging king, nearing 70. Labored breathing. The servant left quickly.

αΘω

The young mother stirred from sleep softly, as if to touch the day with velvet. Noise outside. Horses. Chariots. Shouted commands. Soldiers. The door to their home succumbs to relentless pounding with a loud crash. Her husband's terrified eyes snap open. Cold military professionalism; eyes of steel match that of the steel drawn in his hand. Father sits erect in his bed. Soldier's eyes searching. Father's eyes fearing, glancing first at his wife, then at the sleeping form of his infant son. Soldier's eyes following father's fear. Bronzed, powerful hand takes hold of infant blanket and pulls. Naked child rolls to the floor, exposing male genitals. He awakes in whimpering infant wail, which becomes bloody gurgles as pointed steel is shoved through his heart. Mother's screams are heard in this house and throughout the dwellings of Bethlehem.

"...because they are no more."

XIV

Death of a King

The king lay in his bed with trembling chills. Attending physicians labored grimly. Cool towels applied to his feverish forehead one after another. A nurse held a spoon of cool water to his parched lips. The king was unable to open his mouth to receive the liquid. His face grimaced in pain. Moans, deep and terrible, emit from his diseased body. Foul odors saturated the room. Those attending him wore damp cloths over their mouths. It did little to help.

"Is there nothing we can do?" asked one physician.

"Nothing," responded another. "The king is dying. Each hour he grows weaker." Herod opened his eyes. One eye stared off into space. The other pupil rolled out of control into the corner of its socket exhibiting virulent red veins. Breathing labored and gasping. He tried to speak, but the words were lost in aching moans. His eyes closed tight, his jaw clamped as if warding off the agony. His body convulsed and then relaxed.

"He cannot last much longer."

"Doesn't anyone know what is wrong with him?" The physicians were frustrated, confused. They had never seen this disease, or whatever it was, before.

"His bowels are dead."

"What?"

"His bowels are dead and rotting inside him." The voice came from the shadows of the room. It was a young voice but authoritative, educated.

"Who are you?"

"My name is Lucian, physician to the family of Seth.[3] My name is not important, but I can tell you his bowels are dead. I have seen this before."

"But you are a doctor, then?"

"Of course, I am a doctor. Look." The young man strode to the bedside

3 Father to Annas who later became High Priest who also had a son, Theophilus, to whom Lucian penned his gospel and the acts of the apostles.

and pulled the coverings back from the king. He lifted the king's skirt to expose his abdomen and genitals.

"How can you dare so expose the king of the Jews." This from one of the elders.

The young man looked with contempt at the priest. "You fools concern yourselves with the king's modesty when the man will be dead in a few hours." He turned back to the attending physicians. "Look at his abdomen." It was bloated, distended, gaseous. "For reasons we do not understand, the blood to his intestines has stopped. They have died and are decomposing within him." The clarity of the diagnosis and the young man's demeanor persuaded the other physicians. The priests were incredulous.

"How can one so young know . . ?"

"What can we do to save his life?" asked an attending physician.

"Nothing. He will die soon and there is nothing we or anyone else can do to prevent it."

"You blaspheme the king?"

Ignoring the priest, the young physician continued, "If you surgically incise his abdomen, you might relieve his suffering."

"Cut his belly open?"

"Of course." The young man reached for a small leather case. Untying its strings, it opened to what appeared to be medical instruments. From these he selected a small, sharp scalpel. "Observe," he remarked clinically.

"Stop him!" shouted the priest.

No one moved. Again the doctor, ignoring the priest, deftly inserted the instrument just deep enough to penetrate the abdomen wall. In less than an instant, he had made an incision the entire breadth of the king's body. Gases escaped and the bloating receded. The king, unable to feel the pain of the blade for the pain within his body, sighed in blessed relief. The stench was unbearable.

The doctor toweled his hands of blood and remarked,"Give him heavy portions of wine mixed with myrrh. And cover the windows," he ordered. "Flies. The king will be dead by morning." Abruptly, he turned and left the room. Incredibly, Herod the Great rested comfortably.

The attending physicians looked at one another, stunned. The priests were helpless.

"Who was that?"

"He said his name was...Lucian."

αΘω

The young doctor was wrong. Herod lived three more days before he succumbed. That night, everyone left the king in peace except for the slaves. Sitting by the bed in waning candlelight, the slave awoke to the sound of intermittent buzzing. No one had remembered to close the windows. Since the slave had not heard the young physician, he did not do so. It was not long before Herod's exposed intestines were covered with flies. This condition continued for hours through the next day before someone thought to cover the patient's stomach.

Two day's later, just before the king breathed his last, he awoke screaming. His mouth covered with foaming, bubbling spittle, his words incoherent, his eyes glazed with fear and approaching death, he could not stop screaming. One of the physicians thought to examine the incision. Perhaps, he thought, it was encrusted, causing additional pain. He removed the coverings and the loose-fitting bandage. The stench staggered him. He turned his head in futile attempt to reach fresh air. Turning again to attend the monarch, he viewed the wound for the first time in almost three days. Instantly gagging, he vomited. The king's belly was crawling with maggots. Herod the Great died in his physician's vomit, worms writhing in putrescent tissue.[4]

4 A similar death occurred to Herod's son, Antipas. See Acts 12:23.

XV

Return from Egypt

The weeks in Egypt passed pleasantly stretching into more than twenty months. Once again, they were housed in another's home. The baby walked now, calling Joseph, "Abba." Mary sat for hours playing with the child. It seemed she lived only for him. In her diary she wrote,

> *My life revolves around him. I wonder if it is more blessed to be a parent or to be a child?*
> *Things are a pleasant havoc with him near. Everything has changed. One sweet smile, a hug or even a coo can make a day complete. I burst with emotion when I try to explain the way I feel. Love is not a strong enough word. Maybe adore or cherish.*
> *As I held him for the first time, I did not feel worthy. I look into his newborn face seeing greatness and strength. I wonder if all mothers feel this way or if my baby really is destined for greatness.*
> *I want to help him skip the small steps and boost him into higher things in life but I know he will have to struggle his way through things in order to make him strong. He will have to do almost everything by himself. I constantly fall short of all that I expect from myself. I often feel I have no idea what I am doing. I wonder if he will learn from me or I from him?*
> *I know he is changing me because of the way I feel. He is such a precious gift. The discoveries that are waiting to be found. The potential for joy that one little face holds. His eyes are a clear, empty innocence. Knowing that he will look to me fills me with a need to strive for excellence within myself. I am pulled to him. I revolve around him. He is my sun!*

αΘω

Joseph's thoughts were of a different genus. He was not caught up in the rapture of fatherhood. His musing took a more practical direction. He had protected Mary from the awful news of Herod's slaughter of the male babies in Bethlehem. *How many had there been?* He did some mental calculation. *It could not have been more than fifteen or twenty children,* he thought. This does not make it more acceptable, nor does it ease the horror of the event in the least. But that beast of a monarch could just have easily included the whole of Jerusalem.

Joseph had labored hard through the day in the shipyards of the Nile. Building ships did not tax his skills as much as creating wooden furniture for the homes of the wealthy, but it brought in an income. While he still had the wealth of the gifts of the Magi, he did not want to squander it by not working when there was work to be had. So, he worked and at night, he joined Mary and the child in the home where they stayed, exhausted but feeling good. Life here was not unpleasant. Sated with wine and good food, sleep came easily and sweet. The Egyptian night crept into wee hours. The moon slid down the western sky and disappeared into the horizon.

"Joseph." A familiar voice. In the periphery of his consciousness, he knew what was happening.

"Joseph, it is time. He who sought the young child's life is dead. Arise, and return to your homeland."

It was as simple as that. He did not get up immediately. He lapsed into a deeper slumber and did not open his eyes until the day was several hours old. Mary and the babe were still asleep. His place at the shipyards would be empty that day. There would be no pay. It didn't matter. Gently he stroked his wife's hair until she smiled and fluttered her eyes. They were a deep, sapphire blue. Joseph's were brown, his skin tawny, his face handsome, ruddy and well defined, his beard well groomed. She reached for him, wetting his hairy chest with her milk.

An angel, unseen in the shadows, smiled.

αΘω

Joseph was not a man given to anxiety. As the family neared Bethlehem, however, a feeling of foreboding fell over him. His purpose had been to settle there with his friend, Hermas ben David. He had been born in Bethlehem, he had registered there, he had hoped to build his business there instead of Nazareth where his father worked. There would not be enough business in Nazareth to sustain them both. It was much too economically deprived.

His lips crinkled into a caustic smile when he remembered the popular slur, *"Can any good thing come out of Nazareth?"* Yet, how could he return to Bethlehem now? After what Herod had done? It seemed impossible.

The son of Herod the Great, one Archelaus, now rules in Judea. He is no less a tyrant than his father. It was well known that of all of the sons of Herod the Great, the character and temperament of Archelaus was most like that of his bestial father. Like his father, he was hated by the Romans; yet unlike his father, he held far less power. Later the Romans would depose him, banish him and place their own procurators in power. Joseph feared that Archelaus would attempt to continue the slaughter of children that his father had initiated. Bethlehem was no longer an option. He must lay his hopes and dreams aside for now. The safety and protection of his family preempted all else. That night as he dreamed, his decision was confirmed by the whispers of an angel.

When he reached the borders of Bethlehem, he did not stop. Nor did he stop in the great city of Jerusalem, nor Jericho. Up the eastern banks of the Jordan, they traveled all the way to Galilee and ultimately back to Nazareth. Joseph, Mary and the child were home.

In Nazareth, with the funds provided by the Magi and that of his trade, Joseph could afford a home larger than that he would have had in Bethlehem. Jesus toddled about the rooms with abandon. As the weeks, months and years passed, his little body changed into that of a small boy. He became stronger and seemed wiser and brighter than others his age. It was thought by his neighbors and family that he basked in the radiance of God's favor. There was little doubt that he was a special child.

> *Then a shoot will spring from the stem of Jesse, and a branch from his roots will bear fruit. And the Spirit of the LORD will rest on Him, the spirit of wisdom and understanding, the spirit of counsel and strength, the spirit of knowledge and of the wonder of the LORD.*

XVI

Boyhood Adventures

In the spring following the eleventh birthday of Jesus, came the Feast of Passover. Since the days of Hezekiah, each year the Feast is held in Jerusalem where the Temple is the center of activity and the site of the ritual slaughter of the paschal lamb. Every male from the age of twelve and older was expected to attend Passover in Jerusalem. From all over Israel, hundreds of thousands of men with their families descend upon the city of David. The vast Temple grounds could accommodate in excess of 200,000 worshipers. Filled with the mayhem of celebration, children galloping hither and yon, fathers praying and attending sacrifice, mothers gossiping and tending their babes, the great edifice of Herod the Great swarmed with celebrants.

Excitement crackled through the family like small rivulets of lightning. Jesus would attend his first Passover this year. The family assembled the things they would need for the trip and set out with many others who also made the week-long pilgrimage to the City of David. The highways leading from the region of Galilee south to Jerusalem crowded with people and animals. Clouds of dust rose over roads, and the city itself appeared enveloped in brown mist. This was the High Holy Day. It recalled the most important day of Jewish history, the day in which they were delivered by the hand of God from the oppression of the Egyptians more than one thousand, four hundred years ago. It was a day celebrated each year since then.

αΘω

The sheer size of the Temple and its enclosure overwhelmed Jesus. Struggling with overloaded emotions, he wanted to explore, but did he dare? Suppose he got lost in this monstrous place?

"Have you ever seen such a place?" he shouted to his friend, Eben.

One year older than Jesus, this was Eben's second Passover. He assumed the attitude of an experienced participant, "You haven't seen anything yet. Wait until you get inside. There are doors so large that ten grown-ups standing on each other's shoulders could not reach the top." Jesus did not doubt it.

"Why so large?"

"Well," said Eben with authority, "You have to have large doors to let God in." Jesus looked at his friend marveling at his obvious stupidity.

"God doesn't live here!" he declared.

"Does, too!" Eben shot back.

"Rabbi Abjo-ram said that 'God does not live in a place built with hands.'"

"I don't care." Eben couldn't think of a rabbi to quote, "My father told me that God lives behind the great veil in the Holy of Holies."

Jesus persisted, "I don't see how the God who created the whole world and the stars and stuff could live..." the argument escalated as they passed through the gate and into the courtyard.

αΘω

Approaching twelve years of age, Jesus already had three younger brothers and one sister. The next eldest, James, would be eligible to attend Passover in two years. For this occasion, all but Jesus stayed behind in Nazareth. Eben and Jesus, living next door to each other, had "grown up" together, playing together, doing all the things boys did together. They were "best friends."

While somewhat contemplative and withdrawn, Jesus lived in all respects as a normal child. Joining his friends playing caravan, skipping pebbles on ponds, and chewing on weeds, he sometimes went off by himself to be alone. A casual observer might conclude that the boy was melancholy or morose. This was not the case. Jesus did seem to spend an inordinate time in prayer for an active boy and often surprised adults with penetrating questions or observations that made them look at each other in amazement; never precocious but different; playful, but rarely frivolous. Coarse references in which all boys were prone to engage, for him came less frequently. Other children in the neighborhood liked and accepted him as one of them. Sometimes, one of the larger boys would try to bully him. Jesus did not fight, but he never showed fear. The larger, more aggressive boys left him alone. He never "ran home" to relate his story of woe to his mother. For this, he won the respect of the other children. Most of the children sought to play with him. Some of the older boys were jealous of this respect and wondered that if he would not fight, how could others want to be around him so?

Jesus accepted this respect as though it were an obvious thing for others to offer. It never occurred to him that he was special or, God forbid, that he was unusual. There were, of course, the whispers about how he was born. Jesus did not understand these things and did not care at all to discuss them. On those rare quiet moments with his mother or father, or perhaps with them both, he would ask, "Why do I feel so different from everyone else?" Or, having heard the rumors about his birth he would wonder, *Do I not have an earthly father? Am I really adopted?* Or, when some of the darker rumors would surface he thought, *I am Joseph's son! I am not a child of forni...fornication!* These things passed through his mind as a boy. But the questions did not generate anxiety nor apprehension. He was a secure child. Secure with others. Secure with himself.

αΘω

"Look!" cried Eben.

A covey of sacrificial doves had escaped, forming shapes in the sky among the columns of the Temple as they beat white wings in graceful flurries of motion. How they knew to change direction, all at the same time, how they managed to dodge the many protuberances of Temple architecture, was an amazement and wonder to the boys. Each thought, "If I could only catch one, I would take it home and give it a name, and I would get to keep it!"

People were everywhere. The boys were jostled more than once by unthinking grown-ups, oblivious to their presence. They were bumped, cursed at, frowned upon and ignored. They looked around and discovered that their parents had–*disappeared!* At first, they panicked. Looking about, they searched frantically. To lose their parents in a place like this is frightening even for almost grown-up boys. Still, their panic subsided as boyhood curiosity returned, distracting them.

Wandering through the wall of bodies, they came upon a drainage grate in the pavement. It was ajar, exposing an aperture that gave way to darkness beneath. Jesus wanted to investigate. Struggling, the boys managed to pull the heavy grate open just enough for each of them to squeeze through. Stepping-stones had been chisled into the walls of the cavity that allowed them to descend into its darkness. It was not deep and at its bottom stretched a long, dark tunnel just high enough so that the boys had to get down on their hands and knees rather than crouch.

As their eyes adjusted to the poor light, they noticed another light in the distance down the length of the tunnel, indicating yet another opening to a grate above. "Com'on, Let's crawl to the other grate," Jesus said, excitedly.

"What if we get caught?" responded Eben circumspectly. "We are not supposed to be down here."

"Who's to know?" asked Jesus.

"GOD will know!" shot back Eben.

Jesus smiled, "Yes, that's true, now come on!" With that, he started to crawl toward the next shaft of light. It seemed natural to Jesus that, rather than God punishing them for this adventure, he would be with them and protect them. There wasn't much that frightened Jesus, and as for getting caught doing something of which adults would disapprove, well…In a few minutes they were there. Voices and noise from the floor above drifted down eerily.

"We're exploring a cave," said Jesus as if he had to add imagination to the adventure.

"Maybe we will find some bones or a skull." Eben's imagination quickly caught up. Since they had made it through the tunnel this far, he provoked himself to be a co-discoverer with Jesus.

Another shaft of light beckoned in the distance. Off they crawled. And so it went, from shaft to shaft, from grate to grate the boys explored the tunnels of the Temple until, at length, the next shaft of light was barely discernable in the distance. They stopped. Neither boy seemed eager to proceed.

"I think we should get out now," said Eben.

They sat under the last grate to which they had come. The sounds from above were quieter. They had apparently moved from the center of foot traffic and activity in the Temple to a place of lesser interest.

"This is a good place to escape before we get into real trouble. It doesn't sound like there are very many people around," spoke Eben softly.

Jesus looked above and then peered at the grey light so very far away down the tunnel. "Let's try it, Eben," he grinned.

"I'm not so sure," Eben was afraid but did not want it to show.

"It will be all right, Eben." Jesus coaxed, "God will take care of us." Eben was unconvinced.

"God will kill us!"

"No, he won't!"

"It's a real long way and it looks pretty dark."

"This will be the last one," Jesus said conspiratorially. "At the next light, we will definitely get out of here." Eben's heart throbbed with apprehension.

"Come on," and off Jesus crawled. The other boy had no choice but to follow.

They had not gone far, maybe one-third of the way to the next shaft of light when Jesus cried, "Ay-yah!" and abruptly stopped.

"What happened?" from frightened Eben.

"I don't know. I crawled on something." For the first time, Jesus found himself disquieted.

"Is it alive?" Eben groaned.

"No." Jesus paused as if searching. "There! I've got it. It's, it's some kind of weapon." The light in the tunnel was too dim to see much of anything. Jesus felt the instrument with his hands. "I think, I think...It's a dagger!" Both boys shrieked.

"Oh, no!" cried Eben.

"And it's covered with blood!" cried Jesus.

"Oh, no!" again from Eben. "Murder!"

The boys had not realized it, but the tunnel floor had begun to rise in the direction they were headed. The light they had seen was not the direct light of the next shaft, but the residual light from a shaft even farther up the tunnel. Hearts now pounding with excitement, they crawled faster, knees skinning against stone. From the point where they found the "dagger," the incline increased sharply until at long last, direct light from above came into view.

"Come on," said Jesus, "let's get out of here." Off he scurried toward the light as fast as he could. Eben followed. When they reached the grate from which the light emanated, they stopped to catch their breath. Both boys were panting.

"Let me see," demanded Eben breathlessly. The light was enough now to make out the object of such consternation. To their great disappointment, it was merely a trowel left behind by some worker many years ago. When the boys saw this, they breathed a sigh of relief. "It's only a mason's tool," said Eben. "It's no dagger at all."

Jesus tossed it aside, a look of disgust on his face. "It could have been used in a murder," he replied. "That brown stuff on it really looks like blood."

Light streamed from the grate above. It was a moment before the boys realized that no sounds could be heard. Cautiously, they made their way up the stones in the wall to the grate. The climb was higher here than was their descent into the tunnel. That combined with the long incline of the tunnel indicated a floor level much higher than the place they entered.

Once again, Jesus first. To their thankful surprise, the grate moved easily. In a moment, they were out of the tunnel and standing on—*a marble floor, mirror polished!* The grate opened between two massive tables. There was a large altar with a ramp leading up to a flat surface. A basin, or laver, containing water stood to the left as they faced a flight of stairs. At the top of the stairs there were two golden candlesticks followed by an opening into another spacious room at the end of which hung a thick curtain. The boys approached the curtain hanging wider and taller than anything either of them had ever seen.

Visibly moved by the sanctity of the cavernous structure, the two explorers became quiet. They could hear themselves breathing. The spirit of adventure pounding at their temples, yet not a sound was uttered. His demeanor sober, yet soft, Jesus' face turned serious. He was almost of age, and something inside him exerted itself. He stood looking at the great purple and scarlet curtain. He said to Eben, "Wait here," and without waiting for his friend to protest, he stepped inside its folds. Upon doing so, he instantly encountered another curtain, slightly less dense than the first. In the darkness, the boy calmly bent down, lifted its hem, and stepped under. It was then that young Jesus found himself standing in the Holy of Holies.

αΘω

Except for light filtering in from sources unknown to Jesus, illuminating three stone walls, the floor, the ceiling and the curtain behind him, the room was empty. No furniture, no altars, not even a carpet. Just an empty room. Without realizing why, the boy felt comfortable. He felt as though this were a familiar place very much like home. He knew that this place was a sanctuary, a place for the presence of God, yet there was nothing here. Just an empty, bare room, nothing to suggest even that it had a sacred meaning. He knew intuitively that this room was the heart of the great Temple, the focus and center of worship for all Israel. Crossing his legs, Jesus sat on the floor and promptly forgot about his friend waiting outside the curtain.

αΘω

From the moment Jesus entered the folds of the curtain, Eben felt apprehensive. Only a few seconds passed before he began to call, "Jesus? Jesus . . ? Jesus!" He dared not call above a whisper. He did not want to be discovered here. But Jesus did not hear. The curtain was too heavy, muffling any voice as tiny as the boy made. Eben waited, looking anxiously at the doorways into the Holy Place. It seemed he waited forever while Jesus remained silent inside the curtain. To Eben, it seemed the giant curtain had swallowed his friend. Then he heard voices. Footsteps coming. He had to hide. Behind the big altar. Sure enough, two priests entered the room and walked directly toward one of the tables. The two men spoke to one another of liturgical arrangements while Eben huddled on the floor behind the altar, hoping he would not be discovered. Would they go inside the curtain and find Jesus? What would they do if they found him? He wished with all his heart that he had not been separated from his parents. He closed his eyes and said, "Lord if you let me out of here, I will never..."

Before Eben completed his short prayer, the men were gone. He called to Jesus again. No answer. He wanted to follow his friend behind the curtain, but the fear in him precluded that. He could not move, let alone take a step toward the curtain. *Why doesn't he come out? What's keeping him? Did he leave me and go off on his own? Was he caught by someone on the other side?* "Jesus!" he whispered loudly.

Nothing.

What to do? Since he did not know what had happened to Jesus, Eben made the decision to extricate himself from this situation as best he could. He made his way toward the door through which the men had exited. Peering out into the Court of Israel, he saw people moving about, but no one looked in his direction. He slipped out and down the stairs into the Court of the Women unnoticed. There, miraculously, he saw his father, his mother and his older sister. When they saw him, they were angry.

"Where have you been?" his mother demanded.

"Playing with Jesus," he replied, volunteering nothing more. He still did not know of Jesus' whereabouts. He did not want to betray his friend. Perhaps he was safe with his parents as well. He hoped so.

"Don't you ever wander away from us again," his mother scolded. "You may become lost and who knows who might find you. Some terrible thing could happen to you."

"Yes, mother."

XVII

His Father's Business?

In the dimly lit sanctuary Jesus sat on the stone floor. He did not feel the cold seeping through his buttocks. He did not feel the ache in his knees and ankles. He did not shift uncomfortably. He seemed mesmerized, out of touch with the reality of his time and place. His thoughts consumed him, thoughts uncommon and beyond his age. Deep thoughts reaching back beyond his time. For the first time in his life, he realized he was as different from the rest of humanity as light is different from darkness.

This room. This place where once the arresting patina of glory shimmered.

> *"And there I will meet with you; and from above the mercy seat, from between the two cherubim. I will appear in the cloud over the mercy seat."*

αΘω

"Where is our son?" Mary was occupied with preparations for the journey back to Nazareth. As was her custom, she checked her mental list of items to be secured before they left. All the clothing and food had been packed. All the children in the caravan—except Jesus—were playing games with the children of other families from Nazareth and from other towns along the way. Mary had packed away the last vessel when she had asked the question.

"Playing with young Eben last time I saw him," her husband responded. Mary relaxed. Eben's mother was one of her favorite friends. Often they went to the well together. Jesus was in safe hands. She continued to make ready.

The caravan had traveled most of the day and the sky began to darken. The first star blinked in the waning sunset. Mary spoke to Joseph, "Will you please fetch Jesus now? It is time for him to come home." Joseph acknowledged his wife's request and walked away in the direction of their friend's position in the caravan. When he arrived he saw Eben with his family, but nowhere did he see his son. "Isn't Jesus with you?" he asked of Eben's father.

"Why no. The last time we saw him," he turned to his son, "Eben, weren't you playing with Jesus on the Temple grounds?"

"Yes, father."

"Then where is he?"

"I don't know father." The boy was not about to tell on Jesus. Besides, if he did he might get into trouble himself.

"Where did you leave him?" This time from Joseph trying to hold back the rising tension in his concern.

"I don't know, sir," the boy seemed frightened. "We were together in the crowd and then I couldn't find him. We got separated." Joseph looked with alarm at the boy's father.

Joseph quickly turned to go to his wife. "We must turn back."

"We will go with you!" assured Eben's father.

αΘω

When Mary heard the news, her face contorted with fear. "Oh no!" she cried. "What has happened to my son!?" Joseph tried to comfort her to no avail. *He is not the child's father. How could he possibly know!?* Her fright combined with frustration that privately and unjustifiably burned toward her husband. She wailed, "Oh God, help him. Perhaps he has fallen into the hands of terrible men." She allowed her mind to think the worst. She knew that slavers sometimes kidnapped young boys for unspeakable purposes. Or perhaps he lay dead or dying in a wadi somewhere. All thoughts of future blessing and prophetic fulfillment evaporated before the accusing specter of parental irresponsibility. "Oh, Jesus, my son!" she wailed.

"Hold onto yourself, Mary. Think! You *know* God will take care of him." Joseph's voice suddenly sobered her. Of course, he was concerned. Joseph had never treated Jesus in any other way than that of a favored son. He loved Jesus as much as she. *Oh, strong Joseph! Thank God, he is at my side.*

"Hurry!" said Mary. "Let us leave now! Let us search. I will not leave Jerusalem until he is found!"

"We *will* find him," said Joseph with determination. "Of that I can promise."

αΘω

Jesus emerged from the sanctuary curtain three days later, yet it had seemed for him but a moment fleeting. He felt different than he felt before he entered the sanctuary. No longer the adventurous boy, but the beginning of a man stepped that day from the folds of the curtain. What had he seen in Herod's empty sanctuary? What had he felt? What had he heard? What had touched him? As he made his way from the Temple that day, he only knew that he had experienced something. Encountered Someone. In the deep, quiet eddies of his spirit he knew he would never be the same.

αΘω

Profoundly affected by his solitary experience in the sanctuary, Jesus moved through the Temple in a straight line, noticed by passers-by, but not disturbed. To them, he seemed a strange looking boy. Perhaps lost. An occasional mother wondered if his parents knew his whereabouts. Jesus was not thinking of his parents. Nor had he a single thought that Eben had not been waiting for him. While his mind was clear, his sensitivity to his environs was overcome by his focus. All he could think of for the moment was,...*well, what was it? Contact? In the sanctuary?* He knew something had happened to him, yet he could not grasp it, could not comprehend it. He felt himself glowing inside, almost vibrating with an inexorable quality of transcendence. Whatever it was, it made him feel enfranchised, enabled. He was not afraid. He would never be afraid again.

Soon he found himself among the great marble colonnades of Solomon's porch. He paused, gazed up their graceful lengths and wondered if they might reach to the heights of what he felt inside, and then continued on. In a moment, he heard a voice that penetrated his focus. The sound carried through the door out into the passageway between the columns. It must have been an important voice for Jesus was intensely focused at that moment. He stopped to see. A man with a great beard flecked with grey was holding court with a group of what appeared to be students in one of the anterooms off the side of the porch. Other older men were with them, rabbis and elders no doubt. Jesus listened.

The group consisted of men, or at least, males. Some were boys his age. They sat squirming on the floor, trying to be quiet, but for the most part very bored. The others were a mixture of younger men ascending in age all the way up to the rabbis who to Jesus, seemed quite old. There were maybe thirty in all. They were asking questions about the Feast of the Passover, about why this annual, celebratory trek to Jerusalem.

One young man about eight or nine years Jesus' senior stood, "Did not Moses and the children of Israel eat the Passover in their own homes in Egypt? Did they not apply blood to the posts and lintels of their own homes? Then why must we and our families now come all the way to Jerusalem to celebrate this holy day?"

One of the rabbis, whose beard was black and well oiled, seemed offended at the impertinence of the question and was about to reply with rebuking words. But greybeard smiled. "Do you think the journey too arduous, my young friend? Is such a man of youth and vigor as yourself so easily fatigued?"

Soft laughter from the others. "Do you not recall," greybeard continued, "in the days of Hezekiah, king of Israel, that he sent letters to Ephraim and Manesseh, calling all the priests and Levites to Jerusalem to celebrate the Feast of Passover . . ?"

"That is true, rabbi..." He was interrupted by a very young voice. All eyes turned toward Jesus who was standing at the rear of the group. "Yet do you not also recall that it was Josiah, son of Amon and king of Israel, who established Jerusalem as the place where all Israel should observe Passover?" The rest of the students were stunned that an inexperienced and uneducated child should respond to the rabbis with such confidence and poise. Some of them sucked their breath in surprise. The rabbis' eyes widened. Blackbeard glowered. Greybeard seemed amused. "For do not the Scriptures say," Jesus continued, "that *king Josiah commanded all the people saying, 'Celebrate the Passover to the LORD your God as it is written in this book of the covenant, in Jerusalem?'"*

"Well, it seems I stand corrected!" greybeard smiled. And who might this young scholar be?

My name is "Jesus, Jesus ben Joseph." Spoken with confidence. Spoken perhaps even with a bit of pride.

"Joseph?" said greybeard, raising one eyebrow. "Common enough name." Turning to a colleague, he asked loud enough for all to hear, "Is there a rabbi named Joseph?" He assumed Jesus had learned the scriptures from his father. The implication of the joke was not lost on Jesus and it irritated him.

"He is not a rabbi!" responded the boy perhaps too sharply. "He is...a

carpenter." A ripple of laughter among the students. Greybeard smiled again, marvelously amused. Even Blackbeard smiled.

"Then whence learned you such wisdom?"

"It is not wisdom to remember simple facts from scripture," replied Jesus. It was not said insolently or disrespectfully. He spoke with the innocence of his age, but now the joke was on the ancient rabbi. More laughter among the students.

"My son!" a commanding voice from the rear of the room. An embarrassed Joseph stood in the doorway, his face revealing relief, anger and shock at what he witnessed. A second later the boy's mother rushed by his father pushing him aside. She ran quickly into the room taking Jesus by the shoulders. She hugged him and wept. Then holding him at arm's length she scolded, "Jesus! How is it that you have treated us in this way?" She paused and looked at her son. He seemed totally without understanding of her concern. "Ah!" she cried in strong exclamation. "Your father and I have been in anguish searching for you."

The rabbis and students looked on in curious silence. They were all waiting for Jesus' explanation. Perhaps the rabbis would come to his rescue. Greybeard seemed to sense the expectation of the students. After all, young Jesus was something of a hero to them now. He was looked upon with a favor akin to respect. *Greybeard, say something!* "Madam I," Greybeard was cut short.

Jesus finally found his tongue in response to his intensely emotional mother. "Mother, did you not realize that I must attend to my Father's business?" asked Jesus shakily. Again, the question would appear insolent and insensitive were it not for the innocent tone in which it was asked.

Joseph, however, would have none of these whimsical, pietistic answers from his son who, as far as he was concerned, had done something serious and very wrong. He had with apparent disregard violated the wishes of his parents. This was unacceptable. Taking Jesus by the arm and leading him from the room, he whispered into his son's ear, "Father's business or not, boy, the next time you run off on an escapade like this, you will answer to *this* father!" This time, raucous laughter from the students. Joseph's big, calloused carpenter's hand hurt. Jesus could not remember seeing his father so angry. Suddenly, he was a boy again. He knew he would be disciplined, and he knew it would not be pleasant. He had caused his parents much concern and pain. At the age when he was supposed to become a man, this was not good. He knew that he had violated their trust. He accepted the penalty that was to come.

For, though he were a Son, yet learned he obedience
through the things that he suffered.

His mother, however, despite her fears, pondered the response of her son. It was a response that would haunt her for the rest of her life.

XVIII

Farewell

In all, Joseph fathered eight children. All five boys were master carpenters. Young Judas could handle an adze better than any of the others. The senior Joseph, clearly the best woodworker in the family, observed that his third son and namesake, Joseph, learned quickly. *This one exceeds the others in raw talent for the work,* his father had decided. Possibly exceeding even himself. A fortunate man, all of his sons worked in the trade and, still, they were unable to keep up with the work. The girls, Milcah, Sarah and Rhoda, were a great help also and especially to their mother, his precious Mary.

The house and family of Joseph prospered, enjoying their reputation as the most skilled carpenters throughout the region of Galilee. Jesus, being the first born, was secretly the pride of his father's eye. He'd often watched his eldest son bent over his workbench and his heart warmed to a gentle smile. *My son! Such a man!* His back was strong, his mind sharp; his work was, well, among the finest.

As for Jesus, he loved the smells of the carpenter's shop…the pungent fragrance of pitch, of fresh cuts of aged wood, of the oils used to preserve and reveal the grain of each piece. He loved working with tools, working with his hands and the satisfaction of creating something good and useful. His father had taught him the value of a job well done, whether it was an attractive archway entrance to a home or wheels for an ox cart. And he loved the good fun of working with his brothers and his father, the joking, the teasing and the good-natured insults. They enjoyed the talk of men.

Jesus was, however, preoccupied at times. *He has been preoccupied all his life,* thought Joseph. He remembered with fondness the time they thought they had lost him. *Palavering with the elders in the Temple…*Joseph smiled at the memory. It wasn't amusing then.

Over the last several months, his son had become detached from the family business. Joseph understood. He had understood all along. *I will lose him. The time is approaching.* A terrible ache throbbed in his bones when he thought of it, a permeating pain, from which escape seemed impossible.

In the natural and ordinary earthiness of growing up, it had sometimes been hard for Joseph to think of this son as whom he knew him to be. While a happy child with a quick wit and a hearty laugh, Jesus was pensive at times, preoccupied with things beyond his father's ability to imagine. Beyond anyone's ability to imagine. Despite his terrible uniqueness, Jesus had been a fine son, every inch a source of pride to this father and mother.

He was thirty now. Clearly, his heart was no longer in the shaping of wood.

And then…

αΘω

"My father," Jesus had begun. They had just completed the evening meal. Joseph at the head of the table, Mary at the other end. Things that affected the family were always discussed together. Even the youngest was invited to participate. And Rhoda never let such an opportunity pass. She was always ready to talk, ready to be—wanted to be—involved.

Jesus reclined at his father's right hand. James, the eldest next to Jesus, reclined to their father's left. Sarah to James' left. *Sarah. Dear, sweet Sarah.* Much like her mother in disposition, humble, self-effacing, quiet; and across from her, Simon, who in addition to carpentry, was the family's hunter. Next to Simon, Rhoda, and across from her, Judas. Judas admired his brother Jesus and emulated him in thoughtfulness. To Judas' left, Milcah, the eldest daughter who reclined at Mary's right and who took charge of everything. The family often fondly wondered about Milcah and her mother as to which was really the "woman of the house." To Milcah's left, the boy Joseph.

When Jesus addressed his father, conversation among the family faded. Even Rhoda quieted. All of them knew what was coming. Like their father, they had sensed it for months. Mary swallowed, held her breath and kept silent, tears a heartbeat away.

"My father, I must leave."

The Second Scroll

Water from Water

And God said, "Let there be a vault between the waters to separate water from water." So God made the vault and separated the water under the vault from the water above it. And it was so. God called the vault "sky." And there was evening, and there was morning—the second day.

—Genesis 1:6-8 NIV

I

17 Tishri, 25 A.D.

The Baptist's Shame

The laughter of girls? It came to him on the wisp of a breeze. It was faint but if he listened carefully, *Yes! There it is again!* As certain as someone calling him, beckoning him, he followed the sound. Light-spirited, pleasant laughter has its own appeal. It lifts the heart. It raises anticipation—especially feminine laughter. Especially to a virile young man of thirty who had spent most of his life in the wilderness alone. As he stepped across the grass, around the rocks, through the trees, the laughter grew louder, happy girlish voices. He could hear the splash of water. The ground beneath him littered and soiled with familiar black spots—olives, fallen from their source of nourishment. It was then that he realized he was standing in an olive grove. The earth fell away into a downward slope. He knew it led to the river. He spent so much of his time near the river. It was *his* source of nourishment. He often fished its waters. More often, he bathed there. Now as he stood among the olives, he saw four lovely maidens standing in the waist-deep current. They were as naked as crystal droplets of morning dew upon the grass.

When first he saw them, he averted his eyes and turned in retreat. *Leave them! Leave them their privacy, leave them their innocence,* but he could not.

The scintillating notes of Solomon's Song came flooding upon him as the swelling of the Jordan after a heavy rain,

> *"How beautiful are your feet, O prince's daughter! the joints of your thighs are encrusted with jewels, the work of the hands of a skilled jeweler."*

It was as if an unseen force turned his head and caused his eyes to gaze upon their stunning nudity.

> *"Your navel is a rounded goblet, which wants not strong spirits: your belly is an heap of wheat set about with lilies."*

How is it, thought he, *that God so fashioned the feminine form to be the most elegant and exquisite expression of natural beauty?*

> *"Your two breasts are like twin fawns."*

In creating her, Yaweh must have exhausted his creative resources. Why might he have done that?

> *"Your neck is as a tower of ivory; your eyes like the pools in Heshbon, by the gate of Bathrabbim."*

If sexual feelings are so wicked, so evil, how is it that the Creator himself formed their compulsion?

> *"Your head upon you is as Carmel, and the hair of thine head like shimmering purple glistening in black velvet; it would turn the head of kings."*

How is it that the masterpiece of God's creative genius is the central, the essential core and essence of sexual provocation?

He knew that there is no satisfactory answer to these questions. Apart from his devotion to God, never had he felt such compulsion. But now, his feet refused to move. He felt as though he were invading something private and precious. Guilt and a sense of twisted shame disturbed him, but he could not move. He could no longer avert his eyes and as he watched, he stood transfixed by the scene before him, unable to arrest shameful feelings, unable to stop his despicable behavior. The maidens, however, oblivious to his presence, continued to play in their innocence.

αΘω

John sat on the flat rock in front of the cave that had become his home, legs folded beneath him. His hair, still wet from another of the frequent washings he gave it, dripped water on the stone around him. Grasping a handful of the red-brown strands, he combed vigorously, freeing it of persistent tangles. *Nazirite! Hah!* he exclaimed in silent frustration. As soon as it dried, he would oil it and once again, his waist-length hair would be the talk of all the women in Judea. But he hated it. He hated his lonely life. He hated this cave. He hated the rock on which he sat. Visions of what his eyes had seen persistently haunted his thoughts. Intruding into his dreams, he now often awoke to find that he had soiled himself in the night. Why? What was happening to him? Why would God allow it? His whole existence seemed unnatural and artificial.

His parents had died many years ago. At twelve years old, as other Jewish boys were going to the Temple in Jerusalem, John took a vow to be set apart for the Lord. He had never had wine, not so much as a cool, fresh grape. He had never touched or been near a dead body. John had no one. No friends. He had spent most of his life in this wilderness and he was sick of it.

John was not a man who enjoyed people. He was a man whose judgment of society was usually scornful. He saw others as spending their lives in consumptive living, self-serving and secular. Hence, he became a recluse. He made his way into the wilderness, where he lived in caves and learned how to survive an inhospitable environment.

He held himself aloof from others and enjoyed being alone—at first. He was eccentric. He abstained from just about everything. He was, after all, a Nazirite, dedicated and set apart to God. Although he had blinding desires, he had never, like Sampson, another Nazirite, whose sexual escapades were well known, allowed himself any sexual latitude. That is why his encounter at the river had upset him so deeply. It was a *weakness* in his character, he felt; not to be tolerated in others, and ten thousand times more—not in himself!

αΘω

In the fifteenth year of Tiberius Caesar when Pontius Pilate was governor of Judea and Herod Antipas was a mere tetrarch of Galilee, the word of God came to John in the wilderness.

One could find him in the district around the Jordan river, preaching a baptism of repentance, the symbol of a resolve to leave a dissolute life and live a righteous life. People often referred to John as "The Baptist," likely because he would baptize anyone who would get within arm's reach. "Repent and be baptized!" he shouted. "Change your way of life, stop wasting your lives in debauchery. Come, be baptized as a 'memorial,' as a 'witness' that you will henceforth live for God, for his kingdom is at your very door!" Thousands in and around Judea came to see John. Most came for the entertainment John provided. Some came out of curiosity. Some took him seriously. These, more often than not, submitted to his baptism. And some of these, among them a few scraggly fishermen, became his followers. Many thought John strange because he dressed in camel's hair and wore a leather belt around his waist. His diet included dried locusts dipped in wild honey. However he was perceived by the populace, John the Baptist could not be ignored.

Among the curious to come to see John were many of the religious leaders. Because of the Baptist's obvious popularity, they too, thought it expedient to be baptized by him. They liked John's austerity. They mistakenly thought him to be a legalist, like them, but John was quickly aware that they intended to use association with him for their own ends.

While preaching one day, he noticed a group of them gathered, watching him. Unimpressed by their pretentious piety and dress, he turned upon them and shouted, "You poisonous brood of vipers! Flee from the wrath to come! Are you really interested in repentance? Then show it by living humble, godly lives. Do not suppose that you can say to yourselves, 'We have Abraham for our father.' What is that!? God is able from these *stones* to raise up children to Abraham! *Listen to me!* The woodsman's axe is already laid at the root of the trees. You know what that means. God will cut down every tree that does not bear good fruit and throw it into the fire."

Enraged, these religious prigs sucked in their breath, cursing the Baptist, cursing the insult. They turned away disgusted, muttering among themselves.

II

Repent

Religious authority did not know what to do with John. To them, he was a prophet, but one of nominal consequence. Except, of course, for the fact that he stirred up so much trouble, and that so many followed him. The issues surrounding John must be addressed, but just how to do that appeared difficult. He was an anomaly. Meanwhile, John spoke of something else that was a total mystery to the religious community.

"I baptize you with water for repentance, but there is someone coming after me who is mightier than I." John paused, his voice softened. How *had* he come to start baptizing people? Clearly, it began with his sense of purpose. From a child he had known that God would require something of the hearts of men. His life, he felt, was dedicated—*purposed*—to assist in bringing about that requirement. It is only right that there should be a symbolic ritual. As circumcision indicated Israel's separation to God, so should there be something befitting one's dedication to God, something confirming one's desire for forgiveness. *What could it be?*

John loved water. There is a special spot along the Jordan just south of Galilee, where the water flows fast, sluicing through the rocks with a roar. In that spot, John discovered two pointed rocks protruding from the bottom of the stream which he could grasp. In doing so, he lay out flat against the current while he held on tightly, his body bouncing and snapping as a flag in a stiff wind. The cold water and its roaring froth felt like a thousand thorns pricking his skin. Refreshing, pounding sensory overload; he returned there again and again.

While he wore the most primitive of clothing and consumed the most rudimentary elements for food, he bathed every day, living a life of meticulous cleanliness. He spent his entire adult life in the environs of rivers and streams. Cool waters invigorated him. *Could it be something as simple as dipping a soul beneath the surface of water? Oh, my God, what do you want?* It was a good thing, bathing, feeling almost to cleanse the soul as well as the body. His communion with God complete, the matter satisfied, and so at peace John came, preaching a "baptism" of repentance. Even more provoking for John was that from a child he had struggled with the notion that he was sent by God to prepare the way for Messiah, the Blessed, Anointed One. He believed this, yet it seemed so implausible.

His thoughts momentarily somewhere else. He had forgotten his audience. Emerging from his reverie, apparently assuming his hearers could read his thoughts, he declared abruptly, "I am not fit to remove his sandals," his thoughts continuing, his eyes pensive. They wondered of whom he spoke. "When he comes, he will baptize you with the Holy Spirit and with fire." Again, John's voice lifted, "His winnowing fork will be in his hand, and he will thoroughly clear his threshing floor. Clear it, do you understand!? He will clear it so that there will not be so much as one wisp of chaff left to consider! He will gather his wheat into the barn, but he will burn up the chaff with unquenchable fire." The words poured out of him in a crescendo as though some invisible force were controlling his speech. Visibly shaken and out of breath, the 'Baptist' sat down.

αΘω

The prophetic ministry of John the Baptist had been foretold in the words of Isaiah, . .

> *"The voice of one crying in the wilderness, 'Make ready the way of the Lord, make His paths straight. Every valley shall be filled up, and every mountain and hill shall be brought low. The crooked shall become straight and rough roads shall become smooth. And all flesh shall see the salvation of God.'"*

People were in a state of expectation and wondering about John. Could he be the Christ? This was especially true for the religious authorities. Since they did not know how to discredit this wild man, they had to interpret him to the masses, so priests and Levites from Jerusalem came to ask him, "Who are you?"

"I am not the Christ," said John abruptly as if having already been advised of the real intent of their question.

Where amongst the firmament of heaven and hell would he get that idea? they thought. *Life in the desert has muddled his mind! What magnificent arrogance! Perhaps we should humor him,* "What then? Are you Elijah?"

"I am not."

"Then you must be the 'Prophet!'" they were laughing at him. Moses had spoken of such a Prophet that would come instead of him, someone who would arise from "among their brothers."

"No," declared John.

"Well, who are you, man? We have to give an answer to those who sent us. What can you tell us about yourself?"

John thought about this for a moment. Then he said, "I am just a voice. Just a solitary voice, a voice of one crying in the wilderness."

This made absolutely no sense to them. They couldn't even respond to it. "All right then, if you are not the Christ, and if you are not Elijah, and if you are not the Prophet, why are you baptizing?" They looked at John and at each other with exasperation.

"I baptize because I am a baptizer. Why do you do what you do? You enjoy calling me 'the Baptist.' Well, that is what I do. I baptize in water. It is the best I can offer. But let me tell you something; there stands among you *One whom you do not know.*" He let them think about that. "It is he who comes after me," he continued. "I am not even worthy so much as to untie his sandal." They looked at him with expressions ranging from anger to astonishment. Ignoring them, John turned once again to the crowd and resumed preaching.

αΘω

For however much John was moved by what he had just said, the multitudes were even more. They began to question him, "My God, man! Then what shall we do?"

"Do? You ask me what to do? Are you stone deaf? What have I been saying? Repent! Change your attitudes. Change your way of life. Instead of using his name in vain, ask God to forgive your sins. If you have two tunics, share with him who has none, and if you have a bushel of olives, or a skin of wine, share your food and drink."

The tax gatherers who had come to be baptized also begged, "Teacher, what shall we do?"

"You people are consumed with avarice. You collect more taxes than required and you fill your coffers with the excess. *Stop that!* Clear enough?"

Then some soldiers asked, "What about us, what shall we do?"

Wearily, John responded, "You are in a position of power. Because you represent Rome, you are feared. Therefore, do not take money from anyone by force, or accuse anyone falsely. Be content with your wages."

These practical, everyday matters were the fruit of repentance? Care for poor people? Do not use people for profit? Do not rob, falsely accuse or seek more than you are due? These are the things of repentance? This did not seem overburdening. Yet the impoverished were everywhere. Tax collectors were the richest people in the land. Roman soldiers in charge of enforcing civil law were well known for taking what they want, accusing whomever they chose with impunity and constantly complaining that Caesar did not pay them enough. These were matters, according to this unusual prophet, that interested God. Change in these matters may well indicate a change in the human heart. It would certainly mean a change in human suffering.

III

Baptism

The next day John stood knee-deep in the waters of the Jordan river. His camel-hair tunic lay in a heap on the riverbank, his hairy chest heaving in cadence to his words as he preached to the people congregated on the shore. Unexpectedly, in mid-sentence, his exhortations ceased. In the eerie, echoing silence that followed, one could hear the gentle ripple of water. Hands arrested in mid-gesture lowered to his side. His eyes followed a figure moving in the crowd.

Jesus stepped from the assembly to the water's edge, a smile on his lips. Removing his tunic, he tossed it beside John's. "Greetings, cousin." he said quietly.

It took a moment for John to find his tongue. When he did, he spoke not to Jesus, but to his listeners, "See now for yourselves!" voice trembling just above a whisper. Gesturing toward Jesus his voice straining, "Here standing before us is the Lamb of God who takes away the sin of the world!" Indistinguishable murmuring softly fluttered among the crowd.

For John it all began to come back. He recalled the countless nights when his mother had told him the story of his aunt Mary and the birth of this cousin. Told him of what God had done. Told him of his own special birth to them in their old age. How many times had his father told him of how he was special to God? He had only seen Jesus a few times as they both grew up. They lived too far apart and even when the family came for Passover, the sheer number of people made it difficult for family reunion to take place. But he knew Jesus well enough to recognize him easily. He knew enough to sense and seize the exigency of the moment. He knew that Jesus had come to be baptized, yet...

Incredibly, he thought of that moment in the olive grove. He thought of the shame. Why has *he* come to *me?* It was a question of honest inquiry. *I am the one in need of change. Not him!* Incredulous John. "I—I can't do this," he stammered.

"John, please. This is your hour, and mine. This is the way for us to fulfill all righteousness. It is what the Father wants. You will see in a moment."

They stood together in the river. John lifted his arm to embrace the broad carpenter shoulders of his cousin. Turning again to the crowd standing by he said, "This is he of whom I spoke, 'After me comes a Man who has a higher rank than I, for He existed before me.'" (An odd remark, since John was conceived before Jesus. Was this grizzled prophet somehow aware of Jesus' true origins?) "I did not recognize him at first. But I knew he was coming, and I knew that I was sent to prepare the way for him. Now, therefore, in order that he might be manifest to all men, I baptize him in this water today." Then Jesus knelt in the water and John laid him beneath the eddies.

αΘω

After being baptized, Jesus enthusiastically embraced John and waded out of the water, his body dripping puddles around him. Abruptly, the overcast above parted to allow shafts of sunlight. A dove, wings white with the sun, descended in slow arcs, coming to rest on Jesus' shoulder. There came a distant rumbling in the air like thunder escalating louder and louder until it stopped. And in the silence that followed, a clear voice was heard by all, *"This is My beloved Son, in whom I am well pleased."* Jesus stood there, the dove perched on his shoulder, both bathed in sunlight.

John exulted, "Did you see that!? I told you this was going to happen! I've been telling you for years. Did you see the Spirit of the living God? Out of the heavens He came...*as a dove!*...sitting upon his shoulder! I knew this was going to happen! I knew it because God once said to me, *'He upon whom you see the Spirit descend, this is the one who baptizes in the Holy Spirit.'*

"Now I see with my own eyes, so see you all! I know, and I tell you that this man—is the Son of God!"

αΘω

The journey shaped in the development of one's faith is marked by events terribly significant to its formation. So it was for me when the form of Jesus disappeared beneath the currents of the Jordan. I had heard John speak and preach of Jesus countless times. His reality, though, seemed almost like a ghostly celebrity, a tale of fiction related as if it were true. To actually see that Jesus was real evoked scattered feelings of the ordinary mixed with awe. I was not prepared for the dove nor for the voice from the lowering sky. The nature, tenor and tone of the voice made it clear that no one standing by could have uttered it. Unlike many miraculous events in life, this one left no doubt as to its supernatural character.

It wasn't, however, the deific features of this event that so shaped my intent to pursue this man until my last breath. It was Jesus himself. He certainly had sought no recognition of himself other than that which he had through this act with his cousin, he had publicly committed his life to the worship and service of God. I wish I could tell you what it was that so compelled me, that so made me want to be with him. He was a young man, yet his demeanor spoke of wisdom and depth beyond his years. When his eyes met mine, it seemed that he knew me, yet he had never met me. It was as if he had said, "Hello, Justus, my old friend." Yet beyond his smile, he spoke nothing.

As I write these words now, I try in retrospect to understand my compulsive attraction to him. I cannot, these many years later, I cannot understand. As I write, I know that the bond that occurred between his soul and mine on the day of his baptism is more tightly bound today than ever. I know that we are inseparable—one, together, forever. *How I long to see you again, my Jesus, my friend, my dearest friend!*

IV

The Tempter

He had not eaten for forty days and nights. His body starved, physically weak, he reclined on the barren earth of the mountainside, under a dead tree by the mouth of the cave where he spent his nights. There were perhaps thousands of these caves in the Judean countryside. His body emaciated, the shape of his bones clearly visible, his bowels had ceased to move and were it not for a cool pool of water recessed in one of the inner corridors of the cave, he would be dead of starvation.

This, indeed, was trial by fire. This was his passage, his initiation into the service of God. At the beginning of a new phase of his life, Jesus had been led by the Holy Spirit to this specific spot. It could not have been much worse. He thought with meager comfort of Elijah sitting outside his cave wondering what would happen to him. *At least Elijah had the ravens!* Were it not for the coolness of the cave's interior, he might have perished under the burning sun in this desert place.

Dusk and the hours that followed were blessed relief. He lay for hours staring at the stars. As he communed with the Father, he felt a kinship with these stars that none other would ever know. Now in his earthbound human body, of a mere thirty years, in the periphery of his consciousness he was aware that eons ago each celestial body had something to do with him. In this starved condition, his limited spirit now had trouble comprehending exactly what. On these starlit nights he mused until sleep tugged at his eyelids and he felt his undernourished muscles relax against the stone. He then retired into the cave until the soft glow of dawn began to paint its dreary walls.

Each day came and went. Unrelenting hunger wracked his body. He had long passed the days when his stomach became numb to hunger. Its pain had returned with devastating demands. *"Just a morsel of my brother's venison!"* As he thought about this, painfully bemused, he had a new appreciation for Esau as well as Elijah.

It was then that the tempter came.

αΘω

Hungry, *Son of God?"* It was not a disembodied voice that Jesus heard. The question, a mockery. The title a derision, spoken by the source of evil incarnate. A man stood there dressed in expensive robes, serene, intellectual in appearance, and calm. A man who would stand out in a crowd as someone to respect and to whom others gave deference. "If you are the, ah, *Son of God,* then speak to these stones. Tell them to become bread. Surely God would not object if you took the edge off this insufferable hunger."

He spoke in a manner, matter-of-fact, cultured and self-assured. The words were spoken philosophically, detached, yet hanging cold and demeaning. He appeared refined, polished and in command of himself. Not a man with whom one trifles, accustomed to command, accustomed to respect.

Jesus, his body trembling, making aching and irresistible demands of him, his mind aware of something hard and unrelenting in the deepest corner of his spirit, considered the man—but without fear. On the surface of it, he was thirty years old—young and inexperienced. This fortyish man had an intimidating presence, a polished, professional, experienced, enormous intellect. Yet there was something within Jesus that reached back in time beyond his years. While his earthly eyes had never seen this man before, he knew him. The memory, however dim; he recalled encountering him. Things were different then. At that time, this man was not a man but what . . . ? An authority? It was difficult to remember.

Jesus heard himself speak, "You know well that I could command anything I wish. But I am human now, in a body limited by mortality." *A very hungry human;* a thought he put quickly aside.

"Being human *does* have its constraints, does it not?" The man's lips turned upward, as if to smile, but there was no smile.

"Perhaps you need to be reminded," said Jesus, "human that I am, *'Man does not live on bread alone, but on every word that comes from the mouth of God.'"*

The creature, who looked like a man, seemed amused. He wished to appear tolerant, not insensitive to the younger man's obvious discomfort. There was, however, a flash of calculating cruelty in his eye. *"How profound!"* He remarked with contempt. *"How utterly...mystical!"*

Their transport, something ethereal, transcendent. For in the next instant, they were no longer on the mountain by the cave, but in the city of

Jerusalem, standing at the highest point of the Temple. It was no accident that this particular city and this Temple tower were chosen. Jerusalem, the City of God! What better place to discredit his "Son"! The Temple tower, overlooking the Holy of Holies! What better place to desecrate the Holy One!

"If you are the Son of God," the man said, "jump. You do know the Scripture, do you not? *'He will command his angels concerning you, and they will lift you up in their hands, so that you will not strike your foot against a stone.'* Here in the holy city on the pinnacle of the Temple, could there be a better venue for a divine demonstration? It is only four hundred feet to the ground. Hardly worthy of the *Son* of God. Come now, show your credentials,"

On the surface of it, the challenge seemed rational enough. If the words of the psalmist were true, then there was nothing to fear. Clearly, he was the Son of God. But if not, he would die, and of course, the "Son of God" designation would become moot.

Jesus answered him with confidence, "I do know the Scripture. And I remind you also of the word, *'Do not put the Lord your God to the test.'*"

The man was no longer amused. "*The Lord my God!? Do you say?*" The evil fire in his eye flashed even more brilliantly. He knew then that he would not distract this young man with tricks. *He really knows; he really believes that he is . . ?* They transported again, this time to the highest mountain. From here, the rim of the world could be seen. The man swept his arm encompassing the curvature of the earth and displayed to Jesus all the realms of the world and their splendor—as far as eye could see. "All this is mine, you know. It was accorded to me and me alone. I will give it to you," he said, "if you will give your allegiance to me, if you confess *me* to be the Lord *your* God!"

The absurdity of such an offer apparently had never entered the man's mind. How does one offer the Creator that which he already possesses? How does the Creator worship the created?

Nonetheless, it was out. The real reason for this encounter. This man, this devil, knew when to strike. Strike at human weakness. Strike at the point of doubt. Sometime during the last forty days, angels could have come. They did not. *Why?* Had God the Father deserted him? His cheeks had gone sallow. His body had lost substance of tissue and he was dying. Yet, he could not stop himself. He knew that he must suffer these things. *But I am, after all, human!* But this tempter? And this offer of satiety?

Worship this, this thing? Then Jesus remembered. This "thing" was one

Lucifer, the highest and most noble of all created beings. He, and he alone, was the angel of light. He came to believe that he was the equal, if not the superior, of God himself. And since Jesus had taken upon himself the form of a man, it is not remarkable that this unholy, despicable creature thinks of himself worthy of Jesus' worship.

Stronger than the terrible demands of starvation, stronger than his human needs, finding the strength of his integrity, Jesus said to him, "Away from me, Satan! You know, *you know* what is written: *'Worship the Lord your God, and serve him alone.'* Something, I might add, that you seem to have discarded."

The man gazed at him with accomplished contempt. And then he was gone. Was there a question left hanging? Were there threatening words somewhere in the churning mists of violent hunger that said, *"You will regret this?"* Would there be another time of great suffering when he might once again hear the evil mockery, *"I gave you a chance in the desert, on the Temple pinnacle and yet again on a mountain high. Now look at you. You were dying then. You are dying now, and this time…"*

V

The Lamb of God

Emaciated from starvation, staggering from weakness, Jesus fainted. The terrible hour of torment had come and gone. He desperately needed food. Angels came, finally. Hovering around him, they strengthened him, comforted him.

Dawn broke yet again. He awoke, the smell of desert rich in his nostrils, the Judean sun climbing toward its zenith. The angels gone, weak with hunger, his steps appeared unpracticed and faltering as he made his way down the mountainside. The morning cool warmed. Every few paces, he stopped, leaned against a rock and rested. It seemed forever before the slope of the path leveled. Ahead, along the way, Jesus saw a group of men gathered around another man, listening to him speak. In a moment, he recognized John, that baptist, holding court with anyone who would listen. *Cousin John! Perhaps he would spare a locust.* At this point, Jesus would gladly have eaten a basket of locusts.

John looked up and saw Jesus coming toward him. What John saw on this morning was different than anything he had seen before. Different than when they were children. Different than even the baptism. What did this young prophet see? What was it about Jesus that only John could recognize, indeed had made him leap in his mother's womb; what could John see and feel that others could not? We only know that he whispered slowly as if paralyzed by the spectacle, "Look," he said for the second time in his life, as he observed the awkward, emaciated form of Jesus. *"Look, and behold the Lamb of God!"* Two of John's disciples followed his gaze, and arrested by these words, were compelled to consent.

As it turned out, John was almost as hungry as Jesus. He had no food. He too, looked gaunt and bizarre in his camel's hair wrappings. The two of them made a pathetic tableau, with every appearance of rejection by society, homeless in the world in which they lived. Jesus was too faint, too preoccupied with his own weakness to be sociable. After learning there was no food to be had, he simply turned to leave. The two who had been listening to John speak were fishermen, Simon and John. These two began to follow along after Jesus. Curiously, this continued for a moment and then, turning around, Jesus saw them and asked, "What is it you want?"

Simon and John had heard their prophet speak of Jesus. Times past counting they had heard of the coming Messiah, the Lamb of God. Now he had been identified.

Surprised by the question, they didn't know how to answer. They hadn't thought they would be asked. All they knew was that they were terribly interested in this man. Simon, the more outspoken of the two, responded, "Teacher?" In the momentary silence that followed, he glanced at his companion, eyes shifting nervously, "Ah, . . Teacher , . ?" the question would not come. At length, he asked stupidly, "Where are you staying?"

αΘω

Jesus did not respond. He gazed intently at the men with worn, dark eyes. He considered their eager curiosity. He saw the expressions of anticipation on their faces. At length, he replied weakly, "Come, and you will see." He turned and continued unsteadily down the path. *Come! How inviting the sound when it came from him.*

They had walked together for perhaps an hour, Jesus breathing heavily. Just the act of walking was an incredible effort, sapping him of strength. Conversation spasmodic and uncomplicated. The men were afraid to ask questions or to engage him overmuch, in consideration of his obvious weakness. Jesus abruptly faltered again. He had been doing well. His strength appeared to be holding until at length, he could not continue. Simon's hand steadied him. Jesus looked at him and said, "Thank you. I think I will be fine when I have some food." And then their eyes met. With effort, Jesus lifted his arm to Simon's shoulder. The older man stood still. "You are Simon, the son of John?" It was phrased as a question, but it came across as a statement of fact. Jesus said this as if looking directly into the other man's soul. Simon started. How could this starving man know him? As they had walked, what little conversation Jesus was able to muster concerned his experience on the mountain. Although they did not press him, they sought to know every particular. They were amazed that he had not had food now for forty-one days. *Can he really be the Messiah?* They wondered. Simon needed little convincing. In his heart, he knew what the Baptist had known. His heart was settled. Yet Jesus' gaze penetrated. Jesus saw inside him. Jesus knew him.

"So, Simon." He paused, his hand still on the big man's shoulder. "I give you a new name, Simon; from this day on, you will be called *Peter,* the *rock!*" Simon's heart leapt. In that moment, this follower of John the Baptist knew that he had been changed forever. And that is how it would be for all who would discover intimacy with this unusual man. One's heart, one's mind, one's life is radicalized for the rest of one's days on earth and beyond. A shift occurs. A new beginning. A new birth. Simon became a new person. He would be *Peter, the Rock* forever.

αΘω

As they crested a rise in the road, they observed a group of low buildings from which a small stream of smoke issued. They had come to an inn. The sky had turned gold, the sun dipping into silver western clouds. A calm touch of vesper hours fell upon them. The exquisite aroma of roasting meat adorned the air. Jesus, mouth watering and stomach painfully demanding, said simply, "I must eat."

John, a man of means said, "Teacher, let us stay in this inn and take food." Before Jesus could respond he said, "I will pay the innkeeper, Master. It will be my honor." *Teacher? Master?* So much had happened in so short a time.

Simon (now Peter) and John went back a long time. John owned the commercial fishing business where they both worked, but Peter was the professional. He captained John's boats. While Peter was unlettered, the distance usually maintained by employer and employee had long since disappeared between these men. Their families dined together. Their children played together. Their wives chatted together. Both were men of faith. Both were men who looked to God for the bounty of the Galilean sea. Both had been told of the events in Bethlehem thirty years ago, and both had sought the baptism of John the Baptist.

The talk around the table flowed slowly, each man taciturn and lost in thought. Peter and John wondered about Jesus. In some measure afraid of him, in awe of him, in another measure calmed and at peace for being with him. An odd mixture of apprehension and security.

No one felt like talking. For all of his hunger, Jesus ate modestly. Still weak from his ordeal and travel, he spoke few words. To observe him one might conclude that he thought he was alone. He chewed his food at length and washed it down with red wine. Nominal conversation drifted into long periods of contemplative, quiet inebriation—and yawns.

αΘω

Since the day he told his father and his family, "I must leave," Jesus had traveled alone through the countryside, finally ending up in Judea, a long way from Nazareth, a long way from home. It was in the Judean mountains that he had encountered the evil one. It was on the Judean banks of the Jordan river that he had been baptized. Here, he had met Peter and John, the first of those who were to become his apostles.

Sated, they slept well into the morning, Jesus gathering strength from rest and food. As they breakfasted, Jesus announced that he wished to leave for Galilee. Peter and John, both professional fishermen, were pleased. Galilee was home for them. They had already decided, however, to leave their nets and follow Jesus wherever he went. Life could no longer exist without him. Had Jesus chosen to return to the Judean wilderness, they would just as easily have followed him there. After journeying several days, at length they came to the green, rolling hills of Galilee. As they walked, they came upon a small group of men harvesting figs.

The figs were almost too ripe for picking. Birds had left many of them hanging on the trees with gaping holes in the fruit where they had dined. The ground beneath the trees, littered with rotting fruit. Wasps, yellow jackets, honeybees, lured by the aroma of the summer spectacle, swarmed lazily on half-eaten figs, crawling over each other with apparent nonchalance. Were you there among these harvesters of figs, you would have to be careful where you stepped.

One of the harvesters, stripped to the waist, rubbed his torso vigorously, complaining bitterly of the itching residue the leaves left on his body. When he noticed the watching travelers, he shouted, "Come, friends. Help yourself. There is enough fruit here to feed a legion of Romans." Jesus walked over to where the man stood in the tree, each foot braced against a limb. Accepting a plump fig from his hand, Jesus smiled as if to comment on the good flavor. Then, instead of an elucidation of its quality and flavor, or an expected, "Thank you," he said only these simple words, "Follow me."

Philip, his feet still braced against the forked limbs, laughed nervously. His eyes darted from Jesus to his friend Nathanael, also picking figs. "Nathanael," he said, "step over here," he paused, his eyes now fixed on the face of Jesus, "step over here and meet this man." *Follow me?* Philip pondered. Before Nathanael responded to his call, Philip knew what he would do—what he *had* to do.

As Nathanael approached, Jesus remarked, "Well...here is an Israelite in whom there is nothing false!" It was meant to be a humorous remark, as if finding such a man was rare indeed. The term, "Israelite" was a reference not so much to race as it was to the Jewish religious leadership, most of whom were notoriously false. Smiling, Nathanael asked,

"How do you know me?"

Jesus answered, "I saw you while you were still under the fig tree before Philip called you." He could have said, *"I have known you for a very long time. I knew your unformed substance before you were in your mother's womb."* But he did not say that.

Like Peter and John, Nathanael was a Galilean and a fisherman. He was indeed an honest man, worked hard and loved figs. Like most people of intelligence, however, he did not like to gather them. The stinging insects, the spoiled fruit lying like a moth-eaten carpet on the ground, the prickly leaves all combined to make fig harvesting a delicate and often unpleasant task. In his hands, he held a basket filled with the fruit he had picked. He held the basket out to Jesus who took another fig and savored it.

Nathanael's home was Cana, a small town west of Galilee not far from Nazareth where Jesus grew up. Now, listening to him speak, Nathanael knew. What was it? The quiet, confident tone of his voice? The easy way he smiled? His arresting gaze? Something about this man beyond…what? Nathanael was not sure, but whatever the compulsion, he blurted, "Teacher, you are the Son of God; you are the King of Israel."

Peter and John reacted in surprise. Only Philip knew Nathanael well. Others had seen him among the fishing crews, laughing at coarse and sometimes vulgar humor as fishermen do. Such men are often honest to a fault (if such a thing is possible), preferring to say what they think to anyone who will listen, holding pretense and airs in contempt. But none could have conceived such words coming from this sailor's mouth. They did not believe him capable of such a statement. Nathanael, however, had said what he meant to say. He knew what he knew and had declared it with straightforward directness.

Even Jesus seemed incredulous. "You believe this merely because I told you I saw you under a fig tree picking figs?"

It had not occurred to Nathanael just what it was that justified his blind acceptance of this man or the declaration he, himself, had made. The faith of a child needs no justification. That Jesus had knowledge of him before this moment did not enter his head. He was not certain of what it was, perhaps the force, the power and simple presence of this man. Perhaps an inner revelation. He let Jesus' question hang unanswered.

The silence between them spoke more than words. At length, Jesus laughed, "My friend, you will witness greater things than that." Then he said, "Let me tell you how great, Nathanael; in the future, you shall see heaven open, and you will see the angels of God ascending and descending on the Son of Man."

In decades to come, in moments of triumph and failure, when his hands shook and his eyes were old and watery, Nathanael never forgot this moment, these words.

VI

First Miracle

On returning to Galilee, we came first to Nazareth, where Jesus spent his childhood, and where he had labored as a young man in his father's business of wood. As we approached the family home, we were met with sounds of hammering and sawing. Joseph and the boys were still at it. A smile of familiarity broke on Jesus' face in anticipation of the reunion. Rhoda was the first to notice our arrival. She came running and threw her arms about Jesus in welcome. In a moment, the carpenter sounds stopped and the whole family came upon us. There were tears and laughter, rejoicing and the voices of welcome. Jesus had come home.

At dinner that night Mary and her daughters had set a lavish meal. Joseph at the head of the table, Jesus at his right and the rest of us scattered around the table, which incidentally, was large enough to accommodate every one of us. Joseph had done well in Nazareth. His business thrived. He was not wealthy, but he did operate a successful and profitable business. He did not look well, however, and Jesus commented about it. "You are pale, my father. Are you well?"

"As well as can be expected for a man my age. I will be fifty next month. Perhaps my years and all this work is taking a toll. But I'm all right, son. Don't fret about me. I'll be fine."

The crease of concern on Jesus' brow did not go away. He said nothing more, however, and took another bite of the warm olive-bread prepared by his mother.

"Oh, Jesus," said Rhoda brightly, "Did you know that Abiram ben Zecharias is to be married tomorrow? Our family has received an invitation. I do hope you can go with us."

"Abiram? Married?" replied Jesus in mirth. "Yes! I would love to go. That will be amazing." He shook his head laughing softly to himself.

"What is so amusing?" spoke Mary, smiling.

"Abiram once swore to me that marriage was not for him. 'Never!' he said to me. 'Never will you see me tied down to a woman.' I guess 'never' has come to an end. Who is the fortunate bride?"

"A young woman from Cana," said Joseph, his father. "A delightful girl from a good family. Her name is Sherith. She is the daughter of that…" Joseph struggled with his memory, " that silk merchant, I think. What is his name, dear?" looking at his wife. Mary swallowed, taking a sip of wine.

"I don't know him, but his wife is very nice," she replied. "I see her sometimes at market. We are becoming friends. Her husband is a man of great substance. I'm afraid I don't even remember his name, 'El-Korah' or something like that. I have been asked to help with the wedding. They will be happy to see you, Jesus."

αΘω

The next day, the wedding took place at the bride's home in Cana of Galilee. Jesus' mother immediately disappeared, seeing to the needs of the guests. Since we were with Jesus, we also were invited to enjoy the festivities. Jewish weddings were hardly secluded, private affairs.

The ceremony of marriage was intoned by the local rabbi, vows of fidelity and permanence taken, the announcement of "husband and wife," and the reception begun. Well into the celebration, it became evident that not enough wine had been planned. Or perhaps, since Jesus had brought along his entourage, more guests came than had been invited. In any case, this critical beverage was soon consumed. This was an inexcusable misjudgment that would almost certainly cause embarrassment for the bride's mother on her daughter's wedding day. Mary, deeply concerned over the crisis, spoke to Jesus, "The wine is gone. There is no more to be had and the celebration is far from over."

"Dearest mother," Jesus answered with a tolerant smile, "why do you tell me? Why involve me?" Indeed, what did Mary expect of her unusual son? Were there events in his past where precedents had been laid? Was there a history of reliance upon which she knew she could draw? He paused for a moment and looked at her carefully. She knew him. She knew he could not refuse her. At length he smiled and said, "I know what you want but remember, my time has not yet come." As I thought about this later, I wondered if Jesus knew exactly when his time would come.

His mother, a glint in her eye, said to the servants, "Do whatever he tells you." There was something unique between Jesus and his mother. They communicated at a level that often did not require words.

Nearby, stood six empty, fired-clay waist-high water jars, the kind used for ceremonial washing. Jesus said to the servants, "Fill those jars with water." After several trips to the well, the jars were filled to the brim. Then he told them, "Now pour some into a cup, take it to the head caterer to get his approval." As the servant drew the ladle from the jar, his mouth fell open, and gasping, he splashed red liquid onto the floor.

After a reassuring smile from Jesus, the stunned servants then followed his instructions and took a sample to the head caterer. Tasting the water that had been turned into wine, with no knowledge of its origins, the caterer called the bridegroom aside and said, "You are to be congratulated! At other weddings I do, the choice wine is served first and after the guests have had too much to know the difference, then it is watered down. But, dear Sir, you have saved the best till now! I must know where you purchased such excellent nectar!" The groom thanked the caterer and walked away, puzzled. Since he had no responsibility at all for furnishing the wedding with wine, he had no notion whatever of its origin. Assuming the jars were full, Jesus may have created nearly 150 gallons of wine, aged to perfection! Should all of it be consumed, this was going to be some celebration!

This, the first of his public miracles, Jesus performed at Cana in Galilee. In doing so, he revealed himself for who he was, and it was here that people first began to put their faith in him. Those who did became his followers.

αΘω

Jesus left the wedding with his family and his friends and moved himself and his belongings down from the hill country of Nazareth to Capharnaum (*Capernaum*, the village of Nahum, the prophet) near the northwest shores of Galilee. They came to the home of Peter where they established a headquarters of sorts for their activities in the region of Galilee. Here surged a large spring that watered all of the plain of Gennesaret. As they arrived, Peter's wife, Joanna, (a name as common to women as "John" to men) returned from the spring carrying a jar of water. As yet, Joanna had not met Jesus personally. She knew only what her husband had told her. She could see that Simon was excited. "Joanna!" he exclaimed, "Set your water down. We have just come from Cana where our Lord performed a spectacular miracle." Then he turned to Jesus and gesturing toward the water said, "Here, Master, do it again."

Jesus smiled uncomfortably. "Simon!" rejoined Joanna, "Do not embarrass him. He is not a performer of tricks."

"It was not a trick, Joanna." And then to Jesus, "Lord, show her. Show her now." He looked at Jesus, his eyes gleaming with expectancy.

The others also gave appearance as though expecting Jesus to repeat his act at the wedding.

Instead, he turned to the dining table and sat down. "Indeed I am thirsty Peter. I wouldn't want to ruin that good spring water which Joanna has so kindly brought to us. Please, my friend, sit down and refresh yourself." Nonplussed, Peter sat while Joanna, Mary and the other women served. The water was cool and satisfying. Peter, feeling a bit foolish, spoke to Jesus privately, "Master, why will you not perform a miracle here in my own house?"

Jesus answered evenly, "I do not *perform*, Simon. It should be obvious to you that these things are not done for their entertainment value. They are done to fulfill a need and to give glory to the Father."

"But the wedding?" responded Peter, "There you gave us no teaching of the Father. What you did there was amazing. People will speak of it everywhere."

"You saw that as a performance?" with gathering irritation.

"Well, yes, after a sort."

"Then you have missed the point by a Roman mile," said Jesus, exasperated.

"What then is the point, Lord? Instruct me, *please*." Palpable sarcasm. The others had stopped conversation. All were listening to the dialogue between the two men. Peter pressed Jesus, forcing him to explain, demanding in his tone.

Jesus took another sip of water from his cup. His eyes looked off into space, seeing no one, seeing nothing. He spoke softly, as if to himself, "I thought this part of it was over." Nothing else.

"I am sorry, Lord." It was Peter again. "I do not understand. You thought what was over?"

"When first we met, you and John plied me with questions about my experience with the evil one on the mountain. Do you not remember what I said? Do you not remember that Satan wished me to do exactly the kind of thing you desire of me?" Peter's mouth went suddenly dry. He reached for his own cup. "I expect more of you, Peter. Do not disappoint the confidence I have in you." His gaze fixed Peter, "Do not ask this thing of me again."

Peter placed his cup on the table. "As you say, my Lord."

"You call me 'Lord.' Is this a mere word to you, my friend?"

"No, Lord," Peter now genuinely repentant.

"Then have a drink and refresh yourself." Jesus smiled. Peter laughed, a little more than embarrassed and reached for his cup.

"Yes" said Peter loudly, holding the cup above his head, "To good spring water!" and took a sip. His eyes widened in shock. He glanced into his cup, licked his lips and broke into a huge grin.

αΘω

Jesus lay on his pallet gazing at the night through the window. A small section of cosmos fell away before him. *Who was he? Why had he not so much as flinched with embarrassment at being called the 'Son of God?' How is he able to accomplish these miracles?* These were not questions that truly disturbed him, for he knew the answers. Yet, they haunted him. The dove on his shoulder and the words from the clouds had taken away any doubt as to his identity or his mission. *Whence come these ruminations, these feelings that I have lived before this life? How came I here to live among these who are so like me, yet so unlike me?*

Occasionally the memories of being with the Father were so vivid that he actually thought he was caught up again into the Abode of God. There were flashbacks to certain events that took place, moments when his body, his mind, his heart surged with omnipotence, moments when his intelligence soared beyond anything human. His thoughts shifted, *These three men, Peter, John and James - the sons of Zebedee...*He considered each carefully. *They are so imperfect, yet they have such capacity for belief in me, such obvious and simple love.* These basic qualities, he decided, would be the signature of those who would be his. *Belief and Love. That is all I shall require. Beyond these, the flesh is weak.* His eyes closed. His face bathed in the light of a rising moon, the Son of God slept.

VII

Rage

First rays of a rising sun painted the walls of Peter's home gold. Joanna had been already up and about, preparing for the trip to Jerusalem. Only the men would go this time. She would remain. *I would merely be in the way,* she thought. Joanna was a quiet woman, meticulous in arranging her affairs, not at all like her mercurial husband.

John, her husband's employer and closest friend, was unmarried. John and her husband were inseparable. He was always in their home, even though he had a house much larger and well appointed than theirs. John was a generous man and she and Simon lived well.

But Joanna, for all her faithfulness and support of her husband, was little interested in making the trip to Jerusalem. She would not enjoy the gossiping, the cliques of talk about the importance of husbands or the intelligence of children. She was a woman of great judgment and clarity of thought. She loved Simon, but she did not think him larger than he was. *He stinks of fish too often for that!* Smiling at the recollection.

Sometimes she wondered about her husband's fidelity. He was a man so driven by his passions. That is what she loved about him, yet, it could be his greatest weakness. And this new young man in their home. *Simon and John seem so taken with him. Peter!* She thought of her husband's new name, *I shall never get used to calling him that!* This with some annoyance.

She felt no animosity toward Jesus. How could she? He was so gentle and strong—even concerned for her needs, her feelings. *It is just that, I hope this is not another one of Simon's business flings,* she thought with some desperation. It comforted her that John was also involved.

"Time to get up, lazy one!" she jostled her husband. Peter merely grunted and rolled over pulling the blanket around him. She reached her hand under the covers and ran her fingers along his thigh. Peter awoke with a start!

A wicked grin on his face, he reached for his wife, "Woman, you never give a man a chance. No peace at all. No peace."

"Yechh!" she exclaimed, "even your breath stinks of fish!" For a woman in her early forties, she could still giggle. In the adjoining room, Jesus heard. Amused, he rolled over for another quick snooze.

αΘω

The city of Jerusalem teemed with Passover celebrants. Children bounced gaily in the streets. Beasts of burden, carts, merchandise and merchant booths erected everywhere. It was hard to move about without bumping into someone, or being taken by the arm and guided to a place where wares, both household and cloth, were to be admired and examined.

The trip from Capharnaum had passed without significant event; unusual where Jesus was concerned. Within Herod's Temple, in the Court of the Gentiles, customers argued with merchants over prices of sacrificial animals. There were men selling cattle, sheep and doves, and others sitting at tables exchanging money. Condiments sat about for the taking. Wine, bread, skewered meats, figs, all for a price. The great Temple had ceased as a place of worship. It had become a marketplace, perhaps having once provided a reasonable service to those traveling from far distances, but now had become a floor for exchange, a snake pit of religious commerce. Jesus did not much care for religious commerce.

He entered the Temple quietly, unobtrusively. He was not noticed. Like any other seeker of sacrificial commodities, he wandered from table to table, shopping, as it were. Inside of him, his stomach churned. Fury mounted. One merchant waved the wings of a flapping turtledove in Jesus' face, bidding him to purchase "a worthy sacrifice for the sins of your children." Another grabbed him by the arm, pulling him toward an obviously sick sheep that could be had for "such a choice price." But the worst were those who hawked, "Buy this item, and get a prayer stone blessed by a priest—as a gift." Signs announcing these things and other religious merchandise spread everywhere in profusion. "For a donation of thirty sesterces (Roman coin), we will make a gift to you of this lovely miniature Menorah." Smoke and haze hung lazily in the air. Loud haggling. Merchants discussing with fellow merchants the blatant stupidity of the "bucolic rubes, buffoons" or, those that bought. Customers discussing among themselves the inflated prices. "Robbery!" someone complained. "Predator profits!" exclaimed another.

A richly dressed man of obvious wealth paid outrageous prices for several lambs, each pure white and without blemish, his polished fingernails selecting each one. He selected one for himself and one for each member of his family. "Had I charged him less," said the merchant, "he would not have bought them. Such a man is insulted by cheap prices."

A woman, by her dress abysmally poor, looked at the solitary coin in her hand and looked again at the doves for sale. Closing the tiny disk in her fist she gazed disconsolately at the ground, and then she turned, a tear in her eye, and walked away. "Come back," cried the merchant after her, "when you've enough to pay for your sins old woman!" Laughter. Business was good. Had it not been, he might have negotiated his price. He charged what the market would bear. That was, of course, the prudent thing.

Jesus stopped at the table of a merchant selling leather from the hides of camels. He purchased eight or ten lengths of leather used for harnesses. The leather was thin, but supple and strong. Next, he purchased a handful of bone shards and pieces of metal. These things could be purchased because, it seems, business had a pervasive way of spreading itself beyond sacerdotal requirements. Separately, these items were innocuous enough, nothing more than decorative pretties. Together, they formed the substance for something else entirely. There was money to be made, and wherever this condition existed, greed found a way to be innovative. Finally, he purchased a belaying pin, used in Galilean fishing boats.

Jesus found a shadowed corner of the Temple. Taking his time, he wove the end of the pieces of leather together and attached them to the belaying pin; the issue of which was a respectable handgrip. Then he inserted the shards of bone and bits of metal into the loose-hanging leather strips. Completing his craft, he had constructed a Roman instrument for punishment called a "scourge whip," or "Scourge of leather cords." Where had this man acquired knowledge of such a weapon? How came he to know of it, much less the skill of constructing one? Did he actually intend to use this vicious appliance? If not, why trouble himself with it?

With quiet deliberation, he approached a money changer's table. Jews from Asia, Rome, Greece and Egypt were trading in the Temple that day. The coin of their realm needed conversion to Temple currency—at a profit, of course. The coins were spread by denomination and stacked. This merchant in money had a gleam in his eye. Looking up at Jesus, he did not see the whip. "May I help you, noble sir?" he oozed. Only for an instant did he hesitate, then Jesus placed one foot on the table edge, and bracing himself, shoved. The table fell into the merchants lap. Coin flew in all directions. Before anyone knew what Jesus was doing, children and standers by began snapping up coin pieces for themselves.

Quicker than collective awareness could follow, Jesus moved from table to table shoving and overturning. Where people stood in his way, merchant and buyer alike, he used his whip. Shards of metal and bone tore through clothing. Cages crashed. Doves flapped away, sheep scattered, cattle jumped, lunged and bucked sending celebrants scurrying in every direction. Above the din and through it, feathers and debris flying, the roar of the Lion of Judah could be heard, "Take these things out of here! Move! Now! How dare you turn my Father's house of prayer into a lair for thieves and cheats!" Every door of the Temple that led into the streets opened and people and animals poured out into the city. After a few moments of chaos and confusion, it was over. The Courtyard of the Gentiles cleared of all but overturned tables and tapestry lying forlorn in residual dust.

It didn't take long for the Jewish authorities to regroup. They quickly assembled a contingent of Temple guards, and only then did they approach this warrior with a whip in his hand. With this armed support they indignantly demanded of Jesus, "What in the name of God do you think you are doing young man? Who do you think you are? What credentials could you possibly present that allows you to create such mayhem and destruction? What gives you the right to scourge our customers and colleagues of commerce?" Their anger and bravado obscured their fear. *Had the Romans sent him?* He did not look Roman or as if in the employ of Romans. He appeared no different than the rest of the rabble. No raiment of rank, no military cohort of his own. *Who indeed is this brash young hellion? Does he think himself a prophet? If so, does he perform miracles to support his credibility?* "What miraculous sign *do* you offer that you possess such authority?" They howled, barked and whimpered as hyenas in the presence of the king of beasts.

Miracles! Legalists are very impressed by miracles. They look for miracles under their beds and in every event under heaven. They are titillated by miracles. Jesus surmised their intentions. They hated him for what he had done in the Temple. They wanted to destroy him. They would erect any pretext to accomplish this. *I will give them a miracle!* thought Jesus, sweating and dirty from combat, completely aware of what these clod-headed fools wished to do to him. He struck his chest with his fist in defiance and shouted, "You wish to stop me? Then get you to it! Destroy this temple, and I promise you that I will raise it again in three days."

The Jews, for whom this boast was as enigmatic as the deed he had done replied, "This great edifice was begun before you were born. Forty-six years in its building, and you are going to raise it in three days?" The looks of incredulity were matched only by sneers of scorn and contempt.

They had no concept of what Jesus meant or that he spoke not of Herod's Temple, but his own—the Temple that is his body.

Tossing the whip into the dirt, Jesus turned from his antagonists and walked away. Paralyzed, the Temple guards stared after him in disbelief or, just perhaps, in respect. While he was in Jerusalem for the Passover feast, many people witnessed this act and wanted to believe in him. The excesses of the Temple marketplace had been long despised. This brash young man had done something most had wanted to do for years but were afraid. Jesus placed little confidence in their admiration. He knew it would not last beyond the novelty of the moment. He did not need or listen to the opinions of men about himself or about other men. He himself knew human nature for what it was. He knew that one of the great weaknesses in human nature is greed and that marketing is its exigency. Commerce is the way of man. It is not the way of God. It is secular, not sacred. Place it in the context of worship, and worship is defiled.

A Roman soldier, one of the Temple guards, saw the whip lying unnoticed in the dirt. Idly, he walked over to it, observed it momentarily, bent over and picked it up. He handled it, testing its weight and balance, assessing its grip; satisfied, he disappeared into the crowd, the whip dangling from his waist-belt. It would live to serve another day.

VIII

Nicodemus

The night cold and humorless. An aging scholar stood in the street and waited. Pulling his robes around him against the chill he wondered if his quarry would come out of the house that he had seen him enter the hour before. It had been a curious day. He had watched amused, then terrified, the event that unfolded in the Temple. What an event it had been! How he had felt his blood pound as the young man had usurped commerce in the Temple. Never had he seen such controlled violence, such precise and titillating physical force from one man. The commerce of piety, as usual, had been going on for centuries. But this young tiger, this virile hero, this, this superhuman man, or whatever he was, had completely arrested his sensibilities. And so, he had furtively followed him here. Followed him through the streets and paths of the city. He had listened as he heard the young man speak to those who were likewise curious of his actions. Only one nondescript face in the crowd, so as not to be noticed. Yet insistent in his intent. Determined to meet this man. He would not rest until he had heard him for himself. He could not stop until there had been personal contact. Face to face dialogue. *He is a man, isn't he?*

The light from the windows of the home gave the illusion of warming the night. The man shivered. *What must I do to make him notice me? How shall I approach him? What shall I say? I do not wish to seem like a foolish old man?* With such haunting trivia flitting among his thoughts, he waited and watched.

αΘω

Is there a way, a stratagem if you will, for men to get the attention of God? It is easier to think of this on a mass level. How easy it is to say that "God loves the world." But, how easy is it to say, "God loves me—personally and individually?" And know it. And feel it? More than that, how easy is it to really believe that God notices? That God genuinely cares about the struggles or, for that matter, the whims of an individual?

How curiously satisfying to know that God is my Friend, *my* friend, as distinct, different and unique, say, from being your friend. I have no quarrel with God being your friend or his having as many friends as he chooses. But I want the character of my contact with him to be different than it is with you. I want to know him in a way nobody else does, be with him in a way nobody else can.

Does God actually concern himself that I have a stall for my ass? Does he fret when I am late for an appointment? Do the stars in the sky actually have names that *he* gave them? Are the hairs on my head actually numbered? This one is number one, this one is number two, this one is number three? Does he really notice when a single sparrow falls from the sky? If so, then maybe he needs to find something *real* to do. Why doesn't he notice whole races of people in slavery? Why doesn't he notice genocide? Why doesn't he notice the bulging eyes and protruding bones of starving innocents? Why doesn't he shoo the flies from their nostrils? Never mind friendship with God on the individual level. God has the power and the motivation, one would assume, to address this terrible human trauma. Why doesn't he? While his eye is on the sparrow, while he sees the tiny bird fall, does anyone notice that God does not catch it, that he does not lift it again to fly? Does anyone notice that God lets its carcass rot in the dust? It is enough to make one reject entirely the notion of an omnipotent, loving God. Those of us who think about such things, who ask such questions are often inclined to observe, *If God really does exist, then he must be a monster. He must actually enjoy the killing fields.*

αΘω

The killing fields? And just who is killing whom? And is there a substantive difference between a prescient human and a non-prescient sparrow? In musings and arguments such as these, we forget, or choose to ignore, that humans are created in the Image of God. To put it bluntly, we know exactly what we are doing when we destroy babies in the fire of Molech, or ruin completely the existence of life, or crucify a Lamb. We are responsible for our inhumanity to each other. God gave us that responsibility and will not interfere with our ability to exercise it until his purpose for creation is realized. Meanwhile, he concerns himself with the sparrows until we ourselves become as innocent as they.

Now, therefore, let us sit in judgment of God for natural phenomena such as earthquakes, droughts, whirling storms and floods. Are these not the natural consequences of things he set in order? Of course, they are. Isn't he then responsible for the wholesale loss of life they cause? Indirectly, since he did indeed set them in order, yes, of course. We view these things, however, as disastrous. No doubt they are. Some are witless enough to discern that God is bringing punishment on a rebellious and wicked mankind. Perhaps this is plausible should these events only exterminate the wicked. But they also annihilate the innocents along with the wicked.

It is entirely plausible that God does not view death as we do. If God is real, and if eternal life is a direct consequence of death on earth, it is not unreasonable to conclude that life on earth is temporal. Is massive death so terrible if it is merely a gateway to eternal life? Yes. Massive death is terrible. Life on earth is precious and, other than by faith, some would think that we have no tangible guarantee that life beyond death even exists, let alone exists as paradise. Perhaps this life is the only paradise we will ever know. But it is not just hard, it is impossible for me to accept the notion that Jesus is a liar; or that the appearance of Moses and Elijah, or that his resurrection is all a convenient fiction! Are not these guarantee enough? It is he who has taught us that eternal life awaits those who trust in him. That is enough for me.

αΘω

Similar thoughts as these molested the trivia in the man's mind. He belonged to a self-righteous sect called the Pharisees. He also held membership in the Sanhedrin, the Jewish ruling council. He had too much seen the disregard for human life at the hands of his Roman conquerors. He had seen a gang of unruly soldiers rape his sister. He was fourteen at the time. Repeatedly, one after the other. Again and again. Afterwards, no man wanted her as a wife. She became a hater of men. If they were going to have her body, it would not be without a price. She became a whore. Dear Ruthie! Good God!

He had also visited too often the leper colony where his mother lay dying. Visited as in going to the location, not walking among them. That was unclean. He spoke to his mother by shouting to her across a dividing valley. As a child, he had seen too much pain. After the loss of his mother to that terrible disease, his father's brother took him under his care and educated him. Yet, he knew too deeply the hypocrisy of his own life. He could not answer these enigmatic, morbidly profound questions. Though a respected teacher, an admired scholar, he did not know what to do with the injustice of human torment. And so he waited. Perhaps this young warrior knew. Perhaps this man was of God? Perhaps?

Voices. People at the door. Goodbyes. Good wishes. Thank you's. The Pharisee waited in the darkness. As luck would have it, Jesus came his way. They would pass so close they could touch. The moment came. Jesus was alone. A rare moment indeed.

IX

Israel's Teacher

"Master?" said Nicodemus. Jesus stopped and looked at him. There was no fear at being accosted by a stranger at this unusual hour. Just expectancy. Jesus, always expectant, waited.

"Master," Nicodemus continued just above a whisper, "I am an old man. Just a moment of your time. I intend no inconvenience."

"It is you who are the 'master,' my friend. I remember you from when I was a child," responded Jesus. "I stood among inquirers in the Temple room, you sat upon the dais. I was but a scrawny youth."

"Eh?" grunted Nicodemus, "My mind fails me." For the first time he looked squarely into the face of Jesus. "I—I am sorry. I do not recall."

"It matters not," said Jesus. "For what purpose does the teacher of Israel seek the likes of me?"

"You are too modest," said the old man, "and you honor me more than I deserve. I suffer the curse of most old men; the older I get it seems the less I know and the more useless I become."

"And the more wise," said Jesus with heartfelt compassion for the old legalist.

Emboldened by his reception, Nicodemus said to Jesus, "Rabbi, I know you are a teacher who has come from God." (Better to give him the benefit of any doubt. He had seen with his own eyes what this young man could do.) "For no one could do what you do if God were not with him." For all of his furtiveness, Nicodemus was personally drawn to Jesus. For the first time in his life perhaps, he was seeking something—*honest.*

Jesus did not respond immediately, allowing the question implicit in the old man's flattery to hang. He seemed thoughtful, pensive, as if sensing genuineness. A casual observer to this scene might think that the younger man had a flair for melodrama, for he fixed his gaze on the older man and compelled him, "Look at me!" Nicodemus met the eyes of the Son of God. "Nicodemus. No one can enter the family of God unless he is born into it."

Jesus was not baiting the old man as much as one might think. He knew that Nicodemus was quite accustomed to argument and theological debate. This was but an invitation to such a discussion. *Born into the family of God? A curiously delicious concept!* Nicodemus rose to the bait. "I don't understand. How can a man be born when he is old? Would you have him enter a second time into his mother's womb?" An amusing repartee. The debate was on, good-natured, friendly, a scholar's way of making friends, of knowing one is accepted. Nicodemus smiled. He was enjoying this now. The only thing missing was—well, a flask of good beer!

Jesus felt the camaraderie of intellectual stimulation as well. "No one can enter the realm of God unless he is born of water and the Spirit." *A critical theological distinction.* "Flesh" he continued, "gives birth to flesh, but the Spirit gives birth to spirit. The wind blows wherever it pleases. You hear its sound, but can you tell from whence it comes or where it goes? So it is with everyone born of the Spirit."

"How can this be?" Nicodemus was stimulated. He had indeed come to the right place.

Abruptly Jesus' tone changed. Nicodemus was caught short in his elation when Jesus said, "You are an eminent and respected teacher and do not understand these things? Then let me then speak plainly. Nicodemus, I speak of what I know. I speak of what I have seen, but these things cause you to stumble and you cannot grasp them. I have spoken to you of earthly things and you can't believe them! How then will you believe if I speak of heavenly things? How can I know of such things? Simply this: No one now living has ever been to heaven except the one who finds his origins in heaven—the Son of Man!"

He speaks of himself! The old man was shaken. He did not know whether to rend his clothes or fall to his knees. The crushing weight of his own evil propensities fell upon him. Emotions rushed. He needed to urinate.

"Just as Moses lifted the snake on a pole in the desert, so the Son of Man must be lifted up, that everyone who believes in him may have life. I speak of life beyond temporal life, my friend. I speak of a life eternal."

Jesus stopped. He measured the impact of his words on Nicodemus and felt the warm pleasure of resignation and trust coming from wrinkled and pleading eyes. Nicodemus' head hung in quiet desperation. He had spent his life instructing young men in Torah, Nevi'im and Ketuvim, the three components of Tanakh, the Hebrew scriptures. But never—yes, never—had he considered that a deep, personal engagement with Yahweh was possible. Although he had never admitted it, he sometimes wondered if Yahweh were real, and if the Tanakh were filled with myth, marchen and fable. Jesus reached forth his hand and placed on the old man's shoulder. A moment of silence and feeling passed.

"God loves this world, old teacher, so much so that he gave his only Son."

Gave his Son? thought Nicodemus. As in *sacrificed* his Son?

"Yes" answering the unspoken question, "that whoever believes in him shall not perish but be given this eternal life of which I speak."

"What of Judgment, Master? Isn't that what God does?"

"God did not send his Son into the world to condemn it, Nicodemus. God isn't like that. God sent his Son to rescue and redeem the world. That is the consequence of his love. That is why I am here. I choose to be held accountable for the sins of all people, thus they will not be condemned.

"God loves, but at the same time, he condemns evil. So he sent me to accept and to bear that condemnation. I will become sin for those who embrace evil so they might become the righteousness of God in me. Those who reject me condemn themselves. They are condemned because they refuse to believe that God could love them this much.

"That is the reason I am here, dear friend. The world is full of pain and suffering. The Father fails not to notice this. It causes him pain and suffering as well. So he sent me. The flow of natural forces, set in motion before the existence of human life, will not cease, will never cease until the end of all things temporal. The evil that engenders war, the horrible things men and women do to one another, their children and themselves will not stop so long as evil exists. But that is the reason I have come, to bring an end to all of this, to give men back their dignity and prepare them once again for the eternal family of God; to make them one with me even as I am one with the Father.

"That is the nub of it, Nicodemus; and though you may not know it—*Light has come into the world. I am that Light.* But instead of embracing Light, people embrace darkness. Evil is real. Evil people are real. Evil people embrace dark things. Evil people are afraid of Light. They hate it because Light exposes Evil for what it is. But whoever lives in truth moves freely in Light, and it is clearly seen that his deeds are of God. No shadows are about such a person. Such a person has a spirit that is born of the Spirit. Such a person is born of God."

Nicodemus did not have the answers to his questions, but he had met The Answer. He had let himself become exposed and in doing so became free of his long struggle. But isn't that how it must be? Without vulnerability, there is no relationship with God. He had opened himself to the Son and in doing so found peace.

With this, the teacher of Israel received his first taste of eternal firmament.

X

Two Camp Fires

Nicodemus still very much on his mind, Jesus made his way through the Judean countryside. *What would become of the old Pharisee now that he believes?* How would the Sanhedrin treat him now? *For his sake, Father, let him retain a low profile. Let him not suffer because of me.*

He came to a copse of trees and behind them a campfire. Surrounding the flames, his friends gathered warmed by the quiet conversation as well as the conflagration. It was dark. The dancing glow of the fire dimly bathed Jesus in its golden light. "Master?" Peter inquired in greeting.

"Yes, it is me, Peter. Well." He looked around at his sleepy friends. "I see you are all readying for a sleep under the stars. Have you not homes? Have you not wives? How is it you prefer the smell of sheep to the smell of your wife's bed?"

"I think you know that it is not the smell of sheep we prefer, Lord Jesus," from John.

"Have done with the 'Lord' business, my brother. My name will suffice."

"Yes, Lord."

Jesus looked at his friend, "Why must you persist in this, John? We are every day together. I prefer you call me Jesus. Just Jesus."

John did not respond at once. Flames danced in his eyes; eyes that would in their ancient days see great visions. He seemed distant, staring into the fire, then into the darkness. At length he looked up at the vast array of heavenly bodies. A cricket chirped nearby. "You came from out there." It was a statement that could stand in its own right. In its own integrity. "You are no ordinary man."

"John . . !" exclaimed Jesus in exasperation.

"I wish to speak, Master," John interrupted abruptly. "Please, let me speak my heart. You say to me, 'just call me Jesus.' I am a man of wealth. Almost everyone I know sees me as someone from whom to get something. But you came to me and reached out to me. Your thoughts were for me, not for yourself. Do you realize that I have lived forty-three years and no one has ever done that? No one has ever seen me as a man who *needed to be loved.* No one, except for you. For that all that I am, all that I have, is yours.

"You are much my junior in years, yet you are ages my elder. The things you say. The things you do. I have often thought of those who will come after us, who will not be privileged to walk with you, to hear your voice, to feel your physical touch—and there will be others, Lord. Yes, Lord! To me, you will never be 'just Jesus!' I am just a man. You? You are not just a man. You are that, but you are much more. You are my Lord. Never 'just Jesus!'"

αΘω

Not far from where Jesus slept with his men, another campfire licked the darkness of night. John the Baptist gathered his disciples and spoke softly to them. Unusual for John, for he often thundered when he spoke. But now he wasn't preaching. He spoke from his heart quietly, softly to those who closely followed him. "You have all heard me say, 'I am not the Christ but that I am sent ahead of him?'" John sat, his hands clasped, pensive.

"We have indeed heard you say this but are not sure of the meaning. How is it that you are sent ahead of him? And since you are now here, does that not say that Messiah is also near?"

"It does, but a man can receive only what is given him from heaven. I have received what is to be mine. Now I am done. I must step out of the way. The bride belongs to the bridegroom, not to me. I am the groom's 'best man,' so to speak. A best man attends the bridegroom; he does not take his place. The best man waits and listens for the bridegroom and is very relieved when he finally shows up." John smiled at this. "Now the pleasure of that relief is mine and it is complete." This with satisfaction.

"He will become greater. I am becoming less. He is the one who comes from above and is above all. I come from the earth. I belong to the earth and speak as one from the earth. The one whom God has sent speaks the words of God. He reveals God as he is. All that has ever been spoken or written about God must now be reshaped and understood in the light of his reality. He is the new Lens, the new Prism through which we comprehend and come to know the Father. God gives him the Spirit without limit." John thought about that—he thought of his own limitations. He thought of what it must be like to have the Spirit without limit. The embers of the campfire settled and glowed softer and softer. In time nothing but dwindling smoke remained. John and his men slept beneath the twinkling stars.

αΘω

Much can be told about John. All who knew him also knew that he was a provocateur, an agitator, often tactless and crude, for he spoke what he thought and gave little credence to protocol or propriety. Some said he reminded them of the prophet Elijah who seemed to fear nothing—except, perhaps—King Ahab's wife, Jezebel.

Like Elijah with Ahab, John was not reticent to stride into the palace of Herod Antipas and embarrass him about having married Herodias, his brother Philip's wife. Antipas was Tetrarch of Galilee and son of Herod the Great. Outraged at John's impertinence, Herod locked him up in prison, adding this also to his repertoire of evil, the consequences of which would embarrass him far more than the prophet's preaching. And in prison John stayed, alone without comfort. Alone with the thoughts that he was now useless to God. Alone with doubts. Sometimes in the darkness, he thought of the women in the river; he thought of freedom in the wilderness. Caged men think much of love and freedom.

αΘω

Gentle light from the stars above retreated from the grey beginnings of dawn. Jesus stirred on his bed of woolen robes and grass. As he had laid his head on a roll of clothing, he heard the faint rustle of small creatures making their way through the grass. He had fallen asleep listening to the sound of his own breathing and feeling each beat of his heart reach his temples. Now his eyes opened to the lightening sky with the feeling of discomfort in his abdomen. And so, the Creator of the universe, the Creator of this body he inhabited, had to pee.

His companions lay in scattered array, their chests rising and falling in early morning slumber. Peter could be heard snoring. Jesus smiled. His eyes searched for a quiet spot among the trees, his heart longing for intimacy with the Father; he sat down, leaned against the trunk of a tree and began to pray. Perhaps it was prayer. Perhaps it was just thought of the richness of his life. He thought of his father, Joseph. "Father," he thought quietly, "be very close to my father this day. Help him remember how much I love him. Help him to know how much I appreciate all he has provided for me." He thought of the influence Joseph had had in molding his own character and values. He remembered with embarrassed amusement the day when he was discovered in the Temple. "Oh my God, enrich my father Joseph today, and prepare a reward for him in your realm that his dreams cannot imagine." And then his thought shifted to his mother, and to each brother and sister in turn. Then finally, to the men who were with him. "I know who I am, Holy Father, yet I am uncomfortable when Peter and the others call me 'Lord.' I want them to feel that I am one of them, yet I know they must acknowledge your Presence in me. Sometimes it is hard being your Son. How to be the Son of God and the Son of Man is oft perplexing. And so it shall be for all time a mystery, a struggle for holiness in a world of Pain. Oh God, however much I am a part of you, let me be to them a source of your love. Let me be faithful to them, a counselor to them; let me nourish and feed them." His moment of prayer disturbed by the sounds of awakening men coughing and clearing throats.

XI

The Well Is Deep

The centuries-old Roman road rose from the plains of Jericho, twisting up through the hills on the east bank of the Jordan, meandering toward the cool meadows and vistas of Galilee. Soon, after rising, and crossing the river back into the hill country of Samaria, we came upon *Wadi Farah,* where we paused for refreshment. Jesus regularly sought to get a few miles behind us before we ate. Breakfast consisted of biscuits, dried fish, grapes and water from the *Wadi.* It was early spring in the month of Iyar. The stream gurgled with rushing water. In a few months, the stream would recede and by late Elul, it would be dry again and remain so until the rains of winter and spring came again.

The terrain became one hill after another and rocks on the road made traveling by foot difficult. In the distance, mount Gerizim could be seen. Afternoon sun poured its heat on the countryside and still Jesus and the rest of us journeyed on. At length we came to a town in Samaria called Sychar, near the plot of ground Jacob had given to his son Joseph. Jacob's well was there, and Jesus, tired as he was from walking altogether about twenty miles through hot, rocky hill and vale, sat down by the well.

A focal point of the surrounding countryside, the well enjoyed constant activity. Sychar was only a half-mile away. Women of the town met here early in the day to visit and draw water. The bucket dropped endlessly down into the blackness before they could hear a splash at the bottom. They would often sing as they carried the cool water back to their homes.

There were other travelers, for the ancient well was now the crossroads of several Roman highways. It wasn't the only well in the vicinity and there were many springs from which water could be taken. But Jacob's well was a place where friends met and passed a few minutes or hours talking. Jesus perched himself on the parapet surrounding the well. Had someone given him a push, he would have tumbled into the abyss. Leaving John behind to remain with Jesus, we all went into town to buy food.

An attractive woman approached the well to draw water. As she filled her pots, Jesus, his mouth dry from dust said to her, "Will you please give me a drink?" John stared at him in shock. *What is this?*

The woman glared at Jesus in mock surprise as well. She was not unaccustomed to men approaching her. She had heard more than a few opening lines at this well. She replied with an affected boredom, "You are a Jew." How had she known? One is left to surmise. Perhaps it was clear that we had just arrived from the south via the road that came from Judea. Perhaps there was something in our clothing or appearance that marked us, something thought typical of Jews, by Samaritans. One could easily surmise that the two peoples were, at the very least, lacking in affection toward one another. "How is it that you ask a Samaritan woman for a drink?" She did not disguise her annoyance.

Jesus answered her, "So what if I am a Jew? And why should I not ask for a drink if I am thirsty, of a Samaritan woman or, for that matter, any other woman?"

As the woman allowed the line of the pail to pay out into the blackness, she turned to Jesus and spoke coyly, "Well, how refreshing! I do not often hear such straight talk, especially from a Jew."

"Perhaps," Jesus responded, "if you knew the gift of God and who it is that asks you for a drink, you would have asked him and he would have given you living water."

The gift of God? Who is this man? Whoever he is, he seems rather taken with himself. Incredulous, the woman said with a suspicious smile, "You ah, have nothing to draw with and the well is deep. Where do you propose to get this living water?" She said the words, "living water" with a lilt in her voice as though it was a delightful fancy. "Do you think yourself to be a person of consequence? Perhaps you are greater than our father Jacob, who gave us the well and drank from it himself?" This with playful condescension.

Jesus smiled back, "Is it not true," he responded, "that everyone who drinks this water will be thirsty again?" Without waiting for a reply he continued, "Those who drink the water I give will *never* thirst again."

The woman's eyes widened. She wondered if Jesus were sane, and determined not to be impressed by these wild, reckless exaggerations. She had seen this sort of thing in many men. This fool was obviously desperate.

"Well," she rejoined, "I guess that does make you *special!*"

"Indeed," Jesus went on, "the water I give will become a spring of water bubbling up to eternal life."

"Eternal life? Of course!" Playing along with what she thought was flirtatious comments intended to keep her interested, the woman said invitingly, "Then give me this water so that I won't get thirsty and have to keep coming here to draw water. Give me this water," she laughed, "so that I may remain young and pretty." She was, she thought, in control. She was enjoying this.

Jesus looked at her, his expression flat, compelling her to look back, to respond to him, to stop being coy, to listen without distraction. "Go, *Athalia*," he said, "call your husband and ask him to join us." With this, the conversation took an arresting turn.

"I have no husband," *He should like that,* she thought, *"...but how knows he my name?.*

There was a pause, almost as if Jesus were seriously considering the implied invitation. Even John began to wonder about his Master. Just when he almost said something about the direction this conversation was taking, the poignancy of silence vanished as Jesus said evenly, "You are right when you say you have no husband.

The fact is dear one, you have had *five* husbands, and the man you live with now is not your husband. What you have just said is quite true."

Everything changed.

XII

If You Knew

"*If you knew who it is that asks you…*" he had said. Stunned, she lost her confidence, her sense of control. Flirtation suddenly changed to agitation. In an effort to regain her composure she replied, "Are you a prophet, sir?" *How else could he know about my life?* Then she did something so many people do when faced with the simplicity of truth; she attempted to display a competitive religious knowledge. "Our fathers worshiped on mount Gerizim," her eyes glancing at the towering rise nearby, "but you Jews claim that we must worship in Jerusalem." She was now on the defensive, sparring, dodging to disguise the intimidation she felt. His knowledge of her personal life, his demeanor of authority, the quiet confidence with which he spoke, all combined to give her cause for apprehension.

Jesus did not raise his voice, nor speak with aggression. But the power and force of his arguments were like driving nails into the lid of a coffin.

"Believe me, my dear woman, the time is coming when you will worship the Father neither on this mountain nor in Jerusalem." The first nail. His assertion completely outside the framework of her thinking. Not worship in Gerizim? Not worship in Jerusalem? Where else was there to worship? She was incapable of grasping such an idea.

"You Samaritans worship something about which you know nothing." The second nail. Insulting. How dare he? Who does he think he is? Yet the words, "*If you knew who it is that asks,*" haunted her thoughts, pestering her with anxious questions, *Who, exactly, is he?*

"We worship what we have known for centuries, for salvation is from the Jews." The third nail. Jesus had just added injury to insult. She took this remark personally, as if it were devastating her beliefs, her understanding of God, of herself.

"Yet a time is coming and has now come when true worshipers will worship the Father in Spirit and Truth, for they are the kind of worshipers the Father seeks." The fourth nail. *He speaks as if he knows God, as if he were…*

"He is not interested in places for worship." The fifth nail. Athalia was numb. She did not know how to respond. The whole of religious history contradicted him. She felt overwhelmed, above her meager ability to think clearly.

"God is Spirit, and his worshipers worship in Spirit and in Truth." The sixth and final nail. Her callousness, her coyness, her religious biases, her own disbelief, her questions, all ensconced securely within the coffin, awaiting burial. While she had been conquered, she did not feel threatened by this man. He was not making himself her enemy. He spoke the simple truth, objectively, dispassionately, yet—she was sure—with compassion.

Cowed and trembling she ventured, "I know that Messiah is coming. When he comes, he will explain everything to us." Was it a premonition? Was she fishing for confirmation of what she suspected, *what she already believed in her heart?*

Jesus said softly, lovingly, "I who speak to you am he."

"Ah!" she cried loudly, and dropped her water jar. Water splashed soaking broken clay shards and the surrounding earth. Hot tears leapt to her eyes. The lump swelled in her throat so that she could not speak, could not breathe.

At such a juncture of timing and truth, we all returned from our trip to town. I remember it clearly. There is nothing like the intrusion of irrelevant things demanding attention to rob a moment—of moment. As expected, we were shocked to find him talking with a Samaritan woman. But instinctively, we knew that we had stumbled once again into something beyond our wit. Embarrassed, we tried to step back, but the intrusion had been done. The spell broken.

Athalia backed away from Jesus and the rest of us, holding the back of her hand over her opened mouth, for the first time in her life deeply aware of something much larger than herself, or anything she had ever known, and hurried back to town. Her excitement uncontained, unrestrained, she exclaimed to everyone she saw, "Come! Come see a man who told me everything I ever did! Come! Come now!" To anyone who would listen she said, "He says he is the Christ." People knew this infamous woman who had had five husbands. They also knew Athalia Shimon would not be easily fooled by unscrupulous men. *Could this really be Messiah?* Partly out of amused curiosity, partly because they thought her believable, they followed her from town to see.

αΘω

"Teacher, eat something." It was John, having helped himself to the food we brought from Sychar. Jesus had hardly noticed our return.

Still staring pensively after Athalia, he said to John, "I have food to eat of which you are ignorant."

We were puzzled, "Who could have brought him food?"

"My food," said Jesus, *his thoughts still following her,* "is to do the will of him who sent me and to finish his work."

Sometimes it seemed, Jesus was just plain exasperating. We had traveled hard all day. It had been a hot day. Doubtless, a water jar of sweat had evaporated among us over the hot, dusty, miles. It was time now for rest, for the satiation of hunger, for wine or cool, clear water from this well, and upon finding a proper inn, of sleep. Sleeping under the stars had its benefits, but there were few things more pleasant after a long day of travel than good food, good wine and a gentle bed. Yet, Jesus would not give it up. He could not let an opportunity to "hold court" go by. What was it this time? Oh, yes, he preferred "to do the will of him who sent me," to a savory piece of lamb.

Ignoring the spiritual abyss between ourselves and him, Jesus reluctantly joined us on the grass and took food. He appeared preoccupied, as if basking in the pleasure of what had just occurred.

Many of the Samaritans from that town believed in Jesus because of what had happened with this woman they knew so well. So when they came to him, they urged him to stay with them, which he did. Apparently no one was affected by the chasm that existed between Jew and Samaritan. Somehow, that which we held in common was stronger than that which divided us. Because of his words many believed and became followers. They said to the woman, "We no longer believe just because of what you said. Now we have heard for ourselves, and we know that this man really is the Christ, the Savior of the world."

These were *Samaritans,* a community of people who claim to be the descendants of Joseph, through his sons, Ephraim and Manasseh. They think of themselves as the true "Israelites," as distinct from usurping "Jews." They erected their own Temple on Mt. Gerizim where to this day they worship, while we Jews worship at Herod's Temple in Jerusalem. The two peoples, Jews and Samaritans, have rejected each other, each considering the other apostate. Now, Jesus has reached out, loved and accepted even the Samaritans, the *Cuth'im.*

Although he is a Jew, this man Jesus, is larger than his Jewishness. His purpose and mission is not only beyond Jewry, but beyond Israel itself. This man, this Jesus, is indeed, the Savior of all nations, of the entire world!

"We have much to learn," said Peter to John.

And so, apparently, did Athalia, whose name means, *God is Exalted.*

XIII

Come, Before My Child Dies

It was a journey Jesus made many times in his lifetime. Galilee to Judea, Judea to Galilee and back again. A traverse of about 90 miles depending upon origin and destination, a journey difficult though oft made. His first time to make this journey began in Nazareth in his mother's womb and culminated in the open smells of a stable in Bethlehem. The first sensations of his new body were the pleasant smells of animals and hay. A lowly place, yet a place of warmth and welcome. Such is the nature of low places. May we all know such places, for it is there we are reborn.

Jesus remained in Sychar, among the Samaritans, for two days before continuing his trek to Galilee, another two days travel to the small community of Cana. When he and his friends finally reached their destination, the Galileans welcomed them. They had heard of all that he had done in Jerusalem at the Passover Feast, including his adventures in Herod's temple, and they remembered how he had turned water to wine in their very presence.

Josiah ben Hadad, one of the officials of Herod's court, was in Cana when Jesus and his entourage arrived. His son lay close to death. Like most fathers, Josiah loved his son. Men, good men, are like that. They see more than a bit of themselves in their sons. They know the struggles of boys changing into men. They want to give them every possible opportunity to grow up better than they. A father takes joy in his son becoming an individual in his own right, in his own consequence, in his own persona. And a father's heart breaks when his son is hurt or incapacitated. Like so many others, Josiah had heard of Jesus' power to do extraordinary things. When he heard that Jesus had arrived in Galilee from Judea, he went to him and begged him to come and heal his son.

Jesus, however, was not in a receptive mood. He was tired from the trip, his mind on food and rest. He answered Josiah irritably, "Unless you people see miracles you will never believe!" Is that what Jesus really thought? Was he not aware of this man's profound pain? Where is the compassion? Where is the love? Why such an insensitive and surly retort? Is such a response commensurate with what we know of the qualities of gentleness, kindness and concern for one in pain?

Perhaps he was not aware.

For all Jesus knew, Josiah may have been no more than another of Herod's lackeys seeking a display, a show of magic. Is it not remarkable that the Son of God seemed so myopic on this occasion? But Jesus was human. Completely so. It is not remarkable that he could be tired and irritable. He existed and lived in a human body and was subject to all its frailties. Essentially, the body Jesus lived in while on earth, was no different than anyone's. As I said, he was human. Completely so.

Surprised and anguished, Josiah pleads the more earnestly, "Please Sir, come before my child dies."

"Come—before my child dies!"

A father cannot speak more compelling words. In this town, in Cana, Jesus had turned water to wine. Much has been said of that event. But here, in mortal terms is a far more significant event. A father's child is dying. With that child dies his hopes and dreams. The impending death of Josiah's son meant for him a frustration of the very purpose of God. If this man were of God, how could he not care?

Despite Josiah's sublunary limitations, Jesus was arrested by his desperate appeal. Recovering himself he said, "Josiah…*Josiah, my friend,* it is all right. Be comforted." These gentle words from the Master, these missionaries, these exigencies of peace, this mitigation of agony, the balm of Gilead. "Go now," he whispered, "your son will live." The sun had passed its zenith.

Josiah backed away, his eyes filling, bowed his head and left. He knew he had been heard by someone whose mere word had power to succor. That had been all he wanted. That had been what he had sought for and hoped for. Now he would see. Was this man what everyone said he was? Was he who he claimed to be? *He said my son would live.* He cherished the thought. *My son will live!* As he approached Capharnaum, hoping, anticipating what he would find, he saw men rushing toward him. Familiar men.

They were those in his employ. They had news. *What news? Their animation! The expression on their faces!* The boy lives! Josiah lifted his eyes to the sky and wept out loud. Recovering from wrenching paternal sobs he asked, "When did my son recover?"

"The fever left him yesterday around the seventh hour in the afternoon." Then Josiah realized that this was the time at which Jesus had said to him, *"Your son will live."* So he, and not so surprisingly, his entire household believed. This was the second miracle that Jesus performed, both having taken place in Cana of Galilee.

αΘω

Jesus had returned to Galilee in the power of the Spirit. When the course of events have a story to tell, when things happen in such a way that we wonder if there is something deeper behind them, when occurrences take place that can only be explained by an event larger than the occurrence itself, one concludes that the power of the Spirit is present.

Jesus, of all men only, did not seek such power. It came to him as a natural consequence of who he was—and who he is. With others, it is a spontaneous power that seems at its own whim to be evident or not. One may call upon it, and it will not fetch back. One may be utterly ignorant of it, and be overwhelmed by it. A capricious thing for men, but for Jesus an ordinary spectacle, a common, routine attendance.

Hence, his fame spread. News about him measured through the whole countryside. Repeatedly, he was invited to teach in the synagogues, and wherever he did, he drew enormous crowds and was applauded. Many believed and followed him.

XIV

A Prophet Without Honor

He missed his mother's cooking, his father's wisdom, the frolicsome fun with his brothers and sisters. He missed the smells of home. Nazareth beckoned. Just him and his family. His followers surely had the same feelings and could use some time with their own. The trip would give him some time alone, so he left.

Nazareth, that Sabbath, awoke to a new day. A faithful Jew, it was Jesus' custom each Sabbath, to attend synagogue. Nazareth was his home. He had grown up here. People knew him. Joseph's carpenter shop, where he had spent so many hours as a boy, was still flourishing. It did not seem but a fortnight since he announced his departure from the business, from the family, and from Nazareth. But now he had returned, and to synagogue with his family he would go.

His fame had preceded him. "Come, Jesus," cried his friends, "read to us." The local rabbi placed in his hands the scroll of the prophet Isaiah. All quieted, looking upon their famous son with anticipation. Standing, he unrolled the scroll and found the place where it is written:

> *"The Spirit of the Lord is on me, because he has anointed me to preach good news to the poor. He has sent me to proclaim freedom for the prisoners and recovery of sight for the blind, to release the oppressed, to proclaim the year of the Lord's favor."*

There was a moment's pause and then Jesus rolled up the scroll, gave it back to the attendant and as was the custom for one about to teach, he sat down. The eyes of everyone in the synagogue were fastened on him. With quiet purpose, Jesus said simply, "Today, as you have listened to this scripture, it is fulfilled."

Up till now, except for his baptism and the event at Herod's temple, Jesus had revealed himself only to individuals and very small groups. He had yet to make any public announcement regarding himself. But today in the synagogue, in his hometown, among the people who knew him best, he did.

There were some who, though the power of the Spirit was evident, were oblivious to it. They were taken rather with the pleasure of seeing one of their own become famous and then return to the place where he grew up. Comprehension of what Jesus had just said escaped them. "You can see he hasn't changed," they twittered. "He is still Joseph's son," said another. Though all spoke well of him and were titillated at the gracious words that came from his lips, they also remembered the time when he was five, fell out of a fig tree and went crying to his mother. They remembered him arguing with his brothers over riding up front on the ox cart and being scolded by his father for throwing rocks at another boy in town when he didn't get his way. They'd laughed when, as an awkward fourteen year old, working in father's workshop, he'd tripped over a pile of wood and a basket of nails went flying. They remembered the times when he suffered as he learned the obedience required of a Jewish boy and when as a young man he struggled to become a man. They did not see him as the Son of Man, much less the Son of God; they saw him as the son of Joseph, a local worker of wood. They saw him as a son who had "made good." Some of them wondered if a part of the "old Jesus" was still with him.

"I remember when he wasn't such a know-it-all," said some. "I remember when he was one of us," said others. "He still *is* one of us!" The whispers about Jesus' fame and his roots ran like fire among the hearers.

Nazareth was a town of basics, proud and independent, rebellious. People who spent their childhood in Nazareth were different than the rest. They thought themselves special. No one was wealthy and those who hadn't grown up there were considered "outsiders." They boasted of hard work and simple lives. If the truth be known, most of them were uncomfortable when they left their safe, familiar surroundings. They did not "fit" with people outside their own, and those who did venture away were often scorned. The inhabitants of Nazareth were forever imprinted with a narcissistic character. They even spoke with their own distinctive accent. *Jesus may become famous in other parts of the world. It was natural. What would you expect? He is one of us. But we remember him as he was. We remember...*

Jesus, aware of their pretentious affection, their superficiality, said to them, "You wish me to entertain you with miracles." A statement, not a question. "You would like me to do here in my hometown what you have heard I did elsewhere. Perhaps you will even quote that familiar proverb to me: *'Physician, heal yourself!'* You think because you knew me as a child that you know me now. You don't! You know me not at all! *I am* different from you. I have always been different from you. I tell you the truth," he continued, "a prophet is not without honor except in his own hometown, so it appears that I am without honor among you, for you see me not as a prophet."

They did not expect a rebuff. They were shocked. *So, this is what we get? Instead of showing us what he can do, we get disrespect?! He believes himself superior to us. Who does he think he is? We knew this boy when he was nothing more than an urchin scurrying about the alleys of Nazareth.* "If you are a prophet, Jesus, then act like one! Show us a miracle. Show us a miracle now!"

"There were many widows in Israel in Elijah's time," Jesus went on, "There was no rain for three and a half years and people were starving, yet Elijah was not sent to any of them, except for one poor widow in Zarephath. And there were many in Israel with leprosy in the time of Elisha, the prophet, yet not one of them was cleansed—only Naaman, the Syrian. I did grow up among you. I played with many of you as a child. Because of this, now you cannot see me for who I am. As both Elijah and Elisha were not accepted by the people, so you do not accept me." Jesus looked at them, not with the contempt they deserved, but with pity and compassion. "You are all forsaken, starving in spirit, and like Naaman, diseased. I leave you to remain as you wish to be."

This was not well received. Most in the synagogue became furious, unruly and loud. A large man, Nathan ben Aminadab, walked up to Jesus and *shoved* him. Jesus recognized him instantly. When they were younger, Nathan, because of his size and general meanness, enjoyed a reputation as the town bully. He hadn't changed much. Someone else in the crowd shoved him again. Jesus lost his balance and fell. Unhurt, he stood and tried to leave the synagogue where all of this was happening, but the men in the crowd followed, yelling noisily as they went.

As Jesus, followed by the mob, proceeded down the road out of town, they came to a familiar curve beyond which the road fell away into a dangerously steep crevasse. When they were children, Nathan and his companions would drag the smaller boys to the edge of the hill threatening to hurl them headlong down its steep slopes. On one occasion, they did and the child almost died.

As they approached the precipice, the men physically seized Jesus and dragged him to its edge. Their intention was clear. *They had spent their lives together as children; now they wanted to hurt him!* Just as they were about to catapult him over the cliff, Jesus dug his heels into the earth and shook himself free of the grappling hands of his captors. The crowd, suddenly compelled to silence, stood back, dumbfounded, unable to move. No one attempted to touch him.

Jesus walked with impunity through the crowd and went on his way.

"You know," Nathan murmured to no one in particular, *"he could never do that when he was a kid!"*

Leaving Nazareth, Jesus found his way once again to Capharnaum by the Sea of Galilee in the region of Naphtali. Zebulon lay to the southwest.

XV

Abishag

Just what it was that awakened him each morning well before daylight, Jesus was not sure. He was not unhappy about it. These were the best hours of the day, times to meet with his Father. On this morning, he rolled over on his pallet and stared at the wall. He thought of the events of the previous day. He thought of big Nathan, not with resentment, but with compassion and disappointment that somehow, he had not been able to reach him. *What a disciple he would make!* With that thought in mind, Jesus stood and stretched.

Quietly, so as not to disturb anyone, he wandered out into the courtyard of Peter's home and into the cramped streets of Capharnaum. A dog barked, came trotting up to him and received a scratch behind the ears for its trouble. Jesus smiled at the wagging tail and felt a strange comfort as the dog licked his hand and thought, *Best thing I ever did!* Thoughts like these came with recurring frequency. They disturbed him. The paradox of his God-humanness had become a source of continuing distraction. He could never, it seemed, quite get used to it.

For the past year since his baptism, several of us had tagged along with Jesus but we had yet to draw together into a unit, a cadre of men devoted to our leader and to each other. Jesus realized he needed others in his work, not only to effect the labor of his purpose, but also however lame or ineffective we may prove to be, he had to teach us his way. He had to open our minds to the Father. He sensed, perhaps after the events in Nazareth, *he knew* that his time was short. He had to find others and teach them to carry on his work.

His thoughts wandered from these things and back again, occasionally being distracted by the dog trotting about as he strolled. The stars overhead glistened in the morning chill. At length, he found himself standing at the foot of a pier which led out into the lake a hundred feet or so. There were several such piers along the waterfront of Capharnaum. Fishing boats were tied along both sides bobbing in the gentle waves lapping the shores. Men were beginning to attend the boats even now before the night sky gave way to approaching dawn. In the distance, Jesus recognized the forms of Peter and Andrew. He smiled. He hadn't needed to be concerned about disturbing their sleep back at the house.

There were only a couple of boats tied to the pier where Jesus stood. No one had yet arrived to employ them in the day's fishing. With the dog loping along at his side, Jesus walked out to the end of the pier and sat down, removed his sandals from his feet and felt the cool water embrace them. And there he became quiet with the hush of daybreak. *Father, let your Spirit come.* As the words escaped from his mind, a tingling, burning sensation crept over his skin causing the hairs on his neck to prickle. His thoughts mingled with his eternal roots. From the clear cistern of his Father's Presence, he drank deeply and long. Waves lapped gently at the pilings. The sky turned into an array of color. Jesus felt something touch his feet. He looked down to see small fish playing around his toes beneath the surface of the water. The consummate peace in his heart caused his eyes to fill with glad tears. He was his Father's Son, nothing could change that; a delicious moment of spiritual ecstasy. He was loath to release it. He held out his hands, palms turned upward. The dog, lying next to him, whined. Jesus laughed out loud.

αΘω

His reverie disturbed by the clump of fishermen's feet on the pier. The day had begun. The village waterfront stretched almost 1000 feet along the shores of Galilee. There were many fishermen, many boats. Peter and Andrew had moved to this place from their native Bethsaida precisely because the fish were more plentiful in the northwest corner of the lake. If there was a "fishing hole" in Galilee, Capharnaum was it. The village itself was just that, a 'village' of perhaps 1500 souls about three miles from the place where the headwaters of the Jordan River emptied into the lake. Yet, it enjoyed the privileges of being a border town along the main imperial highway leading to Damascus. The village controlled a much larger portion of the north shore than just its dockings and moorings; stretching from the great spring on the west, later to be named Et-Tabgha, to the Jordan on the east, a distance of almost five miles.

The sun peeked over the rim of the eastern hills, turning the lake into a bowl of shimmering gold. Silhouettes of fishermen casting nets in the shallows created the impression that they were harvesting precious metal instead of fish. Jesus stood from his position at the end of the pier, slipped his wet feet into his sandals and turned to go, his new friend, the dog, following close by. Stepping around and through the fishermen, he reached the foot of the pier. One of the men catching his eye, smiled after the dog. "Poor critter," he remarked, its owner drowned a few months ago in a storm and his widow can't afford to care for it. We all feed it from time to time, but it just runs the streets. Sweet dog, it is."

He watched the dog run instantly to the nearest patch of grass and squat. *A female!* thought the Son of God. *Perhaps I shall give her a name.* He thought about that. He tried and rejected several names. She was a lovely animal, soft dark eyes, a coat of long, black hair generously splotched around the shoulders and face with white, that also ran down the length of one leg. She looked to be a working dog similar to the ones often used by shepherds to work their sheep. After several moments of considering, he thought of a name,...*Abishag! I will call her—Abishag!*

So it was that this abandoned, neglected animal was named after the beautiful maiden sought out to keep King David warm in his old age; the woman who later became the wife of King Solomon.

That settled, Jesus turned to walk among the things that are common among fishing waterfronts anywhere in the world, the smell of dead fish, scattered coils of rope, piles of net and cork. Abishag trotted happily along, sniffing about and occasionally chasing a scurrying rat.

He had not gone far when he encountered Simon in whose home he had spent the night. Simon, whom he had named Peter, and his brother, Andrew, were busy with their nets, casting them into the lake and hauling in their load of denizens. It would be, it seemed, a profitable day. *Good men,* Jesus thought. *Faithful, hard-working men. They would make superb disciples. More than that, they would be my apostles—the carriers of my message to the world! It is just such men as these to whom my work should be entrusted. They are salty, rugged and colorful; the best in all the earth.*

In a moment, they saw Jesus watching them. Leaving their nets for a moment of greeting, they approached. They both sensed something was different about him, a commanding air, a compelling presence. What did they feel? Who knows the hearts of men or how they respond to omnipotent, unrelenting love!? Jesus opened his mouth to speak. The words were plain, simple and straightforward: "Stay with me, Peter." His gaze turned to his brother. "Stay with me, Andrew, and I will make you both fishers of men." While both men had spent considerable time with Jesus to this point, they were aware of something, they knew not what, something different; something that compelled them.

Their nets lay in the water, held afloat by small corks. They took no thought of the nets or the fish they might contain, and they went with Jesus. Other fishermen would claim their nets. Other fishermen looked on as their friends in labor left behind all they had ever known. They never looked back. Neither, apparently, did Abishag.

As he walked the waterfront with Peter and Andrew, he observed the two brothers, James and John, the sons of Zebedee. They were in a boat with their father preparing their nets. He well knew these men. As had Peter and Andrew, these two men had also been with him often during the past year. When Jesus called them, they, too, left their boat and their father and went with their new Lord into the village. Zebedee, his eyes following the departure of his sons, remained behind, pained and speechless.

XVI

Demon in the Synagogue

When Sabbath came, the residents of Capharnaum began to assemble on the large stone pavement where the synagogue stood overlooking Galilee. The building was new, having been only recently erected at the expense of one Flavius Marque, the centurion of the local detachment of Roman soldiers. During construction, Flavius himself could often be seen shirtless, laboring in the sun with mortar and brick. On this Sabbath, Jesus entered the new structure and, as was his custom, began to teach. His knowledge of God and of things spiritual seemed so vast and deep that he could speak for days, revealing the nature of his Father with refreshing confidence. Interspersed in these messages were stories of his own personal experiences, his own struggles, and at times things dark and preternatural. During this particular teaching, his thoughts recalled that mountain of starvation and his encounter with the evil one. He remembered his demeanor, his air of detached objectivity, his attitude of intellectual superiority. "You must be vigilant," Jesus taught, "for the prince of darkness is sophisticated, subtle, cunning."

"Agggh!" followed by the sound of loud retching. Jesus looked out into the crowd to see that someone had fallen. The people around him began to part, pushing their way backward in horror, the disturbance so severe that Jesus could not continue teaching. Attention had turned from him to a stricken man writhing on the pavement of stone. He left his place on the dais and entered the crowd to investigate. What he saw was revolting. The man on the floor had vomited. His mouth coated in red foam tinged with yellow and green bile, his eyes glazed, angry, terrified and in pain, as if beyond human endurance.

Utterly unlike the encounter on the mountain, here there is nothing analogous to a polished professional. Here, there is to be no scholarly dialogue on matters of faith or the meaning of scripture. Here, presents the presence of incalculable evil in all its morbid, repulsive darkness. Here, there exists nothing that would attract men as a moth to a flame. Here, is unvarnished evil, denuded of beauty. Here, is evil revealing itself for what it really is.

His mouth remained locked and open. With neither his lips nor jaw moving, words spewed forth. His face frozen grotesquely in a misshapen configuration, sounds issued forth guttural, screaming, unformed in the manner normal to speech.

"What do you want with us, Jesus of Nazareth? Have you come to destroy us? I know who you are—you are the Holy One of God!"

The sound echoed as if in a corridor, or a deep well. Whatever it was inside him could not make up its mind whether to speak as one or as more than one. It seemed to the horrified standers-by that a chorus spoke, and then a leader, a representative of the rest. The man vomited again, violently emptying what was left of the contents of his stomach, mixed with bright, red blood on white stone pavement.

The eyes of the Son of Man clouded with anger and strength; his lips tight for battle, his visage ominous and totally unafraid. *"Quiet!"* he commanded as sternly and as forcibly as the word could be spoken. Instantly, the screaming stopped. You could not hear so much as a whisper. Still, the tormented man writhed in agony. Bile continued to flow from his mouth, which he was powerless to close. The Son of Man commanded, *"Sons of evil, release this man! Come out and return to your place in the abyss!"*

The man began to shake violently, uttering a wailing howl, a shriek of unbridled agony, and collapsed in a heap on the floor. "He is dead," whispers among the crowd of worshipers. Jesus stepped forward, taking the corner of his robe, cleaned the man's face and wiped his forehead. His eyes fluttered open, his breathing even and unlabored, his mouth and jaw relaxed and without torment. The exhausted man looked up at Jesus first in consummate relief and then in gratitude. The presence of evil was gone.

The dramatic change in the man astounded the onlookers. "What is this?" they said among themselves. "He commands evil spirits *with authority,* and they instantly obey him." The news spread quickly over the whole region of Galilee. The day's sermon was over.

αΘω

Jesus and the others departed the synagogue and returned to the home of Peter and Andrew. Joanna's mother had awakened that morning ill and sick with fever. Involuntary whimpers issued from her mouth. The lines in her face betrayed her better than threescore years. She was a woman whose entire life was characterized by humble, quiet service to others. Ever since she had lost her husband, she had lived with Peter and Joanna. She was fortunate. Many widows had no family to accept them, which usually meant a life begging in the streets.

Peter's house boasted several rooms clustered around an open courtyard, an architectural pattern followed more or less throughout the village. Owing to the warm days in summer, the family enjoyed sleeping on mats spread on the cool stone pavement in the courtyard shade. During rainy season, it was back into the surrounding rooms. The oven was set in the courtyard and it was here that Joanna baked and cooked. It was here also that her mother lay under the open sky. Jesus spoke to her as he and his friends gathered about where she lay, "Tell me how you are feeling, gentle mother."

"Flushed," she responded weakly, "as if my body were burning up inside; very weak, very tired." Peter sat down next to her and took her hand. Joanna touched a cool cloth to her forehead. The elder woman smiled in wan gratitude.

Jesus did not sit. Instead, he bent over and lifted her other hand. "Come," he said. "Get up. It's time you felt better." The moment his hand touched hers, coolness, as clear water from a mountain stream, enveloped her. At first, it hurt to try to rise. Jesus tugged gently at her hand and lifted her arm. She stood dizzily holding on to Jesus lest she faint. Joanna watched quietly with protective concern. Should she try to interfere?

"Feel better?" asked Jesus, as the woman stood on her own regaining her balance. She touched her forehead with her wrist.

"Yes," she said. And then breaking into a broad smile, "Yes! Much better," with genuine relief. The fever was gone. Her strength returned. She felt like a girl. "Yes!" she said again. "I feel deliriously better." And then, characteristic of Joanna's mother she said, "Here, Jesus, let me get you and your friends something to eat."

Joanna attempted to stop her, "No, mother, let…" but Peter motioned her to let her mother do as she intended. Joanna's love for her mother wanted nothing more than to assist her, to do for her, but it also helped her to realize that the older woman felt completely expunged of illness and wanted nothing more than to do what she always did—assist others. And so she did. Jesus acted as if nothing were more natural and routine than to accept a plate of fresh figs from her hand.

αΘω

"He did what?" Zebedee was incredulous.

"It was amazing, father," James continued. "You should have been there. The man in the synagogue was hopeless, obviously possessed by some demonic creature." James was animated. He realized that what he was saying lacked credibility to anyone who had not actually seen what he had seen. "The vile thing actually spoke to him."

"Creatures," corrected his brother. "They, or it, called him the 'Holy One of God.'" James seemed irritated that John would interrupt.

"He spoke to it as if it were a plaything…"

"He *commanded* it!" John interrupted again.

"Do you want to tell this?" said his brother, annoyed.

"You're leaving stuff out."

"Then you tell it!" said James with exasperation.

"Will the two of you stop acting like children?" demanded Zebedee. "Go on, son," he said to James, "finish your story." *Why he would want these two adolescents among his disciples I will never know,* their father thought irritably.

"Well," James continued, "the evil spirit left the man, and he stood as whole and in his right mind as the next man."

"And then there was Peter's mother-in-law," John again. James kept quiet and let his brother relate how Jesus had healed this woman. When he finished, Zebedee sat back in his chair bewildered at his sons. *What is happening here?* He asked himself.

His wife stood by, absorbing every word. She knew Joanna's mother well. How often had they discussed the accomplishments of their sons together? Her sons, she thought, were magnificent. How fortunate this new rabbi was in having them as his friends and supporters. *"I must speak to Naomi."* she remarked absently. With that, she left the room unnoticed by her men. In the matter of an hour, or maybe two, the entire village knew of the events of the day.

That evening after sunset the door to Peter's home crowded with people. They brought to Jesus every sick person in town, every person perceived as demonic. Jesus healed as many as came to him. That seemed to be the way with Jesus. Rarely did he interpose himself or interject himself into the life of another. But to those who came to him, he gave them all he had to give. No one turned away thirsty for more. As it was spoken of him six hundred years before through the prophet Isaiah:

"He took up our infirmities and carried our diseases."

The evil creatures inhabiting the bodies of the tortured and demented were expelled at his command. They knew who he was. However, he would not allow his name to be spoken by them. They were inhuman, diabolical, supernatural fiends whose destruction was certain and total. For such a creature to speak his name would only defile the name it spoke, adding further condemnation and futility to the hideous thing's existence. Not allowing them to speak was an act of mercy, if such a thing can be imagined for such creatures of darkness.

XVII

The Prayer Pond

Very early the next morning, while it was still dark, Jesus' eyes blinked open. He stretched, got up, wandered aimlessly around the courtyard rubbing sleep from his eyes, and wondered if he should go back to bed. Sleep still cob-webbing his brain, he slipped once again between the covers and stretched. Minutes later he was still awake, more so than before. He knew that if he continued to lie there, sleep would not come. Leveraging his weight with his legs, he got up again and left the house.

Morning dew lay upon the countryside. Mists rose from the shallows of the sea. Stars overhead, fading into the dim glow of daybreak, twinkled brilliantly on the earth. Smells of clean humidity. Smells of agriculture and animals. Jesus felt good—invigorated. His heart began to long for his Father and he began to seek a solitary place. He came at length upon one of the streams that fed into the lake. He followed the bubbling current up a slight hill to a place where it issued from a clear pool. The pool was surrounded by mossy walls down through which the water had formed a small gorge, seeking the leaf-covered bottom of the pool. A log lay across the gorge, overgrown with weeds, lichen and shrubs. At its stump, the roots had lost their purchase near the lip of the wady, and had fallen diagonally down to where Jesus stood, offering an inviting place to sit. He sat. He listened to the water. He listened to the small creatures of the night. He listened to the hush of approaching dawn. He lifted his eyes to the stars and whispered, "Good morning, Father."

Jesus lingered at this idyllic spot well into the early hours of the day. Everyone else had risen, breakfasted, and started their day. The family had missed Jesus at breakfast but surmised that he was somewhere, probably praying. They were becoming accustomed to his habits. In time, however, when Jesus did not appear, Peter, Andrew, James and John went searching for him. Andrew, who seemed to have an innate talent for finding people, came upon the stream. And with the others following, in a few moments came upon Jesus at the Prayer Pond, the name it would carry from this time forward. When Andrew found him, he ventured respectfully, "Jesus?"

The Lord looked up from his gaze into the pool. One could easily surmise that Jesus was a contemplative man. And so it is, and so it must be for everyone who seeks to tap his deepest resource of strength. There, deep within the waters or beyond the stars, or in the stillness of the forest, is where one seeks and finds the peaceful comfort of the Creator. Andrew came closer and said, "Everyone is looking for you, Lord!" His time of prayer had ended.

Jesus, however, did not move. As the men gathered around him, taking their places on rocks and clumps of grass, Peter sat down next to him on the log. Acknowledging their presence, Jesus at length replied, "The time has come to go." His voice was low. Quiet.

"Where, Master?" said Peter. "Here," Peter continued with solicitation, "you have my home, food and shelter. Here we have the sea and fishing."

"We shall not always have these things, Simon," Jesus responded. "Before our course is done, we shall have traveled the length of Israel. We will start with nearby villages and expand from there. I must preach. That is why I have come. I must speak to as many as will hear of why the Father has sent me." Jesus spoke with enthusiasm. "Let us be about it! Come, those who need my Father's love await us!"

"What Simon says has merit, Lord," from Andrew. "How shall we provision? How shall we support ourselves?" It was a question that has plagued message bearers since there were message bearers. Who will pay the bills? Where will food come from? Shelter? Sandals and clothing? Indeed, how would they pay the Romans for the privilege of breathing the air?

For the past year, Jesus had lived meagerly owing to the generosity of Joseph, his father. Friends had helped. Zebedee and his sons had provided some sustenance. Peter had offered his home and their trade, fishing, had also provided means. But if they were to undertake what Jesus was suggesting, there would have to be more. One would think there would have to be something regular, sustained and dependable. However, they had little money.

αΘω

It is of great interest to me, on reflection, that during these years of ministry, Jesus owned nothing but the clothes on his back. Throughout this time, he did not work for a living as most men. He had no job for which he received wages. He had no place of his own. "The Son of Man has no place to lay his head," he said. He always stayed in the homes of others, or outdoors during his travels. Everything he had was either given to him or loaned. He paid his taxes from the mouth of a fish! Women collected funds for his work. From the water at the well in Samaria where he was given drink from the hand of another, to the room where he instituted the water and the wine and washed our feet, to the ass on which he rode into Jerusalem. Everything was borrowed, or provided as a gift to him and his work. Yet would anyone say to Jesus Christ, the Son of the Living God, "You do not work, therefore, you should not eat!?"

A dear friend once remarked to me, "How is it that you followers of the Christ, you laborers in his vineyard, are always needing money? Is God so poor that he cannot pay for his own bread?" To this condescending I reply, "How is it that you do not understand that your generosity to those who labor in his service, brings blessing upon blessing to you? Do you think that God will not honor those who honor him? How is it that you cannot see the glory of the lilies in the field? How is it that you cannot know that there are values infinitely more to be desired than money? How is it that God can know when a sparrow drops from the sky, and you cannot?"

αΘω

Jesus rose from where he sat on the log and waving his friends to follow, he strode down the path to the main highway. "We shall see what shall come of this," said he. He left the Prayer Pond with the clothes on his back, his friends, and little else.

So, they traveled throughout Galilee. Amazingly, they lacked little, preaching in the synagogues, healing the sick and infirm and sending demons packing back into the darkness from which they came.

XVIII

The Professionals

Simon Peter's boat had been moored unattended for several months before they returned. Nets needed repair and tending. The bottom of Simon Peter's boat covered with algae, the consequence of warm water from the Tabgha springs. Since Peter was also an early riser, he and Jesus often chatted quietly about the matters of their hearts and the events of the day. This morning, Peter related his need to work on the boat and nets. "Let's go," Jesus responded immediately. "I miss working with my hands."

Together, the two men labored all day until the boat was finally in good shape. They were so absorbed in conversation and work that they hadn't noticed how hungry they were until Joanna came to get them for supper.

The next morning Peter and a few of the others had already gone when Jesus awoke. "I'll walk down to the docks later to see how the fishing went," Jesus thought, smiling with satisfaction at the previous day's accomplishments.

By late morning they had returned with an empty boat, discouraged and grumbling about the day's failure. As they tended the nets, a small group had gathered around Jesus to ask questions. As he taught, the growing crowd began pressing in. Grateful that Peter had returned, he backed away from the crowd and headed for the boat. Stepping into Peter's boat, Jesus asked him to put out a little from shore. Once anchored, he sat down and taught the people from the boat.

"You scurry about quietly as a crab in the night, hurrying this way and that, wondering if you will ever find a morsel, a bit a flotsam in the foaming water, and be nourished. Sometimes you scurry not so soundlessly, sometimes in dark silence the struggle persists. You long for relief from the ache in your belly. And then, at a moment and in a place you least expect, it comes. It comes in such abundance that you wonder what to do with it all. And you are reminded that the Father loves and cares for his children.

"As a small child, when my father visited his friends, he took me along. Sometimes he would ride me on his shoulders. Sometimes, he held my hand as I walked alongside. His steps were so big and mine so small. The path was irregular and uneven, littered with rocks and things to make me stumble. Often my grip loosened and I lost my balance. His hand always tightened around mine, and I never fell. I never skinned my knees, because it was his strength, his love holding on to me. So it is with your Father in heaven. It is he who holds on to you, not you holding on to him. It is his strength, his love that you trust, not your own. As David has taught you to...

> *Delight yourself also in the LORD; and He will give you the desires of your heart. Commit your way to the LORD, trust also in Him, and He will do it. And He will bring forth your righteousness as the light, and your judgment as the noonday...*"

When Jesus taught like this, my heart warmed at his gentle words. It occurred to me that he was revealing the Father by revealing himself in what he taught. They were words of hope that no matter how prone I am to fall, or how grave the dangers of the path, my hand is in his, and even should my grip slip, his does not. The Father will not let go of me.

When he had finished speaking, Jesus said to Simon, "All right, Mr. Fisherman, let's go fishing! Put this thing into deep water and let down the nets for a catch," his eyes still following the people as they dispersed.

Peter thought the idea absurd, a naïve, amateurish notion that revealed ignorance of his profession. He and the others had labored since well before daylight with nothing to show for it. He knew that the fish were running too deep for the nets that day. By now, Jesus should know better. He, Simon Peter, knew what he was doing. They would try again tomorrow. Some days were just like this. Besides, it was the wrong time of day to fish. He knew that. Jesus obviously didn't, or had forgotten. And so he answered tolerantly, as if not to embarrass him, "Master, we've worked hard all morning and caught nothing."

The look in Jesus eye indicated that he remained unconvinced, or that what Peter had just announced didn't matter. One might observe him thinking, *Sometimes, in order to teach the uninformed, it is best to let them learn by their own embarrassment. I will try not to tell him 'I told you so.'*

"All right," Peter conceded, "because you say so, I will do this." Sails hoisted, the boat plowed through the waves toward the center of the lake. Peter was making it as sure as he could that it was not *he* who would be embarrassed. Even the most untutored in this business knew that it was almost impossible to catch fish in these reaches of the sea. At length, Peter dropped anchor. The anchor chain snapped rigid, indicating that it was much too short to reach bottom. Over the side the nets went. It took a few moments for the nets to spread. Then Peter and his crew of professionals, exchanging patronizing looks among themselves, began to pull in the nets.

At first, the nets heaved too easily. That was to be expected. They were empty, obviously, as expected. But as arm over arm of net was taken in, it became more difficult. The looks these experts were exchanging now shifted to surprise. And then bewilderment. And then panic. They could feel thumping and struggling against the nets.

Then they saw them—hundreds of them. Eyes bulging, corded muscles straining, with every ounce of strength mustered, they pulled until they could hear the nets tearing, losing dozens of fish back into the sea. Even with ripping nets, fish cascaded onto the deck of the boat and down into the hold, causing the boat to wallow in the water.

The sons of Zebedee had seen Peter, Jesus and Peter's crew head for open water and had followed, more out of curiosity than any hope of catching fish. Now they could see something. *What are they doing? Arms waving? Signaling?* They came as fast as the wind could bring them until they pulled alongside Peter's boat. It was almost too late. Wavelets were beginning to lap over the gunnels. John, James and the rest of their crew leaped to assist Peter, and then *their* boat too, began to fill. Silvery fish were everywhere, leaping and flopping over the decks of both boats. In a few moments, the men were knee-deep in fish, both boats wallowing in the water.

Peter looked at Jesus. This naive, ignorant of the sea, untutored—*Person*, sat by himself in the stern of the boat, fish flopping all around him, holding himself in repressed laughter. You could see that Jesus was in pain from his mirth.

There was no explanation. Peter, in addition to grossly underestimating Jesus, surely had offended God himself. Seeing this, wading through hundreds of flopping bodies, he fell at Jesus' knees and said, *"Stop it!* Go away from me, Lord; I am a sinful man!" Peter was embarrassed by his own ignorance; in this case, the ignorance of a very proud, self-confident and self-absorbed man, ignorance, no doubt, of who it was who had invited him to launch out into the deep.

Can it be that God would ask impossible things? We, like Peter, who know the futility of such things, know the inherent danger of ruin. We are men and women of discretion, are we not? We define our priorities. We carefully select our battles. We know better than to waste our valuable time in an endeavor promising such minimal value in return. That is the way of the world. We take risks, but only when it is reasonable to do so. Only when the "odds" are in our favor. This is wise and intelligent. It is the way one *should* conduct business. Formulate a plan. Test the market. Validate an idea before committing too deeply. Never strike out on your own. Plan. Plan. *Plan!*

Then said Jesus to Peter, "Don't be afraid, my friend. You have offended no one. You responded exactly as expected. But from now on you will catch men."

Great excitement on Capharnaum's waterfront that day when the boats returned. Fishermen from all around came to help. "Where did you find this?" they asked. When told from the deep, they didn't ask questions but quickly rigged and cast off for the deep themselves. Those that did, did not return empty. There were volunteers to help unload Peter and Zebedee's heavily ladened boats. For their trouble and assistance, Peter and Zebedee parted with some of their harvest. There was more than enough to go around. The income from this catch would sustain them for weeks.

XIX

A Young Leper

Approximately two miles away from Carpharnaum, lay the village of Chorazin. A Roman temple was there erected to the glory of Hercules (Heracles of ancient Greek heroes and gods), who appeared engraved on a wall holding a club. Other engravings such as a medusa and a centaur adorned the grey, stone walls. Outside the temple there hovered in the shadows a man hunkered over, clothed in burlap and assorted colored rags, grey with the dinge common to dirt mixed with outdoor exposure. He sat still and unmoving, head drooped, his hands bandaged in rags. He held a walking stick broken from some unfortunate sapling, still green with ebbing life.

The stick was like the man himself, who could not be more than a few winters past twenty, yet he huddled as if four times that age. The rags on his blackened feet covered with both wet and dried blood, toes protruding, elongated black toenails, what few there were left, trimmed only by the rough rocks of the road. Rheumy eyes glanced furtively around looking for something, anything, someone, anyone to release him from this body of ulcerated skin, bone and viscera; this paralyzed body extinct of sensation, this rotting body of gangrenous flesh and deformation. All who saw him averted their eyes and put as much distance between him and them as possible, as they continued on their way doing their best to think of something else, anything to push his image from their minds and his smell from their nostrils. And then the rheumy eyes blinked.

One of the many dark forms that passed as people borne on their way to assorted destinations had stopped and was gazing at him. This usually happened with children, before their parents yanked them along. This person was not a child.

The man who had stopped took a few steps toward him. Sensing approach through orbs that could barely see, the sick man cried out, "Unclean! Stay away!" This seemed effective. The man halted his approach momentarily and then, ignoring the warning, continued. "Stop, I say! Unclean! I am a leper!"

"You are also a man." Quiet. Soft-spoken. Gentle. Inviting inquiry. "Do you know me?"

Forsaken eyes searched the man's face.

"No," responded the derelict. Apart from mother, father and brother, none of whom had he seen in years, he knew only other lepers; he knew no one else. His only friends were dogs with whom he shared the garbage pails behind inns and other dining establishments.

"I am Jesus, of Nazareth."

The man emitted a deep, guttural sigh. "Oh-h-h." He knew of Jesus of Nazareth. Who in all of Galilee didn't? Especially those in the colony of lepers where he spent most of his days. The talk, the rumors, the gossip.

"He can heal leprosy," some said.

"He is a faker," said others.

"He holds out false hope. He is dangerous!"

"He is of God."

"No,"

And so the talk and rumors of talk continued. The man in rags had heard just about everything that could be said about someone whom others claimed could heal. Now he actually faced this famous man, or infamous, depending on one's perspective.

What had *he* heard? Simple words. But the tone in which they were issued. Could he not hear compassion? Hope? Something beckoning him to believe? "Lord," he said, just above a whisper that began in the remotest reaches of infected bowels. "Lord, if you are willing, you can make me clean." Despite conflicted rumors, despite their uncertainty, the power of hope emerged.

Jesus reached out his hand and took the man's face in his hands; "I am willing," he said gently as if this man was the only man on earth besides himself. And the man heard the words spoken as if meant for no other, "You are clean!"

And so he was.

Odor of disease evaporated. Blighted eyes that formerly could discern only shapes and distorted shades of grey sharpened into clarified focus, now discerned the brilliant, varied colors of the rainbow. Fingers and toes long rotted off, reappeared pink and ruddy; patches of hair fallen away turned from white to dark new growth; disfigured features of face took on definition; sad, rheumy, blighted eyes were now white and blue; parched, flaking lips now soft and supple; the man stooped and bent, the man with rotting flesh, stood now straight and whole! New, fresh vapors filled healthy lungs. The natural order of progressing disease ceased and in its place the natural order of health and vitality stood! Love had intervened.

Then Jesus said to him, "Don't tell anyone about this, but go now." With vehemence, waving his hand toward the pagan temple, "Get away from this place. Show yourself to the priest at the synagogue, and offer the sacrifices that *Moses* commanded for your cleansing." He spoke the word *Moses* with emphasis, indicating clearly the demarcation between the pagan god and the God of Israel. The vehemence in Jesus' tone was not lost on the man. He vacated the pagan temple area instantly and sought out the priest at the synagogue. He did not, however, remain quiet. He could not restrain himself. He told all he met of the healing that had occurred and how Jesus had warned him to avoid the temple of Hercules.

These things did not sit well with the civic leaders of Chorazin nor with the Romans, whose pretense at worship and jealousy of their adopted gods was well known. Jesus knew this. That is why he told the man to remain quiet. He could only bring trouble on himself as well as Jesus by speaking of what had occurred. The Roman authorities required of the locals a certain respect for their gods, and if someone spread notions that they were vacuous deities, then that amounted to sedition.

How quickly and widespread the news traveled was truly amazing—this miracle of the young leper healed on the very steps of the temple of Hercules.

"There is not a trace of it left!" Animated discussion among the people of the village.

"He gives no allegiance to the gods!" Rumors flew.

"He publicly challenges the Romans!" People began to choose sides.

"He is the Prophet," said some.

"He is a seditionist!" said others.

In a matter of hours almost everyone in Chorazin knew of the healing and of Jesus' supposed anti-government preaching. The Romans were angry, the Jewish leadership afraid, the populace agitated. Hence, Jesus could no longer go about freely in this village. He was forced to withdraw.

Frantically, the people in the community sought him out, ferreting about, seeking his spoor, some to be healed, some to hear his teaching, and some to see if he was really insane enough to offend the Romans. It was impossible for Jesus to keep a low profile. So deeper and deeper he went into the countryside, yet the crowds followed still. At length he abruptly turned away from the road to a stand of forest growth, thereby eluding the horde following not far behind. He quickly searched out a place where he could enjoy a hidden moment of privacy. For him, it was a most uncomfortable episode. He had escaped with his life, but had he stayed in Chorazin, he likely would have been killed or imprisoned. He found a large tree, and himself at its root; chest heaving, he buried his face in his hands. When his heart stopped pounding, he prayed.

He would not forget this man, this leper, this town.

The Third Scroll

Let Dry Ground Appear

And God said, "Let the water under the sky be gathered to one place, and let dry ground appear." And it was so. God called the dry ground "land," and gathered waters he called "seas." And God saw that it was good. Then God said, "Let the land produce vegetation: seed-bearing plants and trees on the land that bear fruit with seed in it, according to their various kinds." And it was so. The land produced vegetation: plants bearing seed according to their kinds and trees bearing fruit with the seed in it according to their kinds. And God saw that it was good. And there was evening, and there was morning—the third day.

—Genesis 1:9-13 NIV

I

Which Is Harder?

When Jesus returned to Capharnaum, reports of the leper's healing preceded him. Around the table in Peter's home that night, he seemed unusually taciturn; the features of his face vacillating, often frowning, often impassive, almost as if he were not in the room with everyone else. The dog lay curled at his feet with a sleepy eye lazily blinking open and shut. No one noticed the curious fact that Jesus was somewhere else in his mind, but me. I noticed because it struck me, rather, as strange.

He often seemed pensive, but when with a group of people, Jesus, more often than not, gave them his undistracted attention. Not at this moment. Wherever he was, he seemed disturbed, ill at ease, perhaps upset. As is the nature of man after episodes of apparent failure, Jesus' thoughts gravitated toward discouragement,

> *Resistance builds. How long will it take before they have had enough? In Nazareth, I was almost thrown over a cliff. In Chorazin, my life forfeit to a fiction (Hercules). What is next? And for what? Healing? Preaching? Speaking to them of my Father? No one seems interested. No one seems to care. No one sees me for who I really am.*

Jesus shook his head wearily, as if shaking off consternation. The dog lifted her head and placed a paw on the Master's foot. She looked up at Jesus and was rewarded with a scratch, and Jesus rewarded in turn with an affectionate lick on his hand. The dog seemed to sense his mood and sought to comfort him. Her attempts to communicate her affection caused him to feel gratitude to his Father. Through this loving animal, he was telling his Son that he loved him. Love comes from God, whether through one's spouse, or a friend, or the beauty of nature, sometimes even through pain, but for Jesus at this time, through the adoring affection of this animal.

He thought for a moment of the young leper. *Hardly more than a boy.* He remembered when he was in his early twenties. The woodshop. His brothers and sisters. His mother and father. The smell of freshly shaved wood. He remembered the accident.

Milcah, a lovely child of only nine summers, had scalded her hand when a boiling pot had fallen. Ugly blisters formed quickly, her hand quickly reddened, skin shriveled and separated. She had screamed in pain. Jesus ran to her assistance from the shop and found her holding her wrist, pale and ready to faint. Mary darted about looking for something, anything to help her daughter. Jesus took Milcah on his lap and held her arm. Then he took the injured hand in both of his and held it tenderly. *"Jesus, no!"* from his frightened mother. But for Milcah, it was as if her hand were placed in a vessel of ice-cold water. The pain left instantly, her blisters cooled, the shock to her system evaporated. In seconds, Milcah sobered from her tears. When she looked at her hand, it was as though it were never scalded. It was the first healing. Accidental. Unexpected. He had not thought of healing when it took place. Just a sense of urgency to comfort his sister. It just happened. Another event further defining his difference from other men. It was not a public miracle like the wine at the wedding, just a private family crisis. No one knew except, of course, those who loved him.

αΘω

Abishag suddenly barked, jumped to her feet and trotting to the door. Noises outside. People talking, shouting. Andrew rose and looked out the window. "People are coming. A lot of them," he said anxiously. "It looks like they are led by *Pharisees!"* Before he could finish, there was a sharp rap at the door. Abishag incessant. More loud talking. Peter, excited himself, cried, "Someone hush that animal!" Jesus, unaffected by the clamor, rose to meet the intruders, the dog whined at his side.

Andrew opened the door and there stood Rabbi Asher, splendid in his ceremonial robes, which, unlike the disciples of Hillel, he wore habitually. Asher followed the teachings of Rabbi Shammai, Hillel's great rival and whose school was less popular and associated with extreme zealots.

Shammai was intense, meticulous and foreboding while Hillel never seemed to take himself too seriously. Rumor had it that a gentile wished to be converted. Shammai consented but only on the condition that the poor man be taught the whole *Torah* while standing on one foot. Hillel is reported to have raised one foot and said, "What is hateful to you, do not to your neighbor. *That* is the central truth of *Torah!* All the rest is useless commentary."

This disciple of Shammai sternly demanded to see Jesus. "What for?" inquired Andrew warily. Asher glared at him.

"Let him in, Andrew," from Jesus within the house. "Let us welcome our esteemed visitor from the Sanhedrin in Jerusalem. He has come a long way. Bring water; wash his feet and those of his companions. They are weary from travel."

Asher, surprised at his welcome and hospitable treatment, softened, but not over-much. "Your fame has traveled all the way to Jerusalem, Rabbi Jesus ben…Joseph, is it?" The reference to his father was perhaps an unrelenting reminder that Jesus was, after all, the son of a carpenter, not at all on Asher's level of theological or intellectual sophistication. "I and my friends have come all this way to Capharnaum to hear you for ourselves." His friends were the others in his entourage, other Pharisees, scribes and teachers of the law.

Jesus looked at them and smiled, "Your companions are welcome, Asher. Please," he said, gesturing, "all of you, take a seat here among us." Asher and his friends, the local officials from the synagogue and other rabbis from the region sullenly found places to sit or recline in this house of Simon Peter. Their presence in Capharnaum had attracted a crowd of the curious, but there were many others. Since the dramatic healing of the leper in Chorazin, Jesus' reputation as a healer had increased immensely. His name was on the lips of all who lived in and about the region of Galilee and for many miles beyond. Some came from as far as Tyre and Sidon, coastal cities of the Great Sea in the region of Phoenicia. And, as Asher had said, Jerusalem was aroused as well. Most were merely curious, many were cynical, but some in the crowd wondered; considering the possibility that God, through this remarkable Prophet, was about to bring upon his chosen people some mystical form of visitation.

Rab Asher and his colleagues were to stay well into the night. The people waited outside Peter's home and their numbers continued to grow. They slept on the ground and in huddles, hoping to get a glimpse of Jesus or should their good fortune have it, be actually touched and healed by him. This confluence of seekers outside Peter's home, while Asher and his ensemble were inside, increased to several thousand. They pressed as close to the doors and windows as possible, waiting for Jesus to appear.

The sense of chaotic urgency outside did not go unnoticed by Asher. "Well, young Jesus ben Joseph," he intoned, "You seem to have caused a tumult amongst the people. We haven't had a thing like this since the Maccabean uproar."

"You need not speak to me as if I were fourteen, Asher," said Jesus. "First, you are not that much older than I. Second, I am not a snarling dog, so allay your fears. And third, I have no religious or political interests. I have come to reveal the loving heart of God toward his people. Why should you come all the way from Jerusalem just to learn that?"

"Let me understand," said Asher. "You are the son of a carpenter, isn't that correct?"

"So you keep reminding me."

"How then do you purport to speak for God? Are not all the rabbis, scribes, lawyers and priests in Israel enough? Are not all these learned teachers of the law adequate to the task? How is it that a carpenter's son draws such crowds? Neither Hillel nor Shammai ever achieved such fame in so short a time. How is it that hands so accustomed to labor can cleanse the skin of a leper? Or turn water into," Asher's eyebrow lifted, "what was it, wine?"

"And a quality wine at that," said a voice in the room.

"Is it so remarkable that God who calls the stars by name can do such things with a carpenter's son?" Jesus replied. "Tell me indeed, Rabbi Asher, why are not our synagogues filled with seekers thirsting for God? Why do we not there find the crowds you see standing outside this home?"

"The answer is clear," said Asher. "Their minds are benighted. The people do not appropriately appreciate scholarly teaching. That is why our synagogues are empty. There is no mystery in that."

"I rather think," said Jesus, "the sandal fits better on the other foot. Is it not because they do not find what they come to seek? They thirst for righteousness and you give them platitudes. They hunger for the Father's love and you give theological equations; you give them law."

"Let me quote Rabbi Shammai," said Asher stiffly, "'Never trust anyone who speaks overmuch of love.' You refer to Moses as if his writings were something less than what we have known and followed for almost fifteen hundred years. You speak of the law of God as if it were not to be obeyed."

"*You* have followed Moses?" Jesus smiled benignly, "Come, Asher, we both know better than that." The rabbi's eyes clouded and averted. Suddenly, he was no longer comfortable. Before his discomfort gave way to a defensive retort, he was rescued by a distraction.

II

So That You May Know

There came noise from the roof. Feet pounding on clay shingles. Many feet. Scratches. Blows. Several men were trying to break through the roof of Peter's home. Abishag was instantly on her feet announcing to all who would listen. Dust and debris fell from the ceiling as shingles and stones were removed.

"What are you doing to my roof!?" Peter protested loudly, but to no avail. A break in the ceiling grew into a shaped opening. The men worked with determination and soon they had created a gaping hole about four feet square. Peter tried to go outside, to make his way through the crowd in order to stop the destruction of his roof, but the press was too great. He could only stand helplessly and watch. As he watched, four men swung a large, weighted blanket to the opening. Attached to its four corners were ropes and in this contraption lay a human form. Slowly, they lowered the person to the floor so that it became clear that a severely paralyzed man lay on the blanket before Jesus, debris and dust falling about.

The man's body lay absolutely motionless. He seemed a compilation of flesh and tissue rather than a man, his arms and legs contractured, yet flaccid. His head rolled from one side to the other. He could not close his mouth. One could see the wetness on his clothing directly beneath his chin where, it seemed, drooling was constant. His body deformed and misshapen. His chest heaved in jerks. Eyes glazed, unaware of the crowd. Unaware of Jesus.

The men who had lowered him looked down through the opening above. "Heal him, Master," one of them cried, his voice choked. "We know you can do it. He is our brother, his mother's youngest of five sons." What Jesus saw in the eyes of these men moved him deeply. Their belief in him, their determination, their faith could not be ignored. He said, therefore, to this travesty, to this burlesque of a man on the floor, "Take heart, my son; your sins are forgiven."

The words were spoken only to the sick man but loud enough for all, and especially Asher, sitting close by, to hear. *"What?"* he whispered with alarm to a colleague, *"He blasphemes! Who can forgive sins but God alone?"*

The eyes of Jesus shifted slowly from the man on the floor until he had fixed the disciple of Shammai with his gaze. "You entertain evil thoughts, Asher. Which is easier to say to this poor man, 'Your sins are forgiven,' or to say, 'Get up and walk'?" The Rabbi's mouth opened as if to answer, but words would not come. The possibility of such a pathetic creature actually walking did not exist. Jesus continued, his gaze forcing its way into Asher's soul. "So that you may know that the Son of Man has authority on earth to forgive sins," Jesus turned and spoke to the deformed tissue on the floor, "Get up on your feet, sir. Take your mat and return to your family who loves you."

As Asher and those who stood close by watched, flaccid muscles immediately began to take on tone. The man's mouth that was frozen open, closed. His head ceased lolling back and forth. The expression on his face evolved from blank, inert, semi-consciousness, to awareness and intelligence. Joy and awe flooded his countenance. For the first time in the years since his strength had vanished, it returned. He sat up, and while others gasped, he stood, breathing evenly. He examined his body and extended his arms. He looked at Jesus in wonder. He looked out at the crowd and his mouth broke into a hesitant smile. He tried to laugh. Surprised that he could, he laughed softly. It came easily and comfortably to him. "L-L-Look," he cried shakily. "I-I am whole!" He breathed as if he couldn't catch his breath, and then he shouted in increasing decibels, "Ah! AH!" He exclaimed, "Yes! I am healed! *Praise be to God almighty*!" He fell first at Jesus' feet in gratitude.

"Go, my son," spoke the Son of God, "This is your day. Your hour."

The man took his blanket, gathered the ropes about him, and made his way slowly, to the door. More than once he stopped to look back as Jesus. Receiving an encouraging smile, he turned to go. The crowd parted to let him through. The man who had been paralyzed for most of his life got up and went home, his sins forgiven to the bone.

Some said with amazement, "We have seen remarkable things today," and some felt excited joy that God would give such ability and such authority to a man.

Asher and his friends could only stare—as if this man's paralysis now clung to them.

αΘω

I had a trouble getting to sleep that night. Being near the Son of Man, one cannot escape being witness to remarkable things. How these things are perceived tells a story. They prescribe the life of the perceiver. Small things, everyday things take on special quality, the special remarkable character of shaping a life lived close to him. So I ask myself, "Is my life so contoured?" Painfully, I am like Asher. I must deal with my evil heart. Yet despite my flaccid spirituality, at his voice my bones strengthen, my happy animus sings once again. To be near him, to hear him breathe, to reach out and touch him, I resonate in his presence. I become a remarkable thing.

III

Matthew

Jesus awoke the next morning to the sound of hammering on the roof. He'd slept later than usual. Joanna had breakfast prepared, so he splashed a little water on his face, combed his hair and sat down to the table with her. "Sleep well?" she asked pleasantly. "Things certainly do get interesting when you're around."

"The question is, did *you* sleep well?" he responded. The banter continued. "I'm sure your life would be a little dull without holes in your roof and the commotion of hundreds of people outside your door."

"I'd have it no other way" she smiled. "I've never seen Simon so... alive!"

Peter, Andrew and I, laboring hard repairing the roof, were still reeling from what we had witnessed the day before. Peter did not hide his annoyance. He was not much to hide his feelings about anything.

"Well," said Jesus, after finishing his last bite, "I'd better grab a hammer and get out there to help. It will clear my head to sweat a little. Besides," holding up his hands for Joanna to see, "my well-earned calluses are all but gone. I sometimes miss simple, hard work."

"Why couldn't they just have passed him over the crowd or put him through a window. My roof will never be the same," the burly disciple whined.

"Come, now, old friend," responded Jesus, "by the time we finish the job it will be better than new. Have you forgotten my trade?"

The roof was finished just before noon, and upon examination Peter had to agree that it was hard to see where the hole had been.

αΘω

After we'd had our lunch and a short time to relax, Jesus was ready to give attention to the crowd and he wanted us with him.

We made our way through the press outside Peter's house and walked down by the lake. They all followed him, and he taught them as he continued walking from the lapping shores, and through the streets of the town. Something caught his eye and he stopped abruptly. A question was asked. Jesus didn't seem to hear. His eyes focused on a nearby building as if there was something curious about it. Beside the door there was a sign affixed to the wall. It read:

Office of Tribute
Caesar Augustus

Jesus paused for the briefest of moments and then entered the door followed by as many as could squeeze in behind him. Among them was Asher, the rabbi from Jerusalem. Since the office handled the tribute of all of the residents in the region of Galilee, there were five or six workers, among them, a young Judean accountant.

They all stood in surprise at the intrusion, except one. He was a man in his mid-thirties, olive-skinned, beard neatly trimmed, wearing expensive clothes, Roman style, his neck draped in a golden chain and rings on several fingers.

He was Levi the Jew, the son of a man named Alphaeus. He was also known as Matthew by his friends. Levi had many friends. Oh, I don't suppose you could really call them friends. Levi traveled, you see. As regional supervisor, he went from tax office to tax office throughout the general length of Palestine, collecting tribute from the locations scattered about, intended for the government of Rome. His friends were of the type that gravitated to powerful people, rich people. And Levi was both powerful and rich. His authority bore the stamp of Rome and when he required tribute, he took it by force if necessary. He would not hesitate to use Roman militia for his purposes if the hapless payee was more than recalcitrant.

Tax collectors were allowed one salient luxury: they were allowed to collect more tax than was actually due the government and pocket the excess. The Romans did not care. Levi, however, was losing his appetite for such chicanery. He had learned that wealth is its own empty reward and power a hollow trophy. He did not sleep well these days. He'd dream often of those he'd abused and longed for the simplicity and peace he'd known as a child.

The Jews, of course, hated Levi. The religious leaders particularly hated him. Asher, for example, thought Levi a beast, something less than a cockroach. He took funds, which, in the rabbi's view, properly belonged to the synagogue, which, in turn, was "taxed" by the Sanhedrin for the expenses of the Temple at Jerusalem (or so they said). Asher understood Levi, however, for they were not dissimilar in that both exploited weaker people.

Levi sat at his desk fingering the papyri logs on which were written the taxpaying history of the residents of Capharnaum. His eyes glanced at Jesus but came to rest on Asher. He smiled slightly as if mildly amused at seeing his old nemesis. Owing to Jesus' increasing fame, he also recognized him instantly, but was perplexed as to what to say or how to react to him. He at first thought of Jesus as yet another taxpayer, but then, without understanding why, dismissed the thought as absurd.

"Asher," spoke Levi, quietly ignoring Jesus for the moment, "to what do I owe this dubious pleasure? And why the rabble?"

"The rabble, as you put it, follows not me, publican, but him," pointing to Jesus. "Do you think for one moment that I would allow my shadow to fall upon your lintel? I'd rather swallow swine piss!"

Levi laughed at the rabbi's insult. "Somewhat disingenuous, Rabbi! I mean, after all, you are standing in my presence, in the office of Rome." He could easily have Asher put in prison for such an insulting remark, but would not, and Asher knew it. He continued his veiled taunt, "Since you are here with him, perhaps you, too, are one of his followers?" Levi risked another glance at Jesus. While the other workers in the tax office stood with apprehension, Levi had yet to rise from his place behind his table. His remark was intended to prick at Asher. Levi knew that Asher would never follow this gentle teacher. He knew intuitively that Asher was there merely to watch what would happen between himself and Jesus. About that he felt some concern. Without waiting for the rabbi to respond, he turned to Jesus and asked flatly, "Of what interest is this office to you, sir?"

"My interest is not in your office, Matthew," said Jesus, using the more familiar and informal name. "My interest is in you." He paused briefly and the effect of what he had said registered on the government official.

"You speak to me as if we were old friends," said Matthew rising from his desk at last. Somehow, the words of Jesus had felt to be more of an invitation than a simple declaration. "Have we met?"

"Matthew?" Again Jesus spoke his name. This time, he let the word hang as if it were a question, as if there were nothing else to say, as if it were the beginning and the end of a complete sentence. It was enough to know that for Matthew, it was indeed an invitation, a sweet comfort to hear his name on the lips of this man. Oddly, Jesus' voice provoked memories of his mother and her gentle care for him. The next sentence stunned the Roman bureaucrat. "Matthew, I wish you to come with me. I wish to instruct you in the ways of God. I wish you to be one of my followers."

Unsettled, the publican glanced first at Asher. The rabbi was utterly appalled at the scene; first, that Jesus would have anything to do with this monstrous Roman puppet, and second, that Matthew would be open to the impudence of this indigent prophet's overtures. He distanced himself from what was happening, receding toward the door. The tax official then turned back to Jesus whose eyes evenly connected with his and whose countenance and warmth were irresistible. He still held in his hand the papyri, the list of registrants which he had been examining before anyone had entered the Office of Tribute. It now fell to the floor from disinterested, and now uncaring hands. And then the official of the government of Rome came to Jesus, who put his arm around his shoulders and smiled, "Welcome."

The accountant watched as he observed his employer exit the building with this strange man. He, too, had been struck by the man's compelling demeanor. Unlike Matthew, who was a Galilean, the accountant had come from the town of Kerioth, in Judea, where he had acquired his trade from his father, Simon. Thoughtfully, he laid his writing instrument on his table and quietly followed as well.

IV

Here Is My Servant

The rabbi from the school of Shammai watched in what for him could only be described as a shock of revulsion. He had all he needed. It was time to go.

His report to the Sanhedrin was cold and unforgiving. He spoke of Jesus in profoundly accusative terms as if he were demonized, as if he were Beelzebub himself.

"The very next Sabbath after he cultivated a friendship with that publican," Asher continued, "I saw him cavorting in the wheat fields, his lemmings harvesting the grain for themselves—on the Sabbath, mind you—rubbing it of its hulls and consuming it right there in the fields." Asher became animated. "When Youssef, here asked him..."

At this point Youssef cut in, "I asked him plainly why they were doing what was obviously unlawful on the Sabbath? And do you know what this fool said?" Youssef paused as if waiting for an answer from the Jewish leadership. None came.

Asher spoke again. "He referred to that obscure passage in the first book of Samuel where David and his soldiers ate of the hallowed bread..."

"And he couldn't get his facts straight," chimed Youssef. "He said it was in the days of Abiathar, the high priest, when in fact it was Ahimelech. Open and see for yourself. If he were of God he would know his Scriptures better." In thus saying, Youssef had embarrassed himself. It was indeed in the days of Abiathar's service as *High Priest.* Ahimelech, his father, was simply serving as the Temple priest on the day of David's intrusion.

Asher glared at the younger Pharisee's stupidity and continued, "And then this false prophet said that the Sabbath was made for man, not man for the Sabbath." At that, Nicodemus, who had been listening to Asher's report, chuckled. His mirth did not go unnoticed.

"I see little that is amusing," spoke one of the rabbis. "This man may be dangerous."

"You haven't heard the worst," continued Asher. "His arrogance knows no limit. He actually said, and this is a direct quote, 'The Son of Man is

Lord of the Sabbath.' Did he not use these exact words, Youssef?" Youssef nodded an enthusiastic affirmative.

αΘω

Jesus did absolutely nothing to allay fears about himself. In some cases his behavior seemed clearly designed to exacerbate those fears. Conversely, he did everything to reach out to those in personal pain. He gave no quarter to his critics while sacrificing himself for those who needed him. He did all he could, it seemed, to alienate and annoy religious leadership, those who strictly adhered to religious form, legalists all. Yet he met with compassion and love those whose hearts were open to him.

These things did not endear him to human institutions. Especially those that believed they were instituted by God. In their eyes, Jesus had set himself against God. For them, Jesus was definitively antinomian—*against the Law of God!* He showed no deference to his "religious superiors," and no regard for the traditional laws and time-honored doctrines. Jesus plowed his own furrow. He was thought unmanageable. A maverick. A rogue. A rebel. An insufferably young and foolish renegade.

The good he did was lost on those who could not see beyond his apparent disregard for form and cliqueish theological proposition. In fact, they were enraged by this disregard because it appeared to validate his repudiation of their obdurate rectitude. When he healed, it fanned flames of rage because the institution could not duplicate it. His teaching declared religious form to be vacuous and vain, bankrupt of moral and compassionate values, utterly lacking in authentic sensitivity to God.

Many years later, it would be the same. People would fail to see that he came not to enforce the Law, but to satisfy its demands. What they did not comprehend, was that to fulfill the Law *meant* to satisfy its requirements. Thus, in satisfying its requirements, these demands are at the same time both affirmed *and* resolved. They peal from the holiness of God and are answered in the echo of the crucifixion. Otherwise, there is no point in satisfaction. In its satisfaction, the Law is established; it is credentialed. But in its satisfaction, the Law that reveals human darkness gives place to grace and truth, to embrace human redemption. The coercive force of the Law of God is henceforth met and sated in this Carpenter who calls himself the Son of Man.

Jesus came, therefore, to give to those who would receive it a new Law, the Taskmaster of Love, the Judgment of Grace, the Justice of Compassion.

In so doing, he brought release from religious bondage. He requited the vengeance of a Law that accused.

αΘω

Another Sabbath. Jesus entered the synagogue at Capharnaum and was immediately invited to teach. This was now the pattern wherever he went. The multitude crushed to hear him. The local rabbis naturally resented this, but some welcomed him. Some did not know what to do with him. All extended to him the liberty of preaching and teaching in their synagogues. They would not have dared do otherwise.

On this Sabbath, the Jewish religious leadership had come deliberately seeking a reason to accuse him. They had persuaded a man whose right hand was shriveled to attend the service just to bait Jesus, just to see if the Carpenter would heal on the Sabbath.

The man did not have to be encouraged. He longed to be able to use his hand. When the rabbis approached him, what did he have to lose? So, encouraged, he placed himself up close to where Jesus was teaching so that he could not be missed. At points when Jesus paused, the man gestured, looking at his arm and then back at Jesus, holding it up so it could be seen. He sought not the Lord for worship, nor to learn, but to have his arm healed and perhaps to appease the legalists in the bargain.

Jesus, of course, was not a fool. He surmised what this man wanted and that he had been put up to it. He looked around at the religious prigs in irritation, distressed at their unwarranted enmity. He would give them what they wanted and without equivocation. He said, therefore, to the man with the shriveled arm, "Get up and stand here in front of everyone." The man stepped up on the dais. Then looking directly at the lawyers, Jesus said to them, "I ask you, judicious jurists all, which is *lawful* on the Sabbath: to do good or to do evil, to save life or to destroy it?" He waited. He looked at each one, establishing withering individual eye contact. There was no response. Smiling as if satisfied, he said to the man, "Go ahead then, stretch out your hand."

The man surprised, responded, "What?"

"Stretch out your hand!" Jesus commanded, loudly and with force, his irritation unsheathed. Jesus held unmitigated contempt for burdensome, religious strictures. He seemed to enjoy the public display of such contempt. He did not fear its probable consequences. If the Son of God can be said to hate, he hated these strictures. He rejected with vigor anything that vacated by its very existence the exigencies of human kindness and compassion. Timidly now, with uncertainty, the man raised his hand and as he did, it was completely restored.

The leader of the Pharisees clapped his hands, causing others to do the same. But his applause was a mockery. He was at the same time furious and elated. This witless pseudo-prophet, this absurd pretender had fallen like a ripe fig into his hands. They now had obvious reason to retaliate. He had violated the Law of God with a high hand and with arrogance. This primitive bumbler's days were numbered. Immediately he consorted with his colleagues who in turn began to plan. Jesus, with disgust, withdrew from that place.

All of this resulted in even greater popularity for Jesus. News about him spread everywhere, and people brought to him all who were ill with various diseases, those suffering severe pain, the demon possessed, those having seizures, and the paralyzed. He did not hold back. He healed them all. Large crowds from Galilee, the Decapolis and Jerusalem followed him. The whole of Palestine, it seemed, were streaming toward this young man who held such hope, such promise. When those possessed of evil spirits saw him, they fell down before him and cried out, "You are the Son of God." But he quieted them. And thus was fulfilled what was spoken by Isaiah,

> *"A bruised reed he will not break, and a smoldering wick he will not snuff out, till he leads justice to victory. In his name the nations will put their hope."*

Jesus withdrew to the lake. People followed him, crowding him. Those with diseases were pushing forward to touch him.

A solitary boat lay tied to the dock. "Get me into that boat," he said to Peter. Peter rallied James, Andrew and the rest of us, and forming a wedge, we forced our way onto the dock. Reaching the boat, we maneuvered Jesus into it and cast off. The crowd pressed so that it appeared the dock might collapse. Some actually fell into the water and waded toward him. Immediately Peter pulled the boat into deeper water. "That is far enough," said Jesus intending to continue speaking. He was ignored. In a moment, Peter had raised sail and the boat was gone. Jesus lay back on a coil of rope, exhausted. "They are as sheep," he said, weakly.

"This is madness," said Peter just loud enough for me to hear him.

V

Decisions

Paths formed by countless sheep laced the mountainside like a spider's web. It was on one of these that Jesus walked as the sun descended into the western horizon. Abishag trotted ahead of him stopping from time to time to wait for her Master, pausing to sniff the earth in curious investigation of the animals and beasts that had left their scent.

Jesus had spent most of the day asleep in the boat. The rocking, gentle waves, the light breeze in the sails had restored his sense of peace. Peter loved the water, but seldom went sailing for pleasure. This had been a good day. The men talked quietly among themselves, silently reflecting on recent events.

It was late in the afternoon when Peter had brought the boat ashore. As soon as Jesus' foot touched the dock, he struck out on his own, the dog in his trail. "Master, where are you going?" someone asked. He did not answer. He just kept walking away from us. "He needs solitude," a quiet answer. They understood. They knew him. The rest on the boat had renewed him, and he had now walked several miles away from the water's edge. The elevation of the terrain rising, he continued steady, one step in front of another, his breathing in cadence with his pace as he climbed. He sought a place where he could stop and spend the night. He could use a drink of water. *I need to pray.*

There were several things on his mind. His growing popularity among the people, the escalating hostility generated among the religious leadership, and his sense of need for emotional support, his need to surround himself with a cadre of what?

In retrospect, I often thought about how one who claimed to be one with God could have needs for anything at all! But he did have needs. He needed sleep. He needed food. He needed clothing and shelter. He was capable of laughter, anger and sadness. Yes, he had emotional needs as well.

The sheep trail led over a grassy rise and down into an alcove shaded by several trees, boughs spreading to form a natural umbrella. The effect was the shape of a room, an enclosure, a place designed by nature for the protection of those who may seek refuge. A small creek trickled over rocks nearby. Jesus cupped his hands and drank from it. A dove's soft murmuring. Shepherds, for centuries, had enjoyed this alcove before him. Feeling the strain of the trail in his joints, he sat down, leaning his sweating back against the coolness of a large rock. Pulling his legs up so that his arms rested on his knees, he plucked a stalk of grass, inserted it into his mouth and gazed at the darkening sky.

His mind refocused. He thought of Peter hoisting the sails to remove him from the crowd, protecting him from his own exhaustion, caring for him, ministering to him. These thoughts comforted him. *Who?* His heart lifted to God. He began to pray.

"I need friends; special friends to be with me. I need people with me who will watch over me and each other. What shall I call them? Disciples? They are all my disciples. All who follow me. No, these would be different, set aside to help me in my mission. Messengers of the message I bring. I need friends, Father."

These thoughts comforted him. *Who?* His heart lifted to God. *How does one choose a companion?* Jesus knew who he was and was aware of his own needs—evidence of wisdom and maturation. He was who he was and that would not change. Before one seeks others, one must accept one's self. His friends, his disciples, would need to resonate with that imperative.

What should they know before being chosen? How deeply can they commit themselves and identify themselves with me? What kind of men should they be? And how many? Two or three? A dozen? A hundred maybe? A hundred would be too many. The thoughts went back and forth like that, following no logical order or development. Just thoughts, often disconnected.

Curious how Jesus communed with the Father at these times. It was as if the Father were sitting beside him or across from him chewing on a stem of grass as well. There were no spoken words, only the offering of thoughts which seemed to be exchanged, to interact, as though it were two Minds communicating without the bother of speech. Abishag, curled at his side, raised her head to sniff the air.

VI

The Twelve

Who should I choose? Peter? That choice was obvious. The first thing that strikes one about Simon Peter was his six foot, four inch frame. He cast a long shadow. Almost everyone looked up to him—physically. A natural leader, decisive, clear, forthright and brutally honest; and at times, a formidable presence. His fault lay in his rashness. He too often said and did things he regretted. *Impulsive, perceptive and bright!* He was all of these. Jesus thought about it for a moment. Peter's impulsivity was the direct consequence of intelligence. He saw things. Solutions and resolutions often popped into his head; they were so clear to Peter that he was at once done with it, the conclusion inevitable. Sometimes these conclusions were embarrassingly wrong. But Peter was the earthy sort whom Jesus loved. Peter was his first choice. He could find none better. But Peter had a family. What of his wife, Joanna? Would she understand?

Who do you want, Father? Who would be your choice? Peter? Yes, Peter. What of others?

Jesus considered. His first cousins, James and John, the sons of Zebedee and his mother's sister, Salome, came to mind. He thought of them together, *Sons of Thunder!* A bit silly, he thought, *but literally true*—as we know from their desire to "call fire down from heaven" on a small Samaritan village. They were a family of means. His Uncle Zebedee had owned his own business all his adult life. He was a businessman, a fisherman, as had been his father and his father's father. He allowed himself to consider their wealth. *They would bring financial support to the group. But that is not an issue!* Irritated with himself for the thought, *It has no bearing on the decision!* He dismissed it from his mind. While they lived in different towns, he had known these men and remembered well the occasional adventures they spent together as boys. They were in some respects as close as his own brothers.

The fishing trade produced iron-tough men. Hauling heavy nets soaked with water and filled with fish built powerful bodies and brutally calloused hands. Songs at sea and shouted commands made for boisterous personalities. They were straightforward men. Opinionated. Often intemperate in their language and demeanor. Peter, James and John, sons of sail and sea who stink of fish, were no exceptions. Jesus smiled as he thought about it. *They were perfect!*

My brothers, Father? The other sons of my mother and my father? Should they be included? Why not? James, Simon, Judas and Joseph—good men all. *James seems more sensitive to my work than the others.* He thought, *but if I chose one of them, I would have to choose all.* Again, *Why not?* He considered this choice carefully. *Would they be willing to follow my lead?* He thought of the arguments between brothers, himself included, when they were younger and thought better of it. *No, his brothers would not do.*

The moon hung low in the western sky. A shaded opalescent circle, a dull-orange crescent hanging at its bottom to one side as if anticipating a deposit, a golden, inviting receptacle. To its right several inches, or miles, or eons, or however God takes measure of the universe, hung the brightest star of the sky. Jesus gazed at this sight, seeing beyond it into what for most was stellar darkness, but for him, stellar Light. There he touched the Holy Kernel. There he connected with the Father's heart. With the Father then, both far and near, he prayed into the warm, surrounding Cimmerian shade.

Jesus breathed in the quiet, and then went back to his selection process. *I have three, Father. Who else would you want with me? Peter's younger brother, Andrew?* Another raw-boned, muscular fisherman. Black tousled hair, dark penetrating eyes, inquisitive, a seeker, an asker of questions. His temples and beard flecked with premature grey. His face bronzed, his shoulders broad, his hair tied back in a tail. Active, energetic, and very protective of Jesus. By the look of him, he was perhaps a year, maybe two, older than Jesus. Quick to wrestle and make sport with his friends. *He has a way of making us all laugh, finding humor in simple things. And he knows when to be serious.* Fiercely loyal to his family and his brother, he would fight in a moment anyone who challenged him. He and Peter were alike in this respect. No one would dare face them both. *Good men to have with me, Father.* Number four: Andrew, brother to Simon Peter.

Philip. Consummate cultivator and harvester of fig groves with his close friend Nathanael-bar Tolmai (Bartholomew). Their fruit, both fresh and preserved, could be seen on the tables in the marketplace. "Master," he had once said to Jesus, "I have great respect for John, the Baptist. It requires courage to leave one's family and friends and go off into the wilderness to live alone."

"He is not alone," Jesus had replied.

"I know." Philip continued, "He communes with the Father, and he preaches and he baptizes. I should like to follow his example someday."

"There is only one Baptist." *And perhaps there is only one Philip?* What of Philip? *Another good man,* thought Jesus. Philip had followed Jesus for the past year. A man accustomed to producing fruit.

Nathanael! *An Israelite in whom there is no guile.* Jesus smiled at the amusing memory. While some preferred to think of Nathanael by his ancestral name, Bartholomew, Jesus thought of him as *Nathanael; this is the one to whom I promised that he would see the Father's angels ascending and descending on the Son of Man.* Two farmers, Philip and Nathanael, friends who were loyal to each other *and loyal to me. Do you approve, Father?* His heart warmed with satisfaction. Six.

Jesus yawned and stretched his arms into the air. He felt sleep approaching. He was tempted to lie down in the soft grass, build himself a pillow of fallen leaves, placing a cloth over it to keep the insects from crawling into his ears, and sleep. He had chosen six men to be with him. Perhaps that was enough.

It was not time for sleep. He felt satisfied with the choices he had made but sensed that today's work was not yet complete. He rose to his feet and walked into the darkness observing the path closely. Abishag followed at his heels. After a few minutes of striding in the darkness, on the inclining sheep-path, he felt the blood pounding against his temples and his breathing became labored. His mind clearing of cobwebs and drowsiness, he struggled with the notion that he was not done choosing. Since God's promise to Abraham, the descendants of the twelve sons of Israel have served as those through whom access to the true God was given. Twelve? Yes, he would choose twelve, one for each tribe of the house of Israel. It was settled. It was right. *Who, Father? Who else shall it be?*

Is it not comforting to know how close the Son walks with the Father in choosing who shall be with him? Shuttling between them, adjunct to both, the compassionate and all wise Spirit engaged; separate, yet the same as both Father and Son, without whom no selection could be made. So it was then, so it is now, so shall it ever be. Three Wills, *one Mind;* three Spirits, *one Purpose;* three Persons, *one Symphony.*

Matthew. *A gift from God!* For such is the meaning of his name. If Peter was a captain, a leader, a force to be dealt with, so was this publican. There was, however, a wall, an obstacle to overcome where Matthew was concerned. He was hated by almost everyone. The reality that Jesus himself had accepted him is the only reason Peter, John and the others tolerated him, but they did not trust him. How could anyone associated with the Empire of Rome, let alone a Jew who had betrayed his own people for money, be accepted among their number? But Jesus had loved him, accepted him and embraced him as a brother. The others must learn to do so as well.

Two captains then. Peter, and Matthew. Peter the outspoken, brash fisherman; Matthew the quiet-spoken, objective, pragmatic, perhaps even cynical intellectual. They will go in different directions. Peter will draw the most attention, but Matthew will work his quiet genius for the love of his Master that will impact the world.

Matthew did have one friend among the others; Thomas, called "Didymus," whose name called attention to the fact that he was a twin. Thomas and Matthew were not unalike in their personal constitution. The thing that set Thomas apart was his analytical mind. Thomas thought about things. Measured things. Jesus could not recall Thomas ever making a careless remark. He, like the others, had grown up in Galilee, but like Matthew, he was not a fisherman. The industry seemed repugnant to Thomas who made no bones about disliking fish. *There is a quality of sweetness about Thomas,* thought Jesus. *He has a tender heart despite his need for pragmatism.* Thomas was chosen.

And what of the sons of his uncle, Cleopas Alphaeus? (No relation to Matthew.) Jesus considered the two of them, *James and Simon, the young zealot.* And *Thaddaeus,* the son of James? Cleopas was brother to Joseph, the surrogate father of Jesus. These men, though brothers, were as different from each other as any men could possibly be. Jesus was amazed that they had been raised in the same household.

James was short. It is mentioned only because it was obvious and only because people remarked about it. They called him "James the Less." Because he had been put upon and ridiculed all his life, he had developed a certain toughness, a feistiness and bravado. He would not be pushed around or made to feel inferior because he was short. He had dealt with that all his life. What he lacked in stature, he made up for in arrogance, an arrogance that people did not find unappealing. Perhaps in a short man, such arrogance can be amusing. Incredibly, he was something of a bully. Not many withstood him, for to do so one invited verbal abuse the like of which one does not hear from ordinary men. Moreover, he was irrepressible. His laugh was hearty and quick, often tinged with sarcasm. Yet one did not really feel insulted when James released one of his deprecating invectives. Well, maybe a little. He saw through pretense. He was relentlessly practical and would not brook hypocrisy. *He is delightful,* thought Jesus. *James will keep us all near the precipice.*

Thaddaeus? Judas? Lebbeus? This young man has more names than a thief! Like his father and his uncles, an acerbic soul. Sons of Alphaeus. Sons of hell! Thaddaeus was the son of James and grandson to Alphaeus and, despite his youth, served as a check, or a foil, between the other two. The brothers argued incessantly with unseemly pouts and tirades from James. Usually, it concerned Simon's political ambitions. Young Thaddaeus was no less argumentative, no less a participant in the adolescent fights. But then, the Alphaeus men had been doing this all their lives. Thaddaeus, oddly, seemed the rallying point, the glue that kept the other two from killing each other. Yet, each would instantly give his life for the other. *Choose one of them, choose them all!*

Simon, the most radical, had joined the Zealots, that ragtag army of not so underground resistance against the Roman oppression. He was always spouting off at the mouth. He always had something to say—usually extreme and not well thought through. He held no love for the Romans or for anyone who wanted to try to make the best of that bad situation. He could think only of war. "If this isn't a war," he would opine, "then we are spineless worms." His eyebrows furrowed, his face contorted in manufactured rage. He was bright enough to know that there was little he and his friends could do against so powerful a government, but that did not stop their pseudo-guerilla tactics nor their vituperative rhetoric. James, the eldest, and father to Thaddaeus, just shook his head and rolled his eyes at his brother's recklessness. He often tried to counsel him to be less intemperate, but to no avail. Simon was known to fraternize with some scurrilous people, Barabbas, the murderer among them. How could the Son of God use such an extremist? How could men like Matthew, the publican and Roman sympathizer, and Simon the Zealot ever comprehend one another? How could they ever get along? It was not a good mix. They held in common only their devotion to Jesus—and for quite different reasons. *Only* their devotion to Jesus? It was this singular devotion that held them all together, that bonded them, that made them feel nothing else mattered. So it was then, so it is now for all of us. *I need his passion, his obsession, his youthful energy,* thought Jesus. *I need such a man as Simon!*

It occurred to Jesus that everyone he had chosen thus far came from Galilee. It did not seem necessary for him to select anyone from elsewhere. He, himself had grown up in Galilee. Why look elsewhere? Yet, he felt within himself that he had yet a choice to make. Among the faces that sifted through his mind was that of the young man from Matthew's tax office. Jesus searched his mind for a name, *Judas! Did not he say that he came from a town called...Kerioth. Ish-Kerioth,* a small town in Judea. Judas Iscariot. *The man from Kerioth!*

Like Matthew, Judas had been with those that followed Jesus since that day in the Office of Tribute. *Interesting how a man from Judea has followed along with our Galileans,* thought Jesus. He remembered how this young man had come to him as they rested from a day's journey and said to him, "Teacher, I know you have not invited me to follow you as you have the others, but will you object if I stay? I wish to learn." Jesus noticed that while his lips smiled, his eyes did not. "I believe in what you are trying to accomplish." *An accountant,* Jesus remembered. *It could be advantageous to have such a man among us. Perhaps he will serve a purpose within our group.* What think you of Judas, old girl? He laid his hand to the dog's head and stroked gently. Abishag whined and looked away.

Three years later, the night before his crucifixion, Jesus would refer to Judas as the "son of perdition," the son of eternal doom and damnation. He said that he had "lost" Judas so that the Scriptures would be fulfilled. Yet the ancient prophecies do not mention Judas or a man from Kerioth, nor do they mention the betrayal of Messiah. They speak eloquently of Messiah's death, but do not mention what specific event that precipitated the crucifixion, as Judas' betrayal did. Did Jesus choose Judas with full knowledge of his awful betrayal? Does Jesus select to be an apostle a man foreordained to eternal damnation? John states clearly that he did. Why would Jesus choose someone whom he knew would betray him over someone whom he knew would not?

During the years I was with him, I quietly struggled over why Jesus had done this; why he had chosen Judas and not Matthias or even me or one of the others to be one of the original twelve. Judas had been a relative newcomer to our company, and we had been with Jesus and the disciples since his baptism. It seemed, from my simple perspective, that any of us would have been a better choice than Judas. In retrospect, however, it is clear.

After having preached for a year in the region of Galilee, many people followed Jesus. So, after an all-night season of prayer and a few hours toward morning for sleep, he appointed these twelve—designating them Apostles—that they might be with him and that he might send them out to preach, giving them authority over the forces of evil.

Apostle? What is an apostle? A messenger? An office? A gift? Is there a better understanding of this word?

Whatever it means, it does not mean me. Jesus did not choose me to be an Apostle. Nor did the other apostles when the time came for replacing Judas, even though I was nominated. I was not chosen. The first time, I was not so much troubled. Jesus had a right, I considered, to choose whom he wanted. They were, after all, *his* apostles. There were many of us who followed him who also were not chosen. It never occurred to me then that he would choose me.

The second time, however, was different. There were only two of us, Matthias and myself, from whom to choose. Had Peter and the others made their decision based on what they believed to be the merit of each of us, perhaps my discomfort over the procedure would have been different. But the method by which the choice was made was pure chance. Dice. They may as well have flipped a denary. How could something as significant as this be decided so irresponsibly? It was an insult to the Spirit of God; it was an insult to Matthias who was chosen; it was an insult to me, who was not.

Now as I look back on this singular event, instead of imagining what my life would have been like had I been chosen, I wonder instead what it would have been like had I not known Jesus or spent those extraordinary years with him. It is he who shaped and formed my life. In retrospect, I can state with absolute sincerity, nothing else matters.

VII

Amphitheater in the Mountains

Morning crept through eastern skies. He awoke as the first rays of the sun illuminated the western slopes; he, still among the shadows. Abishag pawing at his arm playfully, whining as if to say "Get up, Master." He smiled, reaching over to pet her, but she was already running back and forth, coaxing him back to the path. Stretching, he rose from where he lay, blinked his eyes several times to clear the fog in his head, and began to descend the mountain on the path he had already traced, the dog now trotting contentedly at his heels.

King David's song swelled into his memory as he smelled the sweet perfume of a mountain morning.

Let me hear in the morning
Of your steadfast love,
For in you I place my trust.
Teach me the way I should go,
For to you I lift up my soul.

With a deep sense of satisfaction with the choices he had made the night before, the song lifted aloud in joy and fullness of heart as, obediently, he followed his four-legged companion down the path.

He heard them before he saw them. A dull roar coming up from the hillside below. The cacophony of many people chatting and laughing one with another. And then they were there, led by his friends, the disciples. The mountainside had played out into a spacious meadow punctuated and surrounded by undulating hills. How came all of these to this place? When they saw him, the roar erupted into cheers. "Master," cried Peter, "we were worried. Are you well?"

"I am! I am well indeed." He waited until the talking ceased and the movement of the multitude halted. "Who are your friends?" he asked. Peter looked around him at the crowd. "Many have come a long way; they come seeking you, Master. You are known throughout Galilee, and because of that, so are we. Having learned of our waiting here for your return, those who seek you came here. But they seek not us. As all who seek to be touched by the Father, they seek you."

Jesus lifted his hands gesturing for everyone to sit down. They settled themselves on the ground surrounding him. The gentle hills rose softly around the plateau, forming a natural amphitheater. When they had stilled, he spoke.

"Some of you look tired," he smiled as he looked into expectant faces. Several of those sitting near nodded in agreement. This crowd was open, receptive. No critics here. They had come in anticipation of something good. As he began to speak, the crowd hushed and became quiet. One could hear a cricket chirp. He did not disappoint them. Discernible compassion attended his voice when he said, "Some of you are impoverished in spirit, your inner resources evaporated. Some of you are sad and broken, you feel hopeless and find nothing in yourselves with which to cope. Be comforted. God understands your weakness and what you perceive to be failure. He knows the desires of your heart. He put them there. Yes, be comforted. Yours is the kingdom of heaven."

Owning these words as nourishment for the soul is not easily experienced. Does God place in our hearts, our thoughts, the desires we possess? I have desires that focus on survival. How I will put food on my table, provide for my family and their daily needs. How to provide for myself when I am no longer able to do so. I have desires that issue from the friends, family and relationships I enjoy. But the most compelling and meaningful desire in my heart concerns my purpose, the reason I breathe, the cause that compels my existence. Why am I here? What was it that prompted the Creator to create *me*?

The answers to these questions take shape around what I am and what I want to be. I would like to think that this predilection of divine rationale and purpose is my central focus. This is what drives me, and all the other proclivities I possess circumnavigate and feed this force, this energy. It is this force that God has placed within me to make myself happen; a force, I believe he has placed within us all. I am certain of it. When it is all done, should there be a footnote to my life, let it be, *"This man was a servant of God. This man completed God's intent for his life."*

Among the assembly were many dressed in tattered robes, patched and repaired dozens of times. Their faces gaunt, resigned, yet serene. These were those who had found contentment in the struggle for survival. Those who understood that struggle is not always a curse. These were those whose lives were simpler, less complex, whose expectations were meager and whose faces were lifted to the Father for sustenance. Jesus spoke to them, "Blessed," he said, "are those among you who must sweat and strain for your next meal. Do not despair. For those who must wear privation as a cloak of honor, yours is the kingdom of God."

Many of these had not eaten. They had no resources to buy food, yet they seemed at peace. They did not complain. How simple it is to cry out from hunger. How honest. How ordinary. How it is to be expected. Yet no hands were out-held. No pleas of "alms" were spoken. To these remarkable people Jesus said, "Blessed are you who hunger now, for you shall be satisfied."

As he spoke, one thing became clear to all. He spoke as one who wished to take them all in his arms and comfort them. As he spoke, some began to weep. One young couple in particular listened to him with painful expressions. Faces downcast, tears streaming down their cheeks. They had good reason to weep. They had just lost their son to illness. They had buried him not two days ago. They sat not far from where Jesus stood. "Blessed," he said, "are you who weep now, for you shall find solace." He had seen them. He approached them quietly, smiling. Gentleness emanated from him. He extended his hand and took the young mother by the chin, and with the other he held the shoulder of the father. "Be comforted," he said, "you shall see him again and you shall laugh." His eyes met theirs. "You shall laugh," he said again. Through their tears an imperceptible smile tugged at their lips.

He strode out among them now. Stopping here to preach. Stopping there to comfort. "The rich," he cried, "live in comfort now. The surfeited, those who revel in food and wine, those about whom all speak well—take care! For suffering and hunger is but a misfortune away, weeping comes in the night and reputations shredded by a solitary, whispered rumor." They were listening, rapt and attentive. Abishag could not be contained. As he moved about speaking and gesturing, the dog danced about happily wagging her tail. Licking one here, nuzzling another there, making eye contact with a child or an old man, seeking to be petted. Wherever Jesus moved the dog moved. All seemed to enjoy the Master's dog as much as the Master's words.

He continued to address those whose tears made wet paths on dust-caked cheeks. "You are in pain now. You are hurting now. You feel the terrible agony of loss. Oh, hear me dear loved ones, you are close to the heart of the Father. Your tears are the blossoms in his fields. You are blessed more than you can now imagine, and you will be comforted." This only intensified the weeping. One could not tell if the tears were of joy or of pain—or of both.

Walking back to his place, he turned and gazed at the crowd once again and then sat down. The hills tenderly echoed each syllable. "Those of you who possess the quiet, non-presumptuous strength of meekness, who have liberty but exercise it with economy and discretion, are blessed indeed. Be encouraged, for you will inherit the earth.

"Some of you hunger and thirst for a life liberated from the evil tentacles of an undisciplined, consumptive life. You will not be sated with anything less than absolute intimacy with the Father. You seek righteousness. You know that there is nothing else truly worth having." Jesus paused and then, "You will be filled." He let these thoughts sink deeply into the kernel of their spirit and then he continued.

"Some of you have learned not to be accusatory or judgmental. You do not exact recompense, or vengeance. You empower others to live constructively. You do not condemn, but you give strength to those weaker than yourself. You have shown mercy; you shall receive mercy."

Who was this man? How came he with such power? Such force of influence? Such poise? How is it that thousands converge on him? He is the eldest son of a peasant carpenter. His life, until recently, unremarkable. Who is he to intrude into the concourse of our lives with such love and wisdom?

I cannot say. I can only lament that I had not known him sooner and rejoice that I live and breathe the same air as he. The mercy of which he speaks? I long to bathe in it, to feel its invigorating life flow over these tired, painful bones. Oh, my God, when I think of my sins against you and against men, how can you redeem me? I think, perhaps—through this man.

"I see purity in the hearts of some of you. Your faith is as innocent and trusting as a child's. When you are weak and fail, you still believe. How blessed you are! Do not fear, for you will see God.

"Some of you, because of your very presence, bring principled and equitable peace and stillness to troubled hearts. It is very difficult to contend with you for your influence calms the violent spirit. You will be called sons of God.

"When you stand strong and are persecuted for doing the right thing regardless of the cost; when you take ridicule and contempt, insult and invective for the sake of another, when you have no need to be right, but possess the rectitude and stamina to defend right; know that you are blessed. Yours is the kingdom of heaven.

"Your life will change as you follow me. Your perspectives will shift. Not only will that be uncomfortable for some of those around you, but some will become belligerent and even hostile towards your new way of life and your new values. They may try to humiliate you publicly, discredit and belittle you. Let joy fill your hearts when this happens because you are in good company."

αΘω

Jesus stood once again. He pointed directly at an individual. "You," he declared, "are the salt of the earth!" And then he pointed at another and another. "And you, and you, and you," he cried. And then he spread his arms, palms held upwards, and with a shrug said, "But if salt loses its flavor, how can it perform its function? It is without worth, no better than dirt. It is no longer good for anything." Pointing again, "So, have salt in yourselves. Do not allow yourselves to become bland and tasteless. Yet, be at peace with each other; and remember salt does not equate to arrogance."

He picked up a small child and held him high, looking at his face. "You, young fellow, are the light of the world!" The baby began to cry. Laughing, Jesus handed him back to his mother. "A city on a hill cannot be hidden," he shouted. "Neither do people light a candle and hide it under a bowl. Instead they turn the bowl upside down and make it a stand on which to put the candle, and it gives light to everyone in the house." He paused as if to invite the next step in logic. "So let your light shine before men. Let them see what good you do. This will bring joy to your Father in heaven."

αΘω

It is difficult to remember all that he said that day. His teachings were like fine wine, not easily appreciated by those with an undiscriminating palate, yet eloquent in simplicity, bold and penetrating in scope. He sat down on a nearby rock, took a deep breath and folded his arms. No one moved. They seemed struck with awe. They were accustomed to the nasal droning of the synagogue rabbis, but this man had spoken to them with animation, self-assurance, force and most of all, believability. Even the dog looked at him in wonder.

It has been many years since Jesus spoke these words; many years since he left us to return to his place with the Father. The apostles have met, indeed meet with some regularity to plan, to consult to lay out the schematic of a budding church. Saul of Tarsus met Jesus on the Damascus road and is now preaching and teaching and planting churches, but I would ask each of them and all of them, upon what foundation are they constructing their efforts? Do they think of these words spoken on this day as they go about creating bishops, elders and deacons? Paul, in his first epistle to the Corinthian church plainly states "other foundation can no man lay, than that is laid, which is Jesus Christ." How came he from that absolute truth to where he now alleges that the Ephesian church is built upon the foundation of the *Apostles and Prophets*, Jesus Christ, being the chief cornerstone? Jesus, the Creator of all that is; Jesus, the Son of God; Jesus the Savior of the world is now relegated to being the chief stone in a foundation of apostles?

I confess. I worry about the church's foundation. Is it being built upon the rock that is Jesus Christ and his teaching, or is it resting on something else, destined to be washed way with the rains and the wind?

VIII

Flavius Marque

Capharnaum. The trek down the mountain to the city had taken the remainder of the day. The light of torches and candles emanated from inside homes as well as boats along the waterfront as they prepared for the next morning's fishing. The noises of the city, a familiar cacophony to all who lived and worked there; it was home. For the most part, it represented for them the security of hearthside and table, bedside and labor.

In the officer's quarters of the Roman garrison in the city, a centurion paced the floor of the room in which his slave lay dying.

Not much longer now.

This thought tortured his mind. He had been a soldier for almost thirty years. He entered the military as a lowly Tirones, playing card games in the barracks with the other members of his contubernium. He had now achieved the rank of an officer, a Pilus Prior Centurion, the highest rank a captain of one hundred could go before promotion to Tribuni Angusticlavii. Having been passed over several times, this was a rank he would never achieve. He was much too close to his men. Because of this, he was thought unfit for promotion to high command. He thought it not "unfit" at all. He preferred to stay close to his men. After thirty years, he would become an Evocarti, a special, long-time veteran who received double pay and exemption from manual labor. The army had always been and still was his life. It was all he had ever known.

During his service, he had seen death dozens of times. He had received numerous decorations for his prowess in combat: one *Battlement Crown*, three *Gold Crowns* and five *Crowns of the Preserver*. Less glorious, and a duty he hated, he had presided over the executions of...*How many now? Fourteen? Fifteen?* Guerrilla monkeys for the most part, the hopelessly ill-trained zealots of the Jewish resistance. But this slave, this servant, this *friend* had taught him that not all Jews were zealots. *He was closer to me than a fellow warrior.* Flavius had already begun to think of him as gone.

He had freed Jonathan seven years ago, freed him because he had served him faithfully and well; freed him because he had become more than a slave. He had become a friend, indeed. But Jonathan would have none of it. *"I cannot leave you, Flavius Marque,"* said he. *"Where would I go? Your home is my home—even if you are a Roman gentile."* The soldier smiled at the amusing memory. He remembered something else. *"You are my family, now,"* the freed slave had said.

The words gave him pain at this time as he watched the last breaths seep from the lungs of his friend. He knelt beside the bed. *"God of the Jews,"* he prayed silently. *"If you are there, if you are real, save this man. Save my friend, save my brother."* He laid his head on the sick man's feverish arm. *"O, Adonai, or whatever it is they call you...please!"*

"Captain, the healer has returned." Adoniram ben Hadad spoke softly so as not to disturb the soldier's grief. Adoniram was a respected member of the synagogue, an elder and brother to Josiah, whose daughter Jesus had healed. He had been present when Jesus eviscerated the demons from the man in the synagogue earlier. Since the healing of his niece and the spectacular exorcism in the synagogue, Adoniram had become a fervent follower of "the healer." As one who, because of his slave, was deeply impressed with the Jewish God, Flavius had been at the synagogue exorcism as well.

"The healer?"

"Jesus of Nazareth, the man who delivered that sorry soul from the demonic sickness. You remember, in the synagogue?"

"Yes, I most certainly do remember." He rose to his feet, a hint of hope energizing the lines of his face. "He has returned? He is here?"

"He has returned to the city from a tour of teaching throughout Galilee."

Flavius remembered indeed. This man who had impressed him more than all others was actually within reach. He knew that Jesus possessed remarkable powers and that he spoke of the solitary God—as his Father—as everyone's Father. He was reminded again of how close he had come to embracing Jewish monotheism. Somehow it made more sense to him than the absurd pantheon of gods the Romans had invented. This God of the Jews was not "invented," of that he was quite certain. And this Jesus of Nazareth seemed to know him well. *Perhaps he could . . ?*

"Please, Rabbi. Go. Fetch him! Beg him to come!"

Adoniram smiled imperceptibly. There were only a few like him; elders and rabbis of the synagogue who realized that this carpenter's son may be the One they hoped for. At least, if he were not, he was surely a prophet of ancient stature. Not all of the elders of the Jews were intransigent legalists. Some were compassionate and some followed Jesus. The others? They were all either old men caught up in the cobwebs of rabbinic haranguing, or maturing scholars intent on getting every nuance of the Tanakh precisely correct, or young firebrands bent on destroying the undestroyable—Rome.

Adoniram found Jesus at the home of Peter and Andrew and presented the centurion's case. "This man deserves to have you come and heal his beloved servant because he loves our nation and has built our synagogue." Adoniram clearly understood the Jewishness of Jesus. He knew that he was not only racially a Jew but that he believed the fathers and the prophets, Abraham, Moses, and Isaiah; yet he need not have argued so assiduously. Jesus never refused a cry for help, "deserving" or not.

After listening intently, Jesus was straightfoward, "Of course, I will go. I will go now."

The military garrison was not far and on nearing the centurion's quarters, Jesus was met by some of his friends. "Master," said they to him, "Flavius Marque sent us with a message for you."

"Yes?"

"The captain told us to tell you not to trouble yourself. He said he does not deserve to have you come under his roof." They spoke this deferentially, although it reeked incredulity.

"What?" with surprise.

The man speaking glanced at the others as if seeking support in the face of Jesus' shock at this humble request. "He said these exact words, Sir, 'I do not consider myself worthy to come to him, to be in his presence. If he would just speak the word from where he stands, my servant will be healed.' He said to tell you that he understands you to be a 'man of authority' as he is. When he tells a soldier to 'Go,' he goes; or to another, 'Come,' he comes; and if he speaks to his servant and says, 'Do this,' he does it." So he believes, Sir, that you may but speak the word and it shall be done."

Jesus looked around at all of us and spread his hands as if to say, "Can you believe this?" This man is a combat officer. He knows command. He is not Jewish. He isn't even religious. He follows no rabbinical teachings. Yet he believes! So Jesus said to the friends of the centurion, "Then go! It will be done just as he believed it would be done."

Flavius Marque waited in silence, brooding over Jonathan's labored breathing. Perspiration beaded on his forehead, minute chills played over his dying form. *I have seen death all of my professional career, but nothing has so grieved me as this.* Deep spears of sadness bled his heart.

His hope that the healer would help faded with each moment in which his friend grew weaker. Abruptly, his servant opened his eyes. *Here it comes,* thought Flavius, *I've seen it many times. That moment of lucidity just before death.*

"My lord, Flavius?" The words were soft, whispered.

"Jonathan, I am here." He expected some last request, some last words.

"I feel better, my lord." He raised his hands to his eyes, massaging them. "I am feeling much better!" He attempted to sit up. Flavius leaped to assist, his face wet with tears.

As I sit here many years later, scratching away on papyri with my Egyptian ink, I turn to gaze at the flame, the soft corona of my candles, remembering distinctly what Jesus said to us who were with him that day. After the men had left, he turned to us and said, "I tell you the truth, I have not found anyone in the whole of this country with faith like this. Many will come from the corners of the earth and will seek to take their places at the feast with Abraham, Isaac and Jacob in the kingdom of heaven. But these supposed 'subjects of the kingdom' will be thrown outside into darkness, where there will be weeping and gnashing of teeth."

I can't help but be amazed at how the rejection of those in spiritual leadership must have hurt him. And when it is placed alongside the simple faith of men like Flavius Marque, who by rights should have no faith at all, it makes the rejection seem even more repugnant.

"Gnashing teeth," indeed.

αΘω

Early next morning before dawn, Jesus rose from his bed and walked outside. He could smell the sentient piquancy of the lake. It is an odor not found in places where there is no lake, an aroma of dead fish mixed with the freshness of crisp morning air. Fishermen were beginning to stir and would soon be on the water with their boats and nets. He found an isolated piling upon which to sit and stared out into the water. What thoughts came to the Son of Man at moments like these? What musings? Perhaps he thought of Flavius Marque and his servant. Perhaps he wondered how the lad was doing—if he had had a good night.

Another day in which to serve You. How may I best do that, my Father? What lies in store for this day? What soldier's servant, what blind beggar, what leprous boy, what widow's son . . ? His thoughts stopped for a moment.

Waves rippled gently at his feet. Only distant sounds could be heard. That, and his own breathing. The sky, yet lowering, had begun to glow in its eastern reaches. Suddenly he was off the piling striding toward the house of Peter.

"Simon!" he cried. "Come, we must be off!"

IX

City of Nain

The hours wore hot into the day. Jesus and his disciples had walked hard all morning. As he went through this community or that, he was recognized and many followed. "Why is he in such a hurry?" Keeping up was a strain and Jesus didn't seem to tire. On he pressed, the hills flattening before his stride. More and more curious hangers-on followed until a great crowd once again stretched out behind him like the wake of a boat under strong sail.

At length he came upon a town called *Na-im* (which some call Nain). It was the ancient town of *Shu-na-im* made famous by another prophet (Nahum) many years ago. Its walls had fallen upon disrepair, its gate dilapidated. As he approached, exiting from the town gate, there came a funeral procession. He ceased his gait and waited for the mourners to pass. The horde behind him gathered around as spectators to some curious event.

When the funeral entourage reached Jesus, he raised his hands requesting them to stop. It was an unusual gesture. Who would stop a funeral procession? Why? Yet, the beasts of burden were reined and black-garbed mourners halted, looking inquiringly at this strange man. Who is he? What does he want? Does he know the deceased? And what means this great crowd following him?

A woman bent with sorrow, walking immediately behind the bier shook with sobs, dabbing her eyes with a kerchief. Jesus approached her. "Her son," said her companion. "She is now alone. Her husband also is dead." Jesus stood quietly as if nothing else existed but this sacred sorrow, the pathetic mother.

He raised his hand and touched her arm. She lifted her eyes to his, "Dear Mother," he spoke in tones soft and comforting, "Do not weep." His eyes fixed hers as he reached to touch the shrouded corpse. "What is his name?" She heard herself reply, "Thomas?" A question, questioning unformed hope. Her eyes followed his hand. *He is touching my poor son!* She did not know what to say, what to feel. Who is this man? Why does he . . ?

"Thomas, I say to you, get up!"

The grey mottled hue of the boy's skin began to take on the flush of life. Shockwaves of murmur throughout the crowd. She heard the words of Jesus but could not accept them. It could not be. This is not happening. The eyes of her son blinked. She saw him raise himself to his elbow and softly, so quiet that only she could hear, this solitary word fell from his lips, *"Mother?"*

She fainted.

αΘω

Simon the Pharisee was among those standing in the crowd. He was enthralled by what he had just witnessed. To touch a dead corpse was something that deeply offended him, but when the boy came back to life, it abrogated any criticism he might have had. He had to know more of this man. There were many standing about him listening to him speak and watching the emotional reunion between the boy and his mother, once she had recovered. Finally, Simon got close enough to speak.

"Sir," he began awkwardly, "the sun is at its zenith. Your disciples advise me that you have been traveling all morning and you have yet to eat. I would be pleased if you and your friends would dine with me at my table."

"I would be pleased as well, sir." Jesus responded, touching Simon's elbow, "Come, lead the way."

There was yet another in the crowd, a woman who also had a son. Her son, however, was a child. And while he had a father, none knew who that might be, least of all the woman herself. She had slept with many men, indeed; that was how she supported herself and her child. She had no husband and no family to help.

First to be considered was her loveliness, her satin-olive face and china-blue eyes, dark hair in soft curls falling down well below her shoulders. She knew well how to dress to please men. Her robe slung low in front, a delicate fragrance, not enough to overpower the senses but enough to turn one's head, escaped from a translucent phial of alabaster, hung about her neck containing expensive aromatic oil. Hanging upon a golden filigree necklace nestled between her breasts, it more than all else advertised her for what she was. The folds of her garments fell about her so as to reveal furtive glimpses of flesh. She was an enticing, beautiful woman who expertly applied all the accouterments of her trade.

Not surprisingly, one of her most frequent clients was none other than Simon the Pharisee. It was no secret. Everyone knew. It was understood and tolerated. Even the righteous Pharisee had to take some comfort now and then.

She had stood that day in the crowd with Simon. Well, not exactly with him but some distance away, far enough so that the connection would not be obvious except to those who already knew. Not many stood close to her. Women avoided her as much as possible. Men stared at her greedily and secretly wished they could afford her. She was long past caring what others thought of her and ignored all of this. But she did want to see this man about whom so many rumors had spread. *An honestly kind and sensitive man?* The incredulity of such a thought amused her. *A prophet?* This only provoked her curiosity. *A healer, teacher or sage?* She was there to see if Jesus approximated any of these things. When she saw a dead boy open his eyes and call for his mother, her breath caught in her throat and tears surged into her eyes.

"Oh!" she cried and fell to her knees there in the crowd. Some glanced in her direction but most were too taken with the event.

X

She Has Loved Much

Women such as this were souls of consummate pragmatism. The salient focus of her life was survival for her and her son. She had to have an income. She had no marketable skills, but the Almighty had so shaped and formed her that she commanded enormous sensual power over men. She simply used that power to survive. This was not to say that she did not find in her trade certain elements of pleasure. She was, after all, a woman. But had she an alternative, she would have leaped at it. She knew what she did was morally indefensible, yet society tacitly tolerated it as it had done for millennia. Owing to her favors to certain members of the Sanhedrin and others of prominence like Simon, she had never been threatened with stoning. Somehow religious leadership was more tolerant of prostitution than of adultery. It was a profession as ancient as man himself.

But the shame inside her was held in check by the prudent necessity of survival for her and her son. Despite her sensuality, she was a mother. She was a good mother. How can such a woman ever be understood as a good mother? The very question itself reveals monumental ignorance of the coercive power of a mother's love. She had lived her maternal life as a she-bear protecting her young from ravenous predators. She did anything she could to protect this son of hers, to give him a life, to give him a future. Now she had witnessed what Jesus had done for this dead boy, only a few years older than her son. She had seen what he had done for this mother.

"Oh, my God! Could he, would he deliver me from this life? Is there some hope for purity of soul, for peace, for a decent life for my son?" Tears rolled down her satin cheeks. Sobs heaved at her breasts. When she saw Jesus speaking with Simon; when she saw him take Simon's arm and walk in the direction of his home, the back of her wrist went to her mouth in surprise. *"No!"* she exclaimed within herself. *"They cannot be friends!"* She followed to see.

Simon's home was clearly the most elegant in the economically depressed small town of Nain. It boasted an open courtyard leading up a step to a lovely veranda and into an entry way with assorted anterooms. There was a kitchen, a small study and, of course, the *Teraglin,* a substantial 15-foot square room. This was Simon's festive reception and dining room. Even the ceiling was exactly 15 feet high. It was into this room that Jesus was now ushered. A long, low table surrounded with leaning-cushions accommodating up to twelve people—four at each side and two at each end—sat in the middle of the room. On it a sumptuous meal had been set. Guests reclined about the table on cushions, their heads toward the table and their feet angling away. Often, when important guests were invited, other guests were welcome to stand about the perimeter, thus giving the occasion an additional quality of significance.

Jesus, however, was not accorded the seat of honor at the center of the table. While he was clearly the reason for the event, Simon himself took this prestigious seat—his seat. It was a slight that the Pharisee intended and one that did not go unnoticed by the other guests. What did go unnoticed was the presence of this woman who slipped in among the others, shawl thrown about her head, partially obfuscating her identity. Everyone who knew her also knew that she was no stranger to this room. Indeed, on occasion she had entertained there. This time, however, she had no intention of entertaining.

Quietly, while all were occupied with the food and banter going on about the table, she moved smoothly and easily until she came to stand at the feet of Jesus. A few moments passed after which, had you been there to see, she began to take several deep breaths; and, had you looked, you could have seen tears welling in her blue eyes. Her head bowed, her tears fell, splashing quietly on his feet. Where the teardrops fell, they formed splash marks in the accumulated dirt and dust, for Jesus had not been afforded the usual courtesy of having his feet washed by the servants of his host. As he felt the tears drop, he turned his head to see. The woman, embarrassed, fell to her knees and began to wipe them from his feet with her hair.

Jesus observed her in silence. He did nothing to encourage her. He did nothing to stop her and that, perhaps, was encouragement enough. As she fell to her knees she moaned, softly wailing and sobbing. Conversation around the table ebbed as she slowly became the focus of attention. She began to kiss his feet and then, extracting the phial from between her breasts, she emptied the entire contents onto his skin. She massaged his feet with her hands, kissing them and weeping in an all-consuming paroxysm of feeling. She now compelled the attention of every guest. Silence in the room except for the sounds of her deep pain. She kissed his feet again. And then again, followed by what may have seemed to the casual observer to be compulsive kissing—almost as if to stop would be to violate the sacred and waste an opportunity for worship.

This was not lost on Simon. How dare this woman come in here at this private, celebratory moment! How dare she make a spectacle of herself and shame him in this way! His anger fueled his skepticism about Jesus as well. *If this man were really a prophet, he would know what kind of woman she is!* These, his unspoken thoughts. In Simon's mind, in allowing this woman (for all of the pleasure he himself had taken of her) to fawn over him like this, Jesus had compromised any credibility he might have engendered previously. However, his doubts about this prophet were about to be challenged.

Jesus turned from observing the woman and fixed the Pharisee with his gaze. "What troubles you, Simon?" he asked. "I can see that you are more than a little agitated." He waited for a response. None came. "Let me ask you something," he continued.

Simon cleared this throat irritably, condescendingly. "Yes, teacher?"

"I heard a story once. It seemed two men owed money to a certain lender. One owed him five hundred denarii and the other owed fifty. Neither of them had the money to pay him back, so he canceled the debts of both." He paused for a moment. "Tell me, Simon, which of these two men will love their creditor more?"

Uncomfortable Simon. He should never have invited this—this peasant beneath his roof. What impertinence! What adolescent arrogance! He was not pleased. He did not want to answer. Chagrined, he wanted to exit. But he couldn't just get up and walk out of his own home. Desperately wanting this whole embarrassing affair to be over, he felt trapped.

"I suppose the one with the bigger debt." So much for stating the obvious. What else could he say? Everyone in the room was listening.

"Well said, Simon!" smiled Jesus.

Then he turned back toward the woman and said, "Do you see this woman, Simon? I came into your house, invited by you, as your guest. You did not give me so much as a drop of water for my feet. Look at her, Simon. Look at her!" It was a command; the Pharisee did not, could not, resist. "She has wet my feet with her tears and wiped them with her hair. You gave me no kiss of greeting, no kiss of welcome, yet this woman has not ceased to kiss my feet." Simon glanced away in embarrassed disgust. "Look at her, Simon!" Simon complied. "You did not put oil on my head. Not a single drop! But she has massaged my feet with perfume. Her sins are many, Simon. You know that better than almost anyone." The Pharisee's face flushed. "She has loved many men. She is forgiven every indiscretion. But as you have noted, he who has been forgiven little, loves little."

Then Jesus spoke to her. "My dear, look at me." She stopped rubbing his feet and lifted her eyes to his. "You are forgiven. You are as clean as snow covering the boughs of the cedars on mount Hermon. Go now. I bless you from my heart!"

Someone whispered, "Who is this who forgives sins? Who does he think he is?"

Jesus ignored them and reached forth his hand to stroke her face. He wiped away the tears. "Your faith has cleansed you," he said softly. "Go in peace."

XI

Mary's Place Revisited

Mary's place. The rain fell in soft sheets. She shivered against the damp chill. She hadn't been here in a while. The flowers were folding under the raindrops. The grass seemed to reach for the moisture. Dark clouds scudded overhead creating a foreboding, but natural sanctuary.

After thirty years together, Joseph was dead. Her heart ached with grieving. The children were at home. Milcah had come, as she always did when her mother needed her, as had her husband and the grandchildren. Thankfully, all of the children had come—except for James and Jesus. They were together, somewhere. So many rumors about Jesus had found their way back to her. It was hard to discern the difference between what she knew to be truth and what was probably fiction. She was glad James was with Jesus and those chosen to be his apostles, but she wished desperately both were here with her now. Jesus would know what to do. How could she get word to him? They were probably not too far away in some town or village, but which? There seemed to be so many. Meanwhile, the body of Joseph lay in her home. With the children and the children's children, it had been too much. She sought escape, solitude. She sought comfort from God.

She sat on the stone where she had first encountered the angel. The angel! Gabriel! She hadn't thought of him in years. She recalled with warmth the exquisite moment of conception. She thought of subsequent events. Egypt. So many years. So much has happened. So little time it seemed. The rain had begun to soak her garments. The chill was growing deeper. Tears surged again. *"Oh, Joseph, my husband! Oh, Jesus, my son, where are you? Oh, my God, please; do not forsake me now!"*

"Mother?" The voice startled her. She thought at first it might be Gabriel, yet again.

"Mother, are you all right?" It was Rhoda, her youngest. She had known that her mother often resorted here. She had not wanted to intrude on her mother's grief yet she herself grieved. She entered the clearing and came to her mother. They held each other and wept. The rain continued to fall quietly. Mary was grateful for the warmth of her daughter's body. She was real. So much reality. So little understanding. *So far from anything good.* She felt a pang of guilt, "except for this child," she said aloud. The rain began to chill them both.

"Mother, I'm cold. Let us leave this place and go home."

"This place is more of a home to me than you realize, my child."

"Come Mother, we will both become ill. The house is warm. Joseph and Simon have come and Sarah. Please now, come home. You must come home and out of the rain."

"The rain brings life to my broken heart," said Mary.

"I know Mother, but you must come now. Let us hurry. Walk fast so our blood will pound. We need to warm up. Come!" Rhoda's voice insisting, demanding. Her mother reluctantly obeyed.

In the absence of Jesus and James, Simon and Milcah had taken charge of funeral arrangements. As many as possible of the extended family were contacted. They began to arrive and soon the house was crowded with family and close friends. The rain had ceased but the ground was wet and mud tracked into the house. Among all the other things she did, Milcah took charge of cleaning the mud as well. Rhoda was left to be with their mother. That was her responsibility. "Just make her comfortable," Milcah had instructed her. "You are her favorite," this without bitterness, but with acceptance or perhaps resignation.

"That isn't true, sister," Rhoda replied, "but I will do as you say. She needs someone close to her now." And then in some frustration, "Where is Jesus? Where is James?"

"He is off preaching and healing somewhere, I suppose," with restrained irritation.

"He is following the Father's purposes sister," replied Rhoda.

"Yes, I *do* know about that," a retort. "You have heard the reports. People are saying he is insane—a madman!"

"Please, Milcah, this is not the time for hard feelings."

"I can't help it! They should both be here helping with our mother. And helping with our..." her voice caught as tears welled into her eyes once again, "helping our father!"

Rhoda put her arms around her sister and held her as she wept but said nothing.

αΘω

Where indeed, has he gone? To what attentions, to what reaches, to what ambitions had this young Warrior escaped? He came into this world from the abode of God, beyond time, beyond the endless corridors of black night. He came to a young woman, to be born not in palaces grand or temples high, but born in an animal stall of straw and smells and warmth and love.

From childhood adventures to healing touches, from ordinariness to miracle, from a boy to a man, he came to us bearing a love so intense, so real that total strangers found his magnetism irresistible, who left all they knew, all they had to follow him.

I cannot speak for others. I can only speak for myself. If others find resonance in my muse, then in gratitude and humility, I invite them to digest the joy I feel at his coming and let that joy nourish their bones.

Jesus has gone to his place. The place ordained for him by the Father. More than ever, now he is employed in his Father's business.

Warrior did I say? Yes, Warrior! Debater! Capable of high scorn towards those who would thwart his purpose of bringing mankind to the threshold of self-realization, towards the meaning of fullness in the Imago Dei. Lover! Lover of those who believe and those who do not. Lover of those who would be gathered under his wings and those who would not.

Fear not, dear Milcah. Your brother has not left. He is not gone in indifference to your rage, to your pain. He knows, he understands. He belongs to you. He belongs to us all. And that, dear Milcah, is where he is gone. Look at your hand. It is whole. It is clean. It is pure and blemish free. Do not forget. Trust.

XII

Horseplay

"*This is impossible!*" Peter's balled fist hit the table so hard its timbers almost split. His cup of wine bounced from the impact and fell over draining into his lap, which only infuriated him more. "My God!" he swore to himself, "Where do they all come from!?" The morass of human faces outside his home dissolved into an annoying, irritating, disruptive mob of needy, belligerent, or merely curious gaggle of abstract individuals.

Though Peter stood over six feet of steel muscle tempered by countless hours of hauling nets, he was weary. Weary physically. Weary mentally. His home in Capharnaum was the third and final stop for the day, yet it was only early afternoon. Jesus sat next to Peter laughing at his friend's outburst and its messy consequence. Between hiccups of mirth, he slurped another bite of Joanna's excellent stew. The guests stood about the sweltering room, pressed together, making it a crushing effort to move around, much less recline at table.

Peter wanted to flee. He was not a man who enjoyed noise and crowds. The amusement of Jesus at his frustration merely augmented it. His beard flecked with white and grey, he yearned for solitude, for the sea, for anything except to be here. This is what it must feel like as a solitary fish caught in my nets surrounded by hundreds of others, all wriggling to be free, yet trapped by the hemp that is celebrity! What a wonder to be a boy again with no concerns, no encumbrances, no fish and no crowds! His imaginative metaphors mixed with reality. To run like the wind, to run out of this room, to run out of this noisy town, to lay in the fields and feel the sun on my old leathery hide...Despite his discomfiture, Peter laughed aloud at the delicious thought of it.

"What tickles you so, Simon?" Jesus asked, through another mouthful of stew. Peter, his face suggesting an impish notion, leaned over and conspiratorially whispered in his ear, "For once, Master, instead of my following you...*you follow me!*"

αΘω

Slowly, they made their way through the press of bodies to a small, unoccupied room in Peter's house. No one had followed them or had taken particular notice of their exit. Peter hurried to a casement that opened onto a piece of earth that, amazingly, the crowd had left pristine. Placing his hands on the sill, he hoisted his frame through it and looked around. No one had seen him.

"What on earth are you about, Simon?" For the first time in memory, Jesus was uncertain, perplexed at the behavior of this strange, impulsive disciple. Jesus couldn't help but recall the Jerusalem Temple adventure he had had with his childhood friend, Eben. He remembered the thrill of it. He felt twinges of it now.

"Allow me this once, Jesus. Come on, let us escape this madhouse!" With that Peter turned toward deliverance.

Jesus glanced back in the direction of the crowds and thought momentarily of their needs and realized how depleted he felt. He could not resist Peter's smile and the prospect of mischievous adventure any longer. He followed the fisherman through the window, piecemeal memories of the time he descended into the sewers of Jerusalem flitting through his brain. Another time. Same excitement. The dog, Abishag, bounded through the window in happy anticipation. In another moment of furtive steps, they were out of sight of Peter's home, leaving the crowd behind. They walked briskly, shoulders back, smiles on their faces.

"Now what, Simon? Where do you want to go? What do you want to do?"

In the distance, Peter pointed to a tree. "See that oak yonder?" said he.

"Yes."

"I'll race you!"

"What? You? Race? On foot?" Jesus laughed. "You're an old man. You'll croak before we run five paces."

"All right, boy. I'll give you a head start." Slapping Jesus on the butt, he cried, "Now off with you!"

Jesus took off. He was not about to let this old codger best him. But it seemed like mere seconds before Peter was running abreast with him. The old fisherman laughed and poured himself into the task of outrunning Jesus. He pulled ahead. Jesus redoubled his efforts—to no avail. Peter was leaving him huffing behind. When Jesus finally arrived at the tree, Peter had already circumvented it and was leaning with both hands on his thighs, breathing heavily. "Old man!? I guess we know now who is the old man!"

Jesus, panting and holding his sides with laughter, sat down and leaned against the tree. "I can't remember when I last ran like that," he wheezed. In the distance lay the lake or, as most call it, the sea of Galilee. From under the oak tree, the water appeared as if painted with an artist's azure brush. Birds whistled in the trees. Leaves fluttered in the breeze. White cumulus billowed into the blue and the siren of the wavelets beckoned.

In a few moments, Jesus and Peter found themselves walking along the edges of the water. Jesus removed his sandals and waded into the lapping shoreline. Peter followed, removing his footwear as well. "Praise God!" he cried for the sheer joy of it. "I think I'll take a swim." Off came his tunic as he waded into the water. In a moment he was over his head, swimming powerful strokes toward the center of the lake. Jesus observed him from the shore, wondering at the silliness of all of this. Two grown men stealing away from responsibility like adolescents. He laughed out loud to himself and off came his robe as well. He could not swim as well as Peter, but he managed to join the fisherman in the deep water. Treading water, Jesus drew back his hand and forcibly brought it forward, slapped the surface, sending water cascading into Peter's face.

Shaking his head and rubbing his eyes, the fisherman growled and came for Jesus. Grabbing the Son of God by his head with both hands, he pushed down with all his might. Jesus sank like a stone. When at last his head broke the surface, it was he who was sputtering and spitting. The Creator of the universe had a surprise for the fisherman. In his hand he held by its tail, a slippery, scaly denizen trying with all its might to free itself from Jesus' grip. Jesus, however, took a swing at Peter with the fish, missing his nose by a whisker. "Take that, you old relic," screamed Jesus with abandon. No sooner had the blow missed than Peter once again came for Jesus. He tried to dodge, but unlike the fish which went flying from his grasp as he swung, he could not escape Peter's big, gnarled and powerful hands from grasping his head, and again Jesus plunged into the depths of Gennesaret.

αΘω

Frolicking ended, the two men lay back on the grass next to the water. "And, how often do you do this, Peter?" Jesus asked as they wrapped themselves in their clothing.

"Not often," was the reply. "Maybe every thirty years or so...starting now."

More laughter. They lay on their backs studying the passing clouds... talking, being quiet. Once breathing had returned to normal, Jesus stood and idly began to skip stones across the surface. Peter watched. "I've lost count of the stones I have skipped when I was young," he offered. Abishag danced crazily, engrossed with her Master's throwing. Excited eyes watched the path of each stone as it sailed across the surface bouncing and skipping. At length, she could stand it no longer and sailed into the waves, chasing the elusive stones. Once about fifty feet from the shore, she became puzzled at the disappearance of the stones. Jesus threw another. It came bouncing out toward her and disappeared a few feet from her nose. Undaunted, Abishag disappeared also, the waves closing over her head. Jesus became alarmed. Peter sat up. The surface of the water was undisturbed by a swimming canine. Then suddenly, her head broke the surface, and in her mouth was a stone. She immediately paddled back to Jesus, dropping the stone at his feet panting happily, looking up at him in anticipation of yet another foray into the deep.

At length, their interlude of horseplay came to an end and they began to make their way back to the chaos of humanity they had left behind. Amazingly, when Jesus and Peter entered the room, it was apparent that they were not even missed. Everything was the same...everything, of course, except Jesus and Peter!

Only scraps of food were left at table and, accordingly, there were vacant spaces and places to sit. Turning to his wife Peter asked, "Is there any food left in our house, Joanna?" Smiling, in a moment she returned with fresh bread, grapes, figs, goat cheese and wine.

As they ate, Peter turned his gaze to those gathering in the room. "So many women," he mused. There was Mary, called Magdalene. Jesus had delivered her from no less than seven demons. Joanna, the wife of Cuza, who managed Herod's palace. And then, Susanna. There were others, so many of them. "A good thing," thought Peter. "Without their help, none of us would be here." These women believed in Jesus. Not in just who he was but in what he was doing. They believed in it so much that they consistently gave of their financial substance to support the work. *"Where do they get the money? Do their husbands know about it?"* He let the thought hang in his head for a moment as he mused. *"Well, that is none of my concern,"* he thought, *"I suppose it is out of gratitude; he has healed just about all of them of something."*

He felt a hand on his shoulder. "So, my friend, what do you make of all these people? I must admit, I am more than a bit weary of it." It was James, the Lord's brother.

"I was just thinking that there are so many women."

"Yes, very loyal," said James. "What would we do without them?"

"Likely not much, considering the demands on our purse," replied the fisherman.

"You are concerned about our purse? Don't trouble yourself. My brother seems adequate to the task of keeping it brimming with denarii. Besides, let Judas worry about it. It's his job."

"That is what troubles me..." Peter did not say these words. He thought them.

XIII

A Grieving Son

The mass of bodies extended outside where the crowd seemed interminable, a sea of faces murmuring, straining to see, wondering when Jesus would come out. Should it seem strange that the crowd could ignore the absence of Jesus and at the same time strain to see him, remember that crowds are made up of people with different needs, different expectations. Loud disturbances arose from time to time, as though clusters of them were being agitated by something.

The excitement level of the crowd indeed required attention. Quietly, Jesus stood and made his way through the hot room to the door. As best they could, people made way for him.

There stood just outside the door, several scribes who had come from Jerusalem to Peter's house in Capharnaum. They were attempting to convince the people that Jesus was driven by evil, perhaps even possessed of a demon. As Jesus emerged someone shouted, "He casts out demons through the Prince of Demons! He is himself demonic!" Shouts of anger and derision.

Others caught their breath in horror and shouted, "Not so! He healed my daughter's blindness!"

"My neighbor's deformed leg was straightened!"

"He speaks of God's love for us! Could Satan do that?"

Jesus held up his hand, quieting the crowd and said simply, "Satan does not cast out Satan!" The words fell so heavy, so final that in the ensuing silence you could have heard an ant making its way to supper. It was as if all were struck dumb. Abishag barked at the sudden quiet, adding punctuation to her master's remark. He continued, "Any government, organization or family that is divided against itself will not stand." Silent nods of assent. No one, especially the scribes, attempted to debate. His logic was inescapable, the clarity and authority with which he spoke, irresistible. "So if Satan has risen up against himself, he, too, comes to an end." He paused, the corner of his mouth raised in a slight smile. Raising one eyebrow he said, "And, as you can see, I am still here."

The crowd jostled and moved about. What was it!? Something in their seeming endless agitation caught his eye. Jesus continued to teach, yet he seemed alerted. Something was wrong. "Soon," he said, "the Holy Spirit will come to live within you. If you are to resist the legions of Satan, his presence in your life is critical. You see, no one can go into a powerful man's house and usurp ownership unless he first overcomes this man. The Spirit of the Living God is not a man, regardless of that man's strength. The Spirit of the Living God cannot be overcome by Satan or anyone, or anything else. Not even your own sins, which are far worse than Satan's influence over you. Never forget that. If the Spirit of God resides in you, you are safe. You are protected. There are three sources of sentient evil: Satan, you and others like you. But the Spirit of the Living God overrules and preempts all three. No force, evil or otherwise, can resist him."

The listeners heard, but it was clear that not many understood. Jesus paused, as if waiting for a response. When none came, he turned and re-entered the house, his expression dark and foreboding. Sitting down, he leaned his elbows on his knees and buried his face in his hands. I heard him utter something...something like, "My father..." It was hardly audible. What was happening? Why was he in such pain?

"James!" he cried suddenly. Jesus looked up, tears in his eyes. "James, my brother!" this time in anguish. I looked around for James but could not see him.

Those standing about began to mutter, "Where the devil is his brother? He is calling for his brother." It spread among those who were near and out into the street. In a moment, James appeared at the door, his face sober. Mournful eyes met.

James began to speak. "Jesus," he said, "our father..." he halted, struggling for words...

"Our father is dead." Jesus finished for him. Suppressing his pain and with surprising determination, his jaw firmly set, Jesus stood.

"He's already in the grave, Jesus. Let us go to him, to mother, to our family. With your powers you can..." Abruptly, amazingly, his brother turned his back on him. Shocked, James cried, "Jesus!"

As midnight in the forest, the silence held them both. Quietly, James realized that there was to be no miracle this time.

"No, James. You go. I cannot. Not just now. I am needed here. My father is...with my Father."

As James, benumbed by his brother's response, turned to go, Jesus stepped back through the crowd. Walking away, seeking release from the moment, Jesus seemed the loneliest I had ever seen him. To this day I cannot explain his reaction to the news of his father's death. Sometimes he seemed tortured by his own existence.

αΘω

I watched him make his way outside and through the crowd. As he moved, the people stepped back to give him room. Many held out their hands to him, and he touched as many as he could. He came to the edge of the lake, the crowd following him and pressing him. He looked wan, weary and for a moment, slightly confused. Nearby lay a small boat. Loosening it from its mooring he stepped into it and pushed. The boat scudded out into the water leaving the crowd standing on the shore. Some thought he would leave them. I did myself. He often resorted to solitude, and I thought he would take the oars and row out into the water, there to sit and be alone. Instead, he took a single oar and put it into the water as one might to pole up a river. The boat went a few feet out and stopped. The lake was as glass. As he sat, he began to speak. The peaceful scene quieted the people. No one spoke and the voice of Jesus carried well out into the press.

"A farmer," he began, "went out to plant his fields. As he was scattering the seed, some fell along a nearby path and birds came and consumed the seed." Jesus seemed preoccupied as he spoke. His words felt empty, disconnected, almost devoid of meaning. What was troubling him? Why would he speak to us of a farmer?

Haunting thoughts penetrated...*My father is with my Father. My family is grieving and I cannot be with them. Why, Father? Why?*

"Some fell in rocky places, where it did not have much soil. The seed sprang up quickly because the soil was shallow." His throat dry, choked with emotion, guttural. It was hard to get the words out. "But when the sun came up, the plants were scorched, and they withered because they had no root." *You have gone too far this time, Jesus,* James had said. *Our mother is suffering, our sisters...and we are not there because...because you insist on being here.*

The boat rocked gently as Jesus shifted his weight.... *but I remain here... with these...these sheep. Your sheep. Oh, my Father, help her to understand.*

"Other seed fell among thorns," Jesus continued, his voice tenuous, "which grew up and choked the plants." *She is my mother. I love her. They are my sisters, Rhoda, Milcah, Sarah. I love them. Oh, my Father, comfort them because...I can't.*

αΘω

"Holy Father, for the first time since he was born, I think I do understand. He is not mine! He never was!" Her heart choked in her throat. Her hand went to her breast. "He is yours! He always was!" What was it the old man had said? Simeon? That day in the Temple? The words came flooding back to her. "'A sword shall pierce your own heart also...That the thoughts of many may be revealed...' Oh Father please...it hurts. It hurts so much!" And then deep within her spirit Mary felt a warmth. A voice, yet not a voice, just involuntary thoughts began to flood her mind, "Yes, my child, he *is* yours, but in a way even now you are just beginning to understand. He is yours, and you are his. That will never change. Be comforted, therefore."

αΘω

"The rest of the seed fell on good soil where it produced a crop—thirty, sixty or a hundred times what was sown." Jesus' head dropped. After a moment he faced the crowd again. "He who has ears, let him hear." This final sentence muttered, as if he had lost the desire for anyone to hear at all.

XIV

Mantle

Abruptly, Jesus stood up in the boat and stepped into the water. It was shallow there so he sank only to his knees. He strode out of the water and onto the shore. Once again the crowd divided as he cleaved through them, his footsteps leaving wet traces on the ground. With determination, he spoke to no one, passing through without incident. No one followed, at least not immediately. Those of us who were disciples, those of us who had been with him since the beginning, looked at one another not knowing what to do. Jesus disappeared into the landscape. In a moment, Peter followed. After a moment's hesitation, the rest of us fell in behind him...

For over an hour Jesus walked, saying nothing. His stride softened into a gentler stroll allowing the twelve and the rest of us to catch up. Walking next to him in silence for a few moments, I ventured a question, "Where are we going, Lord?" He looked at me, smiled and said my name.

"Joseph." He said nothing more for the moment and then, "Joseph, the son of rest, the son of comfort. I am glad you are with me, Joseph. I need your company."

"I will always be with you," I replied. "You are my dearest friend, my Master and Lord. I could no more take leave of you than the sun takes leave of the sky."

He paused, his eyes measuring me, and softly said, "I suppose you wouldn't," walking slower, his arms folded across his chest. "You never knew your father, did you, Joseph?"

"He died when I was an infant. My mother left our home shortly after. I never saw her again." Life without a father, indeed without a mother as well, had not been easy.

"So you managed to grow up with no parents in your home?"

"I was fortunate to have a home," I replied. "I had brothers, sisters, uncles and other older men who seemed to want to help me. But there was no man whom I could call, father; a father whose love would envelop me, and whose mantle of integrity might fall on me. Mostly, I was surrounded by women old enough to be my grandmothers…and one African servant who was more of a mother to me than almost anyone."

"Did you miss not having a father?" I wondered at his line of questioning. Why is he pursuing this? Doesn't he know how it pains my heart?

"Always. I confess I have often envied those who had fathers, even bad ones."

"My father was a good father." He was pensive. "He was a carpenter, Joseph." Then he laughed wistfully, "His name was Joseph, too. What do you think of that, Joseph? And what do you think of a son, Joseph," he said with some emotion, "who is not there for his father's funeral? What do you think of a son who does not hurry to see his family during their time of grief?" The words were clipped, almost angry.

I stopped walking and stared at him. He stopped, too. He turned and looked at me. "I don't know what to think, Master. I would have never done that, but I am not you. You have had two fathers. One is dead, the other will never die. It is that Father's hand that is upon you, his call, his purpose." I took a breath and then added softly, "Sometimes God's purposes are peculiar and, more than peculiar, difficult."

"Yes," said Jesus. "Difficult." Then he turned and walked on.

αΘω

I caught up with him again and asked, "Why do you speak to the people in stories they do not understand?"

"God our Father, my Father," he glanced at me with a resonating twinkle, "has a message he wishes to convey. It is a message of love, a message of invitation…but you know, Joseph, there are people, who because of suspicion or fear, do not respond to an invitation of love. These 'stories,' as you call them, separate those who respond from those who will not."

"But do they not respond because they do not believe the love is real, or because life has treated them so harshly they cannot recognize it when they see it? Would it not be better to make it plain and simple for these people?" The logic to me seemed inescapable.

"It is more complex than it seems. Every man and woman lives life in a cloud of conflicting complexity. This cloud consists of what has been learned from parents, family, teachers and experience. The cloud forms and shapes opinion and character. Each opinion is the result of willful choice based on what is understood from their cloud. The Father will not disturb one's choices—whatever their cloud—he does not force response to his love, Joseph. Nor does he manipulate or cajole. A person still has his own mind and makes his own decisions. So, he who has cleaned his ears of the jaded wax of his cloud will respond to the Father's invitation. Are you familiar with the prophecy of Isaiah?"

"Not very," I confessed.

"Isaiah said...

> *You will be ever hearing but never understanding; you will be ever seeing but never perceiving. This people's heart has become calloused; they hardly hear with their ears, and they have closed their eyes. Otherwise they might see with their eyes, hear with their ears, understand with their hearts and turn, and I would heal them.*

I thought it amazing how he could quote, apparently at random, obscure passages from the sacred writings.

"...But blessed are your eyes Joseph, because they see, and your ears because they hear. Many prophets and righteous men longed to see what you see but did not see it and to hear what you hear but did not hear it."

"I don't teach in stories to illustrate my point or even to make it interesting. On the contrary, I teach in stories so that truth may find a heart predisposed to acceptance. I teach in stories so that truth may be lost on a callous heart. This is not as cold as you might imagine, Joseph. It simply acknowledges the freedom Father has given men to make up their own minds as to what they choose to believe.

"So what do you think of my story now, Joseph?"

"Which one, Lord?

"The one I just finished, Joseph! About the farmer sowing seed. Is your memory that short?" he chuckled.

"I think I understand," I smiled. He returned the smile.

"I grieve painfully for my mother, my brothers and sisters and the rest of my family. But my father, the man who raised me, has known from the beginning that I must be about my heavenly Father's business. Funerals are for the living, Joseph. Such ceremonies help cement the memory of the beloved one lost. But Joseph my father is now with my Father...and his Father. He is at peace and, at the same time, exuberant beyond human imagination. I love my family, but I cannot grieve as they do. Nor can I be among them to comfort them. Nothing stays the same, Joseph. Nothing but eternal things and eternal truths. My father, Joseph, understands this.

He has known it for a long time. My purpose must not be interrupted, not even by his passing."

He put his hand on my shoulder and spoke to me as though he had further explanation to make. He owed me nothing. Least of all, explanations. Yet he went on..."Your name is Joseph," which means 'God will increase.' And you are the son of Sabbas, the son of comfort and rest. Indeed, you are all these things, dear friend, but you are more. You are upright and just. Therefore I give you a new name, 'Justus.' Justus the upright and strong." And then he took my face in his hands and kissed me on the forehead. "You will suffer, dear Justus. You will suffer because you have chosen to follow me. But you will endure and you will conquer because of your trust and devotion. Do not fear, Justus the upright. You will conquer!" He then did something that changed my life more than my name; he removed his mantle and laid it on my shoulders, spreading it about my arms and tugging it firmly in place. "There," he said, "you have your mantle," and then he turned to the others who had begun to stare. "Come, friends" Jesus said. He appeared to be comforted, somewhat relieved. "Let's go back. I am hungry."

So now I am called Justus, and his mantle I have kept to this day. It is worn and tattered and I no longer wear it. I keep it folded and put away for safekeeping. But I do wear it in my heart, and the mantle that covers my heart shall never become worn and tattered. It has become my shepherd, my shroud and my salvation. It has become the mantle of his blood. It shall never be put away.

XV

Weeds

Owing to the fact that we traveled on foot, rather than on the backs of animals or in carts or wagons, our muscles were in good condition and well toned. So, our pace was not hurried, but neither did we amble. This being so, as the day wore on, striding along this way, we began to tire. It didn't seem to matter to Jesus as he once again began to teach us as we walked, keeping our focus on his words and off our weary feet. Jesus continued to speak as we walked, "Consider the farmer who just put his crop in the ground. Exhausted after a hard day's work, he slept. While he was asleep, an evil person came and scattered weed seeds among the seeds of wheat. Men do evil things like this, sometimes for no apparent reason other than the evil satisfaction of hurting others. Sometimes it is 'payback' for the evil they have endured, or for the pleasure they derive from hurting others, just because they can. So when the wheat sprouted, the weeds sprouted, too. The farmer's workers came to him and said, 'Didn't you plant wheat in your field? Where did the weeds come from?'"

"'An enemy did this, replied the farmer."

"The workers asked him, 'Do you want us to go and pull up the weeds?'"

"'No,'" he answered, "'because you might pull up the wheat as well. Let both grow together until the harvest. Then, collect the weeds first and burn them; then gather the wheat and bring it into the barn.'"

I thought of Judas. "Why would Jesus have chosen him? How could he? How is it that Judas could have been with us all this time, and yet…" Not only did Jesus extend himself to a person such as Judas, he sought to include him among his closest companions. He sought to construct a place of eternal honor for him. But Judas would have none of it. *I would have none of him.* That, indeed, may be his epitaph.

"Because the children of God must live their lives among the weeds, they will not find life easy. As you well know, weeds usually choke out the wheat. But you must never lose hope; the Father knows how to preserve and harvest his crop."

The path eventually meandered to a place of rest. A bench of sawed logs had been erected so travelers could sit, and over which a shelter had been built. When Jesus saw it, he made straight for it, sat down, removed his sandals and began to massage the ache in his feet. As it almost always happens, a brook bubbled nearby where those who stopped could cool their feet in running water and those who were thirsty could drink from a standing spring. It was indeed a lovely place, a natural and perfect place for a rest. So we stopped, and after a few moments gathered around Jesus.

He said to us, "I tell you these tales because I intend for you to repeat them to others." We looked at one another in bewilderment. "Does that surprise you? You must understand that I will not be with you forever. I expect you to carry on my work. Learn then the story of a treasure, which a man found in a field not his own. The man's joy at his discovery overwhelmed him. He exploded with pleasure. And then he sought for a method in which to conceal the treasure lest someone else stumble upon it and take it from him. Then, smart man that he was, he found the owner of the field and purchased it from him." We laughed and applauded with enthusiasm.

"Smart move," noted Thomas. "Tell us another, Jesus."

"To seek to be a member in the family of God," he responded, "is like a merchant looking to purchase fine pearls. He stumbles upon one of enormous value, a beauty the like of which he had never seen. So taken was he by this magnificent jewel that he sold everything he had and bought it."

"He sold everything?"

"Everything, Thomas. So great is the value of being in union with the Father. Nothing you have or ever could have compares to it." Thomas was silent. So were we all.

XVI

The Other Side

I watched the sun sink into the western mountains. How odd, I thought, that you can almost see this great source of vision-searing light turn to gold before your very eyes; you can even watch it move...I loved sunsets. They always give a satisfying, final touch to a good day, and a redeeming patina to a terrible one. What happened between sunset and sunset seems almost inconsequential. A nourishing philosophy! I felt content.

By the time we made our way back to Galilee, yet another mass of people huddled close to Jesus. Sometimes they seemed to appear out of nowhere, from behind the rocks, from behind the brush, up the wadis. It was amazing. I have seen great crowds before, especially in the Temple at Jerusalem, and once I attended a contest of sport in a Roman arena. But I have never seen anything like the crowds that followed Jesus. For the most part, they were quiet, many sick and infirm. They had come to be healed. Yet Jesus did not heal everyone. I always thought that strange for one so compassionate. But Jesus did unnatural things naturally. He never made the case for doing extraordinary things outside the current and flow of the ordinary. Thus, he did not go to all the leper colonies and empty them of disfigured tenants. He did not visit all the homes of the infirm and do the same. But he did heal many, enough to make for these huge crowds.

αΘω

Though we had not had a particularly difficult day, Jesus seemed exhausted. He had stopped smiling, his positive, upbeat expression, wan and spent. He appeared desirous to relieve himself of the crowd. A girl-child came to him holding a bouquet of wild flowers in her small, porcelain hand. Jesus, though weary, stopped, took the flowers and kissed the little girl on her head, but kept moving along his way. We reached the waterfront where, tied to their moorings, a small flotilla of boats jostled among the wavelets. The boats themselves were substantial; they could easily hold fifteen to twenty men. Masts stood in each with a single yardarm near the top to which a sail might be fastened.

Into one of these, Jesus climbed and the rest of us followed. Seeing our purpose, the other boats began to fill as well. "What course, Master?" from Peter.

Jesus seated himself on the bench and slumped against the stern of the boat. He arranged a few items for his comfort, a coil of rope and a small cushion for a pillow, upon which he laid his head, closed his eyes and responded quietly, "The other side." In an instant, he slept.

Peter, James and the other fishermen among us raised the sail that filled with breezy winds, as did the rest of the boats, and we were off to the "other side," wherever that meant. I don't think any of us really knew—somewhere, I guess. Perhaps Tiberias. Maybe just an evening sail, but if I knew Simon Peter, he had fishing and deep water on his mind. Yet how could we seriously fish with all of the other boats so close by?

As we scudded away from shore, I looked at Jesus asleep in the stern among the nets and coils of rope. In a few moments, the shoreline was a distant blur. Sleeping there on the aft thwart, he did not look like anyone other than a very tired, very ordinary man. We had all grown used to that. His body, like ours, demanded rest when it was tired. The amazing things he said and did astounded us, but most of the time Jesus was just one of us. He was our undisputed mentor and leader, no doubt of that, but it was difficult throughout the day to sustain the impression that he was extraordinary. He ate and drank with the rest of us, sat around campfires at night and swapped stories with the rest of us. He spoke our language, coarse and distinctly male. Often we spoke of athletes and gladiators, of their feats and prowess. While none of us actually were heroes of sport, we were men—talking and acting as men talk and act. We laughed, joked and with customary male humor, insulted one another; and Jesus, far from reserved and withdrawn, was always a vigorous and integral part of that. We had grown close to one another, our sense of camaraderie intense.

At times, we were confused as to how to act around him. It was a strange mix of the desire to honor him or just to accept him as one of us. At this moment as he lay asleep, it was the latter. We saw him as a very tired man, and we took him as he was. That felt right for the moment.

αΘω

The Sea of Galilee is one of the most unusual bodies of fresh water known to men. Thirteen miles long, seven miles wide, about 150 feet deep in its deepest quarter; its waters sweet and teeming with fish, it is surrounded by mountains, high on the west, lower on the east. At greater than six hundred feet lower than the level of the great oceans, it is the lowest freshwater lake on Earth. Snow-capped Mt. Hermon to the north in the distance. From the cold heights of these mountains, frigid oceans of air spill down to the warm waters generating sudden, intense storms. The fishermen among us knew all about these storms and had endured dozens of them in their professional lifetimes. There was nothing about this sea or the vessels that ploughed it that Simon Peter, in particular, did not know about. Of all the fishermen, he was the most experienced, the most respected for his familiarity with deep water. If a storm came, it would not catch this man by surprise. The storms of Galilee are legendary. No one ventures into the deep water unaware of them. No one challenges Galilee without some measure of anxiety about the storms. Except for Jesus who said simply "the other side" and went to sleep.

XVII

Storm

We were well out from shore, the shoreline a distant haze, the mountains rising majestically out of the wet horizon.

"Strike the sails," Peter clipped in a tone that indicated he meant business.

"Why, Simon?" said another of the fishermen among us. "The night has not yet fallen. The skies are clear. The stars are only beginning to show themselves."

"I smell it," said Peter quietly.

"Smell what?" joked Thomas. "We all know Simon, do we not?" He continued jokingly, "The only thing he smells is the stink on his upper lip." As the laughter began to rise, we heard both anger and urgency...

"Strike the damn sails!"

Instantly, John and the others jumped, reaching for the lines.

The wind hit us like a rolling boulder from the north. The sail could not be reefed quickly enough to avoid heeling over sharply. Matthew, no seaman, almost fell out. The other boats were hit as hard as we. Some did not reef their sails at all; we could hear ripping as they heeled sharply and water gushed over gunnels.

Torrents of cool air tore at the water's surface, which undulated and splashed small whitecaps back, as if angry at the wind for disturbing them. Time arrested itself while these small whitecaps heaved into threatening waves. Another mountainside of wind. Our boat kicked, heaved and heeled as the lake vomited into our boat like a sick sow. Water swirled around our feet, and I could see fear on the faces of those who were not fishermen.

"Bail!" screamed Peter.

I looked for something—anything that would allow me to move water out of the boat. Nothing. No container of any sort. I cupped my hands and began to toss water back into the sea as fast as I could.

"Bail!"

All of us madly began to slap at the water in the boat as it heeled again and a massive amount of water sloshed into it. It was at once obvious: it was impossible to fight this. We were going to sink! Already our boat was wallowing. God knows what was happening to the other boats! It was a figure of speech, an expression of futility. The thought flitted into and out of my head so fast that I did not recognize its significance. The bow dipped into a trough between the waves. Looking up, I saw a wall of water descending on us. Had it hit us full force we would clearly perish.

Oddly, I thought of Jesus. At the same moment I heard Peter scream, "Master!" Then the wave hit. The boat filled with water and began to sink. Again, Peter's voice screamed against the wind, "This is the worst I've seen. Steady the tiller! Bail! Merciful God Almighty! Bail!" With the sea legs of a cat, he made his way aft where, incredibly, Jesus still lay asleep. How could he sleep through this? Mad thoughts went through my mind. Had he taken some kind of medicinal potion? Another wave hit. The boat continued to fill. He slept on, undisturbed, his clothing soaked to the skin.

αΘω

Peter reached for Jesus, grabbing fistfuls of wet robe. Shaking him violently he cried, "Master! Dammit! Master! Wake up! We are perishing!" His eyes fluttered open. I heard Peter scream mere inches from Jesus' face, "For God's sake man, help us bail! Do something!" Then with vehemence, "We are ready to sink like a stone! Don't you care at all? How can you sleep through this?" At this point, under these circumstances, Peter was by default our leader, our captain, indeed, our savior. This was clearly not Jesus' field of expertise. Peter had survived countless storms on this lake. Even though he said it was bigger than any he had seen, we still looked to Peter, not to Jesus, to get us out of this. Our first mistake. But Jesus was a carpenter, not a sailor. What did he know of storms and waves and boats?

I was close enough to see his eyes. He looked at Peter with what at first I thought was rage, but then they softened. He took Peter's wrists and said simply, "Where is your faith, Simon? Release me." Peter unclenched the powerful fists that were filled with the Master's robes. He was bewildered, angry, exasperated. "Faith? While we are drowning, you speak of faith? Where is your sanity, man? Awake now! Get up! Help us bail!" Just then, another wave struck us, heaving the stern of the boat where Jesus lay up high into the wind, which shrieked through his clothes. What was the point of waking him? What could he do now? It would have been a merciful thing to let him drown in his sleep.

Grasping at the rigging, Jesus managed to stand. He looked at the sea heaving and tossing, then into the darkening sky. Spray stung his face. Facing the wind, fist raised at the webbing of lightning spread across the sky, he actually laughed! Into this black, raging storm, he laughed! As if all this were entertainment! As if it were a joyous game! I can assure you, I laughed not. None of us laughed. Why this infuriating smugness? Surely he is aware of the danger? Did he not see that the boat was filled almost to the gunnels with water? Was he mocking us, naively ignorant, oblivious to his own peril? Questions, the absurdities of which were not seen for the madness of our fear. Clouds had obliterated the stars and moon; dark, foreboding and terrible, stabbed with fire, a fitting place for death, not mocking laughter!?

αΘω

In our panic, the other boats were forgotten. Abishag barked, and as was her habit it seemed, only once. The dog! I had forgotten the animal had been sleeping under the bench where Jesus himself slept. Unlike the rest of us, the creature did not seem excited. She looked at Jesus and sniffed at the wind. The Master released a hand from the rigging, the deck wallowing madly, chaotically, and stroked the animal's head.

Turning his face from the wind, he spoke to all of us, "Where is your faith? Why are you all so frightened?" We saw the water in our boat, felt the biting wind and soaked from the waves, wondered again if Jesus had taken leave of his mind.

And then, to our amazement, he spoke to the elements, sentient beings, as if they themselves had a mind of their own. "Peace!" he cried to the winds. Suddenly, instantly, there was no wind. No wind at all. Not so much as an errant eddy. "Be still!" The cannonading, shrieking wind evaporated as smoke from a tallow. He spoke again to the waves. This took a few seconds longer but, in that time, the waves subsided unnaturally, and the surface of the water, undulating rhythmically, became as smooth as glass. For the first time we could see the other boats. Some were swamped completely with men in the water. Abishag barked again, panting contentedly.

Jesus spoke to Peter, spoke to all of us again and for the third time asked of us, "Where is your faith?" *I thought you knew.* The disappointment in his eyes, palpable.

Our minds could not begin to conceive the reality of what had just happened. Had I not seen it with my own eyes, had I not been there to experience it myself, I could never have believed it. Things like this did not occur. It is beyond the capacity of the mind to imagine. Questions flooded my mind. The others questioned as well. "What manner of man is this? Who is this?" Jesus merely returned to his bench, the coil of rope and the sodden cushion. He laid down his head and stared at the sky until his eyelids became heavy once again. Abishag laid her chin in the crook of his arm and blinked sleepily. The boat rose and fell softly at the last vestiges of shifting water. We were becalmed.

We looked at the other boats devastated by the storm and began rescue and repair operations. Jesus did not help. He had done his part. Not a single soul was lost.

I—all of us—were stunned. Later as I thought upon it, and I thought upon it often, I considered: It is impossible to understand or appreciate his teaching or the things that he did if we do not understand and appreciate—who he was. Who he is.

We will not forget this day. I have lived a long and fretful life. I have experienced many extreme moments, visited the valley of the shadows of death more than once, but none so terrible, or so wondrous, as that day on the sea with Jesus and the others.

In the days and years of my lifetime, I have learned that God does not always step in and rescue us from tragedy. Sometimes tragedy overtakes us, accidents happen; a child is crushed under the wheel of a chariot, disease takes a loved one, leprosy is everywhere. Sometimes it seems God has absented himself. But that is an illusion. He is always there with us. He may seem asleep and uncaring, but whether on this side of the valley of pain and death, or on the other, he is very much present, and to all he speaks, "Peace. Be Still." And we are comforted. We are becalmed.

XVIII

Gergasa

There was enough breeze left to gently push us southerly. Traveling from Capharnaum on the north shore, the thirteen-mile length of the lake, to the small town of Gergasa on the south shore, we, at length, brushed our prows into a muddy bottom. The moon had risen high, casting pale light and laying her halo around the shadows. To the right of us steep bluffs could be seen. In the shadows of the bluffs squirmed no less than two thousand pigs which could not be seen from our vantage point, but I was to learn of them. If one is within several miles of 2,000 pigs, one cannot help but be aware of them. In the end, their aromatic presence would add to the already unforgettable memories of this day. But I overreach myself.

αΘω

He lay naked on the cold, dank limestone floor of the cave, bones of the town's dead scattered about; the smell of death pungent and foul. His companion, also naked, lay on the other side of the cave. Their flesh trembled, muscles cramped, festering sores from overlong exposure to uneven, brittle rock, cold pain buried deep in their sinews and marrow. They shifted, turning their bodies as often as they could, trying to find a position for a moment's comfort.

Useless.

Pain intensified with each movement. To be sure, the trembling found its source in the cold, but there was something else to be added to their frigid existence: cold fear. They were helpless before it, or more accurately, before *them*. They had long since given up the fight. They had long since surrendered to the hideous, foul things in their bodies that also had the power to capture and control their minds at will.

Their bodies, bruised with blue welts and running open sores; the pounding of incalculable pain, the cutting of themselves and each other with shards of glass and broken clay pots, engendered relentless screaming.

It lasted several seconds, starting as a low growl and escalating into a howl and then high-pitched shrieks.

αΘω

It didn't fully wake him, but it did disturb him from his own foggy nightmare of existence. He felt the pain in his stomach and then his chest; he opened his eyes to see his companion arched on the floor. Only the back of his head and his heels touched the pavement of cold rock. The rest of his body arched upward like a bow about to loose an arrow. His bloated stomach protruded in the air. His mouth opened wide revealing yellowed, brown teeth, most of which were missing. Open lips issued forth an evil howl and then guttural words, "He comes! He comes! He comes!" Lips remained stretched and stationary, tongue stilled in the cavity that was his mouth, yet words came forth inexplicably, visceral, guttural, from his bowels.

"NO! No, it cannot be! It is not the appointed time." The voice had leapt from his companion to his own mouth. He felt his body stiffen, muscles turning to concrete, lips and jaws immobile. He could not move them yet this horrible sound, these frightened words issued from them. Spittle drooled from his mouth; his bladder and bowels released themselves, filling the cave with noxious odor. He picked up his excrement and flung it at his companion. "Stop it!" he cried, "It is them . ." His voice arrested in mid-sentence, "Hiagggheeeee!" None of this made sense. Clarity of thought ceased to exist.

He stood, every muscle in his body rigid and quivering at the same time. He leaped and fell forward. As his head neared the ground, he tucked it just enough so that his shoulders took the force of striking the ground in a rolling somersault. In a second, his companion was on top of him, pummeling him about the body and face. Blood spurted from his nose and lip. He caught his tormentor's head and bit hard. The man's ear came off in his mouth. Screaming, his companion grabbed his wounded head. This gave the other the opportunity to place his hands on his companion's chest and shove. The man's body literally flew through the air slamming into the ceiling of the cave and falling to the floor, dazed and confused, but conscious. His voice continued to scream expletive after expletive. He stood and stumbled out of the cave. When he saw the moon, he wailed.

αΘω

I heard his scream come from the shadows of the bluff. Jesus lifted his head and looked in the direction of this terrible, mournful sound. The expression on his face became fierce. "Come!" he commanded and strode away in the direction of the sound. We all followed, even the ones who were in the other boats. There were more than seventy of us. He walked directly toward the sound. The dog whined and followed.

"Master, wait," said one of the men from the other boats. "I know what that sound is."

"So do I."

"Master!" the man insisted, "there are two men who live in the tombs up there. They are monsters. Filthy monsters. They cannot be bound…much too strong. They will kill…"

"Stay if you are afraid," responded Jesus. "They are captured in horrible, unholy pain. I intend to release them."

I don't know what made us follow. The danger, clear and evident; curiosity for spectacle, perhaps. I suppose it could have been the storm, or what he did to the storm. We were all apprehensive. All had heard of these two desperate demoniacs. None ventured too close to them. They were insane, obviously. They were more than insane. They were maniacal, homicidal, fierce and dangerous.

αΘω

It was only a short walk to the south of Gergasa, where the steep bluff descended abruptly to a narrow ledge of beach which quickly dropped into deep water. The whole surrounding country was burrowed with caverns and rock chambers for the dead.

After a few minutes of walking in the direction of the howling, we saw two men stumble out of the shadows to meet us. They looked like beasts. Their naked bodies were caked with filth, their beards matted, their skin broken and scarred from wounds that had healed badly. The stench exceeded that of the pigs. In these unclean places for the dead, these unclean incorrigibles had found congenial homes. There was a Jewish superstition that demons dwelt in deserted, lonely places and would come out at night to haunt. These two were no superstition.

In the wilderness, the person of evil had appeared suave, sophisticated, cultured, even academic. Here, foul and repulsive. Night and day among the tombs and in the hills these men uttered cries and cut themselves with shards. When at last they saw Jesus, it appeared as though they would run away. Jesus stopped, his jaw set, his countenance determined. Suddenly, they stopped retreating, hesitated for a moment, and then, incredibly, aggressively, came toward him! When almost ready to fall on Jesus, suddenly they, themselves fell at his feet in total submission. It was a despicable thing to watch. Two grown men, naked, dirty, one of them his mouth bloody, the other with half an ear, the stench of human waste. A foul, foul, thing. A foul thing!

One of them opened his mouth. It formed a misshapen hole in his head. His chest and stomach muscles contracted and heaved as if he were about to vomit. Instead, he screamed loud and long. Again, the lips and tongue did not move except to undulate uncontrollably, yet clear, growling words issued forth, "Jesus! Son of the Most High God! What do you want with me?" The sound reverberated from wall to wall, from rock to rock. He paused, bony ribs and chest heaving, "Why have you come to torment me before the time? Swear to God that you won't torture me! Aaagggh! Aaagggh! Aaagggh!" Each scream louder and more reprehensible than the one preceding it. "No torture! No agony! No unbearable pain! Have mercy!" He collapsed in heaving sobs.

XIX

Legion

How came either of them to know of Jesus? They had never laid eyes on him before this moment. And why did they address him as 'Son of the Most High God?' How could they know? And what is this time of which they speak? And how does this pathetic man speak from his throat without moving his lips?

"You will leave these men." Jesus spoke quietly in great contrast to the screaming going on before him. The man's eyes opened wide, staring at Jesus in morbid fear. Jesus spoke again; this time I could hear a note of compassion in his voice. "What is your name?" he asked. The question was directed at the man, not the howling thing within him.

The man did not, could not answer. His eyes rolled into his head so that only their whites showed. He was locked in this terrible creature's grip, "My name is..." It wouldn't come.

He tried again, "My name is...'Legion!'"

"Legion?" Jesus appeared almost amused. How could he be so calm, so self-assured in the presence of something so evil? I could not understand it. "That seems ambitious," he said. "Are you over six thousand strong?"

"We are many!" the thing replied.

"Yes," said Jesus as though he were bored with this whole scene. "Legion. Well, Legion, what shall I do with you? As you have said, your time has not come, but be certified; it surely will come. Now, where do you wish to go? Back to your abyss?"

"NO!" they screamed. "No! Please!" They were begging. These horrible things in these men were begging. The overwhelming authority of Jesus against their evil power; Oh, I cannot speak it! It is beyond my imagination!

"Send us instead into the pigs."

The pigs, now in plain view, were feeding on the nearby hillside. Jesus considered the sorry spectacle for a moment and then uttered, "Leave these men." And then louder, commanding, "Leave these men at once!"

The two men collapsed on the ground as if they were rags. The pigs, however, began to squeal and mill about. Their agitation became severe, and they began to pile onto one another. Their tenders panicked. Suddenly the herd surged down toward the bluff and the sea below. The water churned with onrushing bodies of helpless animals falling over the precipice. A terrible spectacle. The force and momentum of the stampeding herd pushed those in front of them into the water by the hundreds. They were drowning.

I am a Jew. I do not like swine but I couldn't help but feel a pang of remorse at this waste of life. Their carcasses floated on the surface, owing no doubt to the immense fat they carried. Those tending the pigs ran off. The report they would give found its way to the authorities.

αΘω

When things quieted, Jesus bent over the fallen men. They were unconscious. He touched the side of the head of the man whose ear had been bitten away, ripped from its mooring. When he took his hand away, a new ear had formed. "Help me, John," who stood nearby. John, still wary, hesitated. Jesus gave him a look. Instantly, he moved and assisted Jesus to lift one of the men by the armpits and lean him against the wall of the rock. "Someone get water. Tunics. Clean them and dress them." We passed the remainder of the night around a campfire, tending to these two broken souls.

The effect of the swine herder's news was no surprise. Almost everyone in Gergasa came out to see what had happened. Days later, floating bodies of pigs were found around the shores of Galilee. Fishermen discovered them several miles out into the water. The Sea of Galilee had been polluted with the cadavers of dead swine. Cleaning parties were formed, huge pits dug to bury the carcasses. But in Gergasa, they saw the men who had been possessed sitting there leaning against the rock, dressed, clean and in their right minds. This frightened them as much as seeing them demonized. This galvanized them even more than the spectacle of the pigs. They knew these men. They had heard their howls in the distant night. Incredibly, they began to plead with Jesus to leave their region. It was, I suppose, too much for them. I wondered why no one sought to blame Jesus for the destruction of held property. Then I heard a rumor that Jews owned the pigs, illegally. Jews! I couldn't believe what lengths to which some men would go for profit.

Jesus turned to leave. As he stepped into the boat, the two men came to him and begged. "Lord," they said. How easy this word came to them now whereas before they could utter only unintelligible grunts and moans. "Lord, take us with you. We owe you our very lives."

Jesus said to them, "You will serve me better here in Gergasa. Go home to your families, and tell them how much the Lord God has done for you and how he has had mercy on you." Oddly, they did not argue and appeared to sense no feelings of rejection. They were comforted with the thought that they would actually be messengers of the mercy of God. Perhaps they, who had been such a terror to their fellow human beings, could now bring them blessing and benefit instead.

Word had it that they became quite the evangelists. They preached throughout the Ten Cities (the Decapolis) of all that Jesus had done for them. People were amazed. How many believed because of the energy these two men expended? Only God knows. Even today, decades later, I hear of their preaching and I wonder at the memory.

Now that Jesus' physical presence is no longer among us there is not so much demonic activity. From the baptism of Jesus to the day he was taken from us, demon possession was something to be dealt with. Since the Holy Spirit has come, it seems held in check. I do not understand the purpose the evil one has in making men and women foam at the mouth and cut themselves. It is all so disgusting and unappealing. I only know the power the name of Jesus has over them. It is absolute. It is preemptive. It is final. It is fatal.

The Fourth Scroll

To Serve as Signs

And God said, "Let there be lights in the vault of the sky to separate the day from the night, and let them serve as signs to mark seasons and days and years, and let them be lights in the vault of the sky to give light on the earth." And it was so. God made two great lights—the greater light to govern the day and the lesser light to govern the night. He also made the stars. God set them in the vault of the sky to give light on the earth, to govern the day and the night, and to separate light from darkness. And God saw that it was good. And there was evening, and there was morning—the fourth day.

—Genesis 1:14-19 NIV

I

The House of Matthew

The winds were listless. It took a lot longer returning to Capharnaum than it did sailing to Gergasa. The previous day and night had been more than eventful, and we were all tired. Most of us slept while others took turns at the tiller. Jesus slept, too. The sea was smooth as we approached the city and, not surprisingly, we could see people standing along the shoreline, many of them waving. Word of the healing of the demoniacs apparently had traveled fast. Our little flotilla of boats was anticipated. We docked amongst cheers and applause. The welcome was warm and...well, welcome. The feeling of it was most pleasant. In a short while as the crowd dispersed, I noticed Rabbi Asher and two of his cohorts. What was Asher doing again in Capharnaum?

Despite the celebrations, the day passed uneventfully. We all rested as much as we could. The following evening, Matthew decided to hold a feast with Jesus as his guest. It was at times like this that we were all reminded of Matthew's background. His home gave it away. Well appointed in resplendent furnishings, most of us felt more than a little out of place. He had invited a large number of his friends, tax collectors and other persons of nefarious reputation, most of them government types and bureaucrats. Some of them brought their mistresses dressed in expensive silks revealing shapely contours. The talk, the laughter, the wine all flowed freely. It was a fun party and a sumptuous meal. All were reclining at a large banquet table with Jesus. The Master seemed to be enjoying himself. He was in an animated conversation with one of the guests when Asher arrived and made a grandiose entrance into the room.

The eminent Rabbi had, indeed, been invited by Matthew, but God knows, he was not really expected to attend. A Jewish Rabbi at a social event in the home of a tax-collector? Not now, not here. So when he came through the door with his friends in ceremonial attire, the noise in the room subsided. Both of Asher's friends were scribes. These scribes were not mere copyists of ancient texts as some thought. These men were experts in Torah. They were lawyers, a political sect within the larger framework of the Pharisees. It was clear from the expression on all of their faces that they found the festivities repugnant and worldly.

Taking advantage of the interruption their presence had caused, Asher asked Jesus pointedly, "Why do you eat and drink like a sorry bibber of wine and a drunkard?" He spoke accusingly, as if Jesus himself were actually caught in wrongdoing. "And why are you, a so-called spiritual leader, here in this place cavorting with tax collectors and disreputable people?" Such a pretentious, pontifical question did not offend Matthew's guests. They considered Asher and his crew something of a joke and anticipated no less from him. To them he was a pompous ass. A nothing.

Neither did the question offend Jesus who had a ready response for Asher and his two scribal friends. "It is not the healthy and robust who need a physician, Asher, but the sick. To your mind, no doubt, my friends here might fall into that last group. Fear not, my pious friend, I have not come to call you self-righteous prigs, but those who seek the need for change. So now, you can leave. You are not welcome here. And while you go and think upon this moment, think upon this also: 'Mercy is what I desire and not sacrifice.' Someday the meaning of that may begin to dawn in your thick, prejudiced mind."

Asher left, glaring, indignant and humiliated, he muttered, "What he desires? What does one care for what he desires? Who does he think he is, King David?"

"God, Rabbi," spoke one of the scribes. "He thinks he is God. He quotes Hosea, not the psalmist."

"Hosea?" exclaimed the Rabbi, knowing better than to challenge the scribe. "How so?"

"He applies Hosea's prophecy against Ephraim and Judah to you and, clearly, to us as well."

"I must examine the passage myself." This was Asher's way of saying that he was ignorant of the prophecy, but it did not fool the scribe.

"You need not look it up, Rabbi. I will quote it for you." Without waiting for Asher to reply, he continued...

> *"O Ephraim, what shall I do unto you? O Judah, what shall I do unto you? Your goodness is as a morning cloud, like the early dew it goes away. Therefore, have I hewed them by the prophets. I have slain them by the words of my mouth. For I desired mercy, and not sacrifice, and the knowledge of God more than burnt offerings. But they, like all men have*

> *transgressed the covenant. They dealt treacherously against me. Gilead is the city of them that work iniquity and is tracked in footprints of blood."*

"Well, I have a surprise for this young, self-absorbed god. I am not Ephraim or Judah, nor have I been hewed and slain. And we shall see whose footprints they are!" Asher fumed bitterly.

αΘω

John the Baptist was a Nazirite. He had been one since birth. It was not only a way of life for him, but also a philosophy. It was all he knew. Therefore, in a tangible sense, John had far more in common with Asher and the scribes than he did Jesus. Yet the enormous difference between John and Asher is that John recognized Jesus for who he was, while Asher gagged at this. John believed, and did so thoroughly. Asher and his ilk held Jesus in contempt. John saw himself as closing the old; he saw Jesus as revealing the new.

Not far away, at the same time of Matthew's supper, the followers of John's teaching and preaching and the followers of the Pharisees were deeply engaged in a ceremonial fast. Some of John's people had migrated from his fasting event to Matthew's home, for all of the hilarity going on there. I thought that somewhat odd. Why would someone who is fasting come to a feast? No doubt they were curious about Jesus. Still, it seemed more than a bit incongruous to me.

One of them, David ben Adoniram by name, approached Jesus as he was taking a sip of wine. I recognized him because I had seen him often hanging about in the crowds that followed Jesus. It appeared that he wanted to walk among us, but for reasons known only to him, could not. I know that he, like his mentor, John, believed deeply in Jesus but simply could not extricate himself from John's austere, yet compelling, force of personality. He believed in its "rightness," I suppose. This is reflected in his question to Jesus. An honest one, I thought.

"Why do we and the Pharisees fast often and make petitions, but you and your disciples do not fast? You eat sumptuously and you drink well."

Jesus turned to face his questioner and immediately smiled, "David, son of Adoniram! How good to see you again!"

"Thank you, teacher. I meant no disrespect."

"I know you didn't," said Jesus. "Thank you for asking an honest question. I will try to give you an honest answer."

"Try, teacher? I do not believe you capable of anything other than honesty." This wasn't fawning or flattery. David was such a literalist that it never occurred to him that Jesus was not speaking explicitly. He could not recognize the subtleties of idiom. Jesus smiled again, accepting the plain and somewhat clumsy compliment.

We must realize that David ben Adoniram was at a disadvantage here. He no doubt felt considerable discomfort, not only in the strangeness of his surroundings, but in his empty stomach as well. After all, he had been fasting for several days! Matthew's banquet had been an extravagant affair. There was much hearty laughter, something to which David in his association with the Nazirite was unaccustomed. Jesus, smiling, answered sensitively, "Perhaps you do not understand how profoundly binding tradition and liturgy can be, David. I came to release you from all that, but I do understand how hard it is for you to hear this. You believe too completely that these things have value." Then Jesus shifted his position so that he could face his questioner more directly. "Listen, David, can you make young men at a wedding party fast? Have you ever seen them mourn at a marriage ceremony?" Some sniggering at this, as though some mourning might be appropriate. And then a quiet change affected his expression, as if a fleeting, painful thought crossed his mind. He continued, "There will be time enough for fasting, David. The time will come when the bridegroom will be taken from his bride. They will fast and mourn and make petitions, as you say, then."

By this time most of the noise of the party had subsided. We listened as he tried to illustrate. "You do not tear a piece of material from a new coat and sew it on an old one. If you do that, you will have ruined the new coat. When washed, the patch from the new coat will shrink and pull away from the old and tear it as well. Both are ruined."

Jesus had a remarkable way of coming up with these simple metaphors which in context reveal a compelling truth. He wasn't finished. "Likewise, no one pours new wine into old wineskins." For a moment, I wondered why Jesus spoke of wine to a man who would not touch it. It occurred to me that perhaps David was not yet a full Nazirite, but as I mentioned earlier, he did seem drawn to us. Jesus continued, "When new wine begins to ferment and expand, it will burst the old skins, and both will be ruined. That is not how it is done. New wine is poured into new wineskins so that both may be preserved." And then, as if gently teasing him, "And no one after drinking old wine wants the new, for he says, 'The old is better.'"

David ben Adoniram smiled at that. It won't be long, I thought; this man is near his release.

αΘω

But let us not forget the original question, "Why do you enjoy yourselves and we deny ourselves?" The point Jesus made was that new and old do not ordinarily provide a stable or efficient mix. Put them together and both are destroyed. Let them be themselves and both retain integrity. Jesus was not saying that fasting was better or worse than not fasting, just that one should not encroach upon the other. In the first story, Jesus was not saying that the coming of the new is intended to repair the old. The new is to *replace* the old and accomplish the purpose which the old could not. The new is to connect to that which has gone before, acknowledge it, and move on. His final comment is true of wine. It is also true of him. The old has shown us the holiness of God and the unholiness of humankind. We, who are clay images of the invisible God, cannot and do not successfully approach that holiness. Our failure to do so is old wine. Our brother Paul later put it succinctly, "The Law was a schoolmaster of sorts, to teach us how deeply we are alienated from God and to bring us to our only hope, Jesus Christ." Jesus, his life, his teachings, his character and example is, indeed, New Wine. It easily follows that we who believe are new wineskins. Together, with Jesus within us, we shall become better than the old.

II

If I May Touch

Now, I must speak of a most cherished memory in my time with Jesus of Nazareth. Like zephyrs in the night, one cannot predict the movement of God's power, nor the touch of his grace, nor the brush of his love.

Two little girls knew one another by their mutual attendance at synagogue. And it was within the perimeters of the synagogue that the friendship was confined. Their fathers were well-known to the community, one respected, even celebrated, the other pitied. One dressed in the finery of affluence, the other dressed in poverty. One whose father was obeyed, the other whose father obeyed the best he could, yet begged in the streets.

Damaris and Prisca had known each other for almost two years and were, each of them, twelve years old. Damaris was a lively child, always smiling. Her mother had died in childbirth and she had been raised by her father and uncle. She was always seeking ways to improve her lot and that of these two men, both of whom were blind as a result of Roman brutality. They were poor Jews and failed to pay the taxes Rome had determined was its due. They paid their taxes, therefore, with their sight. When the tax collector reported them to the office of tribute, a Roman cohort arrived at their door a few hours later and cut out their eyes.

Damaris was witness to this. She screamed and cried as would be expected, but she determined that their lives would not end because of this. But life as they knew it did end. Losing their modest income from sandal-making, they were forced to beg to survive. Their home degenerated from a modest hovel to a shack, disheveled and dirty. Damaris did the best she could to care for the two men, but she was, after all, only twelve years old. She led them about the streets of Capharnaum, begging; depending on the charity of others. Actually, her presence elicited greater sympathy than otherwise might be expected, but the income from begging was as nothing compared to having sight and having a home.

Prisca was anything but lively. She tried to be, but her sickness prevented her from the high-energy playfulness common to most twelve-year-old girls.

Moreover, since her birth, her mother had left home as well, owing to what seemed to be incurable disease. Although her father, Jairus, was ruler of the synagogue, he could not give her health, and the child continued to get worse, especially in recent months.

When they were younger, both girls sat in synagogue with Prisca's mother in the women's section in the balcony above the men. During the service, which regularly lasted for hours, the girls would draw on tablets and pass them back and forth to each other. Or they would feign the need of the call of nature and sit outside the synagogue on the steps while services were conducted inside. These things were tolerated in children both by parents and, with disapproval, by the elders. Prisca sometimes embarrassed her father by her behavior in the synagogue, but he could not bring himself to discipline her owing to her illness. His heart was broken that he could do little or nothing for his little girl and her mother...her mother—well that was another story.

αΘω

We spent the night in the accommodations of Matthew's spacious home. The next morning, as Jesus loved to do, we took a walk along the edges of the lake. The previous evening's socializing had taken its toll and the crisp, morning air felt and tasted good. As usual, it wasn't long before people started gathering around us. Of course, they had come to see Jesus, but we were beginning to feel that we somehow, shared in his celebrity. We liked it, but at the same time, we resisted it. We sorely longed for time with Jesus uninterrupted by the needs of others.

A man began to push his way through the crowd toward us. It was Jairus. I recognized him because of his position with the synagogue. A man highly respected in Carpharnaum; as ruler of the synagogue, elders and even the priest answered to him. His face was ashen with grief. He came and fell at Jesus' feet. "My little girl is dying, Lord." He was on all fours, his head hanging. I was struck by the paradox of such a man as Jairus so humbling himself. "Please," he begged, "come and put your hands on her. Heal her and she will live." The response was instant.

"Take me to her," he said simply.

The crowd followed, whispering in anticipation.

αΘω

The woman watched as the crowd approached. They pressed around Jesus. It was a wonder that he could breathe, let alone move through the streets. She saw Jairus approach and shoulder his way through the crowd. She could understand. As ruler of the synagogue, he simply could not be to her what she needed. She was unclean. The flow of her blood had not stopped after the birth of Prisca. For twelve years it continued. The doctors had given her mixture after mixture of herbs and drugs, performing all manner of treatments, but to no avail. She was unclean. She could not even live under the same roof as her husband. Thankfully, he had provided for her as best he could, but the family had suffered greatly. There was just no way. No way. She worried about Prisca. She could not see her as often as she wanted; in fact, it had been almost a year. She assiduously avoided contact with her daughter for the embarrassment it might cause the child. She would often hide if she saw her coming.

Jesus continued to approach. She knew of Jesus. Everyone in Capharnaum did. She knew he could heal, but she despaired that he would ever notice her. *Just let me near enough to touch him*, she thought. Please, dear God, let me just touch his robe as he passes, and I shall be whole. Weak and pale, the blood continued to leak from her body. Twelve years of this humiliation. It was an ugly business. The humiliating stigma of being "unclean" added to her terrible sense of shame. It had weakened her so severely that she did not expect to live much longer. She had lost count of the physicians she had seen. So frustrating. No one, it seemed, could relieve her suffering. At this point, Jesus was her hope—a slim hope, but her only hope.

It was difficult in the press of the people to get close to where he would pass. Suppose he turned aside? Suppose he would not pass close enough? Doubts assaulted her. *No! He is coming. If I can but reach past this person's legs...There!* She felt the soft folds of a garment caress her fingers. She was uncertain that it was Jesus she touched. It could have been anyone. At that instant, she also felt something take place deep within her. Her entire body lost its pale chill and warmed naturally. *Am I . . . ? Am I . . . ? Am I healed?* The realization crept upon her until her sense of wellness was so complete that she could not speak. She wanted to shout but words would not come, only feelings, only spontaneous bursts of tears, relief and gratitude.

The crowd surged on, but suddenly, Jesus stopped. He was silent for a moment looking about him with a peaceful, yet penetrating, curiosity. We all wondered what had caused him to halt so abruptly. Had he stubbed his toe on a rock? He did not seem to be in pain. Was he sick? Did he notice something the rest of us did not see? Did someone shout something that arrested his attention?

"Who touched me?"

Peter, walking next to him laughed. "Master, you see these people crowding against you and you ask, 'Who touched me?'"

"No, wait. Someone touched my clothes. I felt strength drain from me." His eyes darted about in the crowd, searching.

Then he saw her.

And herein are two anomalies. How is it that Jesus could know slender, feminine fingers had merely brushed the folds of his robe in a pressing crowd, and how is it that he could detect that healing energy had been released from him, except that he was exceptional? Except that he had come from God? And over against that, how is it that if he came from God, which I do not doubt, he could possibly not know who had done it?

She was on her knees facing away from us. At first glance, one might think that she had dropped something and was down on her knees looking for what she had dropped. Then slowly, her tear-filled eyes turned toward him, beaming, yet she trembled, a strange mixture of fear and pleasure. He took a few steps and stood before her. Yet it appeared as if she knelt before him. "I am responsible," said she. "I touched you. I said to myself that if I touch the hem of your robe, I will be whole. And I was…I mean…I am." Tears of joy and relief returned, now mixed with anxiety and fear for having been discovered.

Jesus reached his hand and caressed her face. "Dear sister," he said tenderly, "do not be frightened. Your faith, your courage has healed you. Go in peace. You are freed from your suffering."

III

Prisca and Damaris

As Jesus gently continued to converse with the woman, several men arrived. They went directly to Jairus. "Your daughter is dead," they said bluntly. "There is no need to further trouble the teacher." The utter lack of sensitive propriety appalled Jesus. Jairus caught his breath. Stunned and confused, he turned to leave. He looked at his wife, now a stranger. *He healed her with the merest unconscious touch. Why couldn't he . . ?*

The woman looked on, not quite grasping what was happening. And then, in an involuntary action, she cried, "Jairus! God be praised! Do not despair. Only believe. As he loved me, so also he loves you! As he loves you, so also he loves our daughter!" Still on her knees, her hand flew to her mouth as if she were surprised at her own words. She glanced at Jesus, who laid his hand on her head and smiled.

"Jairus," Jesus said, "Ignore these men. Believe your wife's witness. Your daughter will be healed."

The men glowered at Jesus. "You are a cruel prophet," they declared. "You give this man false hope. His daughter is dead. There is nothing anyone can do about that. The sooner our synagogue ruler accepts that, the sooner he can go on with his life and the better our place of worship will be run."

The grieving father looked at Jesus with tentative eyes. "Come," said Jesus. "Let us go to her." We all started to follow. The crowd surged with us.

On arrival at the house of Jairus, Jesus halted yet again, "Wait!" he commanded, "I want no one with me except Jairus." And then pointing to Peter, James and John, he said, "You three come as well." Then he paused, observing the mother and spoke quietly to her, "You come, too." With prescient anticipation and hope, she followed the others into the house.

Inside, there was a commotion. Flute players and professional mourners had already been summoned. They beat their breasts and wailed loudly. Jesus, annoyed by this shallow display of grief, said to them, "Stop all this ridiculous commotion and wailing! Why are you carrying on like this? Off with you! This child is not dead. She merely sleeps." The incredulous snickering that followed was filled with contempt and scorn. They knew full well the child was dead. They did not, however, attempt to resist Jesus. His authority and command could not be challenged. They all retreated from inside the house and stood impatiently outside waiting for reality to prove this trickster wrong. No mere magician could bring a dead child back to life.

He took the girl's parents and those he brought with him and entered the child's room. She had lived but twelve summers. Now she lay pale and lifeless on her bed, her lovely life abbreviated, truncated. She would never be a bride; she would never know the joy of holding her infant child to her breast. The awful sense of irreversible finality was enough to break the coldest heart, to embitter the most joyful spirit. But Jesus took her by the hand, stroked her hair and said quietly, "Sweet little Prisca, wake up. You have many summers yet to fill, many winters yet to brighten." Nothing. Long moments passed. Then, gently her chest began to rise and fall. Her eyes blinked open, clear and crystal. Abruptly, she sat up and swung her legs over the side of the bed. After a moment of orienting her self, she stood. Seeing her father, she ran to his outstretched arms. The raw emotional power of watching father and child holding desperately to one another brought ready tears to everyone's eyes. Even Jesus. The mother, whom Jesus had earlier healed, came and stroked the child's hair and knelt beside their embrace. When the girl saw the woman, she seemed momentarily distant, and then her eyes widened in recognition. "Mama?" she inquired softly. And then "Mama!" she almost screamed; then threw her arms around her mother. They held each other in loving reunion, Jairus looking on. Then he, too, embraced them both. They were together, once again.

The tension broke and Jesus told them to give her something to eat.

Her cheeks wet with glistening tears she whispered to her husband, It is him, Jairus. It is Messiah. I know it. He has come, and we have been touched by the same hand that formed the stars, the hand of love that gives, that brings healing and life...

"There is no need to tell anyone of this," said Jesus to the family. "Keep it and cherish it just for yourselves." But as soon as Jesus left the home, outsiders surged in.

In a moment someone came to the door and loudly announced, "She's alive and well! And the mother has returned, healed and clean!" News of what had taken place spread everywhere.

αΘω

We left the house of Jairus that day warmed with the pleasure and glow of what had happened. Even though Peter, James and John were the only ones among us who were actually present when it occurred, Jesus had done something wondrous and we all felt that we had been a part of it. As we walked, we came upon two men holding on to each other and staring into space. A diminutive girl-child was attempting to guide them toward us. "There he is!" she exclaimed with lights in her voice. "Come!" tugging on them to follow her. She would brook no argument. "Call him, daddy. He can hear you."

Suddenly the older of the two cried out, "Jesus, Son of David! Have mercy on us!" They were thin and gaunt. It was plain that these men, and the girl as well, did not eat very often. They were draped in torn blankets, beards grey and matted. They were a pathetic sight and one not too uncommon in the streets of Capharnaum. The presence of the child, however, arrested our attention. We wondered who she was and what bearing she had with these men. "Shout, Abiud, shout!" said the girl's father. "We must make him stop!"

"Jesus! Lord!" shouted the younger of the two, "Have mercy on us!"

We had arrived at the courtyard of Peter's home. But on hearing these cries, Jesus stopped yet again. He looked weary. "Bring them inside," he said and entered the door. When the two men were brought to him, he asked them, "Do you believe that I am able to give you back your sight? Do you actually believe I can give you new eyes?"

The girl nodded her head affirmatively, tears in her eyes. The men replied without hesitation, "Yes, Lord, we do believe that." The odor of their unwashed bodies filled the room.

"What is your name, child?"

"Damaris, sir." She looked at Jesus and smiled sweetly. "I know who you are. You have come from God our Father."

"How is it you know about this?" he smiled. "And how is it you lead about these two men?"

"This is my daddy, sir, and this is my uncle. Their eyes were cut out by Roman soldiers." She did not answer his first question.

Jesus offered an explanation. "Sometimes a child knows things adults do not," said he.

Jesus placed a hand on each of them, covering their eyes. "According to your faith then, be it done to you." He removed his hands to reveal beautiful eyes with clear pupils, their sight restored completely. The girl's hands went to her mouth in awe. "Daddy!" she exclaimed, "You can see!" "Abiud!" she pronounced the name with a musical lilt, "You can see!" Father and brother fell to their knees in gratitude. The child said gleefully, "I must tell Prisca! The old priest was right!"

αΘω

"First, come with me." It was Matthew. He had in times past seen these men. Indeed, it was Matthew who had reported them to the Romans for not paying tribute. Often, out of guilt, he had given them alms to relieve their circumstances. But it was not nearly enough. Leading the men and the girl-child to his home, he charged his servants, "Bathe these men, give them new robes; place rings on their fingers, and necklaces about their necks. They are my honored guests; treat them with dignity and respect." When they were finished, Matthew came into the room. "Better," he observed. "Come, it is time to eat." Matthew, finished with his meal, pushed his plate aside and drank the last dregs of his wine. "Gentlemen," he began, "I wish to make a proposal which I would be grateful if you were to accept. I have a modest but comfortable cottage in the back of my home which no one is using. The servants have kept it clean and livable, but it has remained empty for years. I would be honored if you would live there and help maintain my home. With all my travels these days, it is hard to keep up with a large house. And," he said firmly but with a smile, "if tax people ever bother you again, I want to learn of it immediately." Such was the turn of events in the lives of those whom Jesus touched. I speak here of Matthew, even more than the men he healed.

Damaris had, in the meantime, been taken aside by the ladies of the household, fed and pampered for the first time in her short life. She emerged a few hours later wearing a delicate blue gown, her hair braided and shining. Now that her father could see, he discovered that she was no longer a young girl but was becoming a lovely young woman. Matthew continued, "I would like Damaris to live in my home and learn from the other women. She needs women in her life at this age. And she will be free to help care for you both."

Matthew turned to the girl with a twinkle in his eye, "Damaris, why don't you visit your friend Prisca, now?" The child bounced up and down and made to run for the door, then stopped. After momentary hesitation, she returned to Matthew and kissed him on the cheek.

"May God bless you, sir, for what you have done." Matthew hugged her gently and then released her. She put her shoulders back, held her head high, and walked with regal grace toward the door.

αΘω

As the two men and the girl-child lived in Matthew's home, they also went about and told everyone and anyone who would listen what Jesus had done for them. All of Galilee heard about it.

As a consequence, others were brought to him as well. One of these was a man possessed of a demonic spirit. He couldn't speak. His eyes bulged, and he shook uncontrollably. Jesus spoke so quietly none of us could hear what he said, but the man's shaking ceased. He opened his mouth and said clearly and distinctly, "Thank you, Lord."

Those in the house of Peter standing about while Jesus did all of this began to murmur, "Nothing like this has ever been seen in all the history of Israel."

But there were a few Pharisees with their attendant scribes, insufferable legalists, who opined among themselves, "This man is controlled by the prince of demons. That is how he has the power to do tricks like this."

These religious functionaries were interrupted by the child standing near them. "My daddy sees," she said plainly and boldly. "My uncle sees," she declared. "How is it that you cannot?"

The men were not unaffected by the big, insistent eyes of the child. "What did you say, my dear?" not unkindly.

"Demons do evil things," she said. "If he was a demon, as you say, how is it that he does good things? How does a demon heal?"

They looked at each other, but said nothing. The eldest of them glanced at the child and gave her a perfunctory, humoring smile. Then they turned and left.

αΘω

It is a marvelously satisfying thing to be so close to God's power, to see it so physically, so concretely at work. Damaris and Prisca became notable women in the early days of the believing community. Damaris served the church in Athens and Prisca in Ephesus. Our brother Paul came to know them well. I wish you could have been there, dear reader. I wish with all my heart that you could have also seen all that Jesus did and said. There was so much more than could possibly be recorded. I wish you could have seen it, smelled it, tasted it. How I pray these pages will help you do just that.

IV

The Prophet

The Baptist watched the rat nibble tentatively at a crust of moldy bread, its tiny black nose twisting and bobbing. He had gagged when he had tried to eat the bread. It crumbled into powder as his teeth bit into it. The water the prison supplied came accompanied with the faint smell of urine. He did not have to imagine what the vessel had been used for. Despite his parched tongue, he emptied the foul fluid on the rat, who didn't seem to mind. Though his mouth was dry, he spat on the cold, damp stone floor as though somehow this would purge himself of the filth around him. He found himself wondering idly where they had quarried the rock and how many had spat on it just as he had done.

Thoughts of rushing green water boiling white over cool rocks flooded his brain, the dank humidity of Herod's dungeon suffocating his every breath. *What I would not give for a cool mountain breeze, wafting over a flowing stream filled with fish!* Thoughts came chaotically and randomly. For the briefest of instants, his mind rested on the memory of naked girls bathing in the stream. *What I would not give...*he allowed himself to envision them once again, and then catching himself, ashamed, forced his thoughts elsewhere.

"Baptist!" bellowed his jailer, his voice echoing against wet walls. Gleaming black eyes accentuated by thick, black eyebrows appeared through the sliding peephole in the iron door of his cell.

The brute had one arm, the other lost in battle in the arena. He had lost the battle, but the crowd appealed to Herod for his life because he had fought well. The king concurred and held his right thumb aloft. His victor extended his arm and pulled the vanquished combatant to his feet. He picked up his severed arm from the dirt and staggered back toward his quarters, until he fainted from loss of blood. Now his gladiator days were over. There is no use for a one-armed gladiator. His assignment to jailor duty had saved him from a life of begging. A humiliating task for a warrior, so he often took his frustrations out on his charges. His brutality was legend. Yet, somehow, John had befriended him.

"This is my kingdom," he would tell the prophet, waving his thick black arm at the surroundings. "I do what I choose. Not even Herod questions me. I take life when I choose. I torture whom I choose and when I choose. I let live when I choose." He paused briefly to let the threat of his power take its desired effect. John did not respond with the anticipated fear. "You will live, Baptist!" He said it like he spit. "But you will not live long. That royal bastard despises you. But if there were water here, by these Roman gods, I would have you baptize me!" No small concession from this man.

"Baptist!" he yelled again. "You have visitors!"

αΘω

The two men were allowed to sit with John while they conversed. "He is preaching in every village in Galilee. Hordes follow him from town to town."

"He must be our Messiah," said John despondently. "Certainly I never commanded such a following." The prophet paused for a moment, then buried his face in his hands. "When I baptized him, I saw…I thought," his words trailed into silence. And then, "Markus, Jannai," the black shadows that were his eyes brightened slightly, "You should have seen it. A magnificent, white dove descended from the heavens and sat upon his shoulder. And the voice…"

"What voice?"

John did not answer. He seemed lost in despondency again. After a few moments he shook his now matted head of massive hair and muttered negatively, "I had thought…I had truly thought that he was the One." He got up from where he squatted on the floor and stared at the wall disconsolately. "I guess I was wrong." The sense of dejection in the prison cell overpowered all three men. Prison has a way with men's minds. Confinement, darkness, cold, persistent dampness, rats, roaches, slugs, inedible food, urine, excrement and inhuman brutality did things to one's mind.

Several moments passed. The two men didn't know what to say. They sat with the broken prophet unable to speak. Jannai broke the silence. Since he was the more reticent of the two, it came as a surprise to hear him say, "I think you are wrong, my teacher. Your heart is so filled with pain that it has colored your judgment. Why would you, of all people, say such a thing?"

John turned on him. Eyes once vacant and empty, now raging with fire. "Then go to him! You think him so unimpeachable, so real, so genuine!"

An accusation of absurdity borne by rage. The bitterness in his voice reverberated against the barren walls of the dungeon. Footfalls of rats scurrying away at the noise. "Ask him why he has not declared himself? Ask him why he does not baptize? Ask him why he has permitted his cousin to rot in this infested dungeon? Do not tell me he does not know I am here. If he were Messiah, surely he would know! So ask him plainly, *Are you he that should come or should we look for another?* Leave no doubt. Then come back here and report to me!" The two men unconsciously clenched their teeth in embarrassment for their master. "And while you are at it," said John shaking, "ask him why he is there and I am here!" The two men turned to leave, the guard having come at the sound of John's raised voice. The door opened and they exited. As they went out they heard him scream, "Ask him why the prophets of an omnipotent God suffer interminable humiliation!" His voice broke into sobs. "Ask him! Ask him! Ask him!" The screams bounced darkly against dank, hollow walls, echoes dying in agony.

αΘω

They found him on the side of a Galilean hill as usual, surrounded by a multitude. The Judean prison lay four days of hard, relentless walking in their train. Their feet were sore, their bones throbbed. They had not bathed in that time and dry rivulets of sweat coursed their whitened paths down their brows and cheeks. Their antipathy toward Jesus had mounted with each step along the way. When at last they found him, Markus acidly remarked to Jannai, "Holding court again! He seems to thrive on approbation accorded by the ignorant, needy masses. How much Roman coin do you suppose these poor sheep give into his coffers?" Thoughts of cynicism and despair surged in their heads.

"He is truly a charlatan," concluded Jannai quietly.

They watched in disgust as Jesus taught the people. He seemed happy. Contented. Gloating, they thought, at the plaudits, praise and words of blessing from those surrounding him. "Why do people flock to him so? What has he to give them? He does not upbraid them for their sins. He does not demand repentance and baptism, as does our teacher. He is jovial, accepting and almost stupidly approachable. Anyone would follow a teacher like that. He tells them what they want to hear!"

"He is a charlatan," again from Jannai.

V

He Is of God

Sudden, loud murmuring from the crowd. Away from where Jesus was standing and off to one side, a disturbance emerged. Bodies began to mill about excitedly; then the cry, "Unclean! Unclean!" And as the parting of the Jordan waters when Elisha struck them with the mantle of Elijah, the crowd fell away, revealing a lonely figure of a girl-child.

She stood there, unmoving. There was no notion of where she had come from. It was quite unanticipated. It seemed as if she had precipitously just "materialized."

She appeared to be eight or nine years of age, dressed in aged rags and leaning for support on a wooden crutch. Her hair was stringy and matted with the brown dust of the leper colony. Her facial skin toughened with what appeared to be scar tissue and the other visible parts of her body, arms and legs, blotched with white surrounded by rashes of red. She gazed with one sad eye at Jesus, for the other was swollen shut with rotting flesh. She stood twenty paces distant. One leg, barefoot on the ground, the other ending in a stump at the place where her ankle would have been. The crutch steadied her on her lame side.

She simply stood there in silence, while the crowd withdrew in horror around her. This disease takes several years to incubate, and it was highly unusual to see a child in these advanced stages of leprosy. She gazed at Jesus in her perplexed silence. The poignant confrontation between the one called the Son of God and this child of creeping death stilled the crowd as they silently watched to see what, if anything, would ensue. Several moments passed in the absence of sound, not so much as a whisper, not so much as a cicada, not so much as the hush of an eddy against the trees.

Standing on her good foot, the child thrust the crutch toward Jesus and lurched a step in his direction. Then another, closing by two paces the distance between them. She whimpered in pain. Not many realize how deeply blazing is the pain of leprosy. It seeps into the joints and bones and makes the sufferer burn white with diseased heat. The staggering physical pain always carrying with it, terrible, disfiguring emotional pain. Such was the daily experience of this sweet, helpless child. While Jesus stood, the girl lurched several steps more. It looked as if she would fall as her weight shifted clumsily from foot to crutch and back to foot.

All eyes were on the child, held transfixed by her struggle to ambulate and crazed with fear for the proximity of such a deadly, repugnant disease. All were paralyzed by the pathos of her plight. No one noticed, but had they examined the face of Jesus, they would have seen eyes filling with tears. The terrible agony of the human condition forever clenched at his heart. The inhumanity of man upon man, the horror of "natural" disaster, the ravages of disease saddened the soul of the Son of Man as much, perhaps more so, as the rejection of non-belief. The child faltered on, closing the gap, one small lurch at a time, between herself and the man from Nazareth.

At last, she stood before him. She opened her mouth to speak, but words would not come. Finally, after a few embarrassed swallows, clear, unmistakable Hebrew language issued from her mouth, "Rab Y'shua, I hear that you know of Yach'weh!" Faces in the crowd turned to each other in surprise; surprise that she could even speak, and to do so in Hebrew instead of Aramaic, surprise that she would say such a thing and surprise that she would so easily speak the name of God. "My father, Othniel ben Ro'bin, is dead. I have prayed for him. I wish for him to be in heaven. Tell me Rab Y'shua, is he is in heaven or is he in hell?"

Except for the sound of the girl-child's voice, the crowd, the universe, remained silent. Nor did Jesus respond at first. He lifted his hand to gently touch her head. Murmured whispers of concern. And then, "Child, your prayers have been heard. Your father in his lifetime walked in faith and love with my Father. Together, they are with you until this day." For the first time, the child smiled as if a burden too great to bear was lifted from her small shoulders.

Then Jesus stooped and pulling the child into his arms, embraced her, enveloping her in his cloak. Sounds of shock and surprise from the crowd. He then stood, holding her still, immobilized. He took the crutch from her and striking it against a rock, broke it. He hugged her tightly and the girl, delighted, threw both arms into the air. Jesus cried to the crowd, "Look, you! See for yourselves the love and compassion of God your Father." When he set her down, from the top of her crown, to the bottom of both feet, the child was completely whole. Instead of hair caked together with filth, she stood with lovely tresses flowing about her shoulders. Instead of rags, she wore fine linen. Instead of whitened and reddened skin, her complexion was a velvet olive; and she saw. She saw with two beautiful almond eyes.

Such an event caused the crowd to fall to their knees. Not a solitary soul of several hundred stood. All were on their knees, as were the disciples of John, Markus and Jannai.

"He is of God!" exclaimed Jannai. His friend merely wept.

VI

His Work Is Done

After they had recovered, they came and stood before Jesus with the child at his side, and said, "We are disciples of John."

"Yes?"

"Our master suffers in Herod's prison." An expression of pain on the face of Jesus. "He is deeply saddened," said Markus. "I think he is afraid. I think he fears that he is of no more use to God. He is surprised and hurt that his life should end this way. He feeds the rats his crusts of bread. He wants to know if you are really the Christ or if he must hope for another?" His tone subdued. He knew the answer to this question but didn't know what else to say.

Jesus glanced at Markus and lowered his eyes. He turned, took a few steps and sat. He seemed stunned and sick at the news of his cousin. "You come from Judea?" This as a way of obliquely responding, acknowledging, indicating that he understood, yet felt as though there was nothing he could do.

"We do, Rabbi. We came quickly, hoping you could come and bring comfort to our master. We hoped, perhaps against hope, that you might find a way to obtain his release. We fear he may not survive."

After a moment of thought Jesus responded, "Go back and tell John what is going on here. Tell him what you have seen and heard. Tell him about the blind, the lame, the lepers, the deaf. Tell him the dead are raised, and the message of the Father's love and redemption is given to those in affliction." The child whom he had healed stood by, watching. He stepped over to her and put his arm about her shoulders. Her eyes sparkled in the sunbeams, her mouth and white teeth perfectly echoed a joyous smile. "Tell him of this child. Tell him all these things. He will be comforted. Tell him that I am indeed who I say I am and tell him not to be afraid." Jesus paused long enough for the two men to think that he had finished. They nodded their heads in assent and turned to leave. "And tell him," spoke Jesus, "that I suffer with him. Tell him that my heart and my spirit are one with his. Tell him...I love him."

αΘω

There were some of us who formerly sat at the feet of John. As the two men disappeared into the crowd, Jesus turned again to us and said, "When you heard John preach in the desert, who did you think he was? What did you think you were seeing? A weed swaying in the wind?" His lips pursed into a grim smile. As anyone who had seen him knew, John was no swaying weed. "Did you see a man dressed in fine clothes?" Again, we blanched at the thought. John's apparel was a contradiction to anything fine. "Those who wear expensive clothes and indulge in luxury live in fine homes and palaces. But what did you see when you saw John? A prophet? Yes, that is what you saw! John is a prophet, and more than a prophet. John is the one about whom it is written: 'I will send my messenger ahead of you, who will prepare your way before you.' I tell you that among those born of women there are none of the prophets, none, that are greater or more powerful than John."

My eyes fell away from Jesus and examined the ground at my feet. There I observed a large beetle lumbering along its way. It is hard to say why such an event captured my interest, or why, these many years later, I tell you about it. The beetle approached a rock buried in the foot of an embankment and covered with lichen and yellow-green moss. Somehow, he found a crevasse and crawled beneath the rock, out of the heat of the sun. I wished that I could crawl under a rock somewhere myself, away from the burning beams of my own shame. How many times had I, how many times had we all made John the butt of childish humor? How many times had we laughed and joked among ourselves of his wild clothing and his diet. How many times had we scorned his poverty? How many times had we made condescending remarks about his thunderous preaching and baptizing anything that moved? How many times had I, myself, shamelessly held John in lofty contempt? Yes. The beetle and I would have been visceral comrades under the rock with the rest of the worms and crawling things.

"John's work is done. And he doesn't understand why. No man who serves God is ever assuaged of the hunger to continue to do so, or to do so in a larger way than he has ever done. It is a deeply troubling pain. He doesn't yet realize his station in the eternal kingdom nor does he realize that he approaches the hour when the Father will reward him beyond his ability to imagine.

"John, also, is suffering under intensely desperate, humiliating conditions. It is not unusual for men, even extraordinary men, in such pain to have times of questioning the goodness of God and seeking release from their pain. Do not judge him. Emphasize with him.

"The prophets of old have continued until John's time. He is the final one. He is the summation of all the prophets before him. And if you are willing to accept it, he is the Elijah who was to come.

"To what shall I compare this society of today? It has all the spiritual sensitivity of children yelling at each other, 'If you won't play by my rules, if you won't do it my way, I will take my agates and go home.'"

"John the Baptist came neither eating bread nor drinking wine, and he was thought odd; much too eccentric to speak for God. Instead, it is said that he is demonic. The Son of Man came both eating and drinking, and you say, 'This man doesn't follow our rules. He too, is demonic. He eats what he wants when he wants. He is a glutton, a drunkard who cultivates friendships with the wrong people; with worldly people. He is much too worldly to speak for God.' When the message of God's prophets do not fit the expected perceptions of what they should say, or how they are expected to act, men pout and sulk like children. They become cruel and inhuman. There is no mystery in this. History continues to repeat itself. Children will always be children. If any of you have the ears to hear this, God help you to hear it."

The girl-child put her arms about him and held him, swaying gently back and forth. Bending over, he embraced her as well. Sweat rolled down his cheeks and into his beard.

Or were they tears?

VII

The Roman

Festivities exploded ninety miles to the south in Jerusalem. People scurried about excitedly, happy faces of children playing, merchants hawking, the dust of the streets, irritating, causing fits of sneezing. Families together taking in the wonder and celebration of it all.

While many of the children and even some adults wore costumes and masks, older men ambled about stately and serene, unaffected spectators. They had seen it many times before. They were amazed but not unpleased at how the younger generation could be so animated, for they yet remembered when they had felt the same. Years have a way of mellowing perspective.

Suddenly a loud roar arrested everyone's attention. It came from the direction of the Temple. Another explosion, a chorus of vocal sound and loud shouting. Some began to move in the direction of the clamor when a man with a booming, visceral voice shouted, "It's the Megillah! Hurry! Be quick about it!" At that, almost everyone in the tumultuous streets surged toward the Temple. The older men, arms folded, smiled in pleasure. Pandemonium! Boos and hisses issued forth, along with the brackish sound of noisemakers. Thousands arrived at the Temple at the same time. The large structure was already packed with people, so all they could do was stand outside and howl when they heard everyone else inside cheer and shriek huzzahs. Amongst all of this, on the podium sat a man reading as loud as he could so he could be heard above the din, "And the king loved Esther more than all the women, and she found favor and kindness with him more than all the virgins, so that he set the royal crown on her head and made her queen instead of Vashti." Wild whooping, applause and jumping up and down. It was the fourteenth of March, known to the Jews as the month of Adar, and this was the Feast of Purim, otherwise known as The Day of Mordecai. It had turned the entire city of Jerusalem into a gigantic carnival. In every synagogue the Scroll of Esther, or "Megillah," was being read. Whenever the name of wicked Haman was mentioned, loud hoots and boos, children waving groggers, the loudest noisemaker one could imagine.

The word *Purim,* is derived from pure, or a small stone used in casting lots, the method Haman used to establish the day in which he would massacre all the Jews. Purim occurs one day after Nicanor's day on the 13th of Adar. This was ordained by a decree of almost 200 years ago, to annually celebrate the defeat of that Seleucid general, by Judas Maccabaeus. The Jewish victors were so flushed with triumph that they cut off general Nicanor's head and his "proud right hand" and displayed them for all to see on the walls of Jerusalem. The Jewish people were ordained and instructed to "keep this great day of gladness" year by year—the day before Mordecai's day. So, the Feast of Purim had taken on a double significance that further intensified the merrymaking. The readings continued enthusiastically, with great drama, punctuated with bluster, bellows, boos and those screeching little twirling groggers. The garish costumes and masks helped the people express their rejoicing in fanatic remembrance of Esther's deliverance of the Jews, though she had to conceal her Jewish origins when she became queen.

αΘω

Jesus made his way through the festivities deliciously alone, having left the twelve and his other followers in Galilee. "Go spend some time with your families," he had told us. "You need them and they need you." He was reflecting, in these words, a very human need within himself to belong, to be loved by people who needed nothing from him except to be with him, as a brother…a son. "Meet me in a fortnight at my mother's home in Nazareth."

His purpose in coming to Jerusalem was private and personal. He desired to see Hermas ben David, his father's old friend. There are few events so heartwarming and comforting than to be among friends whose engagement as family goes all the way back to one's birth. He continued through the city and beyond its walls to Bethlehem, the place of his birth and the home of Hermas, now in his seventies. He remembered coming to this home when his family came to Jerusalem for the many Passovers and other occasions. He thought of the times they had come for Purim, this very celebration. He felt an ache of nostalgia as he recalled happy times.

Soon the house was in view. A fine house, a villa with colonnades and a reflecting pool. Hermas ben David lived well. He was met, however, not by his expected host, but by a Roman soldier of high rank. A tribune, perhaps? A general? Jesus did not know. Military rank had always been so esoteric to him. For such a person to be here was not particularly remarkable, since Hermas ben David was a man of wealth and power.

How had he known of Jesus' approach? It is unknown. He was a man of military bearing, military training, military awareness. Perhaps as an animal senses the smell of prey, this man sensed an approaching stranger. In any case, he was aware, and not only was he aware, incredibly, he recognized the intruder for who he was. The soldier in gleaming uniform, his short combat sword at his side, spoke first, "Welcome, Jesus of Nazareth," he said. "It is good to see you again." He smiled and held out his arm for Jesus to clasp in traditional Roman greeting.

Jesus, a bit nonplussed but in control of himself, said, "Have we met? Do I know . . ?" Tiny increments of recognition began to knit themselves together. In a moment, completely aware, "Urbanus! I—I can't believe it! How long has it been?"

"I believe the last time was when I chased you up a tree. Let's see," Urbanus laughed, putting his hand to his chin as if in somber recollection, "you must have been about twelve. After that you ran off to play with one of your little friends, ah..."

"Eben! His name was Eben. But why did I climb a tree?" he asked, embarrassed that he could not remember.

"I think you were pretending you were a cat, a tiger perhaps."

"And you?"

"A great Nubian hunter, of course!" They both laughed out loud.

"There was an incident. You disappeared for three days, and our families were in an uproar about it."

"Yes," said Jesus with a soberness that approached embarrassment, "I guess I frightened everyone rather badly."

Seeing his discomfiture, Urbanus good-naturedly made the most of it. "What was that excuse you gave?" laughing.

Jesus smiled, "That I was about my Father's business."

"I guess your parents must have loved that."

"They were less than impressed. I'm afraid it was just the beginning of my adolescent itchings." While Jesus understood that this assessment was probably closer to the truth than he wished, he nonetheless remembered the insistent pressure within him on that occasion. His "itchings" had persisted through adolescence, the same holy thing that only intensified as he matured.

VIII

The Soldier

"Jesus!" The voice of an older man came from the cavernous interior of the home. The smile on his face genuine and joyous, Hermas ben David's hair and beard were a dramatic mixture of white and black. Like Jesus always remembered him, he was dressed impeccably but his posture, his uneven gait bespoke advancing years. He held out his arms into which Jesus unhesitatingly walked. They embraced warmly with affectionate kisses on each cheek.

Jesus followed Hermas into the luxurious home; his son, the soldier, came after. A fire crackled in the hearth, removing the bite from the early Spring chill. Through the casement, blue mountains against a light grey sky could be seen on the horizon. Noise from the streets drifted through the windows. The center of the room occupied by a large mahogany table polished to a brilliant sheen, surrounded by silk covered cushions of rich and varied colors. On the table lay certain items that Jesus knew instantly were matanot la-evyonim, or gifts for the poor. This was another tradition of Purim. Jesus knew that there were other gifts as well, or mishloach manot, gifts to be sent to distant relatives and friends.

Julia, now graced with light streaks of grey in her hair, having greeted Jesus with warmth and delight, served the men wine, grapes, bread, fig cakes and hot, melting goat cheese, covered with freshly churned butter and roasted almonds. And then, without the slightest embarrassment, she sat down with the men to participate in conversation. She determined not to miss a thing. Such a bright, intelligent woman could no more be relegated to her quarters than the man Hermas ben David himself. She was, in every particular, his intellectual equal. It was not a fact that Hermas did not notice and appreciate. Indeed, he felt complimented that this woman had chosen to love him, bear his children and be his wife. Any man would be proud and humbled for the blessing she brought to his life. Julia spoke first.

"What brings the son of Mary and Joseph so far from his home? Or should I address you as the Son of God?" The gentle smile on her lips showed no intent of disrespect.

"I see my reputation has preceded me," said Jesus dryly. "Really, Aunt Julia, I am surprised there were no trumpets, heralds or carpets of red to welcome me," he said with mock seriousness. They laughed at the absurdity. A pause, "Actually, I have no business, no purpose, no compelling news to bring you. I think I have come because I know I am welcome, and quite honestly," he lowered his head slightly, "I could use a little of that right now." Julia reached out to touch his arm.

"No one could be more welcome in this house," she responded.

"May God grant this home always your sanctuary, Jesus," Hermas added. Urbanus remained silent, observing, but smiling approval.

Julia continued, "From the day you were brought into our home, almost from your mother's womb, you have been our son as well. You spent almost two years living here. Do you think that you did not find your way into our hearts in that time? Jesus ben Joseph or Jesus ben Yahweh, whoever you are, we love you as we love our own son."

That cued Urbanus, "And I, little brother...I was but a boy with great dreams when you came into our lives. I remember the star, the Magi. You were something of a celebrity then, as you will always be with me." Gripping the handle of his sword, "My protection and my blood are always at your disposal." His mother looked at her son with palpable love and tangible fear.

αΘω

The conversation and pleasantries continued for a time before Jesus realized that Julia had absented herself. She was gone for only a moment when he saw her re-enter the room with a tray in her hands. Odd-looking pastries were on the tray. He instantly knew by the familiar aroma what they were: Delicious, mouth watering Hamantashen!

It was time for Jesus to be excited. "Haman's Hat!" he exclaimed. "I haven't had one of those since I was a child."

"Haman's Ears," corrected Hermas, "or so some say. Personally, I disagree. Ears do not have three corners!" with feigned disgust. The pastries were usually served only at the Feast of Purim. Each had three corners and was filled with sweet prunes and poppy seeds.

"My mother used to make these," said Jesus recalling fond memories.

"As does every Jewish mother. She no doubt still makes them."

Such warm, fervent hospitality touched Jesus deeply. "I have not erred in coming here. You honor me with your love and faith. And my brother," speaking to the soldier, "your sword shall never be drawn in my defense, but it is comforting to know it is there." He waited for the emotion of the moment to pass and said, "Your generosity to me and my parents may never be known..."

"We did not proffer it to be known!" said Hermas.

"I know that, and so does my Father in heaven."

There was a noticeable change in the expression of Urbanus. "You speak comfortably of Yahweh as your Father as if his blood coursed through your veins, Jesus." said Hermas. "Tell us of him. What is he like?"

"I have two fathers in heaven now. My father Joseph is gathered to his fathers. He, too, is in the bosom of Abraham."

"We heard," from Julia. "We were deeply grieved."

"I did not even attend his funeral," said Jesus quietly.

"As you say, Jesus, he was not there. He was in your Father's care."

Jesus considered for a moment. It was odd that this loving family should remind him of the obvious. He knew that Joseph now enjoyed the literal presence of God, yet to be reminded by people who loved him seemed somehow appropriate, yet remarkable. "You know how the scribes and others have intellectualized God. He is the subject of study and ponderous theological discussion. So it is now, and so shall it ever be. In this way, men hold him at a distance. It is perhaps more comfortable for them in that way. But the Father will not be put in a scroll nor confined in theological discussion. My Father is much like any other father. He wishes to reproduce himself. That is why men are created in his image. He wishes to look upon his child, his children, and see himself. To see and experience their love for him, love given freely—of their own choice to do so.

αΘω

"You speak of love as though it were tangible," spoke Urbanus, "as though it were something we could see, feel or touch. Isn't love, as we know it, an unwitting sentimentality? An infatuation?"

"Agh! The soldier has spoken," said Hermas wearily. "My son has become a Roman, Jesus. He speaks of human experience through cold objectivity, as though the issues that sway men were a matter of military precision."

The mood of the soldier shifted from pleasant to irritation. "I have seen love cripple more men than it has ennobled," he quietly replied. "And yes, father, I do enjoy the structure of the military. It plans. It is organized. It gets things done. There is not much quarter for the lack of emotional discipline. My enemy does not ask my permission or inquire as to how I feel about it before he divides my head with his sword. The 'issues that sway men,' as you put it, are best settled by force—the force of a benevolent theocracy." The eyes of the son gazed without blinking at those of his father.

"I have raised an Alexander," said Hermas, looking away into the distance, as if seeking support from something unknown. This was clearly a subject over which father and son had deep differences. "A theocracy, you say? You speak, I suppose, of the divinity of Caesar?"

"If he were not divine, he would not be Caesar!" Urbanus shot back. "How do you suppose one becomes master of the world? There is no army, no force, no bent of will on earth that can withstand him. He is the most powerful man on earth. How can you not revere him, father?"

"You just said it yourself. He is a man, not a god. I cannot revere such a despotic, poisonous ass!"

"Stop it! Both of you!" from Julia. "I will not have the men I love going at one another. Urbanus, I have never heard you speak to your father in that tone."

"It is because of me," said Jesus evenly. "I think what I represent goes against the things that have meant the most to Urbanus. He is not to be faulted."

"I am not sure I understand. Jesus, how do you mean that you go against the things that mean the most to me? Do you oppose Caesar? Do you oppose the seat of power that provides for you, that keeps you safe from enemies of the state?"

"Urbanus, Urbanus, my son! Your heart is afire with naive idealism," from his father.

"Naive idealism!?" The soldier stood, furious. "And what is this drivel that we hear from this man?" gesturing at Jesus. "Naive, you say? This is not naive," grasping the grip of his sword. "This is not naive," bringing his arm and fist forcibly across the eagle on his chest. "These are real, my father. And may whatever gods there be help the pathetic souls who stand in their way!" The fury in his son's eyes would have melted lead. The moment of tense silence in the room seemed more like an hour, then Urbanus abruptly turned, and strode out the door.

"Urbanus!" cried Julia.

"Let him go," said Hermas.

αΘω

Jesus quickly stood and followed him outside. In the yard, the sun glinting on his brass and silver helmet, Urbanus turned and pointed at Jesus with his finger, "Stay away from me, Jesus of Nazareth! We may have been friends in childhood, but now we are men. I am an officer of the Roman court and you . . ? You are a…I don't know what you are! I care not a fig for the silly stories of your birth! But by Caesar, go against me and I'll witness for myself the day of your death!" He stalked away leaving Jesus alone and hurt, wondering how one who so fervently had sworn his defense could turn away so quickly.

Urbanus! Urbanus, my dear brother. So you have spoken, so shall it be.

IX

Family Conflict

It was good to be home again. It had been a long journey with only Abishag at his side. The crowd that followed him from Jerusalem had dwindled to nothing. Sometimes being a prophet…well, it wasn't always what one might expect. One often had to sleep outside and unless one always had a pallet with him, the ground was cold at night. Sandals rubbed blisters, and the dust from the road chafed. One had to move one's bowels behind a rock or a bush. Very unprophet-like.

And so on the day when Nazareth finally came into view, Jesus was once again alone with his thoughts, looking forward to a warm bath and seeing his family. As his feet found the familiar streets, he headed directly for his own home, the dog trotting ahead.

The welcome home was cooler than it might have been. Sarah's heart thudded when she saw the dog and then froze as she saw Jesus following. "Oh!" she said softly, dropping a robe to be laundered, from her hand to the floor. She said nothing else but, remarkably, turned and left the room, presumably to fetch the rest of the family. He heard a small shriek from the interior, and Rhoda came rushing into meet him.

"Jesus!" she cried and ran into his arms. Dear Rhoda, there was nothing to diminish her ebullience. "Oh Jesus!" she said again only slightly more composed. She stepped back as if to take him all in, then joyously hugged him again. Jesus responded in kind, relishing each squeeze. This is what he craved, each moment, each step along the way from Jerusalem.

His mother entered the room, stopped at the threshold of the door and said simply, "Welcome home, my son," and then came to him embracing him tentatively. Jesus sensed a reserve, an aloofness that he had not expected.

"Such a hug?" said Jesus, "What kind of welcome was that?"

His mother stood in front of him; at forty-seven years, her temples greying, the lines in her face deeper. She tried to smile, brushing a wisp of hair from her face. She had gained a few inches here and there, but Jesus marveled that his mother was still beautiful. Her head was uncovered and soft hair fell loosely around her shoulders. Absently, she pulled her cowl over her head.

Her eyes fell away from his. "You've been gone a long time, Jesus. I've missed you."

"Mother, something's amiss. What is it?"

She turned her gaze out the window, toward the lush green hills. "Many years ago Gabriel appeared to me." She spoke of the angel as if he were a dear friend, almost a relative. It was obvious that thoughts of him were familiar to her. "He told me that I would become pregnant without having ever known a man." She turned and her gaze met his. "Since that day, many have spoken to me of you, all through your childhood until this present day. It never ceases."

"Has someone told you . . ?" There was a defensive protectiveness in his tone. He worried that his mother was being harassed because of him.

"No, my son. Most of what people say is intended to bless and encourage, not hurt. Except...except what I have heard that you yourself have said of me—and of your family." Her voice caught. "And you're gone so much of the time, Jesus. It seems as if I...it seems as if none of your brothers and sisters are important to you anymore." The words and the tears started to spill. "I knew you were special to God since before the day you were born. But I never expected that you would grow up and reject us like this..."

Jesus resisted the powerful urge within him to embrace her, to hold her. "I am sorry, Mother. I never meant to hurt you or disparage my family. I love you, I love you all...more deeply than you imagine."

"The things you say," she continued, "and teach. Sometimes even your mother cannot understand," her voice caught again, "...or endure."

Jesus waited until her composure settled. When she was quiet he called out, "Sarah! Rhoda! Joseph! Milcah! Simon! Judas! All of you! Come in here, please." One by one each appeared. All except James, who was with Peter in Capharnaum. All were quiet. Hurt could be seen in the eyes of Sarah, anger in those of Milcah, distance in the eyes of Simon and Judas, expectancy in the eyes of Joseph and Rhoda. "Here is our mother," he began, "hurt and disappointed because of me." He paused. They waited. "All of you know that I am different than you. I hope you understand that I cannot change this. That I was born not of Joseph, our father, is not something that can be altered."

He spoke as if pleading, desiring earnestly to be understood. "But you are my family. I love you and care for you in a manner unlike I care for any of those who follow me or listen to me teach. If something I have said to others has returned to you in a way that makes it appear otherwise, then I want you dismiss it! You are my family!" he said again with emphasis. "I would do nothing or say nothing to hurt you or alienate you from me. I need you..."

His voice broke, "...I need for you to love me. I need you to accept the calling the Father has laid upon me. I...I know it must seem strange to you, as if I did not care, as if you weren't important to me, but I must live out my purpose. I can do nothing else." He hung his head. "Please try and understand this." He remembered the terrible words of Urbanus, "I weary of such pain." He covered his eyes with his hands.

"I understand, my brother." It was Milcah. Of all his siblings, Milcah was the most critical, the most judgmental. She came to him, put her arms about him and held him. In a moment, she was joined by Rhoda, Sarah and his brothers. All of them stood in a circle around him, embracing him, weeping. Mary stood apart and beheld the scene. The tears in her eyes and smile on her face bespoke a relief and a joy she had not known since the day Jesus was born.

"Take us with you, Jesus." The voice was Rhoda's. "Let us follow you and be with you. You need your family with you." Unexpectedly, Jesus began to weep heavily. His emotions seemed lost, out of control. It all came out, all of the pain, the acid debates, the rejection, the hours of deprivation, the healings...everything. It all erupted here before his mother, his brothers and his sisters. They gathered as close to him as possible, holding him as tightly as possible. Mary joined them.

In a moment it subsided. They joined hands in a circle. "We are one," said Rhoda. "We shall never be divided."

"We are one," said they all. Jesus simply stood there, moved too deeply to speak.

At length he managed, "It will be difficult for you."

"We are one!" said they.

The dog whimpered, her tail swishing gently.

X

He Who Receives You Receives Me

The disciples arrived on cue. The two weeks rest had done them well. They were joking with each other, happy and obviously refreshed from time with their loved ones.

The next day Jesus began to teach in the synagogue, and many who heard him were amazed. "Where did he get these ideas?" they asked. "What is this wisdom that he has? Where did he get that? How do we explain these miracles?" (Isn't it interesting how it seems to be human nature never to give a person—any person—credit for a seminal idea? It is always assumed that if another has an interesting thought, that he must have gotten it from some resource other than himself.) They observed Mary and the rest of Jesus' family. "This, the son of the carpenter!? Here is his mother and here are his brothers and sisters! We watched him grow up right here in our streets. He is ordinary. He is nothing special! He is like us. Why did he not stay here among us instead of traipsing around the country? Why does he not honor his own family—and us?" And so, many were offended at his teaching.

Jesus said to them, "It seems that in his hometown a prophet is without honor. In so dishonoring me, you rob yourselves." Jesus, of course, was not unaccustomed to such treatment. Perhaps he expected more from those who knew him from childhood. In any case, he could not do any miracles there, except lay his hands on a few sick people and heal them. He was disheartened at their lack of faith and confidence in him. So taking his leave of Nazareth, Jesus moved from village to village teaching and preaching to any who would listen.

αΘω

It is said that Aristotle, the fabled Greek philosopher who lived more than 300 years ago, walked about, teaching and instructing as he went from place to place. This method of teaching became known as the Aristotelian peripatetic method. Although I doubt that Jesus ever read Aristotle (though one never knows), it seems that he found this method suited his own purpose. He walked from town to town, village to village preaching, teaching and healing.

As always, crowds gathered. To Jesus they seemed disoriented and helpless, like sheep without a shepherd. His heart filled with compassion for them, he said to his disciples, "There are so many. These fields are so ripe. They are plentiful and they are ready for harvest, but there seems to be very few harvesters." Indeed there were only him, the twelve and those of us who followed him. "We should ask the Lord of the harvest to send laborers who can harvest these fields for the kingdom of God."

The "Lord of the harvest?" Wasn't he the Lord of the harvest? Jesus often fell back into his parable mode of expression, even when he spoke of himself.

αΘω

We found ourselves in the hills overlooking Tiberias. Wave caps glistened as the sun rose over the Sea of Galilee beyond the town. We warmed ourselves by the fire Peter had built and breakfasted on warmed barley cakes sprinkled with olive oil and goat cheese. Jesus had dismissed the crowd earlier than usual the night before, and we'd all had a quiet and restful night's sleep.

So, calling together the twelve "apostles," he said "I have a special mission for you. The nation of Israel is God's chosen envoy for the entire human race. For centuries they have been so. It is appropriate, therefore, to give them the opportunity to continue that purpose. Their message to the world is to be the message I bring. Since it is theirs to preach and teach this message, it follows that it is they who must first accept its Messenger, the Messiah, the Son of Man. So I send you, my students, as ambassadors and laborers in the harvest among our own people. For this mission, I do not want you to go among non-Jews or enter any town of the Samaritans. Go only to the lost sheep of Israel. It is they who are being given this opportunity."

"This is the message I want you to preach: 'Hear, O Israel, if you will receive it, the Kingdom of Heaven is here, at your very doorstep. Accept its King; accept his Message and become his ambassadors to all people throughout the world and so fulfill the Father's promise to Abraham."

It is important, indeed critical, to realize that Jesus was not in this act of sending this message to the Israelite nation offering only to them the Kingdom itself. Instead, he was employing them to be his ambassadors to the entire world. It is through the Hebrew nation that news of the Gospel should come. They were to be the carriers of the Message. To them has been given the message of redemption, the message that the Kingdom awaits all who believe, all throughout the world, who will accept its King.

"Now, as you go," Jesus continued, "do not forget to do kind and miraculous things for people. Heal the sick, raise the dead, cleanse those who are diseased and drive away evil. Freely you have received the power to do this, now freely give that power away.

"You need no money; take no provisions for the journey or extra clothing. Do not concern yourself with generating an income for your expenses, for the message you bring is worth what it takes to keep you going.

"Whatever town or village you enter, search for a person of means and tell him you wish to stay at his house until you have completed your mission in that town. As you enter his home, give him your greeting and declare your purpose plainly. If he is sympathetic and receptive, let your peace rest on that home; if he is not, let your peace return to you. If anyone will not welcome you or listen to your words, then leave. Let it be as if you shake the dust off your feet. While it is sad, you are not responsible for the choices of others.

He glanced around the group, his eyes focused on James and Thomas. "Some of you look a bit worried. You need not be. Are not two sparrows sold for a penny, yet not one of them will fall to the ground apart from the Father's knowledge? Did you know that even the hairs of your head are numbered?" Glancing at Matthew's receding hairline, he smiled, "Some have less for God to keep track of than others." Laughter. "So do not fear. Hold nothing back. You are worth more than many sparrows.

"And never forget, he who receives you receives me, and he who receives me receives the one who sent me. If anyone gives to you even so much as a cup of cold water because you serve me, I tell you the truth, he will certainly not lose his reward."

"Now go! Off with you! Do it and do it like I know you can. Let me hear the crowds roar from Judea to Galilee. And know that with every step you take and in every word you speak, I shall be in your heart."

When he finished his charge, the disciples went away two by two, shouting and pumping their fists in the air, enthused by their anticipation of what they had to accomplish. Jesus seemed pleased but sober as he watched them go. With this mission, the nation of Israel will be given her opportunity.

XI

Dancer

What would my father have done? Antipas tried to comfort himself with remembrances of his father, *Herod the Great. He would have slain the Baptist long before I did. He would have never listened to him in the first place.* But Antipas had listened to John and had listened to his message. He might even have been baptized by John, had it not been for his position as Tetrarch of Galilee. Power does terrible things to a man's heart. It causes him to become calloused to such things…or does it? Something had touched him. *Had it not been for that infernal woman I married, perhaps this man of God would have blessed me and I should have prospered and ruled well.* He sat on the side of his bed, his face buried in his hands. He had drunk too much last night. Too late. John the Baptist is dead.

"The Black Fortress," Machaerus, a fortified city on the eastern shores of the great salt sea, eighteen miles south of the place where the Jordan, rich with life, flows into it and dies—as everything does. A forlorn place it was, and an excellent site for both palace and prison. Because of the incessant nagging of his wife, Herodias, Antipas had John arrested, incarcerated and manacled to a wall in one of the prison dungeons. There, also, he had listened to the prophet, at first out of curiosity. He had come to have a modicum of respect for John and his strange message of repentance and was of a mind to release him. But instead, that very night he had murdered this unlikely friend.

The town had another face. Owing to the hot springs in the hills above the sea, the area had become somewhat of a resort, a place that attracted the rich and noble from "Dan to Beersheba," all of it rebuilt by his father, Herod the Great, after it had been demolished by Gabinius in his war with Aristobulus. The hot mineral baths had a magnificent view of the salt sea 3,860 feet below. It was in these hot baths that he entertained his friends. It was his birthday. He had a right to enjoy himself with his friends, hadn't he? Herodias had come to Machaerus as well, to celebrate, as most thought, her husband's birthday. She had something else in mind.

He had made the unfortunate mistake of marrying this insufferable woman, his brother Philip's wife. John had told him on more than one occasion "Your brother is still living. It is not lawful for you to take his wife." This annoyed and embarrassed Antipas, but owing to his curious respect for John, he ignored the remarks. Herodias, however, was outraged that her husband had given this uncouth man such influence or that this strange and ungraceful visionary could utter such words with impunity. That is why Antipas had John imprisoned here, to keep him safe, to protect him from the priests, away from the political and religious arena, and from Herodias. Except now she had intruded herself into his affairs.

αΘω

"She has learned well, my Queen." Herodias examined her daughter with a critical and envious eye; barely fifteen and already a captivating beauty. Her mother recalled her own beauty. She had once had the same sensual body, firm breasts and provocative hips. Salome exceeded her in every feature. Her cascading black hair emitted a bluish sheen in the right light, her white skin deliberately kept from the sun lest it sunburn or, worse, turn brown; those blue eyes that teased and beguiled, not so unknowingly, those who were fortunate enough to attract her glance. Salome was, indeed, exquisite, elegant, and, most of all, useful.

Salome was not Antipas' daughter. She was born to Philip, the first husband of Herodias, whom she had divorced in order to marry his more powerful brother.

"She dances with the grace of a gazelle and the élan of a cheetah," continued her instructor. "She will inflame the passions of any man whom the gods deem fit to indulge."

"She should," stated Herodias flatly. "She is my daughter. And, she's been training with you for how long, Sha-fur? Seven years now?" This was not a compliment. Herodias was not capable of generous gestures. Sha-fur, a mistress-slave of light color and striking beauty despite her years, had served the family since she herself was a child. She had once danced for Herod the Great in his palace in Jerusalem. Now responsible for entertaining the Herodian family, she conducted a school to train dancers, male and female, most of them dark beauties from Africa and Egypt. "Show me," Herodias demanded. "Let me see for myself how well you have trained my vestal virgin-child to boil the blood of virile men."

Herodias, years before, had herself also taken lessons from Sha-fur. Though falling short of Salome's beauty, she was still to be desired. She also knew her husband. His sexual appetites were insatiable. In the past when she wanted something, anything, from Antipas, eroticism had been the way to get it. But recently it had become harder to distract him. Recently she'd seen the way his gaze lingered at her daughter. And now Herodias wanted something. She wanted that disgusting diabolist dead. John the Baptist was not just another religious prophet. He was not just another peasant teacher, peddling idiotic notions. He had the ear of Herod Antipas! He was influencing the Tetrarch of Galilee! She could see it in her husband's eyes, his behavior and his decisions. Moreover, this horrible pig had openly declared opposition to her marriage to Herod. And her husband was listening to his snoutish drivel! This would not do. She knew well that if he persuaded Antipas toward his absurd beliefs, she would be out. Truly out. Philip would not have her back, no one would. She would be destitute. This would not do. Indeed, this would not do!

"Dance, Salome, my dear. Dance as if your very life depended on it." Dance because my life *does* depend on it! A cymbal sounded, followed by the deep throb of African drums. The girl's delicate feet began to move, her hips swaying in soft syncopation with the heavy beat of the drums. Her eyes closed, her lips warming to smile, her pelvis contracting. She clearly enjoyed dancing. She clearly enjoyed its power. Her mother's expression a visage of cold delight.

XII

The Dance

Herod's friends reclined about the tables, their bodies still warm and sweating from the steaming water of the baths they'd spent the afternoon enjoying. These were high captains and many of the chief politicians of Galilee, most of them Roman gentiles. They felt privileged to be here, invited to celebrate the Tetrarch's birthday. When Herod gave a party, one could expect wondrous and unexpected pleasures. The hot baths followed by opulent feasting and flowing wine were powerful tools in the hands of someone like Antipas. He had not his father's penchant for unilateral control nor would that kind of power ever again be conferred upon a provincial king. But this Herod still knew how to play the game. He knew how to get what he wanted from Rome. The affectation of his birthday celebration was a perfect device for such political purposes. Before these men left, he considered, his power in Galilee and perhaps beyond would be consolidated.

And they were his "friends," as much as anyone in his position could possess friends. They at least lent the appearance that they endorsed him. After all, Caesar was far away, and Herod could offer, well, amenities.

An attendant appeared who approached the Tetrarch whispering in his ear as Herod gorged his mouth with a large, succulent, black Medjool date, imported from Morocco. Thereupon he smiled and clapped his hands for attention. "Friends," he announced, "Distinguished guests, dignitaries, tribunes and captains of Caesar's legions. I have just been advised that my wife has prepared a gift for my birthday." Smiling with pleasure, he gestured toward the curtain-shrouded colonnades and said, "May I present to you Salome (he pronounced "Sal-O-May," enhancing the drama), the most exotic flower of Israel..."

Another cymbal loud enough to shock-assault the ears, sounded; reverberating among the marble columns of the palace; and followed instantly by wild beating African drums. Entering the room from both sides, two lines of dark skinned young women moved rapidly and gracefully into a circle, clothed in colorful beads, gold chains, necklaces and ostrich plumes, pulsing to the music of drums, jingling bells and boshghabaks from Persia. After a moment of stunning pageantry, just enough to accentuate the heady sense of anticipation, all of the instruments ceased on precise cue, creating a dramatic, silent, pause. Having formed a circle, and raising dark arms in such a way that it gave the appearance of blossom petals swaying in the wind, the lovely brown maidens kneeled. Suddenly, Salome arose from the center, a white petal, appearing as it were, from nowhere, a vision of shimmering sensuality, her white flesh giving the appearance of a rising, emerging, receptive stigma from the midst of the human flower.

Her hips and legs were draped with sheer, translucent blue silk; a bright gold cluster of olive leaves barely covering the convergence of her thighs held in place by wisps of gold chain. A serpentine strand of gold beads encrusted with emeralds encircled her breasts, and a large sapphire nested in her navel, her silken black hair laced with gold filigree. The illusion of nudity enhanced the fluidity of her hips punctuating each soft throb of a solitary drum breaking the poignant silence. Herod and the men in the room gasped in murmurs of pleasure.

Salome danced. Her lithe, youthful movements rose and fell with what was now a chorus of thumping drums, inviting a feast for aroused eyes, building to crescendo, then diminishing into whisper of movement, tiny bells and silver tassels clinking in syncopation. Slowly and purposefully she danced to each man, pausing, teasing, taunting, inviting. At length, this exotic, dancing apparition approached Herod's table. Reclining on the table before him, she seized his goblet of wine and drizzled the wine slowly, strategically over her body inviting him with her eyes to drink. Blood surging, Herod leaned toward her—breathless…

"Stop!" It was the voice of Herodias, commanding, insistent. Throbbing drums ceased instantly. The girl, as if to tease again, swung velvet smooth legs slowly from the table. "Would my husband take this child in front of the elite of Rome?" Herodias herself appeared, it seemed, also dressed to dance. She was a picture of mature sensuality. "Would he prefer an untested child to seasoned experience?"

In his drunken stupor, Herod was apoplectic. "What do you want?" he said to Herodias, his voice rasping with anger and lust. "What are you doing? I know you seek something of this."

"Is it not your birthday my husband?"

Salome stepped forward moving with deliberation, each step titillating with sensuality. This had its effect. Despite Herod's sense of being manipulated, he was helpless before this display of sexual anticipation. Herodias gestured to the other dancers who then stood. In a practiced move each dancer touched the place where their costumes were fastened, swayed their bodies gently and their costumes fell to their feet. "Happy birthday, darling. These are yours; for your pleasure and the pleasure of your guests."

Herod appeared somewhat a fool as he stood behind the table on which Salome now sat, her legs curled beneath her. "Salome awaits you, my husband." And then she paused, "for a small compensation..."

"Half my kingdom!" roared Herod. His guests howled with laughter as only those who have had too much wine can laugh. "Ask of me anything!" He was now serious and swore with an oath. "By Yach-Weh! By all the gods in Rome, by all the gods who have ever lived, I will give it you!"

The girl turned and looked at her mother, who simply nodded. This is the moment she had been waiting for, planning for, hoping for. Salome knew what was required. "I desire that you give me here at once on a platter of polished silver..." she spoke in soft, sensual tones but so all could hear, pausing for dramatic effect, "the severed head of John the Baptist!" This she demanded with a flourish, as though she had actually asked for half the kingdom.

Despite the wine-induced redness in his face and the heat of his evil passion, Herod paled. He would have preferred she ask for half the kingdom. This he had not expected. Although he had once considered John's execution, his thoughts toward the prophet had changed. He was no longer minded to do this. Herod rose slowly from the cushions. But he had sworn. In front of all these Galilean nobles he had sworn to give this girl anything she wanted. This had become political. He could not now refuse her. His guests looked at him in amused anticipation. As if by magic, the chief of the bodyguard appeared as though expected to be summoned. *The witch is well prepared,* he thought. He waited, not wanting to do this but seeing no escape. At length, he nodded his head to the guard who thereupon left the room.

αΘω

The scene in the prison was quick and merciful. The guard was met by the massive jailer. "It is time," he said in quiet rectitude.

The jailer's eyes fell. Massive man though he was, brutal though his reputation, he had no stomach for this. The blood he had shed in the arena seemed as nothing compared to what he knew he had to do. "Is there no other way?"

"None," said the guard. "Place his head on this," handing him the gleaming platter.

"Oh, my God, no," responded the jailer rolling his eyes. Whereupon he cried, "Baptist! Prepare to meet your God!"

αΘω

Footsteps falling on the polished marble in the corridor. Herod glanced at the entranceway hoping that it would not be, yet at the same time wishing it were, over. The guard entered the room with John's head rocking gently in a pool of blood on a silver platter. Salome's self-assured countenance disappeared. She recoiled in horror. "Take it to her; I don't want it," she shrieked in disdain. "She's the one who wanted it." The child moaned and whimpered as if caught in the act of something she did wrong. The guard set the platter at the feet of her mother. Herodias, pleased that her plot had uncoiled so perfectly, raised her eyebrows with a trifling smile.

αΘω

When John's followers heard of his execution, they came and took his body and entombed it in a nearby cave. They left the prison with a new disciple, his tunic stained with the blood of the prophet. Together, they traveled a week on foot to Galilee, where they found Jesus teaching in the Synagogue of Tiberias, and told him. His reaction was somber. He stared as if in disbelief, his eyes weakening, tears welling. He then lowered his head and whispered, "Then it is done. It was only a matter of time." He looked at the man whose tunic was covered with the dried blood of his cousin. His eyes filled with compassion. Cupping his hand against the ear of the man and holding his massive head with the other, he whispered words no one could hear. In realizing the import of these whispered words, the terrible enormities of his life eviscerated of evil, the old gladiator wept.

The life and ministry of John the Baptist, in contrast with the Hebrew prophets of old, were extremely brief, as were, of course, the life and ministry of Jesus. While these ancient prophets had a lifetime of service to God, into the abbreviated work of our Lord was packed the unfolding of mankind's redemption, indeed, the redemption of the whole of creation. The lives of the patriarchs and prophets were, in most cases, filled with the issues of living, of wives and children. Not so with Jesus and John. What, one wonders, were their expectations of life and ministry? Their lives were filled with followers and friends, but when life on earth ended, they were both hardly into their thirties.

Jesus then withdrew to a solitary place to assuage his grief.

XIII

John Mark

Smoke from burning wicks hung low in the room creating a not unpleasant odor for the celebration going on beneath the candlelight. Moonlight had cast its beams over Genessaret's wavelets and waned, then waxed its silver path again since the tragic execution of John the Baptist. Grief still haunted our hearts when thoughts of his lonely vigil in the dungeons of Herod assaulted the mind. It struck me as a terrible irony that this man who had successfully resisted sensual temptation had been so cruelly slain by it.

The disciples had returned after being away for two months preaching, teaching and being a considerable nuisance, as Jesus had instructed them. An excited, charged ambiance reflected the inordinate joy in the heart of each man. Especially Jesus. They made him laugh as they regaled him with stories of events that took place in their respective adventures. They seemed energized and, at the same time, exhausted. The celebration and the storytelling subsided into a quiet, satisfied silence. "You have done a wondrous thing, brothers. I am proud of you. You have worked long and hard, and it seems you had little comfort along the way. I think it's time for a holiday, what do you think? What do you think of taking a little time away in the mountains to relax and reflect on where we go from here? What do you say?"

"Just us?" asked James, "and you?"

"Yes, just us. I think we are all due." The men flushed with pleasure at the thought of some quiet time away with Jesus alone. What a time of refreshment that would be! As much as they were energized by ministry, the enormous needs of the flocks of people were exhausting. Sometimes it seemed there was little time even to eat. So Jesus took them by boat from Tiberias due North, to a remote place he knew near the village of Bethsaida.

The solace they sought, however, would prove elusive. When they arrived at the place where they were supposed to be alone, a place with rolling green hills, springs and trees, they were greeted by an awesome throng of people. How had they known? How had they deduced where Jesus and his men would disembark? How had they even known that he and his disciples were coming by boat from Tiberias?

Among them were many who were sick and infirm, brought there by caring friends and relatives. They looked at Jesus and the rest of us with anticipation, hoping, praying that they would be noticed; that somehow, they might find a way to be healed of the misery they had endured for most of their lives.

Jesus was, as usual, deeply moved. What a sight they made! Like wandering sheep without a shepherd. God help them! The tiredness forgotten, he welcomed them with compassion and began to speak to them of the Father's love and the special peace of knowing him. As Jesus moved among the crowd, touching this person and that, he healed each one. It was a beautiful thing to watch. The air seemed charged with immense power. Whatever our expectations of solitude and retreat, we were once again invigorated. So we, too, moved among the crowd, encouraging, touching, healing and blessing. Have you any notion of what it is like to see leprous lesions yield fresh, new tender skin with the touch of your hand? The smile on a child's face as a cleft palate closes and heals? The moment was one of magic and enchantment in that remote part of the mountains around Galilee alone with Jesus—and thousands of people.

αΘω

Then I saw him. He could have easily been mistaken for anyone in the crowd of nameless faces, yet he was singular, set apart. A young man, maybe eighteen, perhaps younger, yet he had a countenance about him that stood out from the rest, a bearing that marked him as a person of consequence, eyes of intelligence and inquiry. I might have passed on, thinking little of the moment, except that his eyes followed me and I could not help but return his gaze, however uncomfortable it felt. Introduction, it seemed, was inevitable.

I stepped over to where he stood. "I am Joseph," I ventured, "often of late, called Justus." I held out my hand in greeting.

"I am John, son of Mary. I am often called Mark." How odd, I thought, that he would refer to himself as the son of his mother, rather than his father. Perhaps there was intrigue to this.

"What brings you here today, young John Mark?"

"I wish to inquire of the Master, the Lord, our Messiah." Lord? Messiah?

How could he know this? Certainly the rumor mill had been at work concerning Jesus, but this young man seemed so certain, so sure.

"What, may I ask, is the nature of your inquiry?"

"I was among those in the synagogue in Tiberias. I came by foot to this place."

"Did you know that we were coming here?"

"Yes. I heard it mentioned before you embarked." I wondered who could have mentioned it. Even I did not know where we were going when we stepped into the boat. I was about to ask who had told him of our destination when he said, "I spoke to others of your arrival here, hence this great assembly." Fascinating! We could not have hired someone who would have provoked a crowd like this.

"Come," I said, "I will introduce you to Jesus." When the boy stepped before Jesus he knelt on one knee and lowered his head.

"Gentle Rabbi, my name is..."

"I know who you are, my son." The young man raised his head and looked into the face of his Master. Jesus placed his hand on the boy's head. "Stand, John Mark. You are well-named, for you shall be my warrior of grace." The boy's face flushed with pleasure. "You are young, but like David before Goliath, you shall conquer. You shall be a right arm for the Father."

This seemed a strange prophecy for such a youth, yet I did not doubt it for a heartbeat. Jesus could see in this young man a greatness that others missed. It made me wonder if he sees the same in me or in others. No one knows the steps God plans for him. One may plan, but one cannot determine what God has planned, or where his steps may be guided. This boy, however complimented he felt at Jesus' praise and prophecy, could not have known what lay ahead for him.

That he would become the traveling companion of Barnabas, Paul, Luke and the others; that his mother's home would become the center of the church in Jerusalem; that Peter would be directed to that home upon his angelic release from prison, and that he would put to pen the life and ministry of Jesus were, to his mind, not a part of this moment. He was just a boy. The Master, before whom he stood, knew and with that knowledge, blessed him. Though he could not know it now, his life and work would stand unique and apart from Matthew, Luke and John, and even Paul. The latter was in serious error regarding this boy as he himself, later in his life, found out.

"Now go, John Mark, and let life be your teacher. Learn from your experiences and do not allow your time to be unfocused or disengaged. You are becoming a man of great destiny." Jesus embraced him. "Now be off with you."

The boy backed away, caught somewhere between the great joy imparted by Jesus' words and his intense desire to stay with us. His face contorted with joy and disappointment, he turned and strode away. We watched for a moment. He stopped, turned and looked back at Jesus. His face then creased with a broad grin, and jumping into the air and pumping his fist toward the sky he shouted, "Hallelujah!" Then amongst infectious laughter, he disappeared into the crowd.

Now, many years later, it is reported that John Mark is in Egypt. Alexandria, I believe.

XIV

World's Biggest Dinner

Philip stood beside Jesus surveying the scene. Evening approached and the people milled about conversing in soft but excited tones. One could sense the tension among them. Jesus turned to Philip and said, "They are hungry, and the day is almost gone. They must be fed. What do you think we should do?" I believe Jesus knew all along what he would do. While I have seen him ask questions of people, apparently ignorant of the answer until they gave it, I have never seen him caught by surprise or unprepared for any eventuality. Philip, on the other hand, took the question seriously. His concern was real and, as was customary with Philip, that of a consummate pragmatist.

"It would take more than a year's wages to feed a crowd like this."

Andrew, Peter's brother, overheard the question, and Philip's response. He remarked, "Here is a boy with…let's see, five barley loaves and a couple of fish." He looked at the other two with an impish smile. He was being funny. Jesus laughed. Philip rolled his eyes.

At this point Peter with the others who had not been privy to this exchange came near and observed, "This is a remote place, Lord, and it's already getting late. Send the crowds away, so they can go to the villages and buy food. There is nothing to eat here."

Jesus replied, "They do not need to go to the village, Peter. You feed them!"

"Perhaps you did not hear, Lord. There is no food here. And the crowd is growing restless with hunger," Peter responded with some exasperation.

The child grinned and held up his basket to Peter, more than willing to be of service. The old fisherman managed a fatherly smile and flashed a pleading glance at Jesus. The boy's hair, somewhere between brown and blond, hung ragged and rough-cut just below his ears. His eyes sparkled blue with intelligence.

Jesus held out his hand, "Come here, son. Let's see what you have in that basket." He lifted the soft napkin which covered the food and peered inside. "How many fish did you say you have?"

"Two, sir." he said to Jesus.

"Then how came there to be three?" The incredulous child stepped closer to see for himself. There were three fish, not two. He looked at Jesus. "Mother said she put two smoked fish in there, ready to eat."

"I see, but there are three smoked fish," said Jesus. "Surely she was mistaken."

"My mother? Make a mistake?" The boy obviously thought that unlikely.

"How many fish are in the basket?" asked Jesus again, smiling.

At that moment his mother appeared. "Joash, are you bothering the Master?"

"Mother," said the boy, "You said you put two fish in my lunch!"

"Come now, son. You have caused enough trouble..."

"No, mother," said Jesus. "Joash is no trouble at all, and he is quite right. There are more than two fish in his lunch."

His mother took the lunch from the child and removed the napkin. The count of fish was now four. The loaves were six. The basket was full. The boy's mother looked at Jesus. Her hands, and the basket they held, began to tremble. She fell to her knees before him. He laughed again, took her hand and raised her to her feet. He took the basket and said to her, "All those here thank you, good woman, for the lunch, and for raising such a generous son." He then turned to the disciples, "Peter," he commanded, "you, Philip and the others—have everyone group together in companies of fifty with aisles in between so that you may distribute freely."

"Distribute what, Master?"

"Just do it, Peter, and do not delay." Tightening his lips in exasperation, the apostle did as he was told.

The grass on the hillside was soft, green and inviting. There was minimal confusion as everyone arranged themselves as Jesus had said and sat down. As sparks fly from a snapping campfire, word of what was happening spread rapidly. Lively anticipation stirred among them, especially those with hungry children.

αΘω

Jesus took the lad's lunch and looked toward the sky. "Thank you, Father," he said, "for your abundance." Then turning to the apostles and the other followers he said, "Find every empty basket, carton and crate you can find. Bring them and spread them here before me." Baskets of all shapes and sizes began to appear before him. Jesus plunged his hand into the child's basket and from it extracted quantities of bread and smoked fish. The baskets before him began to fill. As soon as one filled, another took its place. The apostles and disciples hurried to each company of fifty (there were almost four hundred) and passed the baskets to a leader who distributed to the rest. People began to talk loudly and shout. Much laughter and praising God. The air was charged with excitement. Not a few recalled the hail of manna upon Israel in the wilderness.

It took some time to get them all served, and by the time they were done, the afternoon sun was nearing the horizon. People were lounging about, full and satisfied. Several spokesmen came to the disciples and said, "Tell the Master that there is more food here than we can possibly eat. What shall we do with what remains?"

When this message was passed to Jesus, he said, "We are not yet done. Now gather up the leftovers that nothing be lost." So they went about retrieving leftover food. A fish here, an unbroken loaf there. When all were finished, it took twelve baskets to contain all of the broken pieces that were left—all from one boy's lunch.

"That nothing be lost..." Then Jesus said to the apostles, "There are twelve of you, and there are twelve baskets of food. It will remain fresh for a while. Long enough for you to take it to the homes of impoverished and hungry families. Now therefore go, take it to them, that they hunger no more, and give as it has been given to you."

XV

Walk on Water

Zeal out of control creates fanatics. So it was with a small, abrasive and aggressive band of men that had been following Jesus' movements. "Isn't this man the Prophet who is coming into the world!?" they ranted. They knew well the politics of swaying a crowd. And Jesus represented a new leader capable of things others had not represented. It was in their mind to incite the huge crowd and march all the way from Galilee to Jerusalem, demanding that he be made king. Had they succeeded, their ambitious intent may indeed have caused a revolt throughout the region.

Jesus perceived their ambitions and readily saw the threat it represented not only to his purpose but also to his disciples and himself. Fanaticism, once unleashed, is so volatile it can easily devour its own in a moment. Something had to be done swiftly.

"Peter!" he shouted. Among us, Peter had become the apparent second in command. Jesus depended on him to lead us when he could not. "Things are getting out of hand. Find a boat quickly and take our people to the other side of the lake. I'll meet you there." The issue of just how Jesus might do that was never given thought.

"Lord," Peter responded, "I am not going to leave you alone with these people. They might..."

"Peter, do not argue! Go! They will not harm me." And so, while Jesus dealt with the crowd, we got into a boat to go on ahead of him to the other side. At Jesus' admonishment, the mob surprisingly began to disperse, and as they did, he withdrew once more into the mountains by himself alone.

He found a solitary spot, and prayed well into the night. Wind howling through trees, Jesus pulled his robe tighter around him. I often wondered what Jesus prayed about at times like this. How does one pray in a cold wind? How does one pray when pressured and agitated? Did he have specific concerns? Or was it just a moment to touch his Father's face? A moment, perhaps, of nourishment and strength? It would be a good thing to know what went on between Father and Son at moments like this.

It was now dark and the sea was beginning to show whitecaps from the gale coming in from dark, gathering clouds in the distance. Even though the wind was stiff, the sky above remained clear, the moonlight scattered and flashing across dancing waves. Sail was struck, the oars came out and we began to row.

αΘω

I may certify you, we had all had enough of the stormy moods of Galilee. This time we were not dealing with the ferocity of our previous adventure, but it was enough to cause concern. Perhaps, after our previous experience, we were a bit touchy about storms. And, this time Jesus was not among us. Pounded by waves, we rowed into the teeth of the blow, each of us alone with our anxieties. Hours passed. It seemed we hardly moved. We were about three and a half miles from land halfway across the lake. With dawn only a few hours away, we were exhausted, bone-chilled and bone-tired. Backs and arms ached and headway seemed impossible.

Judas Iscariot was the first to notice. Eyes wide with fear, he lifted his arm and pointed with his finger. "Look!" he gasped. The boat tossed. Rowing stopped. The wind quickly turned the boat broadside and swept it away, rocking into the downwind waves. What we saw sent tremors of terror through each exhausted soul.

There was a man in the water. No! He was not in it, My God! He stood upon it! I gripped my oar as if to use it as a weapon, as if to ward off what appeared to be an apparition of sorts, a spirit of...

Thaddeus cried, "It's a spirit!" Fear of the spirit-world gripped most of us, who took mystical beings sometimes too seriously. We did not understand what or who they were. We were frightened because spirit activity was a relatively new thing. A few years ago, few people spoke of spirits. But in these last months, there seemed to be so much spirit activity. Evil spirits. They could do terrible things to people. And just as we were about to throw ourselves into the water and swim for it (inevitable drowning was given no thought), the spirit spoke to us...

"Calm down, men! It's just me!"

Jesus!...came to us, incredibly, strolling along on the surface of the water. And while waves tossed and sloshed, every place he put his foot was straight, firm and level. It was as if there were an unseen road buried just beneath the surface, unaffected by the waves.

He spoke in such a way that told us it could only be him. Our anxieties vanished and in their place, thunderous amazement.

αΘω

Peter, exploding with his laughable, impulsive exuberance, shouted back, "Lord, if it is you, let me come to you on the water." And thus I learned why Peter became our leader. He was magnificent! Bursting with ripping courage none of us had! In his mind, there were no precautionary steps. He took risks. He took no careful consideration of possible consequences; all he needed was an affirmation from his Lord. All he needed was trust, and he had it—at least for the moment—the rest of us had none at all. Sometimes this is just the precise and requisite requirement of leadership.

"Then come ahead, man," Jesus responded. We were astounded. None of us moved. None of us, of course, except Peter. We envied his bravado, or whatever it was that drove him. I guess we forgot that we had just seen Jesus feed thousands of people from a boy's small lunch or, of even greater significance, we had witnessed him turn these very storm-driven waves into calm waters. Had we thought about it, had we realized its significance, we all would have joined Peter—perhaps. We might have frolicked among the white water licking at our knees, never fearing its peril.

Of course, we would not have dared venture out into the waves expecting them to harden beneath our feet, but Peter jumped out of the boat and, amazingly, the water was as firm as cobbled pavement. In this act of simple faith and trust, Peter turned the ridiculous into the sublime. There he was! There is our brother, Peter, standing on the water, just like Jesus! Peter was no stranger to boats rocking in the waves. His sea-legs were as good as, if not better than, any man's. So he stood upright, swayed a bit and then ventured a few steps toward Jesus. Then he stopped, exhilarated, his eyes wide with excitement, and turned to look at us as if to invite us to join him, or just to say, "Hey brothers! Look! Look at me. The old sea-dog still has it in him!" But the water, however capable of supporting his weight, was still wet and slippery. Waves heaving, a gust of wind almost knocked him down. Suddenly, his eyes widened and the "reality" of his situation started to sink in. His balance faltered as the wind whipped his beard into his face. Then, suddenly, his foot slips and he topples into the water with a resounding splash and disappears beneath the foam. It could only have been an instant or two before he bounced to the surface sputtering and sucking for breath. Now Simon Peter was a strong swimmer. So one can only surmise what caused him to cry out to Jesus, "Lord, help!"

Instantly Jesus reached out his hand and caught him, "Ha!" Jesus actually laughed teasingly at him. “Peter the Rock! You live out your name! Will you now sink like a stone?”

It would have been amusing had we not all been in a mild panic. We looked on with some consternation at our brother’s embarrassment. He had played the fool yet again and was getting his deserts. Pulling Peter up to the firm surface and steadying him, Jesus looked at us, lined up against the gunnels grinning like monkeys, watching with intense curiosity and some apprehension at the scenario playing out before us. “Come, great fisherman!” said he, “You who are the only one in the boat with courage enough to come out on the water!” Peter’s fortitude and faith must have impressed Jesus, as our lack of the same must have dis-impressed him. We stopped grinning. “How is it then,” he chided, “that you are so afraid to get wet? How could one such as you have doubted?”

Jesus put his arm around Peter’s shoulders as they walked the distance, arm in arm to the boat, and when they came alongside, the wind abruptly died. We were so excited to welcome them that we didn’t even notice the wonder of the thing. We were confused and so filled with exhilaration that we could only say to him, “Truly, Lord, you are the Son of God!”

“If I am who you say, how is it you all acted so cowardly? How is it that none of you followed your brother Peter? No doubt this story will be told again, repeatedly, in the days to come. But I venture that few will emphasize Simon’s faith and courage. As men will do, he will be criticized for falling into the water. I am not pleased with such assessments, nor am I pleased with grinning over the gunnels at the expense of your brother.”

The rebuke stung. But what he said was true. In the years to come whenever I would hear this story told, it was invariably told with emphasis in the wrong place—on Peter and his failure, not on his courage or our cowardice! Herein I learned, hopefully, we all learned, that it is better to take risks, to launch out in faith, even if it appears we are destined to fail, than not to launch out at all.

αΘω

Suddenly, unexpectedly, the boat jarred as if it had struck something hard. It had. We awoke out of our bewilderment and realized that we had reached land. The bottom of the boat rested on the beach. We were at Gennesaret. How had this happened? The sails were struck. We were not rowing. We were in the middle of the lake and now we were here. Perhaps we misjudged?

The sky turned from grey to a brightening blue as the sun ascended, erupting like fire from the eastern mountains. Air currents swirled softly around us. Fishermen who early tended their nets stood round about, gazing at us in curiosity. Some recognized Jesus and sent word to the countryside. In a few hours, it all started again. Crowds of people bringing their sick and begging to touch the edge of his robe. All who did were healed.

αΘω

We stayed a few days in Gennesaret and then made our way back across the sea to Capharnaum. Sight of the familiar town ahead brought warm smiles to our faces. Joanna was not only a good cook; her knack for making things comfortable made staying at Peter's home an experience to look forward to.

The next morning Peter took a little time to fish, which unfailingly lifted his spirits and recharged his humor. That afternoon he walked in the house carrying a basket of fish, full to the brim. "The fragrance of the flowers in Joanna's garden may sweeten the house, but deep down, I know you all prefer the smells of fresh roasting fish. Here's dinner," he smiled as Joanna greeted him. He handed her the basket. "I cleaned 'em, you cook 'em."

Peter's uncomplicated, spontaneous and sometimes surly temperament kept us all on our toes, but we knew we could depend on him to handle things. And we knew where he stood; he always made that clear. It was this kind of openness and genuineness that Jesus valued in others.

XVI

The Impossible Contradiction

People followed Jesus for many reasons. Some were intrigued by his miracles, others were eager to hear and follow his teaching and some were just plain curious about this person who had created such a ruckus. I, also, was very impressed by all of these things, but mostly I loved him because, being who he was and all, he was so incredibly…human. Now here is a man who clearly demonstrated his divinity for all to see. He is not just a god like the ephemeral Roman and Greek gods; he embodied everything that we understood God, the Father, to be.

One cannot be the same as God without also being God, and he was that. The Father could not express himself any better than in his Son, this Jesus of Nazareth. Yet this, this God is living and doing what God does in a human body. Who could give witness to his humanity more than those of us who were with him day and night? We watched him trim his fingernails, wash his face, eat his dinner and heard him snore. We had also seen him perform miracles and change people in ways that only God could do. It could be said that we had an agenda, that we were prejudicial, but no one knew him better than we did; and we knew by this time who he was… the Son of God, the Messiah, God with us. What an anomaly! What an impossible contradiction!

Yet this incredibly divine Jesus is not too different from me. He was cold, he was warm; he was hungry, he was full; he was tired, he was energetic. He could get irritable, and he was uncommonly sensitive to the needs of others. I'm not too good with this last, but all the rest is very much a part of normal human life. My life. I like that. His being God, the very fact that he is also so human is my point of contact with him. In him is built a bridge between the Infinite and the finite. What a magnificent, loving anomaly!

Another thing that makes me love him is his almost comical aversion to religious pretense. It would be truly amusing if devotion to law weren't so serious or its cause so sinister. I remember when some law teachers came from Jerusalem and asked, "Why do your disciples break the tradition of the elders? They don't wash their hands before they eat!" Jesus almost couldn't suppress his mirth.

These people do not eat unless they give their hands a ceremonial washing, which is, of course, the tradition of the elders. When they come from the marketplace, they do not eat unless they wash. They seem to enjoy making great show of the ritual washing of cups, pitchers and kettles. These things had become "God's standards" for them. What noxious rubbish! We always washed up before meals, but in all my time with Jesus, from the time we all flocked around John the Baptist to this very day, I have never once seen him participate in this kind of mindless ceremony.

αΘω

I understand now that these things were intended to teach Abraham's children, to teach everyone, that adherence to such ceremony and Law alone was a hopeless dead end. A worthless exercise in religious pretense. Jesus helped us see that in the things he said and in the things he did. Only in love do we reflect the true character of Jehovah God.

Jesus' response to these men expressed that very thing: "And why do you break the command of God for the sake of your absurd tradition? In doing this, you nullify the word of God! You see what you want to see and select from the Scripture those parts that best serve your evil purposes. Your hearts are utterly void of compassion toward those who need you most—and you do it all in the name of the Father. Let me tell you that in doing these things you alienate God. You do not draw close to him. The Father has no interest at all in your traditions."

"You insufferable hypocrites! Isaiah was speaking of you when he said,

> *'These people honor me with their lips, but their hearts are far from me. They worship me in vain; their teachings are but rules taught by men.'*

That old prophet was right about you!"

Later that day, over lunch, Peter said, "Well you've done it again, Lord."

"Done what?"

"Don't you know that these legalists were offended? They are furious with you now."

Dear Peter. He could be such a monumental ass at times. I suppose Peter considered Jesus reckless. But Jesus was accustomed to this. People questioning the consequence of his words didn't seem to bother him too much. He was relentless, giving no quarter, no apology. "That's what I do, Simon," said he, meeting Peter with a challenging gaze. "Their fury is evidence that I have spoken the truth. Offense is what I intend. Leave them to themselves."

XVII

The Howling Woman

I am Justus. I am a Jew. A son of Abraham, Isaac and Jacob. An Israelite in whom, unlike my friend Nathaniel, there is considerable artifice and duplicity. My forebear was among the greatest of our Jewish ancestors, none other than Joseph, ruler of Egypt and son of Jacob. As a Jew I have pondered what it means to be among God's "chosen" race. Jehovah-Jireh (The Lord provides, or The Lord sees) has been among us for so many years. Yet we know that he is not just our God. He is the God of all that exists, the earth, the sun, moon, sky and stars, as well as that which we cannot see. He is the God of all. Yet he has chosen a small race of people. He could just as easily have chosen a tribe of pygmies from the heart of Africa or the Mongols of Asia or some people from a distant new world in another time.

And as I ponder, I ask myself why? The answer to this question does not concern our ethical propriety, that we were somehow more deserving. A superficial glance at the history of our race demonstrates conclusively that we are not. Even Jacob (Israel) himself was a man of degenerate character. Abraham? Did he not attempt to prostitute his own wife?

So why indeed? The answer, I conclude, lies not in our merit, but in the purpose implicit in the question itself. God chose us to accomplish a mission. We are his chosen channel of communication to the nations of the earth to bear witness of his love and compassion. And so his Son. That he is the perfect expression of the Creator, that he is the Creator himself, is perfectly consistent with that purpose. So it is appropriate that he is a Jew. It could not be otherwise.

People wonder why God would send his Son to this earth among all the bodies of the universe? Why did he create man here instead of somewhere else among the stars? He had to start somewhere. Why not here? He had to use some nation, some group of people. Why not us? And let there be no mistake: The reason we Jews exist is that we are to be God's vessel of love to the nations, the whole of mankind. We are privileged to be a marker, a waypoint, a sign for the world's inhabitants to know that he loves them. This was made abundantly clear to me the next morning.

We had journeyed northwest into the higher elevations near the borders of Tyre, the capital city of Phoenicia; a special freshness was in the air, bearing a salt edge blowing in from the Great Sea to the west. As on other occasions, Jesus did not want anyone to know we were here. We stayed for several days in the home of Elkanah, a cousin of Peter, who seemed glad to see us. The place was comfortable, almost built, it seemed, for the very purpose of retreat and refreshment in the back valleys of the hills. Elkanah knew the value of privacy and quiet. He lived every day of his life this way. It was a perfect place for the rest and seclusion Jesus sought. However, his desire to keep it all secret, to be hidden away in this quiet Eden, was frustrated yet again.

On the morning in question, as we had just breakfasted, we noticed through the window a woman standing in the grass which surrounded Elkanah's home. She had been there each day, crying and clearly waiting for Jesus to come out. We could tell by her dress that she was not Jewish, no doubt a native Phoenician. Her features looked Greek. We Jews are raised with terrible prejudice. For a race so selected by God to be his instrument to all men, we are a self-absorbed, churlish lot. This woman by her accident of birth was to us worse than a Samaritan.

When Jesus at length went out to her, she fell at his feet and wailed, "Have pity on me Lord, Son of David. Have pity on my daughter. She is sorely afflicted with an evil disease." Lord? Son of David? How came this woman from a gentile nation to know who he is? How came she to be aware of his Jewish ancestry or even the knowledge of the great king she had named?

Here, I thought Jesus did a most curious thing. He reached out and laid his hand on her shoulder as if to comfort her, but he answered her not a word, apparently ignoring her. Turning to us, he raised his eyebrows as if asking, "What do you think I should do?" Typically, we readily volunteered, "Dismiss her! She has been howling around here since we arrived."

Howling? thought Jesus incredulously. Then he spoke to the woman, "I think my friends would have you believe that I was sent only to the lost sheep of the house of Israel."

The woman, utterly ignorant of why Jesus was sent, appealed to him, begging him even more intensely, "Lord, help me!" she cried.

Jesus withdrew from her, distant, aloof, as if this whole scene were distasteful to him. He said with some sarcasm, some would even say contempt, "I am sorry, madam, but we wouldn't want to take the children's bread and throw it to the house dogs." He looked at us, raising an eyebrow. "Would we, gentlemen?" His gaze was weary, as though expecting the usual disdain. The woman was not sure of what Jesus was saying or doing. She had felt the warm assurance of his hand on her shoulder, yet she was afraid of his words. Still, the way he looked at the disciples made it seem as if his words did not carry the brutality of their obvious meaning. It was then that it struck me precisely what Jesus was doing. He was speaking not to her, but to us, his own disciples! *He had known all along what he would do for this suffering woman.* And in the process he wanted us to see our own poverty of spirit, our own demonized attitudes and the insipid paucity in our own self-righteousness.

Suddenly her eyes brightened. It appeared to dawn on her exactly what Jesus was doing as well, for with shimmering delight, she said to him, *"Oh, yes, Lord! For even the house dogs eat of the children's crumbs that fall from the master's table."*

Then Jesus laughed, delighted, and said to her, "Yes! My dear sister, how great is your faith! Your request is granted. It is more than granted!" Then with palpable tenderness, "Go, dear woman, and reclaim your daughter. The disease has left her already." Her eyes widened. Her hands embraced her face with wonder. She could not speak. She merely backed away from Jesus, turned and ran away. A report came back that when she arrived home, she found her child lying in bed, gently asleep. The evil illness was gone.

αΘω

On that day, I learned that the finger of God, through a righteous Jew, could heal the terrible miasma of the whole world.

On that day, I learned that the purpose, the intent of Jesus, was not to make kings and priests of Jews; but his purpose, his intent, was love and compassion for all who need him. He set no value on Jewish precedence.

I also learned that this poor woman's suffering was not a device set upon her by God. This is a very wrongheaded view of the ugly things that happen in life. God does not afflict in order to heal. Nor does he disguise his loving thoughts and purposes in order to bring about some moral or spiritual effect in us. He does not need such prankish means; nor does he use them.

On that day, erroneous perspectives were adjusted both for me and my colleagues. Our understanding of God and his compassion was deepened, our faith strengthened and our hearts were enlarged, because we had witnessed him in action, in the person of his Son.

XVIII

Peripatetic Teacher

Jesus never stopped moving. His itinerant wanderings brought him south and east from Tyre, down to the Sea of Galilee and into the Decapolis, a region of ten cities east of Galilee and the Jordan River. Once I asked him why he moved about so much, why he didn't just settle in any one of the dozens of homes that would eagerly welcome him (the homes Peter, or John, or even Lazarus came to mind) and live there. People would still come to him. He could conduct his ministry with a greater sense of stability and peace.

"Peace?" he said to me. "Do you not think I have peace, Joseph?"

I knew instantly that I had made a fool of myself. No man had more peace and serenity of spirit than did Jesus. Perhaps I was thinking of myself. It was I who was weary of all this scurrying about. The small of my back ached and my feet were constantly sore. I can't count how many times I wished he would stop and stay in one place.

αΘω

We weren't in this region long, of course, before they started to come. A deaf man, who like most so afflicted could barely make himself understood, was brought to him. His words were indistinct and nasal. Those with him begged Jesus to touch the man and heal him. I suppose they were his relatives or friends. Jesus took him aside, away from the crowd, and we watched an amazing thing. He put his fingers into the man's ears. Then he spit and touched the man's tongue. He looked up to heaven and with a deep sigh spoke a single word, "Ephphatha!" (Aramaic for, "be opened").

Instantly the man cupped his hands over his ears as if to stop the noise. Then slowly he removed them and looked at Jesus with eyes of wonder and worship. He opened his mouth and spoke in a plain, distinct baritone, "You are he that should come. You are Messiah!" The words were deep and resonant, clear and beautiful.

"Do not tell anyone about this," Jesus told the man. I don't know why Jesus said such things. The more he told this to those he healed, the more they talked about it. He wanted to keep a low profile, yet he could not but do good wherever it was needed.

Onlookers were stunned. "Is there anything he can't do?" they said. Yet the remarkable thing to me was how he merely spoke the word and healing followed. Sometimes he healed without so much as being present, but with this man and a few others he employed machinations like these.

Thus did I think of the process of miracle working. How to explain this? Did his power to heal change with the severity of the illness? Did it reflect the possibility that his power to heal was affected by how tired he may be at the moment? By his mood? How came this man who calms the sea and the wind with one word to go through an apparently meaningless ritual to bring about healing? It did not seem to depend on the faith of the one being healed, yet he often said that their faith had a part. Perhaps he meant that the faith necessary to come to him precipitated the healing in itself. Yet others obviously had no faith at all—either before or after the healing. Why did Jesus use his fingers and saliva? I confess, I do not know. Perhaps it doesn't matter. Why did he take this man aside from the crowd? I don't know that it is written anywhere that he is required to do it the same way every time. He can do it any way he wants.

αΘω

We continued along the shores of the Sea of Galilee for awhile, and then Jesus ascended a grassy slope and sat down. Once again, incessantly, relentlessly, they began to come, a great multitude bringing the lame, the blind, the speechless, the maimed—people who by some terrible accident or torture had lost limbs and appendages and a host of others. He healed them all. He turned not even one away. The crowds, understandably, were captivated by what they witnessed. One might come to accept the healing of a blind person or the hearing of another. But to see new limbs form where there were none was more than reason could bear. To hear a man speak distinct, articulate words with a tongue that had before been cut out! There it was! It could not be denied. It happened before the eyes of all. And all present, without a single exception, glorified God. We, too, could do nothing else!

XIX

Walking Trees

So, what to make of these things? It was clear to even the thickest mind that Jesus was who he said he was—the Son of God, although he kept referring to himself as the Son of Man. Yet the routine events of the life we all lived virtually precluded our absorption of these facts. It seemed for most of us that the miraculous nature of the things Jesus did was almost to be expected. Commonplace. To be considered among the things of life as it should be.

After we had eaten, Jesus dispersed the crowd and we all went home. They to the various towns and communities from which they came; we back to the shores of Galilee, to Capharnaum, to the warm hospitality of Joanna and Peter. There we spent the night.

We slept later than usual. The sun had risen over the lake, light danced across the ripples. The morning smelled fresh with promise. Then we heard them. A group of Pharisees and Sadducees approached and gathered around Jesus like a swarm of mosquitoes hovering in a swamp, waiting to draw blood.

"Show us a sign from heaven," they demanded. "We understand you've become quite good at it." They enjoyed baiting Jesus, asking questions just to see how he would react. They had no real interest in the answers he gave other than the hope that he might make himself look foolish. They never learned. Instead of Jesus embarrassing himself, it was they who were inevitably embarrassed.

"Oh 'Wise Ones,' how foolish you are! In your religious arrogance, you've become frauds and bigots. You strut and make a show of great powers with your weather predictions, as though they were signs of great wisdom. And then you attempt to use these 'signs' to impress and control the lives of others. You are demented, blind imposters! How is it that you cannot see what even the simplest of men know? How is it that you do not see the presence of God in your midst, that you do not see the clear signs of something of far more consequence than the weather?

Jesus then turned and walked away, leaving them wide-eyed and indignant.

αΘω

We got directly into the boat and headed again for the comfort of Peter and Joanna's home. Good conversation, good company.

Jesus rose early the next morning, as was his custom, and accompanied Peter down to the waterfront. Gentle waves slapped the piers of the dock. In no time Peter had his nets readied for a morning of fishing. "Coming with me, Master? Should be a great day for musht, sardines and biny."

"You go on ahead, Simon" Jesus responded. "I think I'll take some time here." Peter knew better than to argue. Moreover, he respected Jesus' need for private time. He and his colleagues set sail and soon the boat was a speck on the horizon.

Jesus wandered for a time among the boats, nets and cursing sailors of the fishing fleet, the dog trotting contentedly at his feet. Abishag loved these trips to the docks. Jesus would often throw a stick into the water, which she'd swim out to get, and bring it back and then vigorously shower him with water. Then she'd drop the stick at his feet, fix it to the earth with one paw as if to tease him and, hunching down, wait for him to take it from her and throw it. Again and again he'd throw the stick; again and again she'd bring it back, enthralled with the game. This animal, this gift, brought such simple joy to Jesus. Always there, needing nothing, demanding nothing, offering much. They walked the shores together for a while, then turned home for breakfast.

αΘω

A few days later we could tell that Jesus was ready to move on. We gathered our belongings and headed for the lake. Once on the waterfront, Jesus stepped into Peter's boat. We all followed, and Andrew cast off. The sail raised, the brisk air biting our cheeks, the spray wetting our clothes; we felt good! What a great pleasure these moments were—the smell of the water, the loud conversation between men, Peter's shouting mariner's commands. It was wonderful! At moments like these, Jesus did not seem so godlike. He was one with us, one of us, laughing, enjoying the ecstasy of sailing with the rest of us.

After a couple of hours, we were at the shore across the lake. I am often amazed at the smallness of this lake we call a "sea." To sail from one side to the other in a brisk wind easily took less than two hours. After such a sail, we were all hungry for good bread and wine. Maybe a little cheese. But of course, plan-ahead thinkers that we were, we had forgotten to provision ourselves. We depended too much on the women for such things, I suppose.

αΘω

We came at last to Bethsaida, close by the sea; the smells of a fishing community filled the air with rich aromas. Fresh fruit from the market, bread baking, roasted fish. Within minutes we were filling our bellies.

We were not there long before it was known that Jesus had arrived, and soon after that, once again, as it seemed everywhere we went, they began to come. This time, some people brought a blind man and begged Jesus to touch him. It didn't take much begging. Jesus took the blind man by the hand and, placing it on his own arm, led him outside the village. This is the second time he has done this, I thought. So I followed, staying back so I would not interfere with whatever was going on between Jesus and this man. They made a fascinating spectacle. Jesus leading the blind man, telling him where to step, warning him of ruts and stones. The man held tightly to Jesus' arm at complete peace. I thought, what total confidence, what infinite pleasure to know, even though you are blind, that you are being led by him! And then as with the previous deaf man, he did a curious thing. He moistened the man's eyes with his saliva and asked, "Do you see anything?" Why was he doing it like this? Why didn't he just speak the word for the man to be healed? Why his spit? God willing, may he anoint my black heart with his spit!

The man raised his eyes and said, "I think I see people. They look like walking trees."

Once more Jesus put his hands on the man's eyes. When he removed them, his eyes opened; his sight restored. He saw clearly. Tears of joy cleansed the spit from his eyes, ran down his face and onto the ground. He covered his eyes with his hands and uncovered them again. Several times he repeated this. Each time more tears would flow.

I observed Jesus' expression as he healed people. This time was no different. He beamed at their joy. He was fulfilling his purpose, this was why he was with us, these were times when he felt the Father's omnipotence in himself. Jesus patted the man on the shoulder and said to him, "Go home now, but don't go into the village where people will notice you. Hold your words. They will all know in time."

I tried to stop the man, to speak with him. I wanted to know how he felt, what he was going to do. He merely paused, looked at me with flawless brown eyes and shook his head. "He asked me not to speak of this," he said, and then he left. Why? Why did Jesus try to conceal the good things he did? I did not understand.

The Fifth Scroll

Every Living Thing

And God said, "Let the water teem with living creatures, and let birds fly above the earth across the vault of the sky." So God created the great creatures of the sea and every living thing with which the water teems, according to their kinds, and every winged bird according to its kind. And God saw that it was good. God blessed them and said, "Be fruitful and increase in number and fill the water in the seas, and let the birds increase on the earth." And there was evening, and there was morning—the fifth day.

—Genesis 1:20-23 NIV

I

Tabernacles

"Our father would be grieved to see what has happened to us. It's not natural for the oldest son to leave his family as you have done, not to speak of creating such an enormous ruckus everywhere you go. We all know you are different, but I'm sure father would be terribly distressed over your controversial fame." Thus did Joseph, the youngest of them all, express the family's tension that had been building towards Jesus since their father's death.

"I thought by now that all of you understood. But you still misunderstand his expectations and undervalue his wisdom," said Jesus to his siblings. "He has known of me and believed in me since before my birth."

"Perhaps," from Judas, "but he always treated you and loved you as a son. He would have wanted you to lead us, not leave us. We are your family." The resentment they felt, the accusation of neglect stung Jesus. Clearly, they thought he was neglecting them, shutting them out of his life. "You and James both," Judas continued. "The three of us are left behind to tend the business and care for our mother."

He looked from one brother to the other, compassion and sadness in his eyes. "How is mother, and how is the business doing?" asked Jesus, trying to redirect their focus to his interest in and love for them.

"Mother is doing well, but she and your sisters miss you. As to the business, we have more than we can handle," said Simon with undisguised pride. "Doesn't give me even a moment to hunt." Jesus smiled. Simon was a good man, a hunter, a man's man. He looked more like his father than any of them. Sometimes Jesus longed to take bow in hand and go hunting again with Simon as he had done when both were younger...the smell of deep woods and mountain air. What sheer joy sitting still, quiet, waiting by a deer path for who knows what may come along! Jesus looked at his hands. The carpenter's calluses were gone. A feeling of discomfort flickered through his mind. There were moments like this when being the Messiah King seemed, well,...less real, less felicitous than simply working and living like other men...like his brothers. Then he thought of what he had done with the moneychangers in the Temple. It was the last time he had felt the warrior spirit that is in most men. He remembered the surge of raw and holy power when he commanded the legion of demons to leave those two tortured men. He remembered the other thousands of people who'd been helped and healed because he'd been true to his purpose. Such manhood, such a calling cannot be diminished.

His three brothers, Simon, Judas and Joseph, had arrived that day to visit with him and James. We left the five brothers to themselves as they reclined around the table in Peter's home. It was the month of Tishri, and the bite of the wind sent shivers of the approaching winter's cold.

αΘω

Colo shel Moed, the non-sacred half-holy days of the festive Feast of Tabernacles! Five day's journey away, foreign pilgrims from distant countries again thronged the streets of Jerusalem, their contributions swelling the Temple coffers. What was it about this strange, beautiful city that attracted the Jewish faithful from as far away as the banks of the Danube or Asiatic India, from Italy and Spain with unusual costumes bringing refreshing color to its otherwise drab and dusty streets? This City Jerusalem, this City of Solemnities, this City of Palaces, this City of Beauty and Glory welcomed each one and all. Staring at one another in awe and novelty, residents, near-residents from Galilee, and foreigners exchanged pleasantries enough to enhance the flow of money and ideas. They thought each other curiously odd, yet not unattractive. For many pilgrims, their long-coveted presence in this city represented the realization of fondest dreams since being told stories of it in childhood. It was the home and fountainhead of holiest thoughts and highest hopes. It gave an inward sense of victory to many who had, under Roman persecution, felt vanquished. Being here, in this city, converted victimization into anticipated triumph. What a remarkable feast, this "Tabernacles!"

Pilgrims indeed, coming not during the winter for Passover, lest their way be imperiled by snow and freezing weather through the mountain passes, nor yet even in the heat of summer for Pentecost, lest they faint through these same passes. But in the delicious cool of early autumn, they came. As preparation for this particular annual feast, crops of vintage grapes had been harvested years before, crushed, strained and fermented into quality wine. Colors of red and gold had begun to tint the leaves which, when they had said their piece, fell swirling to the feet of the tree they had nourished. Shadows of the marble, gold and cedar wood Sanctuary, standing high on Moriah's mountain, now only a symbol of the wondrous Shekinah Presence of Him who was once the Holy One in the midst of Israel. *Shekinah!*...the word itself evoking the feminine aspect of the presence of God. Priestly hands held out at arm's length, palms facing downward, thumbs touching, the four remaining fingers on each hand forming the letter *Shin*, the emblem for El Shaddai. Fingers were then arranged to form a latticework of 'windows,' through which the Shekinah glory of the Lord would shine and bless the people. Smoke from burning, smoldering, sacrifices rose slowly in ever widening columns, hung in the air between the Mount of Olives and Mount Zion on which the Holy City sat. The chant of Levites followed by solemn responses of the Hallel were borne on the breeze, and the clear blast of the priests' silver trumpets awakened echoes far away. At night, these vast Temple buildings stood out, lighted by the great candelabras and the glare of the torches that burned in the Court of the Women; strange sounds of mystic hymns and dances came floating through the darkness. Well might Israel designate the Feast of Tabernacles as the Feast of all Feasts.

Lodging and hospitality to be sought and found, guests to be welcomed and entertained, all of the things required by the Feast to be readied. Tents had to be erected everywhere, in the courtyards and on the flat housetops, in the streets and squares converting Jerusalem into a tent-city to accommodate the lodging and entertainment for such a vast multitude. Only that fierce castle, Antonia, which frowned even higher above the Temple, was undecked by the festivities, a hateful garrison of Roman oppression with vulgar philosophies and non-Jewish customs, an unwanted anomaly within the fences of sacred buildings and religious ceremony.

On the night of the great Temple Illumination, dozens of Levites crowded the fifteen steps leading from the Court of Israel up to the Court of Women. Out of these stepped two priests with silver trumpets. When dawn brought the first crow of a cock, they blew a threefold blast as they climbed the steps. When they reached the tenth step, another threefold blast. And entering the Court of Women, still they sounded their trumpets as they moved toward the Beautiful Gate. Reaching the gate, abruptly they turned; facing westward toward the Holy Place, they repeated...

Our fathers who were in this place,
Turned their backs on the Sanctuary of Jehovah.
Their faces eastward, they worshiped the sun,
But we? Our eyes are towards Jehovah!
We are Jehovah's!
Our eyes are towards Jehovah!

αΘω

His brother, Judas, spoke for the rest. "You ought to leave Galilee and go to the feast in Jerusalem. Let your followers there see the miracles you do. It doesn't make sense that one who seeks fame stays in hiding and acts in secret. Since you insist on doing these things, go ahead; market yourself to the world."

They do not believe in me either, thought Jesus. "You misjudge me again, my brothers. I do not seek fame as you suggest; I seek the glory of him who sent me. His purpose is my mantle. Whatever I do, and whenever I do it, I do for him. The time is not right for me," he continued. "You may think any time is right, but the Jews don't hate you as they hate me, because I teach that what they do is evil." Abishag came and laid her head in his lap. He stroked it thoughtfully. "You go to the feast," he continued. "I will come later when the timing is right."

Having said this, he rose from the table and stepped outside, the dog at his heels. The green water beckoned to him. The shore was only a short walk away. Traversing the distance, he disrobed and, wearing only a loin cloth, waded into the Sea of Galilee and began to swim. He swam into the horizon until only a faint splashing could be observed from shore. His brothers watched after him. "He'll likely walk back," said Simon half in jest, half in quiet chagrin. They turned to leave. Abishag seated herself at the water's edge and, looking after her master, whined.

II

Jesus at the Temple

The Feast of Tabernacles plunged into its vitality, moved by unseen leverage, both stranger and local caught up in the flow of something larger than differences. Although he was not there among the crowds, in general there was widespread whispering about Jesus. Religionists watched for him muttering, "Where is that man?" Some said, "He is harmless." Others, "No, he deceives people." No one would publicly say anything good about him for fear of the priests and elders of the Jews.

Two days into the festivities, Jesus abruptly appeared, seemingly out of nowhere. He made his way through the dust-charged streets of Jerusalem. His presence galvanized the crowds. He strode confidently into the Temple courts, mounted a few steps and began to address them. Those present were amazed and offended at his presumed authority, at his command of himself. "How came this man to such learning and erudition having never formally studied?"

Arguments ensued. Shouting back and forth. Jesus responded aggressively, "My teaching is not my own! What you hear me speak comes directly from my Father.

"You are hypocritical and self-seeking. You lawyers who self-righteously advocate the standard of law, why do you wish to kill me? Moses gave you the law, yet not one of you keeps the law. Moses actually spoke of me, so why do you wish to kill me?"

αΘω

Some of the people of Jerusalem were aware of the threat to Jesus' life at this Feast of Tabernacles. They knew the religious authorities wished to see him dead. Yet here he was, speaking publicly—no one attempting to stop him. Some wondered if the authorities had actually concluded that he is the Messiah. Then others said, "But we know where this man is from. When Messiah comes, no one will know where he is from."

Then Jesus raised his voice and said, "You think you know me because you know where I grew up?" He paused for a moment. "But the truth is that you are completely ignorant. You have no notion of the place from which I came." His hearers looked at him strangely. Didn't he come from Nazareth? "I am not here on my own. I was sent! He who sent me is true, and you do not know him either. I know him. I know him because I AM from him."

At this, some in the crowd became enraged. How dare he make himself as God! Faces contorted, eyes bulged, much jostling and surging. Some gestured as though to seize him, but none laid a hand on him. His time, as he would put it, had not come. In the midst of all this violence and agitation, one thoughtful soul observed, "When the Christ comes, how can he do more miraculous things than this man?"

"Do not concern yourselves overmuch," Jesus continued. "I will be with you for only a short time longer, and then I go back to the one who sent me." Sharp contention. "You will look for me, but you will not find me. Where I am going, you cannot come."

"Yes, Prophet!" someone yelled. "Just where do you think you will go that we cannot find you?"

"To a place inaccessible to hearts of darkness."

Jesus' presence in the Temple and the things that he said were reported to the chief priests. Immediately they sent the Temple guards to arrest him. When they arrived, he was gone.

αΘω

Five days passed before Jesus appeared again. Finally, on the last and biggest day of the Feast of Tabernacles, Jesus stood once again on the Temple steps. The people gathered to hear him. There were many who hated him. But there were some who loved him and believed, even among the members of the ruling Jewish body, the Sanhedrin. Others were merely curious. To these assembled, Jesus cried in a loud voice, "If you are thirsty, come to me and drink. Believe in me and, as the Scripture says, 'out of you shall flow streams of living water.'"

"Streams of living water. Streams of living water." The words echoed around, reverberating off the walls and casements of the Temple, his voice powerful, clear and strong. This was not the voice of a confident, self-possessed twelve-year-old boy instructing wizened old men; this was a voice impossible to ignore, a voice that arrested the attention of all who heard it.

"Streams of living water," echoing one last faint time around the

perimeters of the Temple. The meaning of this escaped me until later when I learned that he had meant the Spirit. Those who believed were later to receive and understand the powerful presence of such water.

αΘω

With all the commotion surrounding Jesus in the Temple, the guards were sent by the chief priests to arrest him. They came arrayed in military costumes, impressive, intimidating. The crowd parted to make way. Surging to the front, they stopped. Jesus ceased speaking and looked at them. He said nothing to them directly and, after a brief pause, resumed his discourse. The soldiers stood as if transfixed, not knowing what to do and, therefore, doing nothing. In a few moments Jesus paused again, and again caught the eyes of their captain. Nothing. No movement to arrest. No arrest. At length, the captain turned and with low-voiced command took his cohort and returned empty-handed to the priests. "Why didn't you bring him?" they demanded. The guards looked at one another and at their leader. The captain shrugged and said, "No man ever spoke the way this man speaks."

"You fools! Has he deceived you also? Look at us! Have any of these rulers or any of the Pharisees believed in him? Do you see any member of the Sanhedrin here following after this man? No! This mob that knows nothing of the law—they are all children of Belial!" Then to the stunned surprise of those present, one member of the Sanhedrin, Nicodemus, stepped forward, staff in hand. Rapping the end of his staff against the pavement, he demanded attention.

"Does our law condemn anyone without first hearing him?"

The response was silent shock. When it subsided, Ananias spoke, sarcastically asking, "Rabbi, are you also from Galilee?" This was a condescending insult. The region of Galilee was not looked upon favorably; it was a part of the culture of the inhabitants of Jerusalem to look upon Galileans as inferior. "Look into it, esteemed colleague, and you will discover that no prophet comes out of Galilee."

Nicodemus' trained mind immediately thought of the words of Isaiah,

> *"He will honor Galilee of the gentiles, by the way of the sea, along the Jordan—the people walking in darkness have seen a great light"*

Still, their insult stung. *I have met him! He is not just a man!*

> *"...and his name shall be called Wonderful Counselor, the mighty God, the everlasting Father, the Prince of Peace."*

The thoughts of Nicodemus ran together with God's thoughts. But he realized their ignorance of these scriptures was deliberate. Then each one went to his own home, each with his outrage, each with murder in his heart. Nicodemus was afraid.

III

Nor Do I Condemn You

As the lanterns of Jerusalem began to herald the end of another day, Jesus left the rest of us, as he often did, to spend some time alone. He hadn't realized how tired and hungry he had become until the enticing pungency of savory, roasting meat invited him. As he neared the gate of the city, there were booths that sold food to weary travelers. He stopped at one and purchased a portion of flat bread, a special pocket baked into it, stuffed with roast lamb. Drippings of brown juices coated his fingers as he took the morsel from the merchant. While he licked the delicious substance from his fingers, the vendor remarked, "Fine dog you have there," casting an admiring glance at Abishag.

"Female," said Jesus. "She was a stray who found and adopted a solitary human—me. From the looks of her and the way she behaves, I'd say she once belonged to a shepherd. She is one special dog."

"I have some meat scraps and a bone she might enjoy." The merchant added two small raisin cakes and retrieving the stuffed bread from Jesus, bundled everything in grape leaves. A small wineskin filled with sweet wine completed the meal. It was fare for travelers, but Jesus would not travel far tonight. He made his way up to nearby Mount of Olives and found a comfortable spot to spread his cloak where he and Abishag enjoyed their dinner. Stars began to peek through the olive branches. In a few moments, he was fast asleep.

Birds announced the coming day from nearby trees. Jesus stretched, called the dog, who was still gnawing on last night's bone, then made his way down the hill and back to the Temple steps. Even at this hour people still milled about the streets, remnants of the celebrations the night before. They gathered around Jesus as he sat on the Temple steps. We assumed we'd find him there. We joined the group as he began to tell us more of intimacy with God. During this time, Jesus did not lecture. He chatted. He discussed. He dialogued. He responded to questions. His ideas about the Father were fresh and different from those heard from other rabbis. Honest seekers of truth, the curious and the skeptical were provoked to think, to consider.

Suddenly, there was a disturbance. The crowd parted to reveal a group of men dressed in temple garb signifying authority, jerking and dragging a woman along with them, her robes disheveled and torn, hardly covering her body. She looked as though someone else had dressed her without concern for anything but her shame. She had been accosted by these men when she had not expected it. They dragged her before Jesus and threw her roughly at his feet. Trembling and terrified, she wept, embarrassed, humiliated, disgraced.

"Teacher!" they declared with contemptuous aggression. Passion afire, they smelled blood. "This woman was caught in the very act of adultery. In the Law, Moses commanded us to stone such women." Moses again. It is a frustrating perplexity and stupefaction that people so taken with structuralized religion were themselves practitioners of consummate evil. Here they wanted to murder this woman—execute, if it makes one feel better—because she had committed a sin. "But what do *you* say?" angrily challenging him. It was a question and an accusation at the same time.

These brutal men were steeped in false piety. Like peacocks, they arrayed their indignation, dripping with self-righteousness, their hypocrisy blatant and obvious. I scanned the crowd. Where was the male partner in this sordid spectacle? He was not present, or if he was, he was concealed. Perhaps he had fled. More likely, they chose to release him because he was one of their number—yet another religious bureaucrat. In any event, they brought only this terrified woman to Jesus and caused her to cower in public. It was clear that they intended to use this occasion as a transparent attempt to discredit Jesus. They cared nothing for this woman. They cared even less about the alleged adultery or her partner. Jesus was their target, and she the insignificant sacrifice to destroy him.

Jesus then did a peculiar thing. He was in no hurry to respond to their question. He merely stooped to the earth and began to write in the dirt with his finger—ignoring them. Curious at what he wrote, they jostled forward with craned necks to see.

Noadiah...
Hulda...
Anana...

To the profound embarrassment of those who saw, the names of women with whom each of these men, themselves, had illicit liaisons appeared in the dirt.

Sheba...

No one said a word.

Hanna...

None indicated that they recognized a name for fear of revealing their secret.

Jesus stood, erased his writings with his foot and brushed the dirt from his hands. "All right!" he said aggressively, "then let's do it!" He took command, "Each of you! Find a stone. Find a hefty rock, a serious rock, one that will do serious damage, one that if impelled with skill and accuracy, will kill. But not too quickly. We wish her to suffer, do we not? We wish her to die slow and beg for mercy. Quickly now! Find your piece!" Nervously, but confused at Jesus' enthusiasm, they each located a stone. There were plenty available. "Now, arrange yourselves in a large semicircle around this dangerous woman." Fools! They had no clue that he was baiting them. A clumsy circle began to form. "Let's see, how shall we determine who gets the honor of throwing the first rock?" There were some smiles of bloodlust anticipation, some looks of surprise from her captors. Anguished whimpering from the woman who had begun to consider a painful, untimely death. He paused only briefly. "I have it!" he said forcibly, so all could hear, "He who is without sin—let him be the first to cast his stone!"

Silence. No one spoke. No one moved.

It was as if he had thrown ice water on their throbbing excitement and lust for blood. Each man turned and looked at him, then looked quickly away, staring instead into their own condemnation. Again, he stooped down and wrote on the ground.

Sheninah...
Abigail...
Salome...

Names common to many women, but known to these men in intimate, hidden moments.

After what seemed an eternal silence, the dull sound of a stone thudded to earth. And then another and another. A vacancy in the circle. And then another. The semicircle began to resemble broken teeth. One at a time they left the scene—the older ones first (presumably, they had more sins to remember) down to the youngest. Only Jesus and the woman remained. Stilled stones lay scattered on the earth, deprived of their lethal force.

αΘω

The woman still cowed, hugging the earth, grasping at dirt, trembling and afraid, awaiting the first stone. Jesus stopped writing, stood up and said into the air, as if speaking only to himself, "Where has everyone gone?" And then to the terrified woman groveling in the dust, "My dear lady, it seems we are alone. It appears that there is no one left to condemn you."

Perhaps him?! she thought, remembering the apparent brutality of his words to the others. *Some say he has never sinned. If he is the only one without sin, has he reserved the right to kill me himself?* She wondered that if she raised her eyes she would see him poised with a large rock, ready to splatter her brains in the dust. But the compassion in his voice! Her eyes lifted to his. Fixed by his gaze she felt the threat evaporate. And then she knew. "No one, sir," she said, "No one remains."

"Nor do I condemn you," Jesus declared. "Go now. Have respect for yourself. Don't do this again."

"And if you do," Jesus did not say, *"you will still be loved. You will still be treasured. You will still be kept in forgiveness and grace."* He didn't say this, but I am certain he thought it.

In this incident I learned three things. First, that no one is without those pitch black pockets of evil in his years upon this earth. And second, because of this, he has forfeited the right to condemn others. And finally, that Jesus, who has no such darkness, who has the right and the credentials to condemn, does not! If he who has the right to condemn does not condemn, then where does that leave me?

IV

Bethany

The day was quiet. What a relief from the intensity of the past few days! As I reflected on the events of the Feast of Tabernacles, I thought of how controversial Jesus had become. He was receiving more attention than the Zealots. It seemed as if everywhere he went he was surrounded by supporters, detractors and those who were merely curious. But today was different. It was a beautiful, comfortable day.

We found ourselves in the little town of Bethany, less than an hour's journey from Jerusalem by foot. There we came to the home of our friend, Lazarus, and his two sisters, Martha and Mary. The two women greeted us warmly and when Jesus inquired into the whereabouts of Lazarus...

"You have to ask?" chided Martha. "He is at the same place you most likely have been all week, Tabernacles!" She spoke the word in triumph.

While disappointed, we understood. Lazarus was a man of great influence and means. In the old scriptures' sense of the term, Lazarus was one of those who "sat in the gate of Jerusalem." Like Nicodemus, he enjoyed high respect among those of the Sanhedrin. His wealth was of more than sufficient interest to this group. A devoted Jew, Lazarus would not be one to miss the Feast of Tabernacles. Indeed, he likely had much responsibility concerning its organization and function. For all of this, Lazarus was among the closest intimates of Jesus. He was not among the twelve or like me, a daily follower of our Lord. He loved and worshiped Jesus and believed him to be who he said he was. Among others, Lazarus and his sisters generously looked after our financial needs as Jesus and the rest of us traveled about preaching and teaching the gospel.

Does it seem peculiar that the Son of God and his entourage had financial needs? That we had to pay for our lodging? Our meals? Our clothing? Roman Tribute? All must pay for the privilege of the air we breathe. Even the Son of God.

αΘω

This family, of course, could not accommodate all that were among us. Only Jesus and the twelve, Matthais and myself entered into the house. Still, entertaining fifteen hungry men was no small task. While Jesus and the rest of us found a place to sit, stand or recline, Martha busied herself with the problem of how she was going to feed us all. Jesus reclined against some cushions, exhausted. Mary came and settled at his feet, captivated, attentive. As he began to rehearse the events of the day, she sat enraptured, listening to what he said. Martha, however, bustled about with all the preparations that had to be made.

"Mary," she asked pleasantly, "can you go to the cooler and fetch some grapes? These men need refreshment." Her sister did not respond. She merely sat there smiling at Jesus, eyes filled with adoration. It is doubtful that she even heard her sister. "Sister, please," she appealed, "there will be plenty of time for swooning later. Go and fetch the grapes."

"All right," she finally said, "in a moment." But she didn't move. The moment never came.

Exasperated, Martha appealed to Jesus directly. "Lord, don't you care that my sister has left me to do all of the work by myself? Tell her to help me!"

Taking her by the hand, he spoke gently to her. "Martha, Martha, it's all right. Thank you for your concern, and I apologize for all of us unexpectedly landing on you like this. But Mary has chosen the one thing she needs. She thinks sitting at my feet is better than feeding me grapes. Now I can't really take that away from her, can I?"

"So perhaps I will find what is better as well." She plopped herself onto a pile of cushions. Obviously upset, she huffed a few times before she finally relaxed, looked around the room at her company and said "So, what is it that someone else is preparing for dinner? Is my sister the 'virtuous woman' of which Solomon's mother speaks so passionately? It would seem that she was even more industrious and, I might add, a bit more appreciated."

Jesus, knowing he was bested, laughed and said to her sister, "Well, Mary, let's both of us get up and help or we will be in the thick of trouble. Pulling Martha up from the cushions he grabbed her, hugged her tightly and asked, Where are the dishes? I will set the table." And with that, we all began to help Martha.

V

A Man Born Blind

Bethany had been a good place to relax. Lazarus returned home that evening and insisted that we stay. The afternoon of the third day we set to return to Jerusalem.

As we were approaching the city we came upon a blind man who had with him a companion that helped him get about. Jesus stopped to speak to the man. "How long has he been blind?" he inquired of the man's companion. The blind man's sightless eyes did not turn toward the voice that had asked the question. There was no smile on his face. He seemed disengaged, distant, perhaps a bit annoyed at being stopped, at being questioned.

His friend responded, "From birth," he replied. Since the blind man's demeanor was something less than amiable, Matthias asked Jesus, "Rabbi, who sinned, this man or his parents, that he was born blind?" No doubt, this man's disgruntled disposition invited questions of this sort.

Still, Jesus smiled at the absurdity of the question. "How could someone yet unborn sin? If he was born this way, how could it be a punishment for something he had done?" Matthias was noticeably embarrassed. "This man's sin did not cause him to be born this way nor did his parents' sin." Odd how the human mind perceives the pain of others. It evermore gravitates toward finding fault. "This poor man is blind," said Jesus, "so that the goodness of God might be displayed in his life." At this, the blind man laughed bitterly.

Then his expression softened. Perhaps it was the tone of Jesus' voice. Perhaps it occurred to him that the voice belonged to the man about whom he had heard so much and in whom he had dared to secretly hope. It is not known. The man's expression changed.

Jesus spit on the ground and made some mud with the saliva. This was now the third time I have seen him do something like this. I wondered what he would do with this vulgar concoction. He spread the mud on the man's closed eyes. "Now," he told the man, "Go and wash away the mud in the Pool of Siloam."

The towers of the Temple could be seen in the distance to the north. The pool of Siloam was not far, maybe a hundred paces. We could see the light of the deepening sky reflected in the waters of the lower pool.

The man in whose care the blind man had placed himself looked hesitatingly at Jesus, not quite sure of what he should do. Jesus motioned with his hand for the man to lead his friend to the pool. He led him to the upper pool, an oblong reservoir cut in the rock, about fifty feet long, sixteen feet wide and eighteen feet deep. At the southwest corner a crude flight of steps descended into the pool. The blind man stepped cautiously into the water, descending the stairs until he was about knee-deep and then, cupping his hands, dipped them into the water, bringing the liquid to his eyes. Still unable to see, he did it again. He repeated this until every trace of the mud had been cleansed. He brushed the water from his eyes, blinked a few times and peered into the heavens. Venus shone brilliantly against a purple heaven. He gazed a few moments as a child would at seeing a constellation for the first time. "There are lights in this soft darkness!"

αΘω

He turned first to the man who had led him about for so many years, his closest friend. He had never seen his face. He gazed, trying to connect familiarity with recognition. His friend, realizing what was happening, spoke his name, "Ezion?" The man who was blind looked at his friend in wonder. "It is me, Ezion! Rissah!"

"Rissah? Rissah!" Instantly Ezion reached out and held his friend's face in his hands. "It is you, Rissah…I see you!" he shouted with tears of elation. The two men embraced. Rissah looked back gratefully at Jesus still standing some distance away. His friend followed his gaze but did not understand. Ezion seemed agitated. "Rissah!" he exclaimed. "It is all so…so bright! It is more than I can bear. Rissah, you must take me home. I do not know the way. Take me home to my family, Rissah. We must go immediately. My Mother. My Father. We must show them!" His friend took his arm, as he had always done, to lead him away.

As they moved through the streets of Jerusalem, those who had seen Ezion a thousand times in the Temple begging, stopped them and asked, "Isn't this the beggar?"

"The same," spoke Rissah.

"Yes!" Ezion cried, "It is me! I am no longer blind! I see! I see!"

"I don't believe it," said one of those who had stopped them. "This man is not blind, although I must admit he resembles that old beggar. Good joke," they laughed. "Good joke."

Ezion responded angrily, "I am the man!" Everything he said was an exclamation.

"Of course you are!" they responded derisively, "But tell us, how can you now see?"

"The man they call Jesus made some mud and put it on my eyes." Then he realized how improbable this story must sound. But he persisted, "This Jesus…told me to go to Siloam and wash. So I went and washed, and now…I…I see!"

Their faces sobered. They knew about Jesus. "Where is this Jesus?"

"How should I know?" he said.

αΘω

"The priests will want to hear about this." So they forced Ezion and Rissah to go with them to the Temple where the officials were immediately summoned. Now (as one might expect) the day on which Jesus had made the mud and healed the man's eyes was a Sabbath.

A priest examined Ezion from a distance, then stepped forward and peered at his eyes. "I've seen you in the Temple begging." He paused, contempt mixed with condescending curiosity on his face. "How is it that you can now see?"

"He put mud on my eyes," the man replied, "and I washed, and now I see."

"Who put mud on your eyes?"

Ezion did not answer immediately whereupon the question was repeated. "Who put mud on your eyes?"

"I think his name was Jesus…of Nazareth."

"Ah!" exclaimed the priest knowingly. "This man is not from God," his voice rising, "He does not keep the Sabbath."

Someone made the mistake of whispering, "How can someone who is not from God do such miraculous things?"

His inquisitor continued, "What have you to say about him? It was your eyes that he healed."

Ezion replied, "I don't know. Maybe he is a prophet."

αΘω

The Jewish leadership did not believe that the man had been blind. They suspected him to have been faking blindness so that he could survive by begging rather than working. They concluded that he had never been blind and that he and his friend had formed a conspiracy to bilk the public of alms. They conferred among themselves. "So now, what does this man stand to gain by revealing that he can see? What is he trying to prove?"

"It isn't him," said another. "It is that self-styled prophet, Jesus, from Nazareth."

"Nazareth? That community of fools and thieves? There is not a soul of character among them. Why would anyone follow a man from Nazareth?"

"It doesn't matter. This man Jesus is a maker of trouble. He disregards the Law. He exploits people. He conspires and concocts seeming magic to gain a following. And he is succeeding. That is the reason for this thing among us today. This man was not born blind. He has never been blind in his life. This is yet another instance of Messianic chicanery."

"There is a way to expose this thing once for all."

"How?"

"Locate this man's parents. Put the 'fear of God' in them and make them swear that this man is their son. And we shall see if he was born blind." This stratagem was agreed upon, and they brought the man before the priests.

αΘω

"State your name!" they demanded.

"Ezion ben Achor."

"Where do you live?"

"I have been blind my entire life. My parents..."

"You live with your parents? You are a grown man. How can you so burden your mother and father?"

Ezion hung his head. They had touched on the greatest pain of his blindness. He hadn't minded begging in the Temple. He had grown accustomed to being led about. He didn't miss what he had never known. He had never felt sorry for himself. But the pain he had caused his parents was more than he could bear. He could only say, "Until today, I could not see."

"Where do your parents live?" He told them. They nodded their heads to the Temple guards who turned and left.

In less than an hour, the guards brought the parents of the man and presented them to the authorities in Jerusalem. "Is this your son?" they asked. "Is this the one you say was born blind?"

"Yes," said the frightened parents.

"How is it then," they pressed, "that now he can see?"

They looked at their son and for the first time saw his eyes open and blinking. They looked back at each other in wonder and amazement. His mother caught her breath. Her eyes welled with tears. They approached him tentatively, not knowing what to think. "Ezion?"

"Mother? Mother!" the man replied. "You are more beautiful than I imagined."

αΘω

"This is our son," spoke Achor, shakily, "and we know he was born blind. But how he can now see or how his eyes were healed, we cannot explain." Achor looked again at his son, examining him closely. He was met with the gaze of healthy eyes. A smile creased his lips as joy invaded his heart. Turning to the inquisitors, he said confidently, "Go ahead. Ask him! He is of age. He can speak for himself."

Someone in the crowd snickered. "He is afraid," they laughed. It was well-known that anyone who acknowledged that Jesus was the Christ would be excommunicated from Temple worship. But they were mistaken. Achor and his wife came and stood next to their son. It was clear that they intended to share whatever befell him.

They spoke to Ezion, "Then give credit to God. As for this Jesus, we know that he is a sinner."

"Sinner?" questioned Ezion, surprise in his voice. "Whether he is a sinner or not, I don't know. One thing I do know. I was born blind, but now I see!"

αΘω

Word of what happened was brought to Jesus by Rissah, the one who had spent much of his life leading Ezion about. "Take me to him," said Jesus. When at length he arrived at the family's home, he said, "Do you believe in the Son of Man?"

The compassionate voice was unmistakable. Just to be certain Ezion inquired, "Who is he, sir? Tell me so that I may believe in him." Jesus came and stood directly in front of him and said, "Look at me, Ezion." The man stared at Jesus quizzically. Then Jesus stated flatly, "I am he."

"Lord," said this man who was born blind, "I believe!" and he sank to his knees.

"I have come into this world," responded Jesus, "so that you, Ezion, and others like you, may see and those who see but refuse to believe may become blind. This is the judgment of God."

Some of the Temple authorities had been watching Rissah's movements and had followed him to Ezion's house. They witnessed this exchange. When they heard Jesus say this, they asked, "Do you refer to us? Are you suggesting that we are blind?"

Jesus said, "If you were blind, you would not be guilty of sin, but since you claim you can see, your guilt remains." He left them, their mouths opened as if to speak; yet nothing came forth. Utterly confounded, there was no way they could win. It is impossible to reason with this man.

VI

The Good Shepherd

A little to the North of Herod's Temple in the wall surrounding Jerusalem there is a gate where shepherds bring their sheep into the city. Not surprisingly, it is called the "Sheepgate." The flocks are immediately herded all into one pen while the shepherds go about their business in the city. Near the pen there is the "Sheep Pool" where the animals are watered. The flocks mingle together with other flocks and are indistinguishable from all the other sheep. When a shepherd is ready to leave the city, he comes back to the pen and calls his sheep. Amazingly, those that are his recognize his voice and come to him. The others either ignore him or scatter at his unfamiliar voice.

Jesus had come to the fence surrounding the pen. Leaning on the fence rail, he watched them mill about and bleat. A shepherd entered through the gate and called his sheep. Watching what happened was a pleasure. The shepherd's sheep separated themselves from the rest and gathered about him. After counting to make certain all were present, he opened the gate and exited with his flock intact. Jesus turned to us and, smiling, said, "Did you see that?"

"Yes," Thaddeus responded. "It would be amazing if it weren't so ordinary."

"Stand here and you will see this every day. Ordinary indeed," responded Jesus, "yet I never tire of watching them. I tell you the truth," he said, "that sheepgate is the key. Only thieves and robbers enter by other means. The true shepherd comes to the gate and the gatekeeper opens it for him; he steps in and calls his sheep. He calls them by name and his sheep respond to his voice. Shepherds name their sheep. Did you know that? He has named each one, and he calls them out by name." Jesus laughed. "Then he leads them out to pasture. They follow him because they know his voice. It is fascinating that they will never follow a stranger! They run away because they don't recognize a stranger's voice." Most of us were fishermen, not shepherds. Most of this we already knew, but knowing Jesus, we also knew something else was coming.

And it did. Smiling gently, Jesus slowly raised his eyebrows and said, "I am the gate for the sheep." He paused briefly, as if waiting for the impact of his words. "Whoever enters through me will be safe. He can come in and go out and find pasture. All who came before me were strangers—thieves and robbers—the sheep did not respond to them. The thief comes to steal, kill and destroy, but I have come that the sheep may have life. Life! And I want them to have it to the very fullest. Not only am I the 'sheepgate,' I am also the good shepherd. I lead them to the richest pastures to feed. I protect them from predators. They feel the touch of my staff and are in constant communion with me."

"A good shepherd," said Jesus, "will lay down his life for the sheep. A good shepherd feels a sense of ownership for the sheep. He feels responsibility for them and accepts that responsibility gladly. A mere hired hand does not. So when he sees a wolf coming, he abandons the sheep and runs away, leaving the flock vulnerable and scattered. He cares nothing for the sheep."

"I know my sheep," he said, "I know them by name, and my sheep know me. I lay down my life for my sheep. And, of my own accord, with the power and authority given me by my Father, I will take it up again." Before we could think too much about that he said, "And did you know that I have other sheep that are not of this flock?" This surprised us. Where was this other flock? Had he been preaching to others without us? We were puzzled. Then he said, "They are those from peoples and generations to come who will also respond to my voice. I will bring them also; then there shall be one flock and one shepherd."

I must confess that when I reflect on this, I weep. The vastness of God's love...his meticulous care for us all. He gave everything. Through my tears I thought of the shepherd's psalm.

αΘω

The Lord is my Shepherd,
He knows what I want.
He makes me relax and
Enjoy his world around me;
He helps me to appreciate the deep
Dimensions of my life and
Heals the "rawness" of my mind.

He will lead me to do the right thing
Because he has an investment in my life
Which he wishes to protect.

I am not afraid,
No matter how extreme the crisis
Or how strong the force of evil.
For he is at my side,
Feeling it with me.
His power to protect me is absolute,
So why should I worry?

Dear Lord,
You give me a feast
Right where my adversaries can see it.
You let them know
That I am special to you.

I never had it so good!
And this is only the beginning!
It's going to be this way
For the rest of my life!

And I am going to live with you, Father.
Because a Father and his child ought
To be together,
...always.

VII

The Beach at the Great Sea

Jesus sat on the beach digging his toes into sand warmed by the sun. It had felt hot to the bottom of his bare feet as he walked. But beneath the surface of the sand, it was cooler. He dug his feet deeper. Beside him sat Peter, next to Peter, John. The rest of us lounged about the beach. Thaddeaus and Matthew were standing in the surf, letting the waves crash around their legs and gazing toward the watery western horizon. No mountains in the distance here for this is the Great Sea, the ocean filled with leviathan and in depths beyond imagination. If one sailed until he disappeared into the horizon, where would he go? Where would he end up? Where is the island of Crete from here? Where is Italy? Rome? Spain and beyond?

We were at the home of Simon the Tanner, in the city of Joppa. Simon's house was built at a spot only a few feet from the sand of the beach. One could step from his threshold directly into the sand. What a wonderful place to live! I thought about how pleasant it would be to go to sleep every night listening to the pounding waves, smelling the salt in the air. The only distractions were the odors of Simon's trade. It was no accident that he lived near the sea where the breeze is constant.

αΘω

Jesus looked pensively out at the water, sometimes closing his eyes against the wind which often bore with it tiny grains of sand, the smell of the salt water rich and powerful. It was one of those unusually warm and balmy days of late fall. Seagulls drifted overheard mere feet from us. It seemed as if we could reach out and touch them. There, one of them was pure white. I watched as it hung suspended on the wind until its wings cut a graceful arc soaring inches over the pounding surf. What an exhilarating thing it must be to fly, to drift motionless on the wind, to feel ocean spray in your face.

"Peter," Jesus spoke, "I want you to return here often after I am gone.

It is a place of peace. You will find refreshment here, a cleansing and deepening of soul."

"Amongst Simon's hides?" quipped Peter. Jesus smiled. They were quiet for a moment. Then Peter said, forcing himself to suppress his concern, "Besides, there is no place you can go that I will not follow." The thought of coming here or going anywhere without Jesus was for Peter unthinkable. This tall man, hair flecked with grey, powerful fishermen's frame, muscles in sharp definition holding together his athletic body, was, after all, a man consumed with deep spiritual passion for the man he now considered his Master.

Jesus turned and gazed at the fisherman, "Yes there is, Peter."

"Yes, there is, what?"

"A place I can go, a place I will go, that you cannot and will not follow." Peter, frowning, looked into the Lord's face. He did not realize, none of us realized how privileged we were to be able to do that, to look into the face of Jesus the Christ. The Lord looked away, back at the sea. "At least not with me. Perhaps later." Peter did not know how to respond to such enigmatic words. It was enough to be here, now.

"Lord, I don't understand..."

Before Peter could finish, Jesus had picked up a handful of sand and playfully threw it all over Peter. "I said, you can't follow me," he laughed. With that, he stood, shrugged off his robe and trotted toward the surf, gathering himself into an absolute, full-bore run. "Come on, fish breath," he yelled back, "see if you can remember how to swim!" In the next instant, Jesus plunged beneath the waves.

Peter looked after him, astounded. How could he go from heavy ominous words to frolicking in the surf in a moment of time. It didn't matter. Peter shed his own outer garment and ran after him, "I can show a carpenter a thing or two about swimming!" he cried. He knifed into the foaming water as though he had been born there. When they surfaced in waist-deep water, they began swinging their arms at the surface splashing water on each other. In the next instant, I saw Peter tackle Jesus, whereupon they disappeared once again beneath the surf. And whereupon I shed my own cloak as did the others, and we all ran like wild horses to the waves to join them.

αΘω

That night we built a fire on the beach. The wind had softened into gentle breezes but the night had chilled and the warmth of the fire felt good. Flames leaped high above our heads and burned brightly from the dry driftwood we had gathered among the dunes of sand. The sound of crackling fire embraced by deeper sounds of thundering surf produced music for the gods. I checked myself. There were no gods. There was only Jesus. Man though he was, for me his deity was absolute. This wonderful Savior, who could bend the fibers of my soul, who could frolic like an adolescent in the surf with his friends, commanded my every loyalty, my every affection, my very worship.

We sat in groups of two or more, a priceless moment of camaraderie and fellowship. We sang songs and told stories. Just being with Jesus at times like this, just knowing him and having him know us was more than any of us could have imagined. Sitting with him and the twelve around the fire like this, in this idyllic place, was more exquisite than my foolish words can express. It was wondrous. It was euphoric and peaceful.

Laughter and much loud conversation. And as the hours grew upon us and the moon lifted high into its vault, our words dimmed into quiet reflection. I spoke not at all. My gaze focused and rested on the glowing embers of the settling fire. Fascinating how an open fire affects one. I am drawn to it as a moth. My thoughts permeated with the voice of Jesus. His eyes, too, were fixed by the flame.

VIII

The Imponderable

There was a time beyond the way men measure time," he began, "when I and my Father lived together on the other side of the stars..."

What can I say to them? How can I speak to them of love that transcends their capacity to comprehend? How can I tell them that they, each of them, are both the objects and consequence of that love?

"We considered what you might think imponderable. Our love for each other...infinite, eternal, and absolute. I and my Father are One. It is beyond the reach of reality for us to be anything else. Yet in all the endless realms of omnipotent possibility, there was something we did not have and could not possess."

"What could that be?" from Matthew, the intellectual among us. If any of us besides Jesus could wear the mantle of "theologian," it was this tax collector. The irony, as well as the curiosity, was lost on none of us. "How could God, who is wholly contained in himself," Matthew asked, "How could God not have something, anything he could have wanted? How is it that an omnipotent, infinite Sovereign could lack anything he desired? If he lacked something, how could he be all-encompassing? How could he be God?"

Jesus smiled. It was the question he wanted. "One cannot have what is not his to own."

"And what is there amongst all of reality that does not belong to Yahweh?" Matthew looked at Peter to his right and James to his left as if seeking their concurrence and support. He got it. The intense interest in their expressions compelled an answer.

"Your love," said Jesus simply.

A breeze, or something like it, provoked the flames and they leaped slightly higher, illuminating faces. The puzzlement on each face evidenced profound lack of comprehension. "Simon," he said, "You are a tanner of hides. You create fine leather for king's houses. You love the work of your hands, do you not?" Simon thought of the end product of his labors, its softness, its rich fresh leather aroma and smiled in affirmation. "Tell me, Simon," Jesus continued, "does your fine leather love you back?"

Simon's eyes averted, "Well, of course not, but..."

"It may please you, but the pleasure is of your own creation. It cannot think or feel to love you back, yet you cherish its beauty and think it is love. It is not. Love that comes from the object of one's love is not something that can be generated by the Lover—even if the Lover is the Sovereign God. The love of which I speak is not a mere decision, as if it were something one can move, shape or discontinue, as if it were something that can be shut off and on. Love, true, authentic love must come because one feels it deep within himself and expresses it because he cannot contain it. It must spring, irresistibly, from the well of one's being. That is why you have being. You were created in order to love, freely and confidently."

"It is not possible to love without the force of its power within you. You have no power to choose to love, but you do have the power to choose to express it. If it is there, you have the power of mind to repress it. If it is not there, you so not have the power of mind to generate it or choose to express what does not exist."

αΘω

The shadows on our faces flickered with the flames. They were covered by consternation and seeking to understand—no, to appreciate what he was saying to us. "The Father has placed within you the capacity to love him; still, you have the choice to release that love or not. You also have the power to determine by what measure it is released. You are free—free to release love or repress it. You are the only creatures on earth with that power." Was he saying that we were created so that the Father would have someone to love him because the impulse within us was so strong that we could not resist loving him? Such an inscrutable thought was too high for us.

"My Father and I want your love more than anything your minds can imagine," Jesus continued. "Look above you." Our heads lifted to behold a canopy of brilliance spread like a glorious, sparkling belt across a field of velvet darkness. "Can you count them? What you can actually see is an infinitesimal slice of what your eyes cannot see." I thought about that. How could there be heavenly bodies that we could not see? If they were there, why could we not see them? "Before these," Jesus said, "there were angels.

Like you, they were created with the ability to love or withhold it. Those that loved were confirmed in their love. Now they love the Father because the thought that they could not would never occur to them."

It did not occur to me then, on that lovely, starry night, but on reflection I realized that what Jesus was giving us was the very rationale for creation. Moreover, he was telling us why he had come.

"Yet, even they were not created supremely. *They were not created in the Image of God."* He paused only for the briefest of moments, just enough to create a hunger, an anticipation for his next words. *"You were,"* he said. *"You were created more like God than you can now comprehend. Of no other living being can it be said that it was created in the Image of God."* It was too much. Our minds were reeling. We needed closure and Jesus seemed to sense that. "That Image has been corrupted. I have come," he said, "to give the Image of God back to you so that once again, you may freely love the Father and his Son, whom he has sent. There is much to say; there is much to teach you, but this much is enough. For now it is all you can absorb." With that, he rose and shook the sand from his garments. "This day has ended. Let's get some sleep." He turned and walked toward the house. The twelve and most of the others followed. I remained. I needed to think.

αΘω

The days at the home of Simon the Tanner turned into weeks. Before I realized the rapid passage of time, two months had passed. The days were noticeably shorter. We were approaching the shortest day of the year. One morning I rose from my bed while it was still dark. I loved to sleep in the coolness of night, but that morning, my thoughts would not allow me. I rose and stepped from Simon's house onto the beach. The sound of the surf is a beautiful thing. The light of the stars reflected on the water in the distance.

To my left a promontory of rock stood stalwart against the sea, dark waves roaring over and crashing against it in splashing foam and spray. Crashing and splashing. Crashing and splashing in the powerful rhythms of the deep. I felt the spray on my face and the water sucking about my legs as I stood in the surf. The sand around my feet washed away with the pulling water. The sensory response overwhelmed me. I burst forth in deep throated song. The notes of my melody were lost against the roar of the surf. I could not sing louder than the waves, but I didn't care. Tears of joy streamed from my eyes. God could hear and it was to him I sang with all my heart, with all my being.

And then I saw him.

αΘω

Unaware of my presence, he was playing with his dog. I watched as he picked up a small piece of driftwood and hurled it into the sea. Abishag, her barking lost in the crash of the waves, plunged into the water in hot pursuit. After a few moments of surging in the waves and furious paddling, she returned with it in her mouth. Once reaching the firm beach, she dropped the stick and shook her coat as dry as she could, picked up the stick and pranced around him until, after much cajoling, she came to him. He took one end of the piece of wood in his hand, but initially she would not release it, tugging playfully against his grip. After an acceptable time of tugging had passed, she released it and stood looking in eager anticipation that he would throw it again. He did. Again and again. I wondered if they would ever tire.

I considered. This wonderful, wise teacher, this worker of miracles, this loving, compassionate Son of God loved to play with his dog in the hours of the morning, while it was still grey-dark, before anyone else was awake. What contentment he knew. On that morning, in that day, I knew it, too.

αΘω

The shortest day came and went. Biting wind blew from somewhere in the vastness of the great sea onto the land and bowed even the strongest of trees into submission. Amidst the fury came also a peace, a contentment, an awareness of things over which we had no control or responsibility.

The months at Simon's home had given us time to reflect on ourselves and what we knew of Jesus—on the traveling we had done, the miracles, the teaching. The camaraderie we all felt with him and each other flourished. Our beliefs shifted, our thinking recast, transformed.

αΘω

The return trip to Jerusalem was a quiet one, each of us not wanting to disturb the tranquility apparent in the other. Winter was already colder than normal, and we were relieved when we saw the glowing sky ahead, reflecting the warmth of festival.

During this time of merriment, on an especially cold evening, we found Jesus in the Temple area walking among the columns in Solomon's Colonnade. While the Temple was brilliantly lit as it had been during the Feast of Tabernacles two months ago, Jesus halted his promenade, gathered his cloak around him against the chill and sat down on a step. Clasping his hands in front of him, he surveyed the scene of people scurrying about. The expression on his face was serious. Concerned.

We left Jerusalem and set out for Jericho after which we crossed the Jordan to the place where John had been baptizing in the early days. We found a spot to make camp, and there we stayed for a while. Through the cattails and papyrus grass, the sun glinted off the slow current of the water. I could almost see John baptizing and preaching his calls to repentance. I could almost smell him.

Many people came, and Jesus made himself available to each one who sought him. They seemed to enjoy comparing Jesus with John. The consensus said, "Though John never performed a miracle, all that John said about this man was true." Some came to believe in him in this place. As the sun fell into the escarpment rising up to Jerusalem, as the evening purple descended, as the first star of the evening pierced the sky with its brilliance, Jesus could be seen moving among the people who loved him.

IX

You Are the Christ

Jerusalem now lay almost 115 miles behind us, to the south, over a week's journey away. We had taken the usual route, skirting Samaria this time, stopping by Capharnaum for a visit with Peter's family. We stayed there several days, fishing and enjoying the lake. Over all, the trip had taken us twice the time it should have taken. Jesus seemed in no hurry, but it was clear that he wanted to put as much distance between us and Jerusalem as possible. Now even Galilee lay well over a day's journey to the south. This is the northernmost point Jesus would come for as long as I knew him. We were at the foot of Mt. Hermon in the city of Caesarea Philippi, a little village on a pleasing site about 1,150 feet above the sea overlooking a fertile valley at the foot of the mountain.

Under Antiochus the Great, the city bore the Greek name Panion, owing to a cave consecrated to the worship of Pan, the god of nature, and purported to be his birthplace. This is a magnificent cave sinking deep into the bowels of Hermon. Inside there is a prodigious abyss filled with clear water and out of which flows the main headwaters of the Jordan River. There are five niches hewn out of rock to the right of the cave's entrance holding statues which bear inscriptions in Greek mentioning Pan, Echo and the pagan priest, Galerius.

More than thirty years ago Herod the Great's son, Philip, named the town and its famous cave in honor of Caesar Augustus. It became known as Caesarea Philippi. Standing on the road, we surveyed an area punctuated by the Temples of Syrian and Greek gods looking down on us like great lifeless demons in white marble splendor.

It was an odd irony that Jesus chose this place of idolatry and misbegotten faith to be alone with his disciples. One good thing—there were no Jewish legalists here with whom to argue and debate. Maybe, at least, among the pagan faithful he could take a break from derisive, pietistic fools he always encountered in Jerusalem. It didn't occur to me at the moment, but as I look back over the years at this occasion, I can't help but wonder if Jesus, as he absorbed this hopeless scene, was not somehow struck by the massive waste of worship these edifices and statues represented. Aware of his own persona, knowing who he was, I can't help but wonder if the poignancy of this scene prompted his question…

"Who do people say that I, the Son of Man, am?"

In the spirit of the moment James replied, "Some have confused you with John the Baptist!"

"Others say Elijah and still others, Jeremiah or one of the prophets," Andrew added.

"Each of these were good men," Jesus said pensively, "but they are all dead." In the pause that followed, his words struck home. John, Elijah and Jeremiah were indeed dead, but this Lord whom we follow is alive. Everything about him is alive. There is nothing about Jesus that does not resonate with vitality. But he was still a young man. Would he not also die? When his body became old and weak, would it not also give out and his spirit go to spend eternity with his Father? The answer to these thoughts would become clear to us soon enough, but at that time we had no way of knowing, of understanding what was ahead.

"What about you?" he asked of us all, "Who do you say I am? What is your opinion about me?"

αΘω

The wind hissed through the leaves in the distance. There were no other sounds. A hawk traced its silent way through the blue above us observing the crevasses for a marmot or the fields for a mouse. No one spoke. Every one of us wanted to answer him but none could form the words. Finally they came, "You are the Christ, the Son of the living God," from a simple fisherman.

Jesus' eyes searched until they located the speaker and fixed him with their gaze. Peter's eyes seemed to ask, "Am I right?" while all the time knowing that he was. "Peter, the rock!" Jesus exclaimed. "How right you are named!" His affection was palpable, the bond between them beyond our understanding. "Bless you, Simon, son of Jonas," he continued. "This was revealed to you by my Father in heaven." In the presence of us all he said, "This confession of Simon's is the rock upon which I build my church!"

"My church?" A term he had not used before. Was he talking about a new temple, a new place to worship? Or was it something else? Something more than that?

"The strongest powers of evil, even the gates of hell will be powerless against it. I give to you the key, Peter, which will open the doors to the kingdom of heaven. That key is the immense love of the Father and my love for the world. By this, you will be the first to show the way to the nations. Others will follow your lead. Those who return hatred for the love you bring will forfeit eternal life, but those who are liberated by that love will themselves liberate that love in eternity!"

With that, he leaned closer and we were all drawn in to hear what apparently were to be words of great import. He then implored us to not, at this time, share with others what Peter had just declared and what he was about to say. We nodded our concurrence.

"The Son of Man, must suffer and be rejected by his own people and die. The very people to whom he has been born, the very people to whom he has been sent will kill him." He spoke as though he were speaking of someone other than himself. We were aghast at the stark words, our mood shocked into silence.

The intenseness in his eyes relaxed a bit as he continued, "And, in case you were wondering, unlike the prophets and teachers that have preceded my coming, after three days I will defeat sin and death once and for all and rise from the dead."

There. He said it. He was definitely speaking about himself. He spoke plainly and forthrightly about this as if it were a certainty.

αΘω

We were all confused and upset, especially Peter. Perhaps he thought the magnitude of his confession allowed him to take liberties with Jesus. It was clear that he was angry. Taking Jesus by the arm and forcibly dragging him aside he said, "No, Lord!" he exclaimed. "How can you suggest such a thing? This will not happen!" said he, as if willing it so himself. Jesus turned and looked at his disciples. We watched and wondered what would happen.

They do not yet comprehend! Don't they understand that I must subject myself to this? And don't they know that I struggle within myself when I think of it? I feel like I might as well be back in the desert with the Tempter.

Then he looked back at Peter. The look of love and affection in his eyes had evaporated. It had been replaced by a palpable, frightening fury. "Get out of my sight, Satan!" Jesus snapped. "You are much too thick to understand the things of God!" It is amazing how sweetness can turn to bitterness in such a short moment, how one can possess profound theological insight in one glance and be inutterably dull in the next. But a few sentences ago, Jesus had issued upon Peter the sublimest of blessings, and in close to the same breath he had cursed him with the worst of curses. How can this be? None of us understood. Peter was smitten. Never had Jesus spoken to one of his own like this. Never. It would not be forgotten.

This incident also underscored a change in the character and tone of what and how Jesus taught us. This was the beginning of a shift in the content of his teachings about ethical concerns and the beauty of the Father to something more ominous to us but to him inevitable and necessary. He seemed to believe he was going to die, and soon.

X

Mount Hermon

Far above us at the summit, one can stand upon Mount Hermon and view every mile of the Jordan valley. At 9,232 feet, the mountain is so high its snow-laden peak can be seen from the Dead Sea, more than 115 miles away. As its name suggests, Mt. Hermon is a mountain "set apart," sacred to the peoples over which it stands, a maternal sentinel. It felt as if the whole of the land were in antiquity, spawned by this mother of mountains.

Jesus had come to this mountain for a special reason. None of us knew it. In this adventure, as in most, we followed him blindly, not knowing why and not caring as long as we were with him. As it is with me to this very hour as I scribble away under the flickering illumination of these candles, I think of the roads I have traveled, the paths I've walked. I would not in millennia have guessed that I would be here today where I am and doing what I am doing. I had other plans. Other roads.

But...I follow him. My hand is in his. As long as it is, I am never blind. As long as it is, he is with me—always. It doesn't matter my location, my employment, what my hands find to do; so long as he is with me, what he wants is what matters to me.

We were above the city now, perhaps a third of the way up the mountain. The air was thinner and dryer, making us breathe a little harder. The inside of our nostrils felt like rock. We found a spot to rest. Abishag plopped at Jesus' feet, her pink tongue lolling out of her mouth. Taking her head in his hands he asked, "What's the matter old girl?" scratching her ears. The dog responded by licking his hand. We were a long way from Jerusalem, a long way, in terms of how it felt, even from our beloved Galilee.

Caesarea Philippi, a place for Roman and Greek gods. Why had we come here? The day had worn into evening, and the stars were just beginning to glint in the mountain sky. We had eaten the biscuits, goat cheese and fruit we had purchased in the city. Spring water and juice from the grapes helped wash it down. "I must pray," said Jesus after we had settled in for the night. "Peter, you, John and James come with me." The rest of us were not quite at ease about what we perceived as favoritism toward these three.

And why, I thought, would the Master give so much credence to Peter? John I understood. John was the wealthiest among us. John helped fund our little conclave, as did James. No problem there, but why Peter especially after what happened yesterday? And then I remembered, *"You are the Christ, the Son of the living God!"* Why hadn't I thought of that, why hadn't I said it? Reflecting on this event I have begun to consider that, perhaps, it was no accident that Matthias was chosen instead of me.

αΘω

The four of them, Jesus in the lead with Abishag trotting behind, vanished into the tall cedars. The wind rushing through the limbs of the firs above had ceased its thrashing. A strange phenomenon: Late in the afternoon the wind would pick up and blow with sometimes heavy gusts until the sun dropped beyond the surrounding mountains. And then it would suddenly stop, as if knowing with the setting sun that it was time to rest, leaving an eerie silence and darkness.

It wasn't long, perhaps half an hour, perhaps less when I heard the dog bark. That was unusual. Abishag was not a noisy animal. She barked only when genuinely alarmed. We all looked in the direction in which Jesus had gone and were amazed to see a soft illumination through the woods. It silhouetted the trees. I started to run toward the light thinking Jesus and the others might be in danger, but then abruptly the barking ceased and was replaced by total silence, but the light remained. "Wait, Justus," spoke Matthew softly, "this is not for us. It is for him. He will not be harmed." We waited for what now seemed an eternity. The glow from deep within the woods remained.

αΘω

Smoke from the campfire shifted with the remaining soft currents offending the nostrils of whoever it enshrouded with noxious fumes. They had not returned. The rest of us were bone weary and had found comfortable—or at least as comfortable as one can find in the cool airs at this altitude—places to lay our heads and had drifted off to sleep. We awakened with the light of dawn and still they had not returned.

I rolled over and gathered the covers around me to attempt to continue my slumber until the grey of dawn decided I had had enough of sleep. My bladder would not permit it. Clumsily, I extricated myself from my bedroll and stepped behind a convenient cedar, grateful that God had made me a man. It was then that I heard them. The underbrush moved and I saw Abishag loping along, her tongue happily shlepping out of her mouth. And then I saw Peter, James and then Jesus and John emerge from the woods. They seemed unaffected by having spent the night away from the rest of us.

Peter strode into the campsite clapping his hands together. With his foot he jostled those who were still asleep. "Get up!" he yelled. Some protested, gathering their covers against the cool of the morning. Peter was not dissuaded, storming through the campsite, he rolled everyone out of his sleep until all were standing, rubbing the slumber from their eyes. In a few moments, the fire had been rekindled into flame. Biscuits and dried fish distributed.

"You were gone the whole night," observed Thaddeaus. "We saw a light in the woods where you had entered and heard the dog bark. What happened? Surely you saw the light as well?"

Peter smiled. "We saw the light," said he.

"When we arrived at a glen in the woods," Peter began, "Jesus said that he wanted to pray. There was nothing unusual about that. He had just knelt. James, John and I made ourselves comfortable. We were just beginning to nod off when the very air we breathe began to glow with iridescent light. It came from a spot about waist high where its source emitted soft waves of brilliance. Then it grew to such intensity that we had to squint and shield our eyes. We were startled. I was so frightened I couldn't spit."

"My blood pounded like a blacksmith's hammer," offered James.

"As he was praying," continued Peter, "we heard other voices, voices that were not his. Then we saw two men conversing with him. The appearance of his face changed. He himself had changed. He looked the same, yet different. He appeared as through a misty radiance. His face shone with light and his clothes became brilliant. The other two men were also immersed in this same splendor," said Peter.

"Did you know who they were, Simon?" I asked.

"Not at first, but then it became clear that it was Moses, Justus! And the other was Elijah!"

"How did you know it was them?"

"Jesus called them by name." He spoke this with wonder in his voice. "It was the most wondrous thing I have ever seen. They spoke of his departure… from this earth." Peter's voice broke, remembering. "It is supposed to take place in Jerusalem." And looking at Jesus he said, "Soon."

Jesus' gaze continued to be held by the fire.

XI

Moses and Elijah

"Moses and Elijah!" I was captivated. "Moses and Elijah? How could this be?" It isn't that I doubted what Peter said, but I was stunned to hear him say it. Both of these great men had experienced the power of God on a mountaintop. Moses returned from Sinai his face shining as Peter had just described the face of Jesus. Sinai, where the Commandments had been carved in stone by the finger of God. And Mt. Pisgah, where Moses had died, we could look in the distance and see this mountain from where we now stood. I wondered if Moses saw Hermon in the distance, if he thought he would one day visit here, with the Messiah himself? Elijah had, of course, met with God on Mount Horeb and destroyed the prophets of Baal on Mount Carmel. Mt. Hermon could be seen from Carmel also. Now they were here? On this mountain? Now?

He ignored my questions. "I was struck," continued Peter, "by the word the two of them used for 'departure.' It was the word *Exodus!*, the same word which we use to recount the departure of our people from Egypt." Turning to Jesus once again he inquired, "What does that mean, Lord?" The fire glowed in Jesus' eyes. He said nothing.

I had no idea what it might have meant. Both Moses and Elijah left this world in an unusual manner. Moses was buried in a place known only to God. Elijah was conversing with Elisha, and suddenly a chariot of fire appeared and separated the two of them. Elijah went up by a whirlwind into heaven. Was Jesus to leave as well? If so, would he be caught up like Elijah?

Moses and Elijah! Moses died centuries ago and was buried in a sepulcher of unknown location. So far as anyone knows, Elijah never died. Why would they now appear, how could they appear with Jesus on this mountain, in this place? This means that Moses is alive, not dead, and that Elijah is alive with him. Does this mean for certain, that physical death is not the end? I pondered these questions for a moment. Of course, I had always believed in life after death, but if Peter, James and John were to be believed, not to speak of the Lord himself, who by his silence gave approval to what was being said, here with the appearance of Moses and Elijah was living proof that they yet lived! The hairs on my neck rose.

"I don't know how long they spoke with him," continued Peter. "On the one hand, it seemed as if they would stay forever; on the other, it seemed as though they were there and then they were gone. I…I didn't know what to do, what to say…So I spoke to the Master…" He gestured at Jesus still gazing at the fire, but at Peter's reference to him, he simply looked up at us and quietly smiled.

"I said, 'Master, it is good for us to be here. Let us put up three monuments—one for you, one for Moses and one for Elijah.' While I was speaking, a cloud appeared and enveloped the four of us. This was not a normal cloud. It came upon us suddenly and it, too, was luminescent, like it was…like it was alive. Suddenly, a voice came from the cloud, saying, 'This is my Son, whom I have chosen. Listen to him!' And then it was over. Moses and Elijah, the cloud, the light, all gone. There was no one left but Jesus, myself, James and John and of course, the dog. The splendor of it all had evaporated." Peter left off. There was nothing left to say. He looked at us and shrugged. Jesus sat on the log, staring at the fire.

αΘω

After we had breakfasted, we poured dirt on the coals and began our descent. As we walked, Jesus spoke, "I do not wish you to speak of this to anyone."

"Why, Lord?"

"Because what happened here on this mountain last night was private. Meant only for you." And then he said quietly to himself, "And for me." He paused briefly and continued. "There are several reasons why this took place. One of these reasons is to convince you that the dead live. As you have seen Moses and Elijah, you will also see me. Remember this, you will need it to comfort you in the days to come."

"But you are not dead, Master," I ventured. "As the Father has spoken, you are his beloved Son. How can you die?"

He stopped, turned and faced us all. We all stopped, waiting, listening intently. There was no sound except for the wind in the cedars. No birds, no chatting squirrels, no wild dogs howling in the morning light.

"I will die," he said, "before your very eyes." He said it simply, stated as directly and forthrightly as anything could be said. We were incredulous. At least I was. To further stretch our incredulity he added once again, "And as you have seen Moses and Elijah, so shall you see me." With that, he continued walking, leaving us with the silence of our thoughts. The trail gave way to the approaching valley. We had walked in silence for some time, each of us left with his own mental stratagems as to what to do with what he said. I could think of nothing else.

XII

Taxes

Disciples of Jesus. By this time there were a great many. The twelve were not the only ones that were called by that name. All of us had been a part of what our Lord was doing early in his ministry. We had a purpose in his plan and we knew it. We, like the twelve, were meant to be servants of the Father, as was Jesus himself...as were we all.

We made our way to Peter's home where we all, as usual, enjoyed Joanna's hospitality. When Jesus finally joined us from one of the back rooms, his hair had been washed and he was wearing fresh clothes.

αΘω

Shortly after we had returned to Capharnaum, there was a knock on Peter's door. Tax collectors had come to collect taxes. In particular, they were concerned with Peter and the payment of his taxes. None of us were immune to their scrutiny. Amazingly, Matthew had chosen this moment not to be with us. Had he been, perhaps these emissaries of Rome would not have bothered us. Where was Matthew? This was his city, his world. Could he have known these men would come? Then they inquired of Peter, "Has your teacher paid his taxes?"

Peter replied "I wouldn't really know."

"Fetch him," ordered his visitors. Peter closed the door, leaving the tax collectors outside.

When he came back into the house, Jesus was the first to speak. "What do you think, Simon?" he asked. "From whom do the authorities collect taxes—from their own sons and family, or from others?"

Peter laughed scornfully, "From others," he answered.

"Then their sons are exempt," said Jesus with some disquietude. He thought for a moment before saying anything further. Under the Romans, paying taxes was a hard reality. You either paid or were incarcerated—or worse. The Jews they conscripted to collect taxes were the result of a particularly insidious practice. The Romans knew that collecting revenue from the Jewish population could be best effected by the Jews themselves, exploiting their quaint societal structure of rabbis, synagogues, legalists, etc. Those they "suborned," were not exactly unwilling victims, either. In order to provide incentive, the Romans did not concern themselves with collectors who added a percentage on top of the actual tax owed and kept it for themselves. As long as the government received what it required, they considered it an acceptable incentive that their collectors made themselves obscenely rich.

"Walk down to the lake, Simon, and throw out a fishing line. Take the first fish you catch; open its mouth and inside you will find a gold coin. Take it and give it to the collectors for my tax and yours."

Peter stared at Jesus in some bemused amazement. "Jesus," he said quietly, "this is no time for jokes. The greedy pigs are standing at the door."

Jesus looked at Peter with a tolerant but annoyed expression, "I know that Simon. Please, go and do as I have said."

Peter backed out of the room and left through the front entrance. "Wait here," he said to the collectors. "I will return in a moment."

"If you keep us waiting, your taxes will increase. We do not spend our time doing this for nothing."

Peter smiled, "Yes. How well I know. Don't go away, I'll be right back." With that, he strode toward the dock, several hundred feet from his house. Like any good fisherman, Peter kept a container of bait in his boat. He was a commercial fisherman, but on occasion, he enjoyed wetting a hook on a line as much as anyone else. He searched for the worms, extracted a long night crawler from the container and then paused. This is silly, he thought for a moment. If Jesus wants me to make an ass of myself, I may as well be a total ass. He dropped the squirming creature back into the container. He whistled his line and empty hook over his head out into the water. No sooner had the bare hook submerged than there was a strong tug on the line. He was excited now. Added to the thrill of a fish striking his baitless line was the thrill of knowing that this is really happening! He almost couldn't wait until the finny creature lay flopping on the dock.

The fish was about eighteen inches long. When Peter grasped the thrashing, slippery creature, Abishag, who had followed him down to the water, yapped and danced happily. He took the fish carefully in his hand and pried its mouth open with his fingers. In its gullet there lodged a bright, polished gold coin. Wondering for a moment how it got there, or how Jesus knew about it, the amazed fisherman extracted it, tossed the fish back into the water, and walked quickly to the men waiting at his door. When he handed them the coin, their eyes widened.

"This should take care of it," Peter laughed. "Got it out of a fish's mouth!"

It was more than enough for Peter and Jesus. It was enough for all of us and then some. The tax collectors were stunned. However, despite Peter's unlikely tale, they were careful not to reveal that the amount of the payment was excessive.

As soon as they recovered from the initial shock, one of them cleared his throat and said "Well, ah, yes, this should be sufficient, I suppose." They quickly stuffed the coin away, nodded their heads in stiff acceptance and left.

Moments later Matthew appeared at the front door. "Did I miss something?" he said with a grin. He crooked his neck to take another glance at the men as they quickly walked away.

What all of this taught us about our responsibility to our government I am not certain. There is one thing, however, that was quite clear. Jesus had access to financial stores the like of which the rest of us could only imagine. People gave of their generosity to support our ministry, yet the needs of the ministry were already certified. It seems as though any time Jesus needed funds he could make a withdrawal from...well, the oddest places.

αΘω

How do I find the words to speak of God? Yet each day I was with Jesus, it is self-evident that I was with God. How many fish are there in the waters of Galilee? Thousands? Millions? What were the chances of that one fish swallowing Peter's line? It is not so hard, perhaps, to conceive of how a shiny, gold coin came to be in its mouth. If the fish had seen it fall into the water or watched the sunlight dance on its turning, twisting sides as it made its way towards the bottom, that would certainly have provided a sufficient lure. But how could Jesus have known...of that particular fish in all the Sea of Galilee...that it would swim near where Peter dropped his denuded hook or that it would seek out the hook? It staggers the mind.

Further, it seemed a rather blasé way to approach the payment of one's taxes. Does this reflect a bias in Jesus' thinking of the whole concept of a government's collection of revenue? Is it possible that by this act he was scorning the government's right to take a person's livelihood? I know not. But that we walked with someone special, there could be no doubt.

XIII

Faith of a Child

The morning broke bright and happy the next day, as we made ready to journey yet again. Joanna, ever the concerned mother to us all, commanded and directed to make sure that we were adequately provisioned. She even adjusted Jesus' robe and kissed his cheek and said, "You remember to keep warm, young man. You may be God's Son, but you can still catch a cold and run a fever." Jesus smiled tolerantly, then gave her a warm, affectionate hug. Abishag darted about excitedly and wagged her tail so hard her whole back end wiggled. She always seemed to know when we were making for another journey, this time to Judea. We would be on the road for several days.

At length, we were on our way, road dust rising from the movement of our entourage. There were sixteen of us for this trip. The twelve, Matthias, James, the Lord's brother and I, and of course, Jesus. As it is among men who like to talk, it wasn't long before voices started to get loud and an argument ensued.

It happened like this: James, because he was the brother of Jesus, always seemed to consider himself the most privileged among us—even though he was not among the chosen apostles. Perhaps he thought of himself above the apostles. In any case, James never let us forget that since he grew up with Jesus, he was the one most credentialed to manage our affairs and be the general leader of the group as "second" in command.

After the death of Jesus, James did emerge to be become a chief leader among the apostles. Paul even accorded James this honor. But, of course, Paul considered himself to be numbered among the apostles as well. He established his own criteria for apostleship—which did not include, notably, that one had to have been with Jesus since his baptism. But, as we shall see, who was what and how one got there was not something that captivated the mind of Jesus. Still, James' arrogance grated on the nerves of all of us, and I suppose because of his natural leadership qualities, or perhaps, he felt his leadership threatened, it hit Peter the hardest.

As we began our travel for that day, James remarked, "We shall head south and stop first at Magdala and then on to Tiberias. It's the shortest distance."

Peter looked at him with a "here we go again" exasperation in his expression and said, "I think we should take the route around the northern end of the sea and stop first at Bethsaida. The road is better and, even though it's a bit farther, will take less time. Besides, there are good fishing spots along the roadside."

"Simon," James rejoined, "We don't have to think of fishing all the time. There are other things and other ways to consider. All things considered, fisherman, the southern shore is better for all concerned. We will head south." Like Jesus, James was, of course, a carpenter.

"Of course, my captain," said Peter with sarcasm, "we are all highly skilled in those 'all things considered' of which you speak. Perhaps a carpenter's son would be more than happy to provide us with food and shelter with his amazing expertise in the working of wood. The rest of us poor fishermen will watch in awe."

A flash of anger erupted, "I am the one most qualified to lead here, Simon. After all, I spent over twenty years..."

"Yes! Yes, James. We all are aware of that fact. You have reminded us dozens of times. But your status as his brother does not automatically confer upon you competence. You think because you are his brother you should receive special honor. Let me remind you that you are his brother. You are not him..."

"I speak for him..."

"You speak for no one!" This from Judas Iscariot. "I am the one with the money. I am in charge of that. How it is spent is my doing. If we are going to debate who makes the decisions in this group, you would do well to bear that in mind."

"True enough," spoke Thaddeaus wearily, "Judas should be second in command. The one with all the money should definitely be in charge." And so it went. Back and forth, each arguing on behalf of himself or another as to which amongst the group was to lead the rest.

Jesus had been walking contemplatively by himself several paces behind. His concentration was disturbed by the raised voices, and when he saw all of the jawboning and gesticulating, he made to catch up with us.

He spoke with some irritation. He seemed to know what was going on before he asked questions. "So, what is the big disagreement? I would think your mouths would be too filled with the dust of the road to haggle like a flock of crows." They scowled at each other and muttered reluctant acquiescence as children do when required by a parent to stop a fight. Even our respect for Jesus could be clouded when our self-assurance became inflated.

αΘω

Once it was learned that Jesus was traveling through, crowds of varying sizes followed. This day was no exception. Among these stood a mother and a little boy watching the passing of our entourage. Jesus stopped and spoke to the woman quietly. He took the boy by the hand, led him over to us. Sitting down on a cedar log, he placed his hand on the boy's shoulder and said to us, "Look, my self-absorbed disciples! Look and learn! You must stop this adolescent foolishness of elevating yourselves one above the other."

He then picked up the boy, who immediately gave Jesus a huge giggling hug around the neck. Jesus tossed the little man up in the air several times, and by this time both of them were laughing and enjoying each other. Other children playing nearby observed the fun and came to join them. Several of the disciples tried to stop them.

When Jesus saw this, he became indignant. He said, "What is the matter with you men!? Get out of the way and let the children come to me. The kingdom of God belongs to kids like these." We were arrested. "Let me tell you something," he continued, "anyone who will not receive the kingdom of God like one of these children will never enter it. I wish to God my Father that you men were like them! Perhaps you would be at each other less.

"Who do you think is greater in God's kingdom? Did you see this boy come to me with no reserve, no expectations, just innocent, simple trust? Let me be clear; whoever humbles himself as this child is the greatest in heaven. Welcome the little ones in my name and you will please the Father.

"If anyone causes one of these 'little children' who believe in me to stumble or fall, it would be better for him to be taken out to sea, have a large millstone tied to his neck and thrown overboard. Never look down on one of these little ones. Instead, observe them, and become like them. For I tell you that their angels are in constant communication with my Father in heaven. They are not unrepresented."

It was a long night, that night. Each man with his own thoughts about what Jesus had said. Each man troubled, disturbed by the internal struggle with his own ego, his pride, even his "manhood." Where did this fit? Humility! An extremely difficult thing to grasp!

This was not the first, nor would it be the last time this issue concerned the apostles. Repeatedly, Jesus reminded us that humility, not status—even if we had status—is one of the chief traits of those he has chosen to follow him.

Incredibly, after he was gone, the twelve ignored these warnings. As did Paul. As did James. As did they all. Because of this, the first seeds of ecclesiasticism began to take root. Derived from Hebrew tradition, bishops, elders and deacons were "ordained." Status and licensure became the measure of competence and authority, disregarding humility and service. And, in accepting this, they lost the sweet, simple innocence of relationship with him and with each other. It was to become, after the death of Jesus, one the most insidious spiritual diseases of his followers.

αΘω

No doubt, owing to the previous night's uncomfortable discussion, John ventured, "Teacher, we saw a man exorcising evil spirits in your name and we ordered him to stop."

"And exactly why did you do that?"

There was rebuke in the question. John, embarrassed, tried to save face, "Well, Master," he said, in a pubescent tone, "He was not one of us!"

Jesus smiled. "Yes. Of course. How easy it is for me to ignore the obvious." John braced himself. He knew what was coming. "John, you of all people should know better. That was a serious mistake. Surely you must realize that it is difficult for one who does miracles through my name to oppose me or reject my teachings. I have said that whoever is not with us is against us. Similarly, whoever is not against us is for us. Did he stop?"

"Well, yes. I guess he recognized us as apostles."

Jesus shook his head in sad disgust. "Already you are beginning to be full of yourselves. How many times have I asked you to humble yourselves as a little child? How many times must I ask you not to lord it over others? When I am gone, the Holy Spirit will come and raise up a great church in my name. But you will cripple and corrupt it. You will corrupt it with your persistent lust for 'apostolic' authority and recognition. You will be no different than the Pharisees who lay heavy burdens on the people and yet would not lift a finger to help. The only way others will truly know that you follow me is when you love as I have loved you, not when you build an institution."

αΘω

Then Jesus raised his voice, "I am disheartened by the lack of humility and love you show one another. Despite your hardness of heart and insufferable self-importance, the Father loves you and listens to your cries and the pain in your hearts. If only you could agree and be harmonious with one another! Do you not realize that if two of you shall agree on earth concerning anything you ask, the Father will see to it that it is done? And do you not further realize that when even just two or three of you get together in my name, I'll be there with you?"

Peter was upset. Later, no doubt concerned as to how he should now respond to this whole uncomfortable scene, he came to Jesus alone and asked, "Lord, how many times shall I forgive my brother when he sins against me? Up to seven times?"

Jesus answered, "Peter, you miss the point of forgiveness. What if you did forgive him seven times and he wronged you again? What happens then? To carry rancor against your brother, not to forgive him in your heart, is to carry a heavy and unnecessary burden and to invite the crippling disease of bitterness. Because of this you must always forgive. Besides, among men, the one forgiving is even more blessed than the one forgiven.

"Forgiveness is at the heart of heaven. When you withhold forgiveness, you bring destruction upon yourself in addition to whatever suffering you inflict on another. My Father has forgiven all your debts to him, all your sins against him, so how can you do less than forgive your brother from your heart?

"Therefore search your heart and if you find you are withholding forgiveness, then be quick and certain to forgive. Only then will you be able to be free and clean yourself and reap the benefits of God's forgiveness."

Peter asked nothing further. I don't know if Jesus' answer to his question satisfied him or not. He never spoke of it again. I was comforted, however. I had much to forgive and, no doubt, much for which to be forgiven. Jesus' presence with me was strong wine. I felt warmed and affirmed as he spoke.

XIV

Gratitude

The jarring weariness of the road sank deep into my bones. I awoke to the first grey of dawn. Lingering, brilliant points of light still punctuated the sky overhead. I lay there for a moment awake, gazing at heavenly bodies. My eyes closed and slumber claimed me once again. I awoke a second time with a start. Jesus had thrown a small stick that came to rest close to my head. I awoke with the hot breath of Abishag in my face. She had come for the stick but paused to give my face a lick. I sat up abruptly and could hear Jesus chuckling in the distance. The dog retrieved the stick, bounding back to Jesus. Leaning on my elbow, I watched them. Jesus teasing the dog by waving the stick as if he were going to throw it, Abishag lunging for the stick as Jesus quickly tucked it behind his back. She was only fooled for a moment as she circled behind him to find the elusive quarry.

Again, he hurled. This time the stick flew straight to where Peter was snoring. It touched the earth a few inches from his nose. The dog sped toward the stick and slid to a stop, smothering Simon's face with dirt and her dusty belly. He awoke with a shock. "Be-damned!" he cried, sitting bolt upright. Jesus held his sides in laughter. This fisherman was never far from a well-turned profane phrase. The Lord and his dog continued their mischievous game until we were all awake. "Time to be up and about!" he shouted. "Little James" (not the Lord's brother), be about breakfast! My noble beast and I are famished!" His laughter could be heard throughout the vale.

Breakfast of dried grapes, goat cheese and hard bread baked by Joanna tasted wondrous. Jesus and Abishag's antics left us all breathless with mirth. It was a beautiful morning. Jesus was on his feet and gathering his things to start the day's journey. "Come," said he, "we go to Jerusalem. Thomas, Thaddeus, go before us among the Samaritans. We lodge there tonight." We traveled along the border between Samaria and Galilee. With some foreboding, we walked through the morning mists. Samaria is not the most inviting place for Jews.

The two men went ahead of us and arrived at the town of Sychar several hours before the rest of us. Thomas said to Thaddeus, "This is the place where Jesus spoke to the woman at Jacob's well, where afterwards we were treated so well. We will be welcome here." Approaching the man's home where they had lodged before, Thaddeus inquired, "We wish to purchase lodging for Jesus of Nazareth and his disciples this night. He is on his way to Jerusalem."

"Jerusalem?" the man responded. "That whore of a city? What business could he possibly have there?" he growled.

The two men looked at one another. The hostility surprised them. It was a moment before they could respond. "I believe he intends to teach and heal," said Thaddeus quietly.

The man scowled, "If he is going to Jerusalem, he is not sleeping under my roof. Go away!"

Thaddeus and Thomas returned with the unsettling report. Upon hearing it James and John said, "Lord, will you have us to call fire down from heaven and consume them, as did Elijah?" Sons of thunder, indeed. Typical.

Not surprisingly, Jesus spoke sternly to them, "What kind of spirit is in you? Will you never learn? I did not come not to destroy men's lives, but to save them. We'll go to another village where we are welcome." Jesus spoke nothing else as we continued through the darkening hills. I would have given anything to know his thoughts…

I know that these men, especially my brother, will assume authority over the faithful after I am gone. Oh, Father! Would that they not! Would that they could see that I came as a Servant, not as some ancient prophet hurling fire about. How earnestly I wish them to serve each other and by loving, serve the world. But I fear the worst. I fear the worst.

αΘω

Just before we crossed the river eastward into Peraea, descending into the Jordan valley in Samaria far south of Galilee, we entered one of the villages and, in doing so, encountered a group of men. Ten of them, dressed in rags. We could smell their stench even though they stood thirty paces away. They were lepers huddling together in a clump with hardly any space separating their bodies. They distanced themselves from us as if realizing their terrible inertia of disease, yet looking at us with a desperate appeal. Leprosy is an intractable, loathsome malady affecting primarily the eyes and the skin. Two of these men were missing both eyes and several more, missing one. One man's fingers were gone. On another, fingers and ears, on another there was a mass of raw, red and white tissue where his nose once existed. They gazed at us with gaunt eyes; well, those that had them. At length one of them shouted. "Jesus," he cried, "Servant of the most high God; have compassion on us!"

These poor creatures had braved the rejection of society by emerging from the colony to seek him out. It was a pathetic sight. Jesus did not attempt to approach them, for doing so would have only agitated and frightened them. From where we stood he shouted back, "Go on your way. Show yourselves to the priests." His instruction was consistent with the old Levitical Scriptures where Moses required the priests to examine lepers for the severity of their disease and render judgments.

Slowly, the men turned to go, disappointed that Jesus did nothing for them, yet relieved that he had not attempted to touch them. Still huddled together, they moved away from us and in a few moments disappeared from view. I am certain that they were confused at Jesus' instruction. They had no need to be examined by priests. That had been done years ago for most of them. Moreover, they were obviously diseased. As they went on their way, they suddenly stopped. Joash, utterly stunned, looked at his friend Moshe. "Moshe!" he exclaimed. "Moshe, stop! *Something has happened!*" Moshe did not have to be told. Where once a mass of raw flesh appeared with two gaping holes in his face stood a new nose. Where once fingers and hands were gone were new fingers and hands. The pink, the white, the raw, the red—all gone from every one of them. Even the terrible odor of rotting flesh and soiled clothing had evaporated. They were cleansed! Indescribable elation! Now they did want to see the priest. Once they regained their composure, they hurried off.

Except for one. This man, seeing that he was healed, turned back and with a loud voice began to give thanks to God. He came to us and fell on his face at Jesus' feet, offering his gratitude. He was a Samaritan.

With his hand, Jesus lifted the man to face him. "Were not ten cleansed?" he asked. "Where are the other nine?" The man's eyes revealed some apprehension at Jesus' question.

"I - I do not know, Lord. They..."

Jesus did not let him finish, "Were none found to return and give thanks to God except this 'foreigner'?" This he spoke rhetorically—to anyone who might have heard, which, naturally, included every one of us. The moral of his question was not lost. And then in comforting tones he said to the Samaritan, "Rise. Go your way. Your faith has healed you."

"Your faith has healed you?" What faith? This man along with the others were only a few moments ago huddled together in a pathetic gaggle, barely alive within the running sores of diseased flesh, hoping, rather than expecting, that Jesus might let a crumb roll in their direction. Their faith was as pathetic as their condition. Yet, said Jesus, it had healed them. Perhaps this is true of all of us, our faith is as pathetic as our condition, yet…it is enough.

XV

Peraea

Our journey had begun at Peter's home in the north. Given our reception in Sychar, Jesus saw no necessity to continue through Samaria, so on this occasion we took the traditional route through Peraea and avoided the hostile Samaritan countryside. Peraea: a land of protection from the Samaritans, where Jews traveled to and from Galilee and Judea.

There is no more beautiful country in all Israel than Peraea. Gazing west the eye feasts upon a panorama of rolling sandstone hills. This same sandstone provides a base for the slopes of Moab and Gilead and may be found as far south as the river Jabbok.

A white, crumbly mixture of clays and remnants of shells cover the land. These form uncommon peaks above the Jordan valley. In the Spring and Summer, blossoms of flame are plentiful, these joined by the narcissus lacing soft breezes with exotic perfumes. Slopes shady with acacia groves, palm trees, shaggy oaks and in higher reaches, with pines. Streams fringed with towering bushes of pink, white and poisonous oleander. In the lower hills, the tamarisk, lotus and waving canebrakes.

Above this lies hard, impervious, limestone rising to better than 1,500 feet. above the sandstone base forming a porous bed for copious rivulets of water that burst out of the hills into perennial brooks. On the other side of these slopes the country is bare and arid. Water there is supplied by cisterns and deep wells. Plateau becomes desert. On one side, the hill slopes abound in streams, springs and fertility, on the other—wilderness.

Because this province was mainly gentile, Judas Maccabeus found it necessary to move to Judea, scattering handfuls of Jews to insure their safety. Later, under John Hyrcanus, son of Simon, brother to Judas Maccabeus, Jewish influence began to prevail. John was victorious against Antiochus VII and remained in power until his death 140 years ago. Under Hyrcanus, the country enjoyed its greatest political power.

Alexander Jannaeus then took the throne. A tyrant of the first order, Jannaeus headed the sect of the Sadducees against the Pharisees until his death when his widow, Salome Alexandra, became queen. Of the opposite political and religious persuasion, she favored the Pharisees. She governed better than any of the males in the house of the Maccabees. After her death, a civil war erupted between her two sons that resulted in the taking of Jerusalem by the Roman general, Pompey. Since then, there have been perennial struggles between the Jews and Romans, but the land of Peraea as well as the whole of Israel has remained under Roman rule where it is today. This Peraea, this "land beyond Jordan," ranks along with Judea and Galilee as a full province of the land of Israel.

The northern fords and those opposite Jericho in the south afford traverse and converse with Galilee and Judea respectively, so that the pilgrims from any part might go to Jerusalem and return without setting foot on gentile soil. And, what was of equal importance, they could avoid peril of hurt or indignity which the Samaritans loved to inflict on Jews passing through Samaria as we have already seen.

Our having passed through a northern ford, Peraea was now the scene of much quiet and profitable rest for Jesus and, indeed, for all of us.

αΘω

Others, many others, thirsty for his words, had joined us in our travels. We stopped at a cross road. One road led north and south (the one we were on) and the other led east and west. Nearby, stood a small inn reflected in a clear pool of water edged by palm trees, a copse of acacia in the background. An inviting rest for weary travelers; Jesus stopped here to lodge. After a few moments of shade and a cool drink he said, "Select seventy-two men from this crowd of followers. I have a special assignment for them." I was surprised that he would entrust this task to us; nevertheless, we drifted through the crowd looking for likely prospects. Soon we had gathered seventy-two men together and brought them to Jesus.

He told this group, "My brothers, I wish you to go on a mission. It will not be easy. I'm sending you out like lambs among wolves. Do not take money or luggage or even an extra pair of sandals, and do not greet anyone on the road. When you enter a house, first say, 'Peace to this house.' If a man of peace is there, your peace will be welcomed. Stay in that house, accepting whatever food and drink they offer you, as this will be wages for your effort. Heal any of their household who is sick and tell them, 'The kingdom of God is yours now if you will accept it.'

"But when you enter a town and are not welcomed, go into its streets and say, 'The dust of this town we wipe off our sandals! Even so, the love of God is yours now if you will accept it.' If the town still rejects you, the ancient city of Sodom will be more acceptable in God's day than it will be for that town. He who listens to you listens to me. He who rejects you rejects me, and he who rejects me rejects him who sent me."

There were, surprisingly, no protests, no questions and none who declined. They had followed Jesus, believed his message and were ready to do whatever he asked. What was surprising about this was that Jesus had sent none of the twelve to go with them, to train them, to credential them. Yet they were being called upon to represent Jesus, and thus represent the Father. An awesome task for supposedly ordinary men. An awesome task, indeed.

αΘω

We lodged at the inn for several days until the seventy-two returned. They were ecstatic and said to Jesus, "Lord, we have preached good news, we healed those with disease, even the demons submit to us in your name."

He replied, "I am happy with you." He lifted his arms in welcome. "But I wish you to listen carefully." When the noise of celebrating faded, he spoke in a quiet voice, "I myself ejected Satan from heaven. He fell like lightning through the stars. His defeat was absolute and his end is certain." What manner of man could say such a thing? I thought to myself. Can there be any doubt of his true identity? "Now I have given you that same authority to trample on snakes and scorpions and to overcome the power of the enemy. Nothing will harm you." He paused. The awe and wonder of what he was saying overwhelmed his listeners. "However," he warned, "do not be satisfied that spirits submit to you, but rather that your names are written, recorded and sealed in the vault of heaven."

It was clearly a moment of great pleasure for Jesus. These seventy-two men had followed his instructions and had been effective. He told them, "All things have been committed to me by my Father. No one truly knows or understands me except the Father. No one truly knows the Father except me and those to whom I choose to reveal him. I have chosen to reveal him in you. The power you felt, the power you used was the power of my Father." We were all greatly encouraged by these words. Then Jesus extended his arms once again as if to embrace us all and said with great feeling,

"Come to me, all of you who are weary and burdened, and I will give you rest. Take my yoke upon you and learn of me, for I am gentle and humble in heart, and you will find rest for your souls. For my yoke is easy and my burden is light."

In the quiet that followed, you could have heard a falling feather touch the ground. "Blessed are the eyes that see what you see. Blessed are the ears that hear what you hear. Prophets and kings have longed to see what you see but could not see it; they longed to hear what you hear but could not hear it."

αΘω

A prominent lawyer, an expert in the law of Moses, came forward and spoke to Jesus. "Teacher," he asked, "what must I do to inherit eternal life?"

Jesus looked at him with that penetrating gaze with which he was so gifted, "What is written in the Law?" he replied. "How do you read it?" How interesting! He was giving to this man his moment, his opportunity to impress us all with his legal mind. Generous, I thought.

The lawyer was not slow in forthcoming. He answered confidently, "Love the Lord your God with all your heart and with all your soul and with all your strength and with all your mind and love your neighbor as yourself." He answered as if it were a child's question.

"You have answered correctly," Jesus replied. "Do this and you will live." He was not in the least put off by this man for all of his condescension.

The lawyer pressed a finer point, "And who, then, is my neighbor?" He was inviting Jesus to an intellectual exchange of what, from a theological point of view, distinguished one as a "neighbor." The man had his own thoughts about this worked out, of course, through numerous erudite, legal study and discussions. One qualified as a "neighbor" if one owned so many cattle, or held certain political positions or perhaps had been taught at the feet of an eminent Rabbi. Jesus had something else in mind.

"A man traveled from Jerusalem to Jericho," he said, "and fell into the hands of bandits. They stripped him of his clothes, beat him for the pleasure of it and left him for dead. A leader of the synagogue happened to be traveling the same road. When he saw the man, he quickly crossed the road to the other side. So, too, a priest, when he came to the place and saw this unfortunate man, he passed him by, also ignoring him.

"But a Samaritan, who as you know has misguided notions of the Law, came to where the man was. And when he saw him, his heart filled with compassion and concern. He went to him, cleaned and bandaged his wounds, pouring on first wine and then oil. Then he put the man on his own donkey and took him to an inn where he stayed the night with him, taking care of him. The next day he gave money to the innkeeper. 'Look after him,' he said, 'and when I return, I will reimburse you for any extra expense you may incur.'

"Which of these three do you think was neighbor to the man who fell into the hands of bandits?"

The lawyer, lowering his eyes, said nothing. Unable to bear the silence, he replied, "The one who had mercy on him, I believe."

Jesus told him, "So, my friend, would you do as well?

"I can try, my Lord." Instead of testing the knowledge of Jesus, the lawyer had himself been tested.

XVI

The Audacious Frog

Later, as we were resting by a small wadi through which brown water lazily found its way downstream, Abishag took pleasure in disturbing the sunning frogs. There were many of these denizens in this slow moving water. The current there was imperceptible except for the stream escaping from the downside end of a small pool. Abishag approached a sitting frog and attempted to sniff it. When it leaped into the water, the dog jumped back as if it has been stuck in the nose by a thorn. It quickly became a game as she first found and then approached each frog and lunged at it with front paws. When the frog leaped, she barked.

As she approached a large, dark green frog sitting on an outcropping root, she sniffed. The frog didn't move. She tried her trick of splashing down her front paws near the old frog. Still the frog didn't move. It seems oblivious to the dog's antics. At length, Abishag made a large splash accompanied by several barks; still the frog sat perfectly still. She looked at Jesus as if asking what to do. The Son of Man simply shrugged his shoulders and raised his palms upward in response. He hadn't the slightest idea. While the dog's attention diverted, the bullfrog leaped, alighting for an instant on her head. Abishag yipped, turned and fled. Jesus wept with laughter, as did we all. Abishag turned to look at the frog, which had climbed back upon its half-submerged root. The dog had had enough. Insulted by our laughter, she sauntered off and lay down in the shade of a tree.

"This is not an ordinary frog," observed Jesus. "Did you see how it ignored Abishag and then brazenly surprised her when she least expected it? The frog won the day, for the dog now leaves it alone!" Jesus laughed merrily.

"Now suppose one of you has a friend, and you go to his house in the middle of the night and yell through the window, 'Lend me some bread. A friend of mine who is traveling has come to my house and I have nothing to feed him.'

"Then your friend replies, 'Don't you know that it's the middle of the night? The house is locked, the family is asleep. I can't get up and give you anything now. Besides, what are you doing up feeding people at this hour? Can't this wait until morning?' You must admit, this is a pretty brazen request. And though your friend had no intention of getting up to give you anything, even though you are his friend, because of your brazenness, he will at length get up and give you whatever you need."

Jesus smiled and said, "You know, sometimes the Father is like that. He enjoys an audacious frog. He enjoys spunk and audacity. Do not be timid with the Father. Don't be afraid to take what you might think is a risk with the Father. With him, there are no risks. Only certainty. Believe in yourself and trust in him."

XVII

Juliana

Another cold, bitter morning. Every morning was cold and bitter. She never grew accustomed to it. Was it better for the blood to be too thin or too thick? She was not sure. She was not sure if her blood was thin or thick. She was not sure she had blood. Nor did she care. She only knew that every morning was the same. Cold and bitter. Perhaps God provided the cold. She provided the bitterness. Her garments were the latest fashion for women with no visible means of support—rags. They were thin rags, having seen too much wear. It was the Sabbath. A holy day. It was just another day, a day for prigs and priests. She would have none of that fathomless wasteland. A familiar but still odd sensation crawled across her skin. She looked at her forearm to see the hairs rise on tiny mountains of skin. She looked like a half-plucked chicken. She shivered.

Her name was Juliana Hebaav, the daughter of Roman and Miriana Hebaav. Today was her forty-sixth birthday, and alone she languished in a dark cave in this land beyond the Jordan. It was still very early. Grey shrouds of dawn made it slightly possible to see the opposite wall of the cave and to trace the outline of its opening to the fields outside. Through the haze of awakening from a troubled sleep she felt a familiar sensation from deep within her abdomen. It came up through her body like vomit and she began, like she had done a thousand times before, to cry. The feeling inside could only be understood in terms of a relentless, leaden sense of approaching death, something for which she wished every day of her life since…since…

Juliana rose from her bed of sparse straw to her full height slightly above four feet. This is not to say that she was physically underdeveloped. Had she been able to stand up straight, she would have been at a normal height for a woman, a woman whose considerable beauty was marred by almost two decades of unspeakable pain. She was not sure which came first, the physical pain or the unbearable agony inside that made her cry every day of her life. Her tears exhausted, she continued in tearless sobs. Her hunched body was stooped with a backbone that curved in such a way that she lived her life in a fetal posture. What tears she had left remained in her eyes, which continually swam in them, yet they rarely coursed down her dirty cheeks. The times that they did left rivulets of a lighter shade of skin. A close look at her face revealed dark, hollow eyes set in streaked skin. She looked like a sad corpse, dead without really knowing that she was dead—or perhaps she did know it. She whimpered slowly, haltingly left the cave, found a bush, squatted and urinated. She wailed into the mists as the fluid left her body. Had anyone been close enough to hear, they, too, would have shivered.

Brown, matted hair tied back to keep it from dragging on the ground, fell stiffly over her shoulders.. The grey humidity outside the cave turned into a soft but cold rain. She moved as fast as she could back into the shelter of darkness. Finding her bed of straw she lay down and wondered how she would spend the day. Where would she go and what would she do? The cold embers of the previous evening's fire stared back at her. She had let it go out. Starting it again would be a chore with only flint and rock to generate a blaze. Like a bone-chilling shroud, the cold seeped through her skin deep into tissue until she could feel it in the marrow of her bones.

Memories came back to haunt her. Memories that made her gasp with grief. The pounding on the door, the fear, the impassive, determined look on the face of the soldiers—men who had pledged their loyalty to Caesar and were obligated to do the bidding of Herod the Great, Herod the Monster. The shrieking sound of the sword being extracted from its scabbard, the glint of steel, the look of terrified surprise from the bulging eyes of her son as the steel penetrated his tiny body, the abrupt cessation of his scream, his life. Before her eyes and those of her husband, before they knew what was happening, not to speak of why, the life of their child was taken. "By the King's command!" shouted the soldier, pointing the bloody sword at them. It was all over in a matter of seconds. A few seconds that had mercilessly killed her baby, a few seconds that had destroyed her marriage, her mind and her body. Another child never came to ease the pain. The sadness grew so great, so profound. Deeper and deeper her sadness worsened until no longer could she stand erect—now, eighteen years in this agonizing contracture. The sobs came, which she tried to bury in the filthy straw on the floor of the cave.

αΘω

When at last she awoke still shivering, she knew she had to move, to get up and do something. She felt a brief moment of gratitude when she glanced outside and saw the sun drying the foliage. Stumbling toward the opening and stepping clumsily into the sunshine raised her spirits only slightly. The prospects of the day before her were not inviting. She knew she had to beg if she were to live another day. The nearest town was a mile away; for her, a two-hour journey.

Hobbling along the road, she tried to catch the eyes of passersby hoping for any glance of pity or mercy. Eyes diverted, avoiding her entirely. People did not care, or if they did, made no move to express it. They seemed to make it a point not to care. They had their own problems. They did not want the intrusion of eye contact with this disfigured, miscreant woman. Besides, did she care when she had her son, her husband and enough food to eat, a home in which to live? How many times had she walked by a beggar with money in her purse? How many times had she crossed the way to avoid those who looked as she did now? The callousness of those who now passed her by, served her right. She deserved no less. Yet the hunger...the mind-numbing pain of isolation and humiliation. She leaned heavily against her crude stick as her head drooped almost below her waist.

Before she noticed the animal, it had trotted up to her and stopped within an arm's reach. She, too, stopped, amused and strangely warmed by this curious creature. The dog seemed to sense her, to be aware of her misery in a deeper dimension than just curiosity or looking for a handout. A scruffy nose sniffed her extended hand; a friendly lick followed. She suspected the animal was a stray and thought to send it away. She could ill afford to feed a dog. But her heart resonated with its gaze. She saw something in its demeanor that spoke of acceptance, even love, or so she would like to think. This immediately comforted her, and with a gentle touch she patted the animal's head. She stroked the dog's flanks and scratched her behind the ears and was rewarded with more licks. After a brief moment of this, her new friend took a few steps away from her, turned and gazed at her with raised ears. She sniffed again as if trying to find an elusive scent in the afternoon air currents. Abruptly, the creature trotted away. Soon it was out of the limits of her stooped vision.

Mixed feelings flooded her. Struggling with her sense of sadness that the animal was gone, briefly entertaining the possibility of having even a little companionship, the warmth and comfort she felt in the encounter; feeling all of these at once, she whimpered. More emotions to deal with. Would they never cease? Would she ever know peace? She found herself longing for the cessation of life yet again. Her head drooped lower still.

αΘω

Spending the morning in the synagogue was not my idea of the place to be. More and more these days, I found myself resisting the trappings of the Jewish religion, although I have been raised in it all my life. Jesus himself was a Jew, yet he held himself aloof from the Jewish religious system. He taught respect for the traditions. He seemed to hold a special regard for the old prophets, but his disdain for religious order and religious dictums seemed to grow everywhere we went. He had just completed one of his teaching sessions. It was amazing to me that people would come from all over to follow him traipsing about the country, just to hear the things he had to say. This was because much of what he said was repetition to me. I had heard his teaching so many times, yet on each occasion, he did seem to add something new and unique.

So much of what he said was never written down. Many years later, as I thought about it, it is astounding how much he did and said that was never written, never recorded for posterity. How can people think they really can know him from the little that has been written about him? I was thinking about these things when he exited the synagogue. As always, he left a covey of religious imbeciles arguing and dissecting what he had said, what he had taught. Shaking my head, I joined him in the street.

Laughing, he turned to me and said, "Justus!" He slapped my back and embraced me around the shoulders with his arm; "Justus!" he said again. "What do you think we should do with the rest of this beautiful day?"

I never knew quite what to do with this kind of exuberance. I think of myself as the more cerebral sort. I think about things. I was never very good at a quick, witty retort. I just smiled back at Jesus and said, "That is your decision, Jesus; but if it were mine, I think that since we started out for Jerusalem, that is where we should continue to go. Peraea is lovely, but it is time we moved on."

"Always the pragmatic soul!" said he back to me. "Are you the kind of person who never wants to enjoy the trip? Always pressing to get to the destination? Never stopping to rest or enjoy?" He was chiding me with humor. "Shall we stride through the night, Justus? Shall we look neither right nor left? Shall we keep focused on the path before us?" I was getting the treatment. Matthew and Peter were amused. I was saved by Abishag, who bounced up to Jesus and jumped up on him with her paws.

Jesus recoiled slightly and then began to play with the dog. He reached for her to cuff her behind the ears and gestured as if he would run to the left or the right. Then the dog did a strange thing. Instead of dancing around Jesus as was her usual bent when he was in a playful mood, she trotted a distance away and turned back to look at him. "Come, Abishag!" he called after her. The dog came instantly, wagging her tail and exchanging pets and licks. But when Jesus attempted another playful move, she trotted away again and looked back at him.

"Something's amiss. I think she is trying to tell you something, Jesus," said I. For a moment he paused and looked after her. She took a few more steps away from us and stopped, looking back again to see what we would do. Jesus called her to him again. This time she did not come. It was the first time I had seen that. Instead, she took a few more steps and stopped, looking back yet again. Jesus strode toward her, and immediately Abishag continued on her way as if leading us to a destination in a dog's world. What was she doing? Where was she going? Our curiosity aroused, and feeling an inquisitive alarm, we followed obediently. We could not keep up, but just as she was about to disappear, she stopped and looked back. She never let us out of her sight.

After some time, she stopped in front of a stooped creature. It was a woman dressed in faded brown rags. I had seen the poor before; I had seen them lying about, palms outstretched, some of them sightless, some covered with sores, but I had not seen so pathetic a human being in my life as this woman before me now. Abishag approached her gently and licked her hand.

αΘω

She was genuinely surprised to see the dog again. She stopped and reached out to welcome the animal and felt its affectionate lick. The dog sat down. She had decided to do so as well when she saw in her stooped periphery the sandaled feet of a man standing near her. She aborted her intent to sit. The dog seemed to know him as it walked happily about him wagging its tail. "I see my dog has found you," he said. It was difficult to do, but she raised herself enough to look at his face. She did not recognize him.

"I am Jesus, of Nazareth." She stared at him blankly. She hadn't the slightest notion of who he was. "This is my dog, Abishag," he continued. "She has brought me to you."

"And why would your dog do such a thing?" she inquired, not knowing whether to be afraid or angry at this invasion of privacy. Only his eyes told her that she was safe, that he meant good, not evil. Still, life had taught her that good things do not really happen. She felt justifiably skeptical of good. Maybe it happens to others. It did not happen to her. The cold fingers of bitterness had wrapped themselves about her heart.

"Because she knows me, and I think, perhaps, she knows you as well."

"I am an old woman," she responded, reaching once again for the dog who responded eagerly. "Your dog has comforted me with her attention."

"She is good at that," said Jesus. "But you are not old; you are only forty-six. Today, isn't it? Happy birthday, Juliana Hebaav." He spoke her name in soft, musical tones.

The woman was stunned. The look of shock and surprise contorted her streaked face. She wanted to anticipate something good of this, yet she resisted for fear that it would be yanked away, yet another disappointment, yet another rejection from a cruel God, if, indeed, there was a God. *I want no more of this!* It was Solomon who said, *Hope deferred makes the heart sick!* For this sad woman, there was no hope; no hope at all—or so she thought. Waves of fear started in her stomach and she could feel nausea. She whimpered. The dog whined and nuzzled her hand, sensing that the woman needed comfort, needed her.

"Do not fear, Juliana." Jesus took her face in his hands and turned it so that she could see his. He kissed her forehead and then each of her eyes. Instantly, the dark shadows left her eyes and were replaced with smooth, radiant skin. Her eyes took upon themselves the freshness of a younger woman. The streaks were gone and her face and body cleansed as though she had just bathed in a river of rushing, sparkling water. Lifting her face again he spoke, "Stand up straight, Juliana." Before she could respond with "I can't," Jesus exerted an upward pressure on her head. Her back straightened without pain or discomfort. "For eighteen years," he said, "you have been bent over; destroyed by the forces of Satan who took your child, who took your husband, who took your life and left you destitute and alone. Oh, my dear, sweet sister Juliana, know that you are loved by the Son of Man, by God his Father and your Father. Arise and be whole." And then he whispered in her ear, "Be whole."

Almost two decades of morbid sadness evaporated. Her heart leaped within her and she reached out to embrace Jesus. Before our eyes, this person had changed physically from a bent, offensive crone to a stately, mature beauty, full of vitality. Abishag leaped and barked. "I know who you are!" she exclaimed. "You are the one come down from above," she said before Jesus could quiet her. "You are Messiah, the Chosen One of God!"

And then she paused, and said quietly, "My son was slain that you might live." Once again, her heart was in her throat. And then it came pouring out. "After that terrible night, neither I nor my husband was the same. Over the following months we drew apart; he became critical and judgmental of me. And then, the beatings…"

Jesus stopped her, "Don't continue, Juliana, all that is gone now."

"But it is you! I must speak of this." Jesus seemed amazingly dense at times. Only then did he realize that this was a moment of terrible release for this woman. She needed desperately to let this all out.

"Speak, then. Speak, and leave out nothing."

"I was only sixteen when it happened. My son, only two months. For twelve years my husband beat me. He came home drunk almost every night, and after beating me, he forced himself on me. He held no love for me. I would service him, because if I didn't, the beatings became more intense. He blamed me for the death of his son. To this day, I have no idea why. The more he beat me, the more withdrawn and servile I became. I would do anything for him. I was deathly afraid to leave him. He would kill me. Besides, where would I go?" The words came in torrents. However, in a few moments the story was told. She sat on a low parapet facing him. Tears welling in her eyes, yet they were not tears of suffering. They were tears of blessed relief.

Jesus spoke, "These years of your agony are indefensible. There are no words that can compensate for the pain you have endured. Yet in your heart, know that your son lives with your Father and my Father. He is about my age, yet he looks as if he were twenty. Soon I shall see him, and I will bring him your love. Now, go my mother; God my Father shall provide your every need from this day and forward."

But she did not go. She had nowhere else to go but to follow Jesus. We purchased clothing for her in Peraea, and the next time we were in Capharnaum, Joanna insisted that she stay with her and the family. She spent over a year with Peter's family, thriving on Joanna's love and nurturing.

Juliana Hebaav became my wife. She died ten months ago, the love of my life for twenty-seven years. I miss her. I miss her as much as I miss the Savior himself. But she is enjoying her son now. Later perhaps, when I have finished this writing, I will join them as well.

XVIII

The Curse of Eden

As Juliana and Jesus were conversing, several of the elders of the synagogue approached Jesus. One of them, the leader and most senior, said loud enough for us all to hear, "There are six days for work. Why did not this woman come and be healed on one of those days, and not on the Sabbath?"

Jesus shook his head and looked dumbfounded. He could not fathom their apparent need for ritual and liturgy. Why were they driven by these things? What was it about religious form that attracted them? What was it about religious law that made it easy for people to disregard human pain?

Yet it has always been so. Since Adam, like a moth to a flame, men have been attracted to the knowledge of good and evil, the regulation, the order and the rubric from which it naturally flows. The believers and followers of Jesus, after he was gone, were no different. After Jesus left us, the first thing the disciples did was to form a cadre, an exclusive group of *apostles*, who represented the collective repository of truth about Jesus and the Father. Paul spoke of the church being built on the foundation of these apostles, Jesus himself being the chief cornerstone. This is a bit difficult to understand, let alone accept, in that earlier he taught that, *"No man can lay a foundation other than that which is already laid, which is Jesus Christ."* How Paul evolved Jesus from the foundation to a "cornerstone," is inexplicable.

I was almost one of those apostles. Had I been selected instead of Matthias, I might today be writing from an entirely different perspective. At the time, I was hurt that Matthias was chosen instead of me. I felt rejected by God himself. But now I am grateful. I am not the church leader that James, the Lord's brother, became or that Paul became. I had wanted to be, but God had other ideas. I had thought that I was not chosen because of the enormity of my sin, because my character flaws were so preemptive. But I no longer cling to these destructive notions. Each of these men, the apostles, were flawed as well. Paul, himself, was honest enough to admit his flaws, that he considered greater than any of us. Perhaps that is the very reason God chose him.

When a reader examines these pages, if one thing does not stand out, then I have failed to communicate this thing most obvious; it is that Jesus despised this adherence to religious law. He despised it because it limits and curtails the highest principle conceived in the mind of God. It is the principle of loving and being loved. Jesus came to release us from the terrible curse brought on by Eden. It wasn't pride that attracted Adam to partake of the forbidden fruit, it was the need to get at the essence of the tree, to know right from wrong, to know the rules, and hence, to implement them in his own life and in the lives of others. Of course, there were no *others* at that time, but they existed in his loins, and in his mind. He knew his calling was to replenish the earth, he knew there would be plenty of others. From the beginning, control has been the passion of the worst in human nature. One cannot do that without sacred law, hence something called the authority of the church developed. Paul, for all of his great awareness of God and his truth, became the chief progenitor of church authority and officialdom. This should not have been. Jesus never meant for it to be and he taught forcibly against it. Other than the Damascus road encounter, Paul was never with Jesus. He never saw such things as Jesus did with Juliana nor heard the insult and invective of the Savior against the mindless adherence to religious law.

And so, typically, his response to these synagogue officials was to treat them roughly, "You hypocrites!," he cried, "Each of you on the Sabbath will not hesitate to untie his ox or donkey from the stall and lead it out to give it water! You know that you do that. Should not this woman, who has been bound for eighteen long years, be set free on the Sabbath day?" Jesus may as well have struck the poor Pharisee with a stone. He and his cohorts were humiliated and insulted, but the people were delighted. One by one, people with illness and disease came to him to be healed as he sat there next to beautiful Juliana on the wall. He healed each one who came. Sabbath, or no.

XIX

On the Road

We journeyed the rest of that day, and all the next through the towns of Gadara, then down the green slopes to Philadelphia. As we turned southwest toward Bethabara, we could not help but note once again the dramatic change of terrain. The lush green of Peraea became thinner as we descended into the Jordan valley until there was no green at all. Just brown, desert hills. I have never seen the beauty that others say they see in the desert. It is all so denuded, bare of life and freshness. We continued through rocks and gorges until at length, we crossed the river and reached the city situated on the western bank a few miles north of the Dead Sea.

Despite the heat, Jesus busied himself teaching as we made our way through Bethabara, Jericho and up to Jerusalem. Walking and teaching. Teaching and walking. Sweat wetting his clothes. The journey from Jericho to Jerusalem is steep, hot and exhausting. Sweat stinging our eyes, dripping down our necks, soaking our robes. How could he keep up this pace? At times my legs became so sore I could hardly throw one leg in front of another and fall on it. During one of these sweat-drenched teaching sessions, a follower asked him, "Lord, are only a few people going to heaven?" Perhaps as the man felt the raging, burning of the desert heat through the soles of his sandals, the suffocating oppression of the super-heated air about him, his question seemed reasonable.

It is said that Aristotle taught in this peripatetic manner, although he had no experience with the Jericho desert. In any case, people were comfortable asking questions of Jesus. Sometimes the questions had a malevolent motive. These he anticipated and was never caught off-guard. He allowed persons with different points of view to express themselves. In fact, as he began a teaching or a story, he often started (or ended) with the question, "What do you think of this?" For someone with his power and authority, Jesus was remarkably benign and approachable. There was a compelling reason. He simply loved every genuine seeker of truth.

"There are two answers to your question," he responded, "First, it is true that many who assume they have the credentials to enter heaven will try to do so, but will not succeed. Once the owner of a house closes the door after the invited guests arrive, he is not receptive to those who stand outside knocking and yelling, 'Open the door! You owe us!' He answers instead, 'I don't know you or where you come from.' Then they will say, 'How can you say that? We ate and drank with you, and you taught in our streets.' But he will reply, 'I don't know you. Away from me, all of you are seekers and doers of evil!' Indeed, they will see Abraham, Isaac and Jacob and all the prophets in the kingdom of God, but they themselves will not be granted entrance. So yes, there are many who think they should be admitted, but will not.

"But there is another answer to your question. Other people will also come from the east, west, north and south. Far beyond the borders of Israel and far beyond this time, they will come; from every corner of the earth they will come and will take their places at a feast in the kingdom of God. The feast will be in celebration of the marriage of the Son to his Bride. None of these will be turned away because each of them has been invited.

There will, however, be some who think they will be the last and least of those who enter, but will in fact, be first. And of those invited, there will be those who think they will be first and greatest, but who will instead, be last and least. God's criteria for who will be honored is vastly different from the criteria or the expectations of those invited."

On hearing these words, I didn't know whether to be comforted or to be afraid. I felt deeply that I had been invited to this feast, and that I had accepted the invitation. But I dared not consider that I would be accorded a place of honor. As I thought about it, I realized that it doesn't matter. I would be satisfied with a place in the corner of a closet. Just to be there and be accepted among the beloved would be more than enough. Given the depth of evil in my character, it would be far more than I deserve. Moreover, it is not mine to decide.

I know of many men and women I consider far more deserving of places of honor than me. Are there any who deserve it less than me? I do not see how that could be. Whatever murder and mayhem has been caused by others in this world has also played itself out in my own heart. Am I writing these words just so God can see how humble I am? I do not know. How many of us truly know the shadows in our own souls? I can only pray that I am not. Any hope of heaven at all that I hold for myself is based on the infinite love and grace of the Father. I can say this: I do not know how any man can be more ashamed of his sin and weakness than I feel about mine. Is that a thing of merit for God to consider? I cannot say. My hope is in his promise. How far can the grace of the living God reach? I am satisfied that despite my opprobrium, it can reach me.

XX

Salt

It had not occurred to me that it might require something of me to believe in Jesus and follow him. Life is, after all, a series of trade-offs. Choices are made by weighing the benefits against the liabilities and deciding almost always in favor of the benefits. Why would one decide in favor of liabilities? Following Jesus is so rich in benefit, any liability seems negligible and tangibly insignificant by comparison. Almost none, including me and the twelve, had truly evaluated the costs, the necessities of being a follower of Jesus of Nazareth.

"I have come for a reason," I often heard him say. "I have come from the Father of Light to bring Light into the world. If anyone seeks to follow me, if anyone comes to me and is not willing to lay all else aside, he cannot be my disciple. My purpose is too high. The calling is too great to allow room even for family to come before me. Father, mother, wife, children, brother or sister or even one's own temporal life may never be put above this calling. If one is not willing to accept the consequences of following me, though it mean a life of pain or even death, it is impossible to be my disciple.

"Let me be clear about this. Suppose one of you wants to build something. Will he not first sit down and estimate the cost to see if he has enough money to build it? If he lays the foundation and is not able to finish it, everyone will think him a fool. They will say 'this man started what he was not able to finish.' What kind of impression does that give?

"Or suppose a king is about to go to war against another king. Will he not first sit down and consider whether he is able with ten thousand men to oppose one coming against him with twenty thousand? If he decides no, if he is smart, he will send a delegation while the enemy is still a long way off and negotiate for peace. In the same way, you need to measure what it will require of you to come with me. You need to seriously measure the cost. If you cannot sacrifice what may be otherwise gained by not following me, you cannot be my disciple.

"He who would follow me must have uncompromising grit—salt. Salt is good. It adds pungency to your life and those around you. Salt rubbed into a wound can assist in the cleansing and healing of the wound and is often used to keep disease away, is it not? Nevertheless, it stings like fire and is painful when applied. There are some who prefer living with their sores and lesions rather than have the salt applied and be made whole again. So if your salt is not salty, you can be sure that it is not salt! Such salt can do nothing! So what do you do with it? It can't be re-made into salt. It is not suitable for anything, not even for a pile of manure. You throw it out. Some of you will never understand this. But if you have the ears to hear, then hear."

αΘω

Jesus gave little thought to the status of those with whom he associated. He never sought out the wealthy and the socialite, nor did he avoid them. He did seem to take perverse pleasure in annoying religious officialdom.

Jesus truly enjoyed the company of tax collectors, drunks, rogues and other unpretentious people. They in turn, enjoyed gathering around him and listening to him. This left the religious bureaucrats and the teachers of the law muttering to themselves, "This man welcomes dogs and swine. He takes pleasure in eating with them and not with us." It never occurred to them that he might enjoy their company as well had they been willing to enjoy his.

I never figured out how he could do it, but Jesus always seemed to sense what others were thinking about him, or to hear what they said when they were whispering to themselves. Walking over to the synagogue officials he said simply, "Gentlemen, are you concerned about something?" Before they could respond he raised a question he had raised before. It introduced a story he had told and re-told many times.

"Suppose one of you has a hundred sheep and loses one of them?" We nodded at one another. *Here comes the sheep story again.* We smiled. I suspect Jesus knew of our amusement, but it mattered little to him. "Does he not leave the flock unattended and go after the lost sheep until he finds it?" This was a favorite theme of his. "And when he finds it, with satisfaction he gladly puts it on his shoulders and returns it to the flock. When he returns home after a day's shepherding, he calls his friends and neighbors together and says, 'Let's celebrate! I found my lost sheep today!'" It was a great story containing a wonderful truth. "Listen!" Jesus said, lowering his voice and by doing so caused everyone to lean forward to hear, "I tell you that in the same way there will be more celebration in heaven over one sinner whose heart is changed than over ninety-nine self-righteous prigs who think they do not need change."

XXI

A Merciful Father

"One more story," said Jesus, holding up his index finger. I often wondered if Jesus made these narratives up on the spot, or if he was relating a real event. I suspect this story may have been real. "A rich man," he continued, pulling his robes around him and taking a seat, "had two sons. The older son was a faithful, steady sort and was content with his life. He worked hard and loved his parents and the life they'd provided for him. The younger one, as it often is with siblings, was quite the opposite. He was restless, ungrateful and greedy. One day, as they were walking in the garden after dinner he said to his father, 'Father, this isn't the way I want to live. I need to travel and see the world. I need to meet new people, find new and exciting things to do and enjoy myself. I would like for you to give me my inheritance now. I find it tedious hanging around here every day waiting...'

"The father was hurt and grieved, but knew his son would not be happy until he'd learned life's lessons for himself. So he divided his estate between his two sons. Within a few weeks, the younger son got together all he had and set off for a distant country. After traveling for months he decided to settle down in a city near the sea with lush gardens and beautiful buildings. He purchased a villa, enjoyed the company of many beautiful women and invited prestigious people to lavish parties. He had many friends and thought, *'this is the good life'*.

"Soon, though, his wealth squandered, he found himself with nothing. He went to several of his friends to borrow just enough money to get by until he was able to build back his fortune. 'What a humiliating thing to have to do, he thought.' But, they would have nothing to do with him. 'This pauper,' they would laugh 'is a fool if he thinks we'd loan him money. I wouldn't give him a goat.'

"That year there was a severe famine and he began to be in desperate need. He swallowed what pride he had left and got a job feeding pigs. He was hungry and longed to fill his stomach. He would have settled for the slop the pigs were eating, but no one gave him anything.

"In time, his extremity forced him to come to his senses. The thought occurred to him, 'How many of my father's servants have more food than they can eat, yet here I am starving to death! I will go back to my father and say to him: Father, I have disappointed you and I have disappointed God. I am no longer worthy to be called your son, but let me become as one of your servants. Give me a job and let me work in the fields.' So he got up and began his journey back to his father, hoping for mercy.

"For all the years that he was gone, his father would go to the garden in the early evening and watch; just watch, in hopes that maybe...

"One evening as the sun began to fringe the clouds with gold, the old man squinted his wrinkled eyes and looked intently, yet again at the road disappearing into the sunset. He was sure he saw a silhouette walking. As his eyes adjusted, he recognized the gait. *It was his son!* Love exploded into excitement as he ran to the boy, threw his arms around him and kissed him again and again and again. Through sobs muffled by his father's garments, he said, 'Father, I have disappointed you. I am no longer worthy to be called your son...

"But before he could finish, his father called to his wife 'come quick, our son is home! Our son is home!' Then he turned to his servants, 'Hurry! Bring the best robe I have and put it on him! Put my personal, signet ring on his finger and sandals on his feet! Bring a fat calf and slaughter it. Let's have a feast and celebrate! For this son of mine was dead and is alive again! He was lost and is found! My heart is about to burst with joy and thanksgiving!' Everything about this man was an exclamation, so happy was he at the return of his son. So preparations were made and they began to celebrate.

"Meanwhile, the older son was just coming in from the field supervising the workers. When he came near the house, he heard music and dancing. So he called one of the servants and asked what was going on. 'Your brother has come home,' he replied, 'and your father is celebrating because he has him back safe. Come! Join the celebration!'

"'That stinking brother of mine is back? And my father is celebrating? I can't believe it! No! I will not be a part of that!' So in his rage, he refused to go in. His father went out and pleaded with him. But he answered his father harshly. 'Look! All these years I've been slaving for you and never disobeyed. Yet you never gave me even so much as a corn husk so I could celebrate with my friends. But when this...this son of yours who has wasted everything you gave him with whores and wild living; when *he* comes traipsing back, you throw a party for him!? How do you think that makes me feel?'

"'Oh, my son,' the father said with compassion, 'you are always with me, and everything I have is yours. But now, we have to celebrate. Your brother was dead and is alive again; he was lost and now, he is found.'"

The officials of the synagogue were left in pensive thought. The story of this generous and gracious father seemed to touch them. They looked at Jesus and nodded their heads in reluctant assent. Had he touched something deep in their hearts? Something they couldn't process? But then, they abruptly turned and left and got back to the business of their lives.

This, without a doubt, was the most powerful and compelling story that Jesus ever told. To think that this recounting was about the two boys is to miss the heart of the story. It is about God, our Father. It is about his love and forgiveness. The story, dear friend, is about us.

XXII

Old Friends

Well into the afternoon on a warm day we came to a spot where pepper trees, over-hanging the road, offered a bit of shade. Jesus, adjusting himself at the base of a tree, sat down to rest. Putting his elbows on his knees, he held his head with his hands and then rubbed his face and eyes. Soft currents of breeze whispered through the hanging boughs giving the impression of massaging the Son of God. He smiled, looking upward through the limbs as if to say, "Thank you."

There were others about, including a family with a small boy about ten years old. The child approached, carrying a pot of water. He set the pot down and taking a cup offered the Lord a drink. We were all very thirsty and Jesus, with gratitude, accepted the cup from the boy. After serving Jesus, he then served each one of us, and approaching the Master once more he said, "I know who you are." This with a bright smile looking up at Jesus, as though he knew something no one would expect him to know. "You are Jesus of Nazareth, the son of David the king."

It was one of the few times that I saw genuine surprise on the Lord's face. "How did you come by this knowledge, my boy?"

"My father told me," spoke the lad.

"And what is your name?"

"Eben, sir," the boy responded. "My name is Eben ben Eben."

"Eben? The son of Eben?"

"Yes, Jesus," came a nearby voice, "This is my son." Jesus glanced in the direction of the voice and observed the man and a woman standing, staring at him. The man's beard was short, black and rough cut. The woman at his side with golden hair and intense blue eyes smiled back at him. It took a moment, but recognition came. Jesus sucked in his breath like he had been hit in the stomach.

"Ah!" he shouted. A brief pause and again, "Ah! My old friend! What pleasure! What joy!" At once he strode to the man and embraced him warmly.

"Eben!" he cried, "Eben, is it really you?"

"It is I," said the man. "And this is my wife, Miryam."

Miryam bowed as if she were meeting royalty. "I am pleased and humbled to meet the Son of God," she said softly. "I have heard much of you. My husband speaks of you almost every day. His faith in God the Father finds its strength in his faith in you."

Jesus was moved by her obvious sincerity and, no doubt, by her eyes, blue as a deep pool. "I, too, am honored to meet the wife of my childhood friend. But please, to you, I am Jesus ben Joseph, an old childhood and family friend. Come, let us sit and renew our friendship." Not too far from the pepper tree was an inn with a courtyard cafe. Tables were set about where people gathered and refreshed themselves with food and wine. A table was quickly found for the four of them, the boy looking bright-eyed and excited; and when food was brought, he wasted no time with preliminaries. The rest of us either found a table or stayed outside and waited.

"So," Jesus began, "Tell me, Eben, what of your parents? What of your life? And how in the world did you find me? Tell me everything! Leave nothing out!"

Eben smiled, glanced knowingly at his wife and then spoke, "I have found you, my Lord, because I...well, I have a concern. I suppose you could call it a major concern...a need." His voice trailed off.

The expression on Jesus' face changed from excited anticipation to serious interest. With his elbows on the table, he brought his hands up in front of him clasping them. "You bring a man water to slake his thirst after a long journey. You are a friend who was lost and now is found. I am overjoyed with your presence. Tell me, is there a possibility I can help? How may I assist my dearest of old friends?"

"I don't know," said Eben flatly. "I just don't know. Maybe this is a bad idea." He looked uncomfortably at his wife, thinking that perhaps they should not have bothered Jesus. Miryam extended her hand and placed it on his, comforting him. With her other hand she stroked the sandy-colored hair of the boy.

Jesus saw how intensely she loved her husband and how devoted she was to her son. He also saw in her a deep strength of character and dignity. When she spoke her voice was soft, yet commanding. "I will speak for my husband..." She looked wistful for a moment and began to speak. "The winds of autumn are bringing a bitter chill to our home. Eben, my husband, hasn't had a restful night for months. Eben, my son, often finds his father weeping and crying out to God our Father in great agony of spirit. Still, they come. Each week they come. And the days of the week are spent in anguish for their coming and in dread for their coming again." The expression on Jesus face became intense. "They are men, rough men, usually two of them, sometimes three. They come to our home and leave with every denari we have. If we do not pay them, they threaten to take away our son. If our son is taken, we will never see him again, and only God knows what will happen to him." She paused and then shuddered visibly.

"In some respects," responded Jesus, this is a re-visit to our childhood, Eben. You remember that one of the concerns of my parents when I turned up missing in Jerusalem was that I may have been abducted by flesh-peddlers. How did you come to be in debt to such men?"

"We owe them nothing!" exclaimed Eben bitterly.

"Are they doing this to everyone in your community or just to you?"

"I have heard rumors but nothing more. If others are like me, they will not advertise their shame. No one wants other people to think that they in debt to vile men like these. I have seen these same men enter the houses of others. It is as if all are being victimized, and no one speaks about it. But I am very afraid for my son. It is said that the landowner likes…likes young boys."

"Let me make sure I understand," said Jesus, eyes furrowed. "These men are in the employ of your landlord? And they extort you of your livelihood on the threat of abducting your male children?"

"Exactly," spoke Eben. Several moments passed in silence. Jesus' friend appeared drained and in state of dazed emptiness and, yet, still terribly burdened. Abruptly, Jesus smiled, leaned back in his chair and stretched extending both of his arms above his head. When he relaxed and brought his arms back down, he appeared in obvious relief that all things were settled.

"These men will not bother you again," he stated simply. "You may return to your home in peace."

Miryam stared at Jesus with incredulous joy. Eben lifted his eyes from the table and stared but said nothing. Jesus looked back at him smiling, raised his hands palms upward and shrugged. "That's it?" said Eben in agitated disbelief. He frowned and appeared greatly irritated. "I bring to you the most terrible threat of my life and you tell me to go home? Everything will be just wonderful?" Eben's voice rose in gathering pain. "Why do you play with me, Jesus? Why do you mock me, as if I were a fool!?" He did not wait for a response, "I came to you expecting…I don't know what I expected…at least some sympathy, some comfort or perhaps some action from you and your men on behalf of an old friend who loves you. I guess I thought you might confront this landlord and his thugs…if he saw you and your men…well, with your fame and…"

"Eben, please!" his wife spoke. "It's all right. Don't you see? His eyes!"

Jesus looked at Eben evenly. He spoke, "My dear friend, you have heard of my storytelling. Well, let me tell you a story meant for you." Eben rolled his eyes and looked exasperated. "Listen well. There was once a very wealthy man who dressed himself in purple and fine linen and lived in luxury every day. A beggar named Lazarus laid every day at his gate, covered with sores, and would have been glad to eat the crumbs that fell from this man's table. His solitary comfort as he lay at the gate too weak to move was when dogs came to lick his sores.

"Well, this beggar died, and instead of dogs, angels came to him and carried him to Abraham's bosom. The rich man also died and was buried. In hell, where he was in torment, he looked up and saw Abraham far away, with Lazarus by his side. So he called to him, 'Father Abraham, have pity on me and send Lazarus to dip the tip of his finger in water and cool my tongue. I am in agony in this fire.'

"Abraham replied, 'Son, remember that in your lifetime, you in your greed and lust received many things and gratified yourself. Lazarus received the attention of street curs. But now he is comforted here and you are in agony. Besides, there is fixed between us and you a great chasm, so that those who want to go from here to you cannot, nor can anyone cross over from there to here.'

"He answered, 'Then I beg you, father, send Lazarus to my father's house, for I have five brothers. Let him warn them, so that they will not also come to this place of torment.'

"Abraham replied, 'They have Moses and the prophets; let them listen to them.'

"'No, father Abraham,' he said, 'but if someone from the dead goes to them, they will change.'

"He said to him, 'If they do not listen to Moses and the prophets, they will not be convinced even if someone rises from the dead.'"

αΘω

Eben and his family spent a restless night at the inn with Jesus and the rest of us, struggling with this seeming irrelevant tale, disappointment, embarrassment and anger tearing the fibers of his heart. The next morning, after saying goodbye, he began his journey home. He didn't know what awaited him when he got there. It was entirely possible that he, like Lazarus, would die in his suffering. Clearly, for his son's sake and his wife as well, he would have to move his place of residence elsewhere. His family had lived in this house for generations; the house, the land, always owned by someone else, yet they had always gotten along. They had always survived. But not now. He had to leave. He had no choice.

Despite his misgivings, after meeting with Jesus, an amorphous peace began to cool the embers in his brain. He felt in his heart that maybe God did love him after all and would care for him and his family. So he would do what common sense told him: Leave his ancestral home and hope for the blessing of his heavenly Father elsewhere. After all, Jesus did say that the men would not be back. *Or did he say that they would not bother us again?* He was not sure.

Night had fallen when they arrived. The house was dark, and except for the crickets and an occasional tree frog, all was quiet. The solitary lamp that they had left burning was still lit, shimmering in the darkness. It had several days of oil left. But something was wrong. There was a strange smell. The dark shapes of furniture, the dining room table, somehow it all looked different in the shadows of the single flame. Eben took several unlit candles and lit them from the lamp. In a few moments, the rooms were comfortably illumined. It was then that the staggering reality of what had happened seized him. Miryam exclaimed, "What have they done?"

"All of our own things are gone!" cried young Eben.

"Who did this?" from his wife.

"It is all new," said Eben softly. "The odor is the fragrance of newness. Someone has replaced our old furniture with…look! They've placed a silver bowl on the table filled with spices and herbs."

Miryam approached the matched set of elaborately carved myrtle wood settees covered with billowing colorful pillows. Stunned beyond belief, she muttered softly, "It's beautiful."

"And rich," said Eben. "Much of this has been imported from the East. Look at this fabric." He fingered a fine silk, gold woven into its design.

"Who did all of this, and why? Have they given our home to someone else while we were gone?" asked Miryam. She thought surely a home so wonderfully furnished could not have been meant for them.

"Look, there is something on the table," noted Eben. As he approached the table, he noticed that it was made of an exquisite wood he didn't recognize and polished to perfection. On the table lay a document sealed with wax. He held the candle close to the seal. The light from the flame revealed the crest and seal of the house of Habib ben Alouisious, his landlord. He broke the seal, his curiosity mixed with fear, opened the document and read:

My Dear Eben,

In my bed last night, while you were away, I was visited by angels. Perhaps it was a dream. Perhaps they were real. I do not know. But they were terrible. Their swords flashed in celestial light that came from a source I could not see.
I saw also myself, tormented in flame, blisters rising and bursting on my skin, excruciating pain—and then I saw you—a man I have tortured, in the bosom of Abraham. I cried to father Abraham for mercy but he would have none of it. The reason I was in the flame and you were with him is why you see what I have done in your absence.
Please, Eben, the house, the furnishings, the land on which it sits, and the fields you've sown—all of it!—is now yours. I beg your forgiveness. And pray to God my Father for me. I wish to be with you in the bosom of father Abraham, and not tormented in eternal flames.

A single tear made a path down Eben's cheek, losing itself in the forest of his beard. "What does it say?" asked Miryam, terrified.

XXIII

Matthew's Inquiry

We had witnessed the exchange with Eben and his family. How could he return home facing what he must? In the face of the terrible threat that hung like a sword over him, for so long, Matthew was struggling. Eben had not left in peace. In fact, he obviously didn't get the response from Jesus that he'd hoped for. For Matthew, this exchange and the effect it had on Eben was troubling.

"Lord," he asked of Jesus, "How is it that men deliberately set themselves to persecute and destroy one another? It is a troubling question. Eben had done nothing to cause this man to hurt him. Are some men really evil? Is there not some good in every human being?"

"In Eben's case, yes. There is a seed of hunger in the heart of his tormentor that will cause him to repent." Jesus continued, "But it is impossible that unprovoked offenses against good men shall ever stop—at least not in this age."

"Impossible?" exclaimed Matthew. "Are you saying that the heart of some men is so black that it is their nature to hurt others?"

"Precisely," Jesus responded. "But I can tell you this, *Woe* to that person through whom these offenses come. Assault against people less powerful or weaker will not be tolerated or excused!" The expression Jesus wore while saying this could have been chiseled from stone. The look of unmerciful rectitude was distinct and irrevocably final.

"Do not allow yourself to be bullied. If a powerful person seeks to hurt or destroy you, stand up to him. Make him aware that you know what he is doing. It is possible that he will see his offense and apologize. If he does that, forgive him. It could be that his obnoxious attitude is the consequence of the pain in his life and a part of his personality. He may be aware of that more than you. If this is the case, he may have to apologize many times. If he does that, forgive him many times"

"Lord, increase our faith!" declared Matthew. "Otherwise, we shall not have the strength to stand up for ourselves or to forgive *that* many times." Matthew was not one to mince words. Perhaps he asked this of

Jesus—more like demanded—perhaps he asked because of all of us; he was the most pragmatic in his thinking. His logic was often cold and irrefutable. For such a man, faith is based more on reason than trust. Intellectual, erudite, almost always soft-spoken, Matthew could reduce one to an infantile fool with an absolute minimum of words. There is no question, however, that Matthew believed, it was just that some things seemed to fly in the face of his beliefs. He believed in God. He believed in Jesus and he believed that Jesus was in reality who he claimed to be. Yet the doubts that assailed him shook him. It made him question his beliefs and wonder if he had faith at all. Sensing this inadequacy and aware of its impropriety in the company he kept, he sought in Jesus a solution to the conflicts within him. "Increase my faith, Lord! Help me to square my faith with reality."

"Your faith, my dearest friend, is more real, more tangible and dimensional than what you perceive as reality." Jesus saw through the thin veneer of Matthew's intellectual bravado. He knew his friend was troubled and insecure in his ability to trust. "Matthew," Jesus continued, "don't allow the doers of evil to upset you. Do not concern yourself with the magnitude of your faith. If you have faith as small as a mustard seed, you can say to this mulberry tree, 'Be uprooted and planted in the sea,' and it will obey you." Jesus did that. He helped us to accept our limitations and encouraged us to see beyond them. And whenever he did that, it always—always engendered a deeper searching, a deeper questioning.

"A mustard seed?" The tax collector seemed to consider that. "A mustard seed and a mulberry tree. What have the two to do with each other?"

"He could as easily have said an elephant and a jackass!" spoke Peter crassly and nonsensically.

Matthew ignored the fisherman whom he sometimes considered intellectually truncated. He always chastised himself when such thoughts came to him. He genuinely loved this big, vulgar man, but everyone had the same problem with Peter. We all had to deal with his abruptness and ill-manners.

"The two are connected by belief," said Jesus, answering Matthew's question. "Apparent smallness impacts the integrity and stability of the larger reality. A superficial assessment of the mustard seed concludes that it would struggle to produce anything more than a scruffy weed. One must never overlook the potential, or the exponential power of insignificant things, or apparently insignificant people." This was abstract language Matthew could understand and in which he took perverse delight. "Is it not true that weighty issues are often balanced on a small fulcrum?" continued Jesus. "Shift the fulcrum, even slightly, one way or another and what happens?"

"You are saying that we must never underestimate the power of the finite in its effect on the infinite?" It was a question to be taken as an elaboration on what Jesus meant. Matthew enjoyed being the philosopher.

Peter shook his head in confused disgust. "How do you answer a question with a question?" he demanded.

Jesus acknowledged Peter with a slight smile. Matthew's lips pursed, thoughtful, amused and satisfied. Neither attempted to answer.

A loud, throaty, abrasive grunt from the fisherman, tossing his arms in angry annoyance.

The Sixth Scroll

Mankind

Then God said, "Let us make man in our image, in our likeness, so that they may rule over the fish in the sea and the birds in the sky, over the livestock and all the wild animals, and over all the creatures that move along the ground." So God created mankind in his own image, in the image of God he created them; male and female he created them. God saw all that he had made, and it was very good. And there was evening, and there was morning—the sixth day.

—Genesis 1:26-27, 31 NIV

I

Last Words

Light rain watered the earth, making shallow puddles as we made our way through the countryside. As I consider the substance of which I am about to write, my conclusion is this: This was not only the most important and significant event in the life of those it concerns, it was possibly the most significant event in the ministry of Jesus of Nazareth. This is the recounting of an event that establishes forever the credentials of this man who did not refuse or reject the assertion that he was and is the Incarnate Deity. If these events are true—as I myself am an eyewitness—as were dozens of others of both high and mean political estate, then no belief is nobler or more authentic than this.

αΘω

Far away, Bethany lay cold in the rain. The dampness outside made the candlelit room inside feel thick and muggy, the air of sickness and approaching death adding its pall to the flickering flame. Mary sat next to the bed holding his hand. Breathing had become labored and irregular. Sallow cheeks replaced what used to be a firm, aristocratic face, hair tangled and unkempt. Mary brushed away a few strands as her fingers caressed his brow. The silk robe, imported from the East, that clothed him did little to allay the appearance of serious illness. His fever remained high and his skin a deeper yellow than anyone had seen before. One thing was immediately clear: Lazarus was dying.

"He is gone," said her sister softly. Mary's eyes widened and observed his chest rising and falling in a still, then a jerking, convulsive fashion.

"No," she exclaimed, terrified, "He is still breathing!"

"I meant Jarud," said her sister. "He is on his way to fetch Jesus." What she didn't say was that she felt it was too late. Her brother was fading too quickly.

Mary turned tear-stained cheeks toward Martha, "We should have sent for him three days ago. Our brother is…" she couldn't bring herself to say it, "...so very sick." There was a moment's silence between them. Other members of the family had begun to gather. Word had reached friends. They, too, had come, several of them bringing dishes of food. "Where is he?"

"A day's journey away," said Martha, "He was last seen in the town of Ephraim, in Peraea. Jarud will go as fast as he can."

"How will he find him? Our Lord moves about so."

"He will not be difficult to locate. Thousands follow him wherever he goes. Someone will know where he is. Do not worry, sister; he will come."

αΘω

Of what significance are the words of a dying man? Whatever their significance, they are rarely as dramatic or poignant as most of us imagine. Having spoken so many words in his lifetime, he knew they were about to cease. His brain felt lethargic and drugged, incapable of speech, incapable of coherent, linear thought. He knew he would not last the night. He knew Jesus would not come before he was dead. An enormous sadness enveloped him. "If I could see his face one more time," he thought, "just one more word of comfort and peace, just one more moment in his presence." Through the clouds that were his thoughts, he remembered the good times when Jesus visited them. He remembered the laughter, the stories, the embraces, the joy. Suddenly, unexpectedly, everything cleared. Mental clouds evaporated and he felt surprisingly lucid and in control of his faculties. He opened his eyes to see his sister sitting next to him and became aware of his hand in hers.

"Mary," he whispered softly. Words from his dry throat and parched lips came hard, almost as if they emanated from a dried cob of corn. Mary's eyes fluttered from dozing. She awoke, startled.

"Oh!" she exclaimed, "Oh, Lazarus! My sweet, sweet Lazarus!" She didn't know what else she could say, should say. "We sent a servant to find Jesus," she explained. "He is coming. He will be here soon!"

"He will not arrive in time, dear sister."

"Oh, yes! Yes, he will Lazarus," she stammered. "You rest now, Jesus will here soon." Instinctively, she began to fuss over him, straightening his hair, tucking in the covers, pulling them up around his chin. "Would you like some water? Some wine?"

"Mary." he spoke softly.

She looked at him in hopeless desperation. "What!" her voiced choked out the word.

"Mary, call our sister. Call Martha. I have something to say to you both."

"All right," she said. "All right...you rest now. I'll be right back." She hurriedly left the room.

She found Martha in the room where food was prepared and served. She was moving about managing all of the items people had brought, wondering what to do with them all. How could they possibly eat all of this, where was she going to find room for everything? Her sister came to the door. "At last, you're here. Please help me put these things away before they spoil."

"Martha . . ?"

"Oh, Mary, please. Not now. Don't just stand there looking helpless. Here, take these grapes and put them..."

"Martha, he is calling for us. He wants to speak to us."

Her elder sister stopped as if struck by a stone. "He is awake?" she asked. Wiping her hand on a cloth without really needing to, moving another item or two without actually knowing what she was moving, she responded, "Yes. Well, let's go see what he wants." And then anxiously, "There is so much to do. Oh, how I wish Jesus were here..." and then, "But he isn't. He isn't. There is no use fussing about it." She hurried after her sister.

They found him as Mary had left him, lying on his back, eyes staring at the ceiling of the room. It was getting on in the day and the light from the candles was brighter than the light through the window. Lazarus looked gaunt and emaciated, far from the vigorous leader of men that he had always been, far from the educated, erudite counselor of friend and enemy alike, negotiator, man of substance with no small influence and power. Now he lay on his bed, moving persistently toward death. Martha began to do what she knew to do, straightening the covers, fluffing his pillow...

"Sister, sit down!" he ordered, quietly but firmly. Both of them took their places at his bedside. "Listen carefully to my words. They are to be my last..."

"No!" they both chimed. "Lazarus, don't say such things," ordered Martha. You will recover. Already we have sent Jarud to find Jesus. He will come..."

"Quiet, Martha! Let me speak." His sister stopped. Martha caught her breath, quieted herself, and gently sat on the edge of her brother's bed.

"Speak, then," she said softly.

"Wealth and riches are in my house," he began. "Even in darkness light has dawned and good will has been my mistress. I have conducted my affairs with justice. I have tried to be generous and freely lend to those in need. And now, though I face death, I will not be shaken. I do not fear, my heart is steadfast, trusting in the Lord. I have scattered my substance to the poor, and I am ready to face my Maker." He stopped for a moment shifting his eyes. It seemed as though he were searching for thought. After an awkward pause, a pause Martha could endure no longer and was about to interrupt, he found his tongue...

"I am ready to face my Maker...just...not yet."

In the waning hours of the day, the rain ceased. Mary sat still by the bed when she noticed the silence. At first it merely struck her that things seemed unusually quiet, and then she became aware that his chest no longer rose and fell.

II

He Knew

The puddles were still. Drops of water that fell from the heavens had turned into fine mist, and what there was left of light reflected the tops of trees on the surface of the puddles leaving an eerie calm. We were in the home of Bahroud el Hamaan located in the outskirts of Ephraim. Hamaan is a Lebanese merchant who had offered to feed the lot of us. Dinner had been superb, roasted shallots with roasted lamb, which we washed down with a wine the quality of which I had never tasted, except for perhaps… once. The air in the room was suffocating with the smoke of incense. What with a bloated stomach, I couldn't take the dense air another moment. I stepped outside in the darkening mist. As I did, a man stepped from the shadows at almost the same time I exited the house. While he was dressed in the finest of robes, there was something deferential in his manner. He appeared familiar to me, but I couldn't place him. I was certain I had seen him before…

"A thousand pardons, sir," he began. "Is this the home of Hamaan? I seek Jesus of Nazareth."

I am an unassuming sort. I trust people too much, but this night, perhaps it was the weather, I was wary. "Who are you man? What do you want?"

"I am Jarud ben Ahasuerus, servant to Lazarus of Bethany."

I chuckled to myself at the name. Yes! I knew this man. I had observed him on our previous visit to the house of Lazarus, Mary and Martha. He was Lazarus' most trusted servant. His name, however, was a subject of mild amusement. "The son of Ahasuerus!" That was quite a name for a servant.

"What news do you bring, son of Ahasuerus?" I inquired, amused.

"Please," he responded with his head bowed, "I must speak with the Master."

"Then come." We entered the house and then the dining room where all sat. Peter and John had enjoyed the wine a little too much. Rosy cheeks and glazed eyes stared at us with good humor.

"Ah!" Peter cried, "Justus brings a visitor!" Someone must have told a story because Jesus was laughing. That was not unusual. For someone who came from God, he laughed too much. The smile still on his face, he turned to greet us. As soon as he saw Jarud, the smile was replaced with sober anticipation.

All quieted as the servant spoke, "I am Jarud ben Ahasuerus, servant to..."

"I know who you are," said Jesus. "What has happened? What is wrong?"

"Lazarus, my master and friend whom you love, is gravely ill sir. He and his sisters ask that you come."

Thoughts of that dear family came flooding back to me. Mary, dear sweet Mary, who had anointed the feet of Jesus with the finest oil and wiped them with her hair,[5] a woman whose beauty was excelled only by the rose that was her character. And Martha; wonderful, busy Martha. And Lazarus. No finer man lived. Lazarus, gravely ill?

Jesus seemed to have read my mind. "This sickness will not end in death," he said.

αΘω

On the day that Lazarus died, he was buried. On noticing that her brother's chest no longer rose and fell in its irregular spasms, Mary released his hand and stood. Her paralyzing grief did not hit her right away. She went to find her sister. It was Martha, who upon learning that her brother had died ran into the room wailing. Mary, too, wept in her heart, a solitary tear rolling down her lovely cheek. To weep for loss is one thing; to weep for the loss of intimacy is quite another. This was a close family. The two sisters and brother loved each other deeply. None of them had married. They lived together and they lived for each other. They had been inseparable since they were children. No one breached or came between this triad. Only One was allowed to penetrate their bond, and he was miles away.

Not far from Bethany, the family owned a parcel of land of about half an acre in size. It was part of a rugged landscape of hills and valleys where the wealthy often purchased land to bury their dead. It wasn't a cemetery. That was closer to town (although, according to law, never closer than 75 feet) and occupied by those who could not afford the luxury of their own

5 John 11:2

family property. Plots of land like the one belonging to Lazarus were often converted into lovely gardens, gaily decorated with shrubs and colorful white and yellow daisies, myrtle, rose and mandrake. This land was one of the loveliest of these. Within its lines lay a small hill out of which was hewn a family crypt. The House of Silence it was called, or the House of Stone. In its crypts lay the bones of Lazarus' mother and father.

In Galilee the custom was for mourners to precede the body as it was taken in procession to the burial garden. Here in Judea, instead, they followed. Every mark of sympathy and respect was shown to Lazarus and his sisters, as he had been an enthusiastic participant and supporter of the Synagogue. And, as is the case with all distinguished persons, as he lay on the bier before the opening of the tomb an oration was made, an obituary extolling a life well lived and that there shall never be another to take his stead and that his place in heaven was sure and certain. His body, heavily embalmed with wrapping cloths and spices, was placed in one of thirteen crypts in a hewn out vault of nine by twelve feet in area. After the goodbyes of loved ones and friends, a large circular stone, chiseled to the exact correct proportions was rolled across the opening to the vault and sealed. The funeral concluded on Sunday night, the mourners sent home. The next day, Monday, Jarud had reached Jesus.

αΘω

It occurred to none of us to doubt that Jesus was correct that the illness was not life threatening. Jesus loved Martha and her sister and Lazarus. Yet when he heard that Lazarus was sick, amazingly he continued to teach and preach for two more days. I could not help but consider the callousness of it. The sisters would not have sent the servant had the illness not been grave; but Jesus had sent him back with the promise, "We will follow soon."

"Soon" turned out to be two whole days! It was now Wednesday. We were stunned at first, and then just confused. After this time had passed, he said, "Now is the time to return to Judea." We had waited for two days, and now he wanted to go? What was going on? I was thoroughly puzzled. It appeared as though he deliberately stayed the extra time for a rationale that escaped my simple mind. And why did he say "Judea," as our destination instead of the home of Lazarus—as though we were returning to minister to the people of the region instead of the specific purpose of caring for Lazarus? I had nothing but the message of Jarud on my mind for this seemingly interminable time that we waited. I didn't know if Jesus would really make the trip or not. Thoughts of his missing his father's funeral probed my mind. And now he said that we return to Judea?

John seemed to have forgotten about Lazarus, too. Ever the cautious one, he pointed out that "a short while ago the Jews tried to stone you, and now you are going back there?"

Jesus responded with one of his insufferable, enigmatic epithets, "There are twelve hours in the day. A man who walks by day will not stumble, because he sees by the light of the day. It is when he walks by night that he stumbles. He has no light to see. So, while it is yet day, I will walk."

Why does he do that? I wondered to myself. *Why doesn't he just say what he means?* Anyone could speculate what he means. My speculation was that he viewed his life and ministry as his "twelve hour day," and that he intended to busy himself about his work during that time, lest night come with the work unfinished. As I reflect back on the events that occurred, I am certain that he knew full well what he would do concerning Lazarus and that the delay would play directly into that series of events.

Then Jesus said, "Our friend Lazarus has fallen asleep, but I am going there to wake him up."

This was good news indeed. We were relieved and grateful. Lazarus was recovering and healing. "This is good, Lord," said Thomas. "If he sleeps, he will get better. It will do him good." All of us thought that he meant natural, healing sleep. But Jesus meant something else entirely.

"Lazarus is dead."

The shock was profound. Restrained silence. None of us knew what to say. None of us could speak. Grief had stunned all of us, but it seemed to affect Thomas the most. "How do you know that, Lord?" he asked. Jesus gave him a look that sent an inescapable and irrefutable message. Thomas quickly added, "Then let us go, that we may die with him." Dear Thomas. Everything he said was tinged with curious melodrama.

"I am glad I was not there," said Jesus evenly. "Now we will go to him, and God my Father will be honored. It will give you reason to believe."

He knew it. All this time he knew it. He knew it when Jarud came. He knew it while he was on his way. He knew all the time what was happening and exactly what he would do about it. We were kept in the dark because that is where we live anyway. Our eyes could only be opened by the event itself.

III

Lazarus Come Forth!

Thursday. We approached Bethany around the southeastern side of Jerusalem, directly from the road leading up from Jericho. A day's journey from where we started in Peraea. When we arrived, Lazarus had already been in the tomb for four days. Four days! I still could not believe that we had delayed so long in coming. As we neared Bethany, I felt no small burden of guilt. There were still many friends at the home of Mary and Martha from Jerusalem, a mere two miles distant. They had come, of course, to comfort the sisters in their loss. Martha, informed that Jesus approached, came out to meet us. Where was Mary? *Odd!*

"Welcome, my Lord Jesus!" said Martha, her eyes brimming. She embraced him, and he held her in his arms while she quietly wept. With his hand, he stroked her hair. When she had composed herself, she said, "Lord, had you been here, my brother would not have died." At first, I thought her comment accusatory. But then I realized that Martha had simply stated the truth. She knew that Jesus would not have allowed her brother to suffer. He could have and would have easily healed him. "But I know," she continued, "that even now God will give you whatever you ask." *What was she saying? What was she thinking?* In retrospect, I suspect that Martha was much farther along than any of us. Certainly me.

Sensing her anticipation, Jesus said to her simply, "Your brother will rise again." It was a simple something to say that anyone would say to ease the loss of a loved one. Only Sadducees believe there is no resurrection. I was sure that was all Jesus meant at the moment.

Martha replied, "Yes. I know he will rise at the resurrection in the last day." Perhaps she said this seeking assurance. She said it softly, wistfully, as if not daring to really mention what she hoped against hope that he would do. And then, "Oh, Jesus, this hurts. It hurts so deeply."

Jesus took her face in his hands and kissing her forehead he said to her, "Martha, Martha. I am the resurrection and the life. He who believes in me will live—even though he dies--and whoever lives and believes in me will never die." She looked at him not understanding. "Can you believe this—my dear Martha?" still holding her face in his hands.

She nodded her head and whispered, "Yes, Lord, I believe that you are the Christ, the Son of God, who has come into the world." The words spilled out. She swallowed and opened her eyes, returning his gaze. No sweeter moment of love existed than this.

"Then go," he said, releasing her, "and bring Mary to me."

She returned to the house and called her sister. "Our Lord is here," she said. "He asks for you." Mary's heart leaped within her. She caught her breath and got up quickly to go to him.

It took a few moments for all this to happen because we had not yet entered the village. We stood silent, waiting at the place where Martha had met us. When those who had been with Mary in the house, comforting her, noticed how quickly she left, they followed her, supposing she was going to the tomb. But she came instead to Jesus, and when she saw him, she fell at his feet and said exactly the same thing Martha had said, "Lord, if you had been here, my brother would not have died."

Jesus saw her weeping and the friends from Jerusalem also weeping, he was deeply moved in spirit and troubled.

"Where have you laid him?" he asked, voice breaking.

"Come Lord; this way," the friends replied.

Jesus wept.

I had never seen Jesus weep like this. There was murmuring, "Look at that! He must have loved him deeply!"

"Could not he who opened the eyes of the blind, could not he also have kept Lazarus from death? Could he not have protected him?" Heads nodded in agreement and sorrow. I was amazed at how this occasion of great mourning could bring forth so much belief. These things were not said to judge or accuse. They were words of expectancy, of anticipation. They thought Jesus would do something—even yet!

When Jesus had recovered he said again, "I wish to go to the grave. Where have you laid him?"

Thinking that he wished to go there to grieve, a woman said, "Come, Lord Jesus, we will take you there." The women began to gather their things and give instructions for more flowers. The garden lay just outside the town on the side away from Jerusalem. We were there in less than half an hour. Jesus, once more deeply affected as he came to the entrance of the tomb emitted a groan from deep within him. I myself heard it. A deep, whimpering groan. The Son of God grieved. A large stone was sealed over the opening. He issued a single order, "Break the seal and take away the stone."

Reaction to his command was predictable, shock and for some horror. Martha spoke for everyone, "But, Lord, by this time there will be a stench. He has been dead four days." It was a common Jewish notion that corruption commenced on the fourth day, that the drop of gall which had fallen from the sword of the Angel of Death was working its inexorable effect and that, as the face changed, the soul took its final leave from the decaying body. A point well-taken, I thought. I was fond of Lazarus, but I had little inclination to disturb, let alone smell, his remains.

"Did I not tell you that if you believed, you would see the glory of God?"

Why this preachment? What exactly, had he in mind? None of us had the slightest premonition of what was coming. Martha, a bit embarrassed by his remark, nodded to the workmen. It took a moment to break the seal and work the stone loose, but after a few moments of struggling, the sweating men stood aside and the opening of the vault stood dark and ominous almost inviting anyone, if they dared, to step in. Wrinkled noses. Hands covering nostrils. The putrid odor of decaying human flesh was distinctive and powerful.

Then Jesus looked up and offered a prayer just loud enough for those standing close by to hear, "Father," he prayed, "thank you for hearing me. I know that you always hear me. Grant that the people standing here who witness this may believe that you sent me." When he had said this, he gazed at the dark opening of the grave and then he commanded in a voice loud enough for the dead to hear:

"Lazarus...come forth!"

IV

A Step Toward the Light

The sound echoed through the early evening hours and off the surrounding canyon walls. The words provoked an arresting dramatic effect. All eyes turned toward the cave.

> *Warmth. He remembered feeling cold, just before...just before...the memory of Mary's face just above his, bending over, testing, trying to ascertain if he still breathed...then nothing...nothing but peace. Now warmth. The cold was gone...gone. Warmth. Comfort. Peace. His eyelids moved but could not open. Tingling in his arms, as though they had been asleep. His breath came so sudden it almost frightened him. His lungs filled with stifling air. He coughed. More warmth. His muscles flexed, then cramped, then flexed again. He tried to move, but could not. He was wrapped, bound. He could not move, or could he? Slowly, inch by precious inch, his legs shifted toward the edge of the hollowed crypt in which he lay. Then space beneath. He scissored his legs. Some of the bandages loosened. Breathing labored, and then the fresh air from the opening flooded his lungs. Saliva returned to his mouth. His eyes could see light through the bindings over his face. He took a step toward the light...and then another...*

Silence. The wind brushed whispers against the trees of the garden. First stars appeared. A rabbit poked its head around a stem of hyssop. A gentle rustling of...what? From inside the tomb? In a moment, a man, or the figure of a man, wrapped in strips of linen pasted to his body with burial spices, stood in the doorway of the cave that served as a sepulchre. A murmur rose among those standing by. Breath arrested. Noises of fear mixed with joy. The figure of a man stumbled awkwardly, imprisoned by the wrappings, eyes blinded by the cloth around his face. The odor of death had evaporated. I could not help but think of the story of Shadrach, Meshach and Abed-nego, how that when they emerged from Nebuchadnezzar's burning fiery furnace, there was not so much as the smell of smoke on their clothes. All that remained here was the sweet smell of flowers and spices, the fragrance of life, not death. Jesus said, "Help him! Remove the grave clothes so the man can walk!."

In a stupefied trance, attendants mechanically completed this task, and Lazarus stood, naked as the day he was born, his skin fairly shining with life and vitality. His nakedness was only for a moment. His sisters, still recovering from the shock of what had just taken place, were frozen in their steps. Andrew quickly covered him with his own cloak. Jewish legend has it that before a child is born its soul has seen all of heaven and hell, of past, of present and future; but that as the Angel strikes it on the mouth to waken it into this world, all of the memory of those things pass from its mind and it awakes with no knowledge of anything. What was in the mind of Lazarus as he gazed into the eyes of Jesus on that wondrous day? I do not know. After what had just happened, further description of events is superfluous. I sat on a rock, my mind numb. I still cannot speak or write of it without the hair on my neck rippling rigid. My skin still shivers. I still gasp for breath.

αΘω

Most of those who had come to visit the sisters and had seen what Jesus did had faith in him. But amazingly, the hearts of others were hardened. They ignored the voice of the Spirit as he spoke to them in answer to the prayer of Jesus. These went to the religious authorities and told them what Jesus had done. Predictably, they called a meeting. That is what religious authorities do. "What are we accomplishing?" they asked. It was obvious that they felt they were accomplishing nothing where Jesus was concerned. "Here is a man performing outlandish tricks the people consider miracles. If we let him go on like this, everyone will believe in him, and then Pilate and his thugs will come and take away both our authority and our political control."

Caiaphas the High Priest spoke up, "You are as ignorant of history as you are lacking in pragmatism! You know nothing at all! Don't you realize that it is better that one man die than the whole nation perish?" As it is with self-absorbed persons, it was Caiaphas who was ignorant. He was not remotely aware that he was speaking prophetically. Jesus would indeed die for the Jewish nation, and not merely for that nation but also for every soul in the entire world, in order to bring them together and make them one. Caiaphas had none of this in mind. Murder entered his heart and into the hearts of his lackeys.

It is a thing to be noted. From this day forward in the events of our Lord, in the resurrection of Lazarus, his own death was certified. From this day forward, the Jews began to lay their perfidious plans—plans that provided human history with its blackest day. Jesus seemed to sense this ominous specter, and because of the raising of Lazarus, we ceased to move among the Jews. Instead we withdrew once again to Peraea, near the village of Ephraim, where Jarud had found us. In my musings I wondered, *Is it easier to raise one from the death and decay of the body, or is it easier to raise one from the hideous corruption of spiritual morbidity? What difference does it make as to which is easier, if it is true that both are raised?*

V

Barnabas

Ephraim in Peraea was hardly large enough to be called a town. Not many families lived here. It seemed to be a dying community. How it came to be named is a mystery, especially in view of the fact that the land had no historical relationship with the son of Joseph. Peraea was situated on the east side of the Jordan river, just north of the Jabbock, within the ancient tribal territory of Manasseh. The land accorded to Ephraim, Manasseh's brother, bordered on the west by the great sea. I spoke to an old scribe who believed the present eastern Ephraim got its name as a result of Manasseh's wish to honor his brother somehow. At one time, he told me, it had been named Ephron, which some scholars believe to be a corruption of the name Ephraim. I was puzzled by this, however, because the only Ephron (one of three locations by that name) of which I was aware had been located more than a day's journey to the north near Gadara.

It was to this fading community that Jesus and the rest of us came, and it was here that one of the most revealing incidents that spoke to the character and integrity of Jesus took place. These qualities were never questioned among those of us who followed him. But they were not only questioned; they were often maligned by those who wished for him to go away. To them, Jesus of Nazareth represented an aberration, an unpleasant interruption into the routine of the way things should be. He was not a part of the religious leviathan; moreover, he upset it. This was difficult to tolerate.

Even here in this remote corner of Peraea, their spies and emissaries were rampant, observing every move the Lord made, compiling information, reporting back to superiors, plotting, relentlessly scheming toward one objective: his eradication. On occasion, they came close—close enough to frighten us but never close enough to disturb Jesus. In all the time we spent together, I never once saw him afraid or anxious over the manner of events. It seemed he anticipated them, expected them. It seemed that to him, it was all a part of a carefully conceived schematic.

αΘω

The beggar sat by an old well, the water source of which had diminished to a trickle. This was one reason why the community was dying. People could not live where there was not enough water. Most of the dwellers had to walk several miles to the Jabbock for water and it was just too far to be practical. Like all other beggars, when people walked by, he held out his hand, and as I observed him, he sometimes withheld his hand and just sat there staring at the ground, looking miserable in his poverty. Jesus approached him, apparently taking him for what he looked to be, a person burdened by years of unrelenting hardship and pain. For these people, Jesus had great compassion. Most of them had some physical handicap, lameness, deafness, blindness or limitless proclivity to wine. Many could not speak. I thought this man to be among the latter, and I fully expected Jesus to heal him. The Lord came and stood before the beggar, hardly an arm's length away.

The man stared at the ground and as he saw the feet of Jesus come into view, he raised his head. He was filthy, grotesque and smelled of rancid urine. Lines in his face were creased with dust and accumulated dirt had turned his countenance grey. One eye was normal, the other had no pupil. It was filled with a milky substance that gave the appearance of agate. He looked monstrous. His beard matted with spittle and oil-caked with filth. His clothes ragged, torn and disheveled. He looked as if he were on the very edge of death.

"How much did they pay you?" We were at first puzzled at Jesus' question. "Is it enough to slay the Son of Man? For that they should have paid you well." The beggar remained seated as Jesus stood before him and said nothing, eyes glancing in every direction for all the good it did for the blind one. We thought we had misunderstood Jesus. We couldn't have heard what we thought we heard. But the coldness of Jesus' words had an effect. The beggar seemed unnerved, and then in one cat-like movement the man was on his feet, light from the sun glinting on the blade in his hand. Before any of us could react, the razor-edge of a dagger was held at Jesus' throat. One tiny movement would open a critical vessel of blood within his neck. Our Lord was a flick of the wrist away from a certain, bloody death. Peter lunged toward the man, but the others held him in check.

"Stay away!" screamed the beggar, "Or I will remove his head!" We all froze, our feet immobile. The anguish on Peter's face revealed a terrible mixture of fear and rage. The man's right hand held the dagger and his left gripped the front of the Lord's chest. He jostled Jesus so that he fell back against the wall of the well, his knees buckling beneath him, his head held against the parapet. Yet if there was fear in him, his face did not show it. We were powerless to help. The man could easily kill Jesus before we reached him. Despite his appearance, the man was a brute with the strength to move Jesus about with one arm as if he were a sack of salt. Then as if there weren't enough bizarre extremity taking place before us, the dog came calmly forward and sat on her haunches not two paces from the beggar and Jesus. She watched the scene unfold with oddly curious interest. It was as if she were waiting to see what the man would do.

Everything flashed through my mind. All that we ever did together, his baptism, the cold nights and blazing campfires, the wondrous teachings, the healings, the compassion—all of it flooded my thoughts in what seemed like an eternity. Everything congealed as if arrested in motion. I could see myself charging, seizing the man and his blade, thrusting it into the attacker's breast, yet my feet were immobile. I couldn't move, yet the dog sat there, watching as if it were all taking place for her entertainment. The blade pressed deeper into skin. I was amazed that it had not yet cut through and we—all of us—were paralyzed.

Crazily, thoughts of that terrible night on Galilee came to me. The boat was being tossed like a toy. We were taking on water. There seemed to be no question of the outcome, we were all going to die. Yet he lay there, his head on a coil of rope, asleep. I looked at Jesus now. He was not asleep, yet—and this was eerie—he was the one who appeared to be in control, not his assailant.

"Do then, what you have come here to do." The silent, slow motion sequence of events were intruded upon by his words. "Slay me if that is your intent," the voice went on. The words were even, unaffected by fear or rage. There was a moment of poignant silence again. We waited. Would he do it? None of us doubted that he would. Any second we thought we would see an ugly crimson streak on the neck of Jesus. We waited for blood. It didn't come. "Do you need help?" asked Jesus. Slowly his hand rose and approached the assailant's knife-wielding arm.

"Move another inch and you're dead!" screamed the beggar, his voice rasping with emotion. Jesus did not hesitate. His hand continued on its path until it grasped the man's wrist.

"Here, let me assist," he said. Incredibly, Jesus applied pressure. We saw the sharp blade press even deeper into his skin. The dog simply cocked her head. Slowly, the truth began to come to me. Jesus was not going to die. He was in total control of this event. He was in no danger at all. He would not lose so much as a whisker. This was some bizarre event with a surprise ending. The man relaxed his grip on the weapon. Yet Jesus now held his hand in place, the blade pressed hard against his skin. It was Jesus who held the beggar as his prisoner, not the other way around.

"Let me go!" The man cried.

"Why?" asked Jesus. "Did you not come to kill me? Get it over with. This is what you've been paid to do."

"I've not the stomach for it," the man whimpered. He was defeated. But Jesus held the knife in its ominous place.

"You will be hunted down and killed yourself, if you do not kill me." The man made an obvious attempt to pull away, but the powerful carpenter's hands held him firmly in place.

"Please...Master..." When he said that, Jesus allowed the man to withdraw his weapon. He broke into weeping and fell in a heap at Jesus' feet. Peter started toward the man. The knife had fallen from his hand clinking on stone. In one motion Peter grabbed it, took hold of the beggar and would have killed him were it not for Jesus.

"No, Simon." Peter stopped, looking at Jesus with rage in his eyes. "Release him." The fisherman could not believe his ears. "Release him, Peter! Release him now!" Jesus commanded. Peter allowed the heavy body to fall back to the earth. He stepped back sensing that Jesus wished him to do so. The man groveled, weeping at the Lord's feet. The crying escalated into rough coughing. Thick heaves of loud sobs overtook the man, and then he vomited blood bright red. In a moment the coughing and heaving stopped. "Bring him a towel," said Jesus. Stooping down, the Lord took the towel, lifted the man's face now pale with fear and wiped the blood and spittle from his face. The unholy orb that was his blind eye rolled in his head, uncontrolled and wild. At Jesus' touch, at his compassion, the man's spirit calmed. "What is your name?" he asked.

The man's head bowed in shame. "I have no name," he said. "And now I have no life. As you said, I will be hunted down and killed."

"Then I will give you a name," said Jesus. "Henceforth, you shall be known as *Barnabas*, son of consolation. Your life begins today, Barnabas. There is something within you that the Father loves." Jesus laid his hand on the man's eye and massaged gently. When he removed it, the eye was clear and matched the other one. Barnabas could now see clearly in both eyes. Abishag licked the man's hand, the very hand that had held the weapon. Color returned to his face, his shoulders straightened. "Bring garments," said

Jesus to the disciples, "for at the appointed time, this man Barnabas shall serve the living God."

Yes, dear friend, this is the same Barnabas about whom Luke the physician wrote, whose surname was Joseph, a Levite from Cyprus, the same Barnabas who became the companion and mentor of Paul of Tarsus and later the defender and mentor of John Mark.

Barnabas remained with us for about a week before Jesus sent him home. How such a man ever became a murderer for hire stupefied me as his deportment among us for that week was nothing short of enriching. That such a man could have such spiritual insight and use it—without knowing it I might add—to fill the hearts of those who only a few days before were victimized by him was remarkable. He offered no resistance to leaving; it was he who wanted to leave us. What happened in his heart he had to share with his family, who would no longer recognize him, he said, nor would his former friends. Another surprise. How could such a man as he ever have friends? But as the Lord reminded us, buried deep within this Joseph of Cyprus was a sweetness of character that had been covered over by the bitterness and cynicism of poverty.

VI

High Places

We continued for some time in our wanderings without adverse incident and free of care. "With regard to what is possible for God," laughed Jesus, "Look at yourselves! See how he has brought you from the rogues that you were to passably amenable creatures!" His eyes examined us with a look of mild approval. "Simon, you no longer smell of dead fish. What is impossible with men, is possible with God. End of debate!"

Peter was not amused. "We left everything—our work, our homes—to follow you, Lord. It has been difficult." His jaw set. "I have missed my children, time with Joanna, private time, intimate time, for months now. My sandals, my knees, my bones; all worn down by these damnable roads we travel. At times it feels as if we have endured hardship the like of which I have never seen at sea; what then will there be for us?"

Those of us who were non-committal about Peter's clodishness were, henceforth, converted. It had never occurred to me that following Jesus was sacrifice. But then, I was younger than most of the others, had no family, no wife (at this time), no business I had spent my life building. Oh, I know there were those who would later refer to our time with him as sacrificial. Even severe.

For me, however, the day that I knew Jesus loved me and wanted me among those closest to him; was as though I have been given wings. My feet were suddenly released from the sucking mud and set, instead, upon a rock. I felt lifted and cleansed. Now after all these years of hardship and disappointment and that yet to come, I will perhaps acknowledge the point. Yet and still, when I remember the days I wallowed in life without him—if it was, indeed, living—I would not trade a single moment of my present faith for a lifetime of such wallowing. I cannot even yet bring myself to ask, "What's in it for me?" "Come to me," he said, "and I will give you rest." I have found that invitation to be true. I am, therefore, too grateful for what I have—to complain about what I have not.

But his response to Peter was strange. "At the hour," he said, "when the Son of Man is to claim the throne of his glory, you also, who have followed me, shall sit on twelve thrones, judging the twelve tribes of Israel." Twelve tribes. Twelve thrones. Twelve simple men whom Jesus had chosen.

As to Peter, I could not tell what he thought or felt about Jesus' answer. Surely, he must have felt flattered, perhaps humbled, perhaps a bit awed. I did wonder at the time—although no longer—of what of the rest of us. What reward had we? It really didn't matter. Just the thought of eternity in intimacy with him was more than I could ask. As David put it,

> *"I would rather be a doorkeeper in the house of my God than to dwell in the tents of the wicked."*

And now after the deed, after the dice and the elevation of my friend Matthias, I wondered why I was not also chosen. I felt more than a little left out; yet strangely, I felt wondrously disengaged. This odd "sense," if you will, was confirmed some years after Jesus' death.

It occurred that I was in prayer with two men of black skin. Both men dearly loved our Lord and served him without distraction from secular affairs. We sat in chairs, the three of us, and as was my habit, my eyes remained open in prayer. (I've never quite understood why people close their eyes to pray as if God were somehow inside their head.) One of these two men I knew well. We had served the Lord together in preaching and teaching. It was he who had invited me to pray with them. The other man was from his native soil in Africa. What he was doing on our foreign soil I did not know, but here he was, praying in the same room with us.

As I observed him speaking in prayer, it came upon me to lay my hands on his head and pray for him. I resisted the impulse thinking how foolish it would appear when the thought intruded, "If you don't, you will miss the blessing I have for you." Believing this thought to have come from the Father, I extended my arms, buried my hands in his black hair and offered a prayer on his behalf. When I had finished, he opened his eyes and looking at me said, "I have a word from our Lord for you: *'I will make your feet as hind's feet and set you in high places.'*"

Perhaps this would not have resonated so deeply within me had not my sweet Juliana, only a few days before, sent me a missive. It contained these same words from God, *"I will make your feet as hind's feet and set you in high places."* She had heard them in Synagogue the day before. She felt, oddly, that God had let those words be read at that time so that I might know of them and believe them to be a promise to me. Coincidence? Or—confirmation? I am not certain. My faith is too weak.

Since that day I have journeyed many roads in my faith. In the passing summers and winters over the many decades, I have not seen my foot in a single high place. My life instead has often been one humiliation after another. Yet I still seek that high place. If it does not happen in this life, I believe I will find it in the next. Let the twelve have their thrones. God has prepared a place for me as well. A high place—where my feet and my heart will abound. Where no longer will I feel on the outside looking in; where no longer will I have to prove myself—to myself, to others, or even to God. Where at last the struggle will cease.

In the course of my lifetime with Juliana, she would often hold my head to her breast, look into my eyes, smile, and shivers of love would assault my soul. This soft place, I thought, is "high enough."

VII

The Servant

On a quiet evening in the home of a friend, Jesus took us aside and said with compelling directness, "We leave in the morning for Jerusalem." As he continued, he spoke as though he were removed, somehow, from the events to come, yet he was obviously speaking of himself. His expression was intense and deliberate. "Everything written by the prophets about me is about to be fulfilled. The Son of Man will be handed over to the authorities. They will mock him, insult him, spit on him, flog him and kill him. On the third day he will rise from the dead."

We understood none of this. We knew that going to Jerusalem was dangerous business. That point had been made before the affair with Lazarus, but his actually being arrested, persecuted and killed was something beyond comprehension! There seemed to be a deeper meaning, but if there were, it was lost on us. We were concerned about survival, his and ours. None of us looked forward to an encounter with Herod's guard. We were frightened.

Ancient City of God, what demons lurk in your shadows?

αΘω

It was bound to happen. What with twelve thrones governing the twelve tribes, it would not be enough for some. This played out on the way to Jerusalem when we were met by the mother of James and John. The three of them came to Jesus and with pious ceremony knelt down in front of him. I was a bit surprised at this behavior in John. Somehow, it didn't fit his personality.

Such actions always embarrassed me, and I believe, embarrassed the Lord as well. I knew who he was. We all did. Yet his demeanor among us was never one of superiority. We laughed together, wept together, told stories together and, yes, sat at his feet to hear the wisdom and love of God. He was who he was and we were who we were, but still it was he who crossed the line. It was he who made us feel that we were a family, a fellowship of brothers. Though he was different from all of us, he was the same, a man of intellect, passion and action.

But they came and knelt, asking a favor of him. "What is it you wish?" he asked, as if he did not know. Perhaps he didn't. I never did comprehend the depth of his mind. Sometimes it seemed eternal, supernatural. Sometimes not.

Their mother said, "Grant that one of these two sons of mine may sit at your right and the other at your left in your kingdom." She must have been told of the twelve thrones.

Oddly, the request moved Jesus deeply. He placed his hand on her head to comfort her. "You don't know what you ask," he said. He knew, however, that she was serious. He turned to James and John, "Can you drink the cup I am going to drink?"

Without hesitation the brothers answered, "Oh, yes, Lord. We will do anything required of us!"

"You will, indeed," said Jesus, "far more than you now realize. The time will come when you will indeed drink from my cup and wish with all your heart that you had never so much as tasted it."

"Never, Lord!" from both of them.

Jesus merely looked at them, "I cannot grant what you request. To sit at my right or left is not for me to decide. These places belong to those for whom they have been prepared by my Father."

"Who then?" thought I. *If not James and John, perhaps one of us? Simon, perhaps? Me?* I rejected that thought instantly. *More likely Moses or one of the prophets. Perhaps even Adam himself. Who? Was it someone who has yet to be born? Yet to believe? Someone thousands of years hence? How could it be?*

Jesus called us together and said, "Gentlemen. Gentlemen, do not be angry with your brothers. They only know, as you do, of this world. In this world, rulers of the nations lord it over their citizens, and high officials exercise authority over them. *It is not to be so with you.* Authority among men is at its essence and at its best a secular exercise. Let there be no constituted authority among those who follow me. None! No vicars or bishops, no priests and no silly trappings. Let there be no institutions, however beneficent, for their evil is greater than their good. Instead, whoever wants to become great among you must be your servant, and whoever wants to be first must be your slave—just as the Son of Man did not come to be served, but to serve, to lay at the feet of his captors even his very life, so that the world may be emancipated."

The Servant.

That is why he had come among us. To serve. To give of himself for the sake of those he came to redeem. Though he is the Lord of Lords and King of Kings, that is not why he came. Though he is the Son of God, he came as the Son of Man. Jesus did not come to found a great religion. He came to give of himself. He came to serve.

After his death, we all forgot this clear and simple instruction. In this, we did not well.

VIII

Have Mercy

We crossed the river to the western bank and continued along the dusty road to Jericho. In a short time we could see the outlines of the houses and shops in the shadows. With the Dead Sea not far to the South, this is and has always been an inhospitable part of the world. Why anyone would choose such a place to live, I did not know. On the outskirts of the town were many beggars, most of them physically incapacitated in some way, unable to labor, poor, starving. Most of them just sat mute, a terrible symbol to the inhumanity of the terrible fate that brought them to this place. One of these was not so mute, a blind man sitting at the roadside begging. Hearing the crowd that always seemed to accompany us, he asked what was going on. A companion heard his question and told him, "Jesus of Nazareth is passing by."

Instant energy seemed to charge him. He cried out in a voice laden with urgency and anticipation, "Jesus! Son of David! Have pity on me!" He reached for his staff and struggled to stand. In his anticipation, he couldn't quite make his limbs work, and he started to fall. The person who had spoken to him reached out and steadied him.

Those walking at the front of the entourage began to tell him to be quiet, but he cried louder and repeatedly, "Son of David, have pity on me!"

Jesus stopped. "Justus," he said to me, "bring that man to me." I stepped forward and took the man's arm and brought him to Jesus. "What do you wish me to do for you?" It was a question spoken into silence and penetrated the dark realm of this man's meager existence.

I've often wondered what it might be like to be blind. At times I have shut my eyes tightly just to see if I could duplicate the experience, stumbling about. Yet I always opened my eyes again and saw. This man had never opened his eyes. All that had ever stood before him was the blackness of a starless, moonless night in the forest, inside his head. It was as if he had no eyes at all. No. I could not in my childish attempts duplicate that.

Through my musing I heard him say, "Lord, that I may receive my sight."

Jesus, knowing his pain and deprivation more than any other, was deeply moved with compassion. He spoke gently to the man, "Then receive your sight, my friend. Your faith is sweet and beautiful. It has healed you." As he said this, he touched the man's eyes; and when he removed his hands, where once discolored, yellow orbs twisted grotesquely, now clear, perfect blue-green, seeing eyes illuminated his face. Tears of gratitude streamed down his cheeks into his beard as he squinted at the brightness, then peered into the eyes of the Master.

The art of language fails me to properly relate what witnessing such a scene does to a person. I could feel myself shaking. This event took place within arm's length of where I stood.

αΘω

Onward we pressed toward Jerusalem. You could almost feel the tempo of our journey increase, the sense of urgency, anticipating battle, preparing for inevitable agony, surged with the pounding of blood in our veins. We were not aware of what would happen, yet we knew that something would. It was as if we were preparing our stomachs to meet a hideous event. Even Jesus, though outwardly calm, seemed tense, knowing yet accepting with resignation the foreordained destiny that lay ahead.

αΘω

As we passed through the dirty streets of Jericho, curious crowds increased. Here we encounter Zacchaeus, chief tax collector, wealthy and despised. He was as curious to see Jesus as the others, but being absurdly short, the top of his head came to the average man's chest. He could not see over the crowd. So he ran ahead and climbed a tree to see. When Jesus reached the spot, he looked up and laughed, "Zacchaeus, what are you doing up in that tree?" Intoning his voice as if he were speaking to a child, "Come down this instant. I was just on my way to visit with you and your family." Zacchaeus scrambled down at once and welcomed him gladly.

Everyone saw and heard this. Some began to mutter, "Incredible! He has gone to be the guest of this evil creature."

Two issues are clear: First, Jesus ignores criticism of what he considers the appropriate way to think and the right thing to do. He seems to taunt his critics by rubbing their nose in it. Second, he fully expects the effort of good to result in good. And with Zacchaeus, that is exactly what happened.

At dinner that evening Zacchaeus stood up and said to the Jesus, "Lord, here and now I give half of my possessions to the poor, and if I have cheated anybody out of anything, I will pay back four times the amount."

Jesus raised his eyebrows and smiled. Reaching for his cup of wine, he raised it and said, "Today life and deliverance have come to you and your house, Zacchaeus. I toast your generosity and your honesty!" And to those standing by Jesus said, "This man is as much a son of Abraham as any of us, and from now on, you must treat him as such. For the Son of Man came to seek and to save men and women just like him." Not that Zacchaeus could not afford to be so generous. He was a man of extraordinary, ill-gotten wealth and remained so. The point is, he accepted. He believed. In his heart, faith had been planted. We continued at his home for several days before resuming our journey.

With God, all things, indeed, are possible.

αΘω

It seems the world is full of blind beggars. On the other side of the city, as we were leaving Jericho, yet another group of them sat about in the filth of the street holding out their hands, palms up. Two of the beggars became aware that it was Jesus going by. They shouted as did the poor soul we encountered coming into the city, "Lord! Son of David! Have mercy on us!" The crowd was the same as before. They were told to shut up and be quiet. But they shouted all the louder, "Lord! Son of David! Have mercy on us!"

As he did with the others, Jesus had compassion on them and healed them. Yet again, another blind man came. We learned that this one went by the name of Bartimaeus. Like the others, he sat by the roadside begging. On hearing what Jesus had done for his colleagues, he also began to shout, "Jesus! Son of David! Have mercy on me!" Like the others, he was told to be quiet, and like the others he shouted all the more. "Son of David!" he screamed, "have mercy on me!" Had these people no sense of decorum?

Jesus said again, "Call him and bring him to me."

So they said to the blind man, "On your feet old fellow, he's calling for you." Throwing his cloak aside, Bartimaeus jumped to his feet and with help found his way to Jesus.

"Teacher, please," he pleaded, "I want to see."

"Then go," said Jesus, "your faith has healed you." Immediately he received his sight and followed us along the road.

We continued our trek to Jerusalem; Bartimaeus, formerly blind, in our train.

IX

Behold, Your King

Six days before the Passover, Jesus once again arrived at the home of Lazarus, Mary and Martha in Bethany. For a man recently dead, Lazarus looked as healthy as the day he was born. That evening we took dinner in the home of a neighbor and friend, known in these parts as Simon the Leper. The dinner had been given in Jesus' honor. As usual, Martha scurried about orchestrating the servants as they attended to us, while Lazarus was among those reclining at the table with him. Mary sat at the feet of Jesus. With a cloth she gently toweled his feet, bare of sandals from having been washed.

"Simon the Leper" had once been a name repugnant to the man, but now he wore it like a mantle of honor. Simon's healing was one of those many events not told about Jesus. Not that it was being deliberately hidden, just never recorded. Tonight it was not forgotten. The conversation around the table focused on the raising of Lazarus and the healing of Simon.

Simon stood, raised his goblet in toast and said, "Forty and two years had I spent in the caves of the colony." He paused and the next time he spoke, his voice choked. "Forty and two years until the flesh rotted from my body!" He held up his empty hand. "Do you see these fingers?" He wiggled the four fingers of the empty hand. "Before the Lord Jesus came along, these fingers were gone. They had dropped off to bloody stumps. And now, as you can see, they are very much present and alive." All applauded and there were shouts of praise. Simon turned and gazed at Jesus, held out his raised goblet and said, "Thank you, my Lord! I owe you my life! Wholeheartedly, I thank you, my family thanks you, my friends thank you." And then he raised his voice, "To Jesus of Nazareth, from whom leprosy and death flee as if scalded! To Jesus of Nazareth, Son of God, Messiah, Lord of Lords and Friend!" There were shouts of consent and joy. Goblets around the room were raised, clinked, and we all drank in praise of him.

All drank, except for one. I noticed Judas raise his glass in toast, touch the cup to his lips but he did not drink. He returned the vessel to the table and observed the rest of us with black contempt. This went unnoticed, I think, by all except me. Later, I was to discover I was wrong about this. One other in the room knew. Before the evening was over, Judas would reveal his colors.

Judas notwithstanding, the feeling in Simon's house was joyous and convivial. Unknown to anyone, Mary had brought with her an alabaster vessel. Typically, such vessels were reserved for expensive perfumes or ointments. This one was no exception. It contained almost a lavish amount of pure nard. The oil of nard comes from the root of a plant grown only in the distant East and among the foothills of the Himalayas in India. It was rare and costly.

Mary did a surprising thing. With a gentle smile on her lips, she opened the vessel, and poured its precious contents on Jesus' feet and wiped them with her hair. *I knew she was up to something! She had been sitting there massaging his feet, caressing them with her hair since he had first reclined at table.* The house filled with stunning, heavenly fragrance.

Then Judas made his move, "Why wasn't this perfume sold and the money given to the poor?" he objected. "The contents of that vessel *alone* could have fetched enough money to feed a man's family for a year." He then began to upbraid Mary and speak to her harshly. He did not do this because he cared about the poor but because he was a thief. Had the perfume been sold and had some or all of the money found its way to us, as keeper of the money bag, he would secretly help himself. Jesus knew about Judas. It is, therefore, a mystery as to why he allowed him to be treasurer. Had the perfume been sold, Judas would have found some way to profit personally from the sale. *How did this man become an apostle?*

"Leave her alone," Jesus replied. "Why is this bothering you? She has done a beautiful and sweet thing to me. It was intended that she should save this perfume for the day of my burial and she has chosen to use it now. What is that to you, Judas? You will always have the poor among you, but you will not always have me."

This was now the second time Jesus had come to the defense of Mary. And then there was that odd exchange between them when he raised Lazarus. In all of my years of knowing him, Jesus never once gave any indication that he held any romantic interests at all. It seemed his calling transcended that part of human experience. Sometimes I wondered if he had any sexuality at all. Jesus of Nazareth, for all of his humanity, was an unusual man, but how *human* was he? To my knowledge, he never did anything to cast a shadow over his moral integrity. Yet there seemed to unmistakably be something between him and Mary, sister to Martha and Lazarus, that did not exist between himself and other women. That substance in alabaster which Mary used to anoint the feet of Jesus was the same substance of which Solomon spoke in his song of intimacy. I cannot say that his relationship with Mary was like that. I can only say that it was special and unique, reserved, it seemed, only for her.

Jesus stared hard at Judas, challenging him. Judas knew that the poor were perennial and ubiquitous. He cared nothing for them. No one could do anything about the poor. As Jesus himself had said, they would always be here. That is why the money should be his, should it not?

But Jesus did not make this remark because he did not care for the poor, but to honor the worship and adoration in Mary's heart. Nor was he unaware that Judas cared not for the poor. He chose not to allow Judas' real motivation to diminish the significance of Mary's deed.

Then he said something that immediately galvanized our minds, "I tell you the truth," he began. Whenever Jesus said that, you knew something extraordinary was to follow.

He looked lovingly at Mary and continued, "Wherever the message of God's love and forgiveness is told throughout the world in ages to come, what Mary has done this night will also be told, in memory of her."

There it is. Jesus knew even at this moment that the world would never be the same after his life. He knew that the impact of his visit to earth would never burn out. Long after he was gone, people would remember significant events simply because it was connected to him. To this hour, when I think of Mary, I think of this moment. I think of the sweet aroma that filled the house of Simon the Leper. I think of this dear sister, this sweet woman of loving faith.

αΘω

We arrived in Jerusalem at Passover. Thousands had already come from all over to Jerusalem to go through the ritual of purification. The primary subject of conversation and gossip among them concerned the whereabouts of Jesus. While standing on the steps of the Temple, looking over the throngs of people milling about in celebration, Obed remarked to Joash, "What do you think? Will he show up? Will he come to the feast?"

The reason everyone was wondering about this stemmed from the religious officials. The chief priests and the Pharisees had issued a command that if anyone knew where Jesus was he should make it known. They sought to apprehend him; he was sought by the religious authorities like a fleeing fugitive.

When we heard this, we were frightened and wanted to leave the environs of the city. But Jesus would have none of it. Indeed, as he approached the hill called the Mount of Olives, he called for Nathanael and Philip, instructing them, "I want you to go to the village of Bethpage where you will find a colt tied which has never been ridden. Untie it and bring it here. If anyone tries to stop you or asks you, 'Where are you going with the colt?' tell him, 'The Lord needs it.'"

When Philip and Nathanael entered the village, they found an ass's colt, just as Jesus had told them. As they were untying the colt, its owner asked them, "Where do you think you are going with my beast?"

They replied, "The Lord needs it." Amazingly, the owner offered no further resistance.

In those years of journeying with Jesus, traveling from village to village, living like nomads, I had witnessed many wondrous events. More important than the miracles and such, more even than listening to him teach and preach, were the quiet moments with him, just meditating and being with him. I truly loved Jesus, and I believe that he thoroughly loved each one of us in a special way unique to each one of us. This being the case, I was profoundly appalled when Judas did what he did, but that comes later in my story.

The crowds were always there, always seeking, always demanding and as events happened, the crowds today, on the outskirts of Jerusalem, were larger than usual, even for Passover. It was then that I realized that I had lost him. Not really, I suppose, but I realized that Jesus belonged to more than just us disciples, or more importantly, just to me. He belonged to all these people—to all people. He belonged to the world. In what was to follow, I would come to believe and accept this more deeply than before.

When the colt arrived, people threw cloaks on its back and assisted Jesus astride it. People began to spread their cloaks on the road for the animal to walk on. Suddenly, the whole crowd erupted joyfully in praise of God with a deafening voice:

> *"Blessed is the king who comes in the name of the Lord! Peace in heaven and glory in the highest!"*

They broke palm branches from off the trees and waving them, went out to meet him, shouting, "Hosanna! Blessed is the King of Israel!"

Hosanna? King of Israel? I was stunned. I believed this, as did the twelve, but I had no thought that so many had come to believe. Obviously, this did not go down well with the religious authorities. They intended to arrest him but could not because of the crowd. "Control your people, man!" they screamed, trying to make themselves heard. "Make them be quiet! You have no idea that you are riding into a nest of hornets! Be warned, this won't last!"

"If they keep quiet," Jesus laughed, "the very stones at your feet will cry out."

"This is getting us nowhere," I heard one say. "He does not listen to us. Look how the whole world has gone after him! We must find a way to stop this!"

The procession, with the Lord Jesus riding on the back of the colt, made its way through the gates and into the city of God.

αΘω

As he approached the city, Jesus looked above the crowds about him to Jerusalem itself. For the second time since I had known him, I saw tears glistening on his cheeks. The ass stopped for a moment as if it were aware of its rider's mood. Jesus sat quietly on its back and patted its neck compassionately. He looked beyond the crowd to the skyline of the city. "Oh Jerusalem, Jerusalem," he lamented, barely loud enough to be heard,

> *If you had only known on this day what would bring you peace—but now it is hidden from your eyes. The days will come upon you when your enemies will build an embankment against you and encircle you and hem you in on every side. They will dash you to the ground, you and your precious children within your walls. They will not leave one stone on another. This will happen not because of the strength of your enemies, but because you did not recognize the time of God's coming to you.*

In less than forty years, Titus, son of the new emperor, Vespasian, invaded Jerusalem and in five months razed it to the ground, leaving Herod's great Temple a pile of rubble. Those who escaped gathered at Masada.

I traveled back to Jerusalem a few years ago in hopes of revisiting pleasant memories, and perhaps some not so pleasant, but wishing to honor them. What I saw turned my blood cold and ran shivers up and down my spine, lifting the hairs on the back of my neck. Had this been the grand and bustling city I had walked through, worshipped in, and been enthralled by? It felt empty, lifeless, as though its soul had been ripped away.

αΘω

The crowd had hardly quieted when his lips had ceased to move.
Jesus had one week to live.

X

This Is Not Like Him

Events began to unfold to the beat of an imaginary drum, drama increasing with each beat and culminating with that terrible, final cry from the cross. Do not think for an instant that the following events were anything approaching routine. We could not possibly comprehend what was transpiring at the time, but as we recalled it all later, the necessity, the purpose, the immeasurable eternal significance of those events became remarkably clear. We all marveled at how perfectly God had brought it all together. The single focus for the rest of our lives would forever be driven by these events. But, as far as I know, the only ones who gathered as much as they could remember, and as much as could be derived from eyewitness accounts, and then wrote it down were Luke, John, Matthew, Mark and now, me.

Events unfolded to an unbearable rhythm. It began with his arrival on the back of that ass's colt to the steps of the Temple.

Jesus entered the Temple confines and saw it all again. They were back. The money exchangers, sellers of wine, rich fabrics, fruit and nut vendors, sellers of doves and sacrificial lambs; nothing had changed. It was a veritable marketplace. Trinkets, icons, religious symbols, *Stars of David,* all hawked and bargained over like cattle. The bazaar of commerce continued in the place of God's visitation.

Once again rage welled up inside him. Once again his face contorted and once again the violence within him erupted in flying merchandise and kicked over tables. Coin rolled and danced in happy abandon and release on the tiles while merchants cringed at his fury. With his bare hands he drove them from the Temple shouting, "Get out of here!" He roared, "Leave this place! It is written, *'My house will be called a house of prayer,'* but you have made it a cesspool of thieves."

In the shadows, a Temple guard stood, an amused expression on his face. For him, this was nothing but theater. On seeing him, Jesus paused and their eyes met. The guard's hand moved with deliberation to an instrument of torture attached to his waist. Jesus followed the movement of his hand to where it rested on what resembled a belaying pin used in Galilean fishing boats. A flicker of recognition clouded his eyes. Their gaze met once more, and Jesus turned away.

Is there a way to reconcile the enraged, violent Jesus with the gentle friend, confidant and peaceful man whom we all know and love? He could speak peace to the storm and bring healing to great pain. Who is this terrible, wild man shouting insult, invective, kicking things over and scattering them about? In observing this thing, one is stunned with how dreadful it might be to fall into the hands of the living God.

The chief priests and the teachers of the law saw it all. They, too, were frightened. Not so much from the rage of a young idealist but by the crowds that followed him in from the outside. They had to find a way to end this. *There must be a way to destroy this insane man!* Their frustration intensified when the blind and the lame came to him while he was still in the Temple, and he healed them. Children ran about shouting, "Hosanna to the Son of David!"

The priests and the leaders of the Temple could stand it no longer. "Do you hear what these empty-headed babes are shouting?" they indignantly demanded.

"I hear them," he replied. "Only it is not they who are deprived of their wits. It is you! No doubt you have never read the prayer of David, *'From the lips of children and infants you have ordained praise?'* Do you not understand anything you read? Or is it more likely that you cannot read at all?" The priests had, of course, read the passage many times. But the verbal jab stung. The man was insufferably brash, and the notion that he would use such a passage to refer to himself outraged them almost beyond their ability to contain it. Despite the obvious urge to kill Jesus there and then, they restrained themselves because of the crowd. Slowly, as a group, they left him and found a dark corner of the Temple in which to conspire as to how they would rid themselves of this menace—this peasant Carpenter.

Evening came. By then, those who had come for healing or who had come for the spectacle had either left or were sitting about conversing among themselves. Jesus gathered us together, and we exited the city. We walked the two miles back to Bethany where we spent the night.

αΘω

Next morning, we were up at first light. Gathering our things, we once again left the home of Lazarus before any of the family were up; hence, breakfast was not served. It was not long before hunger gnawed at out bellies, but we were heartened when we saw in the distance a solitary fig tree growing in the soil. It was in full leaf. Surely, there would be enough fruit to blunt the edge of our hunger. Fig trees, with their broad, fuzzy leaves, often grow alone almost as if they shunned the company of others of their ilk. This one was of medium size, about eight feet high and as many wide. When we examined it, however, for its succulent fruit, there was none. "Well of course," muttered Peter, "it isn't the season for figs. See, it is just beginning to bud. It will be several weeks before…"

"May no one ever eat fruit from you again." It was Jesus. When we heard him say this we were all amused that he would talk to a tree. But in a moment's passing, as we watched, the tree withered and died. The leaves just shriveled as if held to intense heat. Our chuckling stopped. We were left with open mouths—and still hungry stomachs.

"Why did you do this, Lord?" Peter asked.

Jesus seemed annoyed, "I am famished, Simon, and my expectations of this tree were disappointed. You are right, of course. Figs are out of season. It was childish of me." He looked away, exasperated.

A brief moment while we all waited. He looked back at the tree, evaluating his work. "Yes," he said testily, "Well, if you have faith and do not doubt, you can do this, too. Want to try it?" He looked away at the blue mountains. "While you're at it, say to those mountains, 'Go, throw yourself into the sea!' Do not doubt and it will happen. Go ahead!" he chided, "You can do it!."

Something was the matter. This was not like him. Obviously, he did not mean for us to be take him literally. One does not play with or trivialize the power of God. No one knows this better than he.

This was the first time we had seen him pulled, as it were, in two directions. On the one hand, he was human—still simmering, no doubt, from the blowup in the Temple. Add to this, his shouting, demanding stomach. On the other hand, he was, well, something else; something else that could cause a tree to shrivel and die in seconds. The same power that brought a man back four days' dead, had—in anger—killed this tree. In retrospect, it isn't difficult to surmise why Jesus did this. He knew, of course, that he was about to die an unimaginable, painful death. It would not be human to be emotionally oblivious to one's own impending, tortured death. This apparently irrational act was nothing more than the result of grim anticipation working in painful concert with the demands of hunger and residual rage. This was a human thing, erupting in holy power, something that could have only happened with Jesus. And he seemed almost embarrassed by his own deed.

This was not the first time or the only time Jesus had acted intemperately. But it is the only time, in my recollection, that he did something without an apparent reason—at least insofar as I was able to understand.

"But why did you destroy the tree?" Peter asked. "Could you not as easily have caused it to bear fruit?"

"As I said, I was hungry, and when the tree did not have any figs, I became annoyed," replied Jesus.

"You became annoyed with a tree?" Peter responded incredulously.

Jesus smiled, "I suppose you must forgive me, Simon; I am perhaps more like you than you would like me to be."

Peter did not respond.

We stood in silence for a long moment. Jesus, possibly for the first time since childhood, felt the very human desire for forgiveness, once again identifying himself with mankind.

"And while you are forgiving me," he continued, "forgive anyone—everyone—you hold anything against, just as your Father in heaven has forgiven you."

With this, he spoke again to the tree, "Sorry old fellow, I guess my belly got the best of me." Then he took a limb in each hand and gave them a shake. Suddenly, new leaves began to appear. Tiny green budding figs formed at the tips of tiny shoots. "There!" he exclaimed, "Back on schedule! In a few weeks, maybe you can quench the hunger of a child, or perhaps a widow, or," he laughed, "the birds, wasps and yellow-jackets." And then he paused in his soliloquy still holding the limbs in his hands and said distantly, "I wish I could see you truly perform, but that is not to be."

αΘω

We made our way back to the Temple where Jesus entered the courts and began to teach. Rarely did Jesus simply lecture. He raised questions and asked people to respond. And then he took questions and elaborated in his answer. Today as he taught, the chief priests and the elders of the people asked, "What right, what possible credentials give you the audacity to usurp authority over the commerce of the Temple, as you did yesterday? And how is it that you even remotely believe you have this authority?" Different questioners, same questions.

Jesus replied, "Let me ask you a question. If you answer me, I will answer yours and tell you why I have the authority to do these things." They nodded agreement. They could hardly refuse. They were priests and elders, wise ones who, supposedly, knew all there was to know. "John's baptism—you remember the Baptist, do you not? Where did John's baptism come from? Was it from heaven or from men?"

They huddled and discussed it among themselves. "If we say, 'From heaven,' he will ask, 'Then why didn't you believe him?' Can you imagine taking that strutting, self-absorbed prophet seriously?" There was chuckling at the thought. "But if we say, 'From men'—then everyone here will get into an angry uproar. They all hold that John was a prophet of God." It was a choice between brutal honesty and upsetting the crowd. So they chose a middle ground. They said to Jesus, "We don't know."

"You don't know?" Jesus taunted, "Well then, until you do, I will not tell you by what authority I do these things."

Jesus never allowed himself to be bullied by religious "authority"—or by *any* authority. As I think back on it, I am amazed at his composure. In a few days, he would be dead, yet he handled himself as if he were in absolute control and going nowhere. Nor did he think it necessary to respond to every demand or every question put to him. More often than not, he kept his own counsel.

Since they didn't go away, Jesus continued, "There was a man," he said, "who had two sons. He went to the first and said, 'Son, go and work today in the vineyard.' 'I will not!' the boy answered, but later he changed his mind and went.

"Then the man went to his other son and said the same thing. He very piously answered, 'I will go, sir,' but like many children, he dallied and ultimately forgot to go. Which of the two did what his father wanted?"

"Well, let's see," they responded sarcastically, "that would probably be the first." There was snickering.

Jesus laughed as well and then said to them, "Let me tell you the truth. You have answered correctly, but you are not like that child. You are as the second boy whose words are like the mist that burns off at dawn and has no substance. Tax collectors and prostitutes will enter the kingdom of God ahead of you!" The amusement halted immediately. "John the Baptist came to you to show you the way of righteousness. Don't play with me. You did not believe him. You know that and so do I. The tax collectors and prostitutes did believe him. And you thought, 'If we accept his teaching, we will be just like the tax collectors and prostitutes.' So you turned a cold and callous heart toward John."

This kind of exchange with the Temple leaders continued. It had the predictable outcome of exacerbating their anger and further solidified their resolve to have him put to death.

XI

Fueling the Flame

On another day in this final week in the Temple, Jesus preached a sermon. Not many think of it as a sermon, but that is what it was. It was a sermon that changed something deep inside me. I made copious notes of it as he spoke, and I have kept them to this day. It was many years ago, but I still remember it as if it were only a day away.

They first started calling us *Christians* in the city of Antioch, but now it has become a common name for us. I confess, I do not much like it. It makes one appear as if he is in a society, a religious corpus, and carries its own rather ugly elitism. It was intended to be a snide, debasing term of ridicule. "Little Christs," it meant, as if we were all puppets manipulated by attachments to Christ.

They never saw that our devotion, our allegiance to Jesus was, and is now, not driven by our coercive need to join a movement but comes as a result of his astounding love for us. Isn't a thirsty deer drawn to a quiet stream, or isn't a bear in the mountains drawn to the honeycomb? He gave, he gives, life, nourishment, hope. How could we not follow him!? Whatever leviathan may lurk in the stream, or however painful the sting, being with him mitigates completely all that might cause discomfort or all that may raise a threat to this life.

In any case, unfortunately, Christianity is becoming yet another religion. That is not what Jesus wanted. He wanted his followers to exemplify love and intimacy of spirit with each other and with him, not promote yet another form of legalism and institutionalism. It is through love, based on faith and belief, that rescue and liberation come—not through a stylized belief system.

I've thought, at times when I was younger, that I might have made a difference in the direction the church has taken had I been chosen as one of the twelve. I could have resisted the impulse to organize, to make rules, to institutionalize. I might have influenced James or even our brother Paul.

But then again, maybe not.

Men are drawn to structure. This compulsion to quantify and control, this need to assume the role of Authority, has been a part of human heritage since Adam.

αΘω

Well into this final week, Jesus' sermon took place on the Temple steps. He was ready. He was, as the momentum built toward the crucifixion, building the fire, stoking the flames, fueling the blaze. It seemed that every action, every word at this point was deliberately devised to insure his death.

"You teachers of the law," he began, "and religious officials who sit in the office of Moses. You people set yourselves up as the definers and interpreters of the law. It is a nice arrangement for you. Since your own cultic penchant has allowed you to do this, you must now be obeyed—at least until the liberty of the Spirit comes. But be careful. You are all men of flawed character; you do not practice what you preach.

"Everything you do is done for men to see. You make your religious symbols conspicuous. You love the place of honor at banquets and the most important seats in the synagogue. You love to be greeted in the marketplaces and to have men call you 'A Holy Man,' but you are anything but 'Holy.' There is only one who is 'Holy,' and it is not you. In the quiet of your room, you know this, but your arrogance and conceit is more important to you."

Embers of indignation grew into hot coals as they listened to him preach. They were seething! Crowds began to gather. I was beginning to wonder: *What was Jesus doing?* But he knew exactly what he was doing.

Stirring the seething coals of their anger further, he continued, "Teachers of the law are you? You hypocrites! I say you are all insufferable, pious bureaucrats, because you shut the door to the kingdom of heaven in men's faces. You keep people from coming to God. You yourselves do not come to him, nor will you let those who are trying to come do so. You travel over land and sea to win a single soul, and when you win him, you make him twice as much the child of hell as you are."

Furiously shouting threats came at him from the crowd. Their hatred for him burned hotter with each word. Yet, Jesus seemed to enjoy this. It seemed that all the sanctimonious injustice in the world was being massacred by his words. As we disciples, on the other hand, tried to fade into the crowd in fear, Jesus stood authoritatively, continuing his attack. Metaphorically speaking, you could see the moneychangers tables pushed over, you could see the coins fly, you could feel the lash of his hand-made scourge.

"You are all blind guides! Blinded by your greed! Greed for money, greed for power, greed for status! 'If anyone swears by the church, you say it has no meaning, but if anyone swears to pledge money to the church he is bound by his oath.' You blind fools! Which is greater, the money, or faith in God? You say, 'If anyone swears by the altar, it means nothing, but if anyone swears to place money on it, he is bound by his oath.' Which is greater, the money or the altar that makes the money sacred? Listen! He who swears by the altar swears by it and by everything on it. And he who swears by heaven swears by God's throne and by the One who sits on it. But I say to you as I have said before, *Swear not at all!* You haven't the stomach or the character to make it good."

Another log on the flames.

At this they tried to break through the crowd to seize him; the crowd, enjoying the attack, prevented them from getting near him. The shouting got louder. So did Jesus' assault.

"You clean the outside of the cup and dish, but inside you are full of greed and self-indulgence. Blind, sanctimonious legalsits! You don't even consider that to clean the inside of your hearts will clean the outside as well.

"You are like whitewashed tombs! You spend much time on how you look, but on the inside you are full of putrid, dead bones and stinking flesh. On the outside you appear to people as righteous, holy and pure, but on the inside you are full of hypocrisy and wickedness. Such as you have no part with God." By this time we were terribly frightened. It became apparent that Jesus had a certain death wish. We knew that this preaching would not be tolerated by the powers that be. We watched in fear as he continued, as the flames of his own invective leapt high.

"You make monuments of the prophet's tombs and decorate the graves of the righteous. Then you piously intone, 'If we had lived in the days of our forefathers, we would not have taken part with them in shedding the blood of the prophets.' Yet, you are the *descendants* of those who murdered the prophets! Fill up, then, the measure of the evil of your forefathers! How are you different than they?

"You vicious, poisonous snakes! You brood of vipers! I send you prophets and wise men and teachers and you kill them with your venom! You crucify them; you flog them and pursue them from town to town. So now understand this, upon you will come all the righteous blood that has been shed on earth, from the blood of righteous Abel to the blood of Zechariah son of Berekiah, whom you murdered between the Temple and the altar."

Enough. Enough had been said to accomplish what needed to be done. Enough to keep the flames of hatred burning high.

Jesus stood quietly for a long time. He looked up at the Temple, his eyes slowly scanning the city. A hush fell over the crowd in anticipation of what he might do or say next. Finally he spoke so softly we all had to strain to hear, but somehow we heard every word.

"O City of God, you who kill the prophets and stone those sent to you, how often I have longed to gather your children together, as a hen gathers her chicks under her wings, but you were not willing. Look, your house is left to you desolate. For I tell you, you will not see me again until you say, *'Blessed is he who comes in the name of the Lord.'"*

Exhausted but satisfied, Jesus turned and deliberately walked right through the crowd...unmolested and unharmed. The listeners, for all their wounds, made way for him to pass. We scrambled to catch up as he made his way to a quiet place we all knew.

XII

A Day for the Gentiles

Returning to the Temple, Jesus sat down opposite the place where the offerings were collected and watched the people putting money into the Temple treasury. Many rich people came and made much of the large amounts they gave, as if they could ill afford it, as if God should be grateful for their generosity. But then a woman in threadbare and tattered clothing, an impoverished widow, struggled to the treasury boxes. "Watch this woman," said Jesus. She pulled from her purse two small copper coins. They amounted to a fraction of a penny, little more than a cup of sand. The look on her face was not pious, but joyful. She quietly placed the coins in the box and made her way out of the Temple.

Speaking to us again, Jesus said, "Look at this destitute woman. You may think that what she has done amounts to little, but with God, she has put more into the treasury than all the others. They each gave out of their wealth; but she, out of her poverty, put in everything—all she had to survive...and did you not see her smile? She was joyful, grateful to give."

My thought was why did she do that? Because of her love for God? Or perhaps because it didn't matter anyway. What are two small coins worth less than a penny when you have nothing? They would possibly buy a crust of bread. On the other hand, perhaps she thought that God would look upon her sacrifice and reward her with prosperity or security. It is possible she was trying to get something rather than give. I have given that way. Sometimes it was my substance—albeit not very much of that—sometimes it was my time or myself, which, on balance, God might find more useful than the money. Whatever her motivations, Jesus thought them pure; and, though she would never know it in this life, as long as these words are read, she is a memorial of what it means to give to God. I thought to myself, *Have I ever done anything—anything—that pristine? Anything that he would think worth memorializing?* I think not.

It is worth noting that the money she gave went to pay for the expenses of the Temple; went for the recompense of its priests, scribes and law experts—the *enemies* of Jesus. But in her mind, she was giving to God.

That is what Jesus saw, and that is what he memorialized. Again, it is the intent of the heart that God observes, not the material character of what is given or the material substance of what is done.

αΘω

Curiously, a group of gentiles showed up here in the Temple. Why would they bother? For those who have demonstrated nothing but contempt for our way of life, for our faith, why are they here? What do they want? They spoke with Philip first. "Sir," they said deferentially, "we would like to speak with Jesus of Nazareth." Philip was wary, as were we all.

"What for?" he asked.

"We have heard of him. Some of us have seen his miracles and heard him teach. We want to follow him. We want him to...well, accept us as disciples," this with apparent embarrassment. They were as aware as we of how strange it was that gentiles should interject themselves into affairs presumably Jewish. Philip went to tell Andrew of their request. Andrew and Philip then went together to tell Jesus. Predictably, Jesus' response was unpredictable.

Who would have guessed that he would say, *"So. It has come to this. The opportunity for my people is gone. The moment has now come."* He looked away, as if resigned to the inevitable or, possibly, to absorb the shift of events. Then he said, "Bring them to me, Philip, and I will speak with them."

As the men came before him one of them knelt. "Master," he began, "We are here because we wish to follow you. We do not seek to become Jews, but we believe in the Father of whom you speak and we believe you are the Son of God. Please, accept us as your disciples. My name is Agatone. I speak for myself. I speak for us all."

The open, honest sincerity of the man and the expectant expressions on the faces of the others were troubling. He waited a long time before he replied. "Your name means 'Good' or 'Kind,' Agatone. You are, indeed, a reflection of your name. What you do not understand, and cannot know, is that you have come to the Temple of God because the hour has come for the Son of Man to be glorified."

"Sir?" Agatone responded.

"Unless a kernel of wheat falls to the ground and dies, it remains only a seed. But if it dies, it produces a stalk with many seeds. You and your friends are the first, Agatone. There will be many others." They all looked at him incredulously. Jesus was right. They clearly did not understand. None of us understood. On the surface of it, it seemed to make sense—yet it was enigmatic. Jesus took the men aside and spoke privately with them. I have no idea what he said to them. I only know that they left in obvious gratitude. When they were gone, Jesus appeared disturbed. He seemed thoughtful, introspective. He spoke softly, as if to himself, but it was directed to us. Perhaps to me, "The man who loves this life will certainly lose it. But he who recognizes this life for what it is, will keep his life forever.

"Whoever serves me," continued Jesus, "must follow me, and where I am my servant also will be." It would not be hard, dear reader, for you to think that I am very taken with myself. Allow me to send you this personal message: However vain, trite or pretentious I may be, however wicked, however improperly motivated, however weak, however impotent, I can tell you this—I cannot begin to conceive how any man or woman has lived who wished to serve my Master more than I. Wherever he is, I want to be. I seek to be his constant companion. I wander about in this world existing in this body of death, engaging in a never-ending struggle with moral decay. Yet I have one hope that gives my life in this carrion of existence, purpose and meaning. It is these, his words…"My Father will honor the one who serves me." Yet it is not this honor I seek, but that which comes with it—closeness to him.

These men, the gentiles, these men *not among the "chosen nation,"* left warmly affirmed. Nor am I *chosen*. And yet again, perhaps I am.

αΘω

The entrance and timing of these gentile men into the Temple at Jerusalem had a special significance that no one—not even they—grasped until later. I am now convinced that God must have sent them as a sign that the nation of Israel, as we know it and as the special people of God, has changed. Since the days of Abraham, God has watched over us, cared for us and separated us to himself. Now I am beginning to realize, there may be a new Israel, one that not only includes gentile nations but embraces them and finds its loveliest expression in them. The seeds of wheat of which Jesus spoke would become not just a stalk with its seeds, but many stalks—fields of golden wheat swaying under the nourishment of the Father, caressed by the gentle winds of the Spirit, planted, blessed and fortified by the Son.

Jesus continued his soliloquy, "Now my heart is troubled, and what shall I say? 'Father, save me from this hour'? No, it was for this very reason

I came to this hour." His heart would become troubled much more, and in a few days cry out to his Father for just such deliverance.

These gentile men? They are the first fruits from the peoples of the world. *They* are the reason he came into this world. Then he lifted his voice to heaven and cried, "Father, glorify your name!"

Something stunning happened. A voice came from the sky above, *"I have glorified it, and will glorify it again."* Some said it thundered but there were no dark clouds. Others said an angel had spoken to him.

Our eyes searched the skies, yet the voice just happened, surrounding us, enveloping us. We had no idea of the direction from which it came. We all knew that a new era had embarked. A new day.

"This voice was for your benefit, not mine," said Jesus. "Now is the time for the prince of this world to be driven out and defeated. When I, the Son of Man, am lifted up from the earth, I will draw all men to myself." There it is again: *All men!* Not just Jews! Not just Israel. Whatever covenant or covenants God has made with Israel now belong to all!

As I think about that miraculous day, I am convinced that he said these things to show the kind of death he was going to die. Those listening to him must have understood at least something of what he said, for they asked, "We know from the Law that the Christ will remain forever, so how can you say, 'The Son of Man must be lifted up'? Who is this 'Son of Man'?" They understood that 'lifted up' meant crucifixion. Yet their love affair with the Law had fouled their minds. And could they not see the very Son of Man standing before them?

Once again Jesus did not directly address the question that was asked. If he had, they would merely have challenged his answer and rejected his claim. Instead he said, "You have light now. You will not have it much longer. Enjoy, appreciate and live in that light now, while you have it, before darkness comes. Become sons of light. I have come into the world as Light, so that no one who believes in me should stay in darkness. When you come to know me, you know not only me, you know the one who sent me."

Jesus continued, "As for the person who hears my words but does not keep them, know this: I did not come to judge you, but to rescue and redeem you. However, there is a judgment for the one who rejects me and my words. And these words will come to haunt him at the last day."

With this, Jesus left the Temple. It would be his last time there. It would mark the final time anything resembling the presence of God was in that place. Still, one cannot be near Herod's Temple without being awed by it. As Jesus walked away, James remarked to Matthew, "This Temple is magnificent. It is massive. It is beautiful beyond imagination."

"You are impressed with these buildings, James?" Jesus asked. He called them mere "buildings." I could not believe it. The elegancy and the majesty of the Temple at Jerusalem overwhelm you. Once visited, it stamps its inspiring grandeur on your mind forever.

"Let me tell you something," he said, "Not one stone will here be left on another; everyone will be thrown down." Less than four decades later, these words became the awful truth.

αΘω

Jesus left the vicinity of the Temple and hid himself from those who sought to arrest him. In a few days, he would voluntarily surrender himself. But not now. He had things to do, words yet to say.

XIII

Jerusalem Destroyed

He had dreamed that he was walking along a road. He had felt intense pressure to find those he expects to meet and give them needed information. He seemed to travel just above the surface of the earth faster than a man could run but not so fast that it didn't take longer than he had anticipated or that he wished. He saw the road stretch miles away before him, and he couldn't find the place he was looking for. Someone came along in a chariot drawn by haggard horses, stopped, and with a kindly, inquisitive face, offered to help him. "Can I help you, sir? Can I help . . ?"

He awoke. It was still dark, but the dim night lights of the city vaguely illuminated the drab, nondescript walls of the inn. He thought briefly of the dream before dismissing it. Yet he could not dismiss it. It seemed to float around the periphery of this thoughts screaming at him, demanding he pay attention, demanding interpretation. He felt himself the weary and frustrated traveler, on the one hand, and, on the other, the offerer of helpful assistance. He wondered which he really was. Perhaps both. He had felt the lostness of the one and the knowledge to guide of the other. *"I am both!"* he thought to himself. I know how it feels to be lost and frustrated in purpose and at the same time to have an answer to give.

We had arrived the previous night late. The innkeeper, ready to retire, paid little attention to anything except to what we would pay for a night's lodging. The sounds of the city lulled us to sleep. The dream had awakened Jesus early. There was a basin in the room partially filled with water. He splashed the stale liquid on his face in an attempt to wash the dream from his brain. He moved among sleeping forms and awakened Peter, James, John and Andrew. Together they left the inn and made their way to the hillsides. Finding a rock upon which to sit, Jesus waited under the olive tree lowering overhead. The place was rife with olive trees. He knew what was coming. The men would want to know why he had roused them. They would want to know his thoughts. And, no doubt, they would want to know why he had selected only the four of them. Why not everyone? Was there anything special about the four he had selected? They wondered. He knew that they were wondering. It was not unlike that moment several years ago on the mountain a hundred miles to the north where Jesus was transfigured when only these few were with him. Had it not been for Peter, this incident and the content of what was said would have been lost.

"Tell us," asked Andrew, his mind still troubled by the previous day's comment about the Temple. "When will all of this happen? When will the Temple be destroyed?"

αΘω

The question must be taken at face value. There was no ulterior background from which it emerged. The most ringing thing Jesus had said the previous evening was that the Temple would be destroyed; "not one stone left upon the other," I believe he said. Quite a feat given that many of the stones were larger than the largest chariot.

"I awoke this morning in a dream," Jesus responded. "I have sent you into the world to share the truth I have given you from the Father, yet there will be pain, frustration and persecution in the doing of it. I confess, the road for these past years has been weary and our earthly vessels have been already sorely tried. Now I must speak to you from a weary chariot, and you must listen carefully. Take care of yourselves and beware of men. You have walked with me. You have walked along this lonely road with me every day for the time we have been together. The time has gone rapidly, yet it seems we have been slogging through mud. In this time, we have learned to love and trust each other, depend upon each other.

"But now I must speak to you. I must appeal to you. Let me help you to understand." The dream began to unfold. "I have asked you… no, I have commanded you not to have authority over each other but rather to be servants to each other. But I know you have not heard. I know you have not understood. You will instead become progenitors of a great religion, a highly stylized religion of men controlling men. This I never intended. But this thing that you create will turn and devour you. It will leave in wreckage countless numbers of my followers. It will take upon itself a life of its own. Yet, within it, my people will live and will prosper in their knowledge of me insofar as an oppressive, institutional structure will allow them. In the course of this time you will be delivered to these institutions, these churches with their councils—indeed you will be delivered even to prison.

"A moment, Lord," interrupted Andrew. "My question concerned the destruction of the Temple about which you spoke last night. Of what do you speak now? I know of no plans to start a great religion."

"No. Of course you don't." Jesus paused, pensively, taking a small olive twig between his fingers and placing the end of it in his mouth.

αΘω

"All right, I will speak more of this in a moment. Shortly after I am gone, you will be treated badly by the Romans. You will be scourged in synagogues and dragged before governors and kings. The Jewish nation will be persecuted, and many will be put to death and hated by the gentiles.

"When you see Jerusalem encircled by armies, then know that her desolation draws near. When you see *'the abomination of desolation,'* spoken of by the prophet Daniel, standing in the holy place, when you see the Temple desecrated and destroyed by Roman forces, then it is time to flee to the mountains. Waste no time, for death, destruction and slaughter will come. I have spoken of this to you before. Do not minimize the importance of my words.

"If a man is working on his roof then he should not delay to go down and take anything out of his house. No one working in the field should go back to pack his clothes. For these are days of Roman rage, that all things that Daniel said may be fulfilled. How dreadful it will be in those days for pregnant women and nursing mothers! People will fall by the edge of the sword and be led captive by the Romans. Vultures and beasts will gather to feed on the carcasses. There will be much to keep them busy.

"The city of God will be destroyed. Jerusalem shall be trodden down by the Romans until they are sated, until their time has been fulfilled. But when all is said and done, Israel will remain as a testimony before the nations. My Body will henceforth succor this people and nourish them. My Body will keep the Jewish nation alive and sustain it until I come. Israel shall come to rely on my Body and shall one day become a part of it."

These incredible words! The four of them didn't know whether to feel joy or rage. Jerusalem destroyed? The abomination of desolation? What was that and just how would it come? Clearly, Jesus was describing some future event, not something in past Jewish history. I had thought that the *abomination of desolation* had come during the rape of our nation by Antiochus Epiphanes. I had perceived *him* as that abomination, but Jesus spoke of something yet to come. Was there to be yet another such abomination? And what was the "Body" of which he spoke, and how could it be so powerful as to sustain the entire nation of Israel? Could there be such a power that exceeded even the greatness of Rome?

The walk back to the inn was quiet. These were terrible, incomprehensible things to ponder.

XIV

Criteria for Reward

"I wish to share with you some more joyful things now that should lift your spirits," he said. "In the kingdom of heaven it will give me great pleasure to honor those who have trusted in me. But there are criteria by which the measure of honor will come. By these you will know something of the joy that is awaiting those who believe and love me.

"*First, be ready*. You are the bride—my bride! When I come for you, have your hearts filled with the oil of the Holy Spirit and your lives illumined with light of love, faith and truth. Do not neglect to nourish these qualities. Your preparedness in these things is the first criterion of honor. Remember, you do not know the day or the hour of my return or when any of this will take place. *So be ready!*

"*Second, make your lives count. Invest your time, your gifts, your substance, and your energy for God*. Do not hold back. Very likely what you love to do has been given to you by the Father. Develop it, hone it, share it. You will be rewarded accordingly.

"Finally, let me tell you *how* and *where* to invest your lives. Listen to this story which speaks of the third criterion: When the Son of Man comes in his glory and all the angels with him, he will come as a King sitting on his throne in heavenly glory.

"Then the King will say, 'Come, you who are blessed by my Father; take your inheritance, the kingdom prepared for you since the creation of the world. For I was hungry and thirsty and you fed me and brought me something to drink. I was a stranger and you invited me in to your home, you gave me clothes when I needed them, when I was sick you looked after me, when I was in prison you came to visit me.'

"Puzzled, they answered him, 'Lord, we know of no time when did we these things?' You see, those whose nature it is to do good are often unaware that they do it.

"The King will reply, 'What you've done for the neediest of my people, you did for me.'

"Invest your energy into the lives of those impoverished in spirit or in the necessities of life or who are imprisoned. These may appear to be insignificant people to you, but they are of great value to me. If you do not give yourself to those I love, you do not give yourself to me."

"In these three examples, I have given you great wisdom. *Be prepared in love, faith and truth! Invest your time, your talents and your money into the lives of those who need it more than you. Invest your lives into the lives of the least of these. For whatever you invest, you shall also receive much, much more shaken down and running over shall you receive when you stand before me."*

XV

Passover

"Passover is two days away. At that time the Son of Man will be handed over to be crucified." Crucified? That barbaric, slow, torturous death in which the Romans were so competent? The first to practice crucifixion were the Persians. Later, Alexander and his generals introduced it to Greece, Egypt and finally Carthage. The Romans, supposedly, learned the practice from the Carthaginians. They became consummate masters at it. To think of this particular form of execution now is, at the same time, to think of Roman imperialism.

"This cannot be!" thought Peter in anguish. "Lord, why do you say things like this? Who could do such a thing? How could you allow it to happen?" He spoke for all of us. That Jesus would die any time in the foreseeable future was reprehensible enough, but to die by crucifixion was a thought too terrible to bear.

αΘω

The Jewish Passover Feast known as the "Feast of Unleavened Bread," had begun. The chief priests and elders assembled in the palace of Caiaphas, the high priest. There they made plans to arrest Jesus and then to kill him. "But not during the Feast," they said, "or there will be riots!" It seemed that for murderers, they worried a lot. They were indeed a frightened assembly. They were afraid of the crowd, they were afraid of the Romans, they were afraid of Jesus.

On the first day of the Feast, it was customary to sacrifice and eat a Passover lamb, so we asked Jesus, "Where do you want to observe Passover?"

He thought for a moment and said, "Go into the city. A man carrying a jar of water will meet you. Follow him. He will enter a house. Speak to the owner of the house these words, 'The Teacher asks: Where is a guest room, where I may eat the Passover with my friends?' He will show you a large room on the second floor of the building, furnished and ready. Make preparations for us there."

Matthew, Bartholomew and I went into the city and found things just as Jesus had said they would be. Would we have expected something different? All of us had long since passed the point of no return where Jesus was concerned. What he knew, we knew not; and what we knew not, we had learned to accept and move on at the strength of his word alone. We went about the business of preparing for Passover.

αΘω

We had gathered about the table awaiting the service of food. Frankly, I was hungry and no small bit annoyed that the empty plates held only the promise of a meal. I could have eaten a whole lamb by myself. At what seemed to me an intolerable length of time, the evening meal was served; and just as I began to attack my food, Jesus got up from the table, food steaming before him, took off his outer clothing and wrapped a towel around his waist. Eating would have to wait, something was afoot. Unlike me, apparently Jesus had things other than food on his mind. *The time had come for him to leave this world and go to the Father.*

God the Father had put all things under his power. That he knew. He also was keenly aware that he had come from God and that at the appointed time he would go back to God.

Still, Jesus loved those who had come to him and belonged to him. Leaving them was no small thing. In retrospect, I take great comfort in this. More than twelve men had spent several years of their lives with him. He had come to love them deeply. At this moment he desired to demonstrate the full extent of this love.

We all watched as he poured water into a basin. He kneeled before Andrew and started to wash his feet. Andrew was startled by this action and recoiled, but when Jesus looked lovingly into his eyes, he quietly submitted. Jesus continued around the table and washed the feet of each of us, drying them with the towel that was wrapped around him.

Peter observed all this, frowning sternly, but for once, said nothing. As Jesus moved the basin close and attempted to lift Peter's left foot, the old fisherman balked, pulling his foot back. "Lord, what do you think you are doing? Do you really intend to do this?" The palpable absurdity of it appalled Peter. None of us felt comfortable, but, typically, Peter was the only one to protest openly.

"Simon," Jesus responded. "You cannot comprehend now what I am doing, but later you will understand."

That was not good enough for Peter, "No," he replied, "you shall *never* wash my feet!" Muffled chuckles around the table. Good old Peter. He could always be depended on to meet the extraordinary with peculiar, stubborn resistance.

"Unless I wash you, you have no part with me."

Embarrassed silence. All eyes focused sharply on Simon Peter. An exceedingly long moment passed. When at length he spoke, his voice was shaking, hoarse and forced. "Then, Lord, not just my feet, but also my hands and my head!"

Laughter, the subsequent tension broke. Jesus matter-of-factly answered, "You're already clean, Simon. You are clean because of the word I have spoken to you. The body of a person who has had a bath is clean and needs only to wash his feet which become soiled when you walk. And you are clean." He paused and glanced around the room. Speaking to all of us he continued, "though not every one of you." He had washed the feet of Judas as well, but to no avail. The heart of Judas was not clean and no amount of foot washing could change that. I thought of my own heart, and when I did, I felt hot tears in my eyes.

When he had finished washing feet, he slipped again into his robe and returned to his place. "Do you understand what I have done for you?" he asked. None of us understood. "You call me 'Teacher' and 'Lord,' and 'Master.' Rightly so, for that is what I am. Now that I, your Lord, Teacher, and Master have washed your feet, in the future you also should wash one another's feet.

"Your soiled feet are a symbol of the contamination of life as you walk through it. Support and encourage each other to be free of your weaknesses and the commerce of life by serving each other in selfless humility. I have set you an example that you should do as I have done for you. Serve one another! I tell you the truth, no servant is greater than his master, nor is a messenger greater than the one who sent him. Now that you know these things, be happy and blessed as you serve each other."

αΘω

As Jesus finished tying his robes about him, finding his place at table he said, "I do not refer to all of you; I know those I have chosen. But I say this is to fulfill the scripture: 'He who shares my bread has lifted up his heel against me.' I tell you now before this heartbreaking desertion occurs, so that when it does happen you will know even more that I AM."

Judas sat idle at the table, eyes narrowed under furrowed brows, eating nothing, brooding over his food. Jesus too, in painful symbiosis, did not put morsel to mouth. Their dark moods affected the rest of us. We knew about Judas, yet we did not.

Judas loved money. We all knew that. He was obsessed with it. That is why, I suppose, he became the treasurer among us. His tight-fisted control over our financial resources had more than once left us annoyed and irritated at him. Some of us wondered if Judas secretly kept back some of these resources for himself. But we had at that moment no notion of the immense betrayal festering in his heart. Jesus broke the silence, "Let me say it plainly," he said, "one of you is going to betray me."

Why "one of us?" Why not "Judas will betray me?" Why didn't he just say who he meant? The lack of specificity troubled us. Perhaps that was the point. As usual, Peter initiated a response. Not directly this time. Instead he motioned to John, "Ask him which one of us he means."

John, reclining next to Jesus, leaned over and whispered, "Lord, who is it?"

"It is the one," said Jesus aloud so all could hear, "to whom I will give this piece of bread when I have dipped it in the gravy." As he spoke, Jesus broke a morsel of bread from the loaf; then, dipping the morsel in the bowl of lamb gravy, he gave it to Judas Iscariot. "Here, Judas, my 'friend'; take some nourishment. You seem faint."

Judas did not take the food. His expression showed, what? Contempt? He looked at Jesus and said evenly, "Surely not I, Rabbi?" Jesus continued to hold the bread out to him, dripping lamb gravy forming brown pools on the table. Judas clearly did not want to take it, but the embarrassment of the mess and of being singled out overwhelmed him. Evil does not long endure the light of focused attention. He took the bread.

"You know it is you," Jesus said quietly.

Judas took the bread and slowly moved it to his lips. Inserting it into his mouth he chewed softly, his eyes never leaving the face of Jesus. When he swallowed, he strained and almost choked, as if swallowing a rock.

"What you are about to do, do quickly."

As Judas took the bread, something came over him. To us, he seemed too clean, too innocent. His expression was one of being victimized, unjustly accused. Was Jesus right in what he said about him? There was a not-to-be-unexpected distance between Jesus and Judas, indeed, between the rest of us and Judas. I believe John was right. Satan entered into him, which is to say that Judas allowed himself a certain vulnerability to satanic influence. He did not scream, or howl, or run about naked, or otherwise cut and abuse himself. He did not foam at the mouth or speak in voices that were not his own. To look at him, you would think nothing terrible amiss. He seemed perfectly rational and in control of himself. He was perfectly, well...Judas. He seemed no different than he had always been except, perhaps, for resignation. Judas seemed resigned now, almost at peace, as though some important issue were resolved with him. He was a strange man, and now licking gravy from his fingers, stranger still.

Whatever resolution had taken him, it drove him away from Jesus and the rest of us. The time had come for him to quit, and it was important to do so from a position of power. His leaving was not unlike an employee who decides that the time to terminate his own employment has come. Surely there was a better place to labor. Surely there were better friends and associates. His "position of power" was that he knew the intimacies and the intricacies of the twelve and of Jesus. He knew, or thought he knew, how Jesus operated. He thought he knew his supposed weaknesses. His weaknesses, Judas was certain, were his adversarial posture toward the Jewish leadership. Since they were indentured to Herod, they were in position to do Jesus considerable harm. All Judas had to do was provide them with the information they needed to accomplish that harm. Judas had that information. Judas had that power. Better to sever his relationship with Jesus and the others while he had it, than to risk a moment when he did not. Jesus is, after all, despite his magic, only one man. The Jews had the power of Herod behind them, and Herod Antipas, while not his father, still had the Romans in the folds of his robes. It was time for Judas to move.

αΘω

Did Judas love Jesus? I think in the beginning, he probably did. Some say that there is but a spider-web of difference between love and hate. What could have happened along the way that might have turned the intent of his heart? Of this I am ambiguous, but certainly his concern for money was a part of it. How many times had he objected to the way Jesus had directed him to disperse it. Thoughts of Mary of Bethany come to mind. Further, Judas, for whatever mad thoughts that ran through his head, held himself aloof from the rest of us. He never seemed a part of us. He rarely joined in the laughter, joking and foolishness that we often fell into, including

Jesus. In fact, it was often provoked by Jesus. Is there some juxtaposition of thought, some tangle of worms in the mind that makes a man conclude, "I am not one of them," when every effort has been made to make him feel as a brother? I confess gross ignorance here, but something happened to Judas that caused him to conclude that money was more to be considered than fidelity.

XVI

Thirty Pieces of Silver

There were six of them, two of the chief priests (members of the Sanhedrin), three scribes and one officer of the Temple guard. It would be a mistake to infer that such men were always sanctimonious and ceremonial. They were men. Just because they were devoutly religious did not mean that they were not men. It did not mean that they could not drink too much wine. It did not mean that there weren't moments of relaxation and a total dismissal of discipline. Judas heard the visceral laughter as he stood outside the door of Rabbi Asher. Sounds from inside did not strike him as remarkable. Better, perhaps, to approach them in a mood of hilarity than anger, he thought. He also thought about what he was about to do. Strategy. What would he say? How must he couch his words? He must be discretionary and careful. He must be shrewd. And just as his knuckles struck the door, he thought about betrayal—and feared. But only for a moment.

The knock at the door was almost completely obscured by peals of laughter. "Did I hear a knock?" asked one of the men inside. All eyes turned to the door. Nothing. "Who would trouble us during Passover?" said another. "Passover? Yes, it is Passover—I had almost forgot." More laughter. There was a second knock. One of the priests immediately got up to answer the door. On opening it, they saw a nervous man standing in the doorway, hands held in an obsequious manner.

"My name is Judas...from the region of Iscariot...I am a disciple...ah, *former disciple* of Jesus of Nazareth."

At this, Asher stood. "Judas? I have seen you before, Judas." At first, Asher was incredulous, amazed that one of the Nazarene's disciples would show up at his door. *There is a reason for this,* he thought. *I have heard of this man. I think I know why he is here.* "By all means," said Asher, "Let him in." Judas shuffled in, bobbing his head in deference to those in high office, smiling appreciation. He stood by the table where the men were sitting. "Did you say, *former disciple,* Judas? Are you no longer associated with the Galilean Messiah?" His tone was patronizing, mocking.

"No! I am not." This with more self-assurance. His jaw tightened, head rising in tentative defiance.

"Weren't you one of the chosen?" Asher continued. "Did not this respected Rabbi deliberately *select* you as one of his special...*apostles?*" Muffled snickers of amusement. "Selected to rule one of the twelve tribes of Israel, I believe?" Asher put a finger to his lips tentatively as if he were smugly uncertain of his information. "Yes, I do think I heard that. Tell me, my good man," said the priest generously, "Which tribe is yours?" Loud guffaws from the others. Judas smiled nervously.

"I have information," he said, intensely aware that he was being ridiculed. Asher's eyes narrowed. "I can tell you where to find him," Judas continued.

"And what makes you think we are looking for him?"

It was Judas' turn to laugh. "Do you think I am a fool?" said he in his best sardonic tone. Judas was indeed afraid of these men, but he did his best to conceal it. "I know well that you seek him. I know that you wish to arrest him. I can help you do that."

"And what price do you require for this information? Certainly there is a price; isn't there, Judas?" Quite frankly, this question had not been anticipated by Judas. A fleeting thought, perhaps, had entered his mind that his information was worth money to certain people, but Judas, despite his history of greed and embezzlement, had not seriously considered the possibility of being paid. *He wasn't doing this for money!* His motivation was something...something else. Suddenly, the opportunity of monetary gain was staring him in the face. And, as he said, he was no fool.

"One hundred pieces of silver."

"Surely you jest," laughed Asher. "You could not possibly have information worth that much to us. You are indeed a fool, a silly, arrogant fool! Whatever you have to say to us could not possibly be worth more than a fraction of that sum."

In the few seconds of this dialogue, Judas had been calculating in his mind. He knew that his initial price should be much higher than what he would actually accept. In truth, until Asher had mentioned the possibility of payment, he had been perfectly willing to provide his information for free. Knowing this, he had correctly assessed Asher's willingness to pay.

"Fifty pieces of silver," he said, anticipating that Asher would reject this as well, but the priest had already committed himself to negotiation, and he was now putty in Judas' hands.

"I would not consider it for more than 15," replied the priest. Judas turned as though he would leave. "Wait a moment, my greedy friend. I will give you 20 and not a denarius more."

"I have lowered my price to 50; I have endured your derisive insult and you offer me a paltry 20 pieces of silver?" Judas replied with artificial contempt. He was playing his role. He was good at this and he knew it. Despite Judas's fear of Asher and his cohorts, once the priest had entered into negotiation he had unknowingly entered into his domain. In doing so, he had conceded major leverage. "Priest," said Judas Iscariot boldly, "I will lower my price one last time to 30 pieces of silver, and, more than that, I will lead you to him now. I know exactly where he is. You can accept my generous offer now, or I will go my way."

Asher considered Judas and completely believed that the exchange was over. Judas would not divulge one syllable of his information unless his price was met. "You will guarantee that you will lead us directly to him?"

"I guarantee it."

Asher consulted his friends with a glance and received consenting nods.

"Done."

Thirty pieces of Roman silver; each of them Shekels of Tyre, the only coinage accepted in the Temple. It was the equivalent of about four months' wages for the average worker. For this, had Judas negotiated damnation.

αΘω

Over the years, I have continued to wonder just what might have triggered betrayal in Judas—what made him available to Satanic manipulation? Nothing, it seemed, was more important to Judas than what he considered the appropriate management of money. He was always conniving, always seeking stratagems by which he could generate greater funds. He was not well liked. This he knew. He was from Judea, the rest of us from Galilee. He never really "fit" with the rest of us. Perhaps, had he approached the group as one of us instead of an outsider in judgment of us, he would have been more favorably looked upon. Instead, he became disagreeable and irritable. Only Jesus would have anything to do with him; and, after a while, even Jesus became distant, or, perhaps more to the point, Judas's demeanor and aloofness, he distanced himself from Jesus. Judas became more embittered and more hostile. Ultimately, he rejected us all—especially Jesus. Disillusioned, he sought revenge for what he perceived as rejection. I could relate to his feelings of rejection.

I, too, have felt rejection—yet I could never turn my back on my Lord. I could not do what Judas did! *Could I?*

αΘω

When Judas had gone from the upper room, we each looked at one another and were quiet. There were the "twelve," now less Judas, Matthias and I. The table was low and square and was almost not large enough for us all to recline comfortably. We were silent for several minutes. Jesus spoke, "Perplexing as it may appear to you, in what Judas is about to do, the Son of Man will be glorified, and God will be glorified as well. God will glorify the Son in himself and will do so very soon.

"My friends, we haven't much time left together. I will be with you only a little longer. You will look for me, and just as I told the Jews, so I tell you now: Where I am going, you cannot come.

"Tonight we celebrate Passover. As you know, the first Passover meal was eaten when the firstborn of Israel was spared from the angel of death. Now, you, therefore, are my 'firstborn,' so I have eagerly desired to eat this Passover with you before I suffer. I want you to know that I will not eat it again until it finds fulfillment—when the chosen ones of God are completely delivered—in the home of my Father."

Jesus then took a loaf of bread, raised his eyes to heaven and gave thanks to the Father. He then broke it open. His gaze fixed each one of us intently. Then he passed the broken loaf among us. We were too numb to eat or to realize the significance of what he was doing until Jesus said, "Take this bread and eat it. This bread is my body and it is broken for you." He again watched as we each consumed our piece of bread. As I put the dry morsel into my mouth, in my mind I did not comprehend the meaning of what he was saying, but in my heart, I think I did.

He then took his cup of wine and lifting his eyes to heaven, he again gave thanks and offered the cup to John and from John to the rest of us. "Take this cup," he said, "and divide it among you. Drink from it, each one of you. Know...know that this is my blood. This proclaims a new covenant, which is poured out so that freedom may be given to all enslaved by their own sin." When it reached me, I realized that this is the cup that had touched the lips of Jesus only a moment ago. I drank and in so doing felt cleansed and at absolute union with him. As we were doing this, I began also to realize for the first time that we were not simply observing the Passover that first took place in Egypt. That lamb, that deliverance from the angel of death, was but a precursor of this man, a foretelling of this "Lamb of God," whose sacrifice would deliver us from eternal death, the death of our soul.

"Let me tell you," he continued, "I will not drink again of the fruit of the vine until the house and family of God are manifest."

A somber, reflective hush settled over the room. What could any of us say or do after what had just transpired? But after a quiet period, the silence was broken.

XVII

Supreme Command

Can you believe that around this sacred table there arose yet again the ugly head of greed, power and control? Much to the chagrin and disgust of those of us who did not think this way, James and John began with it again. John always jostled to get closest to Jesus, and to some degree I think he may have succeeded. I'm sure Jesus was not unaware of this and undoubtedly knew the insecurities in John's heart. This would explain why he had a greater need for position and affirmation. This would also explain why he thought of himself as the "disciple whom Jesus loved," as though the Lord cared more for him than the rest of us.

It was at this dinner that that John exposed a pettiness that I'm sure he later regretted. He whispered to the Lord (loud enough for the rest of us to hear), "When you come into your kingdom, Lord, which among us will be the greatest?" Most of us groaned inwardly. We had been through this before with their mother. Before Jesus could respond, James quickly reacted and an argument ensued. Several around the table had an opinion about it, and some of them more was than a little loud and angry.

Jesus endured this intellectually and spiritually bankrupt exchange for a moment and then spoke so that all could hear—with unmistakable clarity, "Leave the struggles for power to kings and proconsuls! Let them lord it over their subjects, but this must *not* be true of you!" This statement was said in exasperation. Within my heart I found myself cheering him on. What profane incongruity! Within the holy parameters of the bread and the cup, these "Sons of thunder," these hopeless wonders, wanted to debate who would be the greatest. Bile wretched within me. I wanted to spit.

After Jesus spoke, arguing and debate ceased. Jesus continued to speak. Authority, power and leadership enveloped each word. *"There shall not be a constituted authority among you. You are not to be like that! Instead, the greatest among you should be as the youngest and least experienced; the one who leads as the one who truly serves! Not in disingenuous word, but in authentic and heartfelt humility and service."*

After a moment of no one speaking, but long enough for his point to be in the forefront of each of our thoughts, he continued, "Who is greater, the one who is at the table as you are now, or the one who serves? Is it not the one who sits at the table? Yet it is I, your Lord and Master, who washed your feet; you did not wash mine. *You did not wash mine!* I have thus set for you an example. See that you follow it!

"This kind of petty squabbling among you must *cease!* This kind of jostling and posturing for position and influence *must* be totally foreign to those who would follow me or wish to be my disciples. You *must* love one another, not seek to have power and control over your brothers. Let me put it more forcibly, in language you can understand: I give you a *command—a new* command—*Love one another. As you have seen me love you, so you must love one another. By this—and this alone—all men will know truly that you are my disciples.* Moses told you to love God and your neighbor as yourself, but what I am saying transcends Moses. I give you, instead, mutuality of love as the *cardinal signature* that you belong to me."

"I have loved you individually, intensely and without limitation, just as the Father has loved me. Now, live your life in my love. This is the only command that is necessary for you to live in complete joy. Follow this command, and you will live in my love, just as I have followed my Father's command and live in his love. Again, let me be clear: *Love each other as I have loved you. I make no other demand of you than to believe and to love."*

Silence.

His expression relaxed, and his tone softened, "You have stood by me in all this time. For this I confer on you a kingdom, just as my Father conferred on me, so that you may eat and drink at my table in my kingdom. But for now, serve each other as you would serve me."

Ultimately, they would forget the *loving servant* part of his instruction. These men, at some level, forgot that they were but men and became instead spiritual "lords." Because of this, the "called out ones," the church, has become a political force, a not too dissimilar extension of the Temple, the synagogue and Sanhedrin, with its priests, scholars, rabbis and scribes—an institution begun in the hearts of men too greedy for power and influence that they could not lay them aside, even for the broken body and shed blood of our Lord. How easily sacred instruction is forgotten!

Perhaps in some sense, there is a bit of Judas in all of us.

XVIII

Show Us the Father

Shadows lengthened into nighttime. Different noises drifted up from the street than those one heard during the hours of labor. Lighter noises. Noises of play rather than work. Noises of release rather than bondage. Nighttime held its own special charm. It was a time not to think about tomorrow. A time for merriment and the shedding of burden and responsibility. A time for relaxation and the gentle inebriation that a cup of wine brings. Around our table, long after the meal had been consumed and the bread and the cup passed around, long after Jesus had washed our feet, he taught us more of what he desired of us in the days, months and years to follow.

Jesus turned to Peter and said, "Simon. Simon, Satan has singled you out to sift you as wheat. He must think you a great threat to him. But I have prayed for you, that your faith may not fail. And when you have overcome Satan's efforts to destroy you, help your brothers with the strength you have found."

Peter replied, "Lord, I am afraid. I do not fear the evil one, whatever his desires or intentions toward me. But you have said that we cannot come where you are going. That is what I fear. That is what we all fear. Where might that be? More than life itself I wish to go with you. Why do you exclude us? I am ready to go with you to prison or even to death."

"Where I am going, you cannot follow now, Simon, but you will most assuredly follow later."

Peter shook his head, indicating how unacceptable this seemed, "Lord, why can't I follow you now? I will lay down my life for you."

"Come, Simon, don't be so troubled," Jesus continued. "You've spent your life trusting God. And now, you must trust me. In a few hours I'll be with Him, and when I am, I will prepare a place for you, my friend. I will prepare a place for each of you. After all, surely you already know where I am going."

Thomas demurred, "Lord, we haven't the slightest notion of where you are going. How can you expect us to know how to get there?"

I understood, all too well, Thomas's question. Here was a man, as human as any of the rest of us, eating the same food, whose beard grew as quickly, whose body got dirty and needed bathing just as we all did, whose feet had calluses just as ours. When he talked of going somewhere, we were all used to his feet being on this earth. Was he going to the Far East, or to Rome, or to a deep part of Egypt? These were our questions. We were men with bodies of flesh. It wouldn't be until after he returned from death itself, and then shortly after rose to heaven, that much of what he'd said fell into place.

Jesus understood our shortsightedness and responded to Thomas: "You already know the way, Thomas. You know me. I am the way." Thomas said nothing, but the crease in his brow did not diminish. "I am also Truth and Life." Thomas's eyes squinted and shifted to one side as if getting ready to respond. Jesus continued, "I bring atonement for the evil of mankind. By this alone will men be reconciled to God.

"If the heart of a man seeks to know the Father, because of my blood, the Father will welcome him into his family."

"Your blood, Lord Jesus?"

"I have spoken to you of this before. The time has now come to drink."

Philip, more taken with the possibility of knowing the Father said, "Lord, show us the Father and that will be enough for us."

"Philip!" spoke Jesus, "Look at me." Jesus fixed Philip with his gaze, "Don't you know me, Philip? Did you not hear when I said that *you do know him and have seen him*? All this even after I have been among you such a long time? *He that has seen me has seen the Father.* Don't you understand that I am in the Father and that the Father is in me? These are not just empty words of my own. It is the Father living in me, speaking in me and doing his work. Think of the miracles you have seen. Ask yourself, do they confirm or deny what I am saying?"

This question is an invitation for cold logic. Jesus fed thousands from a basket of bread and fish. He opened the eyes of the blind. He cast out demonic creatures. He made the lame to walk. He raised the dead. He walked on water and calmed the rage of wind and sea. It does not take a Socrates or Aristotle to ascertain that no man could do these things were he not of God. And though we did not realize it then, his own resurrection from the dead sealed and confirmed his authenticity forever. Of all that he said or could have said about his credentials, this was the most compelling, the most irrefutable.

"Listen," he said forcibly, "Anyone who has faith in me will do even greater things than I have done because I am going to the Father."

How hard it was for us to comprehend, let alone believe such a truth. Was he referring to the miracles of which he spoke? It seems so. Could he be speaking of the spread of his influence through us? Doubtless the efforts of many would result in a greater distribution of the gospel than the efforts of one.

I have watched with my own eyes the miracles of Jesus. Yet throughout the years of my life, I have never made the lame to walk, opened the eyes of the blind or raised the dead—even having been an instrument of the Holy Spirit, who, unquestionably, has the power to do such things through me should he choose to do so. Such things happened through Peter and Paul, but in no way on the magnitude of Jesus.

XIX

You Did Not Choose Me

With my hand I moved the plate before me slightly, feeling like I needed something to do. "If you love me," Jesus had said, "you will follow my instruction to love one another." What *was* this feeling of hopelessness, abandonment and loneliness that had overcome me? Although I had not yet the ability to comprehend it fully, I sensed rather than knew that Jesus was going away, that he was about to die! Love for my brother? What of his love for us? For me? How could he love us, and at the same time, abandon us?

I had been preoccupied with my plate, fidgeting, moving it back and forth an inch or two. Lifting my eyes I saw that Jesus was gazing at me. "I will ask the Father, and he will give you another Counselor, Comforter and Guide, to be with you forever—the Spirit of Truth." I cared not for "another" counselor, however comforting. Who or what could possibly stand in Jesus' place? "Many will not be affected by him, because they neither see him nor know him. *But you will know him,* for he will live with you and will be in you."

Our eyes still engaged he said, "You will sometimes feel orphaned and abandoned, but fight those feelings because they are not derived from truth. Emotional pain is the result of perceived reality, not necessarily actual reality. You are not orphaned. You are not abandoned. In a few hours I will no longer be with you as I am now. But because I live in you, you also will live. There will come a day when you will understand and rejoice. Believe these words. Let your trust be your expression of love to me. If anyone anywhere in the world truly loves the Father, he also loves me and will follow my precepts. You needn't struggle with this. The Counselor, the Holy Spirit, whom the Father will send in my name, will teach you all you need to know in the days to come, and he will remind you of all that I have said to you."

Night deepened into the crisp bite of small hours. I ached from having sat so long. Yet the words of Jesus became more compelling with each passing moment. "Peace is the gift I leave with you," he said. "It is my peace

I give to you. It transcends what others might understand. It is the peace my presence brings. It will give you an awareness of my presence within you. It is a peace that renders evil powerless.

"The prince of this world is coming. But remember, he is but a toothless hyena. He has no hold on me or influence on what happens to me and has no idea that he himself is about to be destroyed. After tonight, I will not speak with you much more."

αΘω

Today, many years after the event described above, my heart is deeply troubled. I have a place to live, for which I am grateful. I no longer have fine clothing to wear. There is food on my table, but I worry at times if there will be enough for tomorrow. My knees hurt when I walk, and my muscles are in constant pain. I forget things.

I have watched over three generations, birth and some death. My grandchildren bring me much laughter but also remind me that much of my life has been spent.

And I tend to grumble and complain a lot.

Worst of all, I once walked in the corridors of important men. The wealthy and powerful listened to my words as did the poor, downtrodden and imprisoned. Now, at times, I feel put away, discarded by God and rejected. Overwhelmed with my own evil and self-pity, I weep with Naomi,

> *"Do not call me Naomi. Call me Mara, for the Almighty has dealt very bitterly with me. I went out full, and the LORD has brought me home again empty."*

In such a state, it is very difficult to feel the peace of which the Master spoke. Yet at times it flickers across my consciousness so profoundly that my body flushes with the joy of the Spirit's presence. Then, in the next moment, it is gone and I return to *Mara*. The daggers of the prince of this world drip with my blood. He has far more influence with me than I wish. Yet in those blissful moments of peace and awareness of the Spirit's presence, the wounds heal and the daggers blunt. And I am whole once again. In those moments and sometimes hours of peace, my heart becomes a garden instead of a humorless field of rock-strewn dirt. "I am the true Vine," he taught us that night, "and my Father is the Gardener." On remembering these words, I acquiesce in the knowledge that I am in good hands.

αΘω

We got up from the table, our heads spinning with his words. Our bodies were stiff. We needed to move. We stretched. Some of us walked outside for a moment to feel the breeze and coolness of the evening and to make sure the stars still shined in the sky, and to clear our minds a bit. I felt a hand on my shoulder. It was Peter.

"Are we ready for this, my friend, whatever it is? I like knowing how to plan. This is hard for me, not knowing what to expect." I resonated deeply with his feelings. The anticipation of dread and foreboding hung in the night air.

Not wanting to miss anything the Master might do or say, we kept our respite short. We gathered again around the table.

"I told you to serve one another, but I do not think of you as servants. You are friends. My friends. I know you wish to serve me, but you serve me not as a servant. You serve me as a friend would serve his friend; the kind of a friend that sticks closer than a brother.

"There are those who emphasize the exaltation of the Father, who speak much of his glory and how 'his train fills the Temple;' how he is 'high and lifted up.' All of this is true, but does it not make him feel distant from you? I am here to tell you that the Father wishes you to be friends, close to him, not distanced. Worship him in the beauty of his holy exaltation if you wish—but know, too, that he wants your worship to be in the beauty of love, as between a child and his father. Remember, you are created in his image. You are his child and his friend. God does not love you from a distance. He doesn't want you to love him from a distance. This is true for no other creature or anything that has been created. Believe me, you are like him and that is why he desires your heart to be with him. That is why he has sent me and why I call you friends and why I do not call you servants."

"Have we not left our homes, our families, our means of making a living and chosen to follow you, Lord? Isn't this proof of our desire to be with you?" Jesus lifted his cup and quietly took a sip of wine. Returning the cup to the table with his left hand, he lifted his right and...pointed. He pointed his forefinger directly at Simon the Zealot who had spoken.

"You did not choose me, Simon. I chose you. None of you chose me. I have chosen each and every one of you," he pointed to each one of us in turn. "I chose you, Thomas. I chose you Bartholomew. I chose you James. I chose you Joseph, called Justus. Each of you may choose to respond when

I extend an invitation to come to me, but it is I who compiled the list of those to invite. It is I who chooses. It is I, not you."

αΘω

"The Father will give you whatever you ask in my name."

Here it is again. Why does Jesus say such things? Were I a child, I would fully expect to receive whatever I ask for. But all too often my earnest requests seem to be spoken into empty silence.

Some claim that unrequited prayer stems from sin in our lives. If that be the case, is there anyone who would get what he asks? I am very grateful that Jesus gave no provision for prayer credentials. He did not say that there is a list of certain requirements we must meet in order for God to hear and respond. Jesus himself suggested no prerequisites to prayer. "Ask whatever you wish," he said. He said this because I am not honestly conscious of my motives when I ask. And if the reason for unrequited prayer were unbelief, then no prayer would be answered because no prayer would be prayed, for the very act of prayer is in itself, an act of faith! Moreover, since faith is a gift from God, one has as much faith as he is given. No more. No less.

I have come to understand that I must ask. No matter what the reason or motivation, the Father wishes me to come to him and ask. The likelihood that I will receive precisely what I ask rests where it should rest—in the will of the Father. It has often occurred to me that I should be grateful that I did not receive what I asked for.

But on a deeper level, he knows the purpose of his own heart with regard to that for which I ask. God is in heaven and I upon the earth. So let God be God; and God help me, I shall be Justus. Maybe there are things to learn that are better than an answer.

I remember the times he *has* given me more than I could have dreamed. He gave me my Juliana. I had vowed to God that I would love her with his love if he gave her to me. And he did. We shared so many years. There is so very much he has given to me; when I think of it all, I am awed.

XX

Abishag Finds a New Master

Jesus stopped talking for a moment, took a bone from his plate and slipped it to the dog under the table. She took the morsel and trotted over to a corner, lay down and began to gnaw. Then he made yet another perplexing remark, "In a little while you will see me no more, and then after a little while you will see me again."

Muttering around the table, and then Peter, "Lord, what do you mean?"

"You are not sure what I mean?"

"No, Lord, I am not. You said, 'In a little while you will see us no more, and then after a little while you will see us again.' I'm afraid I don't understand."

"All right, I will be clear: You will weep and mourn while all others rejoice. You will grieve, but know this—your grief will turn to joy." We still looked at one another with frowns. We failed to comprehend what he was trying to tell us.

"A woman giving birth to a child has pain because her time has come; but the first time she looks into that little face, she forgets all about the anguish because of the precious new bundle she holds in her arms. So with you: Now will be your time of grief; but I will see you again, and you will rejoice, and no one will take away your joy."

We appreciated the maternity lesson, but our question remained unanswered. We were impossibly thick. How could we understand? Looking back, this all now makes sense. But at the time we were all so confused and worried. I guess all he wanted, was to give us information that would encourage us as things unfolded. And I also believe he wanted us to believe his words and trust him.

He looked away. After a moment he said it straightforwardly. "In a few hours I will die," he spoke in a calm, level tone, "and you will grieve. I know you will grieve because you have already shown your love for me. But your grief will not last. Joy will come."

αΘω

Abishag concluded her interest in the bone and began to nose about under the table sniffing at things quite beyond the understanding of the rest of us. On occasion she rested her head on a knee for a scratch behind the ears. When she came to me, she tarried, sitting on her haunches. My hand reached for her head, and she willingly submitted. I believe she somehow sensed the pending departure of her Master, and in the way that only a creature like her could imagine, she had selected me to care for in his absence. In any case, curling her tail, she settled herself at my feet and stayed. I had no idea of the joy and companionship she would bring me in her remaining years.

Jesus was observing me and the liaison apparently being formed between me and the dog at my feet. He did not seem unpleased. "When that time comes," he continued looking away at the others, "you will be in me and I in you. It will always be. There will be times—many times—when you will feel lonely and abandoned, but do not succumb to your despair. You are not abandoned.

"When the Comforter comes, he will convict the world of sin because its people are guilty of it and because men do not believe in me. He will convict the world of righteousness because they have rejected the Righteous One. And He will convict the world of judgment: because the prince—the leader—of this world has already been judged and now stands forever condemned.

"But let those of you who believe in me, those who are accepted and beloved of my Father, never say, 'I am convicted of the Spirit'; for to convict means to adjudicate, to condemn as guilty. You are not now, and never will be, judged or condemned." *It is I who will be judged and condemned on your behalf.* Thoughts unspoken

"From this day forward and forever, every breath you take will be my breath and every breath I take will be yours. You will ask of the Father, and it will be as if I myself had spoken to him. It is no longer necessary for me to ask the Father on your behalf. The Father himself listens to you. The Father loves you because you have loved me and have believed that I came from him. Never forget that."

αΘω

"It is time." The words we dreaded to hear. "In a few hours you will scatter, each to his own home for refuge. You will all leave me alone." He paused, to let this sink in.

"Yet I am not alone, for my Father is with me. I have told you these things, so that in me you may have peace. This world, as beautiful as it is, is filled with trouble and pain. You can't expect anything different. But do take heart. I have defeated the agony of this world."

With that, Jesus stood, gesturing for us all to do likewise. The supper, the observance of Passover, had come to an end. Jesus, in rich baritone, began to sing one of the songs of David. Following the first few notes, the rest of our voices lifted in melody. It was the kind of song that lifted the soul and enriched the heart. We sang each note, each word, robustly and heartily, the voice of Jesus leading:

Praise the Lord!
Praise the Lord, O my soul.
I will praise the Lord all my life,
I will sing praise to my God as long as I live.
Put not your trust in princes, nor yet in mortal men,
For blessed is he whose help is the God of Jacob,
Whose hope is in the Lord his God,
Maker of heaven, Sun, moon and the stars beyond,
Maker of earth, Maker of sea
And all contained therein…
And all contained therein…
Praise the Lord!

The last notes were sung in harmony. As the notes echoed in the room, we gathered our things and began to make our way toward the Mount of Olives, Abishag at my side.

XXI

Two Swords Are Enough

Each house, it seemed, pierced the night with a festive light. The streets were filled with men, women and children well past bedtime scurrying about with laughter and purpose. Passover. The gates of the Temple would be thrown open at midnight.

None of us felt like celebrating. We crowded close to Jesus.

"After I have risen," he said further, "I will go ahead of you into Galilee." After what? What in the name of heaven was he trying to say? He had to know we had no idea what he meant, but he did not respond to our ignorance.

"This very night," he said again, "you will all abandon me because of what will happen. As the scriptures foretell, *'I will strike the shepherd, and the sheep of the flock will be scattered.'"* Why did he bring this up again?

Peter tried again to set him straight. "We will not abandon you, Lord. Such a thought is unspeakable!" he said with scorn. "Even if all do abandon you, I will not." So spoke he for himself, so spoke he for us all.

Jesus stopped, turned and arrested Peter with his eye. "So proud are you of your loyalty?" Simon's face was set as a stone, wild, grey eyebrows set forward and determined, his gaze intense. "Let me tell you the truth, Peter, this very night, as I said earlier, Satan will attempt to sift you as wheat is sifted of chaff. Before the rooster crows a second time, you will on two occasions thrice deny that you know me."

Angry and humiliated Peter stammered, "Even if I have to die with you, I will never deny you! Not now, not ever! You are quite mistaken to think otherwise, let alone actually speak such a thing." All of us echoed the sentiment. The face of Jesus was unresponsive, unsmiling at the rebuke.

"I have prayed for you, Simon. Your faith will not fail."

αΘω

Passing through the north gate of the Temple, we descended into the valley of the Kidron; dark, treacherous and in contrast to the streets of the city, bereft of company as we continued toward the hill called Olivet. Swirling water, swollen from spring rains cascaded down the wadi in torrents. Finding a place to cross safely we turned left where the road led to our destination. Jesus spoke again, "When I sent you without money, baggage or sandals, did you lack anything you needed?"

"No, Lord, we lacked nothing."

"Well, things are about to change. Now if you have money, you had better hold on to it and also take your baggage; and if you don't have a sword, sell your clothes if necessary and buy one. The things that are written about me are about to come to pass. If it becomes known that you follow me, you will need to defend yourselves."

"We have two swords, Lord."

"That should be enough," he replied.

The Seventh Scroll

It Is Finished!

Thus the heavens and the earth were completed in all their vast array. By the seventh day God had finished the work he had been doing; so on the seventh day he rested from all his work. Then God blessed the seventh day and made it holy, because on it he rested from all the work of creating that he had done.

—Genesis 2:1-3 NIV

I

Wednesday, 14 Nisan
Gethsemane

In the western distance, low clouds dance with colors of purple, gold and imaginary flashes of green, yellow and red. Soft, how sweet the night approaches, how deceptively it steals one's soul, how false its raiment of radiance. Somewhere near the twelfth hour from dawn, the most heinous day in human history inaugurates.

We came at length to the Mount of Olives and emerged into a clearing near the garden known as Gethsemane, brightly lit with moonlight, luminescence so brilliant that it cast our shadows on the ground. The world was too magical. Everything was just too…right. Jesus halted abruptly. "Here is a meadow arrayed in light," he said, "Sit here. I will speak to the Father now. I will speak for you. I am concerned for you. I will speak… you listen."

In the presence of us all he looked up at the moon—or beyond it—its light causing his eyes to shine, and spoke to God as he had to us so many times before. He began his prayer casually, as if his Father were standing at his side in the meadow instead of beyond the moon. His words came soft, gentle.

"Father, the time has come."

αΘω

The hours of the night enveloped us with lonely sounds and the gentle rustle of shifting, soft winds. However delicious the fragrance of spring jasmine titillated our nostrils with beguiling perfume and the panoply above bespeckled with diamond lights dimmed by the light of the moon, we were soon to discover that the loveliness of the moment would prove illusory.

A frown clouded his face accentuated by moon shadows. Sorrow and pain enveloped him. "Please," his voice pleadingly appealed to us; "sit here while I enter the garden to pray." He began to walk away, and just as he reached the opening of the low stone wall that surrounded the garden, he stopped and turned. Hesitating with apparent uncertainty, he said, "Simon, James and John, please join me." With these companions to comfort him, he stepped into the garden. Shadows of Mt. Hermon and the daughter of Jairus tugged at my memory. Inside the garden he spoke again, "I am overwhelmed with...cold...sadness. I know I am about to die. Stay here, close to me. I need you with me."

Going a little farther, his knees bent and he fell to the ground, where he lay, his face to the ground. It was hard to see our Master in such pain. Even from outside the garden, we heard him pleading, "My Father, if it is possible, take this cup from me." He began to weep. The quiet weeping escalated until his body shook with sobs and he began to gasp for air. He groaned while tears, mixed with the earth of the garden, formed droplets of mud on his face. In a moment he was quiet.

He remained quiet for a long time, and then softly he whispered, "No. Not as I will, but as you will." A glow, an illumination, materialized from no known source and in a moment Jesus was no longer alone in the garden. A man appeared arrayed in a luminescence that had nothing to do with the light of the moon. He knelt beside Jesus, lifting him into a sitting position, embracing and strengthening him, comforting him. In anguish Jesus cried out again and spoke in loud incomprehensible words. The sweat on his brow coursed its way down his countenance mingling with tears and the dirt caked on his face. Was it drops of blood we saw rolling down his cheeks and falling to the ground?

αΘω

Seeing our Lord there, lying in the dirt cradled in the arms of an angel, should have made us react. It isn't everyday one sees an angel. It isn't everyday that one sees the Christ groveling in the earth. Many of the disciples, including those Jesus had taken with him, Peter, James and John, had closed their eyes and fallen asleep. For them, the wine of supper and the late hour had finally exacted its claim. I did not sleep, however. Andrew and I sat quietly, afraid and awed. I saw the strange, iridescent man look at us or, you might say, stare at us as some of us slumbered and others, oddly curious, yet detached from the event being played out before us. We did not want to intrude. The truth is we were actually stunned into near paralysis.

Sustained by the ministrations of the angel, Jesus ceased his sobbing, got to his feet and returned to find Peter, James and John asleep. "Could you men not stay awake with me for this one lonely hour?" Was that all it was? Seemed longer. Where did the angel go? Jesus' lips tightened. "Stay alert and pray with me, my friends. I need you now. Do not succumb to the need for sleep. I know your body is weak, but surely your spirits are willing. Force yourself. Stay awake with me."

More in possession of himself now, he went back to his place of prayer and said, "My Father, if it is not possible for this cup to be taken away unless I drink it, then your will be done." He said other things as well, but the minds of his men were as if seized with resin. Their heavy eyelids sealed shut yet again.

When he came back and found them sleeping, he simply dropped his head and returned to his place of prayer. He prayed the same thing he prayed before. Three times Jesus had asked the impossible. Three times the plea of God the Son deferred to the will of God the Father. Three terrible moments of potential conflict which could only be, and finally were, resolved by the words, "not my will but yours be done."

As I reflect on this interchange between Jesus and God, it helps me to see it as the struggle between the human character of the Son and the Divine Character of the Father. Does it bother me that the two Divine Persons are One in essence yet separate in identity, with separate and distinct wills? It would if One did not submit to the Other. But he did submit. He did yield. He acknowledged and submitted to the holy Purpose of the Father. He who is God gave himself, his human will, to him who is God and his Divine Will. It would have violated the nature of God for him to do otherwise.

When he finished, he came to us and nudged Peter, James and John gently with his foot, "Are you still asleep? Wake up! The hour is here. I am betrayed into the hands of my enemies. Rise, let us go! The jackal is at hand!"

αΘω

Judas knew about Gethsemane because Jesus had often taken us there to pray and enjoy the beauty of the garden. He first took the officials to the room where they had eaten the Passover meal. When he arrived and Jesus had already gone, he knew he was in trouble. "I thought you said you knew where he was" one of the soldiers barked. Judas nervously searched his mind like a rat scurrying to avoid being cornered. After a long stressful moment, he remembered the garden. He was sure this is where they'd find him. "Gethsemane, that's where he'll be."

The heavy footsteps of a detachment of soldiers soon materialized into an angry crowd of men carrying torches, lanterns and weapons. Among them were the chief priests with whom Judas had dealt, including Asher. Judas, himself, stood at the head of the column.

Judas had arranged a special signal with them: "The one I kiss," he had told the authorities, "is the man. Arrest him." So going at once to Jesus, Judas said, "Greetings, Rabbi!" and kissed him on the cheek.

Jesus looked with remarkable compassion at his disciple and replied, "Judas, do you betray the Son of Man with a kiss?" The terrible irony of his act was lost on Judas.

Jesus, fully aware of their intent, asked the soldiers, "Who is it you want?"

"Jesus of Nazareth," they replied.

"I am he," Jesus said. When Jesus said, *"I am he,"* some of the Temple officials drew back so abruptly that they tripped over each other. One even fell into a bush and awkwardly scrambled to free himself. Why were they so shocked? Given his supposed infamy, that he would readily identify himself? Perhaps. Some had heard of his mystical powers and were afraid. Others suggest he used the name of Yahweh to refer to himself. This would certainly explain their reaction.

Amused, Jesus again asked them, "Who is it you want?"

"Jesus of Nazareth," a soldier replied in the authoritative tone of Rome. The behavior of the Jews was unsettling to the soldier. The steadiness of Jesus intimidated him. He needed the tone of Rome. He needed it desperately. With it his fear could be stayed, and he could do his job. That is why be had brought a full detachment of men.

"I told you that I am he," Jesus answered. On hearing this a second time the soldiers seized each of us, assuming they were about to have a fight on their hands. They forced us to the ground roughly, yelling as though in battle.

"If I am the one you want, then let these men go."

Then ignoring the soldiers, Jesus said to the Temple officials, "Am I leading a rebellion that you thought it necessary to do combat with swords and clubs? Every day I sat in the Temple courts teaching, and you did not arrest me." They didn't respond. "Are you deaf? Have you lost your tongues?

Why do you not speak?" Again he awaited an answer. When it didn't come he said, "You do not speak because you do not know the truth and would not believe it if the Father himself came down with all the hosts of heaven and spoke it to you. Search the Scriptures, and you will discover that the things of this night were foretold by the prophets. You can be sure that every word will be fulfilled. Now, do what you came for." Then, the captain of the guard stepped forward, seized Jesus, and arrested him.

Once they had Jesus apparently willing to "submit" to their authority, they released us. This was a mistake. Indeed, once free, James said, "Lord, don't you want us to fight?" Without waiting for an answer, Simon Peter drew his Roman short sword from his tunic where it was hidden and struck Malchus, the high priest's servant, severing his ear. The man grasped the side of his head where the sword had struck. Blood spurted through his fingers.

As Peter began a second and fatal strike, cold steel words stopped him, "Peter! Stop! Control yourself! Put your sword away! No more of this!" Jesus bent over and retrieved the man's ear from the ground. Brushing the dirt from it, he put it back in its place and healed him.

Peter, embarrassed and confused, lowered his sword. *"Was it not only a few hours ago that he told us to arm ourselves? Did he not say that two swords were enough? Enough for what if not to fight!?"*

Then Jesus said more gently, "This is the cup the Father has given me. Shall I not drink it? If you live by the sword, you will die by the sword." This was not mere philosophical rhetoric. He was not teaching us; he was rescuing us. Had Jesus not intervened, we all would have been massacred in a moment of time, by the Roman detachment. We had two swords between us all. These trained, combat soldiers each had a sword, and some carried lances as well. Hardly a military match. "Don't you think I could call on my Father, and he would, at once, put at my disposal more than twelve thousand angels? But how then would the Scriptures be fulfilled? Understand that it *must* happen this way!"

Peter looked away in disgust. *Rage. "Let me then die! How gladly I would forfeit my life than to allow you to be led off like a witless sheep! Why do you do this insane thing?"* Silent thoughts. Silent accusations. For the first time in his life, Peter felt unmitigated rage at Jesus. At anyone. At everything.

Shaking his head in disillusioned contempt, Peter allowed his sword to fall to the ground, then turned and walked away. *Was this his leader? Was this the man to whom he had pledged his life—and death?* Then all the disciples fled. The captain ordered that Jesus be bound with his hands behind his back and they led him away. I did not flee, but neither did I follow.

The garden, so disturbed by the arrest, became quiet again. Dark clouds now covered the sky hiding the moon and the stars. The night was dark. I slipped away to the shelter of a grassy cove under a small willow. I was exhausted. Perplexed, dazed and frightened by the events of the evening, I curled up, with my cloak around me and soon succumbed to sleep—alone.

II

Betrayal

"Wake up, man!" I felt myself being shaken, but sleep held me like quicksand. "Justus! Wake up! I've been searching all over for you." It was Matthias. His voice was shrill and frenzied.

"Jesus is being tortured, and the same people who paraded him into town with palm branches just few days ago have all turned against him. He may be even sentenced by now. *Now!?* In the middle of the night? And Passover is not even over!"

My head cleared instantly. "My Lord and my God, Matthias! Is he so dangerous that they could not, at least, wait until morning?" I knew he had no answer.

I barely remember the run to town. I just knew I had to be there.

αΘω

They brought him bound, a prisoner, first to Annas, whose daughter had married Caiaphas, the high priest. The most remarkable thing about Annas is that he was old, well past his three-score and ten. And with his antiquity came High Priestly authority. He was set up as High Priest by Quirinius, governor of Syria, about seven years after the birth of Jesus, and then deposed by Valerius Gratus about eight years later. The Roman procurators set up and put down High Priests as they chose. But Annas and his five sons, including his son-in-law Caiaphas, held dread sway over the Jewish ruling body, the Sanhedrin. It was he who set the tone and character of the trials to follow; even more than Pilate, he was the force behind the crucifixion of Jesus. It is amazing how such an evil man can be accorded what is presumed to be spiritual authority. Others were called "High Priest" and so wielded titular authority, but it was Annas who held the real authority among the Jews. That is why they brought Jesus to him first. And, when Annas was done with Jesus, he was taken to the house of his puppet, Caiaphas, where he had the elders assembled. Caiaphas, you remember, had advised the Jews that it would be good if one man died for the people. Peter and John followed at a safe distance, and while Peter waited outside in the courtyard, John entered the house of Caiaphas to stand with Jesus.

Simon stood warming himself from the chill of the early hour by a fire. A bearded man, someone Peter vaguely recognized, approached him. "You are not one of his disciples…are you?"

Peter's response was immediate and with conviction; shaking his head, he said, "I am *not* one of his disciples!" For Peter, that connection died in the garden of Gethsemane.

And then one of Annas' servants, a cousin of the man whose ear Peter had cut off, challenged him, "Wrong! I saw you with him in the olive grove! You drew your sword against a member of my family!"

Yes, and I would that his head had rolled at my feet.

But Peter denied it forcefully. Almost too forceful. It made the onlookers suspicious.

And then a servant girl saw him standing there in the firelight. She looked closely at him and said, "This man was surely with the Nazarene."

"Woman, I don't know this mad prophet!" accompanied by a hushed expletive. In the distance a rooster began to crow.

αΘω

After a moment, John came back and spoke quietly to another girl standing in the courtyard, and she brought Peter inside. Reluctantly the fisherman followed her. And in doing so, the scene of him and Jesus swimming and frolicking in Galilee flashed through his memory. The recollection was like hot coals in his stomach. The thoughts of happier times made him want to retch. He found the high priest interrogating Jesus about his teaching. "I spoke openly to the world," Jesus replied. "You know that I always taught in synagogues or at the Temple, where all Jews come together. I said nothing in secret. Why question me? Ask those who heard me. They know what I said."

When Jesus said this, one of the officials nearby slapped him forcibly in the face. Jesus staggered. Peter's eyes widened. The hair on his neck stood, but he restrained himself. He kept quiet. This was the first clear indication of how much the Jewish leadership bore extreme prejudice toward Jesus. They meant to do him harm. It was most disturbing. "Is this the way you answer the high priest?" the official demanded.

After recovering from the blow, Jesus replied evenly, "If I said something wrong, then tell me what I said wrong. But I spoke the truth, so why did you hit me?"

Caiaphas, Asher and the whole Sanhedrin (except for Nicodemus) sought to manufacture evidence against Jesus. They clearly wanted him dead. A legal pretext for summary execution would work just fine, but they could not find one. Spurious witnesses came forward; two of whom declared, "This man said, 'I am able to destroy the Temple of God and rebuild it in three days.'"

The high priest stood and gently adjusted his expensive robes. He said calmly to Jesus, "Are you not going to answer?" The two men faced each other, both supremely confident, Caiaphas in what he perceived to be total control. "What is this that these men are saying against you?" Caiaphas! Innocent, innocuous Caiaphas! It was not he who brought charges against Jesus; it was "these men." He would have us believe it was not his murderous intent. It was the unsolicited testimony of others. Jesus remained silent. The high priest then became frustrated and raged, "I charge you under oath: Are you the Christ, the Son of the living God?" Silence hung in the air like a fog. Jesus looked straight into the eyes of his interrogator.

"Yes. I AM."

There were gasps among those witnessing this. The eyes of Caiaphas bulged indignantly. A smile tugged at the perimeter of his lips. *This insipid, would-be prophet had condemned himself out of his own mouth before all.* "It is as you say," Jesus said and turned to face the crowd. He spoke so all could hear, "Let me say clearly to all of you: In the future you will see the Son of Man sitting at the right hand of *El Shaddai*—and coming in the clouds of heaven."

Caiaphas, his face grimacing, his eyes filled with fierce fire, brought his hands up, grasped the edges of his be-jewelled robe and jerked. The ripping sound resonated in the silence that followed Jesus' words. "He has spoken blasphemy! What need have we of witnesses!?" He turned to the Sanhedrin, "You have heard this man's blasphemy in your own ears—in his own words. What is your verdict?"

"He deserves death!" from Asher. No hesitation. No ambiguity. No debate.

At this the crowd became unruly. Those guarding Jesus began to mock him, slapping him in the face brutally, using the heels of their hands as clubs. After blindfolding him, one powerfully-built bull of a man stepped forward and with a burly fist, pistoned it squarely into his mouth. Jesus fell, blood spurting from his lip and teeth. "Prophesy, you bastard!" he yelled in perverse satisfaction at his work. "Who hit you?" Laughter. As Jesus lay on the floor, convulsing, blood pounding in his temples, they began kicking him, spitting in his face. After delivering a vicious kick, one man, otherwise a dignified member of the Sanhedrin, lost whatever decorum he had and screamed, "Clean up this pile of dog vomit!" The deprecatory remarks, derision and insults flooded in violent, vulgar, visceral confusion.

αΘω

Peter, sick in his bowels of the scene before him, lurched through the door into the courtyard; where he was recognized by another girl who pointed her finger and in the powerful emotions of the moment screamed, "This man was with Jesus of Nazareth. I know him!"

Peter glared at her, loathing in his eyes, "Foul woman!" he said in disgust. "I swear to God, I don't know you and I don't know this man!"

A companion with her backed her up. "She is right! I know him, too! And he said he was a leader among the prophet's disciples!"

"No!" cried Peter, "You are mistaken! I am not!" Simon lowered his head and gathered his robes around him as if to hide. The expression on his face was one of fear and rage. He had been betrayed, he thought. Jesus had lied. *Jesus had lied,* and he had followed him so faithfully, so naively. He no longer cared what happened to him. *"I am no longer a part of this!"* he thought. Movement on the dais leading into the house of Caiaphas caught his eye. They were bringing Jesus out. He looked terrible, his face and hair covered with blood and spit, his clothes disheveled and dirty. Yet there was something regal, noble and dignified in his demeanor. He could see Jesus plainly.

A group of men who had been standing there listening to the women accuse Peter approached him and said, "Come now, old fellow, admit it. These lovely creatures caught you in the act. Surely you are one of the Nazarene's lemmings. You even have the accent of a Galilean."

"God damn you to hell, man!" Peter screamed. "I don't know this person!" The outburst was followed by a stunned silence as all turned to look at the leader of the apostles. In this silence, another rooster crowed, this one nearby. Jesus turned and gazed at Peter. Their eyes locked. Recognition exchanged. All saw it. It was as plain and as stark as the moon above. All knew that the women and the others had spoken the truth.

"Before the rooster crows twice you will twice disown me three times." The words came to Peter, each syllable thudding into his skull, into his bowels,

into every reverberating fiber of his being. His breath caught in his throat, his eyes welling tears, spilling down his cheeks into his beard. Releasing a pent-up, hoarse, scream, Peter doubled over in pain, appearing as if he would retch. All eyes, including those of Jesus followed his hunched, broken form as he stumbled clumsily out of the courtyard.

III

Deliverance

Biting coolness of the night's dark hours enhanced the intensifying harshness of events. Passover celebrations had continued throughout the night. The house of the high-priest, being close by Herod the Great's Temple for the sake of convenience, emptied as all made their way to the chambers of the elders. There they convened again, this time for the official certification of their accusations against Jesus. The gallery filled, overflowing with onlookers. Caiaphas and the chief priests assembled in their respective designated positions. Jesus was presented before them. This was the sacred courtroom within the Temple. There would be no unruly behavior here. Outbursts would not be tolerated. One of the elders, clearly appointed for this task, stood and required of Jesus, "If you believe yourself to be the Christ, our Messiah, state it plainly for the record." The clerk sat at his desk, papyri before him, quill in hand, waiting to record the words of the accused.

"We've been through this," Jesus responded. "Clearly, you did not believe what I said then." Scratching from the clerk's pen. Jesus paused, surveying the scene. Curiously, he thought of his adventures as a child with Eben, his friend; their foray through the tunnels of the city, the time of silence in the now polluted and empty holy of holies, the debate with the elders in this very room. His eyes searched every corner of the chamber where once as a child they praised his brilliance before settling back upon the official group before him, now accusing him. "What *do* you think?" said he. "Am I the Christ? Am I the Jewish Messiah? Please, render your opinion." No response. "I am not surprised that you do not answer." The clerk scratched. When the scratching stopped, he spoke again. "Now hear me," said Jesus, "and let it be recorded word for word so that there be no mistake, no lack of clarity. *From this day forward the Son of Man will be seated at the right hand of Almighty God.*" The scratching ceased. The clerk looked at Caiaphas, who nodded his assent. The clerk recorded Jesus' words.

"Are you then the Son of God?" said the interrogator.

"I am the Son of God."

This was followed by a definitive ruling from Caiaphas. "There is no need for more testimony. He blasphemes blatantly and with malicious intent in our very faces. We have heard it from his own lips, without so much as a hint of remorse or shame. He is incorrigible," shaking his head, "unredeemable."

Caiphas had seen a lot in his lifetime, but never had anyone declared such things so brazenly. "He is condemned to death! Take him to Pilate who will authorize the execution." They were confident in their ability to manipulate the Procurator. The assemblage was dismissed. They rose and led him off to Pilate.

αΘω

Among those faces in the gallery of the council of elders was that of a special onlooker—Judas Iscariot. When the full import of what was happening to Jesus struck him, he was mortified and filled with paralyzing shame at what he had done. When guilt stuns a man, his heart seizes up, his mouth goes dry and there is a terrible gripping sensation in the stomach. There is also the natural tendency to find or make excuse for one's self—to actually justify horrendous, unacceptable acts. In time, however, the seesaw battle was lost with Judas. Agonized with remorse, he accosted Asher and the others to whom he had betrayed Jesus and attempted to return the amount he had been paid. "I have made a mistake," he said. "I have betrayed innocent blood."

"You have betrayed innocent blood?" Asher sneered, amused. "How unfortunate, but how does that concern us?"

"You are the ones who arrested him! You are the ones who gave me the blood money! If I had known what you would do I would have never..." Judas' words caught in this own throat. He could not continue.

"We merely acted on the information supplied to us. How could we have known his blood was innocent?" They were laughing at him. "Innocent blood? Why, that does indeed seem your responsibility. If he was innocent, he is no longer. He has condemned himself."

With sweaty hands, Judas squeezed the hard coins repeatedly as though they were clay, in an effort to shape them into something less—less mercenary, less saturated with shame.

Rage, guilt and frustration enveloped him. With disgust, he threw the money at their feet, coins violently clinking in all directions. "Bastards!" he screamed, chest heaving, "Swine!" Abruptly, he turned and left.

"He will not be back," said Asher.

αΘω

Judas wandered the streets of Jerusalem for hours. Accusing thoughts prodded his conscience like white-hot needles. How many times had he taken money from what he, the disciples and Jesus had to live on? How many times had he scorned the teachings of the Lord? How many times had he been jealous and contemptuous of the attention people lavished on Jesus. Now the only contempt he felt was staggering contempt for himself.

At length he found himself in a deserted part of the city. Odors of sewage and garbage wafted from the nearby valley of Gehenna. He discovered a rotting stump on which to sit in a lonely field. In this field grew a solitary and sadly gnarled tree. Its leaves were gone, and no buds of new life were apparent. The moon had descended from the night sky preparing for the appearance of the sun. Despite his tiredness, sleep eluded him.

There is a vast difference between being alone and being lonely. Judas was miserable and lonely. *There is no one,* he thought, *there is no one who cares a shekel about me...no one!* He wanted to weep, but his eyes were dry. Tears would not come. "Is there no one to love Judas?" he whispered to the canopy of morning stars. The heavens were as silent as the response in his heart. Could God love him still? *Of course not! Fool! You are no better than this vile refuse.* The thought of dog excrement occurred to him. His chest heaved, seeking air with which to sob. But the sobs would not come. No freedom. No release from the terrible accusation. No release from the unbearable shame. Instead of sobs, he gagged. When he had finished retching, he saw them.

Ropes. Burial ropes. Sometimes, people buried their dead in this field. There were no stones. No memorials. Nothing to indicate that lives, now ceased, were interred beneath this soil. These were ropes used to lower a human carcass—and that is what they were, carcasses—beggars, indigents, those who had been executed and those who had died without known relatives. City employees were the only ones left to pay their respects. They did this by lowering the body—carcass—carefully into its eternal resting place rather than tossing it into a forgotten hole. But forgotten they were. No graves were marked. Were it not common knowledge that this place was what it was, there would be no obvious sign of interment. Except perhaps, for these lonely ropes, inadvertently left behind from a recent burial near the city dump. Near the valley of Gehenna.

Judas gazed at the ropes and then to the tree.

Deliverance!

The light of dawn would silhouette a macabre figure swaying in silence, from a tree in a place called the *Field of Blood*.

IV

An Old Man's Voice

She startled to the fall of horses' hooves and the crunch of chariot wheels on the gravel outside. She had been awake for several hours, having risen before the light of day. Her friends, Hermas ben David and his wife, Julia had yet to stir. Strong steps with military bearing approached the door. Mary stood, afraid to receive such a visitor. The frame of the Roman officer filled the doorway. Gold, brass and white tunic gleamed. Roman eagles glistened. A sword hung at his side in its scabbard. How many times had it tasted the blood of a neighbor or friend? How many times had it tasted Jewish blood?

"How may I help you, Roman?" she asked with the tone of a woman old enough to be his mother. He remained silent, looking at her. The expression on his face did not bear the usual attitude of stone. He did not look through her with superior eyes of haughty disdain. There seemed instead something else.

"Mary?" he spoke, a trace of compassion in his voice.

Throughout his time with his disciples, Mary had tried to follow Jesus. What with a large family and with Joseph gone, much of the time she could not. There was so much to do. Even so, her heart had followed him. She often imagined him teaching others, healing, being the exceptional, kind human being he was. Though she knew he had a unique purpose she thought of him and treated him the same as her other children. Or, at least, she tried to. Given the nature of his birth, it was sometimes a challenge. After all, she had raised him, watched him grow every day of his life through childhood, adolescence and into manhood. Yet she never forgot how he came to be, nor the great honor bestowed on her. To this day, she had never understood it but simply accepted it as the will of the Father. So it was that on this day in the city of Bethlehem, she had come to be near her son at Passover.

It took a moment for her to realize that the soldier had addressed her by her first name. "How is it that you know me?"

"How is it, dear mother, that in this place you do not know me?"

Mary examined the man closer. The dark eyes, strong jaw, the military bearing. Who?

"Urbanas ben Hermas!" she exclaimed at last. "Oh, I am so ashamed!" They embraced warmly. "Oh!" she said again, "You've grown up!" Words no adult likes to hear, especially a man who takes and gives orders; a man who had slain and ordered others to do the same; a man who had rejected his father's religion and accepted the hated Roman gods and Roman ways as inevitable and routine. These words, spoken by Mary, are the words every adult acquaintance who knew you in childhood inevitably declare. But Urbanus did not really mind. This woman, above all his parent's friends, was his favorite. Her son Jesus, his childhood friend, well, that was another story.

Jesus was everything Urbanus was not. The Centurion of Caesar's Court was glad it was so. He had never bothered to understand what Jesus did and taught. He only knew that he had embraced Judaism which Urbanus hated. He knew that Jesus had somehow managed to pass himself off as a teacher of sorts, yet he also knew that Jesus was despised by the Jewish leadership. For this, Urbanus conceded some level of respect and admiration. But it ended there. Jesus traipsed around the country teaching and preaching as if he were some messianic scion, living off the charity of others—a charlatan, in the view of this proud Roman soldier.

"I heard that you had come," said the soldier. "I've not much time. I must return to my men, but I wanted to see you, to welcome you." He waited as Mary told him that she appreciated his attentions and that she knew he was very busy and shouldn't have bothered. "Mary," he began. He hesitated. He did not want to speak the next sentence. "Mary," he began again, "your son—Jesus—has been arrested." The shock and surprise could not have been more staggering.

"Why?" she exclaimed. "How? Jesus wouldn't harm anyone! Who would do such a thing?" Despite the stunning news, Mary knew that she had been anticipating this for years. Anticipation did not lessen the shock.

"I don't know the details, but rumor has it that Herod empowered Caiaphas to take him into custody. I learned about it from a fellow soldier whose men carried out the deed. I don't know how or for what reason Jesus was arrested, but it is a fact." As an afterthought, and probably to get away from such uncomfortable news, Urbanus asked, "Where are my mother and father?"

"I think they are still asleep," said Mary absently. "Urbanus! Are you sure? How can you be certain?" Urbanus looked at her patiently, though annoyed by the question.

"I am a Roman centurion, mother. I know such things." He waited for the effect of his words. "Now, I must wake my father." He disappeared in the direction of his parent's quarters.

An old man's voice in her head: *"A sword shall pierce your own heart also."* Tears welled into the crinkles of her eyes. Her breath came in short gasps. Her stomach recoiled. *I must go to him!*

V

King Meets Procurator

Damned Jews! Damn their insulting customs! The governor was in no mood for tolerance at this ungodly hour. *Why can't this accursed race begin their day in the morning—which common sense dictates—instead of sunset? Why do they go debauching about throughout the night as though it were the light of day? Damn them! Damn them to hell!* He barely glanced at Jesus and as though his fate were utterly irrelevant to him. "What charge!? *Ignorant fools!* What mindless charge do you bring against this man?" demanded the very irritated voice of official Rome.

In Judea, Pontius Pilate had assumed the office of Roman Procurator, or governor, after the deposition of Herod Archelaus. Serving this office for the past ten years, his authority exceeded that of any other Procurator in the empire. His judicial power was supreme, answering to no one but Caesar. He lived not in Jerusalem but in Caesarea where he occupied the palace of Herod. However, this was Passover, and he had come to the city with a force of soldiers 3,000 strong to help keep the peace.

"This man is a criminal," Asher and his colleagues replied. "Otherwise, we would not have brought him to you!"

"Yes. Quite," said the governor. "Why didn't I think of that?" Unconcealed contempt. "Then do not trouble me with your frivolities, take him yourselves and judge him by your own law. I have a real world with which to deal."

"You know we have no right to execute anyone," the Jews reminded him. This was a lie, of course. They did have that right, the form of execution was stoning. Romans crucified their capital criminals, or whipped them to death, or whatever torture suited their perverse nature. The Jewish leadership wanted their prisoner crucified. Jesus had spoken of this. He knew the kind of death he would endure. The Scripture would be fulfilled.

"Execute?" For the first time, the governor looked at Jesus. "You want to execute this pathetic creature?" Pilate looked incredulous. "What on earth for?" He stepped out to the portico overlooking the city. *What a miserable place to serve Rome!* He despised coming to this city. It was so… so…*Jewish!*

Pilate had known of Jesus. Who in all of Judea hadn't? He knew also of John the Baptist. He confused them one with the other. Wild, fanciful stories circulated about a Jewish prophet who was supposed to become their king. The stories had even reached the ears of Caesar. After a moment of pragmatic reflection Pilate said, "I will see this man alone."

He then went back inside, approached Jesus and spoke softly, "Are *you* the king of the Jews?" He was close enough to his face to smell his breath.

"Is that your idea," Jesus responded evenly, "or has someone told you about me?"

Annoyed, Pilate stepped away, and turning to face the casements, replied impatiently, "Look man, am I a Jew? Why would anyone possibly talk to me about you? Do you think I actually listen to the prattle of these foppish priests?" Jesus remained silent. "They are the ones who handed you over to me. Speak up! What is it that you have done?"

Jesus ignored this question. "My kingdom," he said enigmatically, "is not of this world. If it were, my servants would fight to prevent my arrest. My kingdom is from another place."

"You *are* a king, then?" said Pilate, a condescending smile on his lips, as if Jesus had said something humorous.

Jesus answered with straightforward declaration, "I am King." The implication behind the words did not register with Pilate. Jesus paused, letting the words take whatever effect they would take. "I was born to be King and came into the world to declare the truth of it. Anyone who listens to truth," pausing again, "listens to me."

The audacity of Jesus both amused Pilate and unsettled him. "Truth?" asked Pilate with a laugh, "Truth you say! What the devil is truth?" Without waiting for Jesus to answer he strode out to where the Jews stood and said, "What are you vacuous fools doing? There is no basis for a charge against this man! He is a dreamer of ambitious dreams. Nothing more."

But Asher and his men were not fools. Evil, perhaps, but not fools. They well knew what they were doing, and they well knew how to exploit Pilate. The Procurator lent himself to such manipulation owing to his penchant for expediency. The issue for him was one of personal interest and convenience. He cared not for Jesus or the Jews, but he did care about how they might impact his interests. Knowing this, the Jews said simply, "He stirs up people all over Judea. He spreads his abominable teaching throughout the entire region. He is disruptive to the community. He started in Galilee and has come all the way here." Pilate cared little for what disturbed the

Jews. And he wondered as for Rome, what could one deluded vagabond, street preaching fanatic do?

"Galilee, did you say? Is this man a Galilean?"

"Well, yes," replied a spokesman, "he began his sedition there."

"Then take him to Herod! He is in the city for this…this, silly feast of yours. Let Herod decide what to do with this tedious affair."

VI

Condemned

Herod, in a distant section of the palace he shared with the Procurator, had just been advised that Jesus the prophet was being sent to him. He was pleased. For a long time he had been wanting to see this magician. Perhaps he could prevail upon him to perform some fantastic feat of magic. *Water to wine! Indeed!*

When Jesus arrived, Herod plied him with questions, but Jesus did not respond. He merely stood there, his eyes following Herod with what was it? *Sympathy?* Asher and the priests, however, were not so patient and were eager to get on with the process. They were angry and vehemently accused Jesus of sacrilege, treason and anything else they could think of, justifiable or not.

Piqued at Jesus' refusal to entertain him, Herod entertained himself. He let his soldiers have their jokes and mockery.

"An enterprising fellow!" said one of the captains.

"Enterprising?" replied a sergeant. "How can you say a pathetic vagrant like this is enterprising?"

"Well, my good fellow," said the captain, "What have you done to have yourself presented before the governor of Rome and now to the king?"

"Hah!" said the soldier, "I guess I should also proclaim myself King of the Jews."

Herod was amused. "Wonderful idea," he smiled with eyes that did not. "Bring me a royal robe." Dressing Jesus in royal elegance made a powerful statement of mockery. Satisfied, the king announced, "I weary of this mute vagabond. Send the beggar back to Pilate." *What marvelous sport! I should like to see the reaction of the Procurator when he sees this!*

That Herod would return the prisoner to him did not surprise Pilate. His reaction, however, would have surprised Herod. He also found the elegant robe on this hopeless indigent amusing and was somewhat relieved for a break in the tension that existed between them. *That pompous ass has a sense of humor after all!* On that day a respect of sorts ensued. Before this they had reluctantly tolerated each other. In the persecution of Jesus, they had discovered a morbid sense of mutuality.

αΘω

The affair concerning Jesus was no longer tedious to Pilate. Crowds of agitated Jews gathered. The thing had become a dangerous spectacle, disturbing the governor. During the Jewish Passover Feast, it was a Roman custom to release a prisoner as a gesture of mercy and redemption. Mercy and redemption be damned! The gesture had political benefits, nothing more. The Roman militia and governance knew nothing of redemption, and mercy bored them. Pilate was himself inflexible, merciless and obstinate and showed little sensitivity to Jewish idiosyncrasies. Still, the feast carried with it what they called redemption. Hence, the release of the prisoner—usually of their own choice—a token to appease an unruly populace. *Strange, primitive people!*

In his dungeon the governor held an infamous criminal. This troublesome petty thief and murderer Pilate had finally captured and incarcerated. Called Barabbas, he was a particularly odious man, fomenting rebellion using the most offensive and obscene tactics. He was particularly offensive to Pilate owing to vehement hostility toward Rome and, by extension, toward the governor himself. He looked forward with vengeful anticipation to the satisfaction of seeing for himself that this horrible man was crucified. He hated the Passover, the Day of Amnesty for prisoners incarcerated by Rome. It wasn't so much that the Jews treated Barabbas with respect or admiration; he was regarded rather as an embarrassment. For it was Barabbas who had brought such quantities of hostility from Rome toward the Jews and Israel. It was he who had incited numerous attacks on Roman outposts. It was he who had slain Romans without regard to consequence either to himself, those who followed him or, yet, even his own people.

Now Jesus stood accused of this same sedition, but in Pilate's view, this prophet was no Barabbas. The governor would give them a choice. They could not possibly choose a murderer over such an irrelevant religious leader. So he announced in a tone which suggested that he knew the answer already, "Which one of these two do you want me to release to you, Barabbas or this Jesus, who is called your 'Christ?'"

As the Jewish religious leaders briefly considered the question, Pilate knew it was out of envy that they were after Jesus. These intellectually impoverished religious prigs were actually jealous of this peasant. *The man clearly possessed leadership skills. Such things happen rarely among these obstinate, weak people. They could only envy a man like this.*

While Pilate was thus musing on the judge's seat, a boy, obviously a messenger, approached him. "Noble sir," whispered the boy into Pilate's ear, "a message from mistress Claudia Procula."

"Yes boy, what is it?" said Pilate annoyed at the interruption.

"She sent me to beg you, sir, not to have anything to do with that innocent man! She said to tell you, 'I have suffered a great deal today in a dream because of him.'" Pilate massaged the bridge of his nose with his hand in exasperation. *My wife and her dreams,* he sighed thoughtfully, *Great Caesar, deliver me!*

Thus burdened with his wife's superstitions he turned back to the Jews and repeated, "Which of the two do you want me to release to you?"

"Barabbas!" they answered.

Pilate checked himself warily, concealing his surprise. He held the Jews in high scorn and barely tolerated their impertinence. He could not fathom the depth of their consternation with this prophet. How could they possibly choose Barabbas? This murderer had caused him much consternation. He was loath to hand over a hardened criminal. He had been maneuvered into offering something he did not intend to be taken seriously. Yet he must take care or he may find himself being favorably disposed toward someone they despised. These Jews, however their lack of political relevance and regardless of his antipathy toward them, could not be ignored. Better to distance himself. He would maintain a posture of cool detachment.

"Barabbas? Most curious, indeed. Do you mean that you would prefer a criminal such as this jackal to your king?" Pilate smiled. He was most pleased with himself. He knew that it wasn't that they preferred Barabbas; it was that they hated Jesus. The expressions on their faces revealed their contempt. He did not wait further for an answer. "What shall I do, then, with this Jesus, this Messiah of yours?"

The response was immediate. "Crucify him!"

"Why?" asked the governor with mock generosity. "What crime has he committed? What evil has he done?" He was now enjoying this. He loved to see this odd assemblage of religious fools squirm. Pilate was not one to be squeamish about taking a life. Jesus meant nothing to him, and as for Claudia, she knew better than to interfere with in his official duties. She could do nothing more than sulk. Besides, she had long ago ceased to interest him. He was, nonetheless, appalled at what was random, meaningless bloodlust on the part of the Jews.

The distinction of plausible innocence was lost on them. They shouted all the louder, "Crucify him!"

And then, as if it were something he did every day, Pilate gestured to his soldiers to have Jesus lashed with a Roman scourge of cords, the kind commonly used on a condemned criminal. His gesture was a command that they were eager to obey. A soldier stepped forward, a guard of the Temple contingent who had, among others, been given the task of escorting their prisoner back and forth between Annas, Caiphas, Herod and Pilate. In his hands he held a scourge, its leather strips trailing on the ground, its shards of bone and metal gleaming, its belaying-pin handle gripped firmly. "So, prophet, or whatever you are," spoke he to Jesus, "you thought to rid the Temple of parasites; you also will be disposed by the artifice of your own making."

A whipping post about ten feet high stood in the palace courtyard. Routinely, a prisoner was tied to a rusted ring near the top, arms raised above him. To this appliance, they tied Jesus. His back was laid open with the first tearing sting of the whip he, himself, had crafted. A scourge crafted and once used to rid the house of God of evil, now used to expurgate the Temple of God's Son. Thirty-eight lashes later, his back had been reduced to raw, bleeding tissue. Strips of torn flesh dangled grotesquely down his back. What the world, what the cosmos, had it conscious awareness, could not comprehend; that with each stripe, with each laceration came another blow to the pain and disease of humankind, came another stripe by which we are healed. This instrument, crafted to cleanse the house of God, was crafted instead to heal our sins. Cutting him loose, Jesus slumped to the ground and lay in bloody dirt, groaning in pain, marginally conscious.

VII

Crucify!

The soldiers jerked him to his feet. Those not involved in the scourging had twisted together an assemblage of thorns from a nearby jujube tree, fashioning a crude crown. Protecting their hands from the long, sharp thorns with rags, they unceremoniously forced it down on his head. Blood spurted in the usual profusion produced by scalp wounds. Mercilessly, it coursed down his face and neck. They clothed him once again in the purple robe provided by Herod and in mock adulation approached him in a circular line, again and again, saying, "Hail, king of the Jews!" They struck him in the face with their fists, leaving red welts and abrasions and blood on their knuckles. And as he fell from each blow, he was jerked into a standing position again; and as they struck him again, they released him, laughing as he fell in a bloody heap. Big soldiers with powerful, sweating arms. They struck him because they were men of violence and loved an excuse to shed blood. But, in this case, they struck him primarily because of their hatred for the Jews. To them, Jesus had no identity. He was a symbol. An effigy to be despised, demeaned and ultimately destroyed. Pilate watched with a mixture of curiosity and amused disgust.

"So," he continued, arms folded across bronze chest armor, a smile of nonchalance on his lips, an air of authority in his demeanor, "Look here, I find no basis for a charge against this man." *For this he had ordered Jesus to be whipped and unmercifully battered?* Pilate found it titillating to employ this sordid spectacle for his sport. His display of calmness was a mere ploy for political expediency. There were people taking notes of this squalid affair. Notes that would be read by superior Roman eyes. Pilate protected himself while charming himself in the process. The life of Jesus meant no more to him than the life of a slave in the arena, to be wantonly sacrificed to beasts, a life to be forfeited for the sake of entertainment.

The Romans brought Jesus out on the portico before the populace wearing the crown of thorns and the purple robe. Standing between marble columns with Jesus at his side, in theatrical gesture Pilate lifted his arm toward him shouting, "Behold your King!"

Incensed, agitated, the crowd roared back, "Crucify him! Crucify him!"

The governor shouted back, "Then *you* take him! *You crucify him!* As for me, I have no charge against him." Thus, maneuvering the Jews in theatrical deception, he did not realize that he himself had been maneuvered.

This declaration, this charge, discomfited the Jewish leadership. After much conspiratorial and agitated discussion among themselves, the priests said to Pilate, "We have a law! Our law stipulates that this man must die, because he claimed to be the Son of God. That is blasphemy of the rankest order..."

Pilate did not hear the sentence completed. Now it was his turn to be discomfited. Correlating the notion that there was a remote possibility that Jesus might be the offspring of a god with the dream of Claudia somewhat disquieted Pilate. After all, he was not a man wholly insensitive to the adulation of Roman gods.

When he heard this, he turned to Jesus and asked, "Where do you come from?" but Jesus gave him no answer. "Do you refuse to speak to me?" said Pilate, amazed. *This sordid lump of tortured flesh could not possibly be the son of a god!* He dismissed the Jewish superstition completely. "You simple fool, don't you realize I have the power to crucify you or let you go?"

"You have no power at all, Pilate," Jesus croaked from sheer exhaustion, his voice breaking, "were it not given to you from above. Those who handed me over to you are guilty of greater evil than yours."

Pilate was moved. *This is curious. Could this wholly defeated man actually have compassion for me? What composure! He is magnificent! Merciful gods! What am I thinking?* The governor felt queasy. He decided to do what he could, within the parameters of political propriety, to release Jesus instead of Barabbas, but the Jews loudly countered, "If you let this man go, you are no friend of Caesar. Anyone who claims to be a king opposes Caesar."

He had not realized it until now, but Pilate was trapped, caught in an irresistible tide of destiny. He felt helpless as though events were being controlled by a force he didn't understand and could not bring to heel. He moved to the stone pavement where was erected the Roman Judgment Seat. There he sat and slumped. He motioned for Jesus to be brought out and to be stood before him. It was the day of Preparation for Passover Week. The crowd restless, hot, angry.

"Cru-ci-fy! Cru-ci-fy!" escalating to a rhythmic, insistent chant.

"Bring me water," he said to a slave, "in a basin!"

"Take him away! Take him away! Cru-ci-fy! Cru-ci-fy!"

The water came. The slave stood at Pilate's side, holding the basin.

"We have no king but Caesar," the priests shouted.

"See here then," cried Pilate, standing, his regal white and scarlet robe fluttering in the quiet breeze. Holding his hands in the air for all to see he spoke loudly, forcibly, "I wash my hands of the blood of this man—this righteous man!" He plunged his hands into the basin.

The effect was galvanizing. A lone, solitary voice from somewhere in the crowd shouted, "His blood shall be upon us...and upon our children!" Murmurs of approval.

Exhausted and resigned, Pilate nodded assent to the officer in charge and handed the prisoner over to be crucified. He was loath to look into the eyes of this simple carpenter from Nazareth, but something within him forced him. He was met with a gaze that seared him. Eternity seemed to pass in the merest touch of eye contact. With a jerk, the soldiers took Jesus away.

VIII

Place of the Skull

The sun had not yet risen high enough to cast a shadow upon the dial positioned near Pilate's Seat of Judgment. Rumors had it that sundials were now almost as accurate as Cleopatra's Needle, an obelisk which now stood in the city of Alexandria that carefully marked the points of each hour in the day. While the Jews counted days from sunset to sunset, they counted hours from dawn or six hours after midnight. Such are thoughts of the passage of time at a time like this. Each instant dragged into the next, each event unfolding seamlessly into the next. The trial had taken an hour and a half. Yet there were no shadows except for the terrible shadow of this event.

For most, faces in the crowd hold little meaning. They are a blur, a mere passage of scenery, not even registering in consciousness. On that day as they laid the crossbeam on the shoulders of Jesus, on that day as he staggered helpless under its weight—on another day, the weight of this instrument of death would have been as nothing for such broad, carpenter shoulders to bear—but on that day, the weight was laid upon a back bleeding from lashes unmerciful, on that day it was laid upon a mass of raw, exposed sinew and bone and on that day a face was seen in the crowd.

It was the bronzed face of a man who stood head and shoulders above the masses gathering along the streets of Jerusalem as if to watch a parade, for a parade it was. His name was Simon, a son of Cyrene, a town along the northern coast of Africa, east of Namibia and west of Egypt, the father of two sons, one he called Alexander, the other he called Rufus, both of whom were known to the church of later years, one famous, the other infamous.

But they are another story for another time.

The Roman centurion, horsed upon his stallion, seeing that Jesus would never make it to the place of crucifixion allowed his eyes to trace over the mass of faces in the crowd. He thought of Jesus, a man whom he had come to despise and he thought of his mother, whom well he knew. For the man placed in charge of the crucifixion and death of Jesus of Nazareth was none other than the son of Hermas, Urbanus, warrior, Centurion of Caesar,

Centurion of Rome. Urbanus, whose dress uniform bore the medals and ribbons of many campaigns. Urbanus, whose exploits were known even to Caesar, had grown up from the eight-year-old boy under the tutelage of a Nubian slave. Perhaps had the prisoner been someone other than the son of a family he once loved, a family so close to his, he would not have noticed and would have allowed the continuance of the whip to motivate the criminal to work harder. Somewhere in the heart, calloused by continual exposure to inhumanity, lurked a compassion for Mary and Joseph, friends of his own mother and father, and a trace of mercy toward their son who staggered in blood before him.

Seeing the powerful form of Simon standing among the sea of faces, he gave command that his soldiers arrest him and compel him to carry the bloody crossbeam. To this task Simon took willingly, for he himself could not stomach the scene before him. He knew Jesus to be no criminal, for he had seen his eyes not so very long ago. Those who returned the gaze of the Son of God never forgot the moment. One cannot erase from memory such a glimpse of the face of God. Lifting the beam from the stumbling form, he set it upon his own shoulders and felt the blood smear upon his own bronzed skin. *What was that?* A tingle? A rush of *what?* He felt energy surge through his body and lifted the beam as if it were a toothpick. He motioned, commanding that the centurion lead on. Urbanus, commander of a hundred warriors of Rome, obeyed.

αΘω

When one is in searing pain, it is difficult, if not impossible, to be coherent in one's thoughts. One experiences the agony of helplessness at one end of the spectrum and outrage at its cause on the other. Jesus was no less human because he was God. Indeed, the hypostatic Sameness with God guaranteed it. All of the feelings connected with being both in kinetic union assailed him, producing emotions and thoughts consistent with what humans feel while in pain and what God feels when wounded and bruised.

A large number of people followed, among them the women of Jerusalem who wept loudly at the sight of this suffering. Perhaps they were paid for their performances. Somewhere Jesus found within himself enough breath to address them, "Daughters of Jerusalem, do not weep for me," cried he. "If you must wail and carry on so, then weep for yourselves. Weep for your children." This did not seem to help. The wailing increased with each word he spoke. He tried to raise his voice but could not. Rasping and defeated the voice of God whispered, "The time will come…the time will come when you say, *'Women without children are blessed above those whose sons…whose sons play about their feet! Wombs that never gave birth are blessed above those who have felt…such delicious pain! And breasts never graced by the lips of infants are blessed above those…'*" The crescendo of howling drowned him out, but his lips continued to move. God still spoke words of human agony in fusion with holy rage. "Then," envisioning some future horror, "then you will say to the mountains, *'Fall on us!'* and to the hills, *'Cover us!'*" Holding his manacled hands in the air, arms streaked bright with crimson he cried—or tried to cry, "If men do these things when trees are green, what will happen in winter, when trees are cold and black and barren?" He may as well have spoken to a wall, for that is what it was, a wall of faces, of bodies and minds as uncaring and impenetrable as stone.

αΘω

The sun did not rise this day. Instead, the expanse above cowered itself with shame as low clouds scudded in dismal pall. After a trek from the palace of staggering and falling, staggering and falling for almost one and one-half hours, through the Gate of Refuse and up the Hinnom road, at length they came to a vacant expanse of earth outside and south of the city, the place of the Skull, called Golgotha. It was a place of execution, a place for the offal of Jerusalem. Large flies buzzed. The stench of discarded waste haunted the air. Seagulls from the Great Sea came the distance to feast on the carrion.

Why the name, "Place of the Skull?" It owes simply to the long-enduring tradition that the skull of Adam, the first man, was buried here. This is an authentic tradition, reaching back many years before the birth of our Lord, and is, no doubt, the reason for the name. If it were actually true (and it likely is not), how ironic that the Second Man should die here!

Simon the Cyrenean was ordered to place the crossbeam on the ground. Two soldiers fitted the crossbeam, notched at center, to the vertical beam which had previously arrived, brought here by executioner workers. These same workers set about digging holes of the size and shape for three crosses to stand upright with rigidity enough to do their odious deed against three malefactors. Jesus would not die alone. With him were two criminals, each to die for his own crimes.

A Roman soldier extended a cup to Jesus, a solution of vinegar mixed with myrrh intended to act as an opiate for the torture he was still to endure. Jesus, unknowing, with trembling hands, lifted it to his lips. No sooner had the deadening liquid entered his mouth that he spewed it out. He would not numb himself with ought but love to mitigate the pain. Four soldiers took him by the armpits and legs and laid him out on the cross, arms stretched to extremity in each direction. They removed what remained of his garments. His nakedness visible to all. His humiliation evident to all.

One soldier held his arm in place while another took a mallet and crudely fashioned nails. Fitting the point against his opened palm, with a single blow, the soldier drove a nail through his hand and a second nail through his wrist, into the wood beneath. From each wound blood issued, bloodying the hands of the executioner. Wiping them, he went to the other hand. This, a routine detail. If he didn't do it, someone else would. Remarkably, Jesus made no sound, not so much as a whimper. His only response to the wounding was a grimace each time the mallet struck the nail. With each blow of the mallet, the sound of steel penetrating flesh and wood reverberated for however long both in distance and time the noise would carry; and for the hearts of those who heard this terrible, hollow sound, it carried through eternity.

The balls of his feet were pressed flat against the wood as the nails were driven through, scraping bone, penetrating wood. Jesus lay clothed only in clammy sweat, his chest heaving, writhing, nailed to the wood.

Soldiers now took the deadly instrument in hand and with combined strength lifted it while another guided its foot toward the hole in the earth. It hesitated at the edge for the briefest of instants, its lip crumbling beneath the weight, then plunged the three feet to its depth with a jarring thud. Jesus gasped and, exhaling, emitted a low groan. Straightening the cross, two soldiers shoveled dirt back into the hole around its foot, tamping it, making it secure. It stood straight. There they crucified him, and with him the two criminals—one on his right, the other on his left. The Scriptures were fulfilled: *He was numbered among the transgressors.*

IX

Crucified King

Jujube thorns had done their rapacious work. Streaked with liquid crimson, the body of the Son of Man hung crucified between the stars and the skulls, his body heaving convulsively, painfully trying to breathe. He inhaled, holding his breath, pushing against pinioned feet, only to exhale when he could hold it no longer and sink once again into dark oblivion. His clothing lay nearby in a disheveled heap, his purple robe, his undergarments. He hung exposed to catcalls and mockery, an exemplar of all that civilized society despised.

The soldiers who crucified Jesus were rank and file men, not officers. These had yet to campaign. They wore no medals or medallions, no hash marks of years of service. They had yet to see combat other than the minor police skirmishes in and around Judea. They had lifted the cross, they had inserted it into the ground and they had made it secure. They had followed orders. They had done their duty. Observing now the results of their work, they sat as new recruits do and waited for the next detail.

They took note of the bloody clothing lying nearby. "Look at that," said one, "the royal robe from Herod's palace. Cleaned up, it should fetch a royal price."

Another, whom his brother soldiers derisively called "Socrates," offered a more prescient view, "Nor yet is that all to consider," he declared, "Mark, this shall be a day to record. This was no ordinary man. Historians will write of him. Anything he owned will be worth a price."

"The wise one has spoken," a colleague laughed sarcastically. "Are you not aware," continued his tormentor, "that your namesake once said he was the wisest of all men because he knew how little he knew?" Laughter from the others.

Already, they spoke in the past tense. Already, Jesus was to them no more than tissue, a dead thing that would later require disposal. No doubt, they would get that detail as well. Still, they knew of the legend of this man; they knew that thousands followed him, and they had witnessed for themselves the uproar among the people during the trial. "These rags will be valued, all of them, even the underwear."

So they took the clothing and were about to rend it into four shares, one share for each of them. The undergarment was seamless, woven in one piece from top to bottom. "We should not tear this thing," they said to one another. "It will be of less value torn to shreds."

"Let's throw down stones for it." This suggestion excited them. Laughing with anticipation, they threw smooth stones until one of them had won the robe and another the seamless under garment. Thus was the scripture fulfilled, *"They divided my garments among them and cast lots for my clothing."*

From the cross, the battered, bloody prisoner groaned. His eyes on the soldiers and their game, Jesus spoke barely above a whisper, "Father, forgive them. They do not know what they do."

αΘω

Above the head of Jesus, Pilate had fastened a notice to the cross written in three languages, Hebrew, Latin and Greek. It read:

JESUS OF NAZARETH
KING OF THE JEWS

That it was written in Hebrew, no one questioned and required no explanation. That was for the sake of the Jews. Many of them read this sign, which is exactly what Pilate wished. None would miss its meaning. All Jews would know that this is the certain end for any Jewish pretender. Rome crucifies kings. Still the priests protested to Pilate, "Do not write 'The King of the Jews.' This man was not our king. Write instead that this fool *claimed* to be king of the Jews."

"What I have written," said Pilate, "I have written." The Procurator was unmoved.

Latin was the language of the erudite, Roman aristocracy. The message to them was "Take comfort in what you witness on this cross. You have nothing to fear from this rabble. We have the power to destroy their kings and any miscreants' ambitions to be their king. This is the certain end for all the enemies of Rome."

Greek, once the language of nobility, now the language of commerce. The most ignoble of speech. Its message was "Here hangs the consummation of all who oppose Rome. Lift your eyes in some groundless notion of dignity, and nothing awaits you but crucifixion, hence to be conveyed to the valley of Gehenna with the garbage of Jerusalem."

X

Wrath Exhausted

"You who were going to destroy the Temple and build it in three days, save yourself! Come down from the cross if you really are the Son of God!" It would be a mercy that the insults went unheard, but Jesus heard them. To him, they were like spear points brilliant with white heat. He had given the best he had to these people. He had healed their sick, comforted and encouraged, and raised their dead. How often would he have gathered them to himself. How much he had loved them. Words are not supposed to hurt, but they do.

Asher and the most prominent priests, the legalists and the elders of the faith he loved, mocked him. "He saved others," they laughed, "but he can't save himself! Now observe this presumptuous king of Israel! Let him come down from the cross, and we will believe in him. He trusts in God. Let God rescue him if he wants him. He said, 'I am the Son of God.' Then let the 'Son of God' heal his own wounds. Let him blunt the thorns. Let him rip out the nails. Look at what mere men do to the almighty Son of God!"

The four Roman soldiers also mocked him. Leaning a ladder against the cross, one of them climbed up to offer him a flask of soured wine. "So! king of the Jews, save yourself!" Soured wine! Good for nothing but a corpse. His companions thought this hilarious.

One of the criminals also being crucified hurled insults at him. "You claim you are the Christ? Then save yourself and us!"

The insults were withering. Remarkably, relief came from an unexpected source. The other criminal shot back, "Have you no fear of God, man? Look at you! You also are condemned! You and I suffer the consequence of our deeds. But this man is innocent. He has done nothing wrong." Turning his head to Jesus, he pleaded, "Lord, remember me when you come into your kingdom." The sight of these three nailed to their respective crosses was macabre and grotesque. Jesus, in the middle of the other two, was the only one whose body was beat up, bruised and streaked with blood. Their bodies heaved each breath in staggered cadence, their rib cages surging beneath clammy skin. Pushing their bodies against horribly secured feet, allowed them to breathe and as they grew weaker and weaker, each breath became shorter and shorter, until breath eluded them—until they could not breathe at all. Crucifixion is by far the cruelest approach and denouement of death, excruciating pain in each breath, finding relief only in the brutality of forced suffocation. As his lungs filled yet one more time, Jesus spoke, "I tell you the truth...*my friend*...today you will be with me...in paradise." Knees buckling, the weight of his body fell again against blood-saturated wood. The words emitted a hoarse whisper, but loud enough to be heard by those nearby. It was noon. He had been borne on the cross, impaled, for three hours.

αΘω

Near the cross on which Jesus writhed, pushing himself up and down to capture each breath, stood his mother. Mary could not take her eyes away from her son yet could not bear to look at him. She remembered the verdant hills of Nazareth where first she heard the angel speak to her. She recalled the sounds of his gentle sucking at her breasts. She could see his toddler legs running through the meadows and his smile as she kissed and lullabyed him to sleep. The brief thought of having lost him in Jerusalem flitted anxiously through her mind. Had she known her son would end like this, had she known what it would mean for him to leave home, had she known, would she have let him? Could she have stopped him?

When Jesus saw his mother with John standing at her side, he said to her, "Mother, look, take unto yourself a new son." He tried awkwardly to nod his head in John's direction. His body sank to its lowest extremity and then raised again as thigh and calf muscles strained upward. "John," he managed to speak again, "please take my mother as your mother, too." John put his arm around Mary and with great pain looked up at the crucified form, his Lord, his friend, and nodded assent.

For the sake of this word, Mary chose not to live with any of her children. From that moment, Mary would be an honored member of John's family. He took her into his home of wealth, comfort and prosperity where she spent the rest of her days, knowing that her beloved son wanted this for her.

αΘω

Dark, foreboding clouds blanketed the expanse above. The noon of day had turned to night. Heat lightning snapped through the billows giving rise to distant rumblings. It seemed it was going to rain, but not a drop of revitalizing liquid fell from the sky. Like an Angel of Death, darkness crept over the land shaken by an occasional thunderous streak of dancing white through the morass of black and grey. The winds lifted; debris rolled along the fields of Golgotha, urged on by invisible but powerful forces. The body of Jesus rose and fell with each strained, excruciating breath. The sun hid itself from the shame.

"Unhh!" groaned his cross.

"Unnnhh!" louder. His jaw distended, moving as though trying to form words...

"Eli!" The Name escaped his lips in whispered longing.

"Listen!" said a voice in the crowd. "I think he calls for Elijah!" A moment passed. Jesus labored each painful breath. Silence as he hung there. Flies, braving the wind, licked hungrily at his blood.

"Eli - i-i-i-i!!" The sound exploded from the depths of his nearly dead body as he screamed for the first time. He sank again upon the cross. His breath evaporating, diminishing...

"Eli...

"lama sabachthani?" It ended on a soft, whimpering upnote. Confused. Pleading.

"My God, my God, why have you forsaken me?" The meaning was unmistakable. Could it be? Could God the Father actually turn away from God the Son? That his Son thought so is clear. Could not even the eyes of omnipotent, unmitigated love behold such agony? Such shame? Or did this selfsame agony so derange the thoughts of Jesus that he merely felt forsaken? How does one fathom such terrible rage? For rage it was. I came to understand. I came to know, far later than I should have, that eternal Holiness was exhausting its wrath, exhausting all of the pent-up fury, taking violent vengeance against evil in the miserable souls of humankind. There was Jesus, the solitary focus of the wrath of God, exhausting it, draining it of force, emptying it of meaning, sucking it of relevance. Only God could exhaust the infinite wrath of God, and on that day of morbid darkness it happened.

The terrible wrath of God...exhausted!

XI

It Is Finished!

Six hours, moment by excruciating moment, droned through the day. It was not a particularly long time as crucifixions go, but for the heart longing for it to be over, for whom each second seemed to be an hour—like slogging through muck, it was agony unsurpassed. Resignation to death crept into the face of the Son of God. His bruised, sunken eyes focusing, turning to one of the soldiers he said, "Please, I am thirsty." The touch of cool water on his parched lips would have been wondrous rescue. A sip of such crystal liquid would have comforted his dry tongue, and however small, assuaged his pain. Instead, the heartless Roman soaked a stalk of hyssop in a jar of bitter, vinegared wine and lifted it to Jesus' lips.

"Now, you miserable bastard," his laugh dripping with sarcasm, "where is your Jew prophet? Where is your Elijah? Let him come now and pluck you from the cross!"

Jesus received this bitter drink. The foul-tasting liquid had an effect the soldier had not thought about—it numbed the edge of pain ever how slightly. Enough to clear a throat turned to sand, enabling Jesus to say clearly and loudly, *"It…is…finished!"*

Darkness. But for the soft whistle of wind around the crosses, silence. Not so much as a whisper. All who witnessed this terrible scene heard it. His voice, like a clap of thunder, echoed across the valley, penetrating the hearts of both the faithful and the curious, reaching through the corridors of eternity, into the very Soul of Almighty God. His head fell to his breast in final whisper meant for only One, *"Father,"* he spoke, *"I give my spirit into your hands."* His body emptied itself of its final breath, and his spirit was gone. Jesus of Nazareth, the King of the Jews, was dead.

Mary choked back her agonized scream with eyes of desperate horror.

> *"Do not think that I have come to abolish the Law. I came, instead, to fulfill it."*

αΘω

Beyond the lowering clouds, beyond the moon and sun, beyond the stars our eyes could see and beyond the stars we could not see. Beyond them. Far, far, unimaginably far beyond them. If one were to take flight from earth and rise higher and higher, earth would recede as if it were sucked away from our vision. It would shrink to a mere point of light and then disappear altogether. Turning around we see more points of light now streaking across the blackness as we step across the barriers of time, until we reach the edge, the last cluster on the perimeter of the creation, the last star, the last source of luminosity in the blackness beyond. Finally we reach the most distant orb in the heavens, the end of infinity, the extremity of all created: the last stop before we move into the abyss or whatever it is, beyond. Here we pause as we listen, in absolute cold, to silence. From the silence comes a faint awareness of weeping. Somewhere in the black is a Light we cannot see. It is a Place. An Abode. A Home from which comes this awareness of terrible brokenness. Then, at once, a shattering scream, heard not in the vacant cosmos, but in the heart.

An infinite distance away on tiny earth, great granite boulders split as if they were dried bread. The ground beneath those that stood by, the watchers, shook uncontrollably as if in spasm. The cross moved, the dead mass of tissue and bone swaying like a sack of salt. The great curtain hanging in Herod's Temple, seamless and thick, violently rent from top to bottom. There was nothing now to guard the place called the Holy of Holies. The altar, the candlesticks, all laid bare in unholy disarray. In cemeteries round about Jerusalem, great stones rolled away from the doors of sepulchres. Bodies of loved ones, and some not so loved, humans long dead, appeared in their entrances as if fresh from the finger of God. There arose an outcry of great fear. In all of human history, in all of the writings, in all of the stories passed down from ancestor to ancestor, there had never been anything like this...***Wednesday, 14 Nisan,*** a day conceived in blackness, yet brought forth in the light of holiness.

Urbanus, *Centurion to Caesar,* and onetime friend to the family Joseph, sat astride his stallion and stared. For the first time in his life he was afraid. His men, those who had crucified Jesus, who had driven the nails through his hands and feet, who had laughed and mocked and taunted, those who had gambled for his clothing, now fell to their knees. Afraid of what, he knew not. He was not a believer in the Jew God nor any of those manufactured by the Roman government he served. His eyes traversed the happenings around him, his mount shying from the trembling earth. The horse reared, pawing the air, but Urbanus was not unhorsed. His eyes once again came to focus on the dead form of the man he had once thought to befriend. He felt the hair on his neck rise and his body chill. He trembled. He remembered the argument in his father's home. He remembered, *"By Caesar, go against me and I'll witness for myself the day of your death!"* And he remembered Eh-Ret, the Nubian slave. *What had he said?* The words slammed into him like bolts of lightning, *"You will kill, my little friend. In your time. In your place."* Ubanus had, at last, killed his lion—the *Lion of the Tribe of Judah!* Oh, my Lord God! *Oh, my Lord, my friend Jesus, my God! Forgive me. You are righteous beyond my empty ability to conceive. Surely...surely, you were, you are the Son of God!* Hot tears welled in his eyes, coursed down his face and into his lips. He tasted their salt.

αΘω

What is my worth to God? Your worth, dear reader? We are all so pious and glib in saying, "I am not worthy of the least of his favor." Perhaps God, himself, sees it differently.

Now, these many years after this terrible event, my heart is at peace. What am I worth to God the Father? First, it should be said that as humankind knows and perceives, no man or woman alive or dead is worthy to stand before the Son of Man, both now, in ancient times, or forevermore.

What, then, is the measure of my worth to God? Why am I not cast off and laid among the excrement of human evil? There exists one stark and solitary instrument of measure that provides the answer: *those beams of wood on which my Jesus died.*

I'll never erase from my mind the image of my Lord racked with pain, willingly submitting himself to agonizing torture, and finally death, as he did...for me and for you. I cannot recall those hours without remembering the horrible unworthiness that I felt. But God did not mean it so. When I look back upon the cross and the great cost it represents to the Father, I know my worth. It is wholly beyond the comprehension of men that God would allow something like that for no value in return. His value is me. His value is you. Whenever you question your value to God, may I beg you to see again the cross and that horribly agonized form on it. In that form, I present to you the price, the value of your worth to God!

XII

Thursday, 15 Nisan
Sunset

Jesus died on the Day of Preparation, Wednesday, a day that the Jews prepared for Passover, which was a special "Shabbat." The next day, commencing at the twelfth hour, was Thursday, 15 Nisan.

Because the Jews did not want the bodies left on the crosses during Passover, they asked Pilate to have the legs of all three criminals broken and the bodies taken down. The soldiers, therefore, came and with a large, iron club called a *crurifragium* shattered the legs of the first man who had been crucified with Jesus and then those of the other. The intense, brain dissolving pain this caused quickly disposed of their awkward means of breathing by pushing up on their legs; the two men expired in minutes. But when they came to Jesus, they found him already dead.

"This one's already gone," spoke one of the men.

"Yeah, maybe," said another, "but just to make certain..." he pointed his spear toward the ribs and thrust. There was no spurting of body fluid, for the heart had stopped beating. Still, the pressure within the body had not yet drained and blood spilled down his side. To the surprise of these military men, it was followed by and mixed with a clear liquid: A red stream within a clear stream. It wasn't an enormous amount, but it was enough. This was not how it should be. Jesus should have been alive to endure another several days of suffering. Crucifixion was not a quick, merciful death. The soldiers of Rome were shaken.

The scriptures had predicted this. *Not one of his bones will be broken,"* and as another Scripture says, *"They will look on the one they have pierced."* Human eyes had witnessed this event, as it was foretold by David and the prophets, detail by magnificent detail.

αΘω

Pilate sat poring over administrative documents. They had been sent from Rome by the Senate, something to do with how Judea was divided. There were instructions…his mind wandered, confused and opaque. The events of the day wore on his soul, boring in, refusing to go away. He could not concentrate. He regretted allowing the Jews to crucify the prophet. Perhaps Claudia's silly dreams had some merit. It was useless to wail about it now. *He would be dead by now. Yes. He would be dead.* He did not notice the servant who had appeared at the table. When he did, he was awakened out of his stupor.

"Eminent Procurator, there is a wealthy Jew, sir, a member of the Sanhedrin, I think, to see you."

"Another Jew?" said Pilate wearily.

"Yes, lord Procurator, he comes with a request."

"Oh," said Pilate diminutively. Emotionally exhausted, the airs of rank had evaporated. His brain, still filled with cobweb, allowed him to speak with resignation, "Very well, send him in."

The Jew was dressed in expensive robes. There were jeweled rings on his fingers. His demeanor was reserved, deferential, utterly lacking in the pretense that Pilate so despised.

"My name is Joseph, eminent Governor. Joseph of the city of Arimathea."

Pilate did not even look at him. "Yes," he sighed, "Joseph of Arimathea, what do you want of me?"

"I wish to claim the body of Jesus of Nazareth. I wish your permission to remove it from the cross and inter it in my own personal tomb."

"You what?" said Pilate, his senses alerted. "You are among those demanded the crucifixion of this innocent man and now you wish to run off with his body? In the name of all the gods, man, why would you do such a thing? Isn't his execution enough for you bloodthirsty swine?!"

"I do not wish to run off with it, Governor. I wish to dress it with appropriate spices and balm. I wish to bury it in my own personal sepulchre. I will roll a stone over the entrance and seal it with my own personal seal," spoke Joseph calmly. It was clear that he was not intimidated by Pilate. Nor was he arrogant. "And I am not one who screamed for his death, nor did I make a show of washing my hands for the responsibility of it." He said this not in rancor, but Pilate understood the implications. "I wish you no ill, my Governor. I wish only his poor body, to give it a decent burial."

Pilate had stood in rising annoyance. Now he again took his seat, bewildered. He started to speak but then stopped. He closed his mouth, turned his face away from Joseph of Arimathea to disguise the hot tears welling in his eyes, composed himself and said, "Then take the body of Jesus, Joseph of Arimathea. Take it and dress it with myrrh and aloe, and for a shroud...take this." He removed from his shoulders the white, Roman toga which he wore, leaving himself only with his undergarment. "If, indeed, he has returned to his kingdom, perhaps this garment will keep him warm. And by it, remember the evil that I have done."

Joseph, surprised, was helpless to refuse. Nor did he wish to refuse. In this simple way, this hardened man was reaching for the one Man who could save him from himself. He took it gladly. "He shall wear it this night," spoke this wealthy Jew from the city of Arimathea. He turned and left the Roman to his own private ache.

Joseph hurried into the twilight of the evening. Quickly, he strode down the streets of Jerusalem clinging to Pilate's tunic, up a dark alley, through an intersection and down another street, turning right and then left until he reached a familiar avenue. At the third door he stopped and knocked urgently. The passing of a moment seemed to Joseph the passing of an eternity. Just as he began to knock again, the door opened. A woman past her time of bearing children stood before him questioning. "I must speak to Nicodemus," said the man, "please, quickly!" She led him through a room and then another to where the "teacher of Israel" sat absorbed in the pages of the Torah, one of several copies guarded by the Sanhedrin.

"Who is it, Minah?" he inquired, so absorbed was he that he did not realize that Joseph was standing near him.

"It is Joseph, my husband. It seems the least you could do is acknowledge his presence. He is agitated, I think." Nicodemus looked up at last to see his friend standing with an excited, apprehensive look on his face.

"I have seen the Governor, Nicodemus. He is allowing me to claim the body of our Lord. See, he gave me his tunic in which to clothe the body in its death."

"He did what?" responded his startled friend.

"He is allowing..."

"I heard! But Pilate *gave you* his tunic?" Nicodemus could not believe what his ears had heard. "Then we must hurry, before he changes his mind, or before our Sanhedrin colleagues hear about this."

"We will need assistance. Bring two of your servant men. I will send for two of mine as well..."

Nicodemus turned to his wife who was still in the room and had overheard all that transpired. "Minah, inform his mother, Mary, and her friends. I think you will find her in the home of John. And hurry; they will want to be present as we do this."

αΘω

Nicodemus instructed his servants to bring the customary mixture of myrrh and aloe, about seventy-two pounds of it, to prepare the body for burial. Slipping a rod between the handles of the jar containing the mixture, they each took an end, and being strong men, they were able to carry it without difficulty. Joseph of Arimathea, Nicodemus and their entourage of servants made their way out of the city and out to Golgotha, carrying the spices intended for use in burial. When they reached the crosses, they had to present their credentials from the Procurator before the soldiers would let them near the executed prisoners.

They went to work extracting the wooden beam from the earth and laying the cruel instrument of crucifixion flat so they could remove the body. There was no breath; there was no movement except where gravity chose to jerk its weight against the nails in hands and feet. It was a corpse, the mangled, agonized, twisted remains of the man who had claimed to be the Son of God. To see him dead, to see him in this way, churned the waves of nausea, disillusionment and bitterness in those who trusted in him.

Removing the nails required banging them from side to side to loosen their grip in the wood. Once loosened, the servants gripped them with a pair of tongs and pulled. At length they had extracted these ugly things from his hands, wrists and feet. Lifting the body of Jesus from the cross to a hastily assembled bier, they removed the thorns, trying unsuccessfully to avoid being soiled by the blood. *Soiled by the blood of Jesus?* The servants wiped the sticky liquid from their hands onto their clothing. Once the body was ready for transport, they made their way to Joseph's garden and to the new tomb.

Lying upon the earth, they left behind a wooden cross, scarred with nail holes and soaked in blood, an ugly specter of execution and death. Yet this structure, this form, would become a sacred image, stamping its visage on the collective human conscience like no other. When men and women beheld this holy shape, they would instantly know that the world had been changed because of an obscure, peasant Carpenter. They would know that, with the world, their own heart could be changed and delivered into life eternal. Thus an instrument of death became a symbol of life—eternal life.

They were soon joined by Mary Magdalene and Mary the mother of Jesus, who observed where these two members of the Jewish Sanhedrin had placed the body of Jesus. Then they went home and prepared additional spices and perfumes to bring later.

αΘω

The next day Asher, the chief priests and the Pharisees went, as a delegation, to Pilate. "Sir," they said, "we remember that while he was still alive this deceiver said, 'After three days I will rise again.'" Their response to the work of Nicodemus and Joseph of Arimathea was mixed. Some saw it as an act of solidarity with the priests' cause. Some saw it as the Jewish thing to do since bodies should not be left hanging on a cross through the Sabbath, yet others were suspicious of the two men, concluding rightly that they were sympathizers to the cause of Jesus. So they said to Pilate, "Give the order for the tomb to be made secure until the third day. Otherwise, his disciples may come and steal the body and tell the people that he has been raised from the dead. Hence, his last deception will be worse than the first."

Pilate stared at these religious sycophants, despising them and, his mind twisted in a perverted way, fearing them as well. He let them await his answer for several moments. Then he said, "Very well. Make the tomb as secure as you know how." So they went and put the Roman seal on the stone and gave orders from Pilate to the centurion, who posted a guard.

XIII

Sunday Morning

Early on the first day of the week, while it was still dark, Mary Magdalene, Mary the mother of James, and Salome, a friend of the two Mary's, went to the tomb. This was not the same Salome that danced before Herod Antipas. This woman, along with the others, had been a follower of Jesus. The previous day they had purchased spices for the purpose of anointing Jesus' body. They either did not know or had forgotten that the tomb had been sealed by the chief priests. When at length they realized this, they conferred together wondering how they would gain entrance to the tomb. Soldier guards stood by, amused at their quandary. The stone covering the door of the tomb was large and had clearly been cemented to the walls with mortar and bore the seal Joseph of Arimathea and the seal of Rome, for it had been sealed under Pilate's authority. Hence, a double seal, as insurance against molestation, or possible theft of the body, given Jesus' celebrity, and the zealous deception of his disciples.

As they stood debating what to do, the ground suddenly began to tremble beneath their feet, no doubt continuing aftershocks of the quakes of the previous three days. It shook violently for what seemed like an eternity. Buildings in Jerusalem fell, and panic seized the city as people ran about seeking protection from falling debris. The mortar and seal affixing the stone to the tomb cracked and fell away. Abruptly, a large, powerfully built man appeared. His size was accentuated by the raiment he wore. It shimmered in iridescence. His eyes penetrated the depths of the hearts of the three women. They were deeply frightened and clung to one another. The man said, while the earth was still shaking, *"Do not be afraid."* He spoke in a language they did not know yet understood. He moved toward the stone which yet stood against the opening of the tomb. With one arm he rolled the gigantic boulder aside as if it were vapor. As he did so, small wavelets of lightning crackled around the stone and through the surrounding air. He mounted the stone and sat upon it. The guards standing by were helpless and trembling, frozen in fear. Dust at the feet of the guard in command puffed into little clouds, and small puddles formed as a stream of fluid fell from his loins. It was no surprise that they were stiff and unmoving. The intimidating man who sat on the stone dressed in raiment as brilliant and white as snow was an angel of God.

He again spoke gently to the women, *"Do not be afraid. I know that you are looking for Jesus, who was crucified and buried in this place. He is not here. He has risen, just as he said he would."* Despite his gentle manner, the women were terribly frightened and, of course, skeptical. He seemed to understand both their apprehension and their reticence to believe him. *"Come,"* he invited. *"Step into the tomb and see the place where he lay."* When they entered, the body of Jesus was not in evidence!

Inside, there appeared yet another angel. This one was a young man dressed in a white robe. He sat on the right side of the crypt where Jesus had been laid. Once again the women were upset. *"Don't be alarmed,"* he said. *"As you can see, Jesus is not here. He has risen!"*

The women were stunned. As they wondered about all of this, yet two more men in dazzling clothes stood beside them. Four angelic creatures! All dressed in wondrous, dazzling raiment. They could take no more. Their fear drove them to their knees, and they bowed themselves to the ground, overcome by the presence of such holy creatures. Once again the men spoke gently to them, *"Why do you look for the living among the dead? Jesus is not here. He has risen! He told you this would happen while he was still with you in Galilee. Do you not recall his words, 'The Son of Man must be delivered into the hands of evil men, be crucified and on the third day be raised again?'"* As they continued to bow down their faces in the damp earth, the blazing light around them began to fade, at length leaving them in darkness within the empty tomb. Mary (the mother of James) looked up. Slowly the heads of her two companions rose. They were still trembling and bewildered. Once they realized the angels had gone, excitedly, they fled the tomb.

αΘω

As the women disappeared in the distance, the guards recovered from their fright. They ran into the city, stumbling over each other, and blurted out in confusion to the priests the events they had just witnessed. The priests met with the elders and devised a scheme. They would pay each of the soldiers a year's wages in gold with the proviso that they were to say only what they instructed them to say. "You are to say, 'His followers came during the night and stole him away while we were asleep.' If Pilate hears of this, we will satisfy him and keep you out of trouble."

"Are you certain you do not exaggerate your influence with the Procurator?" one of the soldiers spoke without thinking.

"Fool! Your impertinence will find you in serious trouble if you speak another word! Why do you think this man was crucified? Pilate wanted to let him go, but we prevailed." Asher was incensed. They were paying these dumb brutes for a simple deception. How could they question his authority? "He will listen to us. He knows we control the people. Besides," he continued, "do you think he cares a fig for this self-proclaimed prophet? Go now, do as you have been paid. You underestimate us at your own peril."

The priest was convincing. They took the money and did as they were instructed. The deception worked. The story circulated widely that Jesus' followers somehow broke the seal, removed the stone and whisked away the body of their dead leader.

αΘω

Mary Magdalene and her two companions found Simon Peter, John and the mother of Jesus at the home of Lazarus, less than an hour's walk from the tomb. "They have taken the Lord out of the tomb, and we don't know where they have put him!" This is an amazing episode, is it not? Only moments ago, these very same women were in the presence of no less than four angels sent from God, yet they were still convinced that someone had stolen the body of Jesus. Peter and John, of course, knew nothing of their encounter with the angels. The three women somehow neglected to speak of it, at least right away. Their main concern was the missing body of Jesus.

We knew that no one had stolen the body. That was absurd. Jesus' words rang in our numb minds. Could it be possible that he really had risen from the dead as he had said he would?

The two men were immediately on their feet. "We have to see this for ourselves." As the men started for the tomb, it was Peter who could answer this question best. He knew the answer—but that story in a moment. Both men were caught up in the excitement and began to run. John, being younger, outran Peter, for whom this was somewhat anticlimactic, and reached the garden first. He stood outside the open cavity, stooped and looked in at the strips of linen lying there but did not go in.

Then Peter arrived. Peter was not the kind to be cautious. Besides, he knew what to expect while John didn't. He entered the tomb without hesitation. There he saw the strips of linen used to wrap the body of Jesus folded neatly at one end of the crypt. These were the same type of strips used to embalm Lazarus. The shroud provided by Pilate was folded up by itself, separate from the wrappings. Emboldened by Peter's entrance, John also went inside. He saw, and any doubt he may have had was erased.

αΘω

The word of Jesus' disappearance spread rapidly and soon the other disciples arrived at the tomb along with several of the other women. Each one examined the empty tomb carefully, amazed at what they both found and did not find. They stood speaking with each other talking about how it actually had happened as Jesus had predicted.

"But if he is not here, where is he?"

"He said he had to return to the Father."

"But where is that?"

"Heaven?"

"Will we not see him again?"

After a while, the men began to drift away and go back to their homes. There wasn't much left to see. Clearly, Jesus was not here. They were more than a little confused, not knowing whether to wait or begin to make attempts to restart their lives. But Mary Magdalene and the other women were not so quick to leave. They stood outside the tomb talking and weeping. As Mary wept, she looked again into the tomb and was taken aback to again see two men in white, seated where Jesus' body had been, one at the head and the other at the foot. They were not dressed as the angels she had seen earlier; they appeared to be ordinary men. As she looked at them, she was puzzled. Had she seen these men before? She thought not. One of them asked her, "Dear woman, why are you crying?"

She did not realize that they, too, were angels. "They have taken my Lord away," she said, "and I don't know where they have put him." As she said this, she turned and saw a man standing near her. She did not recognize him either.

"My sister," he said softly, "why are you crying? Who is it you are looking for?" The words seemed so normal. The question so routinely logical. In her grief, she simply could not discern that there was something unexpected happening.

She supposed the man to be Joseph of Arimathea's gardener. "Sir," she inquired through her tears, "did you carry him away? If so, please tell us where you have put him, and we will go get him and bring him back. He should be here where those of us who loved him can come and worship." By this time, the other women also saw the man but did not recognize him either.

Then the man simply said her name, "Mary." He had a bemused grin on his face, and his eyes danced in the morning light.

She had heard her name spoken like this from only one person. It was as though her name had been caressed. Instantly she knew. She lifted her eyes to see joy in the eyes of Jesus. "My Lord!" she cried in the shock of joyous surprise.

"Lord!" cried Salome, and the others. They came to him, fell to their knees, clasped his feet as if to restrain him from leaving them, and there, they worshiped him.

Jesus put his hands on their heads and wiped joyful tears from their eyes with his fingers and said, "Don't be afraid; I am not a spirit. I am here, but do not hold on to me, for I have not yet returned to the Father. Go and tell my brothers, 'I am going back to my Father and your Father, to my God and your God.' Tell them to go to Galilee. There they will see me."

Galilee? That was a week's journey from this place. And then, Jesus was gone—released into thin air as though he were a fleeting hallucination. But he wasn't! The women had actually touched him and held on to his feet. You cannot touch or hold onto an apparition.

Excited and exhilarated, the women went to his disciples (he had called them brothers) with the news, "We have seen the Lord!"

XIV

Seen of Cephas

Yes, dear woman, he is alive. Before you, before any in this room, before anyone at all, I have seen him. I have engaged him, or better, he has engaged me!" Peter reclined at the end of the table and did not even rise at Mary's appearance with her marvelous announcement. He was at peace, and his heart glowed warmly at his thoughts.

After the trial, he had not known what to do with himself or where to go. He longed for the shores of Galilee and the familiar smells of fish and nets. He longed for the sound of sail and the sting of wind-driven water in his face, but Jerusalem had none of these things. *"Anything, anyplace I can be alone with my terrible deed,"* his great heart crushed with self-loathing.

Some would say that it was chance that brought Peter to this place of shame and disgrace. But as he thought of it later, Peter was certain that his seeming random footsteps had been guided by the Spirit himself. In any case, Peter found himself staring at the gruesome form of Judas. Judas stared back with glazed, lifeless eyes, his body still swaying gently. Peter, speechless, could not remove his gaze from those eyes and in his stupor saw not the face of Judas but his own.

He stood there for several moments, feeling uncertain. Then, like his friend before him, he climbed the tree and edged out on the limb where the rope was tied. Unsheathing his sword, he swung its edge at the rope. But as he swung the blade, it almost slipped from his grip and he accidently gouged the body of Judas. Peter was not good with a sword, as his experience in Gethsemane and here confirmed. The second swing, however, severed the rope. Taut with the weight of the body, the tree limb swayed upward as the carcass fell and struck the earth in such a way that the stomach wall, weakened by Peter's mishap, opened its contents to the ground.

To a Jew, touching a dead body was to defile one's self, but Peter could feel no more defiled than he was already. He sensed a certain kinship with Judas, a certain vicarious identification with the body of the betrayer. He handled it gently, reverently.

The hills of Judea and around Jerusalem did not want for caves. It was to one of these that Peter carried the body of Judas. He had no spices, no grave clothes. Having labored under the weight of the body through the rocks and hills, he laid Judas on the floor of the cave, and sat down exhausted. Through the awful hours of the crucifixion, while his Lord hung suspended between the dark clouds and the blood soaked earth, Peter sat weeping and whimpering by the disemboweled body of Judas in the cave. Darkness had descended on the hills. Darkness in the cave. Darkness in his heart. His chest began to heave great gulps of the dank air. The pounding of the earthquakes, the dirt and dust falling from the ceiling of the earthen cave were matched by the pounding in his heart and in his head. *"Fall on me!"* a blunted, visceral utterance from somewhere deep within him. It rose like vomit through his intestines and stomach until it erupted again in a violent, throat shredding scream, *"Fall on me!"* and again, *"Fall on me!"* Again and again it erupted from his insides. Racking sobs came. The walls of the small cave echoed lurid, hideous wails of the insane. Two days passed.

αΘω

Peter awoke to the putrid smell of death. Outside, the sky had begun to pale in predawn emptiness. His eyes, accustomed to the darkness, could barely make out the form of Judas decaying in the loose dirt on the floor of the cave. Something scurried at Peter's movement. Somehow a logical thought entered his mind, *"I must find stones for the entrance."* As he tried to stand, he struck his head smartly against the cave's ceiling. "Damn!" he cried. And then he thought, *"Cursing comes too easily these days."*

"You've been doing that your entire life."

At first he thought he had imagined it. "What?" he answered, absently.

There was mirth in what he heard, "Bumping your head against things, never taking into account your own pig-headedness. Trying to walk on water, trying to get me not to do things, the thing with the foot washing, and then cutting that man's ear with your sword, the denials; shall I go on?" Despite the harshness of the words, the old fisherman felt a smile beneath them. Of course, Peter recognized the voice the instant he heard it. His stupefied response had to do with his inability to comprehend the reality of it. He was overjoyed and terrified at the same time. He wanted to fall on his knees and worship but the casual, matter-of-fact manner seemed so comforting, so inviting. Here? In this dark hole? With the body of Judas rotting at his feet? He felt elated…and ashamed. He felt utterly destroyed yet triumphant, immeasurably triumphant!

"Lord, I..." he began, thinking of something, anything, he could say. There were no flashes of lightning. There was no shining glory. Peter could only see a form in the gloom. But the love he felt, the compassion. "Lord..." His knees began to buckle.

"Simon! Son of Jonas, stand on your own two feet!" Simon stood, nailed to his footprints. Jesus came to him, paused within arm's reach, yet another step and took the broken old fisherman into his arms.

Peter never told the whole story, other than reluctantly revealing to a few of us that he had seen the Lord. I suppose he thought none of us would believe him. As to the rest of the details, some have alluded to them, no one has ever spelled them out until now.[6] I am not sure it all happened just like this. Perhaps I dreamed it. Perhaps I didn't.

---

6 Cp. 1 Corinthians 15:5 with Luke 24:34. See also Brown, Plummer and Briggs, *International Critical Commentary* series on 1 Corinthians 15.5, 1911. p.335

XV

Emmaus Road

Sundown, in only a few hours, would mark the end of Sabbath and the end of Passover with all its frolic and celebration. This Passover, however, had been mixed with other excitement, other events. This would be a Passover to remember.

About seven miles from Jerusalem, two of my closest friends, Jonas ben Abram and Cleopas ben Elkanah, were on their way to the village of Emmaus. As they later related the story, they had been discussing everything that had happened. Since they were unhurried, they often stopped beneath the shade of a roadside tree. It was here that they noticed another traveler sitting on a wayside bench, his hands on his knees. They did not recognize the man but exchanged pleasantries just as travelers often do.

Then the stranger remarked, "I could not help but notice that you men are quite preoccupied with something. Judging from the intensity of your conversation, I assume you were speaking of some newsworthy event. May I ask what it is?"

"Are you a visitor to Jerusalem?" asked Cleopas. "Are you not aware of the things that have happened here these past few days?"

"What things?"

"The things concerning Jesus of Nazareth." Suddenly, both men were full of words, each interrupting the other to tell the story.

It was Jonas' turn, "He was a prophet, powerful in word and deed."

"A prophet before God…" Cleopas.

"Everyone loved him…" Jonas.

"The priests and our rulers killed him…" Cleopas.

"Crucified him…" Almost in unison.

"We were all hoping that he was the one who was going to redeem Israel. We were hoping that he was the Messiah." This was said with anguish and disappointment. Both men became pensive and their animation diminished.

"It all happened this last week—just as Passover was beginning. Some of our women told us an incredible story. They went to the tomb early this morning, but his body was gone. They came and told us that they had seen a vision of angels."

"...who said he was alive."

"Then some of our companions went to the tomb and found it just as the women had said."

"He was not there."

"Gentlemen, gentlemen...please, wait a moment. You go so fast my head reels. Think for a moment of what you are saying. Don't you think it a bit foolish not to believe the prophets? Do they not tell us plainly that the Christ must suffer these things and then enter his glory?" And beginning with Moses and all the Prophets, the stranger explained to them what was said in the Scriptures concerning Jesus of Nazareth. They were amazed. A perfect stranger...a rabbi? How came he to know these things? He does not speak as the rabbis speak. A prophet?

As they approached the village to which they were going, the traveler said, "Well, I guess this is where we part. Good day, gentlemen; it has been pleasant speaking with you."

"Wait, esteemed Sir," urged Jonas, "Stay with us. It is nearly evening; the day is almost over. We very much would like to hear more." They spoke with such sincere intensity that he went in to stay with them. As they sat down to dinner, the stranger took bread, gave thanks, tore pieces of it from the loaf and gave it to them.

At that moment they recognized him, and at the moment they recognized him, he disappeared from their sight. Vanished before their very eyes! When they caught their breath and recovered, Cleopas whispered to Jonas, "Didn't your heart burn within you while he spoke to us on the road? When he spoke of the Scriptures, did it not seem that the words themselves had come alive?"

They quickly paid for their supper and without finishing their food or making arrangements for lodging, they returned to Jerusalem where they found ten of those whom Jesus had named apostles (Thomas was not there) and the rest of us assembled in a large room. We could see that these men had urgent news. We locked the door. Then they told us of what happened. When they had finished, James said, "It is true, then! The Lord has risen!" he looked at Simon Peter, "and Simon says that he has seen already. He speaks the truth." Peter said nothing. *Of course, I spoke the truth!*

Exactly how it came to be that Jesus appeared to these men, chatted, interacted and dined with them without their recognizing who he was is a deep mystery to me. Is he now able to appear to us in unrecognizable form? Both of these men had been with Jesus, had been able to easily recognize him prior to his arrest and crucifixion. Did he somehow confuse their perception so that they could not know who he was? It is possible that any of us may meet Jesus anywhere, anytime, and not know that we have done so? It is a mystery I cannot fathom.

XVI

I Am Real Enough!

While we considered the validity of the testimony we'd just heard, suddenly Jesus himself was standing among us. The door was locked. We were all in fear of being discovered by the Jewish legalists. He did not come through the door! How did he get in? To say that we were startled and frightened could not begin to explain our shock.

"Be at peace, my brothers. You fret entirely too much," he chided gently. "Please, do not be troubled and do not doubt; it really is me." We knew it was him. We all knew. There was no question, yet it seemed so utterly preposterous. "Look at my hands and my feet," he continued. "Go ahead, touch me and see. See that I am not a spirit—a spirit does not have flesh and bones, as you see I have." *Why did he not say 'flesh and blood?'* He showed us his hands and feet. The scars were there but had healed completely. His body was gloriously healthy, not a trace of the smell of death or, God forbid, decay. He was as alive and well as a new-born babe.

And then he said something amazing, "I really am hungry. Did you men bring anything to eat?" Stop! Only three days before, Joseph and Nicodemus had removed him—dead—from the cross. They had dressed him with spices and laid him in the grave. They had sealed the great stone on the entrance to the grave, and now he stood here in our presence asking for food? Human food?" *One would have thought that if he ate at all, he would eat something like whatever they eat in heaven.* Bartholomew handed him some grapes. He ate them as if none of the foregoing had happened. He swallowed. He even smacked his lips. "Wonderful grapes!" he declared, "sweet and juicy." We all stared at him as he swallowed. Amazing! "Come, my brothers," he said. "It is all right. I am real enough and I am among you again. I can enjoy good food, good wine, good conversation. Things are not so different on this side of life as you might imagine." Almost together we took a deep breath and began to calm.

When the chatter of excitement and the charged atmosphere began to abate, the Lord looked as though he wished to tell us something. We all intuitively understood and remained quiet, waiting. "The Father sent me," he said, "so now I am sending you. Elisha took upon himself the mantle of Elijah, so now you must take my mantle upon you. I am depending on you to continue what I have started." He smiled. We felt his trust. We knew we would do what he asked. I think he knew it, too. "The Holy Spirit shall be in you," he said finally, "and those who respond to the Spirit will be forgiven." He paused while we waited expectantly for him to continue. And then suddenly he was gone, leaving our expectations truncated and leaving us to bathe in a moment of wonder and awe.

αΘω

Before we departed to our separate purposes, we decided to meet again in this same room a week later. Our mandate was clear. We would organize and make plans to do exactly what our Lord had asked of us. This time we were joined by Thomas, who was not with us when Jesus first appeared to us. Thomas remained unconvinced. When we told him that the Lord had appeared to us, he responded with, "Unless I can see the nail marks…no, unless I can put my finger on the spot where the nails were driven into his hands…unless I can touch the wound in his side, I cannot believe he has come back. I cannot believe he is alive!"

So when we met again, Jesus came and stood among us just as he had done before. The doors were locked, just as before. No one could enter the door unless it were broken down, or opened by one of us. But Jesus didn't "enter"; he just appeared. He just materialized among us, as if easily, effortlessly moving from one dimension to another. He greeted us with the same words, "Be at peace, my brothers!" Here he was again, and we were just as overcome with his presence and excited as we had been the week before. Thomas sat alone and afraid, his eyes wide with apprehension. He didn't know what to do or how to react. Jesus walked over to where he sat. "Thomas," he beckoned gently, "come. Touch me, my friend. Put your finger here. See the wounds in my hands? It is good, my brother. Reach out your hand and touch the wound in my side." Thomas was hesitant, afraid. "Come, dear friend, and do not hold back. Do not be afraid to believe." Thomas started to reach out his hand and then stopped. He fell to his knees, tears flowing from his eyes. From his lips came these whispered words, "My Lord and my God!"

Then Jesus told him, "You have seen me, Thomas, and you have believed. But there are those who now live and those yet to come who will never see me, yet they believe. I say this not to shame you but to encourage them."

αΘω

Once we reached Galilee, not unexpectedly, Peter wanted to resume his fishing trade. He persuaded Thomas, Nathanael (both non-fishermen), James, John, and two others to join him. Some of the others, including myself, decided to tag along. The moonless sky was brilliant with stars. Lights from nearby Capharnaum glowed softly. So we went out and got into the boat and spent the night dragging the nets. Bone weary and sweat-soaked, for all of our labor, we had caught nothing.

By morning we lay about the deck and against the gunnels, exhausted. We were anchored only about a hundred yards from shore, sail reefed, boat floating in the smooth glass of becalmed water. I noticed a man standing there watching us. He hailed us with the words, "Hello, out there. How's your luck? Have you caught anything?" When fishing, how many times had we all heard these words? It was the universal question asked of fishermen everywhere.

"No, not this time," Peter shouted back. I remained silent. I was much too tired to be sociable.

My interest awakened, however, when the man on the shore said, "There is a large school of fish on the other side of your boat. Throw your net there." Peter stared intensely at the man. No doubt his thoughts were wandering back a few months, or was it years ago? He remembered the time when the Lord told them to cast out into deeper water. As these thoughts made their way through our collective brain, our movements became mechanical, driven by a force beyond our comprehension. Without question or hesitation, we did what we were told.

Immediately we felt bumps and pulls against the nets. They began to strain. We felt not only the weight but the thudding of the fish as they struggled to escape the net. We were unable to haul it in. It was too full of fish. Then John said what we all already knew, "It is the Lord!" Like the rest of us, Peter did not need to be told this. As soon as the words broke the air, he removed his outer garment, tied it around his waist and jumped into the water.

Peter was still Peter, still bumping his head. A strong swimmer, the fisherman knew full well that clothing would be difficult to manage in water. Perhaps he thought he wouldn't need to swim. Perhaps he thought he could try walking on water again. There was no storm; this time maybe he wouldn't sink. Who knows what Peter thought?

The rest of us weighed anchor and sensibly followed in the boat; some of us were calm enough to remember the dragging net still full of wriggling fish. We were glad it was not far to shore. Where the prow of our boat brushed against the sand of the shoreline, there was a fire of burning coals with fish already on it. Several loaves of bread lay nearby. Jesus said, "Bring some of the fish you have just caught, so there will be enough for all of us." Bull of a man that he is, Simon Peter climbed aboard and dragged the net ashore. It was full of sizable fish, but even with so many the net was not torn. Then Jesus, as though a dead man now alive happened every day, said, "Come on, let's have breakfast. I'm starved!" *Was he always hungry like this? Is that what dying and coming back to life does to a man?* Rubbing his hands together, he said with obvious pleasure, "There's nothing like broiled fish on an open fire on a crisp spring morning."

Weary from a night of fruitless net dragging and mouths watering, we didn't argue the point. He took the bread and served each one of us and then did the same with the fish. James remarked, "We have no wine."

After a moment's hesitation I said, "But there is a whole lake full of water here." All eyes turned toward Jesus. He took a morsel of cooked fish and flashed a mischievous smiled. It was good.

XVII

You Know That I Love You

Breakfast had been like a feast for hungry fishermen exhausted from lack of sleep. Our conversation had been light, perhaps even a bit foolish. We were all basking in the moment, the pleasure of being around a campfire with Jesus again. This was, after all, how we had spent most of the past years. None of us spoke of the crucifixion. None of us cared to re-live that searing event in our thoughts. At length, Jesus turned to Simon Peter and said, "Come, Simon, let us walk together." Several of us, needing to stretch our legs a bit followed at a respectable distance, but close enough to catch much of the conversation. As they walked, Jesus picked up a small stick that had fallen from a tree. Then he said to Peter, "Simon, do you believe you love me more than the rest of these men?"

I never quite understood why Jesus singled Peter out like this. Perhaps he wanted the rest of us to know the esteem in which he held him and to prepare him to lead. Whatever the reason, it would later give us confidence in Peter and his leadership and purpose.

As Jesus asked his question, he had chosen the most common word for love, a word used by everyone who spoke of love, a word that carried with it the idea of energy; love that caused one to act.

Peter responded, "Lord, I feel more love for you than I can begin to express." Given Peter's history and personality, it did not surprise me that he chose a more passionate word to express his love, a more obscure word, one that captured feeling and emotion. He said it quietly, flatly, as though it was the most natural and obvious thing in the world.

Why would he ask me this? "Oh Lord, you already know that I love you with all my heart!" *No one could love him more than I love him. Surely he knows that!*

Jesus said, "Then, Simon, I want you to feed my lambs."

Lambs? thought Peter. *"I am the good Shepherd,"* he once said. *"Those who hear my voice..."* Peter was questioning, lost in thought. *What could he mean? What is he asking of me?* The fisherman was perplexed.

Again Jesus said, "Simon, are you sure you truly love me?" Again, Jesus chose the more common word.

"Yes, Lord, you know that my heart is yours." *Of course, he knows this!* And again, Peter chose the more passionate word.

Jesus said simply, "Then I want you to care for the sheep as well."

"If I understand your meaning, Lord, you know that I will! Why ask me these questions of love? Why tear me apart? Why address me with these concerns and not the others?" *"Who am I, and what is my house that you have brought me…?"*

Jesus knew that in his absence Peter would emerge as our leader; he intended to charge Peter with the responsibility of caring for those who would follow him. That is why he asked, "Do you love me more than these?" A strong leader must love intensely. Leaders who are afraid to love and be loved are mere manipulators. It is possible to treat people nicely and charitably and go through the motions about it. Very much like giving of one's funds to a worthy cause. This fulfills the meaning of the word Jesus was using. But Jesus wanted more from Peter. He wanted the kind of emotional intensity from which the call to action arises, and engenders commitment to that cause. That is precisely what he got.

The third time Jesus used Peter's word, "Simon, do you really feel love for me?" Peter halted in his tracks, a pained but intense expression on his face. He was hurt because Jesus asked him what amounted to the same question three times.

Simon wanted to take the Lord by his robes and shake him. Had this scene taken place a few months ago, he might have done exactly that. Instead, he said quietly but with deep passion, "Lord, you know all things; you already know how deeply I feel for you. Surely, it comes as no surprise to you that I love you with every fiber of my being."

Jesus laughed, easing Peter's embarrassment, "Then you will do well, Simon, son of Jonas. You will, indeed, feed my flock!"

Feed his lambs? Feed his sheep? Feed his flock? What could he mean? Three times he asks me of my love; three times to care for his people. On two separate occasions, I denied him three times, yet he honors me; yet he chooses to use me! And what does he find so amusing?

αΘω

Then he said to Peter, "But be of great courage, my big friend. As you have followed me in life, so you will follow me in death!" With the stick he held in his hand he drew two intersecting lines in the sand—an inverted cross. I am certain Simon hadn't the slightest notion of what Jesus was trying to tell him because, unfazed, he turned and saw John, myself and others following them.

Pointing to John, Peter asked, "Lord, what about him?" We must understand what prompted this question. John thought of himself as the disciple whom Jesus loved. If this were true, as some us thought it might have been, then what Jesus was asking of Peter should have been directed at John.

"John? What do you mean, 'what about him?'" Without waiting for Peter to speak he said, "What I have said to you does not concern John. If I want him to remain alive until I return, what is that to you? Your concern must be for yourself and what I am asking of you. Stay close to me, Peter." The fisherman seemed disquieted for a moment but, then reassured, determined. "And by doing so, you will, indeed, honor me and you will glorify the Father." It was a powerful moment, a moment of passion, of purpose and clarification.

After this, Peter became our leader. That isn't to say that his leadership was always wise or even good. Peter's personality never really changed. He spent his life "bumping his head" and "stabbing his foot with his spear." But we loved him. We accepted and affirmed his leadership because his simple, uncomplicated heart was with the Lord and with us. Jesus had chosen well.

And then he was gone. Jesus had once again evaporated from our presence. We were not sure if we would ever see him again. John wrote about this in his own book. You must understand that what John wrote about these events is the truth. I know. I witnessed them for myself.

XVIII

Dancing Shadows

Fishing was what most of us knew, and since Peter was the consummate fisherman, we decided to join him in resuming his business, all of us except Matthew. He not only didn't enjoy fishing, but he could not return to being a tax collector. But after much encouragement we convinced him to stay with us and try to learn the trade.

Peter's boat was in serious disrepair after these years of neglect and needed work, so we all helped him refurbish it. It was a job pulling a thirty-three foot boat up on dry land, turning it over and scraping and pitching the hull. After that came repairs of sail and nets. Once everything was sea worthy again, we were on the water every day. After a motley fashion, we all became fishermen. I quickly discovered that it is hard work, not at all pleasant, yet in many respects, deeply refreshing.

After one particularly grueling night of catching nothing, Peter gathered us around him and said, "I've come to believe that this is not what the Lord would have us do. His message and all that he was to us must not die among fishing boats. We should return to Judea." To a man, we all agreed. After a rest, we set off for the South. The ninety-mile trek was not as easy walking as it had been in the past; at least, not for me. I hoped this would not be the plan, to be on the road continually.

Near Bethany, where Lazarus, Mary and Martha lived, we camped. We awoke just after dawn to another crisp spring morning. As we began to stir about, each taking care of his own personal needs and discussing where we might take breakfast, Jesus appeared once again. When we saw him, we were overjoyed. As we gathered about him he said, "Remember the things I taught you while I was still with you. Everything must be fulfilled that is written of me in the writings of Moses, the Prophets and the Songs of David."

As he spoke, it was like the tops of our heads were opened and we began to understand the Scriptures as we had not known them before. At least this was true for me. It seems that once one encounters the fullness of Jesus, the old writings come alive with meaning and power. He told us, "This is what is written. Messiah will suffer and rise from the dead on the third day. As you can see, this has happened. Now, love, grace and forgiveness must be taught to all nations, beginning at Jerusalem. You have been with me and witnessed the things I have done. I have trained you and given you all that I have. In addition, I am going to send you what my Father has promised, the Holy Spirit. He will continue to order your steps and empower you with his presence."

Off and on over the next forty days, Jesus appeared to us, teaching us more of the kingdom of God and those things that pertain thereto. "All authority in heaven and on earth has been given to me," he continued. "Therefore, I authorize you to go and seek followers, do what you can to stimulate faith among men and women of all nations. Baptize them in the name of the Father and of the Son and of the Holy Spirit, and teach them everything I have taught you. I tell you the truth, whoever accepts anyone I send accepts me; and whoever accepts me accepts the one who sent me. And never, ever forget, I am with you always, even to the end of all things. But stay in this city until you have been clothed with power from on high."

There on the Mount called Olivet, near the outskirts of Bethany, he lifted up his hands and blessed us. As he did, his body began to rise from the earth. As we watched, awestruck, he left us and ascended into the golden blue of the morning skies. We fell to our knees with arms outstretched. We worshiped. Oh, how deeply did we worship. And when he had been received up into the clouds, we returned to Jerusalem with great joy.

αΘω

I think once again of the old priest standing before the angel Gabriel. Put yourself in the old man's place. Walk for a moment in his sandals. You have lived better than your threescore and ten years and never once have you ever encountered a heavenly being. You have read about them, studied past encounters between men and angels, but did you really believe it? Did you own the story as if it were your experience and not just some religious quasi-fictional tale from the past? Isn't your faith a bit tempered by the routine day-to-day "realities" of living? I surmise that you are likely not that much different from Zechariah.

I should speak, perhaps, for myself. It is unwise to surmise. I spent several years with the Son of God and his chosen twelve; now well past my own threescore and ten, I wonder sometimes if it were only a dream, an apparition of a mind not entirely tethered. No matter. Whether real or imagined, my dream has shaped the rest of my insignificant existence. Unlike Paul, the famous teacher from Tarsus, I make no claim at having seen Jesus since that day he ascended through the clouds. There have been no visions, no heavenly encounters. Just silence. Only silence.

I'm afraid Gabriel would have more trouble with me today than he had with Zechariah then.

Still, I haven't forgotten my dream. Or my own reality, whatever it was. Deep in the place where I am centered is the unalterable and unshakable truth that I am yet loved by him. And that, my friend, mitigates all doubt. I have visited the portal of death more than once. I confess that when those ominous shadows of the valley fell over me, I trembled. Yet there is, in the core of my being, the certainty that in my flesh I shall see God—yet again. He has been near all these years, yet in my cloudy befuddlement, I sometimes feel I have missed him. It will be a pleasant reunion when once again, I see his face; when once again, I feel his warm embrace. Despite my stumblings here, my heart trips in anticipation.

Many shadows from countless candles have watched me scratch away at these scrolls. Hours upon hours have passed while my heart has savored the memories. Now, I am Joseph bar Sabbas, called Justus, a servant not too far from the end of my days. I will not be able to complete this project, for, you see, this book is incomplete. There are so many things Jesus said, did and taught that are not written here. You can be sure that if every one of them were written down, it would take the lifetimes of many Josephs. There was so much that Jesus taught, so much that he did. So much has been lost and not recorded. But this much is enough for you to believe that Jesus is the Christ, the Son of God; and if you believe, you will have life in his name. If that happens, then the shadows will not have danced in vain.

Some think of shadows as ominous and threatening. A shadow cannot occur unless there is light. It is but an effect of light cast upon an object positioned between a source of illumination and the surface upon which the shadow is drawn. I am that object. The shadow exists because of me. It is I who have been bathed, and who is awash with light. I turn to behold. I see the light. It blinds me with beauty and love. Dance, dear shadow. Dance, indeed. Dance to the music of my heart.

Endnote

Abishag remained the friend and companion of Joseph bar Sabbas, called Justus, for years beyond his rejection as an apostle. At length, the time came when, with his children, Justus buries her in the wood, beneath the trees, wrapped in his garment, with some of the things in her life with which she played.

Epilog

How, you may ask, do I know all of this? It is simple, really. I was there. I saw everything. Heard everything. Felt everything.

When he spoke the earth into existence, it was I who calmed the waters. It was I who contended with the hearts of men before the flood destroyed them. I guided the hands of Bezalel as he crafted the Ark of Testimony. It was I who caused Eldad and Medad to prophesy and who came upon Balaam the son of Beor. It was I who sustained Moses, Joshua, Othniel, Sampson, Samuel, Saul and David. I fed Elijah and gave a double portion of my Spirit to Elisha. I gave visions to Daniel and foresight to Isaiah and the prophets. As you read the thoughts of Matthew, Mark, Luke, John, Peter and Paul and, yes, even Jesus; it was I who prompted those thoughts.

Wherever there is anything good and truthful said about the Father or the Son, it is said by me. Wherever there is any good that is done in his name, it is done by me. For that is my mission. That is my calling.

It is your calling, too. For it is in you that I live and move and have my being.

Exordium

Earth had yet to bathe in first dawn. Coruscating flares glistened immense in reaches of crystal purple. Beyond other earths, moons, eons of light posturing spirals, fulminating furies, on the other side of black night, before the first instance of time, breathed the living Word, a vital supremacy, pulsating rhythmic cadence,

The Word was with God.

The Word was God.

αΘω

Celestial, vacant and vast, created by the Word who lives outside; external, in transcendent reality incomprehensible, and in unearthly dimension, unimaginable. Into this created expanse, he placed all it now contains, a womb; a tangible place of nourishment for that which he would create in his own image, a world prepared as a home fit for the *Imago Dei.*

From an infinite array of assembled specks of brilliance, he selected one. From its sea sand of luminous bodies, he selected the light that rules by day. From that light's orbs, he selected yet another. From the soil of that orb, he formed a man.

In the Image of God created he him.

αΘω

The Word implanted life into the man he created and the man became a living person, yet unfinished and incomplete. Creation was *not yet good.* Therefore, the Word created woman and the woman and the man were one as he is One. *Perfection!* Male and female created he them. Male without female, female without male are each in their uniqueness, incomplete. Together, they are one. Together, they are *good.*

An image is a reflection, a one-dimensioned, but otherwise exact copy of the original. So elegant, so complete this Image, it reflects the power to make its own choices. The Word has that power, and in creating man and woman in his Image, the two of them also had that power—the power to make their own choices. They were reflections of him, yet they were unique. They were the same, yet they were unique; different from him and different from each other. In the quality of their uniqueness, they also reflected him, for there is none like him. This may seem a paradox, but when considered deeply, you will see that it is not.

They could now choose independently of the Word's choices. And this they did. He chose to have them live together in love, sharing intimacy with him and with all that he had created. They chose, however, to grasp for the knowledge of right and wrong, to draw distinctions between good and evil. In impact and in substance, they became creatures of law. A distance larger than that which separates the stars is that which separates the value of a life lived in hallowed love from a life lived in constraint to law. In making this choice, darkness entered the man and the woman. With darkness came death.

The life of the Word became light to the man and when light shines in darkness, darkness cannot extinguish or resist it. The Word penetrated this darkness with light. Its function is to redeem, to release and reclaim the person, the created soul and body, the effervescent spirit formed in the image of God. What is so familiar, the ant, the worm, a soft breeze, the violet, the urge to move your bowels—all appear insignificant and tellurian set against the backdrop of the Infinite.

Yet from this resplendent palace of unspeakable purity, beyond and larger than the eternal, the Word came to live in this world—in a body that *could* die. Such a consequence as to encompass the Eternal God in perishable human frame is incomprehensible. It blinds the mind, turning it to coal and pith. The result is black. Because of this impenetrable darkness, we who live in this world did not—*could not*—recognize him for whom he was. Still, the genius of his power penetrates the impenetrable, reaching any and all malleable souls, any and all who would dare to believe. This marvelous Light of his infinite life permeates and illumines, reaching to the extremities of hopes and dreams, and the gift to be a child once again becomes his irrevocable warrant; a child of the Eternal God, a child born not of natural descent, but born of God.

αΘω

We honor the credibility and affirm the noble magnificence of him who came from God the Father, this Word so full of Grace and Truth. From the great reservoir of his Grace we have all received *life,* and life's continuing benefits, giving reason for perpetual celebration. From the fullness of Truth, we have received illumination, dissipating the darkness of relativism and uncertainty. To teach men the futility of trying to live by knowing good and evil, religious and civil law came through Moses. The Enlightenment and Life that comes by Grace and Truth, however, comes only through Jesus Christ. No one with earthbound eyes, has ever seen God the Father. But this *Word* who lives in the Father's heart has now lived among us. He lives among us still. It is he, who has revealed the Father to us.

To the question, whether this hope (of the Messiah) *has ever been realised—or rather, whether One has appeared Whose claims to the Messiahship have stood the test of investigation and of time—impartial history can make only one answer. It points to Bethlehem and to Nazareth. If the claims of Jesus have been rejected by the Jewish Nation, He has at least, undoubtedly, fulfilled one part of the Mission prophetically assigned to the Messiah. Whether or not He be the Lion of the tribe of Judah, to Him, assuredly, has been the gathering of the nations, and the isles have waited for His law. Passing the narrow bounds of obscure Judea, and breaking down the walls of national prejudice and isolation, He has made the sublimer teaching of the Old Testament the common possession of the world, and founded a great Brotherhood, of which the God of Israel is the Father. He alone also has exhibited a life, in which absolutely no fault could be found; and promulgated a teaching, to which absolutely no exception can be taken. Admittedly, He was* the One perfect Man—*the ideal of humanity, His doctrine the one absolute teaching. The world has known none other, none equal. And the world has owned it, if not by the testimony of words, yet by the evidence of the facts. Springing from such a people; born, living, and dying in circumstances, and using means, the most unlikely of such results—the Man of Nazareth has, by universal consent, been the mightiest Factor in our world's history: alike politically, socially, intellectually, and morally. If He be not the Messiah, He has at least thus far done the Messiah's work. If He be not the Messiah, there has at least been none other, before or after Him. If He be not the Messiah, the world has not, and never can have, a Messiah.*

—Alfred Edersheim

Bibliography

This is a novel. *It is not supposed to be factual.* Insofar as the gospel record is factual (and I suppose you have gathered by now that I believe it is), the novel is at many levels based on fact. To what degree that it is or is not, I leave to the generosity—and faith—of my reader.

Ordinarily, bibliographies are not found with works of fiction. Since, however, some who open the covers of this volume may be students of theology and/or the scriptures, it is assumed that they may wish to know what works of knowledge and research helped shape the theology and ideas found in the present volume. Such a list of books would reach into the hundreds. This should not be too surprising since I am 76 years old (2012) and have spent virtually each day of my adult life in such books.

So the following list is partial and represents those works which have contributed the most toward the formation of the thoughts in this work. It is hoped that the reader might understand that this body of literature helped with the basics. Some of them affirming and supportive, some of them adverse. Some scholarly works of reference, some language helps, some history or some themselves works of fiction. But for whatever their merit or lack thereof, they represent only the pegs upon which I have hung my imagination.

—Paul Morris

αΘω

1. *A Concordance of the Septuagint.* George Morrish. Zondervan Publishing House. 1976.
2. *A Harmony of the Gospels.* A.T. Robertson. Harper and Brothers Publishers. 1922.
3. *An Expositionary Dictionary of New Testament Words.* W.E. Vine. Fleming H. Revell Company. 1940.
4. *Biblia Hebraica.* Rud. Kittel, editor. For the American Bible Society. 1929.

5. *Brothers and Friends.* Major Warren Hamilton Lewis. Harper and Row Publishers. 1982.
6. *Commentary on the Gospel of John.* Frederick Louis Godet. Zondervan Publishing House. 1893.
7. *Commentary on the Gospel of Luke.* Frederick Louis Godet. Zondervan Publishing House. 1887.
8. *Commentaries on the Old Testament,* Keil and Delitzsch. WM. B. Eerdman's Publishing. 1877, reprinted 1969.
9. *God's Pauper, St. Francis of Assissi.* Nikos Kazantzakis. Bruno Cassirer. 1962.
10. *If Grace Is True.* Philip Gulley and James MulHolland. HarperSanFrancisco. 1986.
11. *International Standard Bible Encyclopedia.* WM. B. Eerdman's Publishing. 1915
12. *Jesus of Nazareth, Savior and Lord.* Carl F.H. Henry, editor. WM. B. Eerdman's Publishing Company. 1966.
13. *Jesus of Nazareth, The Hidden Years.* Robert Aron. William Morrow and Company. 1962.
14. *Jesus Rediscovered.* Malcolm Muggeridge. Tyndale House Publishers. 1969.
15. *Josephus.* Flavius Josephus. The John C. Winston Company. 1957 Edition.
16. *Mere Christianity.* C.S. Lewis. HarperSanFrancisco. 1952.
17. *Nearer My God.* William F. Buckley. Doubleday. 1997.
18. *Novum Testamentum Graece.* Eberhard Nestle. For the American Bible Society. 1898.
19. *St. Luke.* Alfred Plummer. The International Critical Commentary. T. & T. Clark. 1896.
20. *Systematic Theology.* Paul Tillich. The University of Chicago Press, Harper & Row, Publishers. 1951.
21. *The Analytical Greek Lexicon.* Zondervan Publishing House. 1967.
22. *The Book of Acts. The New International Commentary on the New Testament.* F.F. Bruce. WM. B. Eerdman's Publishing. 1954.
23. *The Challenge of Jesus.* N.T. Wright. Inter Varsity Press. 1999.
24. *The City of God.* Saint Augustine. The Modern Library. 1950.
25. *The End of Christendom.* Malcolm Muggeridge. WM. B. Eerdman's Publishing Company. 1980.

26. *The Englishman's Hebrew and Chaldee Concordance of the Old Testament.* Zondervan Publishing House. 1970.
27. *The Fisherman.* Larry Huntsperger. Fleming H. Revell. 2003.
28. *The Gospel According to St. John.* B.F. Westcott. WM. B. Eerdman's Publishing. 1881.
29. *The Greatness of the Kingdom.* Alva J. McClain. Zondervan Publishing House. 1959.
30. *The Illustrated Bible Dictionary.* Tyndale House Publishers. 1980.
31. *The Incomparable Christ.* John Stott. Inter Varsity Press. 2001.
32. *The Interlinear Greek-English New Testament.* George Ricker Berry. Zondervan Publishing House. 1958.
33. *The Interpretation of St. Luke's Gospel.* R.C.H. Lenski. Augsburg Publishing House. 1946.
34. *The Life and Times of Jesus the Messiah.* Alfred Edersheim. WM. B. Eerdman's Publishing. 1967.
35. *The Life and Times of the Last Kid Picked.* David Benjamin. Random House. 2002.
36. *The Life of Christ in Stereo.* Johnston M. Cheney. Multnomah Press. 1969.
37. *The New Bible Dictionary.* J. D. Douglas, editor. WM. B. Eerdman's Publishing. 1962.
38. *The Septuagint Version: Greek and English.* Sir Lancelot C.L. Brenton. Zondervan Publishing House. 1970.
39. *The Song.* Calvin Miller. Intervarsity Press. 1977.
40. *Theological Dictionary of the New Testament.* Gerhard Kittel, et al.) editors. WM. B. Eerdman's Publishing. 1964.
41. *Will the Real Jesus Please Stand Up?* A Debate between William Lane Craig and John Dominic Crossan. Moderated by William F. Buckley, Jr. Paul Copan, editor. Baker Books. 1998.

The Internet. This book was begun in 1995, just when the Internet was beginning to encompass the world. In the passing of these many years since, I have consulted only God knows how many websites, sent and received countless emails—all in an effort to research and seek the knowledge and perspectives of others. Some of it was a waste of time; some of it a magnificent investment of energy. Most of it was in between.

CPSIA information can be obtained at www.ICGtesting.com
Printed in the USA
LVOW132053100413

328390LV00004B/12/P